How Blue Are the
RIDGES

A Novel

D1445905

How Blue Are the
RIDGES

A Novel

KEN OLLIS

iUniverse LLC
Bloomington

FIC
Ollis

HOW BLUE ARE THE RIDGES
A Novel

Copyright © 2013 by Ken Ollis

All rights reserved. No part of this book may be used or reproduced by any means, graphic, electronic, or mechanical, including photocopying, recording, taping or by any information storage retrieval system without the written permission of the publisher except in the case of brief quotations embodied in critical articles and reviews.

Certain characters in this work are historical figures, and certain events portrayed did take place. However, this is a work of fiction. All of the other characters, names, and events as well as all places, incidents, organizations, and dialogue in this novel are either the products of the author's imagination or are used fictitiously.

iUniverse books may be ordered through booksellers or by contacting:

iUniverse LLC
1663 Liberty Drive
Bloomington, IN 47403
www.iuniverse.com
1-800-Authors (1-800-288-4677)

Because of the dynamic nature of the Internet, any web addresses or links contained in this book may have changed since publication and may no longer be valid. The views expressed in this work are solely those of the author and do not necessarily reflect the views of the publisher, and the publisher hereby disclaims any responsibility for them.

Any people depicted in stock imagery provided by Thinkstock are models, and such images are being used for illustrative purposes only.

Certain stock imagery © Thinkstock

ISBN: 978-1-4759-9154-3 (sc)
ISBN: 978-1-4759-9156-7 (hc)
ISBN: 978-1-4759-9155-0 (ebk)

Printed in the United States of America

iUniverse rev. date: 07/10/2013

For my wife, Jackie;
For my sons, Kenny and Marty;
For my grandchildren, Shaun, Dana, and Martin;
For my great-grandchildren, Hunter, Katana, and Austin.

PREFACE

For readers, especially those who have not visited or lived in the Blue Ridge Mountains, this book is intended to share with you a part of the history and domestic life of the people who settled in this very unusual place and to tell you about events that were relevant and essential to the people who braved the elements and endured the sacrifices necessary to live here in one of the most interesting and challenging places on earth.

I chose *How Blue Are the Ridges* as the title of this book because I have been inspired by living here in such a unique and beautiful place for over five decades and touched by the lovely people who live here. I have not been forced to live in these mountains. It was I who chose to live here, and I am glad. These mountains and the people who live among them have offered me a sense of what they have, of what I was, and of what could be. The Blue Ridge is a part of me, and in similar measure, it is a part of all of us.

The Blue Ridge Mountains, located in the eastern United States, are famous for their bluish color when seen from a distance, which adds significantly to their beauty. I have observed no other mountains with such unique qualities provided by nature.

The Blue Ridge is a place of memories of long ago. A sense of the past seems to linger here. Lone chimneys stand in the forest where cabins once stood and families were raised, their cabins long ago rotted away. One can only imagine. Time means little in the silence surrounding the spirits that linger here. The mild, moist climate is favorable for large numbers of plant species, including flowers, shrubs, mosses, and lichens species. The diversity of trees is astounding, with over one hundred species.

Bison and elk once grazed on grassland maintained by Indians who set fires annually to keep land open for the animals. Bison and elk have long since been replaced by cattle and sheep. The Cherokee called the Blue Ridge the unending mountains. The memories of the mountains are unending. These original settlers hunted the mountains and ate wild fruits, nuts, vegetables, fish, maize (corn), elk, and deer, to name the most important.

In 1730 to 1740, frontier families began to settle the region. Most of them were of Scotch, Irish, and German descent. Thousands came south, and evidence of these heritages can be observed to this day in the looks and manners of the mountain folks who live in these mountains.

Ravens and golden eagles sometimes soar across the sky, enjoying their freedom to ride the wind and envied by most of us held captive on the ground we must stand upon by the force of gravity.

Rattlesnakes glide through the weeds in abandoned fields, enjoying the warmth while searching for unfortunate prey. Their bite causes agonizing pain to humans, causing flesh to turn soft and decay. Two poisonous snakes live on the Blue Ridges—the timber rattler and the copperhead.

The old gristmills are fading away. Their time has come and almost gone. They still answer the needs of a few for cornmeal and flour, but their functioning for commercial use has ceased.

Cabins built over two hundred years ago usually were one large room on a ground floor with a fireplace at one end. Steep steps led to a second floor where one or two rooms were usually located. Hewn logs were notched at the ends to fit tightly and seal corners from cold air. Chimneys were large and made of rocks picked wherever they could be found and held together with clay. Roofs were made from oak shakes. Cooking was done in pots hung over the fire in the fireplaces.

The first old schools were one room with fireplaces and, later, woodstoves for heat. The seats and desks were rough and usually handmade, with a single desk and seat joined to form one unit. A picture of George Washington or Thomas Jefferson was often very prominent on a side wall. A well-used blackboard was on the wall behind the teacher's desk, with a long shelf beneath it to hold erasers. The first schools used only books and a slate at their desk to write on.

Each community usually had one store with merchandise stacked on shelves behind the counter. Large potbellied stoves were in back with benches and chairs all around and much used, in winter months especially. Usually the store owner's dog would lay closer to the stove than people. Enclosed glass showcases contained candy bars, cookies, and other goodies. Children delighted in looking at the contents of the showcase. Some larger stores sold shoes; overalls; pants; dresses; gloves; heavy, warm coats; and an array of other needed items. A hardware section sold everything from axes to turning plows that were essential to the farms in the surrounding areas.

Churches, usually nondenominational and often called community churches, were essential from the very beginning. They were very much the center of the spiritual and social lives of the community.

It is good to remember such things relative to the past across the Blue Ridges. Memories must suffice, since we cannot revisit our past. As we grow older, those memories often help sustain us, and they appear the strongest as the fire of life dims and closes into darkness.

ONE

The people who first settled the Blue Ridge Mountains came here in 1730, and much of the history of the Blue Ridge can be accounted for back to that period of time. As time passed, farms and settlements grew across the mountains, but the pace of development was not rapid. The first part of 1900 brought about changes, but in different ways from changes brought to other parts of the country. More specifically, the 1929 stock market collapse caused much hardship and poverty.

The people in the mountains knew little or nothing about the stock market crash of 1929 leading to the Great Depression and the resulting devastation it had caused. But they knew things were not good. The collapse of the financial institutions and closing of banks seemed to cause everything to move on a downward trend. The closing of factories and businesses caused masses of people to lose their jobs, which led them to no longer be able to provide for their families. Word of civil disorder, suicides, losses of jobs and life savings, and widespread panic came pouring across the mountains to the dismay of all. The people of the Blue Ridge were concerned that all these happenings might keep spreading and somehow affect them. Their concerns proved to be well founded.

These were strange times indeed, none of which made sense to the mountain folks, especially the suicides. They pondered why anyone would kill themselves because of material possessions or for any other reason. Their families and land and religious faith were foremost in their lives. All else was secondary. Even the loss of land was no reason for suicide. To them, the Holy Bible had the last word concerning such matters—"Thou shalt not kill," and that included one's self. The good people of the mountains knew that. During both bad times and good times, lives must move onward.

Sometimes they are changed in unimaginable ways that create challenges, all of which must be confronted.

They believed that lives are often changed in different ways unique to each individual and the circumstances presented at the time. People in the mountains feared the Great Depression because they were aware they were not immune to events that occurred in places both near and distant. They had participated in the Revolutionary War, the Civil War, World War I, and even the removal of the Cherokee Indians from their beloved mountain homes.

They were well aware that they did not live in a safe haven free from all situations, serious as they may be. Issues continue and time moves on with each tick of the clock. The earth revolves each day, the moon circles the earth every thirty days, and the earth completes its journey around the sun every year. So go the predictable laws of physics that cannot be changed or challenged by humankind. All else concerning humankind is subject to question and change, with few exceptions. These are just a few of the facts evident and accepted by every interested person. Even issues involving happiness or sadness are subject to these considerations and facts.

The mountain folks were aware of their surroundings and the things that must be done to survive and be reasonably happy. They had very little knowledge of the incalculable thousands of laws governing the earth and the universe. But they did know and took advantage of what they had and how to use each thing to their advantage every day of their lives. Common sense made the difference. Weather predictions, planting of crops, harvesting of crops, and physical healing were only a few of the commonsense laws of nature that these intelligent mountain people considered and used; these were the basis of their beliefs and their unbending philosophy of life.

During these hard and changing times, two young people born and raised in the heart of the Blue Ridge Mountains met and touched each other in ways that would alter their lives forever. With odds against them, Millard Watson and Flora Holland decided to be married and make for themselves a happy and prosperous life. Millard was from the small community of Birch Creek. Flora lived in a more mountainous section about ten miles to the north in a place named Bald Ridge. They could not have selected a worse time to begin a new life together. It was 1929, the year of the stock market crash. They were naive and failed to realize the full impact of their decision and how it could affect the remainder of their lives.

Summer had arrived at last, following a cooler than usual spring. Weather permitting, a barn dance would be held every Saturday night and these festivities would continue until autumn. Millard and Flora met at that first barn dance in 1929. At that very first dance, they immediately became attracted to each other. It was "love at first sight" as the old saying goes, but this was only partially true. Flora was beautiful with red hair, emerald green eyes, and a slender body, and she was taller than most women. She was most always the prettiest girl at community gatherings or social events.

Everyone danced, and the moonshine flowed. Flora did not drink whiskey except for an occasional sip to be sociable. Millard did indulge to a moderate degree. Except for very short breaks, the banjos, guitars, fiddles, mandolins, and a bass guitar rarely stopped all night. The band enjoyed playing as much as the dancers enjoyed the fine mountain music. Square dancing was the most popular dance by far, but slower dances were popular as well. The waltz, two-step, and other slower dances fell into place as the hours passed on into morning and everyone was getting tired.

What a wonderful night it had been. Flora and Millard had talked and danced the entire night away. As Millard and Flora left, the sun was beginning to come up. "I am glad we met this night," said Flora, looking at him adoringly. "I have a feeling this is a special night for us."

"It is a night I will never forget," Millard replied, "and I hope we will have many more together."

Flora was seventeen, and most girls her age were already married. Even so, she was not prone to go against her parents' wishes. They had not told her so, but she knew they did not approve of her staying out too late.

"I am nervous about going home so late," she said to Millard, tilting her head up to meet his eyes. Millard was at least six feet tall, with muscular shoulders that complimented his perfectly balanced body.

"Never mind," he assured her. "I will accompany you to the door and accept full responsibility for the late hour."

As they approached her home, Flora could not avoid hoping no one would hear her arrive. The doors were never locked day or night, but her father, Salem, was up early and met them at the door. Millard did exactly what he'd promised to do, and she could tell her father respected him for that courtesy. Actually, after she thought about it later, she concluded that her father had little room to complain. She had been told by more than a few that he had been quite a rounder in his younger days and still was at times. Even thought she had not dated Millard or even spoke to him before that night, that kind gesture from the gentleman he seemed to be made dating him much easier and comfortable for her after their courtship began.

She did not invite him in or show any indication that she wanted to see him again, but she was certain they would meet again soon. He held her hand very briefly and said, "This has been one of the grandest nights of my life."

As he walked down the road from the house, she watched to see if he turned and looked back. He walked a short distance and then stopped and turned around, as though he expected to see her standing there. She had already entered the house, and after some thought, she concluded that it was best to leave things as they were for now. "What is to be surely will be," she whispered to herself. She had heard her mother repeat those words many times, and her mother had probably heard it from her mother before.

Flora immediately went to bed and did not move until after noon. She could not remember ever sleeping so late, but neither had she ever stayed out until dawn. Apparently, everyone had kept quiet to avoid awakening her, or she had slept through the usual quarreling and noise that always occurred each morning among her brothers and sisters. She suspected the latter to be true.

Late sleeping had never been allowed at her home. Much farmwork needed to be done each morning, and most of it had to be done on time. She immediately went to see about her morning chores, but to her delight, she found her brother, Donald, had done them for her. She gave him a big hug and a kiss on the cheek for helping her. He laughed and pretended to try pulling away, but she held him tight.

Flora anxiously awaited the next dance. Sadly, however, she was very disappointed. During the next week, one of those heavy, torrential mountain rains came with a vengeance, causing severe flooding. It rained heavily for three days without stopping. Most foot logs over creeks were washed away, tree branches and forest debris of all kinds clogged every stream, and the few bridges in the area were damaged and unsafe. Soil erosion was prevalent, causing severe damage to crops. Every available person started working to repair and rebuild as soon as the rain subsided enough for the work to begin. The tall corn was leaning heavily, but fortunately most of it, with help, straightened back up and continued growing soon afterward. The hay fields were a mess but also continued to grow after they dried in the warm sun, assuring at least a moderate cutting for the livestock. The farm was carefully inspected for damage, and everything down to the smallest vegetables that survived the storm was replanted with firm soil placed around them. Rocks were carried to fill in ditches and shore up the banks of streams and other things such as grapevine arbor posts and fruit trees.

Flora could think of little else but Millard while damages from the flood were being repaired. She wanted the work to be complete so her life could return to normal. Thinking of Millard was cause for her to work as hard as she possibly could. If only she knew Millard felt the same about her; that would be compensation aplenty for her labor. She was reasonably sure he did have feelings for her as she did for him. It would not be long now before she would find out. The flood damage was repaired as much as possible for now. The men would have to cut heavy timbers before repairs on heavier bridges and structural work could be finished.

But Flora was well aware that, even though the repairs were almost completed, another flood might follow this one. She would allow no more such thoughts to enter her mind.

The following week, the word was out. A dance would be held on Saturday night if enough people showed up. Flora could hardly wait. She knew she would have a pleasant evening, even if Millard did not appear. If he did not come, she would consider that he was not finished with work caused by the flood damage.

Saturday morning, Flora was up early. She peered through the window hoping to see Millard coming up the road. "How foolish I am," she whispered to herself. "If indeed he is coming, he could not be expected to arrive this early." She set about cooking breakfast and helping with the routine chores. As the sun began to climb higher in the sky, she wondered if he was on his way. She peered out the window again and again.

"Looking for your sweetie, are you?" her twelve-year-old brother Donald, who loved to tease her, called out.

"None of your business," she yelled. Normally she would not have yelled so loud, but she was getting anxious as to whether Millard would come or not.

"He would not walk all the way up here to see an old gal like you," Donald continued, hoping to make her mad enough to chase him with a broom as she usually did when he gave her good cause.

She decided to ignore him. Her thoughts were on Millard. *Surely he will be here soon*, she thought. But after all, he had made no specific commitments to her. He could have other plans that he had not mentioned to her for all she knew. Perhaps they had both taken each other for granted. They had not actually talked of going to the next dance together, she rationalized. No date or plans had been made between them.

With these thoughts in mind, she decided to proceed with the day. If she did not see him before the dance, she would go alone and just make the best of the evening.

No sooner had the thoughts passed through her mind than she looked down the road and there he was, walking briskly toward her. He was a ways off, but she could make out the bright smile on his face. What a thrill it was to see him, and she was certain he felt the same.

He called out as he approached. "I hoped you would be here. All this walking without a rest would have been a severe disappointment to me if you had not been here." He smiled.

"I must say, in all honesty, it would have been a letdown for me too," Flora admitted without hesitation.

They sat down in the swing on the front porch for a while, talking about the horrible flood they had just witnessed and all the work it had created.

Millard seemed totally bewildered by it all. "Sometimes, I just don't think it's worth the effort," he said. "Maybe moving off these hellish mountains would be a good thing. Every damn time things get to going well, something like this flood happens. I intend to give the idea serious consideration, and that's for sure."

"I doubt you will ever follow through with it," Flora said. "I have heard other men and some women make the same remarks, but they seldom carry through with their threats. When the days of autumn appear with their beautiful splendor, how does one muster the strength to just up and leave?" she said, looking him straight in the eyes.

"You are probably right, but I might give it a try some of these days. About one more flood like this one, and that could do it," he remarked.

They walked around the farm, talking and observing the beautiful place. It was an unusually well-equipped and organized farm. Fences separated the areas for crop planting, and a vast field for animals was lush and green. Horses and cattle were grazing there, and a small herd of sheep huddled nearby as though they were enjoying a social gathering of a sort. The farmhouse was well situated near a spring at the lower edge of the field. A large pond could be seen below a springhouse where ducks were swimming about.

Many rustic buildings were situated about the farm. A very large barn sat a good distance from the house, along with a hog pen and a chicken coop—their placement obviously due to the flies and the odor of manure. A fine-looking blacksmith shop was near a large apple orchard to the left of the pasture. A woodshed and smokehouse were located near the house.

Millard and Flora were enjoying every minute getting to know each other. Suddenly, Flora realized she was getting very hungry, and she suspected Millard was also. The day was moving along quickly. Supper was almost ready, and Millard did not have to be invited twice when the call to supper came. He had eaten a small amount at breakfast but nothing since. When he sat down and began eating, everything tasted so good and he was so hungry he could hardly sit still while he ate. The cornbread and buttermilk topped everything. Other family members at the table were amused at the rapid pace he was eating.

He soon realized what he was doing and apologized. "I do believe I have completely forgotten my manners," he said.

There was no need to say anything. Probably everyone at the table had been in the same awkward situation before. Besides, they were country folks, and such things were not nearly as important as they were in other places away from the mountains.

After supper, Millard went to the parlor and sat down. Flora went to her room to get ready for the dance. She wanted to look her best for the dance that night. She arranged her hair as close to the current fashion as she could and put on her nicest dress, which she had stitched completely by herself. It was beautiful and fit her perfectly. Like most ladies did during those difficult times, she'd obtained material for the dress from feed sacks. The feed companies used bags with a floral or other pretty print. It improved their sales of animal feed, and women were delighted to receive cloth suitable for making dresses and decorative items for the home.

When Flora came into the parlor where Millard was talking with her father, she could see by the look on his face as she entered the room that he was pleased with her. He could only admire the beautiful girl he was taking to the dance. He was probably unaware that she was delighted to be going to the dance with such a handsome man.

As she sat down beside him, he reached for her hand and held it gently as he looked into her eyes. It was a loving look, a look she would not soon forget. They were so engrossed in each other, they were forgetting the dance.

Flora then said to him, "It would be nice if we could leave for the dance now to avoid having to rush."

They quickly stood and walked out the door, and Salem walked to the door to wish them a fun evening.

As they walked down the road, their pace quickened, as did their conversation. One could hardly finish relating some part of his or her life before the other would tell some happy or sad occasion that affected his or her life.

They walked hand in hand, and soon Millard drew Flora close to his side and placed his arm lightly around her waist. "Flora," he said, "I feel very close to you, and the feeling grows stronger each time we meet."

"I know, Millard, and I realize how fully and quickly we are beginning to care and develop a need for each other," Flora replied.

"It is sad, in a strange sort of way," said Millard. "We have had little happiness in our lives, and just now, we are becoming fully aware of that void in our lives that never should have been."

"I believe that we are now slowly feeling that love that will grow and fill that emptiness," said Flora.

Suddenly there before them was the barn where the dance was to be held. They had walked a considerable distance without realizing how far they had come. Soon, others began to arrive, and excitement was building. Everyone was anticipating the arrival of the band. The barn had been carefully prepared for the occasion. The floor was swept clean for the dancers, and a smaller area was prepared for the band to sit in comfort while they played.

As Millard and Flora gazed around the barn, Flora remarked, "If it were not for dances such as these, what would people do for fun in these mountains?"

"The communities would just be dismal, bleak, morbid places to live, especially for young people, I suppose. As a matter of fact, that's about all there is now," Millard said, winking at Flora as he spoke.

The band was in its place, and the dance was about to begin. The caller was an elderly gentleman named Abe (called Uncle Abe), who delighted in calling square dances and knew just about all the different calls known to anyone. He knew exactly how to pace the dance to make it go smoothly and comfortably and keep in perfect rhythm with the band.

The caller announced that all dancers form a circle and get ready to begin. The band now had their instruments in tune and ready for action. The banjos, guitars, fiddles, mandolins, and the large bass guitar all playing in perfect rhythm seemed to make the mountains ring like magic. The dancers swinging and moving according to the directions called out loudly and clearly by the gracious caller, who took such pride in his job, was a beautiful sight. To the mountain folks, there was nothing more delightful.

It was so wonderful to dance and have fun again. The warm weather and passing of the terrible flood and the end of most of the hard work it had caused was a good reason for an uplifting of their spirits. The barn was filled with the sound of pleasant conversation and laughter and the continuous music.

Uncle Abe knew the folks needed an evening such as this. Their faces revealed stress caused by the flood and the resulting hard labor. They had worked to near exhaustion during the last few weeks, and he knew it. He had witnessed the same many times during his long life. He loved every one of them and wanted to see them happy. Such a good man he was.

Many of the folks enjoyed walking outside between dances. The moon was out, and the stars were unusually bright. It was an excellent time for the couples to enjoy a few moments of private talk and the fresh air. Also, there was no shortage of moonshine whiskey being passed around for those wanting a little "snort." Most of the men did partake, but not too much. They did not want to get drunk. That would be considered unmanly and embarrassing before the womenfolks.

Trouble rarely arose at barn dances, except when someone would drink a little more than they could handle and wanted to get a little feisty. Usually any skirmish was over a girl and did not amount to much.

This was one of those nights destined for trouble and serious trouble at that. About halfway through the evening, a group of about twenty-five men suddenly crashed the dance. They barged in, all smelling of whiskey, and they were looking for trouble.

"We come here to raise hell and have some fun," one of the men yelled. "We want these gals too," he added. "This sow right here is the one for me," he continued, bringing loud laughter from his buddies.

Trouble was their way of having fun. Another fellow, his face red as a beet and smelling like he hadn't had a bath in a month, leered toward a young girl. She screamed and ran like the devil was after her.

The longer the drunkards stayed the worse they got. Many of them started bumping into people and, even worse, grabbing the girls and pitching them upward as far as they could and then catching them as they fell.

Most of the local boys were just teenage boys who tried but just could not protect their girlfriends as they thought they should. They threw some bottles and rocks but to no avail. They were dreadfully humiliated and understandably so.

Millard had been carefully observing all that was happening but had not discovered what, if anything, could be done at that time. Soon, one large, burly-looking devil walked over to Flora and started making nasty remarks to her. Millard asked him to leave several times and to behave himself, but that did no good either. The man had no intention of leaving them alone. Apparently the man interpreted Millard's warning as a weakness and paid him little attention—a bad mistake for him.

Millard could tolerate no more. Suddenly, he leaped to his feet and struck the man squarely on the chin. That was the beginning and end of that altercation. The man fell to the floor, knocked senseless. Several of his buddies had to come to his aid. They lifted him to his feet and helped him outside, thinking the fresh air would revive him. It was of little help. He had to be supported by his buddies and kin to make it home.

During the commotion one of the band members remembered he had a pistol in his saddlebag. He dashed out and brought it inside and fired several shots into the air. That seemed to settle things down somewhat, and apparently unarmed and uncertain whether more shots would be fired—perhaps in their direction—the rowdy bunch started moving toward the door.

Millard seized the opportunity and called out to the others to leave as quickly as possible. He feared the troublemakers might have weapons outside and return to the barn. As the group started down the road, Millard, speaking in a rather loud voice, told the men not to worry or be heavyhearted about the happenings of this night. "We will settle this matter at another time. I think it best now that we go home and not worry. We can meet later and decide what to do about this insult. That bunch from Jacobs Hollow can be brought down a notch or two whether they know it or not. We will take them to task for this, and you can bet your britches on that."

The men voiced their agreement and made their way home.

Little conversation passed between Flora and Millard as they walked toward her home. Although Millard tried, he was having trouble keeping his mind off the trouble they had experienced. It had ruined the entire evening, and he was mad as hell. He walked Flora to the door and told her he would return as soon as possible. After kissing her good night, he quickly departed.

After going to bed that night, Flora could not go to sleep. Her mind was on Millard, and she was not certain why. She knew she did not like the look she'd seen in his eyes before and after he struck the man at the dance so hard. He'd had every reason to do what he'd done; that was not a problem for her. If he had not acted as he had, she was certain she would not have felt proud of him as she now did. She thought that perhaps this seemingly wonderful man with whom she was falling in love might have another side to him that might not be so wonderful. One thing she was sure of; he was not a man to mess with when he was angry. With that thought, she felt the tiredness of the night and slowly drifted off to sleep.

TWO

The following day, Flora was up early. It was a sunny, warm Sabbath day, and she immediately decided to attend church. The church bell was ringing as she left the house. How happy she was that she had made that decision. The very sight of that exceptionally beautiful Methodist church was a comfort to her, and she always felt a calm spiritual feeling as she entered the sanctuary. Sometimes, she wondered why God had favored her that way since she was a small girl. She always went to church early. Other members of her family usually attended as well, but they were usually late.

The sermon was very touching and appropriate and the singing beautiful. It seemed to be a service especially for her. Of course it wasn't, but she was happy being there. The closing hymn was "Just as I Am." As the hymn was sung, the minister invited all those who desired and felt the need to approach the altar and kneel in prayer. Flora felt a tear slowly flow down her check. The desire to follow his invitation was there, but she did not respond.

After the service was over, she walked home slowly, thinking of the events of the previous night and the holy service she had just attended. She wondered why this was such an emotional time for her. The events of the previous night had been stressful to her, and the doubts created in her mind about Millard bothered her still. All these things, along with the flood, were probably taking their toll on her and others. Depression can be a bad thing and that was, no doubt, the cause for her tears. Strange; she was very happy to be at church, yet why had she had a feeling of sadness later on in the service? After the service she wondered why she had not responded to the minister's call as she normally would have done.

For many years, she had always found relief from emotional and troubling situations by praying at the altar. Perhaps God was trying to give her some direction in her life, and she was not listening.

She then decided to leave things as they were for now. Again her mother's words—"what is to be surely will be"—had revealed the usual treasured meaning to her.

Millard had also attended church that morning. His family had always been very devout Christian people, and his mother insisted on him accompanying the family to church. He reluctantly went along, but with little enthusiasm. The night before was still clearly on his mind, and he wanted some time to just sit on the front porch and think. Nevertheless, after arriving at the church, his attitude changed, and he actually enjoyed the service very much. Millard was considered the best bass singer around, and this morning had been no exception. The choir sang so beautifully that, after they had finished their usual number of songs, they were requested by the congregation to sing another. It was the equivalent of a standing ovation. Millard did not particularly enjoy the sermon, but he had enjoyed the singing as he seldom had before.

After lunch, Millard retired to the front porch with his dad as they often did. They would carve away on pieces of wood with their Barlow knives and talk about any and every subject that came to mind.

Dad had learned at church about what had happened the night before. He knew Millard had vengeance on his mind, and he knew from experience that vengeance was a bad thing. "What are you going to do about the trouble with that Jacobs Hollow bunch?" Dad asked.

"I don't rightly know, Dad," said Millard. "I do know one thing though; we cannot let this thing pass as if it never happened." Millard threw down his whittling stick and stood up. "If we do, they will torment us on and on until we will have to face them again no matter what. They will give us no peace." He started pacing. "I heard of them tormenting one community over near Black Rock until half of the people up and sold their farms and left. I don't know whether that is entirely true or not, but that's what I heard. I will be damned if they are going to do us that way. If we have to keep watch over our community night and day, we will just have to do it." By that time, Millard was walking back and forth across the porch, and he'd dropped his knife without realizing it.

Dad could well see he could say nothing that would be of benefit unless Millard was of a mind to listen.

Millard finally stopped his talk of violence and anger and, after retrieving his knife, sat down again. Abruptly he stood again and told his dad he was going for a walk to clear his mind a bit.

"That is probably a good idea," Dad replied.

Off down the road Millard started at a rapid pace and then slowed. He knew he needed to think rather than walk so quickly. The warm sun and the beautiful scenery was just the remedy for him, he thought. He proceeded down the road along Birch Creek, softly singing one of his favorite hymns, "Amazing Grace." His bass voice was beautiful beyond words. For one person to possess such a singing talent seemed miraculous.

Millard kept on walking, much farther than he had intended to, until he came in sight of the home of John Hughes. John was the finest blacksmith Millard or anyone else in the area knew of and one not to arouse to anger. But he was a very kind, accommodating man, and although he was not known to be a religious man, he was, nevertheless, a good man.

John's blacksmith services extended over a large area including Bald Ridge where Flora lived. Most of the farmers had their own small blacksmith shops, but they relied on John for larger, more skilled and difficult jobs. He provided quality, unique blacksmith services not to be found without traveling to a far community or town.

Millard and John seemed to be forming a close friendship without realizing it was happening. Actually, it was not difficult to understand why. Both were friendly and enjoyed the friendship of others. Neither liked rude people, and both men always tried to be kind and respectful to everyone. John was a little taller than Millard and, like most men of his trade, had uncommonly large, strong muscles.

Millard was happy he had made the decision to take the afternoon walk. He did not understand why he had not thought of John before. He should have remembered that, even if John did not want to get involved in any violence at this time, he could be depended upon for some sound advice.

Millard's boots thumped on the wooden porch. As he was about to knock on the door of his friend's rustic house, John answered the door. After handshakes and backslaps, they proceeded to occupy two comfortable rocking chairs near the fireplace. As they rocked, John's chair creaked, annoying him until he pushed it aside and got another one.

"Did you hear about the trouble at the barn," Millard asked.

"No," said John. "What was it all about?" As he glanced over at the younger man, he could see Millard's black hair was framing sternly set features.

Millard related to him the trouble that had occurred the night before, laying out the specifics of the incident. "Do you have any ideas about how to handle the situation?" Millard asked. "I am just about of the mind to lead our men over to Jacobs Hollow and wipe them damn devils out in one big ambush."

John was aware that Millard was just blowing off steam, but he could see that Millard intended to get even. There was no doubt about that. But he also knew the Jacobs Hollow community, located far over a high mountain a good distance away, was full of rough, troublemaking men who would be hard to handle. Birch Creek, on the other hand, was a peaceful community, not accustomed to abusive behavior deliberately intended to antagonize or disrespect others. "What a damn crazy thing to do," replied John. "I think that was one hell of an insult and should not go unanswered. Even though I was not involved, the people around here are my neighbors, and I would be more than willing to help out."

After talking for a while, John brought out a jar of corn whiskey. "This is good stuff. I got it from Horace Blue, who lives about eight miles from here. I did some work for him a while back, and he offered to pay me with this good moonshine instead of cash. I was more than willing to make the exchange. Horace makes the best moonshine I've ever tasted. You can always depend on it being smooth tasting and pure and aged just right." John reached into the cupboard and brought out a couple of glasses and filled them almost full. "Here, take a drink, and you will want another."

Millard was happy to do so and smacked his lips in agreement. "I have never tasted whiskey of this caliber. Tastes like something made in Glory."

A loud hardy, laugh followed.

"Told you," said John.

As the two men continued sitting in the living room talking and enjoying each other's company, they were both hoping their friendship would continue on into the future.

Before Millard departed, they agreed to meet at his home the following evening, along with all the men Millard could muster throughout the countryside, especially those who had been involved with the dance incident.

Millard gave a sigh of relief as he started back home. He knew things would go much better now with John helping them. "What a fine afternoon this had been," he said to himself.

The following afternoon, he located all the help he could find and advised them of the meeting at his home that evening. He was slightly apprehensive about the planned evening. He felt that most of the men would show up, but he was not sure if there would be enough, considering the task before them come next Saturday night.

After supper, Millard went to the front porch to greet all those who came. John Hughes was the first to show. Millard knew he would be there and, no doubt, on time. Soon, about twenty-five or thirty men showed up, which was pleasing to Millard. He now had a strong feeling that many more men would show up from both sides at the upcoming dance. If he was correct, there would be one hell of a fight. He was somewhat worried that so many of their men were very young and there could be serious injuries. On the other hand, however, youth in this situation could be a big factor. The young boys appeared agile and stronger than most boys their age. Things just could turn out very well, seeing how angry these boys were.

After talking about the situation, they all agreed to meet at the same barn where they had been humiliated by the rough men and take all the satisfaction they could. Millard sensed they were not very confident of their ability to defeat the larger and, for the most part, stronger men. Some of these boys had never been in a fight before, other than minor incidents at school or some other place.

Millard stood up. "We can win this fight and send that bunch from Jacobs Hollow back across the mountain where they came from with their tails between their legs if we take heart and keep our heads," he told the men. "I know we don't have much time to prepare for the fight, but we can be far better prepared than we are now. Do everything you can think of to get yourself in shape to rumble. Try stuffing a sack with hay and securing it to a rafter or tree limb and practice fighting it. That will help you hit faster and harder, and you will be less likely to take a hard blow yourself. Hit hard and fast and then duck and move away; circle around the man you are fighting so as not to be an easy target.

"I am no expert myself in these matters, but I know John Hughes here is. I never knew him to lose a fight. John can give us some advice on how best to give an account of ourselves."

John then spoke. "Millard has done very well with his advice and instructions to you. There is much to be learned before becoming a skilled fighter, but most men have little more skill than you. And if you just use common sense and Millard's guidance you can prevail. There ain't much else we can do in such a short time. Just keep your heads and be of good courage.

"It is natural to be a little fearful, so don't worry about that. You will forget about being scared as soon as the fight starts. If you hit harder with your right hand, jab with your left and then deliver your best blow with your right. The opposite is true if you are left-handed. Watch for a good chance to deliver a stout blow to the stomach. That will take the wind out of a person quicker than any other blow."

John paused and glanced over at the assembled men, his eyes dark under his furrowed brow. "One other thing," he added. "I don't advise anything but fist fighting if you can help it. We don't want anyone to get killed or disabled. If you have guns, put them where you can get to them in case of self-defense. If that should happen, get your guns quickly and take cover. Shoot to kill if you have to, but shoot only as a last resort. You can't bring a bullet back once it leaves the barrel of the gun.

"There ain't no more advice I can give you at this point except to tell you to give them all the hell you have in you. Get bear dog mean and don't let up or give them time to breathe. I think things will be all right, but you never can tell when you are dealing with such a rough bunch. Then again, they might get a little rattled when they see what they are up against in such a good bunch of men as you."

Much work needed to be done, and Millard hoped his men would prepare themselves well for the fight that was certain to come about. The week passed quickly—too quickly to suit most.

THREE

Saturday evening found almost all the men walking toward the barn where they had planned to meet. Some walked together, and some traveled alone or on horseback. Although John Hughes had covered guns very clearly, ensuring that all agreed not to use them unless the other side moved to use theirs first, he had not mentioned knives. Many of them figured a sharp knife might just make the difference if things went wrong.

John too was thinking of weapons as the group journeyed toward the barn. He was an expert with weapons, but the young men, some of them with families, had much to lose. Guns and knives kill, and he wanted to avoid that if at all possible.

The men arrived at the barn and were as well prepared as they knew how to be. They knew the Jacobs Hollow men would show, but they were not sure when. The news of what was about to go down had spread well in advance. The Birch Creek men stationed themselves just inside the barn doors so the intruders would not be aware that no women were inside. Some of the men were getting anxious just waiting. Millard was looking around, trying to detect anything that would give them an advantage or cause a disadvantage. Suddenly, he realized things were just too quiet. It did not seem right somehow. Then it occurred to him exactly what could be a strategic mistake. The band had not arrived, and there was no music. Well, there was nothing they could do about it now except hope the gang would not notice.

"Don't worry about it," said John Hughes. "We don't need music to whip their asses by."

That brought on some laughter, and the group loosened up a bit.

After a short while, they could hear the wild devils coming. They were talking and cursing and drinking their corn liquor, no doubt expecting the same fun as they'd had last Saturday. When they arrived in sight of the barn, they stopped momentarily and then moved on toward the barn. "Here they come," said John. "Just keep quiet and let them make the first move."

The approaching men seemed just a little on edge as they approached the barn, as though they sensed something was up but wondered what. The men inside the barn could hear them talking in very low voices. Suddenly they stomped right up to the barn, cursing and ordering the men standing there to move or be walked over. One of them yelled, "We intend to have some fun with them pretty gals in thar."

John and Millard moved in front of the other men. John had done some scouting during the week to see if the men were sure enough coming and what were their true intentions. He found out that the men were not only coming, but they were bringing three other men with them who were large in size and very powerful. One was said to be so strong he could bend a horseshoe with his bare hands. John had not told any of the men except Millard. They were jittery enough as it was.

It looked like a standoff for a few moments until the man named Clem called out in a loud voice, "I want to see the man who hit me with a sneaky punch last week."

Millard spoke up and said, "That would be me, I reckon, but I did not hit you with a sneaky punch."

"You hit me when I was not looking or expecting it you horse's ass."

"You would not have been hit at all if you had behaved yourself and had any damn manners around women," Millard said in a loud voice. "All of you men would have been welcome here, and we could have been dancing and having a great time if you hellish fools knew how to behave. Furthermore, I intend to hit you again, Clem, if you mess with me, or any of us for that matter."

That started the fight of all fights. Clem rushed at Millard and knocked him to the floor. Then Millard rolled to one side just as Clem tried to stomp him in the face. Quickly, Millard jumped to his feet, and the same thing happened as had happened last week, only worse. Millard hit his antagonist twice with all the strength he could muster, and it was all over for Clem. He was down and out as though he had been hit with a sledgehammer.

That infuriated the men from across the mountain beyond words. They all ran inside the barn and every man on both sides started swinging fists, hard and fast.

John Hughes and the so-called strong man named Forest Crump came straight at each other. Both knew very well who they were up against, and Forest appeared confident he had the advantage. He swung at John so hard that John said afterward that he'd felt a strong breeze through his hair. If John had not ducked under the punch just in time, the fight would have been over for him, without a doubt. Forest threw himself so off balance from his hard swing that he almost hit the ground. As he straightened up, John said, "Come on, you horseshoe-bending bastard," and as Forest regained his balance, John hit him with a very powerful punch straight in the mouth, knocking one of his front teeth out and then followed up with another hard one that put Forest down but not out.

Inside the barn, fists were still flying and cursing and swearing could be heard far up and down the road. Blood and sweat and spit and teeth were splattered all over the place, and the fight kept right on going as though it would last the night. Neither side would give one inch.

The local boys apparently were pretty well holding their own, and John and Millard had just about more than they could handle with the horseshoe bender, Forest, and the other two strongmen who'd come across the mountain to help out their buddies.

John Hughes could fight better than any man Millard had ever seen. He had a style of moving his body from side to side and could hit equally hard with either fist. He moved and punched continuously. It confused Forest, who continued to fight very well but was just not fast enough. John kept banging him with stiff, strong punches until he just slumped to the floor, unable to continue.

Millard kept moving, keeping one of the men between him and the other, careful to not get caught between the two men or face both at the same time. As soon as John saw that Forest was no longer a threat, he immediately came to Millard's aid. It didn't take long until the other two men were also lying on the barn floor.

Then Millard and John turned their attention to the brawl going on with the other men. To their surprise, their boys were giving a good account of themselves at that point and maybe a little more. Someone was getting knocked to the floor every few seconds. Both sides were getting tired, and it was apparent the fight wouldn't last much longer. Certainly there was not going to be any clear winner.

After seeing how things were going, John said to Millard, "I think this has gone on about long enough."

Millard nodded his head in agreement. "We have proved our point, and I think them boys might have learned a much-needed lesson."

John shouted in a loud voice, "Boys, let's just stop where we are and go home. We don't need to fight each other anymore."

The fighting stopped almost immediately. Both sides then moved slowly out the door, looking tired and worn to a frazzle. The men from both sides headed away from the barn without looking back, as though they were glad to be headed home. Their mountain pride was still intact, and that was sufficient.

There had been no cutting or shooting, although there might have been if the fight had lasted until it was evident to either side they were going to completely loose and suffer a humiliating defeat.

The Jacobs Hollow men headed back up the road. Some needed to be aided by the others.

The local boys headed in the opposite direction. John and Millard walked behind to make sure they were all right. Fortunately, no one was seriously injured. Two men complained of pain in their ribs and were being helped along. The moonlight and a couple of flashlights as their only illumination revealed cuts and bruises as the men shuffled slowly home, torn shirts and breeches flapping in the breeze. One man had only one shoe, and John and Millard knew it would be hard for him to get another one.

One of the men said, "I wish they had cleaned the barn out a little better. I stepped in cow shit, and my shoes were so slick I couldn't hardly keep from slipping."

John and Millard kept walking with them long enough to assure there were no other injuries among the men. They were glad to see that none of the fractures were in danger of puncturing a lung. They would no doubt be painful for several weeks however.

The entire group walked together a ways before separating and heading to their own homes. Millard and John walked behind them as they talked about the fight. John remarked, "I do believe we might have got the better on this one."

Millard replied, "From what I saw, them old boys looked in worse shape than us. They were a tough bunch to contend with, I'll hand them that. If they had not drunk so much old moonshine on their way over here, we might not have been able to handle them. But, on the other hand, our boys had been badly insulted last Saturday night, and they were determined to even the score. Anger and vengeance can make a lot of difference in a situation like this, and our boys had a lot of both built up inside them. I don't think we will be hearing from them very soon. Does feel good, don't it, John?"

"Sure does, Millard. I believe it was the biggest, roughest fight I was ever involved in—more like a small war than a fistfight. We certainly were lucky though, having that many men fighting without anyone pulling a weapon. Every man there was probably armed, and just one man could have caused a situation that no doubt would have left bodies lying all over the place. I feel both lucky and thankful to the Lord, and that is a fact," John remarked, his voice strong and sincere.

They walked down the road toward the homes of the two men who had suffered cracked ribs. Allen, the one with two broken ribs, moved along slowly. His folks came to the door and thanked them for bringing him home safely.

The other delivery was not so easy. When they accompanied Tim to the front door, his mother, Mary Peele, jumped all over them before they could speak. "You two fools should have knowed better than to get all these boys and men around here to fight them devils from Jacobs Hollow. Now just look at him." She pointed at her son. "He looks like he has been in a hailstorm or something. Tore up his good britches too I see. I can't mend them neither," she added as she turned him around to inspect the damage.

They tried to explain to her the cause of the fight and assure her that no one had been seriously hurt. Her son had a cracked rib or two, but otherwise, he was all right.

"I ought to knock a couple of pump knots on both your heads for taking him off. That's what I ought to do. All the folks hereabouts have been talking of this trouble that was about to happen and have been worried sick about our boys going to fight that bunch from Jacobs Hollow and getting half of their bones broke or maybe killed. Now get along home before I put some knots on your heads like I said before."

As they walked down the road, Millard said, "Hellfire, I'm glad to get away from her. I do believe she might have put knots on our heads for sure."

They chuckled as they headed down the road toward home.

That was the last trouble between the local boys and the men from Jacobs Hollow. The folks from Jacobs Hollow slowly became peaceful, and later, many of them became friends and actually attended the barn dances together the following summer. They did so peacefully, and all brought their own women and minded their manners. During the first dance with men from both sides in attendance, the atmosphere was tense at first, but they soon relaxed, and all soon agreed that dancing was much more fun than fighting. Most people from that section of the mountains were not given to holding grudges for long periods of time, and for the most part, the same continues to hold true today. The Jacobs Hollow men were the worst anyone could recall, but the fight seemed to square things with them, and an unexplainable peace settled across that part of the ridges.

FOUR

Another week had passed since the Saturday night insult that instigated the fight last night. The fight was now over, and it was the Sabbath. Millard was up early, along with his mother. He said little about the fight. He was happy not to be faced with the same situation that had troubled him on the previous Sunday. It seemed like all was well with the world after he enjoyed a nice breakfast and was off to church with his mother. She always tried to arrive at church early and see that everything was in order for services to begin. Other members of the family would be along later.

As they walked down the road, his mother, Sarah, was very curious about what had happened the night before and began asking questions. Millard knew she would not be satisfied until she knew everything about the ruckus, so he started at the beginning and told her everything he thought she needed to know.

She was against the fight from the very beginning after hearing their plans discussed at their home previously. "Are you injured anywhere?" she asked.

"No, but I could have been," he replied. "That's why I am up so early. I am going with you to church this morning to take my place in the choir for some good singing and then hear a great sermon by the one and only Reverend Brown. I believe it would do me a powerful lot of good."

"Well, I should hope so," said Sarah. "Trouble like that usually piles trouble upon more trouble."

"I know and I promise not to worry you like that again," he assured her. "I just want to attend church this morning and have a good, peaceful day."

Sarah replied, "I do pray you will have a peaceful day, but the part about you not worrying me again bothers me a little. I have heard that promise so many times before; I can't help but feel doubts about what you are promising me now."

No more was said, and they quietly continued on to church.

The following week was a busy one. Everyone worked until dark every night, trying to nurse the crops to good health after the storm had inflicted so much damage. It now appeared they might have a better than expected crop, but the rain had taken its toll. All seemed in reasonably good condition by the end of the week, and folks were looking forward to the coming weekend.

On Saturday, Millard stopped working at noon. He had decided to see Flora and go to the dance if she was willing, considering the fight and all. A three-week hiatus seemed such a long time without seeing her. He had few doubts, however, that she would be waiting for him. Noontime found him on his way as planned.

He had been doing some serious thinking lately. Many ideas kept flowing through his mind, but none seemed to serve his purpose. He wanted a different life than what he now had to endure. Love was beginning to enter the picture, and so was marriage. He liked the thought of marriage but not quite yet. He needed his mind to be very clear before embarking on that subject. The idea was making his mind feel a little like summer salad, all tossed about.

With all this walking and thinking, Millard came to a conclusion he had never even remotely thought of considering before. Then and there, he made up his mind that he would raise above his present station in life. He would find a way to become a man of means. He would achieve a position of prominence and break the cycle of poverty to which he had become accustomed. At present he owned only a few shabby clothes, a Barlow knife, and a .38-caliber pistol. He seldom had little more than two nickels to rub together. Of course, all was not sad and bleak. He did not have to go hungry. Nourishing food was always provided, thanks to the farm and hard work, and he had a loving family who had depended on each other since his first memories.

All considered, however, his life had not been happy, and as he saw it, the future revealed no more than the past. The best he could ever expect would be a small inheritance of land from the family farm at some point in time. This would all change. He was determined that, somehow, someway, he would find the door to success.

These were wild, extreme notions and would take much thought and, perhaps, drastic measures to achieve. He did not know why these very unrealistic yet very important thoughts had entered his mind as he walked that lonely, dusty road on the way to see the love of his life. Flora was the love filed in the crevices of his mind, and he was certain his thoughts would prove to be so. She would be an important key to success in whatever ventures he would pursue. He did not discount his own abilities, even though he had only a common school education. But he knew Flora was very intelligent, and with her help, his chances of success would be tremendously improved. No matter what brought these thoughts to mind, together he and his new love could make them far more than mere thoughts.

It had taken miles of walking to set his ambitions firmly in place. At that point, however, they were ambitions only and would require tremendous time and effort to accomplish. He would set aside these ambitions for now. While deeply engrossed in thought, he had covered more distance than he had realized and was now in sight of Flora's home. As he approached the house, he immediately saw Flora sitting on the front porch swing where she had been napping. She seemed surprisingly startled as he walked into the yard.

"Oh!" she said with a smile. "I was afraid you would not come today." Flora stood up, stretching after her nap.

"Are you okay?" asked Millard. "I did not mean to startle you." His brows furrowed as he looked at her, wondering why she seemed so upset.

"Oh, I had a strange dream," Flora said, rubbing her head. "I dreamed that we were together in a strange place—a very large city I think. All I could see was tall buildings and streets and cars and many people walking about. It was a frightening place and not a place of peace. Far down one street, some men were shooting guns at each other as if they were in a war. I cannot imagine why I had such an unsettling dream. I never want to travel to such a place, but you know, somehow I believe we might."

Millard was taken aback somewhat. Normally, he would pay little attention to a dream, but this one was different. He decided not to question her about it. His mind had been racing ever since he had entertained all those unusual thoughts on his way there. He had already discovered that she was different from other people he knew. It could be, her dream and his thoughts during the day shared a common connection. *Who knows?* he thought. He would reserve it as food for thought for a later time. He had had enough brain ticklers for one day.

Flora had known him long enough to realize he was no doubt hungry. She immediately went to the kitchen to fix them a heavy snack of beef stew, potatoes, green beans, and cornbread, all leftovers from dinner. Millard had noticed how well Flora's family lived. They had suffered little from the Depression compared to others. Of course, her father was Salem Holland, who was a very intelligent man with a lush, fertile farm.

FIVE

Evening was upon them and even though no plans had been made, Millard and Flora would leave for the dance. This evening, to their delight, the dance would be at a farm not nearly so far as usual. They had worked so hard since the recent flood, they certainly did not need the exercise. Even after arriving at the dance, they, like some other couples, danced every second dance. They found it refreshing on this occasion to dance less, enjoy the music, and watch others dance who were not so tired.

They walked home slowly, enjoying the quiet evening and, even more, having just a little of their life back. Their conversation was casual and pleasant. When they arrived at Flora's home, Millard did not seem his usual self. He held her hand as though he did not want to let go and kissed her gently.

"What is wrong, dear?" she asked.

"Nothing, I am just a little nervous and tired," he replied. "Do you think your folks would mind if I sleep in your barn tonight. I am a strong man, but everything has just piled up on me lately, and I feel like I should rest before going any farther."

"Of course they wouldn't," she assured him.

He said no more as he moved toward the barn. During the night, she awoke and went to the barn to make sure he was all right and placed a blanket over him. She returned to see about him again at dawn, and he was gone.

With the events of the recent past fading, Millard and Flora resumed their courting. They attended the traditional barn dances, church box suppers, corn-shucking events, and occasional residential parties. After all that occurred, the summer ended on a note of happiness.

Church revival meetings were prevalent during the warm, pleasant autumn weather. Flora and Millard tried not to miss even one if distance and time and weather permitted. Strong-voiced preachers would preach every night for two weeks or more. Group and congregational singing was, without exception, the most enjoyable part of each service. When invited, Millard could not resist participating in the special group singing. As the preaching ended each night, soft music and songs were sung while church members would move forward among the congregation, pleading to sinners to avoid the fires of hell by proceeding to the altar and committing their lives to Jesus Christ. Often, many would go forward and confess their sins and seriously commit their lives to Christ.

Others often followed at the urging of the preachers, who would kneel with each one who had doubts and read scripture to them and pray with them until they were satisfied that confession of their sins and a firm commitment to God was what they should do. Many of them went on to lead exemplary lives.

Soon after the revivals ended, churches would hold common baptismal services for the converts who had been saved during the revivals. The ceremonies were held at a creek or river where the water was sufficiently deep to accommodate submersion of the converts. Each person receiving baptism would be led by the hand into the water by two ministers and, after a hymn and baptismal prayer, fully submerged and then lifted out of the water. Consequently, the attendees followed those gathered with loud shouts, such as, "Hallelujah," "Praises to God," "Glory-glory," and "Amen." Joyful tears were shed and much hugging and praying went on after each converted person was baptized.

Mischievous little boys would often stand out of their parents' sight and shake with laughter after each submersion. They would make remarks such as, "That one looks like a drowned rat; push him down again so he will look a little better." That would bring on even more laughter. Sometimes their behavior would cause strong thrashings by their parents after the service was over.

With summer gone and fall swiftly passing, Millard and Flora were finding themselves very seriously involved romantically. Marriage was rapidly moving to the forefront of their relationship. They both were acutely aware of their deep feelings but had proceeded no further beyond their months of courting. They were both very anxious for a binding relationship. The entire national economy was in shambles, and most families were clinging together for survival. A newly married couple would probably face many problems due to the turbulent uncertain times. They would be totally dependent on their parents for survival, with no end in sight, perhaps for many years into the future. They would have no way of providing for themselves as a separate family unit. They had no land; no home; and, most importantly, no jobs. These were discouraging circumstances for a young couple wanting no more than each other and an opportunity to be happily married and build a strong, successful future together.

After a very restless winter night, Millard was on his way to see Flora. It was a chilly day, but the weather bothered him little. This could be the most important day of his life. *How many times I have walked this road*, he thought as he walked along at a steady pace. He had never actually measured the distance from Flora's home to his own across the line in Fox County. He was certain it was at least ten miles, maybe more. He walked it more often now since the only place he could see Flora was at her home. The thought made him glad he had made a firm decision to ask her hand in marriage.

Most of his life, walking had made him thoughtful, and now his mind filled with his earlier decision to abandon the traditional mountain existence and make for himself a quality life—one filled with the finer things of life. How wonderful that would be with Flora at his side encouraging him and helping him along. *Perhaps a couple of children might be a good thing as well*, he thought. That idea brought a faint smile to his face. He had never thought much about having children of his own. But he quickly decided to put that consideration aside until his plans for the life he was slowly forming in his mind were fully in place. If only he could put an end to the constant walking without rest, it would be a wonderful achievement. His dad always kept one or two horses, but for some peculiar reason, he would only allow them to be used for work. He would not loan them for riding, except in cases of emergency. "One day, I will own a fine automobile," he murmured to himself. He could now see Flora's home.

He reminded himself of his primary purpose for coming to see her this evening. Several times he had practiced what to say, but it had not seemed to come out right. The practiced proposal made him feel a little foolish. Finally, he decided to just relax and let the words flow normally, straight from the heart.

Millard arrived at Flora's at just the right time again. The family was sitting down to supper, and he was quickly invited. How nice! Pleasant, relaxed conversation and tasty food. Who could ask for more after such a long walk?

After supper, Millard thanked the family for the good meal and then went to the parlor. As he sat down by the warm fire, he felt especially happy. He was near the woman he loved and, even more so, a family he had grown to love.

When Flora came into the room, she noticed something different about Millard. He was not aware that he was acting differently, but she sensed a difference in him as she placed her hand in his. They were rough hands, hands with scars and calluses representing years of hard work—hands she loved and could recognize by slight touch. She knew he had something on his mind that he was not ready to discuss.

They just sat quietly for a while, enjoying the closeness and the pleasant sound of the crackling fire.

Finally, he said, "Flora, will you marry me?"

She had not expected a proposal at that time. What should her answer be?

He sat quietly, patiently awaiting an answer. Millard looked into her eyes and said, "I love you, Flora, and I want you to be my wife."

The glow from the fireplace revealed a handsome, loving, caring man. She knew this was the man she had been waiting for. She knew what her answer would be, but she wanted to be certain to choose the exact words she wanted to say. She was acutely aware that the memory of her words would undoubtedly follow her to her grave. The wall clock ticked off the minutes as she looked around the room.

Strangely, the room looked different, although everything was in place as usual. She had experienced these feelings many times since she was a small girl, and they had always indicated something special or out of the ordinary was about to happen. To her, these feelings were ghostlike feelings. She had never welcomed the feelings and wished they would leave and disturb her no more.

Martha had once said to her, "Honey, witches and warlocks once lived in these mountains. They possessed these powers, but they have gotten weaker with each generation since they came from Germany centuries ago. Many remain here, but their powers are about like ours—slowly diminishing. I think we could revive them if we meditated each day for them to be returned to us." Flora knew her special powers were her own, but she had never before admitted it to herself.

"Yes," she said without further hesitation. It was time she married someone she loved and time she moved out of that house and away from quarreling brothers and sisters.

Millard was delighted to hear her answer so directly and firmly. "Thank you for your answer," he said. "You will always be the love of my life, and I will do for you as best I can. If the future proves to be as I want it to be, we will have a happy life together."

The loving embrace that followed was a lasting seal of their love. Such a glorious feeling Flora felt in her heart.

They sat quietly for a little while thinking of what they had just done. Of course they were not yet married, but she knew there would be no going back on their promise.

Suddenly, the same strange feeling came over Flora again, as it had a short while ago. Her eyes immediately focused on the bed, and she instinctively knew that she would sleep in that bed on her wedding night, but not with her husband. *How can that be?* she thought. Wedding plans were yet to be made, but she did not intend to sleep in that house on her wedding night and certainly not in that bed. Now again, she would have to remove another foolish thought from her mind, as she had done so many times in her life, and enjoy the remainder of the evening.

Then Millard, being the thoughtful man that he was, said, "I think we should speak to your parents of our decision. They have treated me kindly, and I want to treat them honorably as they deserve."

Flora agreed, and Millard stood up as Flora promptly asked Salem and Martha, who usually sat in the kitchen after supper until bedtime, to come into the room.

Soon, they entered the room and sat down. Squirming a little in front of the glowing fire, Millard immediately said, "Me and Flora have decided to get married, and we wanted you to be the first to know. We love each other very much, and we believe our decision to be a good one." Feeling a little shy, he sat down by Flora and gently held her hand. "I think we both would appreciate hearing any opinions you might have."

After a few moments' hesitation, Salem replied, "It's fine with me, but I hope you are certain what you are about. Millard, I believe you to be a fine man, and I wish you both the very best always."

Martha, after several minutes of deep thought, replied, "I know you mean well, but I do not have an easy feeling here." Martha had always been very superstitious and had mental powers few people possessed. Flora understood these powers and knew something was on her mother's mind, but Martha would speak no further. She left the room without further discussion.

Martha's abrupt departure from the room left a little tension for a short while, and then Salem said, "Things will be all right. Martha has always had notions that are not easy to understand. Flora, I see no reason why you should not do as you please."

That was the end of the conversation. Millard and Flora decided to be married as soon as it could be arranged. Flora dismissed the uneasy feeling, knowing it would return at some future time. Her need for spiritual guidance was apparent to her now, and she decided to attend church on Sunday and pray at the altar for things to go well for her and Millard.

The following Sunday found her at the altar of the little Methodist church, just where she wanted to be. She not only prayed for a blessed marriage but also asked God to help her understand the strange feeling and premonitions that had plagued her spirit and aggravated her very soul at times since she was a young girl. A sense of relief surrounded her as she returned to her seat, and the church had become very silent. She was now realizing that these feelings might be from the past as her mother had told her and that they wanted to help her as they had her ancestors of centuries past.

Later, one of her close friends, Sally, approached her and asked, "Why did you tarry so long kneeling at the altar?" She hugged Flora firmly and added, "You seemed to have carried a heavy burden with you and could not let it go."

"It was a heavy concern I took with me, but not a burden. Millard proposed to me last week, and I accepted. I came here today to ask the blessing of my God in whom I have trusted all my life, and I now feel that he is pleased with me."

"What a wonderful deed you have done today," said Sally. "Obviously you feel good about the decisions you made last week. I would welcome the same situation as you are in."

Sally was a very pretty girl with an exceptionally pretty face, enhanced by a lovely smile and white teeth. Her hair was brown, and she usually allowed it to flow loosely over her shoulders. She was about five foot seven, which suited her pretty figure extremely well. "Jackson has been hinting of marriage for some time now. I am sure he intends to ask me to marry him, but he is uncertain about the Depression. And sometimes he is a little shy as well. I hope he doesn't wait too much longer. I'm tired of living with my parents and can't afford to go out on my own.

"Let's keep in touch more often. Maybe when I tell him about you and Millard, it will put a spark in him. I love Jackson very much. He is a good man and tough as nails. He was involved in that fight when our boys and the Jacobs Hollow gang clashed."

"Don't remind me of that horrible incident," Flora said. "What a nightmare that was."

Sally agreed and said, "Anyway, visit me as often as you can, and I will do the same."

"I would like that," Flora remarked. "Perhaps we can get together next weekend. Try playing hard to get and make him a little jealous," Flora said, turning and walking backward so Sally would hear her clearly.

"I might just try that if nothing happens pretty soon," Sally replied.

SIX

The following week proved to be a busy one. The days of November had arrived and were speeding along rapidly, and the nights were getting progressively colder. Everyone was busy harvesting everything that could be saved for winter. Apples, potatoes, turnips, cabbages, and onions were stored in cellar bins. Vegetables not to be eaten soon were canned and placed on shelves. Apple butter was made with great care in big iron pots and then canned and carefully stored to be eaten on buttered biscuits on winter mornings. It was considered a special treat by all and given special attention to prevent any chance of freezing. In some cases, potatoes were buried in large holes, covered with planks of wood, and then covered with dirt piled high over them. When uncovered, usually in midwinter, they were well kept and crisp, just as they were when they were buried.

Two or three fat pigs were killed and the meat cured and stored in a smokehouse. Hogs were easy to raise and inexpensive to feed. They were allowed to roam in surrounding woods to fatten themselves by foraging on wild berries, chestnuts, acorns, roots, and other tasty foods until killing time. Some folks were lucky enough to have a cow or bull to slaughter, but not many were so fortunate. Most livestock were used to provide milk and butter and cheese all year. A few farmers kept bulls for breeding purposes or to sell on the market.

All this processing and labor of growing and providing food could cause one to believe all was well with the mountain folks. Not so! Almost everyone had to watch their food stores and use them sparingly. The food they kept had to last until midspring or later. They had no money to tide them over to better times. People who did not prepare sufficiently were in for difficult winters. The Depression continued to run rampant, as though it would never end. But folks knew what had to be done and responded. Neighbor helped neighbor when different situations and needs presented themselves. If a neighbor borrowed and could not repay, that was all right. Somehow, the mountain folk always succeeded in making the best of everything and thanked God for the earth beneath their feet that sustained them.

Two more weeks passed before Flora and Sally could meet again as they had planned. The fall work could not be delayed, and one week was not sufficient to complete it. They met one day in winter. Flora Holland, Millard Watson, Sally Benson, and Jackson Stamey gathered at Sally's home. They were two very compatible couples. Millard and Jackson were close to the same size and age, with Millard being about an inch taller of the two. Sally was almost as tall as Flora and a little heaver. They had attended the same school for several years. They were, indeed, two handsome couples. They talked and laughed and shared funny happenings of times past.

Millard and Jackson had been friends for many years and that made for an even more enjoyable evening than expected. Jackson was not very shy as Sally had described him. Actually, he owned a guitar and brought it with him. To the tune of his good music, they sang about all the songs they knew and enjoyed every one of them. Their voices blended well too. After some practice, it was obvious their music was pretty darn good.

It was well after midnight before they decided it was time to go their separate ways. Flora had noticed during the evening how well Jackson had reacted to the events of the evening. He could hardly keep his eyes off Sally, and Flora knew he was becoming soft as a ripe blueberry and ready for picking. She knew it would not be long before Sally could expect a proposal from him.

Flora's feelings and predictions concerning matters of the heart were rarely inaccurate. Sure enough, Jackson proposed to Sally sometime during the following week. Soon after the proposal, Sally could wait no longer to tell Flora. She saddled her father's horse and came galloping up the road. "He proposed!" she yelled loudly as she dismounted. "He came to the house yesterday and the first words he said were, 'Will you marry me?' He gave me a ring too. I don't know where he got enough money to afford one, but here it is." It was not one of those fancy gold rings with a diamond on it, but she loved it, and Flora could not have been happier for her.

The two new brides-to-be sat on the porch swing, laughing and talking and looking forward to the future and what it might bring. Sally then mounted her horse and trotted back down the road. She kept turning around and waving at Flora until she was out of sight.

Flora stood for a short while thinking of Sally and Jackson and then returned to the porch swing. She had no strong feeling that all would go well for them. They would live happy lives and have children, but she sensed no more. No mention of a long life for Jackson was there. If only she had some feelings about Millard and her future together, how much happier she would be. Her thoughts were still wandering as she dozed off with the breeze moving the swing ever so slowly.

Millard and Flora had briefly discussed some preliminary plans but had made no final decisions. Jackson had bought a car with money he had borrowed from his father. Millard chanced to meet him soon after he had made the purchase. As they were admiring the nice car, Jackson made a suggestion that Millard liked extremely well. Jackson asked Millard what he thought of him and Flora joining Jackson and Sally and being married by a justice of the peace. "I hate church weddings," he added. "They make me nervous just to attend one."

"I am about of the same mind," Millard replied. "Flora wants to get married in her home church, but since it made little difference to me, I agreed. I think going to a justice of the peace is a good idea, and I thank you for such a kind offer. I believe Flora would have no objections, but I will talk to her about it."

"Sally agreed as soon as I mentioned it," said Jackson.

"I think it will work out very well for us. Let's meet at Flora's next Thursday and make our plans and set a date," Millard replied. "I know it will work out," he continued with excitement in his voice.

Millard and Flora were so grateful for their friends, Jackson Stamey and Sally Benson. On Thursday, they had met at Flora's home and carefully planned the details of their wedding. Millard and Jackson had agreed to call the justice of the peace in Knoxville, Tennessee, the following day and ask him if he would be available on Saturday afternoon to perform the ceremonies.

The justice of the peace assured them he would be there and would be honored to unite both couples in marriage. "Please don't forget your marriage license," he reminded them. "It would not be the first time couples have appeared before me with their legal authority left at home."

"That would be a hell of a note," said Jackson as they drove away from the post office where they had made the call. "We would never live down something like that."

They enjoyed a leisurely drive home after stopping at a bar for a few beers.

In 1929, while the financial world was collapsing, Millard James Watson and Flora Jane Holland prepared to be married. With only common school educations, all the talk of hard times and hunger and starvation did not deter them. With only a few dollars, a few clothes, and very few tangible assets, they were hopeful and anxious to live the rest of their lives together. How incredibly naive they were. With all the negative possibilities staring directly at them, they were confident of a bright future and convinced that their love for each other would make it so.

Flora was somewhat disappointed because of her desire for a church wedding. How wonderful it would be if they could be married in her church as she and Millard had planned. "A selfish thought," she whispered to herself. "I have already asked God to bless our marriage."

The following morning, Jackson picked up Millard to begin the big day. Their night had been one of tossing and turning and dozing and dreaming. They had planned to meet the girls at Flora's home and leave for Knoxville from there. Both men were silent most of the way. Millard could not keep from wondering whether this would prove to be the best day of his life or the worst possible tragedy he could imagine. He suspected Jackson was having similar thoughts.

The time passed quickly, and they soon were moving up the road to Flora's home. Jackson drove near the front gate and stopped the engine. The girls were not out yet, as Millard had predicted. He knew Flora would be certain she had every hair in place and her attire as perfect as it could be.

They did not have to wait long until Flora and Sally came out the door and stood on the porch. Millard and Jackson were speechless as they saw the girls standing there. It was very clear to them how much they were loved by two such beautiful women, who had so diligently prepared themselves for their wedding day. They had no motive other than to look as pretty as they could for the men they loved and wanted to marry.

Leaving was a very eventful occasion. Jackson started down the road with Sally sitting by his side and Millard and Flora sitting very close together in the backseat. Very few words were spoken for a while. It seemed as if they were at a loss for words or could not find the proper words to express themselves. But they were comfortable and happy, and just the quietness of the early morning was welcome and quite sufficient for them.

They were all glad Jackson had bought the car and thankful his father had helped him with the purchase. It was a Buick touring car with four doors and a solid top. The bottom half of the doors were of solid metal, with open tops to allow adequate ventilation. Canvas materials for the tops of the doors were stored inside the car and could be snapped in place in case of inclement weather.

Traffic was very light, and the roads were bad. The scenery was not as beautiful as the high mountains and deep valleys at home. However, the view was much more interesting and exciting when riding in an automobile. The trees and plant life had not had the advantage of the heavy rainfall, which caused them to grow less thick and lush as those in the mountains. The sparse presence of wildflowers was noticeable as well. Almost every village was unique, and in each, the farms and homes had a different appearance. Apparently the first settlers from so many different countries had brought their ways of life, as well as their architecture, with them. Almost all of the homes were constructed of stone, brick, or wood, and the influence of the original builders was apparent. Few homes were of brick or stone in the mountains; most were of logs or board and batten. Sally and Flora were busy pointing out places of interest and rapidly talking about things they had not seen before. They stopped only once that morning, to fill the car with gasoline and eat a light lunch at a small restaurant close by.

As they traveled on toward Knoxville, the land was flatter and the farms much larger. The evidence of poverty was prevalent and worse than it was at home. The cattle and horses were thin, and their ribs protruded from lack of sufficient roughage and grain. The mountain homes, for the most part, were well cared for, and provisions for the animals were adequate. Traffic was not heavy, and many pedestrians walked along the sides of the roads. Many carried sacks of apples and vegetables to be sold wherever possible at the markets in towns along the way toward Knoxville. A few dilapidated, old trucks rolled along with cargoes of hay, corn, sugar cane, and various other items to sell wherever they could find a buyer.

Worst of all was the occasional truck piled high with shabby furniture and belongings of an unfortunate family whose farm had been foreclosed, sitting wherever they could find a place among their goods. Jackson and Millard, having experienced such sights and conditions before knew what to expect, but Flora and Sally had seen nothing to compare with anything like this anyplace before. They began to realize how well they were living back home compared with this.

Sally started crying after a while and asked, "Why did we travel part of the way happy and with high hopes for the future and then all of a sudden we encounter something like this?"

Jackson wanted to clear her disappointment by trying to explain what had happened. "We are sheltered by the high mountains where we know how to live off the land and we own our farms debt free. People who live in and around most of the cities probably lived above their means and placed themselves deeply in debt. When hard times came, many could not make their payments, and their properties have been repossessed. When the banks can't get their money back, they fail and have no money to return to people who have placed money with them to save or invest. Then one thing leads to another, until more and more people get involved and, in many cases, lose all they have. That is what is happening now all over this country.

Eventually, circumstances will improve but it will take many years before we totally recover from this terrible depression. Many in some parts of our mountains are suffering also, and things continue to get worse. It is very complicated, and I do not know all the answers, just a few of them.

"Anyhow, try not to worry. Millard and me will take care of you girls. We wouldn't have brought you over here to be married if we didn't have confidence that we could take care of you."

Sally said, "I know many of these things you have told us from reading about this awful depression, but I just didn't realize things were this bad and moving toward our part of the mountains."

Millard then replied, "From what little I know, these hard times might last for many years, but we just can't stop living. We have to go on with our lives and do the best we can. We have no other choice."

Flora said nothing during the entire conversation. She knew her life would be a series of many things, good and bad.

The foursome traveled on, seeing the sights as they went and discussing their observations. Although they had been introduced to the Depression and the sad circumstances of its devastation in a far worse light than they had seen before, all was not bad. They passed beautiful plantations with elegant homes and fences painted white, enclosing large variations of animals. The barns and outbuildings were also painted and very outstanding. The barns were for housing racehorses who were kept separately from the other farm animals. Jackson commented that some of the horses were raced at the Kentucky Derby and other races and won large sums of money when they finished high in the race. No signs of poverty marked these areas, except on the roads.

"You see," said Millard, "when people inherit large sums of money or somehow are fortunate enough to accumulate large fortunes, they can live like this. When we get farther into the city, you will see even more examples of what wealth can bring. Much of it is ill-gotten gains but not all."

On through the city they traveled, passing rows of shabby, unpainted buildings along ugly dirt streets. Most of them looked very similar—one-story homes with sagging roofs and porches and outhouses out back. Thankfully, they gradually passed on through those unpleasant parts of town before coming to a stop in a beautiful neighborhood at a lovely, well-kept home of Victorian architecture. The many homes within sight were of varying architecture and fantastically beautiful and picturesque. The trees and lawns and shrubs all complemented the homes perfectly.

"Here we are," said Jackson.

Hearts started pounding, and Flora and Sally began patting their hair and smoothing their dresses and doing everything they could to make themselves look their very best.

When the foursome got to the front door, the justice of the peace, Blake Carson, greeting them very graciously and invited them into the parlor where the weddings were to be performed. The room was very tastefully decorated, with a clever mixture of antique and modern furniture. The walls were decorated with oil paintings and family pictures and Civil War memorabilia. The paintings appeared to be from Holland and Germany, with scenes of windmills and bright flower gardens and ponds and streams. After some pleasant conversation, the justice of the peace told them he would proceed with the marriage ceremony as soon as they wished.

His wife, Julie Carson, came into the room and offered to play the piano and sing a wedding song if they so desired. She assured them she delighted in doing so and charged no fee.

They gladly accepted her offer and were not disappointed. She played the piano well and sang the wedding song, "I Love You Truly," beautifully. Tears were visible on Flora's cheek, and surprisingly, Millard was misty-eyed.

The justice of the peace then proceeded with the wedding. Jackson and Sally remained completely composed during the ceremony. Perhaps it was the uncertainty of their future that brought a tender touch to Millard and Flora. Jackson and Sally had a successful future practically in place as their vows were being spoken.

After the vows were spoken, Flora and Sally were held tightly and kissed by their new husbands, and true joy was in the air. They were then invited to sit in the parlor for tea.

After they were seated, Justice Carson said in a very kind tone of voice, "You must keep your vows as you have sworn before God that you will do. If you do, he will bless your lives, and you will do well. I will pray fervently for you before I sleep this night that God will bless the four of you until you depart this life."

They were all moved and appreciative of those kind and wise words that this obviously good man had spoken to them. Flora knew she would keep her vows and hoped Millard and Jackson and Sally would also. *I must attend church in the morning and pray at the altar*, she thought. It would be wonderful if Millard would also, but she knew he would not.

They drove away from that lovely, old house with a grateful feeling for having been married there. If they never returned to that place again, they knew the memories they were taking with them would never fade, and the faces of Blake and Julie Carson were the most important part of those memories.

The time was passing quickly. Driving to their destination and completing the wedding ceremony had taken longer than anticipated. And the wonderful way they'd been treated by the justice of the peace and his gracious wife was more than they had expected. They were very glad they had decided to be married this way. The strong talk and wise council they'd received by Justice Carson exceeded anything they might have expected at a church wedding.

The return trip began much as it had started. They talked very little for a long while. The lights in the city were on. Brightly lit signs and the hustle and bustle of people out for an evening of dining and entertainment were awesome to the newlyweds. Few people could afford such lavish living during these depressed times. The wealth of these city folks was apparent, and one could only speculate on where it came from and how they could spend it so loosely and dress so expensively.

As the foursome departed the city, they stopped for supper at a well-lit, attractive café. Neon signs outside caught their attention, and they were very impressed with the friendly attitude of the waitress who welcomed them with a bright smile and seated them at a table with a nice, soft tablecloth. The clean, attractive interior was especially pleasing to Flora and Sally. They had money enough to afford a nice wedding meal, but both couples knew they could not afford to dine as well as they would have liked. They did, however, take time to enjoy a leisurely meal and their own pleasant conversation. The owner became aware that the four of them had just been married and provided them with a dessert of delicious cherry pie and ice cream. They were most grateful and thanked him for his kindness.

Soon, they stopped for gas and departed for home. They would have preferred to remain in Knoxville for the night and dine and party and lodge at one of the nice hotels, but they could not afford the price. Prices were higher than most places along the way. Gas was even fifteen cents per gallon, and they had spent most of their money on food and gas and the cost of the wedding. But they would not change one thing if they could. They were truly satisfied with the events of the day.

As the lights of the city disappeared behind them and the lamplights and candles began appearing in the windows of houses along the roadway, they marveled at how things were so different in different places. This trip had caused them to start thinking more about how their lives would now be. They were more aware now that things would never be the same for any of them again. They were marvelously happy yet cautiously skeptical about the future. The skepticism came from the failing economy, and they all agreed they probably should have been a little more cautious before taking this giant step in their lives. Yet they had planned as carefully and had exercised as good judgment as they could. All agreed that, even with the uncertainty they were now experiencing, they were happy. As Millard had said when they were planning this wonderful experience, "You just cannot sit down and wait for things to happen. Life must go on no matter what."

On down the road, they continued, their spirits somewhat energized. They were traveling the same roads that had led them from the high mountains to Knoxville. They enjoyed the smooth hum of the engine and talked about the events of the day over and over. They encountered very little traffic after darkness closed in.

Suddenly Sally said in a loud voice, "I do not believe we would have been married on this day or under the same circumstances if Flora and I had not been at church on the same Sunday several weeks ago. After Flora finished her prayers at the altar, I approached her. We began to talk of marriage, and she told me Millard had proposed to her. Well, one event has led to another ever since, and here we all are as married as married can get."

They all had a good laugh at her amusing remarks.

"Honestly," Sally continued in a sincere tone, "there might be something to what I just said. I don't know what Flora was praying about that Sunday, but she seemed very deliberate as she prayed."

"I hope she was praying for us," said Millard. "I am certain we will need the Lord's blessings as our lives move along."

"That was exactly what I was praying about," said Flora. "Even though I had said yes to your proposal, I knew I must go to the altar of my little church and pray for guidance. That has been my way since I was a little girl. Christ has a wonderful way of handling our burdens."

Jackson spoke up. "My mom has always been that way ever since I can remember."

"Now we must go home and immediately begin planning our future, and at this point, Millard and me have not decided exactly where to start. I know we will have a hard future at first, but we will succeed, and our burdens will become lighter as the years pass," Flora said, as though she were making a prediction.

Soon they started up the steep mountains. Jackson began having to change gears more and more often, and the engine was whining and sounding louder. It was a comfort knowing they were riding in such a reliable automobile. They were slowly gaining altitude, and the curves were getting sharper. The drastic changes had not been nearly as obvious to them on their way down.

It was far past midnight when Jackson pulled his magnificent, old car up the long driveway and came to a stop in front of Flora's home. Millard and Flora had decided previously to stay the night at her house due to their anticipated late arrival. Jackson and Sally planned to stay at Sally's house due to the proximity, and Jackson had no desire to drive on to his home, which was over thirty-five miles away.

They had a group hug, and now their wedding day was over. They had formed a relationship that day that they would always cherish and keep with them. Although they were going their separate ways now, Flora knew their paths would cross in unexpected ways all through their lives.

Millard and Flora quietly entered the house and went into the living room. To their displeasure, two of Flora's sisters were sleeping in the bed where they had intended to sleep. Millard whispered to Flora, "What a disappointment this is."

"I know, but what can we do?" she replied. "I thought Mama would keep this room for us tonight. She might have assumed we would lodge somewhere along the way as we returned home."

"Knoxville is a good ways off," Millard replied. "This is one thing we left out in our planning before the wedding. Let's just go to bed and straighten everything out tomorrow. This will do until tomorrow, you know."

They kissed and then settled down for the night.

Millard grudgingly slept on the couch.

SEVEN

The following morning, Flora and Millard were up and ready for a new day and what it would bring. It was the first day of their marriage and a new beginning. A few hours' sleep had done wonders for them. They were young and had recuperated well from the previous day's travel.

After breakfast, they told the family about their wedding day, and then Millard was off to check on a small, furnished house several miles away. The house and farm belonged to a family who had moved away to accept work in a city somewhere up north. When Millard arrived at the house, to his surprise, the family had reoccupied it. Millard had paid them rent in advance, and they did not have the money to repay him. They apologized for not having money they knew he needed. Being a compassionate man, Millard told them the debt was forgiven; by custom, the subject was never to be mentioned again. This was one of the mountain traditions.

Thus, he reversed his direction and returned to Flora. He was worried and didn't know what to do or which way to turn. When he arrived much earlier than expected, Flora knew something was not right with him. Before she could ask, he sat down on the front steps and told her what had happened. Soon, Salem and Martha came out, and Flora told them of their misfortune. Obviously, they had no place and it was day one of their marriage, which made it even worse to them.

Martha felt sorry for them and wanted to help. Their situation made her sad, and she felt deeply moved to do something for the children, as she called them. "Stay here for as long as you want to, even though I know you want to be in your own home at such a time as this." Martha smiled at the newlyweds gently and added, "But it is not the end of the world, you know. You will find adversities all through your married life; Salem and me have. By tomorrow, things might take a turn, and all will be well."

To Flora, her mother's words were comforting. Millard continued to worry and think most of the day.

After supper, they were sitting in the parlor when suddenly he told Flora he might have figured out a temporary solution to their problem. "We could stay with my folks. There are two rooms in the rear of their house that might serve our purpose. They need some fixing up, but with some work, we could live in them for a while."

With Salem and Martha's encouragement, Millard and Flora made their decision. Morning came, and they were anxious to depart to the home where Millard had lived all his life. He was disappointed to lose the house he had rented but happy they had worked out a partial solution to their very urgent problem. Flora noticed he was saddened by the situation they were in and tried to comfort him. "I have never seen where we are going, and I have yet to meet your family," she reminded him.

"This is just a temporary adjustment. We will do just fine!" Millard said.

Martha had rushed about and prepared a very nice breakfast. She also prepared some ham biscuits for them to eat so they could have a nice picnic lunch. It was a long journey to their destination on Birch Creek.

Everyone in the house came out to say good-bye. Flora had to run back into the house several times to get items she had forgotten to pack during the excitement. Finally, off they went in a jerk. Millard had borrowed a small farm wagon and horse from Salem to transport his new wife to their temporary home. The sun was warm and the scenery beautiful. Flora was now leaving the familiar surroundings where she had lived all her life. Only twice had she left Bald Ridge. Her first trip was to Morganton, about forty miles from her home, and the other was to Knoxville to be married.

The mountains were always beautiful, but this was an especially beautiful day. Due to the largest variety of hardwood trees on earth surrendering their leaves until spring, the autumn colors—red, yellow, green, orange, rusty brown, and almost every other color imaginable—were of exceptional splendor. The beautiful colors radiated immensely in the beauty of the day—their special day.

They had traveled only a short distance when Millard began telling his new bride about how things were during his youth and growing up years. As he talked, she could detect the sadness in his voice. "We are now in a depression, and a severe one at that. But in many ways, things were worse during my youth than they are now. You know, one winter I had no shoes. The money was just not there. I tried going barefoot but quickly found that would not do. Finally, I found some burlap sacks and tied them around my feet with twine. That kept my feet warm enough for periods of about fifteen minutes outside, but no more. Later, I got lucky and came upon the shoes I had worn the previous winter. They were too small, but I put them on without lacing them, and that's the way I went until spring. When the weather warmed and I started going barefoot, I noticed a difference in my feet. They still felt cramped, as though the shoes were still on my feet. My feet felt somewhat deformed and short. I wondered if they would ever be normal again, but in a few months, they were normal, except slightly shorter than they probably should be."

Flora looked down at his feet and could see nothing wrong. "There is no need to think of it," she told him. "Every person has something about them that probably makes them feel as you do. I have always thought I was too large and gaudy-looking. Other people, including you, do not seem to think so."

Millard laughed at that remark. "Maybe you are right," he replied.

"You are a very handsome man and my dear husband, and don't you forget it!" she concluded.

Except for the continuous stories Millard told pertaining to his youth, they had little to say during the first part of their trip. At one point, they passed a farm where Millard's friend, Homer Mullins, lived. "When we were dating," he said, "I often stopped there to rest on my way to your house. After resting and drinking a cool glass of water or milk, I could walk at a rapid pace and make it to your house in time for the dance or whatever we had planned. On the return trip, I sometimes began to feel the weight of the day. I would stop there for the night and make it on home the next morning. Homer has always been one of my very best friends. He was always happy for me to stay the night and would sometimes walk home with me the next morning and visit with us the remainder of the weekend. I intend to continue visiting him when possible. Our friendship should always remain strong."

Flora thought of many subjects and memories that she would like to talk about, but she preferred to remain silent. She wanted to think of the pleasant things and save memories, good and bad, for another time. This was another day she would never forget, and she wanted only good things for this special day. Memories of the past could wait until later, at a more appropriate time.

They stopped about midway through their journey to eat the lunch Martha had prepared for them. Millard stopped beside a clear stream—a perfect, scenic, romantic place for a picnic. He unhitched the horse to allow him to drink and rest.

After their picnic, they decided to take a walk down the clear, flowing stream to where it emptied into Piney River. There it merged with the tranquil river and continued on to a distant lake. They marveled at the beauty of the place. Giant, stately-looking oak; maple; and chestnut trees stationed themselves about, enhanced by a large variety of smaller trees and shrubs seemingly placed there by the hands of a master landscape artist. Fish splashed about catching insects, birds called from far and near, and a deer cautiously ventured down to drink. A beaver was very busy cutting down a birch tree to shore up his dam on a smaller stream close by and store away food before winter set in. A flock of wild geese in their familiar V-shaped formation glided downstream just above treetop level.

Flora and Millard moved closer to each other and embraced ever so tenderly. They could not stop until they had slowly moved away from the river to a soft, grassy area where the warm sun was shining through the trees. They had not planned such a spontaneous move, but it was glorious and almost indescribable. There and then, with the autumn leaves slowly sprinkling down, they consummated their marriage. It was a perfect experience of love with no thought of embarrassment, and they would cherish this memory always. Circumstances had prevented their marriage consummation in a more traditional way, but this was no less holy and right to them. They were happy it had happened that way, close to God's creation and nature. Flora was certain it met God's approval.

They slowly continued their journey onward, enjoying every moment of the day. Suddenly, Millard stopped the wagon at a point overlooking a magnificently beautiful valley. Below could be seen a farmhouse surrounded by a barn and several smaller buildings. A creek flowed beside the road, which extended along the valley floor. Cattle and horses grazed in a meadow near the barn. In the distance, she could see a beautiful log church with a cemetery nearby.

Millard turned to Flora and said, "Down there is where I was born and grew to the man you are now married to. I hunted those woods, fished the creeks and rivers, and farmed just about every foot of land you see below here. What you see does not show the entire farm. Up the mountain to the right and behind the trees, there is a large field. We allow the animals to graze half of the field and cut most of our winter hay from the other half."

Flora was curious about the church and cemetery. She asked, "Is that where you attend church?"

"Yes," he answered, "and most of my ancestors are buried there."

"It appears to be very old," she commented.

"I don't know how old it is, but the dates on the tombstones go way back. Some graves have no stones, and people buried there have long since been forgotten. Ma promised to tell me many things about the church and cemetery, but she never has. She will get around to it one day. She does not forget promises."

"I would like to be with you when she does," said Flora. "This beautiful valley and your family farm will do just fine for now, and I am happy we decided to come here."

They sat in the wagon for a long while and then slowly moved on down into the valley. The wagon squeaked as Millard pulled on the brake lever to help slow the pace. They were in no hurry. This had been a perfect day indeed, and they were not anxious for it to end. So many changes had occurred in their lives lately, and with the passing of each change, Flora knew their lives could never be the same again. They moved along in silence, their minds wandering in different directions.

Millard was wondering if he could keep the promises he had made before their marriage. He had expected times to improve, but they were continually getting worse. He was starting a new life with a wonderful woman and an uncertain future. He did have notions that had been brewing inside of him for some time now, but those notions must be delayed. He knew he must find ways to make things better for Flora and him. He felt himself losing the confidence he had felt during their courtship, but he was determined not to allow such thoughts to interfere with this day of wonderful memories. He quickly turned his thoughts to the present and to presenting his new wife to his family. This was indeed a good day, and he, at least for now, was exceedingly happy.

Flora, quite to the contrary, had unintentionally allowed her thoughts to revert back into the past to her first memories. Everyone on the farm had been required to do a share of the farmwork. Even at age four, she'd carried water in a small lard bucket from the spring below the house. Filling a larger bucket for the family drinking water had taken many trips. On wash days, she'd had to make enough trips to fill three tubs so the older members of the family could wash their clothes. Lucky for her, most of the family members wore their clothes until they were well soiled. Martha said the men would not wash their clothes until they could stand alone if she did not put her foot down. That thought made her Flora smile.

Suddenly, she was aware of her foolish past reflections at such at time as this. She quickly pulled her thoughts together. They were almost home now, and she began talking again. "How happy I am to reach home but how sad I am for this day to end," she told Millard.

Millard replied, "I am not anxious for this special day of ours to end either, but it is not quite over; just our time alone together has ended for today. Just think of the many days we have before us. You will meet my family now, and we will have supper and sit by the fire. There is a chill in the air now, and Dad will be lighting a fire before long."

When they arrived at the house, Flora was somewhat surprised. Five family members were there to greet them. They all stood in the yard as if they had been expecting them to arrive any minute. "How can this be?" Flora said in a low voice. "We had not planned this at all."

"Don't worry; everything will turn out well," he said.

The family greeted her and Millard cordially, but Flora felt slightly uneasy. Counting herself and Millard, seven people would be living in that house. Fortunately, as the younger children came along, the older children were leaving home to find work or get married, thus making a more even occupancy.

Flora was very pleased to meet the members of the household. Lewis Giles was the youngest and was an adopted child. Both of his parents had passed away when he was very young. He was in poor health but seemed rather happy in his own way. Flora later learned that he had a rare kind of crippling arthritis. His face looked haggard and stressed, apparently from the pain he had endured most of his life. Millard's brother, Lee, was next. He was a handsome young man of seventeen years.

Luther Watson, Millard's father, was a large man who appeared to be easygoing. Everyone called him Dad. His quaint smile revealed his kind nature. Flora liked him immediately. Sarah Louise Watson, called Ma by all, was a petite woman with keen, dark eyes and a very intelligent look. Her quick wit was obvious, and it was apparent to Flora that she was the dominant one of the family.

The senior member of the house was Susan E. Mason, mother of Sarah. Flora later learned that she had been the owner of the farm until she'd deeded it over to Luther and Sarah. By an unwritten, established agreement, she would live there and receive care as needed by Luther and Sarah for the remainder of her years. Such agreements were common practice in those times. It was an agreement of love and trust and worked remarkably well.

EIGHT

Fortunately, in spite of the awkward circumstances, Millard and Flora were somewhat better off than they might have been otherwise. The two small rooms located in the rear section of the house cleaned up extremely well. The bedroom accommodated one bed, two chairs, and one small window. The other room served as a kitchen, with a wood burning cooking stove, a chest with two sections where meal and flower were stored and a lid that fit tightly to prevent insect infestation. Millard and Flora were well pleased to occupy the rooms.

Millard had never vaguely considered living there. He thought things were in hand when he rented the cottage on Birch Creek. But his father and mother, being wise and farsighted, had considered the problems and consequences the newlyweds might encounter during this special time in their lives. They had been thinking of patching up those two rooms for unexpected company and immediately agreed to wait no longer to complete the task at hand. A few days later when they saw a horse and wagon creeping down the hill with Millard and his new bride, they were happy they had a place for them.

After meeting the family and entering the house for the first time, Flora felt less comfortable and a bit strange. Something was not as it should be, and she was aware of it. The farm looked normal for the times, and nothing seemed out of place. Yet, it made her stop and think for a moment.

She quickly dismissed the feeling when Ma said, "Come in, child, and rest from your tiresome journey. You must be worn out. Wagons are rough traveling. Every time I ride in one, I feel shook to pieces after the trip. We will have supper, and you can go to bed as soon as you wish."

After supper she and Millard had an enjoyable visit with the family. It was a very pleasant time, and as Millard had predicted earlier, Dad had lit a nice, warm fire in the fireplace.

Flora and Millard retired to their quarters later than they intended and immediately went to bed. As she started feeling sleepy, she experienced the nervous, anxious feeling she'd encountered upon entering the house earlier. Actually, these feelings were somewhat different from the premonitions she had experienced since childhood. She attempted to discuss her feelings with Millard, but he was unconcerned. He suggested she was imagining things brought about by the events of the day. She accepted his explanation but not completely. She had learned long ago from her mother not to dismiss strong feelings, especially if they persisted. She was tired, however, and allowed the feelings to drift away, and soon sleep was the victor.

The next day in her new home, Flora adjusted quite well and set about fixing and arranging things in their small quarters as best she could. She had no funds to buy things to decorate as she would have liked.

Millard went searching for work but returned with a sad face and no news of success. They ate supper quietly that evening. This was the first meal she had prepared for him. Pinto beans, cornbread, buttermilk, and fatback meat was all they had. She had prepared many meager meals before, but she felt sad that she did not have better for him after a stressful day. She prepared everything she had, however, as tasty as possible for him. She rolled the fatback meat in flower and fried it nice and crisp.

She could not tell how he had appreciated her efforts until he looked across the table at her and smiled. "This is a very nice supper," he said. "It is prepared just the way I like it, especially the fatback. I believe I will have another piece of cornbread and another glass of buttermilk too."

He would never know how well his kind words had made her feel. She was delighted with the meal turning out so well and making his day a little easier. She ate very little herself. It was enough for her just to sit and watch him.

After supper, they talked for a long while, mostly about the details of their day. Suddenly, Millard said, "What have you done with this place? It looks different but very nice."

She knew she had not done very much, but the fact that he had noticed was rewarding to her. He then noted that it would be a good time to get better acquainted with the family and suggested they go into the living room.

Dad had his usual fire going, and the warmth of the fire and interesting conversation proved quite enjoyable. They discussed several subjects, most of which had to do with family history and past traditions. Flora said very little during the course of the evening. She purposefully decided to use this time to learn about and assess the family members.

When she looked at Lewis closely, he looked very tired. She was concerned about him. Her intuition told her that he would die at an early age, probably within the next few years. Lee was rather difficult to read, except that he would be married soon and he would fight in a war. Dad seemed lighthearted and happy, but she detected something in his past that had caused him considerable mental anguish to this day. Ma was very hard to understand. She had a very complicated mind. She also had a bothersome past, but her situation was of her own making.

Grandma was different from all the others. She had been a good woman all her life, which extended back to 1843. Her memories occupied most of her time. She was, by no means demented, which Flora could easily determine as the fire reflected the older woman's pale face vividly, and in her slow, crackling voice, she participated in the conversation very well.

The mental listening-in on the lives of the family was unintentional, as she had not ever wanted to use her mental powers in this way. Even so, on this rare occasion, it had helped her understand her new family and be of help to them in the future.

The family had already stayed up much longer than usual. Flora was mentally fatigued and nudged Millard to remind him of the lateness of the hour. They banked the fire and all went to bed.

After they were in bed, Flora was immediately aware of the strange anxious feelings that had plagued her before, only worse. She heard chattering, unintelligible voices. A vibrating, tingling sensation seemed to cling to her body. And most frightening of all were bright lights everywhere yet nowhere. Then everything returned to normal, just as though nothing has occurred.

After Millard was asleep, Flora quietly got out of bed and looked out both windows. The kitchen window faced the outhouse located near the woods about fifty yards away. She saw nothing unusual there. The bedroom window faced north and up the mountain—the source of something unknown. She heard sounds she had never heard before, and a bright light was shining somewhere up there. One thing was certain; powers far greater than she could ever imagine under any circumstances existed on that mountain.

She watched the light for about thirty minutes and then returned to bed. Millard was restless, and she did not want to wake him. She slept the remainder of the night, but her sleep was restless and uneasy. She awoke abruptly, her mind racing and her ears ringing. *This cannot continue*, she thought. Or maybe it would, and she too could learn to accept the strange phenomenon as the other members of the household apparently had.

She wondered if she would ever know. Others living on that farm very well could have no awareness that they were not living alone here. She knew she had special powers like her mother and could perceive things that others were not aware of. She was uncertain if it would be wise to pursue the matter any further. One thing she was certain of was that she had considered these thoughts enough, and now she must busy herself with being a good wife and helping her husband and the family. The task before her would be difficult. Temporarily, other things of less importance must be put aside until a more convenient time.

NINE

Millard and Flora had been living in their present quarters for one year, and their marriage remained rock solid. They were well aware of the swift passage of time and how little they had accomplished. Their financial and living circumstances were at a standstill with no progress in sight. They had expected much more by now.

Flora diligently helped with the very important farmwork while preparing for the birth of their first child. She had become pregnant less than three months after their marriage and as time permitted, busied herself with making clothes for herself and the coming child. Millard's clothing always needed mending. They could not afford to buy new clothes for him. Obtaining thread for mending things was difficult. It was patch upon patch, but her hopes of doing better remained firm.

Flora enjoyed her present life much of the time in spite of the dreadful situation in which she found herself. She and Millard remained very disappointed with their progress, however. They talked often about their situation and how long they must endure before they could manage to improve their lot. Moving to a city was no option. Lee owned a radio powered by a dry-cell battery, and when it worked, about all they could hear was about the hard times and suffering of the poor. They reasoned that they must remain where they were for the present time and hold firmly to their hopes for the future. They remained convinced that their lives would improve in the near future, and they were determined to make the most of each situation before them.

Their love for each other remained deep and abiding, and that was of great comfort. Millard worked wherever and whenever he could find a job, no matter how small. Fifty cents a day was the maximum pay he could expect to receive.

The stress of not having the adequate necessities of life gradually began affecting their marriage. Living in that household with so little privacy was slowly becoming intolerable. They were snapping at each other at times, which was not characteristic of their lives together.

In addition, the abnormal activities occurring on top of the mountain were causing Flora to become increasingly irritated. She was now completely convinced that everyone in that house was totally oblivious to the occurrences and only she had this knowledge because of her intuitive abilities. Again, these abilities were becoming more of a curse than a blessing, but her mother had told her many times that there was a reason for most things and the reason for this special ability would be revealed to her at the proper time. She had decided not to mention the hellish activities on the mountain or her special abilities unless by some miracle she should meet a person who understood. Perhaps God had a plan for her and would intervene. She always believed that was her refuge and her strength and, in the final analysis, would never fail her.

About a month before their child was born, Millard took Flora to her parents' home, where Martha could see to her needs. He felt she would be well cared for there, and he had noticed that Martha and Flora seemed to harbor a special relationship. The services of a physician were out of the question. Salem had told Millard that Martha was very competent in matters such as childbirth and knew many remedies and manipulations often necessary during deliveries.

Flora gave birth to a very normal baby boy soon after she arrived at her parents' home. They named him Cameron Lee Watson.

Flora returned home to the farm shortly after delivery to continue her life—a life of many disappointments. The crowded rooms where they lived began closing in on her. Despite her obvious depression, she still held on to all she had—her husband and her precious child. The mutual love and respect for each other remained strong, but signs of problems were gathering on the horizon of their lives. This was evident to both of them, and they discussed the issues at length with sincerity.

They concluded that no consideration mattered beyond enriching their marriage. They agreed to keep searching for ways to improve their lives. After Cameron was born, conditions worsened, although he brought immense joy to their lives. He cried a lot, possibly for good reason. He was a bright, lovely child and, even at such an early age, seemed to sense the unpleasant atmosphere brought about by the crowded situation in their home. Two rooms were no longer enough. Other family members would sometimes enter their quarters without knocking. Flora came to resent such intrusions and would speak harshly to them at times. Afterward, she would feel sorry for her actions.

On one occasion, the unexplainable strange activities on top of the mountain stopped for a month or more. When they returned, she knew she would have to take some action or leave the farm entirely. The only person in whom she might confide was Dad. Given the kindhearted, warm person he was, she decided to chance an open discussion with him. They had talked before, and he had always given her good advice.

One day, they were talking and he made a remark about the mountain above the house. She was glad he had opened the subject. "Who owns that mountain?" she asked.

"It is a part of this farm, but there have been so many unusual occurrences up there over the years that we just stopped going up there very often, except to tend a garden or mow hay or do other jobs involving the upkeep of our farm. There is a house up there that used to belong to Joe and Ethel Wise. One night, someone shot them both dead. They were buried without anyone ever looking into the case. Once in a while, I quietly walk up there through the woods, just to see if I can discover what is going on. The door of the house is unlocked, and everything in the house remains in order."

Dad's eyes lingered on the mountains for a moment, and then he looked away, seeming lost. After a while, he turned to Flora and, as if he had come to a decision, took a deep breath, and said in a low voice, "Several times, I have seen strange-looking men walking about up on the upper edge of the field above the house."

"What did the strange-looking men look like?" Flora asked.

"They are short and skinny, with large eyes and small noses and small mouths. Their heads look like they have been shaved," Dad replied. "I do not confront them, and they show little interest in me."

"Did you ever suspect the strange men as being guilty of the murders?"

"At first I did, but no more," he answered. "Murder is not their reason for being here; what is under our soil is where their interest lies." After a long pause, as though he did not wish to continue, he looked into Flora's eyes, causing her to wonder if he was afraid she might come too harm. "Do not venture up there alone is my advice to you, but if you should decide to, ask me, and I will go with you. It is a beautiful place with a view for miles in every direction."

"Why do you not take charge of your own property?" she asked.

"Well," he said with a sigh, "I could stir up a mess, I reckon, but to me, it just ain't worth it.

"At one time many years ago, I farmed that large field up there and pastured cattle between crops. It was a very quiet place, and I enjoyed being up there. Even the livestock seemed to enjoy being there. They would go up there every day that I did not have the fence closed to keep them out of the crops.

"I don't remember exactly what year it was, but everything changed up there. It was no longer a peaceful place, and I came to dread the days I needed to go up there. Even the cows hesitated to go up there. On the days I worked the crops, I would toss in bed all night and sometimes wake up in a cold sweat. No one in this family ever mentioned anything unusual about the mountain, and none of the neighbors down the creek have every said one word. They were all free to go up there as they wished. I know why I don't venture up there, but I have no notion as to why they remain at a distance."

Dad sat silent for a moment, as if wondering if he should continue, and then said, "I wanted to caution you about that old mountain when you first came here, but I did not want to worry you."

"I wish you had," she replied. "It would have been a comfort to me."

"You seemed to be uneasy about this place when you first came. After considering the situation, I decided it best to remain silent. To my knowledge, no one has been harmed up there, other than the two killings. I should have inquired to someone in authority, especially about the murders, but I never did. I attended the funeral. Family and friends were there, but I heard practically no mention of the fact that both people in them caskets had been murdered. Strangest thing I ever witnessed. I felt guilty about my silence but kept easing my mind by considering the house was not on my property. I own almost all the land up there but not the upper section where the house is located.

"The law never did take any action on the case, and the relatives made no complaints. They live far on the other side of the mountain, and I have never talked to them very much. I now believe a conspiracy was involved somehow, and evil decisions were probably made by people in authority and even the family."

"Have you observed the lights and noises at night?" Flora asked with noticeable anxiety in her voice.

"Yes, I know about them too," Dad said with a nod. "Strange lights have been observed across the Blue Ridges since the first settlers arrived, and the Cherokee Indians before them told the same stories. I know nothing of the noises you speak of, though," he added.

She explained the noises to him, and he was amazed that she was the only person he had ever heard tell of such sounds. She did not tell him of her intuitive abilities, which involved both sight and sound. She had heard Martha talk of seeing strange lights, but she did not recall her tell of hearing strange noises.

Dad paused for a moment and then said, "I have a feeling that all of this stuff might have something to do with the enormous amounts of minerals and precious stones and rare deposits that lie beneath the surface of these mountains and cannot be found other places. It must be of great importance to cause so much activity. I have heard stories all my life of strange happenings along these Blue Ridge Mountains, mostly where large deposits of minerals are known to be located far down in the earth. Some say strange people mine deep in the earth at night and make every effort to prevent exposure of what they are about. I don't believe they intend to harm us, or they would already have done something. They could swipe us away like flies if they chose to do so. I don't know what else to tell you to ease your mind except, try to accept things as they are. There is certainly nothing we can do about any of it. It might help you to know that the sightings completely disappear for long periods of time."

Flora decided to allow the matter to rest. She thought that she could accept things as they were now that Dad had shared his knowledge with her. Dad had a common school education, and he was a very wise man. In his day, a common school education—usually about four years with three months being equal to one year—was considered better than most. Flora considered that he had learned much in those four years.

★ ★ ★

Another year passed before Millard and Flora moved from that household. Millard had not held a steady job since they'd married. He had tried so hard to find gainful employment, but there just was nothing available lasting more than one or sometimes two days. It was not unusual for him to rise early and walk long distances just for a few hours' work. His failing pride was constantly pressing him to move on.

One day, he decided to try putting an end to what he felt was a ridiculous and unending situation. He could no longer endure living as he was, and he knew Flora felt the same way. It looked to him as though this damned depression would never end. His mind was set.

The following morning, with his mind in a whirl, he started walking down the road. He had absolutely no idea where he was going. As the sad, lonely, forsaken feeling began to subside and his mind began to clear, he knew he must find his compass and set a course, any course. His first clear thoughts persuaded him to seek shelter. This he would attempt to do first, and then he'd follow with the next step—any step indicating a forward move.

He began looking for a house, with the idea in mind that he would keep on walking until he found one. Many miles down the road, he noticed an empty cabin. It was ugly but appeared structurally sound with a tin roof. Strangely enough, it was much like the small cottage he had rented for Flora and him to occupy after they were married.

Millard knew the owner of the house he had just spotted and immediately went to inquire about it. He was very lucky that morning. The owner permitted Millard and his family to live in the house just to have it occupied. Empty houses just didn't last long, especially beside a creek where it was shady and damp most of the time. Mr. Bowman, the owner, offered to charge no rent if Millard would take reasonable care of the place. Millard thanked Mr. Bowman very kindly and assured him he would take very good care of the house and would help him with his farm chores whenever possible.

Millard had done well that day and decided to return home.

By the time he finally arrived, Flora had become very worried about him. She had noticed his attitude before he'd left that morning. "You did not behave normally this morning," she said. "You seemed to be disturbed about things."

"I know," Millard replied. "I felt absolutely compelled to do something to improve our lives, and I had no intention of returning until I had caused something to happen for the better. My mood changed after walking awhile, and the morning air cleared my head. You will be pleased to know that I found a house for us, and rent free at that. I can't talk any more now; just be happy and let's go to bed."

She was happy indeed. Millard immediately began snoring, something he seldom did unless he was totally exhausted. She also went to sleep shortly after.

Nothing disturbed her until morning. Millard slept well, and she was thankful. He knew she wanted to hear the happy news he had saved until morning. He told her about the events of the previous day, and she was delighted. Maybe it was the first step to an improved life for them. After hurriedly eating breakfast, they set about making plans about what they should do next and how to proceed with what must be done.

They decided the first thing they should do was to discuss the matter with other members of the family. They wanted to leave soon but not without showing their respect to the family and seeking their counsel and advice. They had all lived under the same roof for over two years. It was now 1932, and they wanted the family to always be a part of their lives.

Two years had helped Millard and Flora mature in their thinking and attitude. They were now aware that much of the stress in the family who had provided them with shelter and safety during the first two years of marriage was caused by their presence there. Flora had learned to appreciate the family and loved them all. She was most concerned about Lewis. She had seen no improvement in his condition. He was steadily getting worse, as she had known he would.

Lee was getting married soon to a lovely girl, who also lived on Birch Creek. They planned to live in a house provided by her father, who was well off by the standards of the times.

Dad had changed little, except that he was even more gentle and kind and loving than ever. God had surely blessed her life by allowing her to know him. She did wish he would lose some weight though. He was far too heavy, and most of the weight gain was around his waist. She feared he would eventually suffer ill health because of it.

Ma was still Ma. She would probably never change, but Flora had learned to love her without reservation. Flora sometimes regretted talking harshly to her. She would let bygones remain as bygones and always be kind and respectful to her.

Grandma Mason seemed very sad at their departing. Flora loved her so very much, and she knew that, by the laws of nature, Grandma probably would not live many more years. She was in her late nineties then. Flora could not forget those nights when the family had sat by the fireplace and Grandma would always sit to the side of the fire so it reflected her pale, wrinkled face. It was a truly lovely face and one not to be forgotten by all those fortunate enough to know her.

Flora could not and had no desire to wipe away the memories of the past two years. Even though they would never live in the family home again, they would return for visits regularly, and she knew they would always be welcome there. The old place would always remain clearly etched in her mind.

It had been two days since Millard had found a home for them. They had thought departing would be a joyous occasion, but it was not at all what they'd expected. With their meager belongings on board the wagon, they began their journey to their home.

Flora turned to wave at the family. They looked so sad, just quietly standing there.

Cameron could not understand why they were leaving. Flora tried to explain the reasons as best she could, and he seemed to understand some of what she had to say. He was such a beautiful little boy. He was a joy to them and was the center of attention much of the time. He smiled broadly when his father promised to take him fishing in the creek when he got a little older.

They plodded along slowly down the very scenic road, talking excitedly and enjoying every minute of their travel. After a time, they settled down into some quiet thought. Cameron had fallen asleep on his mother's lap. She covered him lovingly with her shawl and held him close.

Millard soon found himself in deep thought. He hoped he had made a wise decision in moving away from his old home. Times were very hard, and nothing seemed to turn out well for him. If only he could find encouragement in just one of his endeavors, it would be of great significance. His hopes had been fading for some time now, but he was determined to make success out of something and never admit failure to anyone, not even Flora. He had not forgotten his ambitions and hopes and the dreams he'd conjured up in his mind while walking the many miles when he was dating Flora. He had not abandoned these dreams and had no intention of doing so. He had made no specific plans, but he was constantly reading and thinking about many subjects and talking to knowledgeable people who had made their lives a success. New ideas were building in his mind, and his determination would be equal to the talk once he discovered the right opportunity.

As they rode alone in the rough, rolling wagon, Flora began to reflect back to her home and family on Bald Ridge. She had only been back once since she left, and that was to give birth to Cameron. She felt a sense of sorrow that she had stayed away so long.

As the shadows were falling, they finally reached their destination. They were sore from the rough ride caused by the smooth, rounded rocks washed onto the road during stormy weather and floods such as had occurred last spring. As they rounded a curve in the road, there was the house sitting beside the stream.

"There is our new home," Millard called out in a loud voice. "It don't look like much now, but we will have it in fine shape in a few days."

"I certainly hope so," Flora mumbled to herself. She had seen many barns that looked more inviting. Moss grew on the roof of the small house, and vines covered most of its outer walls. The front porch looked solid, but the front steps looked as though they might fall down at any time.

The family descended from the wagon and began moving in. Flora would have much preferred cleaning the place up first, but she had to make do, at least until tomorrow. She swept the floor in one room and made a quilt pallet. The three snuggled close and slept quite well.

They were up at the break of dawn the following morning. Millard knew he must find work and find it soon. They had only one dollar and enough food in the house to last for a few days at most. He had heard rumors about a large mica mine several miles away that would be hiring soon. He walked very briskly without rest, hoping he would get there early enough to be hired. When he arrived at the jobsite, several company men were in the office, but none would confirm the hiring rumor. He sat down by the front door and waited.

At the house, Flora worked feverishly to clean the place and put things in some kind of order. She carefully arranged the few furnishings they had to show the cabin to its most favorable advantage. They'd brought the table and chairs and the tightly built chest for flour and meal and a cooking stove that Ma had given them. The other room furniture consisted of two beds, a small floor rug, and a few assorted wooden chairs.

They had no heating stove, but fortunately there was a small one that looked very functional already in the house. One chest of drawers and one mirrored dresser with drawers filled out the room, making it look much better than she had expected.

Now came her most difficult challenge, and her job would be complete. She could never abide a house with no curtains or something to cover the windows. She had none, but after some thought, she found some cow feed sacks she had saved with the idea of making herself a dress. They were made out of the traditional printed material. Flora found barely enough to cover the windows. She had no thread among their belongings, but she did find some small tacks and a hammer. She cut the material to size and tacked them carefully to the top of the windows. Again, she was pleasantly surprised. They looked rather nice and dressy she thought. At least she could live in the house without feeling that someone was peeping in.

Flora had worked so hard that day, she was not aware of how quickly the day was passing. Working inside and keeping watch on Cameron outside made the day very tiring, and she still had supper to prepare.

Darkness was now rapidly approaching, and Flora was becoming concerned that Millard was not yet home. Usually he was home much earlier, unless he had found some work that day. Soon she could see him coming down the road. He was walking slowly and appeared tired. When he got close enough, though, she had seldom seen him with such a pleasant smile on his face. She knew he had found a job.

He gave her and Cameron a big hug and told them of the good news. His wait at the company office had paid off. They were hiring, and he was the first in line. He worked all day and was as happy as a man could be.

She knew he was very hungry and immediately put supper on the table. He ate heartily and was so happy it brought tears to her eyes.

He told her that the mica company had received a large order; enough to keep the mine open for three to six months. "If it stays open only three months, it would be wonderful. Six months would put us in a financial position we have never experienced before, and it would permit me to take advantage of other opportunities before the mine closes again. I am anxious to move on to bigger and better things I know will come about sooner or later."

Flora listened intently. She knew his ambitions were high, and she would not discourage him. She believed what he said was true, but she thought he would have to wait a while longer.

This had been a good day, and they went to bed happy.

The following morning, Millard was up at five o'clock after dreaming about his new job all through the night. Flora quickly prepared breakfast for him, and he was off. She felt sorry for him that first day on the job. He must walk the entire distance to the mine, and he dared not chance being late. Many other men were waiting for any vacancies, and Millard knew that lateness, even once, would not be tolerated by the company. He thought that he might arrange a ride with one of the very few men fortunate enough to own an automobile.

Sure enough, he met a man who lived not far from Birch Creek and owned an old Model T Ford. The man agreed to provide him a ride to and from work for five cents per day. Millard could hardly afford the price, but he also knew he could not hold up to walking such a long distance every day over a long period of time.

Several days passed, and a normal routine began to develop. Flora was looking forward to taking a small amount of money each week to buy essentials for making new clothing for the family. All their clothes were so worn and threadbare that Flora knew they were too thin to last much longer.

Cameron had adjusted to the new home and spent much of his time playing near the creek. At last, things were going well for the Watson family.

* * *

After a few weeks, Millard was off to work as usual. It was a routine day until he returned home in the evening. Flora knew something was wrong as soon as he came through the door. The sadness in his face told the story. He had been laid off indefinitely. The company had lost its large order and could no longer afford to remain open. The company that had placed the large order had gone bankrupt.

Finally Millard said, "I don't think I can take this anymore. I have no way of caring for you and Cameron. If it wasn't for this damned Depression Hoover started, we would be doing well. Maybe you should take Cameron and go live with your folks until things open up around here or I can figure out something. We can't go on like this; something has to change. It might take a while, even months, but I am tired of this, and I intend to make something work out for us. You and Cameron do not deserve this kind of life, and sooner or later, I will make our family prosperous and happy."

Millard could not brush away the memories he was now having of the many times he walked from his house up that long, dusty road to court Flora. He remembered the many promises he made to himself to press onward with his life and depart from mountain traditions and the acceptance of poverty. He would be a man of wealth and distinction, just as he had seen others more fortunate than him previously do. He had not reviewed those thoughts very often since that period of time, but he was aware the thoughts were there waiting to persuade him to fulfill his ambitions. He had been entirely engrossed in trying to just exist and support his family. But he knew there was a formula for success that would work for him, just as he had seen it work for others. He had always wondered why such a divide existed between the rich and the poor. A middle ground should exist somewhere, but he knew it didn't and doubted it ever would. He was determined to take the high ground. Life was not fair, and for most of his life, he had accepted that cliché, but no more. He would force life to be fair for his family. All hell would not keep him from his objective.

Flora had been sitting quietly in the living room, feeling sad and hoping Millard would open up to her so they could discuss their worsening situation together. She could understand why he was deep in thought and low in spirit. He loved them and did not know what to do next. She was beginning to worry about him, though. He was more in a trance than mere thought, and she wanted him to stop. His behavior was different, especially at times when he felt worried or uncertain about circumstances he considered beyond his control. She had been aware of that part of him since they first met. She remembered considering the fact that he might be capable of drastic action when pushed too far. He was being pushed too far now from a socioeconomic point of view, and she was reasonably certain of that fact. She loved him and respected him and harbored no fear of his actions.

Finally, she spoke, talking as if she was not aware of his trancelike state. She was not sure he realized he had been quiet for so long. "I know I would be welcome, but I just can't return to my parents' under such circumstances. When we left there, I made a promise to myself that I would never return to live there again. They are not doing well during these times themselves. I noticed how things were deteriorating the last time I took Cameron up there for a visit. No! I just cannot do as you want," she told him. "We will not leave here until we can leave together. I married you for better or for worse, and I refuse to leave you here alone because things are worse."

Millard was no longer in a trance and had heard what Flora had said. "If only we had sufficient food to last for a few weeks maybe, I would feel better about the three of us remaining here awhile longer but not much longer," he replied. "We can't go on like this, and you know that as well as me. I intend to end this perpetual torment; I just need more time."

Flora could see he was brokenhearted and suggested they go to bed and continue their discussion in the morning. They quietly left the porch where they had been sitting and went to bed, but Flora knew they would sleep very little that night.

Flora awoke to meet the day with a dreadful feeling. Millard was already up and sitting at the foot of the bed, staring out the window, a look of desperation on his face. He immediately turned and said to her, "Flora, I have made a temporary decision. We will remain here until all efforts are totally exhausted. I will continue taking whatever work I can find as I have been doing for years now. We have no other choice in the matter. What worries me now is that even the small jobs that we depended upon before are becoming harder and harder to find. I thought about what you said last night about our marriage vows, and you were right. We will take one day at a time."

"You have made a good decision, and I feel better," she replied.

Millard looked at her fondly and continued, "You must realize, however, Flora, that I have been searching for a way out for us. It might be something that you do not expect, but drastic times take drastic measures, as I have heard before. Depending on how things develop over the next few months or even a year or two, I will put a plan into action that will prevent us from ever being poor again."

He then ate a quick breakfast and was off to what he hoped would be some kind of work. If he found anything at all, it would be in mining or government-sponsored construction. That was about all there was and precious little of that. The farms, of course, were still there, but even they promised little relief to the farmers or anyone else. A late frost had caused severe crop damage, and food was scarce everywhere.

Flora continued to hang on to her religious faith, which came to mind often, and to her mother's words of confidence when things went awry. "God bless this day," she said quietly.

One day seemed to run into another for a while. Millard usually managed somehow to bring in enough money to keep them going. They continued to make every day count and were barely hanging on. Some days were pleasant, especially where Cameron was concerned. He explored the grounds around the house and creek constantly. One of Millard's friends gave him a nice bulldog, who immediately took on the responsibility of watching Cameron. Cameron named him Pet because of his good nature.

One day, Flora heard Pet barking and growling. When she went to investigate, there was Pet pulling Cameron away from the creek by the seat of his pants. A recent rain has washed the creek a little deeper than normal, and Pet would not allow Cameron to go near that part of the creek.

Sadly, one day when Millard was desperate for money, a man had offered him one dollar for Pet. Millard had no choice but to sell the dog. A few nights later, the man's house burned, and Pet did not escape the flames. Millard blamed himself for Pet's death, and Flora could tell he was grieving the loss of the poor dog. Millard had planned to buy him back as soon as possible. Cameron could not understand where Pet had gone and remembered him long afterward.

Pet's death saddened Flora also. It caused her to question why such things happen. That wonderful dog was born innocent, lived his life innocent, and died a horrible death. She prayed that Pet had suffered no pain, and perhaps he didn't. He could have been overcome by smoke and escaped the heat from the deadly flames. If only she could confirm that thought in her mind, it would help. Her intuition did not help as it often did.

It was 1932, and times were not getting better for the Watson family. Actually, they were becoming rapidly worse. The only food in the house was some flour, lard, and a few essentials such as salt and pepper. Work had all but disappeared. They had almost experienced such a disastrous situation once before when the mine closed and Millard lost his job.

When Millard came home that evening, Flora told him of their plight. She had tried to avoid discussing the matter with him until all hope of continuing to live in their little cottage was gone. Of course, they were in no danger of losing the cottage because of Mr. Bowman's generosity in allowing them to live there rent free, but Flora knew very well that they could not make it there any longer. She told him they must move no later than the following day. She knew of nothing else to do but return to either the home of his parents or hers and remain there for a while. They had no options left; so they planned to move the following day as early as possible.

They found no sleep or comfort that night. Little did they know, tomorrow would bring them good fortune and hope.

Twilight found them sitting on the front porch trying to make emergency decisions. Suddenly, they heard a noise up the road, and a weasel came by chasing a rabbit. Millard quickly got his shotgun. He had only one shell and knew it must count. He took careful aim and fired, killing the rabbit. The unfortunate weasel ran in another direction. Flora fried the rabbit nice and brown and used the grease and flour she had to make gravy and biscuits. They had a delicious breakfast, which was totally unexpected.

The nice breakfast was only the beginning of a day that would affect them for the rest of their lives. As they were preparing for their planned move, they heard a wagon approaching. Millard quickly opened the door. "It's Dad," he said loudly with a broad smile on his face. They knew something unusual was up when they saw him coming. He was not one to visit his children very often. He considered it family interference if he did so without reasons.

After he'd cared for his horse, Dad came to the porch and greeted them each as was his custom—a hug for Flora and Cameron and a big handshake for Millard.

"Well! What persuaded you to come this way?" Millard asked.

"I came at Grandma's request. She wants you to come up and spend the night. She did not reveal the reason for her invitation. I am happy to be here. I have missed you all so much since you left us, I could hardly keep myself from coming down for a visit. I traveled without a rest, and I am just about tuckered out."

"I thank you for coming," said Millard. "I guess we will find what this is all about soon enough. Sit down, Dad, and rest yourself. A cool drink of water might help. That is about all we have to offer you; we are a little short of everything right now." He failed to tell Dad that, if he had not come when he did, they would have soon been gone. He had already arranged to borrow a horse and wagon from his neighbor. Dad had realized, however, what they were about by the appearance inside the house.

Flora was delighted Dad had come when he did. She dreaded leaving their home, and now maybe they would not have to leave. She felt strongly that Grandma had something important in mind that would be beneficial to them and that it concerned their home.

Millard had Flora and Cameron sit in the wagon. He then led the horse, not only to relieve the burden on the horse but to help quicken the pace. Dad followed behind. They arrived home at dusk, the outlines of the rustic, old house just visible beyond the boxwood bushes.

When they opened the creaky, heavy wood door, they could see Grandma sitting by the stone fireplace in her creaky, old oak rocking chair. She looked a bit pale but her smile and voice indicated she was doing well. The weather was warm, and no fire was burning. She just enjoyed sitting there in her favorite spot. She was happy to see them, and there were plenty of hugs to go around.

Ma and the rest of the family were overjoyed. Ma served them leftovers from supper, and they ate every bite. Their breakfast of rabbit had long since gone, and Dad had brought very little food with him when he'd come. He had not expected to find them so destitute when he arrived.

With their hunger pains gone, they relaxed and enjoyed a period of delightful conversation. No one even thought of going to bed until they caught up on all the news, good and bad.

They finally remembered that Grandma had had a purpose in mind when she'd sent for them. She had ways of finding out things, and she already knew that, if something was not done soon to help Millard and Flora, they were not going to make it. She feared it might even affect their marriage. They had been married for over two years, and that is a long time without something going well. She had deep compassion for them.

Everyone except Grandma and Millard and Flora soon went to bed. Staying up that late was not a habit for Grandma, but she wanted to discuss things with them before they slept. She was never one to put off important issues that needed immediate attention.

TEN

Grandma slid her rocking chair closer to Millard and Flora, and in the firelight, they could see her eyes were bright. "Children," she said as she leaned forward a little. "You have been having a hard time since you were married and especially since you moved away from here. I know very well how difficult situations can be when things beyond your control cause loss of hope, and you can find no solution to your problems. My husband, Moses, went off to fight in the Civil War after we were married, leaving me with two little boys and Sarah and this farm, which was only partly cleared. This farm was not far from the edge of the frontier in those days. Wild animals prowled all around. At night, we could hear them come right up to the edge of the woods. I was scared that we might be attacked by them, and I was scared we might starve or freeze to death during the winter.

"We had no neighbors within miles, and I knew it would be hard to find help if we became sick or injured. Thankfully, we remained healthy, and injuries were few. Nothing happened to us that we could not overcome on our own."

As her grandmother-in-law spoke, Flora fully realized that Grandma was a perfect example of one with practically no education but wisdom aplenty to make up the difference. She had taught herself to read a little and sign her name.

"We could see Cherokee Indians pass through. Most all of the Cherokees had been pushed far to the west, but a good many were still hid up in the higher mountains all across the Blue Ridge. I have heard of a great march called the 'Trail of Tears' that was forced upon them by the government for no reason except they wanted their land."

"I have studied about those times," said Flora.

"I have read about it and studied it also," Millard added. "Many thousands were forcibly relocated westward into Indian Territory, I think, sometime during 1838 and 1839."

Grandma continued, "During that march, thousands of them died of disease and exposure and starvation.

"We knew many of them were living in the mountains high above here. Occasionally, a group would pass by our farm. We did not bother them or tell anyone they were up there. They never seemed to mean us any harm, and I was never afraid of them. I don't know where they would go after passing here, but in a few days, they would return and go back up into the mountains. They were a mystery to me and the little ones. We would wave at them, and they would wave back every time they passed. I guessed they had always been here and would always remain, but that was not to be.

"One day, a group of fifty or so came down together. We could tell something was different by their behavior. Men, women, and children were among them, and they all carried bundles of their belongings. I knew they were leaving for the last time, and it bothered me. This time, they did not go on by as usual. They stopped and looked our way, as if they wanted to say something." Grandma paused before continuing.

Flora and Millard had been listening intently. Millard asked, "Why have you never told us these things before, Grandma? We would like to hear more."

"I intend to tell you more," Grandma replied. "Just be patient. I need to catch my breath a little." Soon, she continued with her story. "When they did not speak, I motioned for them to come up to the house, and they did. We all sat down under a big tree in the yard. One of the men, who spoke English very well, told us they were leaving the mountains and would not return. I asked why they were making such a move and where they were going.

"'Yesterday, a messenger came and said that what was left of our main tribe was in the hills of Kentucky and wanted us to join them,' he told me. 'They are going on west after we arrive to join the main body of the Cherokee Nation in Oklahoma. They say we have no other choice. It saddens us to leave. Many other small groups such as ours are hidden across these mountains and say they will never leave. We talked much of the night trying to decide what to do. Finally we decided, by vote, that we cannot survive here much longer. The winters are very harsh, and we are too poor and helpless to remain here. If only we could go down into the valleys and build a village and plant crops and hunt and fish as we once did we would never leave.'

"'Oh my Lord!' I said to him. 'How will you make it with so little food and warm clothes?'

"'We will live off the land as best we can,' he said. 'But our chances are better to go than to stay. Sooner or later, some white men will come and demand that we move off their land. We might fight and kill them, but soldiers would then come, and that would be the end for us. We leave with sadness. We shall walk these Blue Ridges no more. The endless mountains will remain forever, and we bid them farewell. We must go.'

"By that time I was crying and wringing my hands. My mind was racing, trying to think of something I could do to help them. 'We have little food, but I will give it all to you,' I told them. 'No,' he told me. 'You are a good woman, but you have no man to help you. You are little better off than us.' Suddenly I thought of a cured ham I had been saving. I ran into the house and got it, and while I was there, I thought of several quilts I had stacked in a room. I took them out and placed them in his arms and refused to allow him to return them to me.

"They all stood and, to my amazement, sang, 'Rock of Ages.' Then, without another word, they walked away without looking back. I cried, off and on, and worried about them for many weeks afterward. The grief was almost too hard to bear. I have never stopped praying for them and their descendants every time I think of that awful day.

"You see, with very little cleared land, we could only farm a few acres of grain and a garden of about one acre. We had no farm animals, so I traded our grain for food or anything that would help us survive. We were left here alone to live the best we could off the useable land and the small garden. I did have a musket and enough powder and shot to kill small game sometimes."

Grandma paused for several minutes, as she did from time to time. She gazed into the fireplace as though giving her memories time to catch up before continuing. Flora and Millard were almost completely mesmerized by the amazing story and by hearing Grandma reveal parts of history like they had never heard before. Not wanting to interrupt Grandma's train of thought and miss something she wanted to say, they made no reply.

"The little ones were very young, but they helped all they could. You would be surprised how those children could sense what a predicament we were in. They pitched in and worked all day long as I did, without ever complaining. Somehow we survived those many years we were alone.

"Finally, one day when we were trying to clear a little more land we could use, I looked up, and there my husband stood at the woods' edge. He looked half-starved and was wearing a gray uniform, half torn off his body. He was almost crazy from all the suffering and fighting he had endured. We had no quarrel with the North or South, and we owned no slaves. But several soldiers came by one morning and ordered him to join the Southern army. The soldiers forced him go with them and fight so they could keep their slaves and get rich in other ways as well, I guess. We mountain folks knew very little about the war and what it was all about, just some of it.

"Moses slept for over two days after he got home. He would not tell me much about where he had been and what all had happened while he was away. I tried to persuade him to talk about it, thinking maybe it would ease his mind a bit. He would have crazy spells at times, usually at night. He would wake up soaked in sweat, hollering and yelling battle words that I did not understand. I would try to calm him by cradling him in my arms, much as I would a child.

"After he'd been home for a while, he told me he did not want to ever talk about the war again because he was ashamed of helping kill so many men and destroying so much property and even burning houses with women and children around watching, knowing they had no other place to go. He said he had not known whether or not he would find us alive when he got home. I asked him what happened to our only horse, which he'd taken when he left, and he said it had been shot out from under him.

"Gradually we all worked together and finished clearing this farm and made a pretty happy life for ourselves. The children and me did all we could to help Moses return to his normal self. It still took years before he got over the war though. I doubt that he ever completely did. Right up until he died, he would sometimes sit for hours and stare off into the distance."

At this point, Millard could not help but realize how he had taken this lovely farm for granted, by not recognizing through the years the work and sacrifice that had gone into the development and how Grandma and his uncles and mother had made it possible.

"Oh well! I could go on for days talking about those terrible times we had and the good times too, but I will stop, at least for now," Grandma said, still lost in thought.

With her voice faltering a little, she continued. "Now I will talk to you about the reason I asked you to come here today. You see, after Moses died, the government started sending me a small amount of money each month. It came in the mail just as regular as that old clock over on the wall there chimes. I used most of it to help keep us going here on the farm, but I hid a little bit away. I just had a feeling that someday there would be a need for it, and I followed that feeling. Now I know what that feeling was all about."

"What was it all about?" asked Millard.

"You children are in need. I have watched you struggle to get by since you got married. I knew when you moved away that things would probably get worse and worse, through no fault of your own. It's just that this old depression keeps hanging on and won't let go. Roosevelt has kept us going as best he can, but the Depression had a severe hold on us before anyone around here knew much about it. It's like a wildfire; if you don't get it stopped quickly after it gets started, you can't hardly get it stopped at all.

"Well, I think the time has come for that little bit of money to be put to use. You were meant to have it; I know you were. I heard of a small farm the other side of River Valley that was for sale. It's only about four acres, but it is good, fertile land and nicely cleared. I have already bought it, and the deed is clear. There's a two-room house on it, and I believe you will enjoy living there. I do believe it will give you a start, and you can go on from there. Later, if times ever do get better, you might buy more land in the surrounding area and make a nice, larger place and live well.

"It is too late to plant a crop, but next spring, if I were you, I would plant all I could. For now, I will give you the remainder of my savings to help see you through the winter. Millard, you are smart and clever. You learned to read well in about four months after you started school. All you ever needed was a decent chance. I know you will make do all right, especially with such a good woman as Flora by your side."

Flora could not keep from crying, and Millard was filled with joy. He had never expected such a generous gift. "Grandma," he said, "I will pay you back someday, but I can't say when that will be."

"No you won't!" Grandma said in a stern voice. "I told you how I felt about this money, and I will not accept one penny in return. I think God urged me to save it, and now I know why. Accepting repayment would go against God's intent and my joy of giving it to you. Take it with my blessing and do the best you can. Now, it is late and I am very tired. It is way past my bedtime."

Millard and Flora immediately retired to the same bedroom they had occupied for over two years after their marriage. They were so excited they could hardly close their eyes. They now had a home of their own. Both were wondering what they would do next. What would tomorrow bring? Neither of them had ever seen the place Grandma had so generously given to them. They discussed their situation until long after midnight. Both realized what a unique opportunity they now had and how important it was. What a wonderful day this had been. They had gone from nothing to being property owners. They discussed the many options they had and how thankful they were to a wonderful, benevolent grandma.

Soon, they closed their eyes for a much-needed peaceful night's rest, still thinking of what tomorrow might bring.

ELEVEN

"Let's go see our new home!" Millard said as soon as he awoke the next day.

Flora thought for a moment and wanted to say yes, but after considering all they had been through lately, she said to Millard, "Perhaps we should allow ourselves a day's rest. Tomorrow would do just as well, and we can relax and make some plans. We owe ourselves that much, don't you think?"

"Yes, you are right as usual," he said and then kicked the covers onto the floor.

"You are so crazy," she said, giving him a big shove out of the bed. This brought on laughing and wrestling around on the bed until others in the house wondered what was going on.

The day proved to be joyful. They walked around the old farm and discussed plans for moving into their new home. Soon, the entire family gathered on the porch with them. Ma served tea and gingerbread as they reminisced. Everyone enjoyed the presence of Cameron among them. He moved from one lap to another, spreading his joy and laughter. Millard expressed his pleasure at being home and how he looked forward to returning often. They planned to leave the next day, leaving Cameron with his grandparents.

Millard and Flora were up before sunrise. Ma was already up and getting things together they would need on their trip. Before they ate a short breakfast, Ma spoke a prayer. "Father," she said. "Guide and bless these children as they go on their way. Help them to be of good courage and keep them close to you and out of harm's way. Amen."

As they were walking away from the house, Flora thought, *What a meaningful and beautiful prayer. I shall try to remember it always.*

They walked at a quick pace all morning, stopping only once at a roadside spring for a short rest and to eat the lunch Ma had prepared for them. It was after noon before they arrived at their new home.

They discovered that the house was situated in a small valley. There it was below where they were standing, looking like a jewel to them, even though they immediately could tell much work needed to be done on the house and the property surrounding it. It was located half a mile from Barber's Store at the junction leading to the main road. Millard and Flora stood there hand in hand for a while and then continued down the road that bordered the front and upper side of the farm. They went through a wooden gate and down the path that led to the front door of the house.

On the left side of the hill in front of the house was evidence of a potato patch, which obviously had been fallow for several years. On the right side was a large garden space that looked rich and fertile. The house was situated on the rear portion of the farm with a spring on the upper rear side that flowed swiftly down behind the house into a swampy area about twenty-five yards away. The entire farm was fenced nicely with locust posts and barbed wire. Millard was especially attracted to that feature of the farm. He said it added a comfortable feeling about the entire place.

The house was most interesting to them. It had two rooms and a cellar and looked strong and sturdy. It was constructed from oak lumber and baton strips. It had only corner wall studs; however, the thick oak lumber nailed vertically from the outside floor joists to the rafters held the roof nicely in place. An uncovered porch on the front of the house squeaked and looked unsafe. The house showed no evidence of ever being painted. However, it was well proportioned and looked quite nice. The roof was well slanted to compliment the house, but the tin covering needed replacing. The general appearance of the outside revealed an attractive cabin common to that era.

Inside, hewn roughened surface planks, the looks of which were not unattractive, covered the walls and floor. A hatch leading to a cellar was visible in the living room. Upon inspection of the cellar, they discovered a thick, sawdust-insulated floor leading to the outside. There were shelves for holding canned food and bins for storing potatoes, apples, and other food items that would otherwise be in danger of freezing during winter months.

The two rooms were adequate for the present. The living room had two double windows in front and one on the lower side. A door led outside to the porch. In the kitchen, one window faced the swamp below the house, and a door on the upper side provided easy access to the spring.

As they were looking about Flora asked, "Do you suppose there are snakes around? The cellar looks snaky to me."

That brought on loud laughter from Millard. "I doubt there are any in here, but there are plenty outside I'll bet. There was a huge forest fire in this area. After such fires, the large trees are destroyed, leaving room for smaller shrubs and berry bushes. Blueberry and other berry bushes reappear in great numbers. Birds flock in for the berries, and of course, snakes come in large numbers to catch the birds. But most of them are harmless. Blacksnakes are the most common variety, and they are helpful in keeping rodents and harmful snakes such as rattlers away."

"What a story you tell," said Flora, "but it does not make me feel much better."

"I would not mind if they leave."

Flora said, "Plenty of rattlesnakes are in the area where I lived, and they scare me to death. Our cats kept them away from the house though. I think we should get some cats when we move in here."

Millard had no fear of snakes of any kind. He had a way of throwing them aside when he wanted to and making it look easy.

They worked around the house until dusky dark and then went inside the house for the night. Millard lit a candle he had brought and they enjoyed their meager supper by the pleasant, rather romantic glimmer of its light.

They were most anxious to accomplish as much work as possible before leaving for home the following day. They brushed the dust from inside the house with an old broom they found and then piled fallen limbs and brush laying around on the property.

They worked and looked over the farm until the sun began its descent and then walked the property just to feel the joy of ownership and get a view of the place from every angle.

For now, they were satisfied and began their return journey to Dad's, talking all the way about what they should do next. They still had many problems to face, but the future looked brighter. Millard did not have regular work, and winter was rapidly approaching. They concluded that facing each day and doing their very best was all they could do for now.

Millard, however, would keep his lofty ambitions in mind and would never give them up. The money Grandma had given them would be of great help. If Millard could only keep finding small jobs, things would be tough, but they were now confident they could make do.

That night the family sat by the fire and talked until late. All wanted to know about Millard and Flora's trip and what their plans were. They explained to the family they would move soon.

Dad could sense the uncertainty in their voices and wanted to help them. He said, "Decide your moving date, and I will help you as best I can." Dad was indeed a gentleman, and his mind held a wealth of wisdom, as Flora knew well. Millard and Flora listened intently, hoping he would have more to say, and he did.

He stared into the fire and paused as if not wanting to say something hurtful. "I do not see any reason in moving until spring, knowing you will suffer through the winter. If you are determined to move, I believe you should do it soon and get settled as soon as possible and store up provisions like a squirrel stores up nuts and makes a warm nest. If the winter is long and severe, don't despair. You can return here and live out the remainder of the winter. Then, you could return home and plant crops and proceed to make a good life for yourselves. I have no doubt about you working hard. You have already proven your willingness to do that. That is what I would do if I were in your place. Of course, the final decision must be yours."

Millard and Flora both agreed with Dad, except Millard expressed his determination that, after their move, he did not want to return again. "We must make this move work."

Flora did not agree with him, but at first she said nothing. After careful thought, Flora was certain Millard should have not talked about not wanting to return. He had made such a statement before, and they had not been successful. She scolded him for being so blunt.

"I misspoke, but this time we are moving into our own home," Millard replied, "and that should make a difference. I meant no disrespect at all, and I do know that Dad does have the best answer to all this mess. I just do not intend to return here and am determined not to do so. I thank Dad and Ma and Grandma for their help and thoughtfulness. If they ever need help, we will be there for them, I promise."

A period of silence filled the room as though their minds were thinking in concert.

Flora then remarked, "Tomorrow is another day, and God willing, we will make our move."

Millard slowly nodded his head in agreement.

"Then let's all go to bed for a good night's rest," Ma said, a smile on her face.

"Amen," Grandma said loudly.

They all laughed and retired for the night.

After Millard and Flora were in bed, Flora realized there were no bright lights on the mountain, and she felt very normal. She slept well that night and with a compliment of pleasant dreams.

When she awoke, she had to think a moment before realizing where she was. The other family members were up and almost ready to depart. Lee had made himself available to help with the move. Flora was very pleased that he was going with them. He was strong and would make the move much easier. She hurriedly ate breakfast and was ready to help.

Dad had hitched the horse to the wagon and they were ready to depart. They must stop for their household items at Birch Creek and haul them to their new home. Flora and Cameron rode on the wagon, and Millard led the horse. Dad and Lee walked behind. They knew the day would be tiresome, and the burden placed upon the horse would be heavy.

Flora turned to wave good-bye to Ma, Grandma, and Lewis. He looked so sick and frail. His health was deteriorating rapidly, and she knew very well he would live only a short while—not even as long as she'd thought when she'd first noticed the severity of his illness. If only he could see a physician and perhaps be taken to a hospital for treatment, it might ease his pain and even prolong his precious life. Her intuition told her it was not to be. He would endure the pain as always and then die within a short while. Tears swelled in her eyes as she silently asked God to take care of him.

TWELVE

They moved along at a rapid pace down Birch Creek and quickly loaded their belongings onto the wagon. Now empty and abandoned, the cabin had a sad appearance. Flora was thankful for the time they had lived there and thankful to the good man who had allowed them to occupy that lovely little place rent free.

After they pulled away, Cameron looked at the house and wanted to stay. Obviously he was remembering the pleasant times he'd had there. "Home, Mama, home," he said.

Flora told him they were going to a new home that belonged to them and that he would like it much better. Obviously, he did not understand fully, but he did not question the reasons for leaving the place he would always remember.

By noon, they were much farther along than anticipated. They stopped for a brief time to eat their bagged lunch and allow time to care for the horse.

They quickly moved on, wanting to reach their destination soon. They must put things in some sort of order at the house before dark. Shadows were falling as they reached Barber's Store. They stopped to buy food to last a few days and then hurried on to the house.

Immediately, they unloaded the wagon and placed everything haphazardly in the house. Flora would arrange everything to her satisfaction on the following day. After supper, they all bedded down with quilts.

It was wonderful to be in a home they could call their own. They knew they would sleep and rise early to greet a new day and a new era in their lives. What a wonderful opportunity Grandma had provided them, and they marveled at the prospect of owning their new home, paid for by money from the great Civil War. Millard and Flora decided to repay Grandma even though she had made it quite clear she wanted nothing in return. Flora quietly decided, in her own mind, that if ever Grandma was in need, she would go to her side.

The following morning began a little slower than the previous day had. They all slept later than intended, doubtless a result of the mental and physical fatigue they had endured. Flora rapidly prepared breakfast, which consisted of a bowl of oatmeal. As they hurriedly ate, she silently gave thanks to God for Grandma.

Millard thanked Dad and Lee for their help, shaking their hands in a grateful way. Everyone seemed to have no time to waste. Dad and Lee quickly departed for home, and Millard left as usual to look for work. Flora could tell he was anxious. He desperately wanted to find work, and he would be searching in places he would not ordinarily be looking. She felt uneasy about him, as she often did, and wished he would have waited another day to start.

Flora and Cameron set about putting things in place. Cameron did the best he could to help out. Even though he was small, he could carry water and do other small chores. Flora washed all the walls meticulously to rid the house of spiders and ants and other unwelcome creatures that might cause problems. She would stand for nothing short of a completely clean house. That was her way.

Afterward, she placed each item of furniture in place, hung curtains, and made beds. Her curtains were made from feed sacks with printed patterns as before, but this time, they were nicely pleated and placed on homemade rods. Fortunately, her decorating work was not a difficult task. They had accumulated little during their marriage; thus, the arrangement of what they had took little time.

She was very proud, however, as she stood back and admired what she had accomplished. "One more thing," she remarked to Cameron. "We must sweep the porch and yard, and things will be completed for now. Later on, we will find ways to do much more."

As soon as she was finished she began to prepare supper. She wanted everything to be in place and a good meal ready when Millard arrived.

As darkness closed in, supper was almost ready, and as she looked toward the road, Cameron asked, "Where is Daddy?"

"I am sure he will be home soon," she replied. "I know you are hungry, but I would very much like for him to be here to eat with us."

Long after dark, she could hear people coming down the path. She knew something was wrong and rushed to the door. Four men were carrying Millard on a makeshift stretcher. He was pale and unconscious and groaning constantly.

"What has happened to him?" she asked anxiously.

"Mine cave-in," one of the men, John Beam, replied. Flora knew all the men. They were just like Millard, trying to find work each day. "Almost completely buried him, but thank the good Lord, we were able to uncover his face in order to save him. We all knew that old mine was unsafe, but we shored it up some and decided to see if there was any mica left worth mining. Turned out, there was more mica left in the mine than we had hoped. I guess we got a little excited and careless. Millard ain't hurt much like it seems. He don't have any broke bones, but the soft dirt packed him in pretty tight. He's mostly bruised, and a rock hit him in the head is the reason he looks so bad. He was knocked out by the rock, but he is coming around now."

The men laid Millard on the bed and then left for their homes.

Shortly, Millard began to mumble and then opened his eyes. "Where am I?" he asked.

Flora told him he had been injured in a mica mine accident and had to be carried home.

"Oh, so I did," he replied.

He started to return to sleep again, but Flora would not allow him to do so. She knew one should not sleep soon after receiving a blow on the head. She remained by his bed until morning, and then she made him a cup of tea from wild mountain tea leaves. That seemed to make him feel better.

After eating breakfast, he was able to sit up, but he remained at home for several days to allow his bruised body to recover.

Feeling reasonably well, Millard returned to his routine of taking odd jobs while searching for steady employment. He heard of a man who needed someone for two days to help dig shrubbery to sell up north. When he arrived, the job had been filled by another person. Millard was accustomed to such days, but somehow this day made him heartsick and very disappointed. He reasoned that the mine accident had had more effect on him than he'd thought. It was too late to look elsewhere, so he went home. As he walked, he thought of past disappointments, and it came to him for the first time that, perhaps, he might just figure a way to become self-employed. The more he thought, the more he was refreshed by the idea.

When he arrived at home that evening, earlier than usual, Flora could see he was deep in thought and that his attitude had changed somehow. "Something wrong?" she asked.

"No, nothing is wrong," he replied. "Actually, something might be right if I can determine what it is. After supper, I will talk to you about an idea I have and see what you think."

She nervously hurried supper so they could talk. Something good was about to occur. Her intuition was at work again.

After supper Flora could wait no longer. "What do you have on your mind," she asked.

"Well, maybe nothing, but I did a lot of thinking today as I walked home. What would you say if I started working for myself?"

Flora looked in amazement. "What kind of work would you be doing?"

"Mica, if I can manage it," he said.

Flora could not believe what he had just said. "You were almost killed in a mica mine only a few days ago, and you are thinking of going into the mica mining business!"

"Don't get so riled up about it before you hear me out," he said. "We just got careless in that mine the other day. I don't intend to make that mistake again. You know, that old mine we were working in is on government land, and they will allow me to mine it if I pay a fee for the quantity of mica I mine. What's more, I can pay for it after I've sold it. I overheard some men who are heavy into the mica business talking, and that's the way it works. I would have considered trying it before now, but those men know how to wheel and deal in such matters in a big way. I doubted that I would be capable of competing with such knowledgeable men and be successful at it like they were. They have political connections and heavy equipment and such. I dismissed it from my mind at the time, but today it came to me again.

"I have the same rights as them men, and I intend to give it a try. I have always been able to just about smell mica before I see it, and I smelled it in that mine we were working when I was injured.

"There is just one catch; I must have enough money to get started and abide with government regulations. Those men I just spoke of have the money and the knowledge to get started properly."

Flora asked, "If you were injured on government land, why were you working there?"

"Desperation is about all I can say. I won't do that again without prior arrangements."

After a period of careful thought, Flora was obviously skeptical about the whole idea. "We have no money to invest except the small amount Grandma gave us to help us through the winter," she said.

"I thought about that," Millard replied as he studied her face to get her reaction. "I believe we should take the chance. I know winter is coming soon, and I also know the money Grandma gave us will scarcely last us into February. We have to do something, and we can't wait until the last minute—until we are desperate—again. I will go to the government office tomorrow and tell them my plan. If they agree, I will begin work the following day. I know you are worried about my safety, but I know how to keep a mine safe. I'll use heavy timbers and go slow. I'll work alone at first and then hire help if and when I need it."

Flora could see he had convinced himself that his plan could work. After a pause and more thought, she agreed. She concentrated deeply and sensed no negative feelings about this important change that might come into their lives. She also was aware that her psychic abilities were not strong enough to guarantee anything.

Shortly after breakfast, Millard was off with his packed lunch in hand. He walked to the government office as quickly as possible. Nervously, he stopped to catch his breath and calm himself before entering the door. He could feel his heart pounding as never before.

The official on duty listened with interest to Millard as he presented his plan. The gentleman seemed very impressed and wasted little time in giving his approval. "I wish you the best of luck in your venture," he said as he shook Millard's hand. "I have seen so many good men walk out that door with papers in hand and never return. They either get themselves killed from lack of experience in mica mining or just can't handle the more complicated issues involved in running the business end of their operation. The government began this project to create jobs during this depression. It has been a tremendous success for some but a disappointment and sometimes death for others. They were just good men desperately trying to get by."

Millard thanked the gentleman and immediately headed for the mine. He wanted to look things over again before opening it up again. He found many strong bracing timbers and several mining tools that would serve him well.

Those who had worked the mine previously must have been unfortunate men such as the government agent had warned him about. He then thought of how things could have turned out when his friends and he had started to explore the mine several days ago. He inspected the mine carefully and organized everything neatly. *Tomorrow I will be ready to begin without delay*, he thought. "God help me; this has got to work," he whispered to himself. So far, he was very pleased.

When he arrived home, Flora was very happy for him. She could sense that he had been to the mine by the sheepish smile on his face. "I am ready to start, and I can hardly wait," he said.

The next morning he was up even earlier than usual and off to his mine. Flora knew he would not be home early, and she was correct.

Just before dark, he came down the path with something under his arm. It was a large chunk of mica about two or three feet in diameter and of considerable weight.

Flora immediately began asking questions about the mica and everything that had occurred at the mine. Millard was tired but he happily related the events of the day to her. "First thing this morning, I shored up the front section of the mine and began shoveling. Within the first hour, my shovel struck something, and I could tell instantly in was mica. It is worth at least five dollars or more, and I believe there is much more quality mica there. This is the most money I have ever earned in one day."

They were both delighted. It was a lucky day, and they were extremely thankful. Cameron could tell something good had happened. He laughed when Millard told him what it was. Cameron did not understand, so he asked Millard if he could go with him to work one day and see what it was like. Millard promised to take him one day soon.

THIRTEEN

It was now 1933, and things seemed to be well in hand. Millard and Flora began having notions, not heretofore considered, about the purchase of an automobile. Flora was skeptical about the idea, but Millard was extremely excited at the very thought of owning a car. When he reminded her about how it would provide a way to church and town and visiting relatives, she soon agreed.

She loved the idea of having a car, but the expense of two hundred dollars seemed prohibitive to her. They had been so poor all their lives, such a huge jump was frightening to her. She continued to think about the purchase, though, and decided it was definitely a smart thing to do. She thought of Millard and the endless miles he had to walk almost everywhere he went, and it had always been that way for him. That alone was enough to convince her of how deserving he was of this thing he wanted so much and how selfish it would be for her to object. Of course, he could have proceeded to buy a car without even consulting her, but that was not his way. That evening after supper, she and Millard talked at length about how far they had come in such a short time and how the purchase of a car would undoubtedly have an impact on their lives.

Among their recent accomplishments, Flora considered the resumption of her religious life and how it would be of great comfort to her. It had always been of great importance to her life as far back as her memory could reflect. Millard and Cameron were the joy of her life. Millard was the husband that had made all the material achievements of their lives possible. He had never been willing to completely give up, although she knew how close he had come so many times. Little Cameron was the product of a loving relationship she and Millard had refused to abandon through all the disappointments they had encountered since their wedding in Knoxville, Tennessee, with their beautiful friends, Jackson and Sally. What a joy it would be for him to own an automobile. Just the thought of it made her happy.

Now that the decision had been made, Millard immediately decided to begin searching for a suitable car for the family. The following morning, he walked up to the store, hoping by chance that someone he knew might give him a ride to Spruce Willow, a town about ten miles away and the county seat of Fox County.

Shortly after he arrived at the store, a familiar-looking Buick pulled up in front of the store, and Millard could hardly believe his eyes. It was his friend Jackson Stamey, and the car he was driving was none other than the one they had driven to Knoxville to be married.

As soon as the car stopped, Millard ran to meet his old friend. They were so happy to see each other, they could hardly stop shaking hands and back patting. "Where on earth have you been so long?" Millard said in a loud voice. "I have been to your house more times than I can count, and you were never there. I inquired all around as to your whereabouts but got no answers. None of your neighbors knew, or they wouldn't tell me anything. To be truthful, I have been worried, but not to the extent that I thought anything bad had happened to you. I knew you would show up sometime, but I never stopped hoping it would be sooner than later."

Jackson smiled. "I have missed you, old friend," he said, "but my absence has not been totally voluntary. You know my old man and his money. Well, shortly after we returned from our wedding in Knoxville, his business was going sour. He saw it coming and sold out. He had another business he was in the process of buying, and it fluttered out too. He was frantic, for no reason! He had enough money and property to last him for the rest of his life. No matter, he has never been content unless he was making money. He had never understood the Depression and feared it. Anyway, to shorten a long story, he decided to start selling white liquor and demanded that I help him. I resisted but finally agreed to work with him, and I will tell you now I have been in a hell of a mess since I last saw you."

Jackson filled his car up with gas, and they both went inside the store and returned with an RC Cola and a MoonPie to enjoy while they sat on the front porch, relaxing and talking.

"What have you been about since I last saw you, Millard?" Jackson asked.

"I have had a good marriage, and I have a fine little boy. Until about eight months ago, it has been a tough row to hoe for us, though. We have just about gone through hell and back again. Finally, I got a government contract to operate a mica mine on their property. Since then, I have made more money than I ever thought possible for me. Also, my Grandma gave me a small farm. We've fixed the place up pretty well since I found a successful way to make a little money. It is located just over the hill above the store here."

Millard looked over at Jackson's car and said, "I have never owned a car, but I intend to change that situation soon. I am tired of walking every damned place I go. I was hoping to catch a ride to Spruce Willow to buy one when I saw you drive up. Damn, it is good to see you again, you old rascal."

"Me too," replied Jackson. "I haven't met many friends since I got into the whiskey business, if you can call it a business. It has caused me to break more laws than anyone I know of. I don't know how I have stayed out of jail. It is one way to make a lot of money fast though."

Millard immediately picked up on that remark. He had not forgotten the past promises he had made to himself about his poverty-stricken life. He was reminded almost every day in one way or another. "Jackson, for years, I have thought of rising above the poverty that has always imposed itself upon my family and me, as well as most folks along the Blue Ridge. I have been more successful in my mica mine business than anything I have ever tried before, but mica mining is unpredictable. It is doing remarkably well now, but Monday morning, I might very well find that it is like a well gone dry. I had never tried mica mining before, although I do know these mountains are full of the stuff and precious stones as well. The trick is to find it and know how to make the business work for you."

Jackson said, "I worked in an emerald mine one day, and that was enough for me. I guess I have a phobia about working underground. I was scared as hell all day. I didn't even return to get my check for that day's work."

Millard laughed. "It just takes getting used to. Don't bother me at all, although I have come near to getting killed in them a couple times. We all have our fears of one thing or another, I suppose.

"I've had no choice but to put fear and danger behind me years ago," said Millard. Hell, you can't make a living in these mountains without skirting fear and danger nearby. I get around it by keeping alert and taking no unnecessary chances. I worked at a sawmill once when a conveyor belt broke and knocked me directly toward the saw. I came within one inch of getting my head sawed off. I was afraid of everything for months after. It was then I decided that I could not live that way all my life. Now I do not fear danger in any form, including killing or being killed. I love my life, but I do what I have to do."

"You are an interesting man, Millard," replied Jackson. "You explained it in a different way, but I am much the same way when faced with reality. No wonder we have been such good friends."

"How is Sally doing?" asked Millard.

"She is a fine woman, and we get along well. We found two jewels when we found her and Flora, I do believe," Jackson replied. "Sally and me have no children yet, but we keep trying. Sally does not approve of my way of making a living at all. She scolds me all the time about it. I can't say I blame her, but that is the nature of the business I am in. I accepted that fact when I first went into the business, and I intend to stick by that decision. I am aware of what is involved in selling moonshine. But I make a hell of a lot of money, and she don't seem to mind that," he added with a laugh.

Millard and Jackson sat quietly for a while. They had been friends since they'd attended school together at the old, red school located not far from Birch Creek. They had helped each other out in boyhood fights, fished together, hunted together, and gotten married together. They did not want to part company soon and then go several more years without meeting again.

Jackson then said, "Millard, I sure would enjoy spending the rest of the day together. Didn't you say you were headed to Spruce Willow to buy an automobile?"

"Yes, and I had better be on my way," said Millard. "It will probably take me a long while to find one. I have little experience with cars and want to find a reasonably good car at a price I can afford."

"I'm no expert," said Jackson, "but perhaps I could drive you over there and we can search around for one together. If we can't find one, I have some friends who can fix you right up with whatever you want."

"What a lucky day," said Millard. "I could never meet another friend like you."

With that remark, they were soon headed for Spruce Willow, like two boys on a new bicycle. As they cruised along, much faster than they should be going, Millard said, "This is the same car you had when you drove us to Knoxville, and it seems in better shape than it was then."

"Yes, and it runs better now than it did then. The boys I told you about completely overhauled the engine, modified many parts to increase speed, and even installed overload springs and shock absorbers to allow heavier loads to be carried without being noticed."

"I see what you are doing," Millard replied. "You can carry heavy loads of moonshine without being noticed and also outrun anything on wheels that might try to catch you. But Prohibition is over Jackson."

"Yes, but moonshine remains in big demand here in the mountains and other places," Jackson replied. "The repeal of Prohibition didn't change things much and won't for many years to come. White whiskey is less expensive to manufacture and the taste is better than that of legal whiskey in most cases."

"I see your point all right," Millard said.

The two men were enjoying the ride and the pleasure of being together. Millard was fascinated with Jackson's car. "I have never seen anything to beat this. It appears ordinary, yet it's crammed full of modern gadgets."

"That is exactly what I had in mind when I took it to the boys before they started rebuilding it. I had electric windshield wipers installed to keep the wipers from slowing in rainy weather like the vacuum wipers did every time I went up grade and the engine slowed, put in a heater that blows warm air from the engine to keep the car warm and moisture off the inside of the windshield, and got solid metal construction to replace the original fabric on the upper half of the doors. When I agreed to help my dad work this business, I knew there was a chance that I could end up in trouble, like jail or, even worse, prison for a year to two. I decided to give myself every chance possible to avoid such a situation."

At that point in the conversation, Millard decided to ask Jackson more about the whiskey business. The subject had had his attention since Jackson first mentioned it, and it had remained in his thoughts since they'd left Barber's Store on their trip to town. The notion of having money and a pleasant place to live felt good. He did have that now on a small scale, but he could not escape the gnawing feeling that his mine could give out without warning. After hesitating for some time, he decided to ask Jackson about working for him and his father. It could be a chance he would never have again to find his place in the sun—the position he had wanted and that had eluded him for so long.

Jackson had been observing Millard as he stared out the window deep in thought. He suspected he would have something to discuss soon. He knew Millard would say what he had to say when he was ready and not before.

As they approached town, Millard spoke up. "Jackson, I would like to work for you and your father. I will admit right off that I know little about your business, but I am a quick learner. I don't expect an answer now, but I would appreciate your consideration of my request."

"I will do just that," said Jackson. "I am glad you asked. I already have a good feeling about it, and I think the old man will go along."

Millard asked, "Do you have any other men hauling for you?"

"No," said Jackson, "but we would like to expand our operation if we could find one or two more good men like yourself. Let's just say you are in and be done with it. I will help you find a car if you want me to. You will a need a faster car than you had in mind when you first mentioned it earlier."

"I was already thinking of that just before you spoke," replied Millard.

Jackson suggested that he and Millard go by the home of his father, Walter Stamey, a man Millard knew and had always admired.

Walter Stamey was a person who seemed to always succeed in his endeavors.

Jackson thought it best to consult with Walter to assure that Millard knew exactly what he was getting into and the expectations of his performance. Soon they pulled into the driveway of Walter's home. It was not the same home Millard had visited years ago. Large columns supported the full-length front porch. It was of antebellum architecture and was graced with a huge, well-manicured yard with statues, water fountains, and well-trimmed shrubs, all surrounded with a beautiful brick and iron fence. A front gate provided both security and beauty.

As they exited the car and walked toward the house, Millard said to Jackson in a low voice, "I didn't know such a place like this existed anywhere in this county. Do I get one of these if I go to work for you and Mr. Stamey?"

"I'm afraid not; I live just like everyone else around here myself. He is tight, but I am going to loosen him up a bit if he expects us to do the heavy work."

They walked to the front door and rang the doorbell. Mr. Stamey soon opened the door. He looked amazingly like Jackson. He had aged considerably but appeared strong and healthy. He was a handsome man, a little taller than Jackson, and his shoulders were still as broad as Millard had remembered him. "Is that you, Millard?" he asked.

"I'm afraid so," Millard replied as they shook hands.

They passed through an unbelievably luxurious living room as Mr. Stamey led them into his den. "I am pleased to see you, Millard," Mr. Stamey said, motioning for them to sit down. Millard sat in a very comfortable chair; it was a Queen Ann-style, upholstered in a chintz fabric imprinted with a floral design. The remainder of the room was elegantly furnished with furniture of equal beauty and comfort and adorned with appropriate, original paintings and other artwork of classic and antique design. "I haven't seen you in several years. I can't recall exactly how many. How have you been doing? I know you and Jackson went all the way to Knoxville with your ladies to tie the knot."

Millard said, "Well, to be truthful, I don't think I could have done worse if I had tried. This depression has been knocking me down every time I get up. I finally got lucky about eight months ago and things have been much better. I succeeded in obtaining a contract to work a mica mine on government land, and it has paid off well so far. I have a fine wife who has stood by me all the way and a fine little boy. We have a small farm between here and Birch Creek, which Grandma gave me. That was a good break for us. Other than what we have accomplished during the last year, things have been tough."

"This depression has been tough all right. It almost put me down. I think it would have if I hadn't sold my old business and found another way of making money," replied Walter.

Jackson spoke up at that point and said, "Pop, Millard wants to work with us. I have talked to him, and he understands what we are about. I need help in running the heavy end of the business, and I know of no one more qualified than Millard here. You and I both know that we'll be expanding as soon as practical and Millard could be the third man from the top."

Walter walked to the window and looked out over the garden, giving himself time to think before proceeding further with the conversation. As he turned from the window, Millard knew by the pleasant expression on his face that he had come to, at least, a partial decision. "Jackson, he said, I need to talk to Millard privately for a few minutes. Would you mind going to the dining room and bringing three glasses and a bottle of that good peach brandy while we speak a few words?"

"Good idea," said Jackson. "This is serious business, and I knew you would need to speak to Millard before any permanent decisions are made."

As Jackson left the room, Walter leaned forward, touching Millard on the shoulder. "Son, are you sure you want to be involved with this?" he asked, his dark eyes holding Millard's gaze. "You have a fine little family from what I gather, and you seem to be getting your feet planted in safe, secure ground. You could lose it all in one day, you know. This business, as we intend to run it, is about as illegal as you can get, short of armed robbery or some other such high crimes. I would be delighted to have you aboard with us but not at the expense of ruining your life. I have a lot of money, and I can get Jackson and me out of just about anything without going to prison. I might be able to give you the same safety, but I can't guarantee it. If we decide to hire other men as we expand and get busted, it could cost five thousand to pay our way out. That's a lot of money, even for me.

"It's also a greedy business. One dishonorable person in our group could ruin us all. Think about it a few days if you want to, or the three of us can make a handshake agreement right now. I advise you to take a few days to make up your mind and discuss it with your wife. No need to try keeping it from her. It had caused some disharmony between Jackson and Sally, but I think they have come to grips with it. They are still together and seem to get along for the most part."

Millard listened carefully to Walter. He had great respect for his friend's father and knew him to be a wise and honest man. He would never try to take advantage of others, especially his friends, for the sake of making money. Millard had made up his mind before Walter had finished talking, although he made no indication to Walter that he had done so. He thanked Walter, and they waited for Jackson to return to the room.

Soon Jackson returned with the fancy glasses and brandy Walter had requested. Jackson was anxious to know the outcome of the conversation between his father and Millard, but he asked no questions. He uncorked the bottle and filled the glasses almost to the brim.

"This is the finest brandy I ever tasted," Millard said after he had taken a few sips.

"This is special stuff," replied Walter. "I know of only one place to buy it and that is in Johnson City, Tennessee. Help yourself to all you want. I have a wine cellar and keep it pretty well stocked with wine. I also keep many brands of whiskey and stacks of the whiskey we sell illegally. We are very careful to test our white liquor before we move it to our customers. One load of poison whiskey and we would be out of business. Some suppliers make whiskey using few precautions to ensure the whiskey they bottle for sale contains no lead or other impurities. Lead poisoning is usually fatal, and we make sure our whiskey is clean and safe to drink."

Jackson could wait no longer to continue with the business at hand. "Did you come to any conclusions during your conversation?" he asked.

"We discussed very little except how our business might affect Millard and his family should he decide to come in with us. I have advised him to discuss this with his wife before he makes a final decision."

"I have made a final decision," said Millard, "and nothing would please me more than to work with two of the finest gentleman I know."

Walter and Jackson were both pleased but not surprised. Walter smiled and said, "I do believe you made your decision while we were discussing the matter."

"Actually, I did, but I sincerely wanted to hear what you had to say before revealing my decision to you."

"Good thinking," said Walter. "I probably would have reacted the same way."

"Now, we three know what this is all about, so we might as well complete our business without delay," said Walter.

"I agree" said Jackson. "Millard was on his way to purchase a car when we first saw each other this morning."

"That's just fine," said Walter. "The first order of business is to persuade Millard to leave off the Mr. Stamey and just call me Walter. No need for formalities here."

Millard was happy with that decision but said nothing.

"Next," said Walter. "We keep no formal records. A verbal agreement and a shake of hands are our contract. You'll furnish your own car, but mechanical and service work is done by the same garage we have selected. We do keep a few things in writing. We must keep a list of our customers and their addresses but nothing else about them. Monies received are to be kept on your person. Don't worry about the amounts of money you have.

"Give the customer the benefit of any doubts or disagreements as best you can. You will keep his trust and more than make up for the loss later on. If you get caught with a load of whiskey in your car, hint at a bribe with the officer but don't actually offer one. If you can make a deal with him, do so. Give him as much of the load as you see necessary and maybe some money as well. If no bargaining can be achieved, just go to jail and get word to me as soon as possible. Keep your mouth shut and wait for me and my lawyer. I keep a good one at all times. As we expand, as we hope to do, I cannot offer the same protection to others. I think it would be best to keep this information between the three of us. Jackson and I have been using the same routine for some time now, but we will probably expand our routes soon and organize ourselves well. We will then know precisely what to expect at all times."

From the excellent way Walter explained things, mainly for Millard's benefit, Millard and Jackson were happy with the agreement. "Millard will need to find a car today if possible," Walter continued.

"I would prefer that you get a 1932 Ford V8," Jackson added. "If you can manage to get one today, we will get our boys to start modifying it tomorrow."

"That would be just fine," said Millard.

"You will need a car that will outrun the law and will handle well on curvy roads, whether dirt roads or, in some cases, hard-surfaced roads," Walter commented. "Millard, you will be a part of all the details and plans as you will be a part of it all as we go along. We might even use trucks later on. Now you boys had better try to find a suitable car."

Millard paused to shake hands with Walter and thank him for the job and for his kindness. Millard and Jackson quickly left the house and drove away in Jackson's car. The day was passing, and they knew they would be rushed to find a suitable automobile and possibly make a deal before days end.

They drove about ten miles where Jackson pulled onto a side road that led to what appeared to be a fine working farm. It was a working farm, but that wasn't the only operation on the property; the barn was a virtual speed shop. As the owner of the business saw Jackson's car coming down the road, he opened the barn door for them to enter.

Millard had never seen so many tools, car parts, welding machines, tooling machines, and anything you could think of that could be used to build fast cars. The mechanics could even make their own parts if they could not purchase one from a factory. They gave Millard a strong suspicious look, however, until Jackson indicated to them that all was well. The farm and shop in the barn was not illegal. They just wanted to run their operation without interference from suspicious people, and their customers needed their work done confidentially.

Millard got out of the car as the owner of the establishment approached them. Jackson introduced him to Millard as Lawrence Davis.

"Glad to meet you," Millard said to him as they extended hands.

"Same here," said Lawrence.

The shop was in full operation as Millard could tell by the sounds of body hammers and cylinders of engines being bored out to make room for larger pistons to fit into the holes and the smell of metal being welded together.

Jackson immediately began the conversation between the three of them. "We apologize for rushing in here like this," he said, looking at Lawrence.

"Heck, that's all right," Lawrence replied. "What can I do for you fellows? I suspect you are looking for a fast car; you want it yesterday and at a very reasonable price."

"Not so fast," said Jackson. "We do want a car but not just any car. We are looking for a 1932 V8 Ford with overload springs and shocks and modified to run like a scalded dog."

"Well," said Lawrence, scratching his head. "I do have one that is almost like that. Knowing your dad's line of work, I will have to do a few more things to it. For example, we will need to do some welding of the springs and a few other places to make it hang a curve well without swaying much. Otherwise, it's almost perfect the way it is now."

"When can we see it?" asked Jackson.

"Now if you want," replied Lawrence. "I have it stored here in the barn." They immediately walked to a stable where Jackson said Lawrence used to stable a fine racehorse.

"I hope that will be a good omen," said Millard.

Lawrence removed a cloth dustcover from the car, and what a beautiful machine was sitting there. It was solid black, but not a noticeably shiny black that would draw undue attention. "That is the best car I have of the model you asked for," Lawrence remarked, shifting his feet and crossing his arms. "I like that one myself. I prepared it for a man from Kentucky, but he never came for it for some reason."

"That is exactly what we're looking for," said Jackson as he turned his eyes toward Millard to get his reaction.

Millard was very pleased, as Jackson could see. "We are definitely interested," said Jackson. "When can we try it out?"

"Well, I think you can take the car now and keep it the remainder of the weekend; then Monday morning, we will complete the modifications I spoke of and do the paperwork. Just don't drive it hard until the car is yours. Of course, I know you will need to give it a full trial run before we complete our business."

Millard had not contributed much to the discussion. He wanted to listen and learn as much as possible. This business was new to him, and he knew he would have to learn quickly if he was to succeed. At this point, he decided that he should intercede to a limited extent. He started by asking some questions that would indicate that he was actually the person who, in the final analysis, would be the owner of the car. "On Monday," he said, "we will make every effort to have the money in full with some to spare. It will all depend on cost and the expense of getting the car on the road."

Jackson then looked at Millard and, in a kind voice said, "Don't worry about that right now, Millard. We will discuss these details at a later time, tonight or tomorrow."

Wallace handed the keys to Millard and said, "Seems that we are all in agreement sufficient to last until Monday at least. Drive carefully and take good care of that beauty over the weekend. I think you will discover what a fine car you will be getting. It will, indeed, run like a scalded dog to say the least."

Millard started the engine, and all he could hear was raw power under the hood. He exited the barn with great care and followed Jackson home. As they drove along, Millard could hardly believe what he was doing.

When they drove up to Walter's home, Walter was standing there with a smile on his face. "I knew you boys would strike up a deal and come home with a fine automobile just as we talked about."

"Lawrence took a liking to Millard right away," Jackson said. "We talked things over, and he allowed him to take the car with him. Millard will return on Monday to complete the deal we have been discussing."

Millard said, "I have never owned a car, but I have driven one enough to know this one is a tiger. We have not discussed the price of the car. Maybe I should have talked money with Lawrence, but for some reason I decided to wait until I talked to you first," he said to Walter.

"You see how much cash you can come up with, and we will go from there."

These were comforting words to Millard. He had never had a person so well-off treat him with such kindness.

Millard did not want to take Walter for granted, however, and he wanted to be perfectly honest with him. After Walter went into the house, Millard turned to Jackson with a worried look on his face and said, "I think I have been putting the wagon before the horse. I should have known more about the cost of buying this car. Guess I just got carried away for a while. I do need an estimate of the amount of cash I will need, or come Monday, I am going to be one embarrassed man."

"Let's sit in the car and do a little figuring," Jackson replied. After entering the car, Jackson began writing and figuring in a small notebook he pulled from his pocket. Soon, he wrote one large figure on a page and handed it to Millard. "That's a rough estimate, but I think it is reasonably accurate and will do for now."

"I don't know about this," Millard said. "I had no idea automobiles cost so much."

"They do," Jackson replied. "A regular family car doesn't cost anything like this, but you are buying a superfast machine that can make you rich."

"This figure of $500 looks larger every time I look at it. I have some money hid away but not nearly that much."

Jackson replied, "I think my dad intends to help you out, or he would have not proceeded with this. He knows when to take a chance and knows how to read people more than any man I ever knew. He probably has the situation already figured out. Just drive this jewel home and think about your decisions over the weekend. The way I see it, if you want to go through with the deal, when you return on Monday, we will complete all the details at that time. If you feel it's too much to tackle now, just let us know your decision and that will be that. There will be no hard feelings, and you can come in with us at a later date. It won't bother Pop much, but I can't say he won't be a little disappointed. I can tell he likes you and trusts you completely."

"I will do exactly as you say," said Millard. "I want in this business, and it's now or never. I dread going home and discussing this day with Flora though. She won't like it at all, I can tell you that."

Jackson laughed and said, "Oh hell, Sally didn't like it at first either and still don't, but she don't mind spending the money I bring in. Flora is very religious I know, and it might become a very sticky subject with her, more than it was with Sally."

Millard got in the car at that point and started the engine. "Wish me luck, Jackson. I will probably have hell for breakfast in the morning."

They were both still laughing as he reached the end of the driveway. He headed on up the road with a feeling he had never had before—a feeling of fulfilling his old dream of changing from poverty to prosperity and becoming a man of means. *I will do this thing in spite of hell*, he thought. *This will be my last chance. I can feel it in my bones.*

FOURTEEN

What a stressful day this had been for Millard, even though it was a day of hope he had never felt before. He knew of a roadside café located ahead and decided to stop. A bar was located in the rear of the building, and he stopped for a beer or two.

He eased the car down the narrow path to the house about midnight, the beer from the bar having fortified him enough to greet Flora, who he knew was waiting up for him. He saw the dim lamplight shining through the window. He was very careful to steer clear of the briars and bushes, which were spread out close to the path. He wanted no scratches put on that beautiful car.

As he turned off the engine, he immediately saw Flora looking out the door. It was too dark to see the surprised look on her face, but it was there. She opened the door wide, and he kissed her on the cheek as he walked into the house. "Sorry to be so late" he said, "I have had a long hard day trying to find a car as I set out to do. I think I have been successful, but it will be Monday before I can close the deal. It ain't mine yet, but I think it will be."

"I haven't been very concerned about a car," she replied, "but I have been concerned about you. I have had an uneasy feeling about you all day. Is anything wrong? Why are you so late? Tell me what has been going on."

"There are important things we need to discuss but nothing that can't wait until tomorrow," he replied as he sat down.

Millard started snoring as soon as he closed his eyes. Flora blew out the lamp, but very little sleep came for her. She could sense things were not as they should be. The smell of alcohol on his breath did not necessarily indicate anything was wrong. Nevertheless, the remainder of the night for her was a mixture of dozing and bad dreams.

She was up with the sun and cooking breakfast. Millard was just beginning to stir, but only after Cameron climbed up on the bed and was sitting on his chest, urging him to get up by pulling his nose. Soon they were eating breakfast.

Flora quickly cleared the table and put the house in order. She suspected this would be an unusual day and probably one to be remembered.

Millard insisted they dress nicely. He wanted to take them for a ride in the new car and celebrate all day long. Even if the car was not officially his, he knew it would be. He would find a way to make this another leap forward for him and Flora and Cameron. They went out the door to begin the day with a thorough inspection of the car. Cameron immediately climbed into the driver's seat and began turning the steering wheel and jerking the gear shift.

Flora walked all around the car and then inspected the inside with care. "This is a new car, isn't it? It smells new." She liked the car very much, although she sensed there was more to it than just buying a car. "Millard, this car is beautiful, but how can we ever pay for it. Couldn't an older, less expensive one do us just as well for now?"

"I know you have many questions about yesterday and this car, and I will answer them in due time. Let's have a nice, enjoyable day and save discussions until evening. We do have some serious matters to talk about, and I don't want to mislead you into believing that I have no concerns. We will talk things over when we return. I need more time to think."

Up the path they went and turned onto the dusty road that led them across the hill and to the narrow concrete main highway. With no specific destination in mind, Flora made the decision without hesitation. "Let's drive up and visit with Papa and Mama for a little while. We haven't been there since I don't know when."

Millard nodded his head in agreement. "Can't think of anything better," he said. "I care very deeply for your folks, and I hope we haven't hurt their feelings by staying away so long."

Millard headed up the highway to the road where he had walked so many times when he was courting Flora. As he drove up the road at a moderate pace, he remembered the many times he'd thought of his determination to breach the barrier of poverty. These notions were as fresh in his mind as yesterday. He could now sense a trace of reality and hope just ahead. He would not give up now. He would find a way to pay for this car and drive it to prosperity for his family and himself. He had entertained these thoughts more times than he could remember. His confidence was increasing, and he considered that he would become a man to be reckoned with.

They shortly arrived at Flora's old home. Things had changed very little from all appearances. It was a beautiful, old, two-story house painted white, with large porches extending the full length of the house on both sides. Hanging swings gave it a warm, welcome look. What a sight to behold as the family came out to greet them. Salem and Martha were especially pleased, and Flora's brothers and sisters who still resided in the home were all smiles. Many hugs and handshakes were exchanged. This was a wonderful reminder of what a fine family Flora had and how much he felt a part of it. They had always treated him with such kindness, and he loved every one of them.

He and Salem decided to sit on the porch while lunch was being prepared. Salem wanted to know all about how they had been and whether life was treating them well.

Millard told him of the difficult times they had encountered and the obstacles they had overcome. "Salem, sometimes we felt like giving up, but we just kept on fighting," Millard told him.

Salem said, "I might have been able to have helped you out some if I had known. No one told me about your situation. I wasn't here when you brought Flora here to give birth to Cameron."

Millard did not respond to Salem's willingness to help. He sensed that Salem was sincere in his desire to see them do well.

"From the looks of that fine car you are driving, you seem to have improved things," Salem added, pointing at the Ford admiringly.

"Well, you might not approve when I tell you about what I plan to do, but I don't mind telling you about it at all," said Millard. "I am about to get into the white whiskey business, big-time, you might say. It's a chance of a lifetime, and if I don't get in on it now, I might not have another chance. To be honest, I could end up in prison. Or I could very well become wealthy or very well off. I am tired of being poor and dragging Flora and Cameron around like an old cat moves her kittens. The head man lives in Spruce Willow. He is very rich and knows what he's about."

"You're talking about Walter Stamey, ain't you?"

"True," said Millard, "but how do you know about him?"

"He was born about two miles from here. He sold his farm and moved away a long time ago. I used to run into him occasionally, but he never did mention where he was living. He was a peculiar sort of fellow. They had one son, and that would be Jackson. It was rumored that he started some kind of business after he left here and made a lot of money. Likeable old rascal, as I recall."

"Sounds just like Walter and Jackson," said Millard. "Of course, you remember Jackson from a few years back. He drove the four of us to Knoxville to be married."

"Yes, but I didn't know he was Walter's son at first."

"What do you think about me going into business with them?" asked Millard.

Salem thought for a while and then sharply remarked, "I think it's all right. If I were younger, I might ask to be a part of it. I know how the business works, but I am too old to try anything like that now."

"I wish you could," said Millard. "Wouldn't that be something? Martha and Flora would probably not speak to us for six months."

"You are probably right," Salem agreed as they laughed at the thought of it.

"Martha would accuse me of leading you off to the devil." Millard then expressed his concern about the car to Salem. "We intend to finalize the deal Monday if I can arrange to pay for the car. It's the fastest car on the road I do believe. It will cost about five hundred. That's a lot of money, but with any luck at all, I'll make more money with it than I ever dreamed possible for me."

"I hope you make it, son," said Salem, a serious look on his face. "I know you're a good man, and I have been afraid this damned depression might break your spirit. How much money do you have to put down?" he asked.

"Two hundred dollars that I have saved back from working the mica mine, and I think Flora might have some hid back that I might persuade her to let me have."

"Tell you what; I have a hundred dollars hid in the woodshed to buy grain for the livestock next winter. I will give it to you with no strings attached. If you succeed in your business, you can pay me back. If your plans don't succeed, you need not worry about it. You just keep in touch with me every chance you get, and I will help you in every way possible."

"This whiskey business could make me wealthy, but it could cause me prison time, as I said before. I am not overly concerned because Walter more or less told me that he would stand by me if I get into trouble with the law, and I know he will. That causes me to not worry much about getting caught hauling whiskey, but I am a bit concerned about the bad places I will be going into. If push should come to shove, I might have to fight or shoot my way out of some situation beyond my control."

"I know about such things, but I have a feeling you will come out to the good," Salem said encouragingly.

"Say! I didn't tell you about the money I have made working my mica mine," said Millard, folding up his whittling knife. "I got a government contract to work a mica mine that everyone else thought was worked out. I felt certain it hadn't been, and I was right. It was the first moneymaking break I ever got and still is, but I think it probably is just about worked out now. That gives me even more reason to go into the whiskey business."

After lunch, Millard indicated to the family how happy they were to visit and promised to return soon. Salem motioned to Millard to follow him to the woodshed, where he handed him the money he wanted him to have.

Millard was grateful and told him so. "If what I told you works out, I will repay you with plenty of interest well before winter. I would like to stay longer, but I best hurry home and work my mine as late as I can this evening and all day tomorrow. I might get lucky as I have before in that mine and find enough mica to help on the car. Monday morning, I will settle up with the government office and go to Spruce Willow ready to do business. It makes me somewhat nervous though when I get to thinking about it."

"You have a good head, Millard. I believe you will be successful," Salem remarked.

"I will come by soon and let you know how things are going," Millard assured him.

Millard hurried Flora, and after the usual parting words with the family, they headed toward home.

"Why did you insist on leaving so quickly? We might have hurt their feelings," Flora said, a worried look on her face.

"I explained everything to Salem. He will set things right," said Millard as he increased his speed.

"Then set things right with me too," spoke Flora, a little sarcasm in her voice. "And why have you not mentioned stopping to see your folks?"

"Listen, Flora, before this evening is over, I will tell you everything that has been going on since yesterday morning. You know I do not try to hide things from you."

Millard was too busy thinking to pay much attention to Flora. He wanted to go to his mine as soon as possible. As soon as they parked in the yard, he asked Flora if she would fill a lantern with oil and go with him to his mica mine. "Don't ask any questions now; just please do as I ask."

She did as he asked and was ready in a few minutes. Millard did not want to chance scratching the car, so they walked to the mine. When they arrived at the mine, he told her that he wanted to work there as long as possible. "You just watch Cameron, and I will do the work."

He immediately began working with his pick and shovel, careful not to miss even the smaller pieces of mica. He would work about thirty minutes and rested ten. "I can work at this pace for long periods of time," he told Flora.

She watched and admired how thoroughly he sorted through the soil as he used his pick and shovel alternately. He worked for about two hours with little success. He then began to slow as his pick hit something solid. "Sounds like mica to me," he said, parting the dirt with his hands, and picked up a chunk about two feet in diameter. "This is worth several dollars," he remarked. He held it up for Flora and Cameron to see. "This might be the last chunk of mica I will ever dig out of this mine, but I am thankful for what I have achieved here. I only hope that I will never have to mine any more, anywhere, for anything. I want to do things more in keeping with my ambitions and plans for a brighter future and aboveground, with fresh air and under sunny skies."

"I think that you will do just that," said Flora before he could say more. "This has been a good day."

FIFTEEN

It was getting late, and Millard decided to take his little family home. Cameron was getting sleepy, and Flora had a tired look about her. "I will return tomorrow after church and dig as much as I can. I will need every cent I can make to pay on the car."

His remarks made Flora even more suspicious about the events of the day.

When they arrived home, Cameron was sleeping soundly. Flora quickly put him to bed. She could hardly wait for Millard to answer the questions that were burning in her mind. "Where were you all day yesterday and what were you doing out so late? And where did you get that automobile, which we obviously cannot afford?"

"Now wait a minute before you explode," said Millard." You knew I was going to look for a car to buy. Well, I ran into Jackson Stamey up at the store, and he agreed to help me, not only with the car but with other things as well. I spent most of the day with him and his father, Walter, talking business. We then went to a garage outside Spruce Willow that specializes in modifying cars. I found a suitable one, and the owner offered to let me drive it over the weekend. I stopped for a couple of beers on the way home to relieve some of the tension that I had built up during the day."

Millard stopped to get his breath and then continued. "Now I will tell the part you will probably not agree with. Walter almost lost his business due to the Depression. He sold it just in time to keep from going bankrupt. He and Jackson decided to go into the whiskey business. They operate all over these mountains and intend to expand and need some men they can trust and keep silent about the business. They asked me to be their first employee, and that is where the car came into the picture. Your suspicions about the car are correct. It is expensive and is built for speed and stamina. It must hold up at a high rate of speed. It is priced at five hundred dollars. I have two hundred that I've been saving, and your dad agreed to loan me another hundred. I am certain Walter will loan me the other two hundred. He is wealthy, as you know, and he more or less has assured me that, if I should get into trouble, he will do his best to get me out."

"I do not agree with any of what you have told me," said Flora, solemn-faced and determined in her conviction. "It is a cauldron of trouble, and I can feel it. You have been doing so well in your mining operation, and I want you to continue with it. We have never known such happiness and prosperity, and I don't want it to end. Please don't go through with this. Maybe I could get a job taking in washings or something to keep you from having to work so hard. I will do anything you say to help out. You have always carried the heavy load since we married."

"Flora, I know what you say is true as you see it, but one major mistake, and you and Cameron would have to face this hard cold world alone. I have been noticing indications that the mine might be close to becoming unproductive. Then I would have to abandon the operation or chance digging farther into the mountain searching for more mica. I have never told you the dangers that really lurk in mines, but you know many of them. It is hard, backbreaking work, and I don't want to lose my health or maybe my life in that dark, foul-smelling place. Some days when I work there, I can almost sense death lurking in the shadows. I know that is just my imagination, but I do know I can't continue working there much longer."

Flora sat silent for a while, and then with sadness in her voice, she asked, "Have you considered another type of work or another mine that is not so hazardous?"

"I don't give a damn about other work. There ain't any other work, and I don't intend to work in mining ever again."

She knew Millard had made his decision, and there was no reason to argue with him. After hearing him speak as he had about the mine, she did not want him to continue working there even for one more day. It was his love for her and Cameron that had caused him to take such chances, and she loved him for it. Her Holy Bible told her that women should obey their husbands in such matters, and that sealed the decision for her. He had never demanded anything of her or ordered her around, and she would now follow him as she always had.

After they had gone to bed and blown out the lamp, Flora realized that her intuition had been active lately, which was a signal to her that something was about to change in their lives—something that would change their entire direction forever. She had ignored it and forced it to vanish. Now she knew that, perhaps, the change Millard had proposed was something that was meant to be. And too, she was not always right.

She knew Millard was apprehensive about his decisions and probably worried about failure as he often did. Even so, she had something to tell him that would probably add even more to his concerns. She had planned to wait until a more appropriate time, such as after a well-planned supper, but she knew it would be best to tell him now. It might provide him with information that would have some impact upon his current decision and perhaps on into the future.

She knew he was not asleep as she moved close by his side and kissed him on the cheek and stroked his hair. "Dear," she said, "I have something I must tell you that is very important."

She hesitated briefly as he quietly listened, knowing she was about to hit him with something heavy. Otherwise she would not be acting so strangely.

"I am pregnant," she whispered.

"What!" he said as he sat up in bed. "Did you say pregnant?"

"Yes," she said, "and I shouldn't have brought it up at this time." She thought she had angered him.

"Why haven't you told me before? This is the best damn news I have had in a long time. I have wanted a little girl a long time now. Light the lamp while I get that bottle of brandy Jackson gave me the other day. I want to celebrate. I couldn't go to sleep now no matter if I wanted to."

Flora lit the lamp, and Millard jumped out of bed and hugged her so tightly she could hardly breathe. They laughed and laughed and then sat down on the edge of the bed and sipped several ounces of the brandy. She was so happy now that she knew the news was such good tonic for him.

After talking for a while they returned to bed. "Thanks are to God," she whispered to herself as sleep overcame her. Beautiful dreams surrounded her all night.

The next day being the Sabbath, they were off to church. They had not been attending church regularly for several months. They enjoyed church but could never attend regularly since they had been married, except during times when they lived close enough to walk. They had the nicest car around now, and not only were they happy to have transportation to church, but going also allowed Millard a chance to show off his fine automobile.

As usual, the sermon was fiery and the music was uplifting. Not a sour note was detected in the choir, and the old organ never sounded better. Millard's bass, as always, was beautiful beyond words and carried far. It seemed to just ring down the valley. This was one of those special Sundays when everything went right and all was joyful.

After services were over and everyone gathered in the front of the church to exchange greetings and a certain amount of gossip, everyone headed home to enjoy what was usually the best meal of the week. Millard, however, would not leave until all the men had had an opportunity to admire his car and he'd answered all their questions.

When they reached home, Flora hurriedly fried delicious bologna and made hot biscuits and gravy. Millard and Cameron ate their fill and licked their fingers. Flora was always happy when they were happy, whether it was because of a meal they liked or something they enjoyed doing together.

After lunch, they played ball until Cameron became tired and was ready for a nap. They had allowed him to win the ball game, and he was happy as could be.

Millard and Flora retired to the front porch. They both knew there were issues at hand that must be cleared up. Their mood was relaxed, which always made talking easier.

After a few minutes Millard asked, "Are you still satisfied with the decisions we made last night?"

"Of course I am," Flora replied. "I know if anyone can make such a drastic change in their life and cause it to work, you can. You well know how I feel about liquor and the harm it does when used in excess, but that does not change the way I feel about supporting you in such important decisions. You and Cameron are my life, and I know you always have us in mind and want to make us secure and happy."

"I know this mine operation and our gift of this little farm were our first breaks, but I truly believe my chance meeting with Jackson Saturday morning will prove to be my best and perhaps last big chance for success. I still remember almost every thought that went through my mind while I walked to see you and go to those wonderful barn dances."

Millard sat upright in his chair, looked at Flora, and said, "When Cameron awakens, let's drive over to the mine and look around a bit. I need to retrieve my tools as well." Millard was silent for a few minutes, and then, in a shaking voice, he added, "Pray for me, Flora. You are a good woman."

"You don't have to make such a request of me," she said. She put her arms around him and held her head close to his chest. "I love you, and every day, I think of you often while you are away. Every thought causes me to be close to you."

"I can't make it in this world without your help and prayers," he said in a low, soft, convincing tone. "I have always known that, even though I have never told you in so many words. I know the whiskey business is not what you want and you consider it sinful. Perhaps it is, but consider it as a way to make up lost years and hard times. You and Cameron and the little one you hold inside you deserve more."

Just then Cameron awoke, and the family headed for the mine.

Cameron was quick to recognize the surroundings as they walked to the mine from where they had parked. He kept repeating, "Dig, dig, dig," over and over.

Millard entered the mine to look around once more. After all, it had been good to him during these difficult times. It was a dangerous place, no doubt about it. He had been lucky, and he knew it, especially working alone as he had been doing. What he was about to do was dangerous as well, but if something happened to him, it would occur in the open, and he would not be buried alive as could have happened here. Actually he had come very close to death the first time he'd entered this mine. That incident was something he would never forget.

He picked up his tools and carried them to the entrance of the mine, where Flora and Cameron were waiting. As they started toward the car, Millard said, "Wait a minute, Flora. You know, I had planned to work over here today in hopes of finding at least one more valuable piece of mica. I am going to need every cent I can come up with to help me close the deal tomorrow. I believe I should work one hour before we leave."

Before she could voice her objection, he had entered the mine and she could hear him digging. She did not like this place anymore. One hour passed and then another. Cameron had been playing in the dirt with his toy shovel, but he was getting tired now. Flora called to Millard, and he was quick to respond.

Then out he came again with his tools and laid them down.

"Are you ready to go now?" she asked.

"Yes, if you can wait a minute for me to retrieve my loot," he said as he entered the mine again.

Back out he came with an enormous grin on his face. In his arms, he was carrying a large hunk of mica. "This is a fine chunk," he said. "It's good quality mica, and it's heavy. I believe that it might be worth over five dollars," he said. "Let's keep what I have found today and yesterday in case something should go wrong with my plans next week."

Flora stepped forward and put her hand on his shoulder. "Listen to me, Millard, no matter what, don't ever enter that mine again. I had a very strong sensation as you were walking out of the mine just now. Promise me you will do as I say."

"Okay, okay!" he said. "I had no intention of ever entering that place again anyway."

As they were returning home Millard suddenly drove past the turnoff and continued on toward Spruce Willow. Flora did not question where they were going or why; she knew she and Cameron would know soon enough. There was a small café in Spruce Willow that Millard knew well. It was a lovely place, with beautiful country curtains and tablecloths that complemented the soft, cozy atmosphere. It was kept spotlessly clean and the walls were covered with a combination of matching wallpaper and a pleasing off-white paint. Millard had decided they should have a treat, and that was where he took them.

It was a rare occasion for them and a very pleasant one. After Millard washed the dirt from the mine off his hands and face and brushed the dust off his pants, they sat down and ordered a large hamburger and a Coca-Cola. For dessert, they had a delicious piece of chocolate cake. What a wonderful, spontaneous occasion it was.

Of course, Cameron probably enjoyed it the most. He ended up with chocolate cake all over his face. Millard and Flora could not hold back the laughter; he looked so funny. All they could see was his eyes until Flora cleaned the chocolate from his face with a table napkin.

As they were driving home, Flora said, "What prompted you to take us out like this? What a nice surprise it was."

"I just did it," he said with a smile.

All the way home, Cameron kept saying, "I like chocolate cake; go back, go back."

Millard assured him they would go back again.

When they arrived home, it was almost dark. Flora lit the lamp, and they put Cameron to bed. Their day had been delightful and happy. Millard especially wanted it that way. He knew tomorrow would begin a new way of life for them, and he was not certain of what to expect come morning.

Millard and Flora were not ready for bed. They both knew they should talk before sleeping. Flora began the conversation by asking Millard if he still felt comfortable about his new undertaking.

He could not force himself to tell her anything but the truth. "Flora, I do not know anything for certain, but I do know this will be my last chance to fulfill my hopes and plans that I have already told you about. Most of tomorrow will involve completing the deal on the car and taking care of business, I think. No doubt Walter will have a long talk with me about my part of his operation and what he expects of me. Jackson no doubt knows everything well. It will probably take all day to get me trained and ready for work. That's all I can think of for tomorrow. I will probably be home before dark, but if I'm late, don't worry."

"We have discussed little about our new baby," said Flora. "He or she is already beginning to move a little."

"I have not forgotten about that baby girl," Millard quickly replied, knowing he had no control, and kidding Flora a little. "I will leave that decision up to you now, if you don't mind. We will do what is necessary as time gets closer to the big event. Things are in hand now, and we will keep them that way."

"Your words are always comforting in such important decisions," Flora replied, placing his hand on her stomach.

Sleep came quickly, as did the dawn.

Millard was out of bed and half-dressed before Flora woke from a sound sleep. He quickly shaved and was ready to go. Flora prepared breakfast for him, and he was off, a tin cup of coffee in his hand. This whole thing was getting too much for her. She was feeling nervous about everything. She could muster no cheer for this day, until the sun filtered into the valley and Cameron came bouncing out of bed. What a joy he was.

Millard pulled onto the highway and headed straight for the mining office to cancel his contract and sell those splendid pieces of mica he had. The government employees at the office were happy to see him and appeared sad that he was canceling his contract. They assured him of another contract if he should decide to continue in the business later on.

Since he was running earlier than expected, he decided to drive over to the mine for a last look at the place where he had spent so many days. He was feeling sentimental and just could not resist going there once more. As he walked to the entrance of the mine, he had a strange feeling that he did not like. He continued on a few paces, and then decided he did not like that feeling at all.

Just as he started walking away he felt the ground shake and heard a sickening noise. "Hellfire," he said, "I am getting out of here."

He quickly turned and could not believe what he was seeing. The entire mine was caving in, and dirt and rocks kept falling until no opening remained. It was as if something inside had completely sealed the entrance.

Millard was visibly shaken when he returned to his car. Never before had he seen such an occurrence in a mine. He remembered his promise to Flora not to enter that mine again. *I will never understand how she can predict when and where danger lurks,* he thought as he entered the highway and headed toward Spruce Willow.

He was certain that he would now be dead if he had gone into that mine again after her warning. "That mine must be the entrance to the devil's quarters," he said out loud to himself.

Sixteen

Soon, Millard was knocking on Walter Stamey's door. Walter opened the door, still in his robe and holding a cup of coffee in his hand. "Good morning, Millard," he said.

"Good morning to you, sir," answered Millard. "I hope I didn't rouse you too early."

"No, I usually arise much earlier. I didn't sleep very well last night, so I decided to rest a little later than usual. I feel well and rested now though, and I am ready for a good day. Come on in and have some coffee. Jackson will show up soon and we can get down to business."

Walter and Millard were talking and enjoying their coffee when they heard Jackson enter the driveway. He came into the kitchen, poured himself a mug of coffee, and sat down at the table. "I thought you two would be working hard at something by now," he said. "Sally would not allow me to leave the house this morning until I did a host of chores she had wanted me to do for some time. Of all mornings, I wanted to arrive early and visit with Millard before we started with a busy day."

"Not to worry," said Millard. "I was too anxious to prevent me from being on time. To be truthful, I wanted to make a good impression, and Flora knew it."

Jackson and Walter laughed. "That is a sign of a good, conscientious man," Walter said as he looked at Millard with a sincere expression on his face. It was evident that he was very impressed with Millard. "We work hard, but we try to have a little fun too," he added as he shifted his chair forward.

"Well, Millard, how did you like the car?" Jackson asked.

"I have never driven anything so fast. I took it easy so Flora would not be afraid for me to drive it. I did open it up once when I was alone up on the highway. It handled great, and I was very pleased with everything about it. I am not afraid of it, but I did find that the roads around these mountains are not advanced enough to accept such speed safely. Still, I decided I'd rather have something fast and dependable in our line of work. Better to have something that will leave everything else behind and keep me out of trouble. I have little fear of being caught, but I do need to improve my driving abilities. I want to be an expert driver and keep this car in good shape."

"The first order of business to begin the day, I suppose, should be to get that fine car of yours in your name," Walter said, looking at Millard as though he wanted Millard's approval.

Millard nodded in agreement, and the first day of a new life for Millard had begun.

"How do you want to work this arrangement, Millard?" asked Walter.

"I have $380 to pay down on the vehicle. That leaves me $120 short. If you could advance me enough to complete the deal and hold the title as collateral, I sure would appreciate it," said Millard.

"Fine and dandy," Walter remarked, "and there is no need for me to hold the title. Your word is enough collateral for me. You can repay me a little at a time as you can afford it, and that will be that." Walter then reached out to shake Millard's hand. "The deal is made, and we need not mention it anymore," Walter added, patting Millard on the back for good measure.

Soon, they all were in Millard's car, headed for Lawrence Davis's place to finalize the deal. Their business did not take long. Lawrence was expecting them and had things ready. They paid cash for the automobile and received the title. A mechanic completed the springs and made other necessary adjustments on the car. Walter and Lawrence talked over some mutual business concerns, and now the car belonged to Millard free and clear. This was strictly a business trip, and they were all too busy to get involved in chitchat.

They immediately returned to Walter's home to iron out the details necessary to orient Millard to his new job.

As they relaxed in the den, Walter talked to Jackson and Millard. "Boys," he said, "as soon as Millard gets the hang of this new job, I intend to step back and run the business end of things. I am getting too old to be driving up and down these mountains and through hollows and gaps and the like. I am going to turn over my outside duties to you, Jackson. And, Millard, you will take over Jackson's part of this operation. I have decided to hire three more good men, and that is all for the foreseeable future. Maybe we can take on one or two more sometime later as we see the need."

Millard wanted to learn more details and specifics of his immediate duties, but he decided not to ask questions at that point in the conversation. He knew Jackson was listening and would give him all the help and instructions he would need.

Walter continued, "Millard, I should have explained to you more about the bad parts of the liquor business we are in before we got this far along, but I thought you probably already knew much of what it was about, and I let it go at that. We are in a dangerous business, and you will have to be alert at all times. We distribute our liquor to cafés, honky-tonks, roadhouses, backroom gambling houses, private residences of all classes of people, and many kinds of places you would never suspect. I even take a full load to a preacher about once a month. We don't know what all of our customers do with it, and we ask no questions. Two important things keep us well established with our customers. One, they know we keep our mouths shut no matter what we hear or see. Two, we sell clean, quality, fine whiskey consistently. We run a classy operation, and they all know it.

"Jackson and I have been all alone with this so far, but we have moved a lot of booze and made a considerable amount of money since we started. You will need a good pistol for self-protection, and don't be afraid to use it. Carry it on you at all times when you are working and leave it on you until you get home. Find a way to conceal it and, yet, get to it quickly."

Millard replied, "I have a .38-caliber Smith and Wesson, but it might be difficult to conceal. I might manage to tuck it in my belt and wear a loose shirt over it. If that don't work, I will manage some other way."

Walter turned to Jackson and asked, "Do you have more to add to what I just said? I know there are many things I have not covered, but we can coach him along. Allow him a few weeks, and he will be fine."

"One important point we need to discuss now is money," said Jackson. "Millard needs to have some idea of what to expect. He has a family to support."

"You are quite right," Walter said. He looked at Millard. "Would thirty dollars a week do until you are familiar with your route? Then we'll consider salary and commissions again at that time?"

Millard smiled and said, "More than satisfactory to me." He did not want to appear foolish, but he was elated. He considered himself a professional now and wanted to behave as one.

Walter's wife, Mary, called from the kitchen to inform them that lunch was ready. Millard felt very much at home and perfectly at ease as he followed Walter and Jackson through the dining room to the kitchen table.

Mary greeted him with a nice hug and welcomed him into "my part of the house," as she called it. A large plate of delicate-looking sandwiches was on the table, and glasses of delicious lemonade stood by their plates. This was like living in another world to Millard. He was already feeling like the man he had always wanted to be.

The afternoon was essentially uneventful. Jackson and Millard had planned to cover a small part of the route Millard would be covering in his new job. Instead, Walter decided they should just sit around and exchange ideas and future plans. He seemed to want Millard to feel totally at ease with his change in both lifestyle and occupation. They decided that Jackson and Millard would leave the following morning at ten o'clock for parts of the Blue Ridge that were most unfamiliar to Millard, yet close enough to return home before dark.

Evening shadows were falling as Millard arrived home. Flora and Cameron were anxiously waiting his arrival. Supper was ready, and they went inside to enjoy the deliciously prepared meal and a pleasant evening.

Millard and Flora retired to the porch after Cameron was tucked into bed. The stars were out, and a very slight, warm breeze was stirring. Millard could hardly wait to share events of the day with Flora. They sat holding hands quietly before Millard began.

She listened closely as he described to her what seemed like a different life from anything she had ever known. Obviously, it was a life based upon money; luxury; excitement; and, perhaps, danger. She was happy for him but hoped the uneasy feelings she was experiencing would depart.

"My duties will begin Monday morning," Millard told her. "Jackson will travel with me until I become familiar with the first phase of the operation. I intend to concentrate on learning that part of the business quickly so that I can relieve Jackson of that responsibility. I don't know how long it will take, but I do know Jackson covers a large territory and many miles. I think he has been working too hard trying to keep up, and hopefully, I will remove much of the burden and stress he is now carrying." As he spoke, he noticed his wife staring off into the distance.

"Flora, your silence bothers me. I sure hope you're not about to reveal another premonition such as the mica mine cave-in. That one just about scared the life out of me. If you have something to say about all this, tell me now, and I will surely listen. I will make no bones about that. I can still hear the rumbling of that old mine as it collapsed and belched out all that dust. No, can't ever forget that."

"Nothing I can say now would have any meaning," she remarked. "All I can say at this time is that I do not have a comfortable feeling about something. It might have nothing to do with your new job. Perhaps something will come to me later. If it does, I will tell you."

✳ ✳ ✳

It was Sunday morning, and church services were about to begin. Millard was seated at his place in the choir and appeared happy as could be. Flora and Cameron were in the front row. It was a beautiful day, and the church was full. Two lively songs were sung at the beginning of the service, with the choir director moving both arms and keeping them in perfect rhythm. Cameron started clapping his hands, keeping time, and Flora made him stop.

Reverend Brown was standing in the pulpit and sounded amen loudly several times during the singing. It was a wonderful Sabbath day and a wonderful service. Flora considered the sermon the reverend delivered to be exceptional. She was a Methodist and preferred a more orderly service, but this one was just fine.

After the service was over, they drove Dad and Ma home. Grandma and other members of the family were not at the service. They did not stay for lunch and, after visiting for only a short while, soon departed. Millard wanted to get home and relax and prepare for the coming day. They promised his family to return soon for a long visit and to take them for a nice drive in their new automobile. The family members were satisfied and seemed to understand. Flora and Cameron wanted to visit all afternoon, but Flora did not pressure Millard to stay. She knew he was already beginning to feel a little pressure about his new job, although he made no mention of it.

After lunch, Millard took a long nap, which was uncharacteristic of him, especially on a Sabbath day. Later, Flora saw him on the porch cleaning his gun. She asked him if he was expecting trouble.

"No," he told her. "Walter just told me that I needed to carry a gun in our line of work. He said it might come in handy, as I would sometimes be going into some bad places. I am taking him at his word."

That night, they went to bed early. Millard placed his hand on Flora's stomach and patted gently where he could feel the baby moving. "Don't worry about me and my new job," he said. "Things will be all right. I have two very savvy, experienced men as my guides. I would trust either of them with my life."

Flora made no reply.

Morning came, and Flora was awakened abruptly by the sound of a car engine running. She rose up in bed and pulled the curtain enough to see Millard tucking his pistol under his belt and extra ammunition in his pocket. *Oh my goodness*, she thought. *How did he manage to get out of bed and ready for work without me hearing him moving around?*

Within seconds, he was in the car and driving away. "Dear God, bless this day and keep him safe," she whispered quietly. She then realized why she had slept so soundly. The child she was carrying probably needed more rest now that it was growing so quickly. Being aware of her delicate condition, Millard had made a conscious effort not to disturb her.

As Millard drove away from the house and up the road past the crest of the hill where he hoped to build a fine new home in the future, he could picture in his mind how it would look. He would face it so it overlooked the valley and river below; the rear would face the highway in the distance. He enjoyed the wandering thought but had little doubt that he would eventually make this specific thought a lasting reality. He turned onto the highway and headed on toward Spruce Willow and what he hoped would be the life he had kept in his heart and in his dreams.

Walter was standing on his front porch as Millard turned into the driveway. To his surprise, Jackson's car was already there. The day was about to begin, and Millard's heart was pounding a little as he approached the porch.

"Good morning," said Walter as he turned toward the door.

"The same to you, sir," Millard replied.

The two men went inside to find Jackson sitting at the kitchen table finishing his coffee. "Have some coffee and something to eat," Jackson said.

"No thanks," replied Millard. "I have had breakfast, and I am too excited to eat anything else."

"Anxious to get on the road, huh," Jackson said with a smile.

"I have looked forward to this morning since last Friday," Millard answered.

"Well, we might as well get with it then. Drive your car around the house to the basement entrance, and we'll load it up."

"Load your car up as well if you don't mind, Jackson," said Walter. "I will drive it and catch up on some of our longer runs where we are behind schedule."

Millard drove his car around to the large basement garage door, proceeded inside, and closed the door behind him. He was amazed at how well the driveway and door were hidden from view. The high wall in back and the shrubbery and trees made the landscape look very natural. The massive basement was stacked high with many cases of bonded whiskey of varying brands, and the massive amount of white liquor in half-gallon mason jars was unreal. Strong, handmade crates held four jars each and were constructed with four slots to house each jar securely and prevent breakage. Millard marveled at such a well-organized system.

Jackson and Millard quickly loaded the car to capacity, careful not to place their cargo in such a way as to be easily noticed. They stacked several quilts and pillows on top to further conceal their load from anyone looking in the window.

Millard was careful to drive at a moderate speed as they headed down the road leading through Spruce Willow. They went north up a road that was unfamiliar to Millard, and within a mile of Spruce Willow, they came to a very ordinary-looking country store. Jackson motioned for him to back up to a side door toward the rear of the building.

The store owner quickly opened the door and held up two fingers. They carried in two cases of white liquor and placed them behind some sacks of cow feed piled loosely near the door. The store owner paid Jackson and turned his eyes toward Millard. "Who is your friend?" he asked.

"His name is Millard Watson, and he will be working with us now. This fine man is Blaine Houston, a good, steady customer, Millard," Jackson said.

"Glad to know you," Millard said as he and Mr. Houston shook hands.

As they drove away and continued up the same road, Jackson said, "I noticed you were very observant back there—memorizing every detail."

"You are right," said Millard. "I wanted to be able to recognize him and remember his name anywhere."

"I do the same thing and always have since I first started this job," replied Jackson. "That policy has served me well. People like to be called by name, and that is especially true in this business."

They continued on down the road several miles until they came to another general store, very similar to the last one. The transaction was very similar as well. They sold one crate and carried it to a small room in back of the store and, again, placed it among some sacks of cow feed.

Millard could hardly believe their next stop. It was at the home of a widow who was slightly elderly. She ordered three crates of white and two pints of bonded whiskey. They carried her order about fifty feet behind the house and placed it behind a spring in a clump of bushes. Millard had seen her before but did not know her name.

Jackson always introduced him at every stop during the day.

At midday, they had sold about half of their load. They stopped for a large bologna sandwich and a soft drink at a large country store that sold everything from farming equipment to hardware. It housed a post office, and one room contained work clothing and sturdy-looking boots and brogans. An enormous potbellied stove sat in the middle section of the store. Millard had never seen a stove so large.

They sold four cases of white whiskey and several pints of bonded, which Jackson said was the store's usual order. The owner showed little concern about who might be watching as they carried his order from the car and placed it in plain view inside the store. Millard considered that he probably moved it to a less obvious place later.

As the day progressed, Millard listened and observed carefully as Jackson explained the whiskey business and the delivery route for that day. They delivered to all their customers within a ten-mile radius of Spruce Willow, going up and down each road and taking care not to pass even one road where they had a customer. "You have to be very methodical about each route each day," Jackson explained. "A customer passed by is a customer lost, unless you have a very good reason. Each day we cover a territory, and we complete the day's run even if it takes until after dark to get through. I don't like that part, but if you want to stay in business, you have to be dependable."

As they made their last stop, dark was closing in. They had only one case of white whiskey and two pints of bonded left. "That's the way we like the day to end. We had enough to service everyone, with just a bit left over. Today was perfect."

SEVENTEEN

Soon after they arrived at Walter's, Millard left for home. He was not physically tired, but he could not say the same for his mental state. The chore of memorizing all the roads they had traveled and the customers they had served was taxing to him. He knew he had an excellent memory, but he was not entirely satisfied that he remembered them all. He was not about to run the risk of losing customers due to forgetfulness. He then decided on the only alternative. Contrary to Walter's policy about the danger of keeping records, he would do just that. He was nearing the café where he often stopped for a beer; he pulled up and went inside. While he was drinking his beer, he carefully recorded each customer he had met that day. *What a relief*, he thought, *and this will be my secret alone.*

It was well past supper when he arrived at home. Flora was getting Cameron ready for bed. She had kept supper for him, and he was glad. His bologna sandwich had been gone long ago.

Flora could smell the alcohol but made no mention of it. That was evidence to her that his day had been stressful.

Only after they had gone to bed did he reveal the events of the day to her. "I enjoyed the day, even though I had to be very alert to everything that happened. It was exciting, and as I become familiar with all the details of the job, I know I will do well. Jackson is a good teacher, and that made things easier. I'm glad I made the decision to go into this business, even if some folks do believe it's evil. It is unlawful I know, but with times the way they are, a man has to do the best he can for his family. This is one lucky break for us.

"Speaking of family, how is the new one coming along?"

"Kicking more every day," answered Flora. "I do not have many months to go. I believe it will be another boy, because he moves about exactly as Cameron did before he was born."

"That's all right," Millard replied. "I would like a girl, but whatever God gives us will be satisfactory to me."

"You are such a good man, Millard. You just be careful each day when you are working. These old mountain roads are dangerous, and I know you will go into dangerous places as your work requires it."

"I hope you are not trying to tell me something," said Millard. "You are not having another bad view into the future are you, like your last one about the mine? If you are, let me know ahead of time for gosh sakes."

"I will," she assured him.

"I won't wake you in the morning. You need to rest, and I know Cameron will have you up soon enough. I will find breakfast in Spruce Willow."

He soon began snoring—another sign of a stressful day.

The following morning, Millard and Jackson loaded the car soon after Millard arrived at Walter's. Walter was standing on the porch as they drove away. From the way he was standing, he looked as though he did not feel well.

Millard mentioned it to Jackson, and he had noticed it as well. "I think we need to train you on your route as soon as possible. I think the old man should continue to supervise and work from inside. I believe his days on the road are about over. We probably need to proceed with hiring two more good men and also more good moonshiners. Suppliers of good whiskey like we require are hard to find, and the way our business is picking up we will have to keep pace if we want to remain in business."

"I think I can help out when you give me the word," Millard said. "I know one of the best whiskey makers around and another man who is a blacksmith. Both are good men and might be interested in working with us. John Hughes is the blacksmith; he fought with us when we tangled with that Jacobs Hollow bunch."

"Heck yes! I remember him. He was one hell of a fighter as I recall."

"That's him," Millard replied.

"We will discuss the matter again later," Jackson said.

"Today we will move in a circle, much as we did yesterday," Jackson said, motioning with his arm. "The only difference being, we will extend about five miles farther out. Otherwise, our day should be about the same. We will be stopping at a couple of honky-tonks, but they are peaceful places, as opposed to some we will stop at later."

Their day went well from start to finish. Most of their deliveries were to country stores of all sizes and shapes. Three stops were made at private homes. The two stops of most interest to Millard were the two honky-tonks. Both establishments ordered many cases of white whiskey, and between the two, they took almost all the bonded whiskey he and Jackson had in the car. The honky-tonk owners, like the large store on the previous day, cared very little about concealing their deliveries. Millard quickly came to the correct conclusion that all law officers and public officials who were a threat had been bought off.

At days end, he and Jackson had sold their entire cargo and could have sold more.

"Damn, what a business," Millard remarked.

"It is that," replied Jackson. "Now you see why I wanted you to come into business with us so badly. You were perfect for the job, and we needed you long before now." He then pulled a roll of money from his pocket for Millard to see. "I will turn this over to Pop as I always do.

"It will take the remainder of this week to cover the entire route," he added. "Next Monday will be your first day on your own—that is, if you feel you are ready. I need to replace Pop as soon as possible. He is still in good health, and I want him to stay that way. But you and me both know he needs to retire from the heavy work and all the driving required every day."

"I understand," Millard replied, "and I will contact Horace and John about working with us whenever you want me to."

"Go ahead and do it this weekend if you can," said Jackson, a sense of urgency in his voice.

That night, Millard slept soundly, but Flora was awake much of the night because of uneasy feelings.

When Millard arrived at work the next morning, Jackson was ready to leave. They loaded the car quickly and were ready to depart when Walter came out and held up his hand for them to wait. He wanted to express his gratitude to them for looking toward the future for the business and gave full approval of the plans they had been making. "Jackson informed me about the discussion you two had yesterday, and I approve wholeheartedly," he said as he looked at Millard with a pleasant expression on his face. "Just keep planning things, and we will have a meeting soon and work out the details."

Millard thanked him kindly and promised to help out in every way he could.

They did not encompass Spruce Willow again. Their route stretched farther out, and the roads went in every direction. Most of them, however, were familiar to Millard and that made recollection of them much easier. They delivered to private homes, honky-tonks, and country stores, much as before.

One stop was at the end of a very narrow road, which must have been five miles off the beaten path. As they drove into the yard, a huge man with enormous, long, muscular arms and a thick, heavy body walked off the porch to the car. Jackson called him Ed.

When Jackson introduced him, Millard got out of the car and shook hands with him. He knew this was no time to act timid. Ed had a very nice handshake, and after exchanging pleasantries, Millard had a very good impression of the man.

As they drove down the road, Millard said, "I didn't know about that man when we first drove up to the house. Judging from his looks, I thought he might get a switch and give us a whipping."

Jackson laughed loudly and said, "I should have prepared you for that one, but he is such a nice man, it didn't occur to me. He has a building out back of his house that's a gambling joint. It looks like a large woodshed, but it is far from that. Gambling men flock in on weekends, and they play poker big-time. He will eventually show you around when he gets to know you a little better."

They made only a few more deliveries until they'd emptied their load and then headed back to home base.

Walter was in the yard when they arrived. "You guys are returning a little early today," he said.

"We ran out of booze and had no choice," replied Jackson. "I am convinced that we have to expand and soon."

On Thursday morning, Millard headed down the road to Spruce Willow feeling happy and ready to work. It was his fourth day on the job, and he was already feeling comfortable in his duties. He was amazed at how quickly he had become so involved with the inner workings of the business. He could visualize nothing in the future but success, and what a wonderful feeling it was.

As soon as he arrived at Walter's, he drove directly to the basement entrance and began loading the car. Jackson arrived soon, and they were on their way.

"Where was Walter?" Millard asked.

"Mom said he left before dawn this morning. I don't know what got into him. He is unpredictable like this sometimes. We have been running behind a little, and he is probably trying to help us catch up today," explained Jackson.

This day was much the same again. The pattern of delivery was the same, but the area extended far beyond Spruce Willow—beginning where they had left off the day before. The terrain was more mountainous, however, and the people were somewhat different. The evidence of social deprivation and poverty was more prevalent than Millard had seen all week. The distance between customers was farther, and he very soon could predict that they would be later completing their route.

Jackson made a special effort to orient him correctly throughout the day. "When I first began working this area, the hills and hollows and everything else began looking the same," Jackson explained. "I made myself a map and took notes for a long time. You might want to do the same if you want to."

Millard smiled. "I was just thinking about how convenient that would be," he replied. He had already been taking notes, although he had not gone to the extent of drawing a map.

"Hell, go ahead," said Jackson. "The old man ain't always right in his thinking. I always listen to him and then do pretty well as I please."

"Well, I might do just that," replied Millard.

Sure enough, they were much later returning from their run. They had no whiskey left to return to Walter's cellar.

Walter called from the front porch as they started to leave and told them he wanted to meet with them the following evening. They acknowledged that they'd heard and kept on going out the driveway. It was already dark, and they were both tired and hungry.

Millard stopped for his usual two beers and to record the day's route in his small notebook while everything was fresh in his memory.

Flora had managed to keep supper warm, and it was delicious. Cameron sat close to his father and chatted constantly about all he had done that day. Flora sat across the table and smiled as he tried to listen to Cameron and pay her some attention at the same time. She had become accustomed to his late arrival each day. That was a part of the job, and she knew it would continue to be that way.

The following morning when Millard arrived at work, he was surprised to find Jackson already there and loading his car. "What's going on?" asked Millard.

"Pop wants us to make a delivery to one of his customers on our return trip this evening. It's a large restaurant and dance hall that always takes a large order of bonded whiskey. Your car will not hold such a large load," Jackson replied.

Millard began helping, and soon they'd filled Jackson's car to capacity.

"This will be a long day I think. I will drive, and maybe that will speed things up some," he continued, a look of disgust on his face. "After our meeting, we will be lucky to get home by midnight."

Millard did not reply. Jackson was obviously aggravated with his father, and he had no desire to become involved.

They wasted no time in getting started up the road, gaining altitude as they went. Millard had never been in that section of the mountains before, and all seemed very unfamiliar to him. Steep, winding roads, deep, dangerous curves, and often, deep ravines and streams far below became the norm. Every few miles, however, Jackson would turn up a side road, and there would be a store and many houses in sight.

Millard never knew what to expect as they climbed farther up the mountains. He reasoned that he would find out soon why they were going into such a forbidding territory. As they reached the top, he was amazed at what was there: a small town named Smithville surrounded by many tourist attractions. The views were far-reaching, showing deep, wide valleys with many streams flowing in different directions; high ridges abundant with healthy forests; and large cliffs streaked with many varying layers painted by time and looking as though they had been there forever. Fenced pastureland was dotted with cattle, sheep, goats, and horses grazing lazily in the warm sun. Farm ponds were well situated to provide drinking water for the animals and perfect for geese and ducks to swim in safety. Garden spots could be seen on each farm. The homes were well kept, and there seemed no reason for anyone to experience hunger when living in such a well-developed place as this. Surely this place was developed by people of wealth for people of wealth. The Depression had no place here, and no signs of poverty were evident at any of the places they stopped. They made stops all over the town and proceeded to cover much of the surrounding area. The people were very friendly, and the few law officers they saw paid absolutely no attention to them, other than to raise a greeting hand and smile.

Millard was soon surprised to realize that he and Jackson were only a few miles from the Tennessee border.

"I thought I was reasonably familiar with these mountains until this week," Millard said to Jackson as they were returning the same way they'd come.

"You probably do know more than you think about the places we have covered so far today. We just traveled in different directions and circled round in ways that are confusing the first time you take this route. The more we travel, the more you will reason things out."

When they neared the bottom of the high mountains, Jackson took another direction and headed into another section, which led to rolling hills. They passed farm after farm before entering a small town named Edgemont. It was obviously a farming town and nothing more. The residents of this peculiar town looked stone-faced as they went about their business. Not much conversation was going on. They passed men on horseback and more horse drawn buggies than Millard had ever seen in one place. From appearances, it was like stepping back in time and never wanting to leave.

Harpers Hardware Store received the largest order in town, followed by two barbershops whose orders didn't amount to much. They exited the region the same way as they'd come in.

"This is a strange section of the mountains," remarked Millard, looking at Jackson with a puzzled expression.

"I know what you're thinking," replied Jackson. "This place was first settled by a group of Amish people long ago, but the settlement wasn't successful. Somehow, they mixed with the regular mountain folks around here, and that was not acceptable to the dyed-in-the-wool Amish. They left for other places, leaving this place just as you see it now; strange as hell to have a mixture of Amish and regular mountain folks. I have never seen anything like it anywhere. They seem to get along very well, and you see the evidence of a fine community. Pop likes the place or I wouldn't come here for such small orders. We are returning the same way we came in because there are no roads beyond the far edge of town. Nothing but thirty miles or more of wild rugged wilderness extends beyond that point. Many people who dared venture into that country were never seen or heard from again. Pop is fascinated by unusual places and things like we have seen today, and I am too, I'll have to admit."

Their day was winding down. They had only one more delivery to make—the delivery Walter had directed them to make for him that day. They had other deliveries, but they would have to be postponed until later, as the delivery for Walter would require the remainder of the white and bonded whiskey. The last delivery was at a large honky-tonk and gambling joint far off the beaten path about twenty miles from Spruce Willow.

They ended the day unusually tired. They had watched everything but the gas gauge during the day and, as a result, ran out of gas and had to walk over five miles to a filling station. Millard had relieved Jackson by driving much of the day, but they had covered many difficult miles, talked to many people, and sold a full load of whiskey.

When they returned home, they found Walter waiting and anxious to discuss future plans. They did not share his obvious enthusiasm but tried not to reveal their true feelings. Millard knew things were about to change. His week of training was over, and from this day forward, more would be expected of him and his responsibilities would multiply. He also was aware that he was on the razor's edge of becoming a wealthy man. He would just have to hang tight and perform as he had never done before.

Walter immediately asked them into the house as they knew he would. "Set down, boys," he said. "Let's have a mixed drink or two and relax a bit before we talk. I am very happy with the progress we have made this week. You are both to be congratulated on a job exceedingly well done."

Jackson made no reply but Millard responded very promptly with a, "Thank you kindly, sir."

The meeting was relaxed and went very well. Walter reaffirmed both his plans to hire three more men and his intention to remove himself from delivery work and concentrate entirely on the business part of their operation. He would consider himself president of the illegal and unnamed cooperation, and Jackson would be second in command. As third in line, Millard would keep himself informed of all components of the business and be prepared to respond in emergency situations. Jackson would train the new employees as they were hired.

Millard agreed to ask John Hughes and Horace Blue about working with the organization as soon as possible. He told Walter that he was reasonably certain they would be interested.

"Monday morning will be a new beginning if all goes well," said Walter, a tone of confidence in his voice. "Millard, try to get Mr. Hughes and Mr. Blue to be here Monday."

"When they see what we have going here, I feel certain they will want to work with us," Millard replied. "I will talk with them tomorrow."

"If they are definitely interested in working with us, we will be in a very good position," Walter noted. "Try to be here by six o'clock Monday. Now I know you boys want to get home to your families after such a long day. I thank you for your extra time this evening, and I hope you have a restful weekend."

After bidding Walter a good evening, Millard headed home, stopping only once to update his notes, as was now an established habit. As he drove into the yard, the house was dark. Flora and Cameron had gone to bed hours ago, but Flora was awake and lit a lamp. The soft light was a comfort to him and a loving reminder of the two people inside he held so dear. Supper was cold, but he ate some pinto beans and cornbread. Flora knew he was tired and hungry and felt much compassion for him.

Morning brought a cloudless sky and a warm summer sun, a perfect day for fun and play. The breakfast Flora prepared was fantastic, and Cameron wanted to go fishing. Flora had little to say. She knew Millard had things on his mind that would probably require most of the day, and she was right.

Millard had already decided to approach John and Horace without delay. He told Flora what he must do, and she agreed that he should take care of business first and perhaps they could have family fun later.

EIGHTEEN

Millard wasted little time in driving over to see John Hughes. John was working in his blacksmith shop and did not hear Millard drive up. He was repairing a hillside plow that required the fashioning of a new swing hinge, and Millard did not try to disturb him until he was finished. The hinge was red hot, and John was hammering it into shape when he saw Millard standing in the door.

"Damn, it's hot in here," he said as he dipped the new hinge in a large tub of water to cool and temper it.

"I can't disagree about that," replied Millard.

They laughed and shook hands.

"Sure is good to see you, John," said Millard.

"It is mighty good to see you too, Millard. I think about you just about every day. Have you been in any fights lately?" John said with a laugh.

"No, I'm glad to report."

"I ain't either," said John. "I ran into Forest Crump a while back, and he was friendly as could be. We talked for a while, and he gave me a drink of good whiskey he had in his coat pocket. I do believe we parted as friends. That's the way things should be."

"You are right, John, and I believe we come to realize that more as we get older," said Millard.

The two men exchanged pleasant conversation for a while, and then Millard got down to business. "We have been good friends for a long time, John, and that's what brought me here this morning. A while back, I started working for Walter Stamey. He is in the whiskey business and wants to expand his business as soon as possible. He wants to hire three more men that he can depend upon in any situation. I immediately thought of you as soon as he told me his plans.

"He also needs one more supplier of good-tasting, yellow corn whiskey that is both clean and safe. I instantly thought of Horace Blue as the man who could produce whiskey that would more than meet Walter's standards. If you and Horace are interested, I am certain he would like to have you men in his organization. You are exactly the sort of men he is looking for—men of intelligence and integrity. It is not a shoddy operation."

"Well, I don't know what to say. I have been a blacksmith since I was a teenager. Don't know if I could or want to do anything else. You will have to let me think about this and talk to my wife before I give you an answer."

"I knew you would need some time," replied Millard. "If you don't mind, I will drive by tomorrow after church and talk to you again. Walter has his plans in mind, and if you and Horace are interested he wants to see us early Monday morning, along with the other man he intends to hire. One more thing, John, there is a lot of money involved."

Millard had already stood to leave when he realized he did not know where Horace lived. Millard asked John to come with him, and John agreed. "Oh hell, why not. You have already ruined my day so far as my work goes. I might just as well have some fun with you and Horace," John replied.

John was soon ready, and they were off with a spin of the tires. "Where on earth did you get this set of fast wheels?" John asked.

"I had to wheel and deal to get it, but you have to have a fast car if you work for Walter. You will find all about that later on if you decide to talk to Walter about the job."

They wasted no time before arriving at the home of Horace. As one might expect, Horace lived in a very sparsely populated section of the surrounding mountains, among the densest forest Millard had ever encountered. Horace had cleared very little land around his rather large log house. Several springs cascaded down the slope behind the house, converging into one rushing stream. "What a wonderful place to live," Millard remarked as they pulled up in front of the porch where Horace was sitting with his feet propped up on the porch railing.

"Yeah, especially in his line of work," John replied as they exited the car.

"Come on up and have a sit down, boys," Horace said, motioning with his hand. "Reckon you would be Millard," he said as he stood up to shake their hands. "John has spoken of you so many times I knew it was you before you pulled up. He says you like the taste of my whiskey pretty well."

"Best I ever tasted without exception," Millard replied, "and I am mighty glad to make your acquaintance."

Horace was a stout-looking man about the same size as Millard, except he had a large belly. His arms were large—no doubt from stirring mash and lifting kegs of whiskey. He looked about fifty years of age and had a pleasant look on his face.

Horace immediately went into the house and returned with three water glasses almost full of whiskey. It was clear and beaded up nicely, a very good sign of fine moonshine whiskey. But the quality is in the tasting, and Millard was not disappointed as he took a large gulp.

No chaser needed to follow the taste of this good stuff, thought Millard. It tasted just as it did the first time he'd tasted it at John's home. Millard knew Horace had his formula well developed, and he had no doubt that all the whiskey Horace produced was of consistent quality, just as Walter wanted.

As they emptied their glasses, John spoke up. "I am glad you brought this fine whiskey out," he told Horace, "because your whiskey is exactly our purpose for coming to see you today. Millard came to me earlier today to tell me Walter Stamey wants to talk to me Monday morning about coming to work for him. He wants to talk to you as well. He intends to expand his whiskey business, and Millard recommended us to him. There's a lot of money involved, but as with most things like this, there are risks. I am going to think on it and let Millard know tomorrow. What do you think about what I have just said?"

"I suppose it wouldn't hurt to talk. I know old Walter is a clever man and has a lot of money. I'll go over there with you and hear him out. It will have to be something pretty good though, 'cause I do pretty well here, and there is nobody around to bother me. But I take some chances too. I make whiskey, and that's against the law."

"You put that well, Horace, and I don't think I need to take any longer to make a decision. I have decided to talk to him as well.

Millard, do you have anything more to say about this? I have been doing all the talking without even asking you about things, and you are the main man here."

"That's just fine, John," Millard replied. "Walter wanted me to arrange a meeting with you men, and that has been accomplished well and good. Actually, I haven't worked with Walter and Jackson very long, but I sure am happy so far. I am anxious to see how the reorganization works out. I believe it will be even better after the changes they have planned are completed. If you two decide to work for him, that will make five of us. Walter wants seven, and he has two other men that he wants to hire soon."

It was past noon when the conversation ended, and they agreed to meet at Walter's at seven a.m. on Monday.

Millard drove John to his house and then headed on home. When he arrived, Flora and Cameron were waiting impatiently. They wanted to leave immediately to visit Flora's family. He was looking forward to a late lunch but made no mention of it. They were soon headed up the highway with Cameron slapping his hands gleefully.

Visits with Flora's folks were always delightfully pleasant. This one was no exception, with Cameron getting most of the attention. Flora exchanged the latest news with her sisters and, of course, her mother. Millard and Salem retreated for some men talk at their favorite spot in the woodshed. Millard paid Salem twenty-five dollars of the car loan he owed. Salem was very pleased at the progress Millard had made since their last conversation. "My age prevents me from trying to work with you boys," Salem said as he twisted his mouth in a way he often did when he felt displeased with himself. "It would be nice if I could."

"I wouldn't worry much about that if I were you," Millard replied. "You seem to have done well in life and live well now considering this depression. But if you ever need help with anything, you can count on me to help out."

Salem knew Millard meant what he said and thanked him for such a sincere remark.

Martha insisted they stay for supper before leaving. They all gathered around the large kitchen table and enjoyed the fine supper and every minute of their time together. They were indeed a family who knew how to make the most of every special occasion.

Flora, Millard, and Cameron departed, and Martha stood on the front porch and watched them drive away. Flora could only wonder what her kind mother was thinking as they left. She knew it was something important.

It was dark when they arrived at home. Millard was very tired but decided to sit with Flora on the porch before retiring. "I don't believe I will go to church this Sunday," he said. "I need some time to just sit and rest and think."

"Please take us to church, Millard; don't stay away from church, not this Sunday!"

She needed to say no more. "We will go," he said without hesitation. "And we might just as well stay the afternoon with my folks after church," he added.

He had no way of knowing, but that was precisely what she had in mind.

Sunday came, along with dark clouds and heavy rain. They all slept late but managed to get ready and make it to church on time. Cameron's hair stood up in back, a condition commonly referred to as a rooster tail. Flora licked her hand several times and pressed it down until it finally stayed in place. Cameron then saw Dad seated on the opposite side of the church and called loudly to him to get his attention. Dad was quite amused and acknowledged him with an adoring smile. Flora had a deep desire to pray at the altar when the invitation came but gave up after so many distractions from Cameron.

She also had a deep desire to pray for Millard's family and looked forward to visiting with them that afternoon. Immediately after church, Dad, Ma, and Grandma Mason were anxious to leave. They were happy to have Millard drive them home.

Flora could sense things were not right when she entered the house. Lewis was in bed, and Lee was holding a cold compress to his head. Flora felt the boy's face, and it was evident he had a dangerously high fever.

As soon as Ma saw him, she began treating him, using every remedy she knew that might help him, and she was successful in her efforts. Lewis soon looked much improved, and his lovely smile returned. Ma lamented that she had left him but had detected no signs of fever when she'd left for church.

Flora knew that he would have died had they not returned in time to treat him. She tried to convince them that he needed to be treated in a hospital, but to no avail. They did not believe in hospitals, and she knew that trying to persuade them to change their minds would not help. Lewis had suffered from a severe case of crippling arthritis since he was a child. The condition was terminal in most cases. His joints would swell and become inflamed, causing his body temperature to rise to dangerous levels. After his fever was lowered, he would feel much better.

Ma prepared lunch, and Lewis was able to leave his bed and join them.

The rain had stopped, and the sun was shining brightly, permitting all to gather on the front porch.

The remainder of the afternoon was spent in pleasant conversation and joy and laughter. Grandma Mason was as keen minded as ever as she joined in the fun. Millard thought of giving her some money, but he knew better. He knew she would not accept it and would scold him for the offer. Perhaps sometime, under circumstances acceptable to her, she might accept such a gift from him, but only if she was certain he was not trying to repay her for what she had done for him in the past.

Flora focused her attention on Lewis, and she did everything she could to make the afternoon enjoyable for him. His smiling face gave her a feeling of much joy, and knowing that perhaps she had helped bring a spark of joy to his day was a comfort.

After many hugs and a promise to return soon, Millard and his little family departed for home.

Darkness once more found Millard and Flora sitting on the porch. Millard knew the following week would probably be another busy one. Even though he was happy with his job, Flora knew he was experiencing a little dread and leaned her head against his shoulder. "Fall is approaching and our new baby will be here soon also," she said in a soft voice. "It will bring joy to our lives just as Cameron has. I can hardly wait for the baby to arrive, and I know he or she will be another true blessing in our lives."

"I think about it every day and still hope it will be a little girl."

Flora laughed and hit him on the shoulder in a kidding sort of way.

Millard had bought a Big Ben alarm clock, and it reminded him early the next morning that it was time to head for Spruce Willow. *What a terrible noise*, he thought as the alarm went off. He shut it off quickly, hoping not to arouse Flora or Cameron. He quickly shaved and dressed neatly before departing for work. There was no need for a bath since he had taken a full bath Saturday night in one of the large, galvanized washtubs, which had a dual purpose—bathing twice a week and the weekly washing of clothes. He wanted to present himself well at the meeting Walter had scheduled. Dressing nice was a pleasure now that Flora had bought new clothes for him since they could afford them. She kept the shirts ironed and his pants well pressed.

After stopping for a breakfast sandwich, he drove quickly on to find Walter sitting on the front porch alone. None of the others had shown up yet, much to his surprise. Millard had arrived earlier than usual, and Walter did not fail to notice his promptness. "Good man," said Walter as Millard closed the car door. "The others will be along shortly I'm sure," he added. "The other two men I mentioned will be here. I talked to them again over the weekend, and they were keenly interested in coming to work for us. They are two nice, friendly men, and I think they will work out well."

"John and Horace will be here this morning also," said Millard. "We were together most of the day Saturday, and they agreed to meet with us, but I am not certain about either one of them accepting employment here. They are laid-back and pretty satisfied with their lives as they are. They are two very fine men, and if they decide to join us, we will be lucky to get them."

"Sounds like I might have to sweeten the pot a little for them if necessary, especially with the whiskey maker," Walter said, a sly smile on his lips.

Momentarily, Jackson drove up the driveway, and as he exited his car, John and Horace showed up. They had driven over together.

Millard introduced John and Horace and the men proceeded into the living room at Walter's invitation. Within a few minutes, the two men Walter had invited knocked on the door, and Jackson welcomed them in, introducing them as Clyde Thompson and

Clifford Anderson. The expression on their faces revealed their amazement at such an impressive, eloquent home in such depressed times.

Walter wasted no time in proceeding with the business at hand. As soon as everyone seemed comfortable and at ease, he explained in minute detail how the business operated and his plans for the future. Millard listened closely, even though the orientation was almost exactly as it had been explained to him before. Even the plans for expansion of the business were familiar to him. As he watched the faces of the four new men, he felt certain that Clyde and Clifford had already made up their minds and were ready to work. He was not at all convinced that Horace and John would do the same. Walter would negotiate with them and probably get them to at least try things out for a week or two.

All the new men owned automobiles and pretty good ones too. Walter explained the importance of a fast car in hauling whiskey. "We will make arrangements later on to have your cars modified," he told them. "You will not need your cars today since you will be riding with Millard and Jackson learning your routes. Clyde and Clifford will go with Jackson, and John will go with Millard. If Horace is willing to consider his role in the operation, I will spend the day with him. If all you good men will take the job for at least a week, we will load up and start delivering immediately. This evening when you return, we will talk salaries and commissions and all the particulars and get you to feeling at home in this business. We have a special place where experts will modify your cars during the week. If you have doubts about working, please let me know as soon as possible, and that will be all right. You are a fine-looking group of men, and I hope things will work out for the good of all of us."

To Millard's surprise, Horace and John agreed without questions or objections to everything Walter had said. Of course Walter would call them together later and probably make special arrangements with them. They were very clever men, and Millard knew that things would be settled soon.

Jackson, Clyde, and Clifford loaded up and headed out for a long run. Jackson would teach them much about the whiskey business that day, and they would probably sell their full load.

Jackson was exactly the man they needed to be with that day, and Millard knew it.

Millard and John were happy to be together as they drove up the winding road, fully loaded with white and bonded whiskey. "I am taking you on the same route as Jackson took me on my first day," said Millard. "It's a good route, and I think you will enjoy the day. I hope you will decide to join our group of whiskey peddlers."

"Whiskey peddlers, did you say? Now, that's a new name for it I think. Peddlers come by my house selling everything from Watkins Liniment to work boots, but I never had one come by peddling whiskey."

"We are more daring than house-to-house peddlers, but I think we are peddlers just the same," Millard replied.

Their day passed very smoothly.

"I am not certain, but I think this route is the easiest one we have. Write down addresses and customers' names if you like. Walter says no, but Jackson said do otherwise if I wanted to. It is very important not to pass customers by on your route and to remember their names as well. Makes good business sense to me, and I do it. I just don't let Walter know, and I keep all written notes well hidden."

John and Millard did indeed enjoy the entire day and ended up with no whiskey left. As they were returning from their day's work, Millard pulled off the road near a lake where they could talk. "John," he said as he lowered his window for fresh air. "We can make a lot of money in this business Walter started, and he intends to expand it all through the Blue Ridge Mountains and to several other large cities—maybe even Chicago." Millard paused and looked out across the lake as he thought to himself about what lay ahead. "Even though prohibition has ended, people have little inclination to stop the flow of illegal whiskey," he continued. "But this is not fun and games anymore. I can see that we are organizing and going into the business big-time. We are getting into organized crime and might have to not only fight other organized groups but evade the law in places as well."

John was listening to Millard, but Millard was not certain he was getting his message through to John. John was looking across the lake at a hawk fighting with four crows. "Damned if that hawk didn't kill two of those crows, and the other two flew off just in time," said John.

"Have you heard a word I said, John?" Millard asked.

"Yes, I have," said John, "and I understood everything you told me."

"Well," Millard continued, "I don't think that will happen for a while yet, because Walter is smart and ahead of the game so far. The reason I am telling you my feelings about this is to make you aware that, if we move fast, we will become wealthy and be in a position to legitimatize our business. These are my thoughts and nothing more," Millard assured John. "Walter has mentioned nothing like this to me, but I know his mind is working overtime figuring all these things out. He probably don't want to scare us away, and he wants to hire and keep the best and smartest men he can find. I am third in line now, and no doubt you will move up quickly too. I can see that Walter likes both you and Horace."

John had not made a definite decision about joining the operation, but he was getting pretty close to making up his mind. The lure of such money was very exciting, and he was wondering if he would be doing himself a disservice to refuse such a position, illegal as it was. He loved being a blacksmith, but his work had been gradually slowing ever since this damned depression started. He knew Walter would pay him well, and there would be few other options. "I am going to take the job if Walter still wants me," he said to Millard, after staring into the lake for a few minutes. "To refuse would be foolish considering these hard times."

When they returned, Walter and Horace were standing in the yard close to the basement door. "Horace is going to work with us, Millard," Walter spoke out with a satisfied look on his face. "Things are coming together well, and within a few weeks, I think we will have a first-rate organization."

"Did your day go well John?" Walter asked.

"It did indeed," John replied. "So well I believe I will just stay for a spell."

"Splendid, I'd hoped you would," said Walter. "We will discuss the particulars of everything shortly, and I believe you will be even more pleased."

Jackson, Clyde, and Clifford had not yet returned. They had covered two routes, and dark would probably overtake them before they completed such extensive territory.

"I believe we can complete our new organizational plans before the day's end if the other boys come in before too late," said Walter as he paced about anxiously. "Jackson and me will answer all questions and come to salary agreements I think. That won't take long. I will take the cars to have them modified tomorrow, and we should have them back by the week's end."

Walter was methodical and foresighted, always planning and looking at his plan from every vantage point. That the men had already gained tremendous respect for him was clear as they watched and listened to him talk. They knew when he spoke that words of importance were about to be spoken.

"Training everyone on the routes we now have established will be the next item of importance. That will then put us in an excellent position to begin branching out all over the Blue Ridge Mountains and beyond. We will move carefully and methodically, yet not get too big for our britches. I can see it all coming together," he said as he stood, paused briefly to look about the room and ascertain how the men were receiving his message.

He enjoyed making short and long-range plans with goals in place. Walter was indeed a man ahead of his time. "We will make every effort to make a lot of money reasonably fast while exercising caution. Then if things should start going sour, we can get out of the business as fast as we got in, and with considerable wealth stashed away for us all."

"Hellfire, what a plan," said John. "I'm glad I said yes; after hearing your plans I feel very fortunate to be involved in such a well-oiled organization." He glanced at Millard, feeling very appreciative that Millard had already provided him with almost the same information.

Millard decided to depart for home. It was obvious that he would have very little to contribute during the evening. Walter would talk with the new men and prepare them for the next day and clarify any concerns they might have.

As Millard drove home, he thought about his responsibilities in the organization. Although he had not been with Walter and

Jackson very long, he would have to continue to learn quickly and make important decisions. Much would be expected of him beginning tomorrow, and he was determined to live up to all expectations of him.

After his usual beer stop, he arrived at home. Flora and Cameron were already in bed. Flora was not asleep and seemed worried. "Supper is still warm on the stove," she said to him as he sat down on the bed beside her.

"What is bothering you?" he asked. "I hope you are not having any trouble with the baby."

"No, the baby is fine, and so am I," she replied. "It's Lewis I am concerned about. Lee came by today, and Lewis is much worse than he has ever been before. He is unconscious and breathing heavily. We must see about him soon."

"I can't stay out of work tomorrow, but if you can, we will get up very early in the morning, and I will take you there. I will come over there as soon as possible tomorrow evening."

The following day would probably be difficult and plagued by uncertainty. Millard knew Walter would have plans for the day carefully in place, but the best of plans are often difficult to accomplish. Millard soon went to bed and held Flora closely until they were asleep.

In the morning, Millard drove Flora and Cameron to Dad's, where she could help with the care of Lewis. He went inside with Flora and Cameron to find Lewis critically ill, as he had expected. It was a very sad situation to witness. He felt guilty that he would not remain and try to be of help, but he knew there was nothing he could do. The day would be a day of worry and stress, but he would return as soon as possible.

Millard was late for work for the first time. All the men were present. Clyde and Clifford were loading the vehicles while Jackson was talking to Walter. They were soon to service two more routes unfamiliar to Millard. He and John would probably learn those routes as soon as Jackson was available to go with them. Millard and John would cover one of the other routes familiar to Millard.

Walter had decided to spend another day with Horace. He wanted to view Horace's operation and test the quality of his product.

After a day at Horace's, Walter was very impressed with the location and the entire business. Horace knew what he was about all right. The place was a pleasure for Walter to see, and he congratulated him on such science in his operation. "Horace, I am happy you are joining our operation. The only question concerning me at present is the capacity of your operation; what would be the maximum volume you could produce on a regular basis?"

"I can produce as much as you will ever need," said Horace. "As you can see, I have a wealth of clear, pure water; the farmers I know can furnish me with any amount of corn; and as we are talking, I have several thousand gallons of whiskey stored about, sealed and aging in gallon jugs and some in fifty-gallon barrels. I will have to hire some help, but that won't be a problem. After talking with you, I am ready and anxious to get started. No sense in having plenty of good whiskey around when there are plenty of fine customers who want to buy it. I have never sold whiskey on a large scale before. Usually, I just sell to people I know in the surrounding area."

"Let's go to my house and finalize the details and get started selling your product," Walter cheerfully remarked.

It had been a good day for Millard and John too. Millard knew the route well, and John was familiar with most of the territory they had covered. Both Millard and John had been around and were aware of the surprises that could come out of these hills and hollers. They knew things would get rougher and tougher as Walter expanded his business. They agreed that kind, gentle people occupied most of the mountains, but they also knew they could encounter trouble in the dangerous places they would have to travel through.

Millard left for Dad's soon after his arrival at Walter's. He drove swiftly up the road, not knowing what to expect.

Lewis was gravely ill, and the family members were doing all they could. Millard, without thinking, demanded that he be seen by a physician or taken to a hospital. Dad and Ma said no. "We can do more for him here, and we have no money for such foolishness."

"I have money," said Millard, "and I am going to take him now." He placed a blanket around Lewis and started to pick him up but immediately saw that he could not do so. Lewis yelled so loudly that

Millard quickly returned him to his former position. "Well," he said, "perhaps I could go and fetch Dr. Burleson."

"Dr. Burleson is very sick himself, so I have been told," replied Dad.

"I suppose we will just have to help him as best we can here then," replied Millard. "He is so critical and in such pain I don't think he could survive the drive to a hospital. Ma and her remedies will have to do."

After an hour, his breathing improved, and then he began breathing normally.

Flora appeared overly tired and very worried. Cameron was sleeping on the floor. Millard decided to take his family home. Nothing more could be done. He would return Flora in the morning, as he knew she would want to be here. Grandma said that she would stay by Lewis's bed that night.

The night was one of restlessness and light sleep for Millard and Flora. At daybreak and without breakfast, they drove directly to see about Lewis. Astonished, they found Lewis awake. He even managed a weak smile as they approached his bed. Grandma was asleep in her familiar rocking chair.

Millard departed for work completely amazed at how anyone so sick could escape the cold fingers of death as Lewis had done. He took some comfort in knowing that Ma and Flora were with him and would see to his needs as best they could and provide comfort and prayer.

He arrived at work on time, and everyone was ready to load the vehicles and depart their appointed ways. Millard and John took another route that Millard was familiar with, and they had another excellent day.

They arrived from their daily route earlier than usual. Jackson, Clyde, and Clifford would probably not return until much later. Even so, Walter was waiting and wanted to talk with them collectively. Millard wondered what was on his mind. He had earlier suspected that Walter had a master plan in mind that he had not revealed to anyone, probably not even Jackson. Millard was curious and hoped the others would arrive soon.

Unfortunately, it was totally dark before they drove in.

Walter wasted no time. He immediately asked everyone to come into the living room for drinks and talk. "Men," he said, "I have completed my plans for the future of our private cooperation.

"First I have succeeded in paying off all political officials and law officers that will take a bribe. This depression is driving people crazy, and they are having hard times just as most everyone else and do take bribes.

"Second, Horace can produce and supply us with the finest corn whiskey money can buy."

"I can vouch for that, sir," said John. "With your permission, we will continue to sell bonded whiskey to our customers who want it, but our white whiskey will be our primary product. That's what's most in demand everywhere I go—not just any white whiskey but the white whiskey made by Horace. When they taste it they want no other."

That brought delightful laughter from the group, and Horace looked very pleased. The men within reach patted him on the back to show their appreciation.

After waiting for the laughter to die down, Walter cleared his throat and continued. "Third, all cars will be modified to run as fast as possible after each new man is hired. We have experts who do all repairs and modifications, as you all know."

"Mine is superfast, and it's in perfect condition inside and out," Millard replied.

"Fourth, I will continue to furnish everything you will need in your work except cars and weapons. You will need to keep your cars in top shape. That will help keep you and everyone in our group out of trouble. A good pistol will do fine while we are making deliveries around the places where we are already well established. But when we begin expanding into territory farther north, you might need to rely on other types of weapons. If necessary, we will use .45-caliber submachine guns or something similar."

"Where can we buy one of those?" one of the new men named Herman asked. "Are they legal?"

"Hell no, they are not legal. Nothing we do is legal; you are not legal now that you are tied up with us."

Everyone in the room laughed at that remark, and Walter quickly apologized to the young man for replying as he had done.

"Son, I am just fooling with you. After you have been here a while, you will get accustomed to our crazy ways. We have to have a little fun as we go along. We all are happy to have you with us. And we have a black-market gun dealer who can furnish us with all kinds of weapons and ammunition.

"We intend to extend our territories farther north and south and probably on into the Midwest. No final decisions have been made on that part of our expansion," said Walter.

"Sixth, we will pay you well. I have already talked with each of you about salaries for now. We will cover that subject again later.

"Seventh, Jackson will establish new routes. When he has established five new routes, I will hire a new man, and that will be the territory assigned to him. Incidentally, Jackson is in charge of all field operations. I will take care of the office and oversee our expansion.

"Eighth, Millard is third in line and will keep himself informed of all routes and assure all customers are serviced efficiently. He will be the troubleshooter in case of unexpected happenings. And if someone must be absent, he will temporarily cover for them. If you have problems, take them directly to him. He is a fine man and will treat you fairly and honestly. Should Jackson be unavailable, he will be second in command. Changes and promotions will be made as we go along. John is next in line for a promotion."

Walter was an excellent speaker. His manner of speaking was firm and sincere, but at the same time, he was an entertainer. His style captured the attention of his audience, and the way he looked about the room made everyone feel comfortable as though he was speaking to each of them individually. What a great talent for a wonderful, kind man.

"That is about all the mechanics of our operation that I can share with you at this time. Many other things that will need our attention will come up along the way. We will just have to consider them as they present themselves. One thing, however, that I need to say that is very important to me. You all have families, and I do not want anyone to get hurt or killed. But there is danger on the road we are taking, and you should make your wives aware of the hazards of your work. Although I intend to pay you well, that will be of little comfort to your family if something happens to you.

"If all goes as planned, we will stay in this business for a long time and make a lot of money—enough that, if something should force us to retire the organization, we will be secure enough financially to live well. That is my plan and my hopes for you gentlemen and for me."

Millard and Jackson smiled when Walter was looking away. They knew he had more money than anyone in the county even if he retired today.

One thing was certain; everyone there knew all about Walter's organizational plans now. No one could deny that he had not informed them and warned them. They were all very impressed and were happy to be associated with such an outstanding man.

Millard quickly left for Dad's after the meeting. As he drove along the familiar road, he wondered about Lewis. Flora came out to meet him as he drove up.

"How is he?" asked Millard.

"Just as he was this morning," she replied. "I have never seen anyone so determined to live. He smiles often and attempts to get out of bed. Just act as you normally would when you enter the house. I know he will be happy to see you."

Lewis was very happy to see Millard and smiled brightly as he approached his bed and hugged him. Ma wanted all the family to have supper together. All said a prayer after they sat down, except Millard who took a seat at the table but was not one to say prayers aloud. Even Cameron said, "God bless Lewis."

Flora had helped Lewis with his supper hours ago. The family talked for a while before Millard, Flora, and Cameron went home. They felt somewhat better about Lewis, but Flora reminded Millard not to expect miracles. "Lewis has a very short time to live," she said as tears gathered in her eyes.

The remainder of the work week went smoothly. All the men had proven themselves and could make many of the runs on their own. John was competent to make all five runs he had made with Millard now and had much knowledge about the business, especially after hearing Walter's informative talk. They all received their wages and were happy. Clyde and Clifford were exceedingly happy. Millard had talked to them briefly during the week, but he knew they were hard-pressed for cash. He knew that feeling from long experience and hoped this job would be the beginning of a wonderful life for them. Millard knew they must take advantage of every opportunity.

The café where he often stopped on his way home was brightly lit, seemingly beckoning him to stop. He'd ordered a beer and begun updating his notes when he realized his notes read like a diary. *Not a bad idea*, he thought. These notes could come in handy sometime in the future. He decided to order another beer and just relax for a while.

One beer led to another until he lost count. What an unwise decision he had made and one he would not forget. As he stood to leave, he quickly realized he had consumed too much alcohol. He staggered as he walked to his car.

Flora saw him drive up and was shocked to watch him walk to the door in such an unsteady gate. He tried to keep control, but he knew he could not fool Flora. She said not one word to him as he entered the door. He went straight to bed and immediately began snoring. She had watched her father and brothers too often in that condition and sensed trouble.

It was still dark when they were awakened by a pounding on the door. Millard quickly got out of bed, staggering from his night of drinking. It was Lee. "Lewis is dead," he said. "Ma went to check on him during the night, and he was gone. Dad came to get me and I came straight on over."

Lee left immediately to be with the family.

The sadness of the message caused Millard to stand straight but unsteady. "God, what a lousy bum I am," he said. "Half drunk at a time like this. I am glad you answered the door Flora."

Flora got up and got dressed as though she were moving in slow motion. She thought about awakening Cameron, but when she looked toward his bed he was already sitting up. *Strange how death seems to announce itself*, she thought. The night before her brother was killed in a dynamite explosion, a flame about the size of a candle had appeared in a corner near her mama's bed. It had burned for a short while and then went out as quickly as it had appeared. Her mama had known it was a sign that her son's life would soon be snuffed out, just like that flame.

Suddenly Flora was aware that she was just standing there reflecting upon the death of her brother so long ago. Millard soon reminded her that they should get ready to leave. "This will be a sad day, and I already have a feeling of dread," Flora replied. "Dear sweet Lewis is gone."

The sun was peeking over the horizon as they arrived at Dad's. As they entered the room where Lewis lay covered with a sheet, all seemed very still and quiet and peaceful. No one was crying in the house as might be expected. Flora sensed that all were saddened beyond words, yet they felt relief knowing that Lewis's pain was gone forever and he was at peace.

Grandma was rocking softly in her chair beside the fireplace. One could only imagine her thoughts. She had witnessed so many happenings and deaths and tragedies during her long life; her thoughts and memories were probably quite different from those of others.

Soon after they arrived, the neighbors began gathering to help and show their concern. The family withdrew to the kitchen to plan the funeral and burial. They sat around the kitchen table and planned each detail to proceed in an orderly and dignified manner. They wanted nothing left to chance.

The men obtained materials and constructed the casket from the finest mahogany wood available. Every joint was cut to perfection. Some of the men were skilled in carving and carefully carved designs on the sides and lid of the coffin. Millard had never seen such beautiful craftsmanship outside this region. He had taken this ritualistic practice for granted up until now, at a time when death had come to his family to claim Lewis. While the men carefully finished it to bring out the wood grain and color, the ladies fashioned a soft, feathered mattress for the bottom and then lined the insides with soft padding complemented by a covering of silk and handwoven lace. Each person working on the casket had a specific duty and, through the years, had become extremely skillful at performing that duty. Their beautiful work of art was completed within one day.

Lewis's body was carefully prepared and placed inside. A silk-covered feather pillow was gently placed under his head. Such gentle, loving care that went into the handiwork of that casket and care of the body was amazing and admired by people within and without the region. Lewis had died during the previous night, and the entire community came by on Saturday to bring food and show their love and compassion to the family. Being such a small community, they were all deeply touched and mournful. They had watched Lewis live a life of pain since he was a small boy. Now it was over. Lewis stayed his last night in a dimly lit room with his family near.

The funeral was at two o'clock on Sunday, and after sad songs, a lengthy sermon, and much grief and crying, the beautiful casket was carried to the cemetery upon the shoulders of his best friends. It was then lowered into the grave using strong ropes. Last rites were delivered by Reverend Brown and then the grave was filled. Each shovel of dirt was softly and lovingly tossed into the grave. It was the last thing his friends could do for him, and they were deeply saddened. Lewis now belonged to the ages where eternity reigns.

NINETEEN

Walter was there when they returned. He had traveled about a hundred miles that day, edging his way along the right outer rim of the Blue Ridges, where he had more contacts than other places. Apparently that was going to be his pattern, and it had worked for him before. He would establish routes and communications in several areas and then rely upon those people of goodwill to suggest other potential customers. Moving cautiously, he would be less likely to intrude into territory established by others.

Jackson, Clyde, and Clifford soon arrived, and Walter invited everyone in for drinks and conversation. He was very interested in the new group and proud of his new organization. He reaffirmed his dedication to them and congratulated them on how well they were doing. "This will be the last week Jackson will be doing route work," Walter said. "He will spend the remainder of this week training Clyde and Clifford. I hope to have at least one new area established by week's end, and Jackson will take over from there. Of course, I will have to show him the new area I have developed. If all goes well during the coming month, we should have our basic organization in place. I think we will have at least five new areas with five routes per area. I will hire one new man for each new area. We will have roughly fourteen men in our organization at that time. As we turn west, who knows how things will turn out? We will talk again as new developments or changes occur."

As soon as everyone departed for the day, Jackson remained behind to determine whether his pop had anything else on his mind. He was glad he stayed.

"Jackson," Walter said, "I have not been feeling exactly as I should lately."

"What is it, Pop?" Jackson replied, a concerned look on his face and a degree of alarm in his voice.

"I have been feeling a little washed out lately. I am getting some age on me, and I believe it is time for me to admit it and turn things completely over to you. Next Monday, the entire organization is yours. I will remain in the office doing things and giving advice as you request it, and I will always be interested in what goes on. I do want to see our new reorganization completed and running smoothly and reveal to you some secrets about the business that I kept to myself. If you need help in hiring new men, I will be there if you need me, as long as I am able. There might be times when you will need my intervention. Otherwise, I look forward to sitting back and enjoying the progress and changes that occur in our fine organization. You have two good men with you now. Millard and John will never let you down. I have observed them closely, and I am certain of their loyalty."

"What a shock this is," said Jackson. "I am happy for you to retire and enjoy life and do things that are interesting and fun to you, but I don't want you to be sick." He then looked at his father and said, "I would like to come for lunch Sunday."

"I will look forward to Sunday," said Walter.

★ ★ ★

Soon after Jackson and Sally had enjoyed a delicious dinner and a wonderful visit with Jackson's parents, Jackson and Sally decided to visit Millard and Flora on their way home. Millard and Flora were pleasantly surprised to see Jackson's car, and Flora ran to Sally as fast as she could go. They hugged and began talking so fast that all Millard and Jackson could do was smile and pat each other on the back.

They all eventually made it to the porch and sat in the shade. Millard went to the spring box and brought a watermelon he had purchased. He split it into pieces, and with Cameron's help, they ate every bite.

Flora could hardly wait to show Sally inside the house. She told her about the condition of their little farm and house when they'd first moved in and pointed out all the improvements they had made. She was very proud of what she and Millard had accomplished since they moved in.

"It is a delightful place," said Sally. "Our house is larger, but we have had to work on it as well. Your garden is very beautiful also. I have a garden much like yours, and I spend much of my time working it."

"Cameron likes to help me with mine. He loves to work with the hoe most of all," Flora replied.

"Jackson told me you were expecting again. I am very happy for you and Millard," said Sally.

"Our second one will be along in a few months. As you can see, I don't have too long to go," said Flora. "I will be glad when the baby gets here. I don't want any more after this one, but Millard wants a girl. If this one isn't a girl, there won't be one if I can help it," she continued with a laugh.

As the women visited, Jackson asked Millard out to the car. "I need to talk to you, Millard. Friday evening after work, Pop told me he was not feeling well, and after this next week, the business will be turned over to me. I suspect he is worse off than he cared to tell me. Anyway, he has much confidence in you and John. He recommended that you be second in the organization and John third.

"I know I've told you he's announced his intention to step down before, but I really did not think he was fully sincere. He says he will be available for advice and will run the office. I thought it best that I contact you soon and not spring things on you in the morning when we will all be busy. We can tell John later on during the week. What do you think about what I have just said?"

"I hope nothing is seriously wrong with Walter, but I definitely would be honored to work closely with you, and I am reasonably certain John will be happy as a pig in poop," Millard replied.

"Don't say anything about this yet," Jackson added. "Pop will probably talk to our group again and make his decision known when he feels the time is right."

After a very nice visit, Jackson and Sally departed for home.

"What was that all about?" asked Flora. "I knew Jackson wanted to talk about something important when they first came."

"Oh, nothing we need to discuss now. I promised him I would not reveal what he said, and we can talk about it later."

"It is important though," said Flora, determined to get in the last word.

The next morning, Millard awoke thinking of what Jackson had told him. Millard knew Jackson was worried about Walter, and he was concerned about the stress of the coming week. *No more of this*, he thought and slid out of bed and readied himself for work. He moved quietly, but Flora was peeking through the curtain when the car engine started.

When he arrived at work, things were much better than he had anticipated. Walter seemed to be his usual self. He immediately headed north and took John with him. He wanted to finish establishing another area, his final one, and John would be ready to begin servicing each route within the new area immediately.

Jackson and Millard quickly organized the day, making certain that all routes would be serviced. Jackson and Millard worked two routes, making everything come out just fine.

The following day went just as the previous day had. Walter and John came in later as the others were about to depart for home. Walter called to the departing men and asked them to please remain a short while. He beckoned for them to come into the house.

"This won't take long, boys," he said. "I just want you to know that I have definitely decided that Friday will be my last day working. After Friday, this business will belong to Jackson. Millard will take over Jackson's duties, and John will be the third man."

John was startled as he had not been approached about the job. Walter quickly apologized to John for the oversight. John told him that it was all well with him and thanked him very kindly for showing such confidence in him.

"I have other matters to share with you good men very soon but nothing for you to be worried about. That is all I have to say for now.

Millard knew things were not as they should be with Walter. His hands were shaking slightly, and he seemed unsteady on his feet. Jackson had noticed it also and expressed his concern to Millard as they walked to their cars.

"I am going to return later this evening and see just what is going on."

"Let me know, Jackson," said Millard. "I am worried. He is like a second dad to me."

Flora and Cameron were in front of the house to greet Millard as he drove up. They had been gathering vegetables from the garden to can the next day. The garden had produced well, and Flora was proud of the many baskets of vegetables they had harvested. Millard bragged on their hard work as he carried the baskets into the kitchen. "I bet there will be much work going on in here tomorrow," he said to Cameron. "You see what hard work will do?"

"Yes, I do," said Cameron, "and I will do more and more work to help Mama. I like to work with Mama. She shows me lots of things, and she says we will eat all this stuff when winter comes. We don't bother the snakes though."

"You are a very smart boy," Millard replied.

Needless to say, they had delicious vegetables well-seasoned and perfectly cooked for supper. Even cornbread and milk were not needed to make their supper complete.

All went well that week up until Friday. Walter and John had almost established another area consisting of the usual five routes. The last place they approached was a large restaurant with a dance hall upstairs. The owner, Mr. Bill Johnson, immediately arranged for a delivery every week. The taste of such fine whiskey could not be refused. He was quickly convinced that such whiskey would increase his business, especially on weekends.

Mr. Johnson took Walter and John upstairs and introduced them to the man in charge of the dance hall and bar. His name was Wheeler Zimmerman. It became immediately evident that Wheeler was a man with an intemperate disposition. He was a tall, muscular man with a large chest and arms. Mr. Zimmerman walked with Walter and John down the back stairs where Walter presented him with a pint of whiskey as well. That seemed to irritate him more than ever. He stood up straight and told them that, if they ever came around that establishment again, he would bash their heads together.

"We want no trouble with you, sir, and you have no reason to threaten us," said Walter.

"You heard what I said. Now you two jackasses get before I get mad."

John then stepped in front of Walter and told Wheeler that, if he made one more threat, he was going to get his ass kicked. Wheeler looked very surprised but, without hesitation, took a hefty swing at John. John was expecting such a move and knew exactly how to handle things. He ducked under the blow and knocked Wheeler head over heels.

With blood coming from his mouth Wheeler jumped to his feet, but before he could steady himself, John kicked his legs out from under him. Wheeler then tried jumping forward at John and tackling him. That was a bad mistake. John stepped aside and kicked him flush under the chin. That was the end of the fight.

Walter rushed inside and told Mr. Johnson what had happened. Bill came outside and, after taking one look at the defeated Wheeler, told him he was fired.

Bill said to Walter, "I was going to fire him soon anyway, so don't feel bad about this ruckus. He has been stealing money from me and taking kickbacks from whiskey dealers from Wilkesboro and other places for some time now." He told Wheeler to never come there again or he would have him arrested for embezzlement or put a bullet in his ass, whichever he preferred.

"Man, what a stop that was," said Walter. "You handled that like it was nothing, and that man was much taller than you."

"He was a nothing," replied John. "People like him are usually cowards. They use their size to bully people and often make a living at it."

"Well, I sure am glad you were with me, and I appreciate what you did. When I was young, I could handle myself pretty well, but nothing like I just saw you do. Now let's go home," he said with a loud laugh and a clap of his hands.

When they arrived, Walter was elated. He could hardly wait to tell what had happened. "What a way to end the week," he said as he walked across the yard. "It makes me want to reconsider my decision to quit traveling the roads."

The men all went into the house, and Walter proudly told everyone about the fight. "I knew we had a fine group of men, and now I am even more certain of it."

Before they departed for home, Walter reminded the men that Jackson would be totally in charge on Monday and he wanted them to support him in every way. "I know he has been running things for the most part, but having full responsibility is different." He thanked them for everything they had done and assured them he would still be around to help out a little.

As they walked to their cars, Jackson motioned for Millard to stop. "You and John and I need to talk about some things. After work Monday, we will meet some place if you agree. We need to exchange new ideas and information about anything that comes to mind."

Millard nodded and said, "I anticipated that you would have new ways of doing things, and I fully agree. I will drive over and tell John tomorrow."

The weekend proved to be very peaceful. Millard visited John on Saturday morning as he'd told Jackson he would do. The remainder of the day was devoted to having fun, mixed with some garden work. The families attended church on Sunday and then went home immediately to rest and take it easy. Millard and Flora enjoyed the day. It gave them an opportunity not only to rest but to discuss their unborn child.

As they sat on the porch, Flora reminded Millard that she wanted to have this baby where her mama could be close by just as when Cameron was born. "I know I will feel safe and comfortable with her near. She will look after me and see that all goes well."

"We will go there when you think the time is right," said Millard, "and I will stay with you as much as possible. We are in a much better position now than we were when Cameron was born. I have a car and money, which we did not have before. If you will agree to be delivered at a hospital, I will take you there."

"No, somehow I know I will feel much better with Mama. I know how competent she is in such matters and trust her completely."

Millard and Jackson were worried about Walter when they returned to work on Monday and checked to assure that the day was as well organized as Walter would have had it. Jackson intended to keep the operation well organized just as Walter always emphasized. To do less would cause the organization to fail.

After the men had departed, he sat in his vehicle thinking of the many responsibilities with which he was now charged. He then departed to cover one route that had been overlooked. Discovering the oversight made him even more acutely aware of the importance of double-checking, just as Walter had been doing.

Millard and John had left for the area Walter and John had established the prior week. John knew the route very well, and in keeping with his position, Millard knew that it was very important for him to become familiar as well. Millard was well aware that his performance and ability to establish new areas would mean success or failure in the planned expansion of the organization.

They returned home to find the others clearing their vehicles for another day. Clyde and Clifford seemed extremely happy. Their cars had been modified beyond their expectations, and they enjoyed making their runs. Walter certainly had hired two good men, and Millard could see they were going to perform well.

As the others departed, Jackson, Millard, and John decided to remain and check on Walter. They entered the house with the pretense of reporting to Walter how the day had gone and how they had missed him. He seemed happy for them to visit. Jackson asked him how he was feeling, and he reported a good day except for feeling a little tired.

"I haven't been out to greet you men because I know I must resign myself to a new lifestyle. If I start coming outside and nosing around, I would most certainly be interfering. Jackson, I know we will have to yet spend some business time together, and we will do that in a day or so; or if you have time tomorrow, come in and we will go over some important issues.

"Millard and John, you are welcome here anytime."

After bidding Walter a good night, the three younger men made their way to the café Millard had suggested for their meeting. As they entered the café, Jackson asked Millard if there was a private table or room where they could discuss business and also drink a few beers and have something to eat.

"Sure, they even have poker rooms all around," Millard replied, "or they will place a table wherever we want. I had that in mind when I suggested this place."

They went upstairs to the bar and were provided a nice table in a far corner of the room. "This is a perfect spot," said Jackson. "I had rather not be closed up in a small room."

"I like this better too," said John.

While they were waiting to be served, Jackson said, "We can't cover everything, but we can get started. First, I want us to work closely together. That goes without saying. I'm no smarter than you guys. I do have more experience in the business, but that is only because I have been lucky enough to have a father who is very smart and has taught me many things. We are already in the midst of expanding our business. I think we should continue our present plans as they are. But I think it would be unwise to move too fast or expand too large. I don't think we should have over thirty men in our organization unless we see a very important reason to do so later on. I fear the larger our organization becomes the more attention we'll draw to ourselves.

"Others are in this business but not close around here. Pop has managed to gain control of the organized whiskey business for at least fifty miles around."

"I know," said Millard, "and we are starting to move farther along. Walter told me once that he would like to expand over the entire Blue Ridge Mountains. That's a lot of territory. They begin near Gainesville, Georgia, and end near Carlisle, Pennsylvania. A map I looked at showed them extending to Blowing Rock, Chattanooga, and the Tennessee Valley. To the north are Shenandoah, Cumberland, Pulaski, and even Gordonville, Tennessee. It also curves back east toward Washington."

"I believe you have done your homework," said John as they all chuckled.

"I don't think we are so ambitious as to try going that far," said Jackson.

"I don't want to go south much farther than Asheville myself," John remarked. "It gets too hot down there, and I never hear of much going on in that section of the country so far as illegal whiskey operations are concerned. I did have an opportunity to travel with Walter last week and hear some of his opinions. The impression I got from him was that we should go north as far as possible, feeling our way along. If we start encountering trouble from any source, meaning the law or other whiskey-running people, we should back off a little and reevaluate our situation. I sensed the main thing as he saw it was the money we could make being worth the effort. He doesn't want to risk a serious confrontation, yet he doesn't want to back down from some unprincipled bunch of rowdies."

"Walter is right," said Millard. "I suggest that we move right along with our expansion by going north as far as we want to go, and then, at the proper time, we can start making long hauls." He took a sip of beer and added, "We should also consider buying a couple of large trucks for hauling very large loads."

"At that point, we should consider going west, as we've discussed before," said Jackson. "We might begin by making trial runs to Knoxville and Nashville and Memphis. Later, we might even consider runs to Chicago. I hear that folks in the city like our mountain whiskey." He smiled and continued, "That brings me to Horace."

"We need to include him in on our discussions," John remarked. "I don't think he has much interest in distribution or organizational work, but he likes to produce fine whiskey and enjoys being a part of our group. Walter really likes him, and I suspect Walter will spend time with him in the future just for fun."

"Well, boys, we have had a fine supper, discussed a few important points about our long-range whiskey distributions, and consumed a considerable amount of beer," said Jackson. "We need to meet again soon, even tomorrow night," he continued. "I will not only notify Horace of our next meeting, but I'll also invite our entire group of fine men. One or two more sessions like this, and I believe we would have our organizational feet planted on firm soil."

"Let's do that," said Millard. "I prefer to get things as well organized as we can and then move on with our expansion as soon as possible."

"Let's meet here tomorrow after work just as we did today," Jackson said as he ended the meeting.

✷ ✷ ✷

The following morning, Jackson was at his post seeing to things much the same as Walter had been doing. This was his second day, and he was already learning that filling the shoes of his old man was not an easy task. Everyone quickly readied themselves and their vehicles for the day.

One welcome change was in place. One of the men Walter had been recruiting to work with them had lost his job and had come to see Walter about accepting the position if Walter still wanted him. Knowing that Walter had a very favorable opinion of the man, Jackson immediately hired him. After talking with the new man briefly, he assigned him to travel with Clyde that day. Normally Millard would have made the assignment, but it was necessary for him to spend the remainder of the week with John, in keeping with organizational plans now in place.

At the end of the working day, the entire crew proceeded to the café where the leaders of the organization had met the night before. The café owner provided them a nice, large room with more space and privacy.

As the meeting progressed, it was obvious the men had been giving much thought about the future of the organization. They would miss Walter and his sharp mind and could not keep from wondering if all would be well with him away. Finally, Clifford Anderson asked if Walter's retirement would interfere with the progress of their expansion or in any other way that everyone should know about. "Of course, I am speaking for myself only, but with such a big change in leadership, it would ease our minds if you wanted to tell us anything we need to know."

"I know what you are getting at," said Jackson. "You are concerned whether Pop is definitely retiring, and the answer is yes. He will do some paperwork in the office as needed. I believe we will all feel somewhat insecure at first, but that is natural. Don't worry about it. I am filling his shoes, and Millard and John will be with me. They are two of the best men I ever met, and I know we will do well.

"There is one point he has talked to me about, however, that cannot be overlooked or overemphasized. He has paid a lot of money in return for favors. Some goes to people in political offices and some to people who are just in powerful positions. The payments are made every six months. He will not reveal their names to anyone under any circumstances, except to me. It is a matter of respect and loyalty. He does trust the people in our organization, but names can be spoken and conversations overheard that could cause irreparable damage. It could destroy our organization, destroy reputations, and possibly cause people to receive prison sentences. He keeps the names in a secret place, along with the names of our people. He has revealed the place to me and instructed me to reveal the names to Millard, since he is next under me. There is always a chance that something could happen to me, and in that case, you fine men could carry on.

"That is all for that important subject, so let's not mention it again to any additional employees. My dad has always held his employees in high regard, and I intend to keep that policy in place.

"As we hire more men, we no doubt will change duties around a bit and delegate responsibilities as necessary. Let's talk about expansion now as we agreed," continued Jackson.

Millard then voiced his concern about continuing expansion to the north. "I believe strongly that we should keep spreading in that direction as we go, probing to the left and right to the edge of the Blue Ridge Mountains. I have heard that powerful organizations operate beyond those boundaries. They have little interest in the places we intend to cover because of rough terrain, and the population is sparse compared to the heavily populated areas they cover."

"Makes sense to me," said John. "We could work within the Blue Ridges Mountains from Asheville northward, a maximum of about two hundred miles. That's a good chunk of territory, and we won't run the risk of stepping on the toes of the people farther north."

"Let's not forget our westward move," said Jackson. "If we could establish several delivery points to Knoxville on to Memphis and even Chicago we might move more whiskey than even Horace could produce without expanding his operation. I'm thinking of heavy truckloads, boys, just as Millard suggested last evening. That could bring in more cash to our organization than us mountain boys could imagine."

"I can see all this succeeding very well if we stick to our plans and don't get greedy," said John. "If Millard and I do our jobs well as we work our way north, that will allow Jackson to boss our organization without much worry. And if we can establish a western move, we would have our expansion completed. Of course there is always the possibility that we might have to pick different cities as we move along. We can cross those bridges as we come to them."

"I believe we have a clever plan," Jackson said, looking very pleased. "You guys are putting a lot of thought into this organization, and I thank you. We have only one thing left to discuss now, and that's manpower. We have discussed eventually having forty men. I still think that will suffice, but if we need more, we will consider that also as we expand. We will need two men to handle one truck route and two more if we should be fortunate enough to put two trucks on the road. These issues will have to be dealt with as they present themselves. In any case, I believe we all agree that what we have planned is big enough. We want to remain peaceful and profitable, and if we keep that in mind, I think we can have it both ways."

"Now let's have a few beers and go home," said Millard.

The men finished their supper then finished off too many bottles of beer.

It was eleven o'clock when Millard arrived home. Flora met him at the door looking tired and with a mean look on her face. Her large belly was showing prominently, and her red hair was disheveled as though it had not been combed all day. "Tomorrow night, I want you to come home much earlier. Cameron has been asking where you stay so much, and Grandma is sick, and I might be having some difficulty with the baby."

"Is Grandma bad off?" he asked.

"No," Flora said, "but she does need attention."

"What about the baby?" he asked with alarm in his voice.

"I don't know," she replied, "but I don't think things are as normal as they should be."

"I will be home as early as possible," he said. "I'm sorry to be so late, but we had a very important business meeting regarding the expansion of our organization."

"Yes," replied Flora. "I can smell it all over you."

Millard quickly decided it was time for him to get into bed.

✶ ✶ ✶

The next evening, Millard arrived at home earlier but not nearly enough. Every day he traveled farther and farther away from Spruce Willow, which caused him to arrive home later each day. Flora understood his predicament and tried to be patient. She had known when he first became involved with Walter and Jackson that their lives would change. He was making much more money than ever but at such a sacrifice, and their lives were much more complicated recently. When he arrived home, things were not as bad as he had anticipated; even though he had had a few beers on the way home, Flora made no mention of it.

Grandma was much better, thanks to Ma's remedies. Flora's condition had not improved, but she had determined that she had been suffering from gastritis. The baby was doing fine.

Millard played with Cameron and promised to take him fishing. Everything was settled down for the time being.

After going to bed, Millard held Flora close and said to her, "Flora we are in the midst of expanding and reorganizing our organization. If everything goes as we have planned, you and I could end up very wealthy. I have repaid Walter and Salem the money they loaned me on the car. Thanks to Grandma, we own our home. What a wonderful feeling it is to be debt free. Soon, I intend to help our families. We are doing well, but this depression is still wreaking havoc everywhere. Our families deserve help from us, and I intend to help them as they have always helped us."

Flora snuggled close to him, and they were soon asleep.

Millard awoke with a mild headache. *Too much alcohol,* he thought and turned over to rest a little longer. He was wide awake however and decided to ease out of bed and go to work earlier than usual. His headache cleared almost immediately, but something was on his mind—an idea or something that wanted to surface and couldn't.

Just some foolish notion, he thought as he started up the hill. Just as he approached the crest of the hill, there was his foolish notion. It was the beautiful antebellum style home he had imagined so many times before. He had gradually allowed it to escape to his subconscious mind, where it had been since he had walked the long road to court Flora.

"Damn!" he said to himself. "I am making good money with a very good chance of becoming wealthy, and I am forgetting my plans for using it."

He stopped his car and looked around the countryside. He visualized owning all the land in sight—all the way to the river. And he saw his splendid home facing in that direction. The opposite side of the house would be facing the highway, making it necessary to design that side to look much as the front. Large columns would be necessary on both sides to project a fantastic appearance from any direction. *If all goes well with our organization all this could become a reality in the not-too-distant future. I will dwell upon my future plans more often,* he thought as he entered the highway and headed on to Spruce Willow.

The remainder of the week passed quickly. Millard and John finished organizing the area they had been working, and Jackson kept everything in good shape elsewhere. Millard reasoned that Jackson was a chip off the old block. He was a natural-born organizer. With his leadership and John and himself putting forth their best effort, their current organizational plan could possibly be in place within two months.

On Monday, Millard headed north, bypassing Blowing Rock by about twenty miles. He kept a small compass in his pocket, which often helped him keep oriented and within the bounds of the Blue Ridges. Today the roads were a series of constant curves. He was beginning to question whether this section of the ridges was worth organizing into a route.

At one place, a mean-looking bull was in the middle of the narrow road and refused to move. He honked the horn, and soon a bearded, old man peered over the fence above the road. "Go on up against him right easy, and he will move on off. He has been hit by a car once before. He knows what they can do but still ain't learned a thang. Just mean and ornery, I reckon."

Millard did as the old man suggested, and sure enough, when the front bumper touched the bull, he moved out of the way, and Millard went on his way. No point in asking the old man to keep his bull fenced in. "Now there," Millard said to himself, "I wasted twenty minutes of my busy day on that damn bull."

Many miles up the road, when he least expected, he drove out into open country, with homes and farms everywhere. From experience, he knew there would be a town or village close by. As he drove along rather slowly, he kept watching for businesses where he might find customers. He passed on by the first one he noticed. It was very shabby and inhospitable-looking. A building like that was seldom worth the effort of stopping and could be troublesome. Not much farther along, however, he noticed an establishment that looked like a prime target. The rather large building had been freshly painted, and it was nicely furnished inside.

Millard approached the man who appeared to be in charge and, in a firm, pleasant voice, told him about his product. They stepped into a back room, and he handed the man a complimentary bottle to sample.

The man smiled. "Best whiskey I've ever tasted," he remarked. "Can you deliver the same quality stuff regularly?"

"As often as you want it," Millard replied.

The gentleman replied, "I own four places just like this one, about every ten miles down this road. I will give you a note. You stop at each place, and my boys will place an order with you. Furthermore, a friend of mine has several places up and down these old roads, and he would probably be interested. We can get whiskey around here but nothing like this. What we are used to is mostly rot gut."

By the time Millard had followed all the leads passed on to him from one establishment to another, it was late afternoon. He had established one full route and part of a second route. *What a day,* he thought as he drove home at a speed much faster than usual.

It was late evening when Millard pulled into the driveway. He knew Jackson would be worried, but Millard hopped out of the car and did a little jig. "I've had a very successful day."

"What caused you to be so late?" he asked. "I was getting concerned enough to begin looking for you as you mentioned this morning."

"I know that I asked you to make sure I got in safely in the evening, given that the territory I'm working through this week might be hostile. I thank you for watching out for me, but the pickings were so good I just couldn't seem to make myself leave as soon as I should've," said Millard.

"Well, that's a good reason," replied Jackson, "but I wasn't about to leave without knowing everyone was in and accounted for."

"I thank you, Jackson. I established one full route and a part of another one. People in the area near Virginia that I've been covering are crazy about our whiskey. They like it and want plenty of it."

TWENTY

Today was a beautiful Sabbath day—not a cloud in the sky. The church was filled to capacity. The worship service was wonderful. Dad and Ma and Grandma were present, and even Lee and his wife, who normally did not attend church, were there. The choir sang several songs in perfect rhythm. Strangely, Flora was especially sensitive to Millard's clear beautiful bass singing. It seemed to her that it carried clearly and vibrantly all the way down to the end of the valley below the church. It caused a special feeling through her body, and she did not understand. As she stood in the church yard with the church bell ringing, sounding the end of worship, the feeling did not go away. She was convinced it conveyed some meaning that she wished she could interpret. She could not and put it out of her mind as best she could.

Before Millard left for work the following morning, he gently awakened Flora and told her that he would be late coming home again. A very important meeting was scheduled, and probably another one again for tomorrow evening. After that, they would only meet as often as necessary to keep the organization progressing and address important issues.

Another new week, thought Millard as he drove to work. *Wonder what this week will bring.* He had been thinking of ideas that would be of value in expanding the organization—things that he wanted to discuss at the meeting that evening and that might be an asset in speeding up the process of their expansion.

He arrived at work earlier than the others. Today would be a long day and one that could be full of surprises. He wanted to leave before the others. He left a note for Jackson and felt confident that would be enough. It was a comfort to know that the men now working knew their jobs and could make their runs without instructions. One new man, who would require training, would be hired each week, but even that was becoming routine. As of today there would be ten men in the group. Every man would shift up one space, and the new man would begin training on the oldest route in the oldest area. Millard could foresee hiring at least thirty more men. If they started using trucks on long hauls, there might be a total of forty-five more men before they considered their expansion complete. That is considerably more than first anticipated not very long ago. Millard headed to the place where he had left off on Friday. He wanted to continue in that direction and the surrounding territory until he completed four more routes, which would make two more nicely connected areas. These would be the best territories yet outside the Spruce Willow areas that were already established. He continued on throughout the day, establishing the two new areas he had started on Friday. He made accurate notes and even drew maps to use in teaching the two men who would be working the areas.

Jackson, Millard, John, and Horace were present at the planned evening meeting and wasted no time in getting down to business. Millard suggested that two more men be hired as soon as possible. He told the others that he was having no trouble at all establishing new areas and was reasonably confident he could establish many more areas within the next month.

Jackson then reminded them that they must remain a secret organization in order to remain in business and stay out of trouble.

John said he believed they should consider moving the business to a different location. Walters's basement was getting overcrowded and so much activity about might invite trouble and exposure.

Jackson said he had been considering doing just that. "I have talked to Lawrence Bowman about purchasing five acres on the rear section of his farm, which has an unused barn that would suit us quite well. The building would need fixing up and a room added on for office space. It is perfect for our needs. The barn is made of thick logs and stays comfortable during all seasons."

Horace reported that he was doing quite well. He was confident that he could continue keeping up with demand, although it had been necessary to hire two men. "I intend to keep making the same fine whiskey and have fun doing so." That remark brought laughter from the other men. He told them about Walter coming over the last week and staying all day one day. "He had so much fun; I have been expecting him to return."

Millard asked the group's opinion about his ideas of area expansion. "So far," he said, "we have succeeded in grouping our areas. I think we all know that works well. We are moving to the north very well, but perhaps we should set some limits. Personally I do not want to go farther than Galax, Virginia, in that direction and no farther south than thirty miles beyond Chattanooga, Tennessee. We could establish areas from Galax by working our way methodically between the eastern and western slopes until we decide upon a boundary south of Chattanooga. The slopes along the edges of the Blue Ridge Mountains look like good pickings to me. From what I could see from a distance, the roads look in good shape. I hope you men will think about this and give me your opinions next week or sooner if you can."

"We have a lot of things to discuss next week," said Jackson. "For now, let's finish our supper and drink some beer."

There were no objections to that statement. They were becoming very good friends, and they all sensed the bond of closeness. Flora was not feeling well when Millard arrived home. "I wish this little one would quit kicking so hard and settle down some. I don't want it to arrive early, but I will be pleased at the passing of the next two weeks. I told Cameron that he should expect a new baby in our home pretty soon. He said he was glad but asked few questions. I was surprised at his calm attitude."

"I should be here to help you more, but my work is at a critical point right now. I might even have to be away all night sometimes. I never dreamed when I took this job that I would be second to Jackson in charge of the organization. Walter has completely retired, and Jackson and I have our hands full."

The next day, Millard kept working his way north toward Galax, Virginia. He was anxious to develop several more areas rapidly. He was not as successful as before but did manage to develop two areas near Galax. He still had no desire to proceed beyond that point of the Blue Ridge. He decided to return home, intent upon working his way south the following day. He was more convinced than ever that going farther north would be a mistake. It was too far away from home and would either require increasing the size of their planned organization or cause some of the men to endure exhausting travel.

When he returned, Jackson was still there winding up the day and planning for the next. Millard briefly reinforced his opinion about not proceeding farther north than Galax. Jackson did not comment on the subject. He looked too tired to consider the matter. Millard wished he had not bothered him. The expansion would be up for discussion at the meeting next week, and that would be soon enough.

As he drove home, he became acutely aware of the home he aspired to build. He passed by the great-looking site where he intended it to be and could not avoid the wonderful feeling he had as he envisioned each phase of construction as it was being completed. He decided that very evening that he would build that home as soon as it was financially practical. *I have made this promise, and now I am committed*, he vowed to himself.

The evening passed swiftly, and after spending some time with Flora and Cameron, Millard went to bed early. He was very tired and knew that tomorrow would be another rough day.

Millard busied himself the remainder of the week working his way south, crisscrossing back and forth from east to west, developing areas as practically as possible. The terrain was rough, and most of the roads curvy. They had been constructed by the Civilian Conservation Corps, a government-sponsored organization designed to provide work for poor, unemployed young men suffering from the ravages of the unending Depression. Millard circled on around past this section of the mountains. It was beautiful country, but he saw nothing but abject poverty in every direction. In some places, roads were currently under construction. The men worked with hand tools, such as picks, shovels, and mattocks, and moved loose dirt with horse drawn drag pans. He felt deep sympathy for the people in these places and hoped their plight would soon improve.

By week's end, he had carefully covered the territory from Galax to about thirty miles back down into North Carolina. He had developed another area sufficient to keep one man busy and had found no competition. One important consideration that had not been addressed in their expansion plans had surfaced this week, however, and that was the crossing of state lines. Laws were different across state lines—an issue they would have to consider. Or maybe they wouldn't. They were already breaking every law on the books.

Friday was a welcome day for Millard and probably the other men in the organization as well. After talking with Jackson about the week's progress and occurrences, he and Jackson headed for home. The hour was late, and the other men had long since departed. Millard stopped at his usual cafe and updated his extremely important notes. Without them, he doubted that he could train the man who would be working that section of the mountains. He finished his notes much more quickly than expected and then ordered a beer to help him relax. One beer required another until he had consumed many more.

A waitress shook him on the shoulder and told him the restaurant would be closing soon.

"Damn, what time is it?"

"It's eleven o' clock," she answered. "You have been sleeping over an hour. You seemed tired, so I didn't want to rouse you. Maybe it would help if you started relaxing more and not working so hard," she added as she massaged his shoulders with her right hand.

"I have never gone to sleep in a public place before," he remarked.

"We could relax together sometime," she said with a cute smile on her face.

"I can't think of anything right now," he said and headed for the exit. *If she has something on her mind, I will be hearing from her again*, he thought as he crossed the parking lot to his car.

He drove home at a normal speed, uncertain what he should say to Flora when he got home. He could not believe it; Flora and Cameron were asleep. *What a lucky break*, he thought. *Now I won't have to lie.*

Saturday and Sunday passed, and the Watson family had enjoyed every minute of the weekend. No church; just play and relaxation. After they were in bed Sunday night, Millard reminded Flora not to expect him until late the following evening. He would be driving all day and had a very important meeting after work.

Millard headed for work very early the next morning. A new week had arrived, and he hoped it would see their organizational expansion jump to new levels. He had his car loaded and ready for the road before anyone else arrived. Jackson, of course, was not too far behind. They had little time for small talk. Both knew what was at stake with so many changes taking place almost simultaneously.

"If you agree, I will take Isaac with me this week and get him oriented on the most northern area," Millard said.

"I believe that would do well," answered Jackson with a nod of his head. "He's a good man, and we don't know what to expect until we learn our people and their ways and habits."

"If he does well, maybe we could assign that area to him permanently," Millard remarked. "I will test him out good this week and let you know how things turn out."

Millard could see Jackson liked the idea.

TWENTY-ONE

Isaac and Millard were well prepared for the day. They headed north to begin delivery to the routes Millard had recently established. Isaac was amazed at the beauty of the hills and valleys. He had never been to that section of the Blue Ridge Mountains before, and he was very excited. Millard advised him to pay close attention to the roads and landmarks and memorize everything he could along the way.

"Some of the places we go into are rough, and you need to be prepared to defend yourself. Carry your gun with you at all times." Millard's firm voice emphasized his point. "You cannot take anything for granted in this business."

"I will do exactly as you say," said Isaac, "and I won't let you down. I need this job badly, and I will do whatever it takes to keep it. I'm tired of living on the edge of starvation through this damn depression."

"I think you will be all right," Millard replied. "You have about the same attitude as I did when I came to work for Walter and Jackson."

Millard covered one route with Isaac that day, slowly and methodically showing him how to complete the route without missing a customer and stressing the importance of making friends with the customers and people within the area.

The scheduled meeting was on time. Everyone had something to contribute. Jackson announced that they would be moving their base of operations to the property just purchased from Lawrence Bowman within a couple of weeks. "And I have contracted some men to build a large storage room on the rear of the barn," he added.

"This is a great place to be associated with," John remarked. "All decisions and changes since I have been working here have been good ones."

Millard gave a report on Isaac. "I think we can depend upon him to handle our northernmost area beginning at Galax. He is a very capable man and a lot of fun to be with."

Horace said that his whiskey-making operation was working just fine. "I don't believe the entire population of the Blue Ridge could drink as much whiskey as we are capable of producing," he remarked.

"The Jacobs Hollow men might drink that much," said Millard.

All the men laughed loudly at that remark.

"I don't want us to get too far ahead of ourselves, but I have been giving further considerations to a few long-haul routes," said Jackson. "I am confident that is where fortunes can be made. We have briefly discussed it before, and I want everyone to be thinking about it. Now, I am ready as usual for a steak and a couple of beers."

In unison, everyone yelled, "Amen!" The meeting was now over.

As Millard drove home that night, his headlights beamed upon the site where he intended to build the house of his dreams. *When should I plan on building it?* he asked himself. The answer came immediately to mind. *I will break ground after my finances are stable and I have a very sizeable bank account. The cost of labor and building materials will probably be very low at that time. I will build it in my mind, and then I will begin building.*

Isaac and Jackson were in the yard when Millard arrived at work the next day. Isaac had his own car loaded and was ready to get on the road. He was anxious to try it out fully loaded as he knew it would be today and many times in the future. This gave Millard an excellent opportunity to canvass the roads and countryside as they continued along. They began the second route of the area at a very pleasant country store that sold about everything as most country stores did.

Isaac found it difficult to accept just walking into an ordinary store and delivering an order of illegal whiskey like you would a bushel of potatoes. Few people even noticed; if they did, it made no difference. Millard had already made an arrangement with the local law enforcement officers when he'd organized the area.

In some areas, the powers that be couldn't always be depended on to look the other way, but they usually did. This was the busiest and most successful week the business had ever had. They were moving through the mountains like a storm.

Millard and Isaac were making deliveries rapidly and making friends everywhere they traveled. Isaac had a very pleasing personality, and Millard had already determined that he would be an asset to the organization. They wasted no time during the entire week. Each morning, they started early and finished the route early, using the extra time checking places they might have missed. Millard wanted to leave Isaac well established in this section of the country. He could see many possibilities in this beautiful, friendly place.

At the end of the week, Isaac and Millard had established a close friendship, and Isaac knew without saying that Millard was a man he could count upon if the going got rough.

After talking over the progress of the week with Jackson, Millard went home. He had no need to stop for beer or any other reason. He felt relaxed and happy. As he crossed the crest of the ridge above his little home, he stopped for a moment. The warm glow of the lamp was such a welcome sight, as it always was. He drove very slowly down the hill.

Before he stopped in front of the house, he heard an unfamiliar sound. It was guitar music, and whoever was playing it was pretty good. He opened the door, and there sat Flora on the bed playing a beautiful tune. Cameron was delighted as could be. Flora immediately stopped playing and smiled as Millard stood there looking at her in amazement.

"I didn't know you could play music like that," he said.

"I used to play and sing with Earl and the boys and Papa when Earl was alive. After he left, I never had the desire to play again. Papa came down today and brought this guitar to me. I have been banging on it ever since, and Cameron has been mesmerized by it. He has tapped his feet to the rhythm constantly."

The guitar was an old flattop Gibson and sounded like new. Millard knew enough about music to realize that instrument was a real prize. "I don't feel up to it right now, but later I would like for us to try singing some songs together," he said.

"I think I might like that," she replied and gave the idea a brief thought. "Just allow me some time to adjust to having this guitar with me again. Papa brought it to me and a lot of memories too. Most of the memories are good ones though. It's just the memories of Earl that make me a little sad. I loved him so much. For a month after he was killed, I stopped remembering things. I take comfort in knowing I will see him again someday."

After they went to bed, Millard held her close until she was asleep. He knew that time did not always completely heal things, and the guitar apparently had brought back both happy and sad times.

Another week had passed, and Flora packed a picnic lunch first thing that Saturday morning.

"Just where are we going to eat that?" asked Millard.

"I know," said Cameron. "Down by the river. Then we are going to visit Grandpa and Grandma. Mama says this weekend we are going to be the boss."

"Is that a fact now?" Millard said. He picked Cameron up and tickled his belly until he could hardly stop laughing.

After a tasty lunch they headed up the road to visit Flora's parents. As usual, they all enjoyed a delightful afternoon. They pitched horseshoes and played hopscotch, hide-and-seek, and jump rope until they were tired out. Millard and Salem played penny poker in the woodshed. What a wonderful day it was.

Just as the sun was sinking, Millard and Flora decided to leave in time to stop and visit with Dad and Ma. Millard sped along rapidly, hoping to get there before supper.

They were warmly welcomed when they arrived and lucky enough to get there while the family was eating supper. Ma quickly fixed a place for them, and they all enjoyed the meal she had prepared.

"We had no idea you children were coming today," Dad said. "Is something special going on?"

"Yes," said Millard. "We are getting to see everyone here. That is always special to us. We just came from visiting with Salem and Martha and had a good visit there."

"We played horseshoes," said Cameron. "Would you like to play horseshoes after supper, Dad?"

"No, I think not," answered Dad. "It is getting late, and I am not limber enough to throw a ringer any more. You know, I used to play horseshoes, and I was pretty good at it too."

"Well, we could play then," insisted Cameron.

That brought a chuckle from Grandma.

After supper, they all gathered in the living room and talked for a while. Millard did not comment on his work; he just stuck to family subjects. They knew what he was doing, and he knew they did not approve. They had made that clear to him before. He sat close to Grandma and slipped a ten-dollar bill in her apron pocket. She pretended she did not notice, but he knew there was no need to say anything.

Money meant little to her, but she loved him for his kindness and generosity.

It was getting late when they left the old family home. Millard promised to give them a ride home from church the next day if they were there.

"We will be there if it don't rain," said Ma. "Some clouds are moving in like it might shower us a bit."

Sunday morning came, and the rain was pouring down.

"I knew it," said Millard as he rose up in bed. "Ma always could forecast rain, as though she can feel it in her bones or something. I don't think we should try going to church. The road out of here looks so muddy I might get stuck trying to get out of here, and the road leading up to the church is probably in even worse shape."

Flora began making dough and patting out biscuits. Soon, they were enjoying a leisurely breakfast. Millard looked out the window, wondering if this was the beginning of one of the famous mountain floods. The rain was slacking, though, and as he looked up to the crest of the hill, he began to think about the home he was planning to build up there.

"Come here, Flora," he called. "I want your opinion about something I have in mind."

She quickly came to the window where he was standing.

"I am going to build a beautiful antebellum-style home on that large flat spot on top of that hill."

"My word," Flora replied. "Just when do you intend to bring this about?"

"We will begin construction just as soon as our plans are complete and our bank account large," Millard answered. "We will plan it together. I want you to find a book with pictures of that style home that will help us with our plans. That is all I will say about it now, but I believe it will give you plenty of food for thought while I am at work during the day."

"It certainly will," she said. "I will do as you say, but it will take me a few days to get over the shock. I guess I assumed we would keep living here always, but I have thought of adding a couple rooms to this house. Cameron and me will go up there tomorrow and look around. My goodness!" she exclaimed as she returned to the kitchen. "What will you think of next?"

Another week arrived, and everyone in the organization was anxious to get started. The previous week had primed them well for even more success. Jackson had to get everything organized in a hurry. Millard could readily see he needed help and felt compelled to remain with him until everything was in order. Millard knew he had a long day ahead of him.

He helped Jackson and then immediately headed south from Glendale Springs working his way down to Boone and then west to Johnson City. That was a large territory and he easily captured many areas.

Even though he had never been so successful in one day, he might have found his first problem. A car had kept following him during the day while he was in and around Johnson City. Since no move was made against him, he decided to wait and see what happened toward the end of the day. When nothing aggressive happened, he stopped and decided to make notes and draw maps as was his habit.

At the end of the day, he had organized five areas. Johnson City was the most lucrative place he had encountered since he had worked the whiskey business. Now he decided it was time to go home.

He arrived back at home base after dark, and everyone was gone except Jackson. They briefly discussed the events of the day, and Jackson seemed very encouraged when he told him about the new areas he had organized. "Jackson, I want to get this expansion completed as soon as possible, and I know you do too. I know we don't want to get ahead of ourselves, but I feel trouble on the way. And I believe, if we can get our organization in place as we have planned, we might be all right. Walter warned me of the dangers in this business, and I think he was right. The same car keeps showing up in too many places where I go for it to be coincidental. We have been spotted by someone, and I am being followed. Could be they are trying to see just how far we intend to expand. They probably have their territory and don't want us to cross their line, yet they have no interest in working in our part of the country with so many curvy roads and rough mountainous terrain."

"Could be you're right," replied Jackson. "Just keep a close watch and don't go any farther than Johnson City tomorrow."

"I have been thinking the same thing," said Millard. "I will keep you informed, but I won't say anything to the other men."

With that exchange, he drove home. He was tired and harboring an uneasy feeling.

Millard drove near Johnson City, the small farms giving way to a dusty town set in the rugged woods now familiar to him. Suddenly, Millard did a double take in his rearview mirror. The mirror revealed a slow-moving black Model T. His heart began to pound, and he pulled his pistol from his belt. It was the same car he'd seen yesterday. He checked his pistol and placed it in his lap where he could reach it quickly if necessary. A few miles into Johnson City, he turned left in the direction of Asheville. He watched in his rearview mirror, and the car did not turn back until Millard was almost out of sight. He was more than certain now that someone was giving him a message. This occurrence could be a matter for consideration later on.

Millard continued toward Asheville, working his way back and forth and taking care to keep on the outer fringes of the areas they were already servicing. The territory he was now covering was vast and rugged and the population sparse. He found several mountain hamlets that he did not know existed and numerous coves and hollows and valleys that looked promising. He found most of the people to be cordial and prepared to do business.

A few, however, were very rough-looking places with men inside who looked even rougher—places where the wrong move or wrong body language could get your throat cut. Most of such places had a rough bar and rough booths along the walls. The center of the floor was for dancing. Back rooms provided places for gambling and sex. Several drunks were usually sitting in the booths, and loud, rough-talking men most always was the sign that a fight was about to take place. Hamburgers and jars of pickled eggs and pickled sausages and crackers were available from a small kitchen behind the bar.

All day, Millard traveled over bumpy, curvy roads. Most of the roads followed along streams or rivers, except in the higher elevations. He traveled through many places such as Erwin, Tennessee; Roan Mountain, Bernardsville, Weaverville, and Black Mountain; and on into Asheville. It was dark at that point, and he decided to travel on to Black Mountain and then head back to Spruce Willow.

It was long past dark when he returned to home base. He checked in and proceeded home immediately. Tired as he was, he remained up and talked to Flora about the events of the day. She knew he was overly tired and listened carefully and spoke kindly to him.

"I was determined to finish that rough section between Johnson City and Asheville before the day's end," he remarked. "Now I have surveyed a very large section of our planned territory. Tomorrow I will double-check where I went today and make sure I have every part of my day's work organized properly. I have never felt it necessary to recheck myself before, but I might have neglected to record all the places where I found customers. If I don't accomplish that successfully, I could ruin much of the progress I have made today. I am happy to be home and now I am ready for bed."

Millard hurriedly ate breakfast the next morning before rushing off to work. This was an important day for him. First, he wanted to tell Jackson that the car that had followed him the previous day had shown up again. He also wanted to inform him that the entire section from Johnson City to Asheville had now been completely searched for possible areas. "I was disappointed in covering that much terrain without organizing more areas than I did," he related to Jackson. "However, I believe I found about everything that could reasonably be organized."

"I know that country very well," replied Jackson. "The customers you did organize probably will prove to be stable and reliable for many years to come. Did you encounter any trouble along the way?"

"No," replied Millard, "but I did enter some places I didn't feel right about and got out of them as quickly as possible. I used the tactics you taught me about such places, and they worked."

"I told Pop about the car following you, and he thinks we have very little to worry about. No organizations such as ours exist anywhere near Johnson City. There might be some people who have found out about us and would like to get in on the action. We have set our limits without being greedy, and if they want to run a business such as ours they are free to do so.

"They won't get any of our customers, not as long as we have Horace Blue making our whiskey. We won't bother them, and it would not be wise for them to bother us. Let's just keep this one car incident to ourselves."

"They would have to make another move before we could take any action against them or even determine who they are. How are you progressing on moving into the new quarters?" asked Millard.

"We will be moving in on schedule I think," answered Jackson. "Millard, you have been knocking yourself out recently. Why don't we spend the day together? We can talk about things and exchange ideas and both work on organizing the new quarters, if you like."

"I would appreciate that," replied Millard. "I need to review the work I did yesterday, and it would help me to review our future plans again."

The day passed quickly. It was a very successful working day. Jackson and Millard agreed that it would be beneficial to arrange a day such as this on a regular basis. After all, the responsibility for the success or failure of the organization was upon their shoulders.

Millard went home. "This has been a good day," he told Flora. "Jackson and I worked together most of the day getting things ready to move into our new headquarters. It also gave us time to exchange ideas and opinions about our expansion efforts. Jackson and I work well together and have since the very beginning. We seldom disagree and have never had a harsh word between us."

TWENTY-TWO

After due consideration and thought, Millard made a calculated decision to extend the southern boundary to Hendersonville, the county seat of Henderson County. It had become apparent to him the previous day when he was reviewing the progress of his work that Henderson County, which was south of Asheville, was home to many small towns and tourist attractions. It was just too big a temptation not to scout it out.

Immediately he departed for that section. He had no desire to encompass Hendersonville. Instead, he began stopping at the attractive-looking nightspots located near the quaint little towns and villages, where tourists would likely frequent and the local population as well. He visited places such as Fairview, Skyland, Reynolds, Arden, Gorton, Bat Cave, Chimney Rock, and many others. Every place he went was wide open for his kind of product. Everyone he met loved the whiskey and wanted more as soon as it could be delivered. He organized four perfect areas before he decided enough was enough. He thought it might be advisable at some later date to stake more areas down there, but he knew their organization could not promise to service many more places for the time being. He headed back toward Asheville and on to Spruce Willow.

Jackson seemed overwhelmed when Millard reported to him where he had been during the day and the remarkable progress he had made. "I knew that mind of yours was working overtime yesterday during our conversations," remarked Jackson, revealing his obvious amusement and pleasure combined. "You are moving faster than I had anticipated. We will have to hire more than one new man a week to keep up with you. You are putting yourself entirely into completing our expansion, and I thank you for it. Just don't overdo yourself."

"I believe we are thinking along the same lines without actually saying so," Millard continued. "We have our plans and goals for expansion, and we both want to put them in place soon. This depression is as bad as ever, if not worse, and we never know what will happen next. Luckily, we are doing exceptionally well here in the Blue Ridge Mountains, probably because others like ourselves and organized crime organizations in the Midwest just don't want to do business in these rugged mountains. They like it where they are. I hope they remain that way, but if they don't, it is essential that we have our organization firmly in place and be ready to defend our boundaries without interfering with anyone else."

"You are right. Pop and me have been talking along the same lines. He reads the newspapers, including *The Wall Street Journal*, to keep himself informed. The country is going to hell right now, he says. People in the Midwest are doing everything from robbing banks to operating mobster type organized crime. Notorious people like Machine Gun Kelly, Bonnie and Clyde, Baby Face Nelson, John Dillinger, and others are robbing banks and shooting and killing everywhere. The law seems powerless to stop them. Pop says the soup lines in the cities are worse than ever, and even Mother Nature has turned against the people in the farming states in the Midwest. The winds have started blowing with such force that the top soil is being lifted into the sky, and rain has ceased to fall to help keep what is left of the crops alive. Ships in the Atlantic Ocean report sweeping soil from those states off the decks of their ships. Farmers are just giving up, packing their belongings on pickup trucks, and returning to where they came from in the first place. An alarming number of people are becoming extremely poor and dying of disease and hunger. We don't want to become one of them."

"We won't be one of them if we can help it," said Millard. "I would like to help them if I could. I know poverty firsthand."

That ended the conversation, and both men departed for home.

After making such progress and this being Friday, Millard decided to head for Chattanooga, Tennessee. He knew the terrain was not too rough and the roads were pretty good. If he could find a reasonable number of good customers and establish some goodwill along the way, he would be satisfied. At the end of the day, it would be nice to get home in time for supper for a change.

Establishing a solid, well developed route all the way to Chattanooga and the southern end of the Blue Ridge Mountains would take about two more days. That would conclude the current planned expansion of their organization, except for long hauls, which had yet to be planned. They would need to develop strategies before such an extensive undertaking could begin.

He had Chattanooga on his mind, and in that direction he was headed. From Spruce Willow, he traveled through Newland, and after losing some altitude, he drove through Elizabethton, Tennessee, but stayed to the left of Johnson City. All of the territory he had traveled through was already being serviced by their organization.

To begin, he decided to work in and around Greeneville and then check out most of the small towns and villages down to Sevierville and Pigeon Forge. It was a rather lucrative area. The dirt roads were curvy and the countryside was littered with farms. As always, when he was scouting territory such as this, he would look for country stores and buildings with gas pumps in front of what appeared to be honky-tonks. If nothing eye-catching appeared for several miles, he would just pick a large, nice-looking farmhouse and stop and inquire where people around there went to have fun. If he received a positive response, he would often tell them he sold the finest whiskey in the world. His technique quickly became a class act, and he was becoming very successful at it.

When he arrived at Sevierville, he had contracted over three areas, and each area had many routes and would keep one man busy working the routes and finding new customers as he went. He counted the day another success and headed for home. His car was running very well and was very efficient. He could burn the road up when he needed to, and this was one of those days when he was wanted to retrace his way back home in a hurry.

Along the way, he realized a very important aspect of his business. He had not contacted even one law officer and had not seen one. He had remembered Walter's instructions about the law when he first came to work for Walter and Jackson. Since then, they had refined their ways of dealing with the law. On Monday, when he returned to this section to work, he would rectify this error and become the law's best friend. This depression and a little money should fix everything. Walter had every officer and public official within fifty miles around Spruce Willow bought off, but now that Walter had retired, the chore had fallen upon Millard's shoulders. So far he had done the job well.

Darkness had caught Millard again before he had arrived home. Jackson was waiting when he returned to Walter's. Everyone in the organization was aware they were moving to their new quarters next week, and they needed everything moved and ready for business on Wednesday morning. Jackson also needed to hire more men because Millard had pulled in so much new business. They had all had a hard week and needed to be rested for an even harder week coming up.

"Let's go up to that café of yours and drink a few beers before we go home," said Jackson.

"I had planned to get home earlier, but at this hour, it don't make much difference," replied Millard. "A cold one or two sound mighty good to me and even a steak wouldn't go bad since we have probably missed supper anyway."

This was a very nice restaurant. It was clean, and the food was excellent. The lighting was soft, and the tables were attractive with nice tablecloths. A café like this was rare across the Blue Ridge Mountains, Johnson City being the place that another as nice as this could be found. Jukebox music could be selected from the booths along the walls, and there was plenty of room for dancing.

Live music was being played when they arrived at the café. They took a seat at the bar and ordered two huge steaks and two mugs of beer. After eating, they ordered another beer and then soon lost count. The same waitress who had winked at Millard the last time he was there waited on them. She kept giving him the eye, and then another good-looking waitress decided she wanted to get in on the action. Millard and Jackson were almost drunk when the bar closed, and when they left the bar, both girls were with them.

They decided to drive up on a high mountain not far from Spruce Willow and view the sights below. Not many lights were to be seen, but the heat was building up inside both cars. One thing led to another, and before they drove the girls home, both Jackson and Millard considered they were in big trouble if someone they knew had spotted them and decided not to keep quiet.

They were lucky. No one mentioned their indiscretions. The girls could have caused problems, but they did not. The only problem they had was that, when they got home, their wives gave them hell for coming home near dawn, drunk as they could be.

The weekend went by swiftly. On Saturday, Millard, Flora and Cameron went shopping in Spruce Willow. Flora had her hair styled in a beauty shop for the first time ever, and Cameron talked Millard into buying him a little red wagon—one that was big enough to ride down the hills around the house.

Sunday was a great day. Most of the Watson family was at church, and afterward, Millard drove them home, where they ate lunch. Dad Watson was especially happy and jovial. They all walked down to the creek and waded in the water. Even Grandma sat on the bank of the stream and dangled her feet in the water. Cameron fell down, and there wasn't a dry thread on him when Flora picked him up. He looked so funny, everyone laughed, including him.

Monday morning was like getting ready for a horse race when Millard arrived at work. Jackson had hired additional men, and everyone was anxious to begin work. Jackson had done well in his hiring. The new men were all poor and had been through hard times, but Jackson had not hired one man he did not consider intelligent, capable, and trustworthy. The success of the organization depended largely upon that principle.

Jackson looked directly at Millard as they approached each other, both thinking the same thoughts. "Are you in trouble from Friday night?" he asked Millard.

"No, nothing but catching hell, and it didn't amount to much. How about you?"

"She threw a pot at me and just barely missed."

"I have felt guilty though. There we were with two women and our wives at home. We should not do that again," said Millard.

"Yes, I know," said Jackson. "The devil made us do it," he added as he walked away.

Millard headed toward Chattanooga, Tennessee, like a ball of fire. He knew he would be helping Jackson the next day, and he wanted to complete organizing all the areas possible in and below Chattanooga. That would be the end of their expansion plans to the southern tip of the Blue Ridge Mountains. He decided to be cautious and deliberate, however, and not rush things. The territory he was about to cover showed good development potential, and he would take as long as necessary to do a good job there.

The territory was sparse until he reached Maryville and then things began to show good promise. It was an excellent place to work his way south. Using his established pattern, he succeeded in developing four new areas with many routes within each area. He worked his way down to Athens and stopped there. He studied his maps carefully at that location and decided it would take two more days to completely develop and stabilize the many places he had covered the last two days. It would be necessary to train the men who would be working that territory very well and also establish good contacts with the law and possibly bribe some officials. He had a good feeling about his recent accomplishments and had good reason to believe he would be just as successful on down to Chattanooga. The people were very hospitable and gracious and seemed to have no objections whatsoever to the sale of good whiskey.

As Millard returned to Spruce Willow and parked near the basement entrance, he was reminded of the first day he'd come to work at this wonderful place. Now he was aware that this would be the last day he would report to work here. Tomorrow, he and Jackson would complete the organization of their new headquarters, and from then on, all business would be transacted from that location. They had grown and expanded so rapidly; Walter's lovely home was not a suitable or proper place to carry on such a shady, illegal business. It was time to move on, and he was glad.

Everyone had reported in and left for home when he arrived. Jackson walked up and patted him of the back and asked him if his day had been a good one.

"I have found more places to sell whiskey than you would believe, and I still have about two more days before I cover all the territory down to our stopping place just past Chattanooga."

"Let's take a quick look at our new place," said Jackson. "It has turned out better than I expected."

Millard liked the place immediately. The log barn was clean, with new painted shelves constructed on the walls. And a large office had been added in front next to the parking area. Inside the office was plenty of room for meetings, social events, and all kinds of activities. "This should do just fine," remarked Millard as he looked all around. "I will be here early in the morning."

"It will be a busy day," said Jackson. "We will need to stock the shelves and get everything organized for the men to start their day Wednesday without too much confusion."

Millard went home with his mind racing. He had never dreamed of getting into something like this so soon after coming to work for Walter and Jackson. Barring unforeseen circumstances, he could see no limits to what they were about to accomplish.

This will be a big day, thought Millard as he entered the highway and headed to work the next morning. Jackson had asked the men to report to work very early and leave on their routes to allow him and Millard a full day to prepare their new quarters for opening day.

Jackson and Millard went immediately to the new quarters where Horace was waiting with a full load of whiskey. They quickly unloaded the truck and returned to their old center of operations and began transferring their remaining stock. It took Horace many loads to move everything from Walter's house. After everything had been moved to the new quarters, it took them most of the afternoon to stock the shelves and complete other jobs. Horace was a lifesaver. All three men worked all day without stopping and finished just in time before the delivery vehicles began arriving to unload any unsold whiskey they had.

The work was tiring, but the day had gone wonderfully well. The men, returning from their routes, jumped right in and helped complete the move. Jackson and Millard kept on working until they were certain every part of the move was complete and they were prepared for the new day. The office looked very professional, with new furniture and office equipment in place.

As they stood admiring their work, Millard realized they had no name for their illegal business. "We should now give our business a proper name," he suggested. "We have been calling it anything that comes to mind."

"What about Newbarn as our official name?" said Jackson.

"Newbarn sounds great," replied Millard. "We don't want anything that stands out to anyone except those connected to the organization."

They quickly found a board and painted NEWBARN on it and nailed it above the office door.

When Millard arrived home, Flora was still up even though the hour was late. He knew something was wrong, or she would have been in bed. "Dad is not well," she said. "He began having heart pains this morning and refused to see a doctor. When the pains continued to increase, he finally did agree to see Dr. Burleson. He had not had a heart attack but was very close to having one. Dr. Burleson said it was a very strong warning and put him on medication and a diet. No more ham or other such salty foods that are bad for his heart. Lee came over this afternoon to tell us."

"Maybe I should go over and check on him," Millard said. "I don't want anything to happen to Dad. I worry that he will not follow Dr. Burleson's orders, and Ma will try to talk him out of doing so."

"Lee said the pains have stopped, and he is resting well. There is nothing anyone can do for now," Flora said.

They went to bed, but Millard could not sleep. He got up and drove to see for himself how Dad was doing. Millard found him doing well and sleeping soundly. He returned home and slept the remainder of the night.

When Millard returned to work, he went to Athens, Tennessee, and continued to work south. The country was somewhat rural at first but soon turned into choice territory. He traveled in and around Big Springs, Riceville, Mount Vernon, and Etowah before stopping to eat lunch. To his surprise, he made the largest agreement of the day at the café where he ate two hamburgers and a soft drink.

News must travel fast around here, he thought as the owner came over and introduced himself as Dwight Taylor and said he had been hearing of a mountain man with the best whiskey available and at a good price. Millard confessed to being that man, and they soon had a gentlemen's agreement for a large once-a-week order.

He headed south at a rapid speed, sometimes going faster than he should. He was anxious to reach Cleveland before days end. He was careful, though, not to move so fast as to miss places he felt certain were good markets for his whiskey. He scouted town after town and made wide berth around each. Regularly, he stopped to make notes on the places he had organized, taking great care to be precise in his record keeping. Finally he saw a sign that said, Cleveland 20 Miles. He decided to stop there and complete his route south tomorrow. His hard work that day was rewarding to him. He was now confident he could complete the territory down to and around Chattanooga in one more day.

He turned his car around and headed home, feeling tired and a little sleepy. He decided to stop in Maryville and get a sandwich and black coffee to go.

Just outside Maryville, a car pulled out of a side road and began following at an uncomfortable distance. Millard decided to speed up and see what might happen. The car also increased speed and followed even closer. Millard could see a man driving the car and that he was following him with a purpose in mind. He pulled his pistol from his belt and placed it on the seat beside him. The car continued to follow even though he lowered the window and motioned the driver to go around him. Nothing seemed to deter the car from following him.

Millard decided to just increase his speed but take no other evasive action. He continued to watch the driver closely. He intended to take action if the fool did not back off soon. Millard decided to wait until he got to where the road was very sharp and curvy several miles ahead. He just wanted things to remain as they were and cause no trouble of any kind. The car continued to follow until it was obvious to Millard that he should do something. Besides, he was getting damn mad at that bastard, whoever he was.

Soon he saw a deep curve ahead and knew this would be the best place to make his move. He pushed the accelerator downward and went around the curve almost sideways. The driver behind him tried the same maneuver but was not very successful with the heavier car. Millard immediately began to pull away. It must have been obvious to the other car that he could not keep pace with Millard. Before they headed into another curve, the driver slowed his vehicle and fired a pistol. Millard had no way of knowing the intentions of the driver, but he was taking no chances at this point.

He pointed his pistol out the window and returned fire. Millard was not fooling around; he aimed at the windshield. The car continued the chase but with only one headlight.

The message apparently got through. After Millard pulled out of the curve, he saw the one-eyed vehicle no more.

It was three o'clock in the morning when Millard arrived back in Fox County. He quickly got into bed and immediately went to sleep. Flora asked no questions. She knew something unusual had happened, but she did not wish to worry him and knew he would explain the situation later.

Flora was very surprised the next morning to hear Millard driving away at a fast pace. He was well aware as he left that she was awake by now and watching him leave. He hoped she would not worry, but he was extremely pressed to talk to Jackson and continue his business in Tennessee.

Most of the men were preparing for the day when he arrived at the new headquarters. They were all excited about their new workplace and the convenience it afforded them—they could drive their vehicles into the barn and load up effortlessly. Jackson was watching with interest how everything was working out. He appeared to be very pleased.

Millard waited a short while before disturbing him. As the men were departing, he told Jackson he needed to talk to him in the office. Jackson knew it was something important, so he wasted no time in going inside.

"Jackson, I don't know what this means, but I don't feel good about a problem I had near Maryville, Tennessee, yesterday evening." He told Jackson about the chase and the man firing his first shot. "I don't know who the damn fool was, but he was playing a dangerous game. By that time, I was mad and returned fire," he concluded.

"Well," Jackson said, "I know how accurate you are with your pistol, and the man is lucky to be alive this morning."

"I aimed at his windshield but missed and took out one of his headlights. He apparently got the message. After I went around the next curve, I didn't see him anymore."

"What do you think about it?"

"Let's have a cup of coffee while we think on it a bit."

As they sat quietly for several minutes, Jackson checked his pistol as though he intended to use it soon. "It is puzzling, but I think he was trying to kill you Millard," Jackson finally said.

"I know," replied Millard, "and if it happens again, I won't cut him or anyone else any slack. Actually, I wanted to turn around and give chase and blast him off the road, but I knew that would be a foolish move."

"We have discussed the possibility of trouble during out expansion, but I didn't expect trouble this soon," said Jackson.

"Especially since I have been working around the friendliest people you could ever expect to meet," Millard added "That is a prime area for our business and I don't want to do anything to harm our chances there."

"Anything I could say to you now would be only guesswork. Wait until I talk to Pop about this. He is an expert in dealing with situations such as this. Just go on with your day and complete the Chattanooga phase of our expansion. If you encounter a bad situation, get away as fast as you can. I doubt anyone could outrun you in that fast car of yours. If you determine you are in danger, defend yourself. We will talk to Pop soon. He will have good advice for us."

Millard was soon on his way toward Chattanooga, driving much faster than usual. He was determined to complete his plan for the day as quickly as possible. When he reached the beautiful country about twenty miles from Cleveland, he began making his familiar pattern.

It was a successful day but not as much so as he had expected. The Depression seemed to have a death grip on the area, and money was scarce. He did, however, establish three areas that were located in proximity of each other, thus providing easy delivery. Millard started to return home.

Suddenly, Millard saw two shadows nestled in the hill. His heart raced, and he gripped the steering wheel. Two cars were waiting for him.

TWENTY-THREE

He pressed the accelerator to the floor, and the race was on. One of the cars was the same one that had followed him the day before, but the other car was a smaller car and the same make and model as his. All three cars entered the first curve wide open. When they came out of the curve and headed down the straight section ahead, Millard could see the large car quickly dropping behind. The smaller car, however, kept right behind Millard.

The next curves will probably prove to be more interesting, thought Millard. He went on around several curves with the car behind almost touching his rear bumper. Millard remembered the next curve to be very sharp, and that was where he made his move. Just as both cars were in the center of the curve, Millard tapped his brakes once and then twice more. The third tap did the trick. The car behind him was forced to brake much harder to prevent a collision. Millard saw his pursuer start losing control. He tried desperately to stay on the road but completely lost it. The car spun into the left-side ditch, and when he tried again to gain control, the car came out of the ditch, went across the road, and headed down a bank.

Millard could only see bending trees as the car went through the woods below. It was difficult not to stop and render aid, but he immediately dismissed the idea when he thought of the car following farther back. He decided they could look out for themselves. After all, them sons of bitches were trying to kill him. He drove several miles as fast as he could go and then headed on toward home at a more comfortable pace.

"Damn!" he said to himself. "I wonder what Walter and Jackson will think of this."

Again he was late getting home, but it was Friday night and he could sleep late in the morning. What a week it had been, and he did not know what to expect next week. It had been a successful week, and normally he would be very happy with his job achievements, but the car chases were bewildering to say the least. He had no way of knowing for certain whether someone wanted him killed or scared or what, but he believed that they meant to kill. He was comforted in the knowledge that he had Walter and Jackson to help him solve the problem come Monday morning.

He went to bed and did not wake up until midmorning. Cameron wanted him to get up immediately and take him to the river and then to get ice cream. Flora quickly made him stop. She knew Millard had been through a long, hard week by the late hours he had been coming home.

Soon after breakfast, the family went to visit Dad. Millard had been concerned about him even though he had been very engrossed in his work. They were happy to see him sitting on the porch as they arrived. To their delight, he looked healthy and rested. He immediately motioned for Cameron to sit on his lap, and Cameron wasted no time in doing so. He seemed happy and talked of the large amount of work he needed to do the following week. Millard advised him to just rest for a week or two before resuming his chores, but he would not hear of it.

Ma and Grandma soon came out on the porch. Ma indicated she wanted them to stay for lunch. She did not fail to tell them what she had prepared—ham sandwiches and other salty foods that the doctor had instructed Dad not to eat.

Millard reminded her that she was going contrary to Dr. Burleson's orders.

She immediately got fiery mad. "What I prepare for Dad will not hurt him," she replied in a snappy voice.

"What you prepare for Dad could very well kill him," Millard replied.

"Dad wants his ham and eggs each morning for breakfast, and I intend to see that he gets them," she snapped.

"Heart attacks can kill, and he came very close to having one." Millard replied. "Why go to the doctor and not obey his orders."

"You and Dr. Burleson would just let him starve to death, I guess."

"He can't eat much if he is dead," Millard said, trying to get his point across.

Ma looked at Millard angrily, went into the house in a huff, and slammed the door behind her.

Millard turned to Dad and said, "I don't want you to be worried in any way, so I just think we will leave for now and return to check on you tomorrow after church. Ma will have cooled down by then, and things will be all right."

Grandma had said very little since they had been there, but she nodded her head in agreement.

As they drove away, Millard said, "I don't want to get mad at Ma, but damn it, there are times when she just can't keep her mouth shut or listen to anyone."

Upon entering the highway, they turned in the direction of Bald Ridge. After driving a few miles, Millard turned around and headed toward home. Flora made no objections. She knew they needed to return home and just lay back. Millard had been on the road almost the entire week and appeared very tired now.

When they arrived, Flora cooked for them what she described as breakfast for supper. That meant eggs, bologna, gravy, and hot biscuits with plenty of butter and jelly. That gave them all a boost, and they had a very pleasant evening talking and playing the games Cameron liked most.

Sunday came, and Millard had no desire to attend church. But after thinking of Dad and putting up with some nagging from Flora and Cameron, he slowly got ready, and to church they went. It was a joyful service. Communion was served, and Millard did not hesitate to partake of the Lord's Supper. After such a violent week as he had been through, he felt a need for spiritual comfort.

They went to visit Dad after services. He was taking a short walk in the pasture. He greeted them with a smile, and they returned to the front porch together.

Sure enough, Ma was full of greetings, and Grandma was her usual self. Ma quickly invited them to lunch, but they decided not to stay. They wanted to pay Salem and Martha a brief visit, and Millard wanted to return home soon and do some thinking about the coming week. They promised to spend a full day with or maybe an entire weekend with the family soon.

Sitting on the porch and leaning against the wall felt grand. The evenings were warm, but a little nip of fall was in the air. The katydids were sounding their mating noises. Millard repeated the old saying that when the katydids called there would be frost in six weeks. Flora was washing the dishes, and Cameron was playing in the dirt. The days were getting shorter too. Everything seemed to be happening so soon and so fast.

Soon Flora came out to join him. She knew Millard was enjoying the evening, and she wanted her share as well. They sat quietly for a while.

"I need to tell you a few things," Millard said, frowning as though he dreaded to relive the previous week over again. "I had trouble over in Maryville, Tennessee, last week. Friday evening, two cars started following me. I took off like a wild turkey around some sharp curves. When the first one came up very close to me, I hit my brakes, causing him to run off down a bank and into the woods."

"I am happy you were not injured," Flora replied. "I am afraid for you much of the time, given the dangers in your work, including the possibility that you could get into serious trouble. Do you know the condition of the man who wrecked?"

"To hell with him," Millard said in an angry voice. "After all, I didn't invite them to start trouble with me. I don't know what will become of it. Jackson and Walter will help me sort it all out."

"In a way, I wish you had not told me about it." Flora said, moving her chair close to his side.

"I don't want anything to interfere with our business," Millard continued. "We want to be totally reorganized before winter, and we are making good progress. We moved into our new quarters last week, and that was a big step forward. I completed developing our southern territory all the way to Chattanooga, and that was another big move. I think we will have our expansion plans complete and everything operating normally in about a month. If we are successful, we will be far ahead of schedule and have a near perfect business running smoothly."

"We have another tiny little consideration coming up soon," Flora remarked, placing his hand on her stomach.

"My goodness, what a kick," Millard said with a laugh.

"I know," Flora said. "He does me that way all day long sometimes. I think he will be earlier than we first thought."

"When do you think I should take you home to be close to Martha?" he asked.

"Probably in about two weeks," Flora replied. "I want to be there in plenty of time in case the little one does come early. I will feel more at ease knowing she is close by. Cameron will have a great time following Papa around."

Millard got out of the bed the next morning dreading the day for the first time since he had been working for Walter and Jackson. He knew he would feel much better after talking with them.

When he arrived, most of the men were there and loading their vehicles. Some had already left. It was always a pleasure to see the men work with such enthusiasm. Jackson had been hiring new men and making rapid changes, which had been very necessary because of their rapid expansion. His efforts were showing off too. He no longer looked stressed this morning as he had before. Everything was falling into place, which showed good training of the men and excellent forethought.

Jackson came over to Millard, smiling as he got closer. "You brought in a lot of new business, Millard," he said. "I can almost see the end of our planned expansion of the Blue Ridge coming into view."

"I think we will have it in place in two or three weeks," Millard replied. "Then I hope we can begin including the long hauls we have been thinking about. I would like to have it all in place before cold weather. That would make our efforts much easier I think.

"For now though, I have some news that might spell trouble for us. I was chased again Friday evening, only by two cars this time."

"Damn, what happened?" Jackson asked in an excited voice.

"They took after me like a couple of coonhounds, and one of the cars was about as fast as mine. The fast one got right on my tail, but I took him into a bunch of sharp curves that he couldn't handle. When I hit my brakes, he lost control and went down a bank and through the woods. I kept right on moving and didn't stop until I got home."

"Hellfire," said Jackson. "I didn't expect this."

They went directly to Walter's house.

Walter was in his den reading *The New York Times*. "My goodness," he said as he lowered his reading glasses. "What brought you two victims of hard times over here so early?"

"We need to talk to you, Pop," Jackson immediately replied without giving Walter a chance to say anything more.

"Sit down then and let's hear it," Walter replied.

"Tell him Millard," Jackson said, motioning with his hand.

Millard started by filling him in on the events of the week—first the successes he'd enjoyed followed by the dangerous troubles he'd encountered.

Walter listened intensely, taking in every word. Then after a few thoughtful moments, he slapped his hands together and said, "I know exactly who is behind this. It's that damned greedy Homer Cash. He once was an honorable man, and we have done a lot of dealing together. But he is no longer trustworthy and will invade your business and take it over given the opportunity. When I went into the whiskey business, I agreed to keep within the Blue Ridge Mountains except for possibly establishing a minimal amount of customers in a few of the larger cities such as Nashville, and he agreed not to seek any business within the Blue Ridge Mountains but would also do some business elsewhere. He lives in Maryville and probably wants to cut into our territory, especially if he has learned that we are prospering and expanding. He knows me well enough to know I keep my word and expect others to do the same. I will contact some of my friends and investigate this matter, and I'll let you know something soon. I hope you men will nail his hide to the wall," Walter added in a loud, angry voice, striking his fist on the den table. "I despise a man like that.

"Jackson, you are doing a fine job running things since I decided to step aside, and you couldn't have a better second than Millard. Millard, you handled that situation perfectly. You tried to keep free of trouble and also hold your own. That is the only way to handle things in the business we are in."

"I thank you kindly," replied Millard.

When Jackson and Millard returned to the Newbarn headquarters, they sat down in the office to discuss business in a very serious way. They were both aware they were at a turning point in the expansion of the organization. They were proud of what they had accomplished and wanted things to continue orderly and ahead of schedule.

"What do you think about things at this point?" asked Jackson, sitting down on the opposite side of the table from Millard. "You just had the first encounter of the bad side of our business."

"I don't think we should let it rattle our chain too much, but we do have to take care of our territory toward Chattanooga. To lose control would be like plowing a rich field and then letting it lie fallow. I know Walter will give us good advice, but we can't wait more than one or two days. I believe those boys who chased me meant business, and we must head them off without delay."

Jackson leaned back in his chair, looking much like Walter, and said to Millard, "Would you go over there in the morning with a man of your choosing and straighten that place out? Stay all week if you need to, but put a stop to their nonsense. I agree with you; we have to let them know we mean business and that is our territory. I can handle everything else on this end. I have hired enough men, and everything is organized well enough to service all of our areas without missing a route or even one customer. I intend to hire two more men today. I don't actually need them just yet, but we will need them soon. They will be well trained by the other men by the time we have routes ready for them. My main concern is your safety in doing the job I asked you to do."

"Hell yes, I can do that," said Millard. "They already have me mad at them anyway. I would prefer John to go with me. He is a man who knows how to handle trouble; of course you already know that. If you need another man to handle some unforeseen responsibilities while we are gone, I recommend Isaac. He shows signs of being a good leader, and we are leaving you with a heavy load. You tend to work too hard sometimes, and I am concerned about you at times.

"Do you realize we have used up almost half of the day, Jackson," Millard said as he looked at his pocket watch. "It is too late to start selling whiskey. If you don't mind, I will work around here with you the remainder of the day. That will give me an opportunity to have Sam Burns tune up the engine of my car. I drove it hard last week, and with what John and I might encounter the next few days,

I might need all the power and speed I can get out of that fine car. It sure is a good one."

"That's a good idea," replied Jackson. "We can get everything around here in top shape. Horace will be coming in with a full load of whiskey this afternoon, and we can help him unload too. Did you know Pop goes over there often and helps Horace make booze? He likes helping make the stuff, and he thinks a lot of Horace too. I think Pop still has much of the old mountain boy in him. He had a pretty hard time when he was growing up, and the work ethic is still there."

"I am glad that he is enjoying his retirement and can do as he pleases," said Millard.

Millard waited until John came in before leaving for home. He wanted to explain everything that had been going on and ask John to leave with him for Tennessee in the morning.

As Millard approached, John suspected he had something important on his mind by the frown on his face.

"I have something to discuss with you, John. I had some trouble over in Tennessee last week, and I need to settle it this week as quickly as possible. I apologize for not coming to you sooner, but you know how fast things can happen when trouble starts, and this trouble could possibly affect our business if we don't end it quickly. We have all worked too hard to build an organization that is making us wealthy to allow it to be taken from us."

"Oh hell, Millard, get to the point," said John. "Knowing you, the trouble probably involves fighting or shooting, you old reprobate," he said, a wide grin on his face.

Millard explained what had occurred the previous week and what Jackson wanted done over there.

"Sounds to me like you handled things pretty well yourself," said John. "What do you need me for?"

"Oh, you know what I want, John," Millard said as he placed his hand on John's shoulder. "When trouble starts you and me always end it. Jackson knows and he wants us to leave early in the morning for Maryville, Tennessee, and stay all week if it takes that long. Walter is looking into things also. We will go by his house before we leave. He might have some information that could prove valuable to us."

"Let's meet here at six o'clock then," said John, "even though I haven't agreed to go yet, you know."

"Yes, I do know; you wouldn't miss out on the excitement this might bring for anything."

They departed with no need for further discussion.

"Bring an extra pair of drawers," Millard called out.

Millard drove home just in time for supper and related all the news to Flora. She did not like the plans that had been made. She feared the trouble that was brewing and wanted Millard to have no part of it.

"I can't just pull out of a bad situation. I told you when I went to work for Walter and Jackson that we were going to expand the business and things could get rough in the process. But I also told you I had an opportunity to make a fortune if things went well and we could at last escape the grips of this hellfired depression. Hard times have not departed, not at all. I see so much suffering every day I have become accustomed to it. You can't imagine how fortunate we are, and I cannot let it just slip away. I won't. If it takes fighting, I will fight."

Flora had witnessed him in these moods many times before and said nothing more. After she had packed some clothes for him, she just held him close. They both knew Dad could get sick again and the baby she was carrying was awaiting delivery. There was no need for further discussion. What would be would be. She would watch after Cameron and await his return.

TWENTY-FOUR

As usual, Millard eased out of bed slowly, not wanting to awaken Flora, yet he did not want to leave without holding her close before he left. She was fully awake and knew he was sitting there in silence. He reached and hugged her tightly and, after kissing Cameron on the cheek, quickly departed.

It was enough. They had exchanged thoughts without saying one word. She felt a sense of peace as he drove away and all was silent again.

John was at the barn when Millard arrived. Jackson arrived soon after. They decided to drive Millard's car. It was such a fast car, and they knew they might need the speed. They were taking no whiskey. This trip was intended to revisit all their customers and reassure them that they would return in a few days and fully stock them with all the good whiskey they needed.

Millard could tell Jackson was a little nervous. He shook their hands and warned them to be extremely careful. "I talked to Pop last night, and he wants to talk with you before you leave. He has been in touch with some of his business contacts and has some information for you that might be helpful."

As they got into the car, Millard saw John place something in the rear floor and cover it over. Upon looking closer he saw it was a 12-gauge pump-action shotgun. "What are you going to do with that?" Millard asked with amazement.

"If you are expecting trouble, go prepared, and this is the protection I know of. Sometimes pistols are not enough for heavy duty."

They went directly to Walter's and knocked on the door.

Walter was waiting for them to show and quickly motioned for them to come in. "I was concerned that you fellows might forget and head on to Tennessee. I couldn't find out as much information over the weekend as I wanted, but I have enough to be of value to you. I contacted one of my best friends who lives near Maryville, and he confirmed that old Homer Cash is causing plenty of trouble over there. He wants all the business and all the money. He has somehow learned that we are expanding our business and reorganizing in a professional way and making plenty of money. He intends to take over our territory and began feeling us out last week. You might have more trouble with them soon. They are probably angry at the way Millard bested them the way he did."

"I don't want trouble, and neither does Jackson," said Millard. "But if they do start anything, we are prepared to take care of ourselves and our business interests."

"I knew you boys would feel that way," replied Walter.

They shook hands with Walter and were on their way.

This might be a week they would never forget, but they were prepared to face whatever might befall them. They hoped trouble was not awaiting them and that they could settle any adverse circumstances in a friendly way. Both men were a comfort to each other. They were raised to be honorable men and they knew without a doubt that they could depend upon each other.

It was a beautiful day, and Millard's car was humming along with his hands expertly steering it around curve after curve. They were fortunate to have such an outstanding automobile during what could be a dangerous journey. John had never ridden in a car capable of so much instant power and speed. He had a fast car himself but nothing like this one.

They crossed the Tennessee line and continued on well south of Elizabethton, passing through many small towns and villages. The ravages of the Depression were evident along the way. They kept the course that Millard had set, which kept them in a direct southern route leading on toward Chattanooga. Millard stopped along the way at places where he had established customers. At every stop, they would take time to enhance their friendships, being certain to never give an impression of being in a hurry. Millard explained to every customer that he and John were driving through the area to assure them of prompt delivery service beginning the next week and that all their whiskey would be of the same fine quality every time. He was straightforward and very believable. Their customers seemed very happy to have his friendship.

As they approached Newport, they decided to stop for lunch and to fill the gas tank and check the oil level. They stopped at a store that sold a little bit of everything. The gas pumps were in front, and gas had to be pumped by a hand lever. The cost per gallon was fourteen cents. The glass container at the top of the pump held five gallons and had to be gravity drained into the car's tank. While Millard pumped the gas into the container using the lever in a back and forth motion, John went inside and ordered each of them a bologna and cracker sandwich, a cheese and cracker sandwich, and an RC Cola to wash them down. When the store owner sliced the bologna and cheese, the slices were half an inch thick or more. They were absolutely delicious, and when they paid the bill, the sandwiches cost ten cents each and the RC Colas were five cents.

After sitting a few minutes on a bench in front of the store, they continued on down the road. The car's gas tank and their bellies were as full as could be.

"Why did we eat so much back there?" said John. "I don't think I will want any supper."

"I didn't want to eat so much, but the old gentleman was so generous with his cuts, I didn't want to hurt his feelings," Millard replied. "Maybe we will burn it off in a few hours."

They both laughed loudly as John patted his bulging stomach. Millard burped twice, and they laughed even louder.

They continued toward Chattanooga, using the same route Millard had established and visiting with each customer along the way.

As they approached Maryville, Millard alerted John to keep watch for anything suspicious.

"I have been watching for several miles," John replied.

"I am keeping watch for the law as well. You never know what to expect from them. I know we try to keep them on our side, but I'm not sure bribes would be successful around here. Remember how Walter told us to handle them when they stop us?"

They continued on through Maryville without a hint of trouble. "This don't seem right somehow," said Millard. "Something is up, and I can smell it. But all we can do is to continue on and not get caught off guard."

They were covering every area that Millard had canvassed, and Madisonville was not far away. "We have already come farther than I thought we would today," Millard commented. "I believe we would be wise not to travel after dark. Let's go down to the left of Athens and spend the night. We don't have any customers around there, and it is a quiet, peaceful place. I do remember seeing a café and a boardinghouse when I drove through there. Sound all right to you, John?"

"It does," John replied.

Millard was correct in his assessment of the place. They found two nice rooms at the boardinghouse, and both had bathrooms. The café was nice enough, and after a pleasant meal, they headed for the bar. Actually, they ended up drinking several beers but not too many to prevent them from staying alert.

Although they slept in a comfortable home, their night proved to be one void of sound sleep and suggestive of hearing voices and people calling their names. This happened often as they were drifting off to sleep. It seemed as if they were neither asleep nor awake.

They discussed these strange phenomena as they ate breakfast but they considered it no more.

They continued their journey, driving at the same constant speed and stopping to talk with each customer along the way. "We will arrive at Chattanooga sooner than I expected," said Millard. "We should be there no later than midafternoon. Since we are making such good progress, let's cruise all through the city and the surrounding countryside. I would like for you to become very familiar with the place, just as I already have. It is a very interesting place and I believe it will prove to be very valuable to our business," explained Millard.

"I have heard much about this place, and I look forward to doing as you say," said John. "Perhaps we could catch some of the honky-tonks tonight."

"Now don't get started on that subject. We are here on business, you know," Millard reminded him.

"Yes, I do know," said John, turning his eyes sharply at Millard. "Business like you and Jackson had a while back I suppose you are referring to," he said with a slight smile on his lips.

"I suppose there is no denying anything," replied Millard. "Somehow you find out about everything. Just wait until we find a place to lodge tonight, and then we will see what happens next."

John's face revealed a full smile as he looked out the side window.

Even sooner than expected, they were only twenty miles from Chattanooga. They drove on through the city to the end of the territory Millard had established. Before quitting for the day, they had visited every area and route around and beyond the city limits.

They easily found a nice, plush hotel with deep carpets and matching window draperies; bedrooms with feather beds; and a dining room with beautiful china and silver near the entrance to the lobby. The hotel was near the heart of the city. It was a large, two-story building with full-length porches and well-kept lawns. After a delicious supper, they decided to cruise around and see the sights.

They decided not to stop at any bars, although there were many. Some of them looked like trouble might be lurking inside, and they did not want to chance stopping at any of them. The hotel was a very inviting place, and they decided it would be wise to return there. After drinking a beer and listening to the radio in the lobby for a while, they went to bed.

Early the next morning, a breakfast of ham and eggs with biscuits and hot coffee prepared them for the events of the day. They wasted little time going to every place in Chattanooga where clients were located. They were well received everywhere they went, and comments on their fine whiskey came from every client.

They had completed their entire mission by noon. Goodwill had been spread from Spruce Willow to Chattanooga, and now it was time to head for home.

Just outside of Chattanooga, they stopped for lunch and gas. Millard took time to check the car over very carefully. He looked for oil leaks and faulty vacuum hoses and anything that might cause trouble.

As they proceeded down the highway, he seemed very thoughtful and quiet. John decided not to call any attention to his change in attitude. He knew Millard would speak when he was of a mind to.

Millard soon looked over at John and said, "Do you know what I have been thinking about, John? How in the hell are we going to get home alive?"

"You know more about that than I do. So far, we have had a successful trip and a little fun too. But I have known all along that our return trip probably would not be so easy."

"You are right, and I believe our trouble will start somewhere around Maryville. That is where it all started," Millard said.

"I think we would be wise to be prepared for trouble well before we drive through that part of the country. You are better at defensive strategy than I am, so let's get our heads straight and figure out a plan. If they are expecting us to come through Maryville tonight, maybe it would give us some advantage to throw them off guard. Let's stop for the night about thirty miles from Maryville and wait until tomorrow morning to continue on home. They might stay up most of tonight waiting for us, and tomorrow night they probably won't know whether or not to expect us."

Millard suddenly drove off to the side of the road and parked. "Can you think of anything else that might give us an edge?" he asked.

"Nothing but have our guns ready and plenty of ammunition."

They didn't have to drive far until they found what they were looking for—a big country store. Inside the store they found guns and ammunition of all kinds for sale. Millard bought several boxes of shells for his pistol. John already had plenty of ammunition for his pistol but did spot boxes of shotgun shells, which were for bear hunting. He bought six boxes. They were loaded with large slugs capable of taking the head off a bear.

"Damn, John," Millard remarked. "I wasn't thinking of starting World War II."

"Well, I am," John replied. "This stuff will stop a tank."

I guess we are ready—for war I mean," chuckled Millard. "I knew you would come through with something like this. You do have a knack for knowing what to do in times of trouble."

"I probably will think of something else if we actually get into a fight," John said.

They soon found a small boardinghouse and settled in for the night. The lady who owned the place fixed them a sandwich and a dessert when she became aware they had not eaten.

They did not sleep well, but the rest they did get did them much good. They drove only a short distance after leaving the boardinghouse the following morning before spotting a pool room—a perfect place to hang out for a few hours. They parked the car as inconspicuously as possible. They knew that there was no telling who might be looking for it.

Late in the afternoon, they decided to drive on toward Maryville. They had no desire to reach the place where they anticipated trouble. Deep inside them was a desire to pass through peacefully and proceed across the mountains to their homes and a warm bed. An air of sadness seemed to fall upon the scene involving the two good men. Everyone should be allowed to travel the public roads in peace and without fear.

When they reached Maryville, they decided to eat supper and then proceed on with no effort to conceal their movements whatsoever. If they had to fight, they were ready. Millard increased the speed and made no effort to detour around the route he had been driving before. They had driven peacefully for about twenty miles or more when Millard suddenly said, "Oh shit! There they are, sure as hell."

Several cars were parked at the edge of a hay field. Only the tops of the vehicles could be seen. Millard immediately swerved into the field and drove around them and back onto the road. They did not have time to pull out and block the road in front of Millard as was their obvious intention. They recovered quickly, however, and John counted four cars chasing them like a pack of bloodhounds. They were fast cars and were actually keeping up.

John called to Millard in a loud voice to be heard over the noise created by the engines, "At the next curve we come to, I am going to go across into the rear seat, and at the next sharp curve after that, slide the car sideways in the middle of the road and stop."

Millard was so busy handling the car he had no time to ask questions. He did exactly as John said.

When John was situated in the rear, Millard put the car in a skid at the first sharp curve he came to. Just as he stopped, John slid out of the right rear door with his shotgun and fired at the first car behind them, taking out the right-front windshield. The car turned to the left with the right side of his car exposed, and John blew out the window of the right-rear door. The driver managed to get his car turned around, and as he did John took out the rear window.

The other cars chasing them fired several shots before they saw what they were up against and turned around to get away. As the car John had been firing at was leaving the scene, John fired one more shot at the rear of the car. Apparently a slug penetrated the gas tank; a fire and then an explosion followed. They heard a loud yell as the car rolled away completely engulfed in flames. John and Millard were horrified at the sight and struck with fear at the thought of a man burning alive inside the car.

Millard and John left the scene with their tires spinning. As they drove away, they tried to see where the yell had come from. It was the driver of the car that was on fire. They saw him running away from his car, and he did not seem to be injured. They returned to Newbarn thankful that the man was not cremated in that burning car.

★ ★ ★

Early the next morning, someone knocked on the door. Flora quickly peered through the curtains, and there was Jackson standing on the front porch.

Millard hurriedly jerked his pants on and reached for his pistol.

"You don't need that," Flora said as she unlocked the door for Jackson to enter. She had her housecoat on and went into the kitchen. She had no desire to hear another story of shooting and fighting.

"What are you doing out so early on Saturday morning?" asked Millard (as if he didn't know).

"I came to find out what happened last night. Pop's friend over in Maryville called and said all hell broke loose over there late yesterday evening. Is there something about it that we need to discuss? Were there any injuries or killings?"

"No," Millard answered, "but there could have been if John hadn't had his shotgun along. They were going to ambush us, and when I drove through a hay field to evade them, they were intent on chasing us down. Good old John opened up on them with that shotgun of his and turned them back. If John hadn't exercised restraint as best he could, it probably would have been much worse. John did not want to kill anyone. He just blasted the cars. So far as I know, he did not injure anyone." Millard explained the action in minute detail to Jackson and gave him a full report of the successful part of their trip.

Jackson looked worried as the conversation continued. "Millard, we both know that sooner or later, if something is not done, bullets will start hitting their mark and people will start falling like bowling balls. It could ruin our business."

"I know," Millard said. "It has me worried a lot.

"Our customers like us and our whiskey over there, and we are scheduled to start deliveries on Monday morning. I can't tell you any more than that. I hope you and Walter can find out what those fools who are causing the trouble are about."

"Pop and me will contact some people and determine what should be done before things get completely out of control. You and John did a fine job in keeping things in hand as you did, and I thank you both. I am going to Pop's now. I would like you to come with me if you feel like it."

"No, Jackson, Dad has not been doing well. His heart has been bothering him, and I need to see about him."

"I can certainly understand that, and I hope his condition has improved," said Jackson.

"I will stop by later today or tomorrow and talk with you and Walter. Maybe I can be of help, and I would like to be prepared for Monday morning," Millard said as Jackson left.

Flora did not know what to say about all she had just heard. She decided to keep quiet and prepare breakfast. Millard would bring up the subject when he chose to do so.

Cameron was awake, and their day was off to a fast start. They drove down to the river and washed the car first thing. It sure was a mess from all the dusty roads it had been through during the week.

In a nice, shiny car they were off to visit Dad and Ma and Grandma.

Millard was so delighted to see Dad he shook his hand and began asking questions faster than Dad could answer. Dad assured him that he was doing just fine. He had experienced one small episode of chest pain, and that was all.

"Have you been eating plenty of ham and eggs?" Millard remarked as he turned his eyes toward Ma.

Ma made no remarks, but she did not quarrel either. Dad evaded the remark by picking at Cameron. Millard looked closely at Dad and was satisfied that he could see improvement in him since last week. His color was much better.

Flora quickly turned her attention to Ma and Grandma. Ma went to the kitchen to prepare some refreshments, and while she was gone, Flora, talking softly, asked Grandma her opinion about Dad.

"He's made no improvement at all," replied Grandma. "He eases around all the time like he is in pain, and I believe he is. No need to give advice to him or Ma. They do exactly what they want to do. When Dad falls over dead, maybe they will take notice. Dr. Burleson came by last Wednesday. He is concerned about Dad, or he would not have made a trip over here. He don't usually make house calls anymore. He is getting old too, and riding on a horse doesn't do him any good. His horse looks about as old as he does," she remarked with a low mirthful chuckle.

They had a delightful day sitting on the porch and walking slowly through the pasture. Cameron made himself busy picking and stuffing himself with Concord grapes, which grew along the pasture fence. Millard took his family home in the late afternoon after they were satisfied things were reasonably normal. Flora did not have a comfortable feeling about things but was slightly more satisfied when she learned that Dr. Burleson had prescribed some nitroglycerin pills for Dad.

As they drove toward home, Flora whispered to Millard and asked him to drive to Spruce Willow where they could get a bite to eat and buy Cameron a cone of his favorite chocolate ice cream. "He has missed you so much this week and so have I. He did not understand why you were gone so long."

"I have a good idea," Millard replied. "You both deserve a treat after such a week as I put you through."

On they went at a faster speed to a very nice evening at a café in Spruce Willow. On the way home everything got very quiet. The supper and all those grapes and ice cream had got the best of Cameron. He was sound asleep for the night.

After they arrived at home and were preparing for bed, Flora said to Millard, "Do you want to attend church tomorrow?"

"Yes," he replied, "I very much want to attend worship services. Perhaps I will receive some guidance there. The good Lord knows I need some. As you know already, I will be away for a short while tomorrow afternoon. We need to prepare for the coming week and decide what to expect after the trouble we had Friday. I will return as soon as possible."

It was a beautiful Sabbath day. The choir sang beautifully but not with the enthusiasm usually present. Millard was not his usual self, and it was very noticeable to Flora. He was always the one who pulled the choir together with his beautiful voice.

Millard left shortly after lunch to meet with Walter, Jackson, and John.

Walter started the session by telling them what he had found out. "We all know what happened last week, and I know you gentlemen are anxious to know what is causing problems for us. Well, Homer Cash is the center of it all, just as I told you from the very beginning. I have been in touch with my friends in Maryville, and they report that Homer has hired about forty hoodlums and has linked up with some highly organized gangs all through the Midwest, including Chicago. He has not started murdering people, but the gangs he is affiliated with are quite willing and capable of doing so." Walter looked around at each of the men and continued, "I have known for many years that the best way to deal with someone like Homer is to go straight to the source. If we are all in agreement, we will do just that. Millard, John, and me will make a trip to Tennessee tomorrow when Homer will least expect us and talk to that bastard face-to-face."

"I hope we can stop going to war every time we cross the mountains," said Millard.

"We will certainly bring up that problem when we talk to him," Walter replied. "Jackson is the boss, and he needs to remain here and keep our operation going smoothly while we are gone. I will talk to Homer and try to work something out with him, but we will settle this business one way or the other tomorrow night. It might take return trips over there, but make no mistake; we will get the job done. We will take a load of whiskey and begin servicing customers over there just as if nothing has happened. I will follow Millard and John at a distance. After dark, as we start our return home, we will make a quick detour straight to Homer's house. I hope we can have some positive negotiations. There will be no hard feelings if you don't like this plan. If you have a better solution, we will discuss whatever you have in mind." Walter looked around the room giving the men a chance to respond in some way.

They were being very attentive but voiced no opinions or suggestions.

"We will leave when we feel the time is right, probably after seven."

"Just one thing," said Jackson. "Things could get rough over there, and with all due respect, I don't want you to get hurt. You are retired, and I want you to enjoy yourself. You are the only pop I have."

"Thank you, son," replied Walter, "but nailing old Homer's hide to the wall will be a joy to me. Don't worry about me. I have thought this over, and I will probably do plenty of talking but no fighting."

"That makes me feel better about things," Jackson said.

Millard could detect that Jackson's concern for his father was deep enough to have touched that soft spot most everyone has.

They completed the details and, after a glass of wine, departed for home.

It was late when Millard got home. He had not intended to be away from Flora and Cameron this long. Flora had kept Cameron up late so they could have some time together. She did not ask Millard about the coming week. She knew he would tell her just what he wanted her to know and no more.

After they were in bed and Cameron was asleep, Millard told her about the plans that had been made for the coming day and that he might not be home Monday night. He held her closely and told her not to worry. "We are going to Tennessee to negotiate with Homer Cash, the man behind all the trouble we experienced last week. Walter is going with John and me, and he is a very wise man. He knows how to handle situations such as this. If everything goes as planned, I will return tomorrow night."

"Thank you for easing my mind a bit. I feel like demanding that you stop participating in all these dangerous, foolish actions, but I know it would do no good, I do understand why you men at Newbarn are taking such chances. All I can do is keep you and your friends in my prayers."

"I know you will," Millard said, and sleep came.

Millard had parked his car farther away from the house than usual to keep from waking Flora so early.

She wondered how he left so quietly, and then it became apparent to her what he had done. She could not help but smile when she thought what a sweet, thoughtful thing he had done for her.

It did not take long for Millard to arrive at Newbarn. He wanted to receive any last instructions Jackson might have. Jackson was there, and so were John and Walter. They loaded both Millard and Walter's cars to assure they would have enough whiskey to service all the routes for the day.

Before they departed, Jackson said, "Take good care of Pop."

Walter turned quickly and replied, "You had better take care of things here, young man. I will be all right."

"I hear you loud and clear," Jackson replied.

They were both smiling at each other as they spoke.

TWENTY-FIVE

The three tough mountain men headed on across the Tennessee line and turned slowly southward following the same route Millard had been following since their expansion to Chattanooga first began. It was a very pleasant day, and they were enjoying their journey. They expected no problems until later in the day and hoped none would develop at all. But for this day to be void of problems would be a failure of the mission at hand. Homer must be dealt with, and today was the day to settle accounts. Whatever presented itself, be it good or bad, they were prepared. John had his shotgun and pistol, and Millard and Walter were armed with pistols.

Millard and Walter were in the first car, and John followed. They had decided they did not want Walter driving in a car alone, and Walter was happy not to do so. They followed their routes very methodically, taking care not to miss one customer. Their fine reputations had preceded them, and they were well received. The trio stopped for lunch and gas, and after checking the cars, they proceeded on their way. After lunch, they began to keep a careful watch for anything unusual that needed a second glance. They did not want to be caught unaware under any circumstances. They continued on until late in the afternoon, passing on by Maryville and ending their deliveries precisely on time. They had sold almost all their whiskey. What they had left was bonded. Everyone wanted that fine Horace Blue moonshine and nothing else.

After the last delivery, Millard motioned for John to pull over behind them. They all knew they needed to talk before proceeding on toward Maryville.

"Walter, tell us what to do," said Millard. "I know we have business to attend to before we head toward Newbarn."

"I know," said Walter. "John, I will show Millard the way to Homer's house. When we turn, you keep close behind us. There's a circular driveway in front of his house. We will pull up in front of the door and knock. I am sure he will recognize me and invite us in. We will be very friendly with him and see how things go from there. If other cars are parked there, we will continue as planned unless he does not answer the door. Otherwise, we will not tarry. We'll leave as though we suspected nothing and return later."

After filling the cars with gas, they sat down in Millard's car. They were all of the opinion that they should not leave without attending to business just as they had planned, no matter if they had to stay extra days.

After some thought, Walter decided upon a change in plans that he thought might work better than driving up to Homer's house without casing the place first. "Let's park in the woods close to the house and see what happens," said Walter. "If only one or two cars are there, we'll drive on up to the house as we first planned. If many cars are parked outside, we'll wait until later."

"If the cars leave, they might be going out to set up an ambush for us," remarked Millard.

"That is certainly a possibility," said John.

"If everything looks normal at Homer's, we'll get the information we want. If we have to shake it out of him, we will do it," said Walter with noticeable anger in his voice.

As usual, Walter had planned every move, and even the changes he made were very logical. He was very careful to not lead them into more than they could handle. They had been somewhat anxious about this maneuver but no longer. They had not looked forward to having to fight a dozen or more men. On to Homer's house they proceeded and parked well out of sight from the house.

Millard got out of the car and eased his way close enough to see if cars were there. He returned soon and reported seeing only one car.

"Gentlemen, I believe we can now proceed to pay good old Homer a visit and, hopefully, a pleasant one." Walter seemed to look forward to this venture, even to the point of having fun. The anger in his voice was now gone.

They drove slowly up to the house as originally planned. Homer came to the door and greeted Walter in very gentlemanly fashion.

"I haven't seen you in quite some time, Walter. You and your friends come in and feel welcome."

"Thank you very kindly, Homer," said Walter.

They were asked to sit down, and Homer immediately directed the maid to serve them a glass of brandy. They sat down in the very elegant parlor, which was superbly decorated with expensive furniture and appropriately placed antiques of seemingly priceless value. The parlor walls were covered with wallpaper that complemented the décor perfectly. A large, crystal chandelier hung in the center of the room and made the walls look even more spectacular. The stone fireplace with hand-carved mahogany mantel was most impressive.

Walter immediately made it known what their visit was about. "Homer," Walter said, "we came on business and I believe it would be improper for us to accept your offer of brandy until we have talked about why we are here. I am sure you recall years ago we made a territorial agreement about whiskey distribution, and I feel certain you remember exactly the terms of that agreement. I will not insult you by repeating all the details. Fact is, I have received reliable information that you have violated that agreement to the extent of recently ambushing some of our men. I assume that you are making a move to force us out of business in and outside the Blue Ridge Mountains, where we have every right to do business. What say ye about this naughty behavior from someone I considered a friend?"

Homer shifted about in his chair and seemed to have difficulty in answering Walter. He was edgy and turned his eyes toward the den in the adjoining room.

John, who was sitting closest to the open entrance, took notice and was ready to make any move necessary.

Homer finally gathered his wits and denied involvement in any sort of ridiculous activity as Walter was describing to him.

"I am a man of honor," Walter said. "If I find that you are not being truthful, you know I will demand satisfaction. As it now stands, I think you are a damn liar. But I make no threats at this time in respect to our past friendship and give you a chance to make amends."

At that moment, a large man appeared in the doorway leading from the den with a pistol cocked and ready to fire. He hesitated, and as he did, John grabbed his arm and took him down hard. The man was strong and held on to the gun but to no avail. John twisted the gun out of his hand and hit him once on the head but not too hard. John did not think the circumstances warranted injuring the man severely. Homer motioned for the man to back away.

Millard kept watching the surroundings for any other trouble. He had been suspicious about the car in the driveway, whose owner could be a bodyguard or someone else that might cause harm. The maid looked in the door and then hurriedly stepped back.

"Perhaps we could have that drink of brandy now," said Homer. "I have been out of line and would like to make amends. No one in my organization will interfere with your operation again. I had ordered no shooting, but I found out a few days ago that some gunfire had occurred. Your people practically destroyed two expensive cars of mine. To be clear, I did not realize you were still in business. No offense, but I assumed you had retired and this was a new bunch coming over here."

"Well, you know now, Homer, and when I am certain that you are being truthful, we will have that drink of brandy. But make no mistake, if this happens again and you are to blame, we will return in force, and it will be hell to pay. We have a good operation set up here now, and I hope you will not try to destroy it. If there is no more trouble and you mean what you say, I will stop by in a few months, and I will be delighted to have a brandy with you. For now, let's just shake hands, and we will be on our way."

As they got in their cars, John spoke up. "I am ready for a plate full of something good to eat," he said.

They stopped several miles up the road for a good meal and then headed back toward Newbarn. They encountered no trouble as they departed Maryville.

Even though it was four o'clock the next morning, Millard was happy to be home. Flora was awake and heard his car drive up. Bed never looked so good to Millard, and he quickly undressed.

As he snuggled under the warm covers, Flora hugged him and placed his hand on her stomach. "I know you are tired, but I need to tell you about our baby. Something is not as it should be. You need to take me home where Mama can care for me. I know the baby is not in the correct position, and I feel pressure that I have not experienced before."

"It will be daybreak in a few hours. We will leave as soon as we awake," he said as he started to reach for the clock.

"Don't bother to set the clock," she said. "I will be awake before dawn, and that will be soon enough."

Even though Millard was tired, he slept only about three restless hours. They left for Flora's old home with Cameron wrapped in a quilt and still asleep.

When they arrived, Salem was up and about as usual. He quickly came to the car to greet them, although he suspected something was unusual for them to appear so early.

Martha knew it had something to do with Flora and her delicate condition. "What on earth is wrong, child?" she asked Flora.

"I just do not feel right about the baby. I think something is wrong."

Martha took her to the bed in the living room to assess her condition. They were not in the room long before returning to the kitchen area.

Martha had quickly determined that nothing was seriously wrong. "Flora will be all right for now I think. The baby is positioned precariously, causing her to feel abnormal pressure. I have seen this happen before. The condition usually corrects itself within two or three days. I hope she will remain here until delivery. I would feel better about things if she does. I do not think she is much over two weeks before delivery anyhow."

Flora looked very much relieved, and Millard was happy she was where she wanted to be. He knew it was important that she feel safe and secure.

Millard needed to be at work soon. Many ongoing issues needed his attention and input. He asked Salem and Martha if Flora could remain there and assured them he would return each evening and stay the night. They happily agreed with his request. He shook their hands and left in a hurry.

He arrived at work late, but a quick explanation was all that was needed. Jackson understood his situation very well. Sally was expecting soon, and he knew that he and Millard would probably have to stand in for each other during this period.

Jackson had all the delivery areas covered. All customers would be served without exception.

When they arrived at Walter's, John was already there.

"This meeting won't take long," said Jackson. "I have been trying to continue our expansion, and with a few exceptions, everything is now organized. The route to Chattanooga completed our plans for the Blue Ridge Mountains. I want us to think about these very important long hauls for a few days. Pop and I have connections in all the major cities involved, but we need to move slowly and methodically in moving into these places. What we need to think about now is precisely where, when, and how to proceed."

Walter stood up and stretched his legs as though he had a cramp in one or both of them. "I thought I had retired, but it looks like you fellows want to put me back to work whether I like it or not."

They all laughed at his remark.

"Well, things haven't changed that much," said Walter. "The leadership of our fine group remains the same. I am retired, and Jackson is your leader."

Jackson asked for input concerning the long anticipated hauls to large cities.

Millard immediately gave his opinion as to when they should start. "We have just cleared our route to Chattanooga. I think we should go on from there to Memphis, Tennessee. Memphis is directly west of Chattanooga and less than two hundred miles away. We should go there first and wait until we feel secure and well established before selecting the next city."

The room was quiet for a few minutes after Millard spoke.

"I believe that is the perfect way to proceed. I am pretty sure our Chattanooga route is safe and I suspect everyone knows we intend to keep it that way. If we move quickly on to Memphis I think all will go well," Millard added. "Since John and me know that area pretty well, maybe it would speed things up if we made the first run. Later, Jackson could hire two smart, robust men to service Memphis and the surrounding area. That would take care of our first large city."

"Sounds good to me," said Jackson. "This meeting was easier than I expected.

"Millard and John are all clear to head for Memphis in the morning if they are ready. We have a new truck already loaded and parked in Newbarn. One change I didn't mention; when we use trucks, we'll load them at Horace Blue's place the day before and store them here until time for delivery. It would be difficult to store so much booze here at the headquarters and even more difficult to load a truck and get started early."

"I will be here early," said John with excitement in his voice.

"Yes, and we thank you for allowing us to make this first long haul," Millard added.

When morning light penetrated the room, Millard was awake. He was at Salem's house, where he would spend the nights with Flora until the baby was born. He kissed Flora and left in a hurry. He had told her the night before where he was going and how uncertain he was about the trip and when he would return.

She said a prayer for him as she heard him drive away.

Salem saw him leave and hoped he would have a successful day. He knew Millard was a very busy and determined man. Salem admired him very much and was proud to have him as a son-in-law.

When Millard arrived at Newbarn headquarters, John was already checking the truck. The bed of the truck was enclosed, and John wanted to make sure their load was secure and would not shift as they went around the curvy roads they'd be traveling.

Off they went at a steady speed. They wanted to draw as little attention as possible during the entire run. They were both armed with pistols, and John had a shotgun behind the seat.

TWENTY-SIX

Millard took the first turn driving, and he was very careful to change to a lower gear as the heavily loaded truck came to a steep downward grade. Since they had to make no deliveries, they expected to reach Chattanooga by day's end.

They arrived in Maryville later in the day and decided to detour around Sevierville to avoid trouble during this first run to a large city.

Upon entering Chattanooga, they found a nice restaurant. The owner informed them he had a few guest rooms for travelers, usually truckers. They asked for one and drove the truck in front of the assigned room. They slept very well, and after breakfast, they headed for Memphis.

They stayed the night in Memphis and then began selling their load of whiskey the following day.

Walter and Jackson had provided them some contacts in Memphis. They decided to begin with those places first and then proceed from there. The first contact was only a few blocks from where they had stayed the night. It was a warehouse that rented space and also sold things people needed but were not available on the open market. They were well received as they introduced themselves to a cigar-smoking man of obvious Italian descent named Antonio Vitally. Antonio, a nice-looking man who appeared to be about forty years old with black hair, a tan complexion, and a medium build, had obviously been expecting them. He admired the truck and especially the cargo neatly placed inside.

Jackson removed a quart and handed it for him to sample. He shook it to see how well it beaded and then removed the lid and took several swallows in succession. It looked as though he was going to drink the entire jar, but he stopped after consuming about three inches of the fine liquid. "Damn," he said. "I believe I could sell this entire load within a week. I know you don't want to sell the entire load, so how much can you unload for me now? Walter called me and said you would be attempting to establish a market for this special product, and I told him I would help you out."

"Well," said Millard, "we want to treat you well, so we will let you have enough to do you until we return in a week or so. You are our first customer here, so it is almost impossible to predict the exact date and time we can make another delivery to you, but we assure you it will be at the earliest time possible."

Mr. Vitally gave them directions to the other places on their list—a total of six large bars and another warehouse much like his. Actually, he owned an interest in that warehouse also.

Each place gave them names of other businesses or prospective customers, and they had almost emptied their truck by noon. They saved enough to give samples to other contacts, and only a few failed to request regular deliveries.

Millard and John stopped at a hamburger place for lunch and then continued as before. They decided to travel around the city and call upon at least a few prospective customers in the north, east and south sections of town, keeping the new clients several miles apart. The west was wide open for business, but they decided not to cross the Mississippi into Arkansas. Their samples were almost gone, and after giving out their last jar within sight of the river, they headed home.

As they cruised along enjoying the sights of the city, John remarked, "I would not want to live in this place, but it sure is a great place to do our kind of business."

"Yeah," replied Millard. "We spread our whiskey all over this place like planting a field of corn back home and without one hint of trouble."

John looked out the window, his eyes scanning the rolling hills dotted with small farms. "Seems too good to be true," he said slowly, his finger stroking his upper lip.

The sun was low in the sky as they headed back east toward the mountains. They decided to drive until after dark and keep on going until they felt the urge to stop. On they went, past Athens and Madisonville, before stopping to eat and gas the truck.

"I never expected to cover so many miles this fast," Millard said.

Me neither," replied John. "It is probably because we unloaded all that hellfired whiskey. Our truck weighs less, but Memphis is a lot heavier now."

"You are exactly right," said Millard, and they laughed loudly.

"I'll bet Memphis is a lot drunker now too," replied John.

"We have talked very little on this trip," said Millard. "I guess we have just been a little on edge, not knowing what to expect."

"This is serious business we are involved in," replied John. "And we have both been very alert at all times. We might be developing a habit of looking over our shoulders watching for trouble."

"If we are, let's get out of that habit damned quick. Being in fear every time we go on a trip, especially long ones, is no way to live."

Millard sat in silence for several minutes before agreeing that John was exactly right. "You know, we are making money hand over fist now, and I hope we can continue. But it causes me to feel guilty at times."

"I know what you mean, Millard," replied John. "I made a pretty good living in my blacksmith shop business, but when you told me about this organization, I knew this was the way to go. I thank you for being such a good friend and thinking of me when you did."

"Let's try to look on the brighter side of our trip and forget the bad side. We have traveled through some beautiful country and happy-looking farms."

"I saw some herds of cattle on some of them farms large enough to make one consider they were in Texas," said John. "If we do succeed in making a lot of money and retiring, I would like for the two of us to make a trip to Texas and other states out west."

"I would especially like to see the Rocky Mountains," Millard replied with excitement in his voice. "Dad worked on the railroad through the Rockies in his younger years, and you ought to hear some of the stories he has told me."

On they rolled at a good, steady speed. John was driving now, and Millard was dozing. Much sooner than they realized, they were approaching Maryville.

John shook Millard to make sure he was awake. "We had better be on close watch again," he said.

"I know," said Millard. "I have been thinking of that hellish place. Maybe it would be better if I drive for a while. I don't intend to drive around that place again. I'm going straight through, and if we spot trouble anywhere, I know you can handle that shotgun of yours much better than I can."

They slowed the truck as they entered the city and made their way without notice from anyone except a policeman in a patrol car, who gave them a second look but continued on. They were happy to move on through and head on toward Sevierville.

Within a few miles after leaving Maryville, Millard noticed the headlights of a rapidly approaching vehicle. "I don't like the looks of this," he said. "Keep your shotgun ready."

When the car came close to them, the driver slowed and continued to follow at the same speed.

"I don't know what to make of this," John said. "I think it's that police car we passed in Maryville."

"I'm certain it is," Millard replied, glancing in his rearview mirror. "It has the same dent in the side as I have seen before, and I don't like it."

"Homer Cash probably has him watching things for him, and there are two men in the car now."

The patrol car continued to follow them for several miles and then, suddenly without warning, began firing pistols at them.

John quickly opened the window between the cab and bed of the truck and fired both barrels of his shotgun into the car. The entire front end of the police car seemed to explode, and a terrible flashing fire came from under the hood.

Millard speeded up as fast as the truck would go, and the last thing they saw was the hood of the police car bouncing down the road behind them. Both men were speechless and trying to determine what was going on with the car; they lost sight of it when they rounded the next curve.

Finally John said, "I guess that will break them from farting in the church choir. I should have told you; this is not my old gun. I bought a 10-gauge and loaded the shells with slugs and extra powder."

"Damn, I wish you had warned me," Millard replied in a loud voice. "My ears are ringing like crazy. Why didn't you just bring a cannon with us and be done with it?"

"Well, it shook me out of the jitters at least."

On up the road they went, traveling at top speed. They passed through Sevierville as though it wasn't there.

"That settles our plans for the rest of the trip," said Millard. "We need to get home and hide this truck inside the barn. It might be dawn before we get there. I have got to slow this new truck down or risk blowing the engine. Jackson would shit if we ruined this truck. We probably have bullet holes in the back, but I hope we can fix them at your blacksmith shop."

"I can easily repair them," replied John.

They continued to make good time and arrived back at the Newbarn headquarters shortly before dawn. Jackson arrived shortly after and was surprised to find them there. Millard was placing a large amount of cash in the hidden safe. Both he and John were exhausted, but they took time to explain the happenings of the entire trip to him.

"Seems you had a very successful trip to me," Jackson said. "Go home and get some rest, and we will try to find out what caused your trouble by the time you return. You know Pop; he will find out what happened and what to do about it soon."

Millard went directly home and to bed. He thought about Flora and Cameron, but he was just too tired to drive up to see them.

When Millard and John arrived at work the next morning, they found Jackson and Walter working on the shooting situation from the previous night. Walter had contacted his friends in the Maryville area, and they knew nothing about the incident. Walter was convinced that Homer Cash was involved, but he could not figure out why his men made such a stupid attack on the truck.

"We will just have to wait and see," said Walter. "Those who were involved removed the police car from the area in a hurry and cleaned up the place. No one has reported what happened, and apparently neither of the men in the car was injured. For now, we will continue with business as usual until we can figure this thing out. We had best tell all of our men and warn them to be alert when they are making their rounds."

The disappointment was evident as the men discussed the situation. The three days Millard and John had been away would have been perfect except for the attack, probably by the Maryville police. Jackson and Walter were delighted with the overall success of the Memphis trip, but Millard and John were worried about the shooting and what the outcome might be.

Jackson could see the worry in their faces and suggested they take the remainder of the day off. "Rest up and relax with your families, and tomorrow we will begin planning for the other two cities we have in our long-range plans. You men did such a splendid job on this trip. I think you have put Memphis in our pocket. I think we might use your same strategy in expanding on to St. Louis."

Millard was pleased that Jackson had given them some relief. He drove directly to Salem's house to visit the entire family and check on Flora's condition. He knew Cameron was probably happy as could be.

Flora was doing very well, and the baby was now positioned normally as Martha had predicted. She was very happy to see Millard. They decided to walk up into the pasture as they had done many times before. She kept hugging him as though he had returned from a long time journey. "I worried about you very much last night," she told him. "I sensed you were in danger or something. Was I right?" she asked.

"No," Millard replied. "John and me had a very successful trip and sold enough whiskey to make the entire city of Memphis drunk." He had no intention of causing her to worry, but he was well aware that she knew something had gone wrong. Situations such as this had been going on for a long time now, but he knew nothing else to do but keep lying to her when he had to and keep his family as secure and comfortable as possible. They were prospering, and that would have to do. He would avoid talking to her about his work and concentrate on pleasant subjects that would please her. They sat down among the broom sage at the edge of the field.

"Flora, I am making more money than I ever thought possible. There is a panic going on, and people are suffering everywhere I go. But here we are prospering at every turn. All of us are! Walter, Jackson, John, Horace, and me are doing the best, but the other men who have been hired are doing well too. I don't know how people afford so much whiskey, but they do—Depression or no Depression. I suppose poor people make their own whiskey, and we sell ours to the wealthy who can afford it."

After supper, Millard and Salem went to the woodshed, their favorite place. Millard updated Salem on the events that had occurred since they'd last talked.

Salem was amazed. "What did you men intend to do about these happenings?" he inquired. "If it continues, people will get injured or killed."

"My feelings exactly," replied Millard. "Walter and Jackson are working on the problem now. They will probably have something figured out soon. I will keep you informed, but I don't want to tell the others in the family."

"Maybe you ought to get out of the organization, Millard," said Salem with a look of concern on his face.

"I couldn't do that," replied Millard. "I am making too much money to get out now. If I stick with it, I will be a very wealthy man. No, I just can't do it."

Salem made no attempt to persuade him to do otherwise. They sat comfortably on two large blocks of wood, pausing occasionally between subjects. They had developed a closeness that required little small talk. Just whittling and looking up through the pasture and listening to the animals and birds were enough, but they usually had plenty to talk about. Even the world news came up at interesting times.

Soon Martha called that supper was ready. Before they left the woodshed, Millard reached over and placed a ten-dollar bill in Salem's shirt pocket.

"That is not necessary," said Salem.

"I know," said Millard. "Just take it and say no more."

That ended their pleasant woodshed visit, and they both felt a little closer.

This was a very pleasant evening for Millard. The mood of the family was wonderful, and as always, he felt very welcome there. He tried not to think about tomorrow and the worry it would no doubt bring. Helping to build and expand an illegal business was not an easy task, but he intended to stay the course until his goals had been accomplished. He would take stress over poverty no matter how difficult and stressful the job became. It was like powerful gain over painful loss.

As usual, morning came all too soon. He slowly removed his well-rested body from under the warm covers and soon headed toward Newbarn, anxious to meet Walter and Jackson.

When he arrived at Newbarn, Jackson was there alone. He immediately noticed that Jackson was happy to see him.

"Where is Walter?" asked Millard. "I expected to find him up and raring to go."

"That is just it, Millard; Pop is not able to keep up the pace anymore. I told him to stay home and do what he is most capable of doing—using that smart head of his to help us keep a sense of direction and give us advice. He agreed and, to my surprise, seemed very happy. He thought he could come out of retirement and resume his old slot, but we both knew that I had made a decision that was right for him. And I believe he can continue to provide us with valuable information not available to us from any other source. So that's the way it is; you and me are running the place."

"Damn," Millard said, "I don't know where to start after so much has gone on lately. I have been so caught up in the Chattanooga and Memphis expansion."

"That's all right," Jackson replied. "Later today, I will bring you up to date on everything that is going on, and we will go from there. John will need to meet with us also, and while we are together, we will need to plan the next stage of our expansion."

"The men are loading up and headed out on their routes now," said Millard. "Every car is fully loaded and speeding away. I did not realize how fast we've been growing until I saw so many men and cars."

"They all work in unison, helping each other as needed. They all know what they are about too," replied Jackson. "That's why we need to keep things going and well organized."

John came in just as the men were leaving. "I know I'm late, but it couldn't be helped. Someone has been breaking into my blacksmith shop and stealing my tools. I had to make some strong bars and locks and chains to keep them out. I also had my brother-in-law come and stay with my wife during the night when I am away until I determine if what I have done works. I have tools in there that can't be replaced."

"Blast them with that big shotgun of yours," said Millard with a big laugh. "That will get their attention and a place in the cemetery. My ears still haven't completely stopped ringing. That must be the biggest shotgun in the world."

"No, there's an 8-gauge, but they are hard to find," said John.

"Please don't ever buy one, and if you ever take that 10-gauge on a trip with me again, I want to know you have it before we leave so I can stuff cotton in my ears before you start to fire it."

John and Jackson laughed heartily at that remark.

"You boys must have had one hell of a time the other night," Jackson said. "I am glad I missed all that fun."

"What kind of mischief do you think we might conjure up for next week?" John asked.

"No mischief, but St. Louis would be great," replied Jackson.

"I think we should head that way Monday morning and put it in our pocket just like we did with Memphis this week," Millard added.

"If all areas are covered here today, I think we should make plans for next week," said John.

"Good thinking, boys," Jackson continued. "John, would you mind taking the truck? Have the boys at Horace's load it and then park it in the barn. I need to show Millard some of the duties here in the office to prepare him for times when I am away. Later, we will need to train you also. This evening, we will sit at the table here and plan exactly what we need to accomplish next week."

John and Millard both voiced their approval and were ready to make this a good day.

Jackson and Millard immediately set about cleaning the dusty, unkempt office. Soon Jackson began showing Millard the fine, intricate points that actually made their business hum like a well-oiled machine. "Pop started all this and was wise enough to realize the necessity of keeping things orderly and accurate."

The employee files primarily contained background information, dates of important happenings, and salary status, but Millard was quick to detect sensitive information in each file—information that could be used to make life very uncomfortable for any employee who tried to sabotage the business.

More importantly, the files revealed information on law officers, elected officials, lawyers, and even court judges who had been paid off.

Millard knew about the large safe built into the wall that was almost impossible to detect. It was enclosed in a heavy wall with a false wall in front that displayed only nice mountain pictures. A latch triggered by firmly pressing the end of the third plank from the ceiling allowed the wall to swing open. It housed large amounts of cash, which was for operating expenses; a list of banks where accounts were kept; and even secret information on the bank executives.

Startlingly enough, Millard found a large diary with daily entries and even a list of friends and enemies and potential friends and enemies. Any information that would be important in operating an illegal whiskey business could be found in that safe.

Jackson could see that Millard was aghast at what he was seeing. "When I am away, make sure to carefully update everything in this office, especially the information kept in the safe. Pop has always been a man of order and detail in his business dealings. That is exactly why we are prospering so well. He leaves no stone unturned. With your help, I intend to keep his established policies in place."

"I will make every effort to keep things as you say," Millard replied.

Early in the afternoon, John drove up with the truck with its cargo of whiskey inside. He immediately opened the door and pulled the truck in the barn and closed the door. They were ready for Monday morning.

When he came inside the office, the trio sat down at the table. John began the conversation by suggesting that Millard and he take that load of whiskey to Memphis and make deliveries to their customers in that city on Monday and Tuesday. "I believe we can accomplish that in two days, and it should make them happier than they already are. We could then promptly return here, load up again, and head for St. Louis. Of course, we would have to rest before the St. Louis trip."

"I don't know if you could do both cities in one week," said Jackson.

"We have already agreed to work St. Louis just the way we did Memphis. Maybe we could service Memphis just as John said—make our customers there real happy with our deliveries and then see where we stand," Millard suggested.

"That would work," said John. "That way we won't be too rushed."

After some back and forth, the men decided that aiming for a second visit to Memphis and a first to St. Louis would be pushing too hard. Millard and John would take their time in Memphis and, as Millard pointed out, barring no trouble, be back by Wednesday or Thursday, leaving them plenty of time to prepare to storm St. Louis.

"You know, that might just work out very well," said Jackson. "We need to buy another truck, and I could have it ready for the road next week."

After the trio had discussed other, less important issues, they saw that the day was swiftly fading and the men were returning from their routes. Millard stayed late to help Jackson get everything in order.

After assuring that all was secure around Newbarn, they left for what they hoped would be a happy weekend.

Millard headed straight home when he left Newbarn, and after resting for a while, he went directly to see Flora and Cameron.

He could smell a good supper as he got out of his car. No one had heard him drive up, so he headed straight for the kitchen. He knocked heavily on the door and asked, "Is there anything to eat around here?"

Everyone in the kitchen laughed, and Cameron came running and locked himself around Millard's legs. "No supper here for you," he said.

"Oh yes, there is," Millard said as he picked Cameron up and headed toward the table.

After supper and some lively conversation, Flora and Millard went out and sat in the porch swing. Millard laid his hand very softly on Flora's stomach. "Is all well with the little one and you?" he asked.

"Everything is going normally," she replied. "I believe baby will be here very soon, and I can't wait. I am just about kicked to death."

TWENTY-SEVEN

Millard brought Flora up to date about his plans for Memphis and then St. Louis and about the trouble that had found him and John recently, assuring her that he and John expected no danger in Memphis. "Flora, even during these hard times, the more business we get, the more money we make. It is hard to understand, but it's true." Millard was slowly moving the swing with his arm and softly holding Flora, attempting to help her feel excited about his work.

Flora knew what he was about and sat silently, wondering how long the dangerous business he was in would last and whether he would survive long enough to fulfill his determined goals of wealth and prominence. *I had rather have him than all the gold and fame in the world*, she thought.

Their talk turned to more pleasant subjects until the eleventh hour before they decided it was past time for bed.

Sunday morning and a day to worship came. Flora roused Millard when breakfast was ready, and, of course, Cameron and everyone else in the house were already up. Flora immediately told Millard she wanted to attend her old church this day. He readily agreed but hesitated when she asked him to sing in their choir. She wanted her church to hear what good singing was all about. She looked so pitiful when he hesitated that he immediately said he would not only go but would sing his very best. Such a smile on her face he had seldom seen before.

The congregation at the church warmly welcomed the family. Flora had not attended services there in a long time, and several of the attendees did not know Millard. He soon became involved in conversations with different people, and Flora quietly approached the choir director and asked him to invite Millard to sing, telling him of Millard's splendid bass voice.

The choir director immediately complied with her request, and Millard was soon sitting in a prominent place in the choir. The choir director was quite familiar with the excellent singing in Millard's home church and informed Flora that he had participated in the singing at that church many years ago. He seemed very excited to have Millard there.

The choir director introduced Millard and informed the congregation that they were in for a treat this Sunday. "We are going to do some lively singing this morning that I am certain you will enjoy."

When the organ began playing and the choir began singing, the entire church was filled with joy. The choir director chose songs that highlighted Millard's deep bass, and Millard's voice blended in with the beautiful voices in the choir just perfectly.

The minister could hardly contain himself. He patted his foot and shouted amen over and over. After two songs were sung, the minister preached a short sermon and then asked the choir to sing several more songs before the benediction. "Let's just make this a singing service."

Before he could continue to say more, the congregation shouted its approval with a loud, "Amen." What a happy service!

Flora was so proud of her home church and her husband she hardly knew how to react. They were invited to return at every chance. Millard told the congregation what a pleasure it was to be there and promised he would return soon. Cameron had enjoyed the service also, but his joy was centered on the other children his age, especially the pretty little girls.

What a wonderful Sunday it had been. With a fried chicken dinner, games of horseshoe and baseball, and watermelon eating, who could ask for more?

All things must come to an end, however, and evening shadows ended with tired adults and a sleeping Cameron. After a supper of leftovers, everyone gathered around the kitchen table to catch up on conversation that was most interesting. Just about everyone told of recent events that had occurred. Millard had very little he was at liberty to tell about, but all knew the reason.

When they went to bed, Millard and Flora were surprised to find they were lying on a new mattress stuffed with new, goose down feathers. It was so soft and comfortable. Flora had to shake Millard several times to get him up in time for breakfast and off to work on time.

Flora knew Millard was in for a hard and maybe surprising week. As always, she said a prayer for him. She hoped the baby would not come until he returned. He would be so happy to witness its birth.

He began thinking about the baby as he drove to work and his hopes were the same.

Routine was setting in at Newbarn now. Everyone was arriving at work at about the same time. Each man knew his duties, and soon all had loaded their cargoes and headed out to their familiar routes. Some men were being trained, and Jackson had arranged every detail to fit into place. Everything was working perfectly.

As soon as Millard and John were certain that Jackson had things in hand, they drove their truck out of the barn and headed out on their long haul to Memphis. Jackson watched as they went out the gate and could not keep from wishing he was going with them. Leading Newbarn was a lonely role at times. He missed Millard and John when they were away and was well aware of the difficulties he would encounter if he didn't have those two rascals behind him. Of course, he did not discount the hard work of Horace Blue and the other very fine employees. What a lucky man he was and how very much he appreciated every one of them.

As usual, John and Millard experienced a certain amount of excitement as they departed on a whiskey run, and it lasted until they had put several miles behind them. After then, all was routine and quite enjoyable. Millard and John were looking forward to having some fun in Memphis as well as making a very large wad of money for the Newbarn organization. They drifted on down the steep mountains onto the flat country before stopping for food at the same little café where they had stopped before.

As they were eating they discussed possible problems that could occur. John cut his steak and spoke of his concerns about Maryville. "Let's turn north around that hellish place as we did before. I don't mind coming through it on our return trip, but I know this is a very important trip, and I would like to avoid all chances of trouble we can."

"You are exactly right, John," Millard said. "We need to get this load of liquid gold delivered in Memphis safely."

John put down his knife and smiled. "I am glad you agree. This is expensive cargo we are hauling, and after we make our deliveries, I think we will feel much better driving home with our truck empty."

"We probably won't have one jar left after we have served our customers," Millard replied.

On around Maryville they went without a second glance from anyone. They were in terrific moods and talked and laughed and enjoyed the sights all the way to Chattanooga, where they went directly to the restaurant where they had stayed before. The owner, who recognized them, informed them he had a room available if they needed one. They wanted to stay but were a little skeptical because of their load of whiskey and did not want to take turns guarding the truck all night.

They told the owner their problem, and he immediately gave a solution. "I have a truck just about like yours. I will park it directly behind you, and I don't think anyone would attempt to move my truck in order to get to yours. Besides, if anyone comes around here at night, my dog lets me know."

After such reassurance they thanked the gentleman and proceeded to their room for a very sound night's sleep.

Feeling very rested, they proceeded on toward Memphis early the following morning. They decided to get a good start before stopping for gas and breakfast.

As they were eating, they noticed a man sneaking around behind the truck and attempting to open the door.

"I am going to check on that rascal," said Millard as he checked his pistol. He was out the door before John could reply.

As Millard walked swiftly toward the truck, the man turned toward him, showing little concern that he was about to be challenged. "You had better move on away from the truck and keep on going if you know what's good for you," Millard said loudly.

The man just stood there looking dazed. Millard did not show his gun or threaten the man, as he could readily see that something was wrong with him.

The man said in a shaky voice, "Mr., I know you have liquor in that truck. I crave the stuff and can't help it. Please let me have just one bottle. I can pay you fifty cents; that's all I have."

The man was obviously a physical wreck, and Millard felt great pity on him. "Oh hell," said Millard as he opened up the truck door and handed him a pint.

"Thank ye, thank ye," said the man.

Millard locked the truck door and handed the man a dollar. "Now go in the café and wash up and eat some breakfast," he said. "Just sip along on the whiskey during the day until you can get sober. You ain't going to live long if you don't get a grip on yourself. Try hard to rid yourself of this hellish habit. It will be hard, but you can do it." Millard shook his hand and returned to finish his breakfast.

"What was that all about?" said John.

"He's a drunkard, and I think he was about to go into one of those fits they have when they go off the bottle too quick," replied Millard.

"You just did a good thing," said John. "I don't mean to sound mushy, but I'm glad you're my friend. Now let's head on to Memphis and probably add to the number of drunkards in that place."

"You are a little crazy, you know," said Millard.

"No worse off than you," said John, reaching across to pat Millard on the back.

They reached Memphis in record time and immediately began delivering to their customers in their prearranged order. Their first stop was at the warehouse of their first Memphis customer, Antonio Vitally. Antonio was delighted to see the good friends he had established the first time they had met and receive his order of whiskey. They carried his order into the warehouse and then sat down to exchange pleasantries. They were in no hurry, knowing they were well ahead of schedule.

Antonio asked them about the mountains, and they told him about how things were up there. "We don't have so many hungry people, but this depression is up there too," Millard told him. "People hunt and fish and plant crops and live off the land. Wild berries and nuts and roots are plentiful. They are useful in making medicine for many diseases and making good tea," he continued.

"We found that many people like our white liquor, and we sell as much of it as we can. So far we are doing pretty well, but who knows how long that will last?" said John. "Generally speaking, we live one day at a time and do the best we can to survive."

Antonio shook his head, and his face showed a look of disgust. "Some people, like me, do all right here in Memphis, but for most, it is often a house of horrors. Be careful as you make your rounds. Trouble can jump on you before you realize it's there. You can get your throat cut by just being at the wrong place at the wrong time. I don't mean to scare you. Just be careful. If I am any judge of people, though, I would guess you two fellows could handle yourselves very well in just about any situation," he concluded.

After a very pleasant conversation with Antonio, they continued on to make several more deliveries before supper time. Before leaving Antonio, they promised to bring any unsold whiskey to him, should they have any left over after completing deliveries to their other customers.

"I will take all you have left even if it's half a load," he said as they drove away.

At the end of the day, they found a very nice boardinghouse in a very nice neighborhood. The houses were brightly painted and their lawns well kept. They were allowed to keep their truck parked just outside the window where they were sleeping. That, along with a gated driveway, was a big relief. They settled in early and were up at dawn.

By midafternoon, their deliveries were completed. They had two half-gallon jars left when they finished and took them to Antonio's warehouse, giving them to him without charge. He was very appreciative and gave them a firm handshake before they left.

"That gift will pay off for us," said John.

"I know," replied Millard. "When you make a customer happy and serve him well, you have a friend who will stick with you as well as help you locate more business."

"It gives me a good feeling to deal with someone like Antonio," John remarked. "This is the most successful trip we have had since we started making long hauls."

"Better not say that just yet," Millard quickly reminded him. "We still have the return trip to contend with. That's where we just might run into all kinds of problems. Surely old Homer won't sic his dogs on us this time."

"Now you have ruined my good feelings about the day," said John.

"Can't help it," replied Millard. "Maryville has been bad luck for us every time. I have cotton in my pocket just in case you shoot your big gun."

Silence filled the truck immediately, and Millard knew something was up. "What is it, John?" Millard asked. "You got quiet all of a sudden."

"I've got a bigger gun this time. I found one of those 8-gauges like I told you about—you know, the type that is hard to find."

"Oh Lord," said Millard. "I probably don't have enough cotton to protect my ears from that one."

"Hellfire, Millard, relax," John said with a laugh. "This one don't sound much louder than the 10-gauges. Step on it a little bit. I am ready for a big steak."

"All right," said Millard. "I'm getting hungry too. It will probably be my last meal where I can hear anything."

At that remark, John laughed until he could hardly stop.

They soon came upon a nice-looking restaurant. They went inside and ordered two large steaks and a large mug of draft beer. The meal was a delight.

They had planned to stay the night in Chattanooga but when they reached that city, they realized they were not the slightest bit tired. After a brief discussion, they decided to proceed on, driving and sleeping until they felt like stopping.

Their plan worked perfectly. They encountered little traffic, and their trip thus far had been very comfortable and enjoyable. As they began to gain altitude, however, they decided that it was time to become alert and carefully observe anything unusual or just anything that made them feel uneasy. Cars following them or parked near the highway were of particular interest. They were not to the places where they might encounter trouble, but when they started seeing signs indicating they were approaching such towns as Athens, Sweetwater, and Madisonville, they knew trouble might be waiting not too far ahead.

"This don't seem true," said Millard. "Surely someone would have shot at us by now; they always have."

"Don't be too certain just yet," John said as he peered through the rear window of the cab. "A car is following us at a far distance and staying at the same speed."

No sooner had John spoken than the car suddenly sped up and came at them like a bullet. Its engine was very loud and supped-up, but its body seemed in bad shape. It had scrapes and dents all over, and the headlights were extremely bright. The driver seemed to be toying with them, racing the engine and blinking his headlights from bright to dim over and over.

"What do think, John?" said Millard.

"They are beginning to annoy the hell out of me. They could be just teenagers having a big time, but I don't think so," replied John. "Not many teenagers could afford such a car as that. I have been hearing of bootleggers driving cars like that lately."

Millard could see that the car was getting on the wrong side of John as well. He certainly did not like the bright lights and loud engine right on their bumper.

"I don't know who they are or what they want but I am going to put an end to this shit right now," said John and reached for his shotgun.

"Damn, don't shoot yet," yelled Millard. "Wait until I get some cotton in my ears."

"Hurry up then; hellfire, I can't wait forever," John said as he turned his head to determine if Millard was prepared for the blast.

"Go ahead then; I am as ready as I will ever be."

John quickly pointed his big shotgun out the rear window and fired a blast directly into the front of the engine. The car immediately stopped, and the headlights went out.

No sooner had the car stopped then four men jumped out of the car with rifles in hand and began firing at the truck. Millard had pressed the gas pedal to the floor as soon as John fired the shot and none too soon. A dozen or more bullets pelted the truck, one of which came through the rear window, passed between Millard and John, and went on through the windshield.

That made John madder than ever. He quickly reloaded his shotgun and fired another quick shot, aiming directly at the front of the car again. That shot must have severed a gas line; as usual, they left the scene with a car engulfed in flames.

"Sons of bitches!" yelled John out the window, shaking his fist at the fleeing men.

"I hope you didn't kill anyone," said Millard.

"I don't think I did," John replied.

Both men remained quiet for a few minutes. Neither of them had ever been shook up to that extent before.

"They had better not cross us like that again," said John. He was so angry his voice was shaking. "I didn't shoot to kill them, but they did us."

"If I knew who they were at this point, I would like to go after them," said Millard. "I sure am glad you had that big gun. It might be as loud as a Civil War cannon, but it got the job done and might have saved our lives. Remind me not to complain about the noise of your shotgun again."

TWENTY-EIGHT

Millard kept driving the truck on toward Newbarn as fast as he dared without abusing the engine. After they had reached a safe distance from the incident, they slowed down and proceeded to their destination.

It was past the break of day when they pulled into their headquarters and parked the truck inside the building. Jackson was in the office and suspected something was wrong when he saw Millard and John go directly to the loading area. He went out to see what had happened, and the hole in the windshield told him something had gone wrong. He had no intention of saying anything to Millard and John that might be offensive to them or hurt their feelings. He knew that whatever had occurred, those good men had handled it as best they could and had been the instigators of nothing wrong.

"Looks like you had another good time like you did during your last trip," he said with a slight smile on his face.

"You might say that," said John while Millard nodded in agreement.

Jackson had never seen them so disgusted. He decided to give them time to gather themselves, knowing they would explain everything. He felt perfectly at ease with them, as he always did, and wanted to help.

"We had a very successful business trip," Millard remarked. "We made friends and new customers all over Memphis. We don't have a drop of whiskey left. All went perfect until we reached the bottom of the mountains, and then all hell broke loose. Would you mind if we wait until later to give all the details? We are awful tired and would like to go home a few hours and then return and explain everything. Could we meet at Walter's when we return? He might have some notion as to what we are up against. I think the four of us need to put our ideas together and come up with a solution."

"That's true," John added. "You and Walter always have expert opinions, and with input from Millard and me, maybe we can put an end to this continuing aggravating situation."

"Of course you guys should go home for a while. If you feel like it, we will meet at Pop's at six o'clock. I can probably have this place closed down by that time and can meet you over there."

Millard and John wasted no time in heading for home. John wanted to see if all was well at his blacksmith shop.

Millard was very anxious to check on Flora's condition and rest a little while. That truck was a good one, but it wasn't the easiest vehicle to drive on the curvy roads he and John had been traveling since the previous afternoon.

Driving his comfortable car again was a pleasure. He headed straight to Salem's house at Bald Ridge to see Flora and her folks.

When he walked in the door, he got the surprise of his life. There sat Martha rocking a beautiful, little, fat baby boy.

Millard hardly knew what to do or say. Martha placed the precious little fellow in his arms to love and hold. She anticipated his next question. "Flora is in the bed where this little fellow was born. She is resting well but will require much rest for a few days. The delivery was a difficult one. He was so large we could hardly get him out, and the afterbirth came out first and was entangled about his neck. We had to work hard and quick to save him and Flora. By the time we completed the delivery, she was very weak. But he is perfectly healthy and strong and will no doubt grow up to be a fine man like you."

Millard walked softly to the room where Flora was sleeping. She was sleeping very soundly, but she was pale from the ordeal she had been through. He decided to allow her to rest without interruption. He returned to talk with Martha and hold the baby.

"He was born yesterday morning at three o'clock, give or take a few minutes," she told him. "We were so busy no one thought of watching the clock. I think we have the time just about right though."

"I am not much of a praying man," said Millard, "but I truly thank God that all is well." He decided to sit with Martha and talk until Flora woke up.

Martha could see that he was worried and ill at ease. "Is something bothering you other than Flora's condition?"

"Well, yes," Millard replied. "Don't tell Flora, but we had some trouble on our return from Memphis last night. There was some shooting involved, and we don't know what it is all about. I need to return to work this evening for a meeting to try to sort things out. I don't think anyone was injured, but we have got to determine what is going on before things get worse."

"I can see the importance of what you are saying and that you don't want to leave Flora." She patted him on the shoulder and said, "You go to your meeting. Don't worry about Flora. We'll take good care of her while you're gone."

Millard leaned back in the rocking chair he was sitting in and quickly went to sleep. He wanted to be awake when Flora woke up, but that was just too much to expect. Martha put a blanket over him and hoped Flora would continue sleeping until he'd had time to rest.

Over two hours passed before Flora awoke. Martha gently roused Millard, and he went to her bed. "How are you feeling now, honey?" he asked.

"Tired and weak," she replied, "like I've been hoeing corn all day with a bad cold." She gave a slight smile.

"I see the color has returned to your face. Do you feel like a light hug and a kiss on the cheek?"

As they gently hugged, the weakness in her arms indicated to him that she had been through much during delivery. Just holding hands seemed sufficient for the time being.

When it became apparent that Flora wanted to talk, he told her about the long trip but did not mention the trouble. He did, however, tell her that he needed to attend a meeting soon but that he would return as soon as the meeting was over.

"You had some trouble while you were gone, didn't you?" said Flora.

"My goodness, Flora, how did you know that?"

"Your hands told me," she replied.

"No use lying," he said. "We did encounter some trouble but nothing that cannot wait until later to discuss. There is nothing for you to worry about," he told her as he fluffed up her pillow and helped her into a more comfortable position. He decided to just sit quietly beside her and hold her hand. She dozed off for almost an hour, leading Millard to believe she had undergone a very difficult delivery.

He looked at her adoringly as she awoke, looking a little more rested. "What are you going to do with that cute, little, fat fellow in the kitchen?"

"Just let him play with Cameron and get dirty every day, I guess," she said with a smile.

"He looks like he might be hard to handle later on," Millard said jokingly.

They were both very happy the baby was here.

"Let's not have any more children," said Flora. "Two is enough I think."

"Agreed," Millard replied. "You had a hard enough time with this one. I don't want any more close calls."

"I need to go now," he said as he kissed her on the cheek.

"Be thinking about a name for the little, fat boy," she said.

That brought a happy smile to his face as he left the room.

He arrived at Walter's just behind Jackson and John. Walter was standing on the front porch looking very fit and happy. Jackson had told him they were coming but had not explained the reason.

"Come on in, you law-breaking bootleggers," he boomed, a wide grin spreading across his face. They shook hands and told him how happy they were to see him. Inside the lovely home, they were served delicacies—olives, cheeses, soda crackers, huckleberries, gingerbread, and pickled beans—and great-tasting wine. What a cordial greeting from a wonderful man who they admired so much.

After some pleasant conversation, Jackson began the informal meeting by telling Walter that Millard and John had had some serious trouble on their return trip from Memphis and that they all wanted his input and advice about the matter. "We consider it serious because Millard and John believe that attempts were made on their lives last night."

"What happened, boys?" Walter asked.

"Well, our trip went perfect until we got back to the foot of the mountains this side of Maryville, where trouble always starts," said Millard. He told Walter about the car with the loud engine and the bright headlights and how they'd tried to let it pass them.

"I think they wanted us to pull over and stop," John said. "I could see four men in the car," he continued, "and there was no doubt in my mind but they had a place somewhere ahead where they intended to pass us and cut us off and shoot us. I think it was attempted murder; that's what I think.

"After it was evident we had no other choice, I got my 8-gauge shotgun and fired directly at the engine. It stopped the car, and all four men jumped out and began shooting at us with high-powered rifles. I fired another blast at the front of the car. I guess I ruptured a gas line with the first shot, and when the next shot went home, the car was immediately engulfed in flames. Millard got us out of that place quickly. The last we saw, the car was a ball of fire and the four men were running for the woods."

Millard then said, "You should have heard that shotgun. It sounded like a Civil War cannon going off. John did not want to kill anyone. We just wanted them to leave us alone. They probably got the message. But the thing of it is, we cannot imagine who they were and what they wanted. It confounds us."

"And to me and I am sure Jackson as well," replied Walter.

"That don't sound like something Homer Cash would do. That is just not his style—that is, of course, unless he's changing his ways."

Walter sat for a while as if in deep thought and then said, "Boys, you have stumped me on this one. Did you hear any names called or anything that might give us some idea as to who they were?"

"Nothing," said Millard.

"Well, tomorrow I will make calls to everyone I have done business with from here to Memphis. In the meantime, if that don't reveal any clues, I believe we might do a little spy work. Perhaps we could send a couple of men down to the Maryville and Sevierville areas for a week or so and see what they can come up with."

"Pop," said Jackson, "I have an idea that might just work. The people that we encounter always come up from behind and do their dirty work. I believe we could pick the most likely place where they might get behind us again and have some of our men back their car off the road there. Then when they pass, our boys could follow them and, when they make a move on one of our vehicles, come up from behind and box them in. Even if they leave their car and run, we could have a good chance of finding the person who owns the car."

"That leaves us three possible ways of catching these cowardly devils," said Millard. "Let's try one of them at a time, beginning with Walter's idea first. If he wants to make his calls tomorrow, this will give us time to reorganize things after what we just went through."

"John, do you have any other suggestions?" Jackson asked.

"No," replied John. "I think we have enough ideas for now."

"If we are all in agreement then," said Jackson, "let's go home and start again in the morning."

As Millard was driving away from the meeting, he suddenly realized that he had not told his best friends about the birth of his new son. *How could I have forgotten such an important event?* he thought as he continued on to Salem's farm. *I will stop at the store on my way to work in the morning and buy enough cigars to pass out to everyone at Newbarn. That will be a good way to make sure I tell everyone.*

When he reached Salem's, the entire family was there, as if they were waiting for him. Everyone seemed very happy and was taking turns holding the baby. It was Flora that Millard wanted to see. He knew there would be plenty of time later for the baby. Cameron had fallen asleep at the supper table and had been tucked into bed. No doubt he had worn himself out playing hard all day.

When Millard walked into the bedroom, Flora was sitting in a chair beside the bed. She looked almost fully recovered. "You look much better now," Millard said as he kissed her on the cheek. "Just a little hollow-eyed."

"I feel much better too," she replied. "If I keep improving, I think we can return home in a week or two."

"Please don't try to push yourself. Just concentrate on regaining your full strength, and then we will consider going home."

"Are you in some kind of trouble?" she asked.

"We had some trouble on our return trip from Memphis but nothing that cannot be taken care of. I will tell you all about it later on."

Millard returned to the kitchen to see if there were any leftovers from supper. He was very hungry. The snack food at Walter's hadn't lasted very long. Salem was sitting at the head of the kitchen table eating stew. He had been visiting with a neighbor friend of his and stayed past suppertime. "Any leftovers from supper for a hungry man?" asked Millard.

"There is some stew on the stove. Help yourself. But first, I have to shake the hand of the new father," he said as he gave Millard a firm handshake and a pat on the back.

Millard got a big bowl of stew and began eating rapidly, as was his habit when he was tired and hungry.

Salem continued, "That baby sure is a handsome little fellow. A little heavy for his age, but he will run the extra pounds off in a few months."

"I am very proud of him," said Millard, "and I thank you and Martha for keeping Flora here where she feels so safe and secure. I wonder if she and the baby would have made it through such a complicated birth if she had not had you and Martha taking care of her."

"We did have a midwife, who is Martha's cousin, present, and she helped out, but I don't think she could have handled it alone. I believe Martha and me knew more about delivering babies than she did. Even so, we were very grateful to her. The three of us got the job done, and that's what counted."

Salem finished his bowl of stew, and after eating a biscuit filled with jelly, he scooted his chair away from the table.

"I have a situation I want to discuss with you, Salem, sometime this weekend," Millard said after he had finished his stew. "It is too long and complicated to go into now, but I need your opinion about it when we get a chance to talk. I would like to go to bed now if you don't mind. I have had a long week, and it is beginning to catch up with me."

"I'll be around when you need me," Salem replied. "You take good care of yourself on that job of yours. I know things can go wrong in that business and I do worry about you at times."

When Millard returned to Flora, she was still in the chair beside the bed. He helped her get into bed and then got in himself. "What about the little one?" he asked her.

"Mama will insist that he sleep between her and Papa. Don't worry; he will be well cared for."

"What are we going to name him?" asked Millard.

"I have been thinking about that today," replied Flora, "and I want you to name him. I named Cameron, and now it is your turn."

"If I am going to name him, allow me a day or two before doing so. That will be a big chore for me."

"Just take your time and make a good choice," she said with a cute giggle.

The next morning, Millard left for work a little late. He wanted the store where he could buy cigars to be open.

When he reached work, the first thing he did was start passing out cigars and telling everyone about his new son. They all seemed happy for him, especially Jackson. "Why didn't you tell us about this event at the meeting last night?" he asked.

"I just plain forgot," Millard replied. "I guess the importance of the meeting just took my mind away."

"I am getting anxious for our baby to arrive," Jackson said. "I hope it is a boy, but if it's a girl, I won't mind one bit."

John soon came in the door of the office. He too was a little late coming in and looked sad and worried.

"Is something troubling you, John?" asked Jackson.

"Well, I had to follow up on that thief who has been raiding my blacksmith shop. He had not taken more tools, but my brother-in-law caught him trying to break in the shop again and identified him. I looked him up and slapped his head a couple of times. I don't think he will return. I have felt sorry about hitting him for some reason. A good talk would have done just as well. I am thinking of apologizing to him when I see him again. His family might have been going hungry, which caused him to steal things he could sell for food. If I find that to be true, I will help them out."

"You are a damn good man, John," said Jackson. "Not many people would be so kind."

John, looking a little embarrassed, thanked Jackson. "It gets to me when poor people go hungry," he said.

"Today is Friday, and I hope Pop will have some answers for us sometime today about the shooting incident. I expect he will come over here later in the afternoon. In the meantime, let's start planning for our expansion on to St. Louis. We can't allow our momentum to slow. We will no doubt have more incidents, but I think we can hold our own."

"I have been thinking about this last shooting incident," said Millard. "We should keep on with our plans for Newbarn, but we will have to deal with the men or whoever sent them after us. It's like a radio mystery. There is an answer, but we will have to find it."

After pausing a few minutes in thought, Jackson said, "I have another truck ordered, and it is scheduled to be delivered Monday morning. As soon as we get it ready and everything seems to indicate the timing is right, I would like for you two to head for St. Louis. We know, of course, that leaves only St. Louis and Chicago."

"I am willing and anxious to head out," said Millard.

"I am ready to go too," John remarked. "I have a little dread about Chicago, it being such a large city. But I think we might enjoy organizing St. Louis very much." He moved his chair so he could see who was coming up the road. "I believe that is Walter coming now."

"It is for sure, "said Jackson, "and I am glad. Maybe we can make more concrete plans now that he is here."

Walter soon came in the door with three bags of what smelled like fried chicken. "My good wife thought you might be getting hungry about this time and sent you some lunch to eat while we talk."

"Hand it here quick," said Jackson. "I know the smell of Mom's fried chicken, and I also know it is mighty good."

"Start eating then," said Walter. "I know we won't get much talking done until you guys finish off that chicken."

That brought laughter from Millard and John.

Jackson began the discussion by asking Walter if his phone calls had revealed any information so far.

Walter said that he had called everyone he could think of and had even gone through an old diary he had kept when he'd first started the whiskey business but had discovered practically nothing. "One old friend in St. Louis, Jim Anderson gave me some information that might be of value. Jim used to live in Spruce Willow, but we did very little business together. We just became good friends and have kept in touch over the years. He moved to

St. Louis to take over the family business after his father passed away. He told me that a mean group who live between Memphis and St. Louis in a place called Dexterville have made it known they intend to take over everything relating to the whiskey business for hundreds of miles around. He didn't know where they get their whiskey or whether it was white or bonded. He said they intended to organize in our direction all the way to Asheville, North Carolina. Jim and me agreed that such a bunch might be too stupid to organize anything, or they would not be announcing their intentions so broadly. That's like announcing their plans for failure.

"What do you fellows suggest we do now?" Walter asked. "I won't be doing anything, but you three will be handling everything. I will continue to glean all the information I can and pass it on to you, along with any suggestions I might have. I admire you men. You have more guts than just about anyone I have ever known."

"You are the one to be admired," said John. "If it were not for you, we wouldn't be here making good money and dodging this hellish depression."

"When out new truck arrives Monday, I will have it checked over in the garage and then load it for a haul to St. Louis," Jackson remarked. "If we can find nothing further about the last trip, I believe it would be best to wait until Wednesday to depart."

"That will allow me time on Tuesday to repair all the bullet holes in our other truck," said John. "Did you see the holes in that nice truck we drove on our last trip, Walter?"

"No, I haven't, but I will take a look at it as I leave."

"I will be prepared to do anything that comes up on Monday," said Millard. "I know we will all be thinking hard from now until Monday for a solution to our shooting problem. We have to solve this thing, or we are going to end up killing someone or getting ourselves done in."

Walter then went home to continue making calls to anyone he knew who might remotely be of help in providing a clue about those responsible for such dastardly deeds.

Jackson, Millard, and John spent the remainder of the day at Newbarn preparing for Monday and what the day might bring.

TWENTY-NINE

Two days till Monday and who knows what then? thought Millard as he drove on his way to see his family at Salem's. He was aware that he and the other leaders of Newbarn had much to consider before then. They did not know who their enemies who hated them enough to try to kill them were, and they did not know what to expect on their trip to St. Louis. Jackson had Newbarn to be concerned about, and John seemed more concerned than the others. Millard knew he was determined to see their mission accomplished. If it took a small war to achieve their goals, then let it come. John had never backed down from anything yet that Millard knew of, and he knew he would not shirk from this responsibility.

Shortly, Millard was holding his new son. Millard smiled as the boy yawned.

Cameron was not jealous at all. He called him his baby, and he had all manner of things planned out for the two of them to do. "What is his name?" asked Cameron.

"Oh my," said Millard as he glanced at Flora. "I will tell you his name in a little while."

He motioned to Flora to accompany him outside to sit in the porch swing. She suspected that he had forgotten to think of a name, but he had not forgotten. The name had been in the back of his mind off and on all day but not enough to come to a solid conclusion. When they sat down he paused shortly and then said, "How does Walter Jackson Watson sound to you? They are my wonderful friends. I think it is a pretty name, and it will honor them."

"Well, I never would have thought of such a name, but it has a nice sound," she replied. "It is just perfect, and I know very well why you selected the name. We could never repay what Walter and Jackson have done for us."

When they returned to the kitchen, Millard sat down on the floor beside Cameron and said, "Your little brother's name is Walter Jackson."

"That's a nice name," Cameron replied. "I will just call him Jackson."

The other family members liked the name as well.

After supper, they all sat around the kitchen table and had a wonderful evening.

After they went to bed, Flora reminded Millard that, first thing in the morning, he should go tell his family and take Cameron with him. "I would love to go with you, but I think it best for Jackson and me to stay here a few more days before going out much."

After breakfast the following morning, Millard and Cameron did as Flora had said, and he was happy they did so. Dad, Sarah, and Grandma were doing very well and were joyful about the new baby. They were extremely glad to see Cameron.

"I will bring Flora and Jackson here as soon as possible. She had a very hard delivery. Walter weighed over ten pounds, and the afterbirth was entangled around his neck. We could have lost both of them if she had not had excellent care."

Flora went to bed early, and that gave Millard an opportunity to talk to Salem, who had been sitting at the table since supper. "Too dark to sit in the woodshed," said Salem with a familiar smile at the corner of his mouth.

"Sitting here is just fine," replied Millard. As he looked about, he became very aware that this was one of the most comfortable, usable kitchens he had ever seen. It had a very large table that could sit a dozen or more people and a cast-iron cooking stove with a large stovepipe that gave off as much heat as did the stove and protruded several feet and then elbowed into the chimney. The windows were adorned with simple but beautiful floral printed curtains made from feed sacks that matched the tablecloth well. The floors were of solid, unfinished oak planks tightly fit together and double layered. Two corner cupboards held large stacks of bowls and dishes and silverware, and several attractive chests sitting on the floor housed pots and pans among other kitchen items. An attractively built, upright-standing chest held flour and meal.

"I built this as an all-purpose kitchen, knowing most of the family would be spending more time in here than any other room in the house," Salem said, noticing that Millard was attracted to the kitchen.

"I hope you had a successful trip to Memphis," he added.

"It was a very good trip, except on our return trip, four men tried to kill us. John, with his 8-gauge, put a stop to that. We don't think anyone was injured, but the incident has us thinking. I honestly think they we trying to murder John and me," said Millard. "We have got to find those devils that are after us with such determination."

"Well, Millard, you men know far more than I do about such happenings. The way of doing things seems to be changing and leaving me behind. One thing seems clear to me, though; those bastards want in on your business or to run you out of business and completely take over."

Millard could tell the subject was bothersome to Salem and cut the conversation short. "I will keep you informed about our progress," Millard said.

"Be careful, son; damn, be careful!"

"I will," Millard said as he turned and thanked his father-in-law. He went to bed quietly, not wanting to wake Flora.

Millard wanted to go to church the next morning but didn't know whether he should leave Flora and Cameron. He felt ill at ease and could not go to sleep for over an hour. *Morning will tell if I should go to church*, he thought as he finally drifted off to sleep.

There was no question about attending church services. Flora told Millard to go and take Cameron with him—not a request but a direct order, which he had no intention of disobeying.

Since the little Methodist church was only a mile or so away, Millard decided not to drive. He took Cameron by the hand, and they walked the entire distance with Cameron talking the entire way. Millard just walked and listened, enjoying every minute.

When they entered the church, the choir director immediately asked Millard to sing with the choir. He wanted to very much but did not know what he would do with Cameron while they were singing. The choir director said, "He can sit by you. I will place a chair there for him."

Millard was not certain, but he suspected the choir director had selected songs that his voice would complement. If true, what an honor it was. He loved that little church, which was so well kept and pleasing to the eye both outside and inside. Bright candles set off the beautifully finished chestnut interior and altar dressings just perfectly. The windows were slightly tinted, just enough to enhance the beauty of the interior and allow all who entered to witness the awesome love of God's Holy Spirit. How could one enter such a beautiful little church like this and not feel that only good resided there?

When they arrived back at the house, Flora could not wait to hear about the events at the first church service for Millard and Cameron without her. She had almost predicted everything, except Cameron's behavior while Millard was singing. She was well aware that Cameron was very capable of talking out loud during church services. After Millard gave her a full report, she was so happy she gave them both a tight hug and a big kiss.

Sunday afternoon was a fun time as usual at Salem's, and the day seemed to pass quickly. Millard retired early in anticipation of a hectic Monday.

Everything was normal at Newbarn on Monday morning. All the well-trained men set about loading their vehicles and readying themselves for their route deliveries. Millard, John, and Jackson went into the office after the men were on their way.

"Everything is going mighty well," said Millard. "You have done a great job in training the men how things work here, and it is obvious to me they have caught on quickly."

"You tell them or show them how their work is to be accomplished and that's all you have to do. They listen closely and do exactly as they are instructed," Jackson explained.

"We are moving along well," said Millard, "and when we complete organizing ourselves in St. Louis and Chicago, our expansion will be complete."

"I do not want to expand anymore," replied Jackson. "I know there's always a chance we might change our minds, but I've been studying our maps, and we will have enough territory to keep us busy until we are old enough to retire. Millions of people and small towns and hamlets are all over the maps between here and Chicago. We have a good plan, and I believe we should stay with it."

"I do too," said Millard and John at the same time.

"I am expecting our new truck to be delivered anytime now," Jackson said as he looked through some papers concerning the truck. "As soon as Lawrence delivers it, we will have Sam Burns check it carefully, and then we can load it up for your trip to St. Louis on Wednesday."

"I repaired the holes in the back of the other truck. It looks just fine, except I couldn't get the paint to completely match," John reported. "It is in the barn and ready to go. I will take it over to Horace's and load it if that's all right. I'll put it back in the barn, and it will be ready for the Memphis run by Isaac Whitfield and Frank Center in the morning."

"I have been hesitant about who to send on that run," said Jackson. "You two decide who you think would be best for that haul, and I will agree with your decision."

"I think any of the men could make the trip just fine, but Isaac Whitfield and Frank Center have the most experience, and this is a very important haul," said Millard.

"I believe Millard is right and he knows the men better than I do," John quickly replied.

"We have one more decision we must now make, and it's a big one that I suspect we have all been thinking about over the weekend. Pop has not been successful in finding any additional information. We will have to decide based upon what we have. I think we all want to box the bastards in and beat the information we need out of them."

"Maybe it would be best to make the haul just as we did the last one," said John. "If anything happens this time, we'll go at them with full force. We haven't involved any of the other men yet in any fights, and I hope we don't have to. I know Isaac and Frank might have trouble on their trip to Memphis, but I am confident they will do fine."

"Good point, John," said Millard.

"It's settled then," said Jackson. "I would like to have Pop's opinion, but I hesitate to bother him too much with this."

"Let's just do this one on our own," said John. "We will do it in such a way as to not hurt his feelings. Let's pay him a short visit on our way home this evening though. His mind works overtime, and he might have talked to someone or come up with a valuable idea. It would please him to know how much we continue to respect his opinions and ideas."

The day had been very successful and happy. They had made many important decisions. Their evening visit with Walter was very nice. He was very pleased with their recent decisions and was especially agreeable with their decision to proceed with their expansion no matter what. He also had favorable comments on the selection of Isaac and Frank for the next Memphis haul. "I wish you the best of luck and Godspeed," he said as they were leaving. "The next few weeks could make or break us so far as Newbarn is concerned." He stood on the porch with a somewhat sad look on his face until they had departed.

Millard had not expected such a good day at work. It had been one of those days when everything just seemed to go well. Only two concerns lingered in his mind. He was not completely certain that Isaac and Frank could handle a confrontation such as he and John had encountered. *They are young and need a little more experience*, he thought. The other concern, of course, was the attack on him and John. If he just knew who the attackers were, he would feel much more confident about the two upcoming trips to Memphis and St. Louis during the following week.

When he got home, Cameron was all over him. "Where do you go and stay so long?" he asked. "I want to go with you sometimes," he continued.

"Well, maybe I can take you with me sometime."

That was a satisfactory remark; Cameron said no more.

Flora and Jackson were doing great. As they were eating supper, Millard became acutely aware of how happy he was when he was there. Millard wondered why he had not noticed how wonderful it was being here. He knew Flora was tired of the place when they were courting, but he considered that she was like most all young folks, wanting to spread her wings.

Millard and Salem decided to go sit on the porch swing before going to bed. It was a cool evening, and the stars shone brightly.

That Salem was concerned about the events of the day was obvious to Millard. He was happy to relieve his father-in-law's mind to some extent. But when Millard explained the two matters he had thought about on his way home, Salem still seemed concerned.

"We will be leaving for St. Louis on Wednesday morning with a full load," Millard told him. "It will probably be Sunday before we return—a little earlier if we don't have any trouble."

"I won't rest easy until I see you safely home," said Salem.

Millard walked swiftly to the car and brought back a quart of whiskey. The two men sat in the swing and passed the jar back and forth several times while they talked of more pleasant subjects.

"This sure is good stuff," said Salem as he smacked his lips.

"I am told that every day," replied Millard with a laugh. "Here," he said to Salem as he handed the jar to him. "Keep the remainder of this for later. I will bring you more all along."

When he went to bed, he apologized to Flora for not paying anymore attention to her since he'd come home, but there was no need for that. She knew Salem liked Millard, and she did not mind them having a manly talk. It was good for both of them.

"I will be leaving for St. Louis on Wednesday and won't be home until Sunday," he told her. "After that, we will return to our own home if you are ready. Don't hurry though. You have been through too much, and there is no need for us to rush home," said Millard.

THIRTY

After kissing Flora and Cameron very lightly, Millard was off to work. He knew it would be a busy day, but he looked forward to a day without going on the road.

Isaac and Frank were preparing to leave on their Memphis trip. They were a little nervous, but their spirits were high. They considered being selected for the trip an honor, and actually it was. They were aware that their truck was already loaded and thoroughly checked. John had been thinking about them and had placed one of his 10-gauge shotguns behind the seat of their truck. They were very thankful for what John had done and were very surprised when he handed Isaac a full box of ammunition to go with it.

Millard briefed them carefully about the trip, alerting them of the many dangers they might encounter along the way and providing some helpful precautions, including varying routes and shortcuts they could take to avoid trouble in certain places.

They thanked everyone for their help and were on a trip they would probably never forget.

John and Millard immediately began helping Jackson catch up with the tremendous workload that was obviously becoming a burden to him. As their organization had grown, so had the volume of work in the office and, along with it, added responsibilities as well.

By noon, they had the place in reasonably good shape. The outside looked very neat and orderly. The office and meeting room was a different matter. Jackson had been running the business by memory and handwritten notes placed here and there. Jackson knew Millard and John wanted to help and took the opportunity to show them the minute details of how the business was run.

Millard could hardly believe how complicated things had become since Walter had retired. Jackson had to rely upon keeping several journals, something he and Walter had never done and had never intended to do. But after hiring so many people and monitoring such a large cash flow and keeping detailed maps and records on each customer, record keeping became a necessity that could no longer be avoided. When they had moved the organization from Walter's basement to the current Newbarn headquarters and given it a name, they had wisely purchased a very large heavy safe and placed it in a thick, walled room with iron bars for extra protection. No door led into the vault room; the wall was the door, and a cleverly constructed mechanical lever built behind the baseboard at the bottom of the wall allowed entrance. Chances of even a professional burglar getting into the vault room and into the vault would be highly unlikely.

As Jackson explained the vault, he emphasized that its primary purpose wasn't just keeping money. "We do keep a considerable amount of money in this vault, but the most important purpose is to protect the confidentiality of our accounts and customers, among other things, which I will show you at a later date. Our customers depend upon us, and we depend upon them. We all must keep that in mind. All men who work here now are aware of the importance of keeping detailed information so that a new employee could locate any customer and make a delivery even if he had never been there before. We routinely make cash deposits to our bank accounts located many different places. We have many secrets, a few of which I cannot reveal to you at this time. Later, we will have another session like this, and then I hope that, if anything should happen to one or two of us, business would not be interrupted."

Both Millard and John expressed their approval of the changes Jackson had made, and John repeated his appreciation for being appointed third in line, even though, he said, "I am not well educated."

"Maybe so, but you are smart and quick to learn, John," said Jackson, "and that makes the difference."

"If you don't mind, I would like to stay here and help and observe things until after the end of this business day," Millard said.

"If it is convenient, I would too," said John. "There might be things you don't want me to observe until later."

"Both of you can stay as long as you like. The things I don't want to reveal to you are hidden where you would not see them, and the only purpose for not revealing them to you now is that I need to check with Pop first. After I have informed him of the changes we are making, I think he will appreciate what we are doing."

The day ended with Millard and John feeling a lot smarter and much more like businessmen. As Millard was driving home he thought about what a pleasant day this had been. He and John might go through hell the rest of the week, but this had been a good day. He could vision most days as being like this one once they'd complete their expansion and reorganization. He let his mind rest with those thoughts.

He arrived at home just as everyone was sitting down for supper. Chicken and dumplings were sitting in the middle of the table and steaming hot. "I thought chicken and dumplings were a Sunday treat," Millard said jokingly.

"Since you might not be here in time for dinner Sunday, we decided to pretend Tuesday was Sunday," replied Martha.

"I am glad you did," Millard said as he was filling his plate with vegetables and a portion of the main dish.

Flora sat beside him, amused at him making himself so much at home.

Cameron remarked, "Daddy sure does eat a lot."

"All right, young man," said Millard. "I am going to tickle your belly good after I finish eating."

When Cameron saw Millard's plate almost empty, he jumped down from his chair and hid behind the cooking stove. Millard pretended to search the kitchen but could not find him.

The family sat in the kitchen, and talked for a while after supper and then went to bed. Millard wanted to get an early start for St. Louis in the morning. Cameron slept well, but the baby cried some during the night. Millard did not mind though. It was a strong cry from a beautiful, little boy.

As Millard was discussing his upcoming trip to St. Louis, Flora reminded him again to be very careful during his trip.

"Why?" he asked. "I hope you are not having one of your premonitions."

"I have been feeling a little uneasy, but it is probably nothing," she replied. "Don't worry and enjoy your trip. I will take good care of the babies, and we will go home next week."

When morning came, Millard and John double-checked everything remotely related to their trip to St. Louis. They left nothing to chance. Millard again made sure he had cotton for his ears, in case John had to shoot those two large shotguns he had placed behind the seat. And he could hardly believe what he was seeing when John brought a thin, steel plate from his blacksmith shop and placed it behind the truck seat to help protect them in case they were fired upon from the rear. It shielded the entire back of the seat. "John, you always amaze me and in a good way. Who else but you would think of armor plating our truck like a tank?"

"Heck, Millard, you are so clever in other ways you make up for things that normally come natural to a blacksmith."

"We just make a damn good team."

With that remark, they headed down the road toward St. Louis, Missouri.

They were twenty miles down the road when the sun appeared above the trees. "I am glad we are getting an early start," Millard remarked as they moved steadily along, their speed interrupted only when shifting gears, mostly on downgrades.

"It would be great if we could make it to Chattanooga today, or even farther," said John. "The sooner we arrive in St. Louis, the sooner we can get our cargo sold. It will take more time, you know, this being our first delivery trip and establishing new customers as well."

"I know," replied Millard. "I always dread the first run like this one. Some of the nicest customers you find want to talk on and on. It takes some tact in trying to move on without offending them. Almost always, things turn out just fine though. I am confident we can finish by Saturday evening or maybe sooner."

"This should be an interesting trip." John said. "If we can finish our work on schedule without any trouble in St. Louis and then battle our way back through Tennessee, we should make it home by late Sunday night."

"I know," Millard replied. "It would be wonderful if we could have just one nice haul without any gunfire on the way back home. We have yet to get through Tennessee without firing a shot."

They continued to make good time and enjoy the scenery and good conversation. They were within fifty miles of Chattanooga before they had to stop for gas. Their tank was almost empty, and their stomachs as well. They ate sandwiches and filled the gas tank at a country store. A country store with a gas tank in front was always a good indication of a nice place to stop.

They rested awhile and then continued on, intent on passing through Chattanooga and continuing on to Lawrenceburg for the night. Their efforts were successful, and they easily found a nice-looking home in a well-kept neighborhood. The home was two stories, painted white with shuttered windows. It was nicely decorated inside with handmade wall hangings and oil paintings that were very pleasing to look at but not overwhelming. Lovely items such as antique wall clocks and shelves with very old items that appeared handed down from years long past gave a soft, warm look.

The bedrooms were nicely decorated also, with much-appreciated high-bedpost feather beds. A sign in the yard read, "Sleep well and have a good breakfast."

They did exactly what the sign said and, after a good breakfast, were on their way toward Memphis early the next morning.

"Boy, did we ever run into some good luck back there," John remarked.

"Them sausage and eggs and hot, brown biscuits were mighty fine," replied Millard as he patted his belly.

"We should make it to St. Louis this afternoon fairly early," Millard said as he looked at a roadmap. "We could begin work immediately after we get there. You know, changing drivers often as we do makes a big difference."

"That's right," agreed John. "We cover more distance and don't get so road weary either."

Knowing Memphis well, they were successful in getting through the city with ease. With Memphis far in the background, they decided to stop and eat lunch and gas up early. They wanted to stop at another country store, but after not passing one, they stopped in a small hamlet with a small café and a gas station close by. They wasted no time in that place and were soon well on their way to St. Louis.

"I think we are going to arrive even sooner than we anticipated," John said as he looked over the map, "and I am not one bit tired."

"I'm not tired either," Millard replied, "and I feel great. If our luck holds, we might have a considerable amount of time to look the city over and get some quality work started."

It was midafternoon when they arrived in St. Louis. It was a beautiful city with wide streets and nice-looking homes in many places. Signs of a depressed economy were present, but the Depression did not seem to have affected St. Louis as much as it had many places. The main business section had extremely wide streets paved with bricks. Many important-looking business establishments and factories were scattered about. The Mississippi River was a great asset to the city, providing a route for all kinds of commerce.

Millard and John were astounded by this grand and old city. After they had driven around for a while, they hardly knew what to think or say. Finally, they collected themselves and began talking. "We can only cover a small part of this vast city. I can determine that before we start work," said Millard.

"You are right," John replied. "I hardly know what to do or where to start."

"Well," said Millard, "let's drop back a few blocks and circle around until we find a place that looks and feels good to us and go from there."

"Sounds good," said John. "We'll just let our instincts be our guide. I have a feeling we will know where to begin when we see it."

It was a good choice. The business establishments and bars and hotels and everything looked much less intimidating now that they had made a plan.

They had gone only a few blocks when they spotted a welcome-looking café and bar. The café was very clean and neat looking with smells of hot, delicious food coming from the kitchen. A wide door led into the softly lit bar, which also was clean looking, and the mirrors behind the bar reflected the smooth, maple-paneled walls perfectly. John and Millard walked into the bar with a nice feeling and a desire for a frosty mug of beer.

The bartender wore a white shirt with the sleeves held above his wrists by decorative rubber bands. A nice-looking apron was tied around his waist, and he was just finishing up drying the shot glasses and beer mugs with great care.

Millard and John sat down at the bar and ordered a beer. When the bartender brought two mugs of ice-cold draft beer, Millard took a drink and immediately started a conversation. "This is a great tasting beer," he commented.

"Thank you," was the reply. "It is made right here in good old St. Louis."

"I am Millard Watson, and this is John Hughes. We come from the Blue Ridge Mountains of North Carolina. Our organization makes and sells the best clean corn whiskey available anywhere. Recently, we made a decision to expand and sell some of our product to a few cities here and there. We just arrived in St. Louis, and this is our first stop. If you are interested, we would be glad to bring a jar in and let you sample it for yourself."

"I don't know if I would be interested or not, but bring a jar in," the bartender replied "I would like to see it and take a sip. You mountain people are well known for your good corn whiskey."

John immediately brought in a sample, and the bartender took a small sip. He was quick to recognize the value of what he had in his hand. After looking at it carefully, he took two large swallows. "This is the best whiskey I've ever tasted, white or bonded," he said as he took a second look at the jar. "By the way, my name is Jim Cooper."

After thinking a few minutes, he said, "I am the owner of this place, and I have ten other places just like this one. Could you make a delivery once a month to each of my establishments? I want it to sell to my best customers, who will have a lot of fun sipping good-tasting whiskey from the mountains and also know how to keep secrets."

"Sounds good to me," said John when Millard looked at him for an opinion.

"We make agreements by handshake only," Millard told the owner.

"I know how you mountain folks seal a deal by handshake, and woe is the one who breaks the agreement."

They all laughed at that remark.

"We are not hard to get along with and we value friendships too," said Jim Cooper.

They shook hands, and Millard and John brought two crates through a side door leading to the kitchen. The owner immediately came in and paid them.

"There is no charge for the jar we brought in," said John. "It's a small gift to what we believe will be a lasting friendship."

"I thank you kindly," said the owner. "Now here is a list of my other places and all the information you will need to make transactions with the managers. They will be expecting you. See you soon, men. I wish you well and hope to see you next month."

"Damn," said John. "I didn't expect to get a start like this at our first stop. We might be able to make the ten deliveries before the day is gone."

"I think we will, John," said Millard. "Our deliveries are all to places that I am sure stay open until late in the evening."

"We need a map of the city," John said after looking at Jim's list. "The addresses don't look like they are close together."

They soon located a store, where they got a map and learned many ways to find their way around the city. It was of tremendous help.

The city had a street pattern that was very evident when using the map. Soon they were making deliveries, one after the other, and learning more about the city every time they stopped. Every store manager was very cordial and seemed to enjoy talking with them. Their mountain dialect was appealing and quite different from the city language they were accustomed to, which had the makings of good conversation.

Millard and John completed their deliveries at eight o'clock. They ate supper at the last stop, and luckily, there was a small hotel nearby. It had been a good day and a tiresome one.

They went to bed soon after securing the truck. John had reinforced the rear doors with double locks and a super strong iron bar. They also removed a part of the engine to prevent theft of the truck.

They slept soundly and just a little late. They ate breakfast at the café where they'd made their last delivery the night before. They immediately started circling the city, working their way around as they had done when they first arrived in the city.

Suddenly John said, "I have an idea. Let's drive down to the Mississippi waterfront. I have heard there is a lot of activity down there. It's mostly commercial, but we might just luck up on something."

"Fine," said Millard. "I have never seen the Mississippi."

On they went, trying to look at everything. The city of St. Louis was a very interesting place.

As they came in sight of the river, they noticed a commercial-looking warehouse, much like the one they had found in Memphis. They decided to stop and see what type of business it was. Sure enough, it looked almost exactly like the place in Memphis.

A large man came out of an office as they started inside.

"Good day, sir," said John.

"Same to you," the man replied.

"We are in the whiskey business, and one of our finest customers in Memphis has two buildings there that look much like this one. He stores and sells all kinds of things, including the finest corn whiskey available, and we supply him regularly. We noticed your place here as we were passing and decided to see if you run the same type of place as the one in Memphis."

"No, I deal in storage for river traffic," the man replied. "I used to sell a lot of good, white corn whiskey, but my supply ran out. Nobody makes it around here anymore that I know of. Where are you boys from?"

"We are from the Blue Ridge Mountains of North Carolina," said Millard. "We sell our product up there, but we heard that, since the Depression, the cities are selling all they can get. We now sell it in quart jars with six jars to a wooden crate. If you are interested, we can make a delivery to you once a month."

"I might be; bring in a quart and let me take a look at what you have."

John went to the truck and brought a quart for sampling. They introduced themselves, and the gentleman gave his name as Weaver Clark. He had a nice smile but seemed very businesslike. He opened the jar, and things happened just as usual; he took one sip and then several swallows. After waiting for his palate to completely enjoy the flavor, he said, "This is fine whiskey. I will try ten crates, and if you stop by next month we might do more business."

"We will give you two quarts to sip on until we return," John told him.

"We look forward to seeing you next month," said Millard.

"If things don't work out, I will take several crates and drink them myself," Mr. Clark said with a husky laugh.

"That sounds just fine with us," Millard said, and John nodded in agreement. "Mr. Clark, we are glad to make your acquaintance," continued Millard as he was paid in small bills. "We look forward to seeing you again next month. However, we are just getting organized; if two other men should make the delivery, don't be alarmed. They will be honest, dependable, polite men. We screen new employees carefully and hire only the best men available."

As they exited the area, Weaver was waving good-bye and smiling.

"We did well there," remarked John. "We have sold about thirty crates in two stops.

"Where do you think we should go from here, Millard?" he asked.

"I think we should stick to our old pattern, which has worked well so far. Circle the city from the inside and work our way toward the outer limits."

"I agree completely," John replied. "Let's return to the last place we stopped yesterday and go on from there."

Soon, they were circling the city as best the streets would allow and stopping about every mile. They had long since decided to keep a reasonable distance between customers to prevent any possible conflict. They had never seen such a place so wide open for mountain moonshine. The stuff sold itself. They just located likely establishments and introduced themselves to the person in charge. That was the way to do business in St. Louis.

They would just let it be known that they were Blue Ridge Mountain boys and were selling the best clean corn whiskey available anywhere. A good sampling of their product, and almost always the sale was made and handshakes sealed the deal. All transactions were recorded immediately and marked on the map in keeping with their tradition of ensuring they would never miss a delivery to a customer. By late that evening, they had sold every crate and could have kept on going if they had more to sell.

Both men were tired after such a busy day, and they decided to wait until morning to head home. They found the same place where they had stayed the night before, and after supper, they turned in for the night.

The next day started out beautifully and gave every indication of remaining so. They switched drivers every hour or so to prevent road stress and increase their chances of getting well past Memphis before the day's end. They passed Memphis and kept going after deciding to proceed until they came upon a suitable place to eat and stay the night.

Memphis was two hours behind them when they came upon a pleasant place that appeared to have food, lodging, and gas pumps at the corner of the building. The food was delicious, and two bottles of beer made for an excellent stop and a sound night's sleep.

So far, their return trip could not be better. At the rate they were going, they would pass Chattanooga and continue toward the mountains. Neither man had been talking very much. They had not had a return trip from outside North Carolina yet without trouble, and the dread of a confrontation was on their mind.

"I hope we continue all the way home with good luck and avoid the kind of luck we've had on past return trips," Millard said, looking over at John to see his reaction. John was always looking ahead and seemed to sense when things were not as they should be.

They arrived in Chattanooga in record time and decided to stop. They stopped at a place where they had stopped before, and again, they were well pleased. After a tasty breakfast the next morning, they headed on at a steady speed. They would not need gas for several hours, so they continued on.

Finally John spoke up. Lowering his window a little to let in some fresh air, he said, "Millard, I feel trouble and plenty of it."

"Oh hell, don't say that," Millard replied. "I am going to pretend you didn't say them words."

"I don't pretend to be a psychic or something like that, but sometimes I do sense trouble when it is somewhere about. I hope I am wrong and there's no reason to worry," he continued.

"I will just change the subject," said Millard. "One thing that always worries me when I am on the road is the sad and hungry, dejected people I see along the way. It is even worse when I realize that I am beginning to pass them by without a feeling of shame and sadness, especially when children are involved."

Just then they passed a patch of woods and could see a family huddled around a fire in front of a tent.

"Try to not let it get you, Millard," said John. "I have gone through the same situations as you have, and it has brought me to the point of tears. We just have to go on and do the best we can. We can't carry the burdens of the world on our shoulders. Sometimes, I do stop and give money when I come upon situations that appear totally hopeless. All this will pass eventually, and everyone will go on with their lives, but scars will probably remain with them as long as they live."

"I have been on the edge several times myself," said Millard, "enough to understand what they are going through. I remember when we traveled to Knoxville to be married; the girls were pretty upset at what they witnessed on that trip. They settled down as Jackson talked to them. Seems like a long time ago, and it has been a good many years."

John and Millard had continued on for another hour or so when they came upon a large general store and immediately decided to stop for a short rest and perhaps have one of those delicious sandwiches such stores were famous for.

Just as they were about to enjoy their cheese and cracker sandwiches and RC Colas, a fancy, new-looking sedan pulled up in front of the store and four men, all dressed in expensive suits and broad-brimmed hats, got out and came inside.

John and Millard spoke to them in friendly tones, but the men only glanced at them, not speaking or smiling; they just walked around the store as though they were looking for someone.

"If you are looking for the owner, he went in that room in the front near the post office," Millard said to them.

One of the men walked over to them and said, "We are looking for you two hillbillies we heard were traveling through here peddling that damned old mountain whiskey. You ain't welcome around here, so just be on your way. And you won't return if you know what is good for you."

The remark made John as mad as a hornet. "Like hell we will," he said. "This is a free country, and you best leave us alone. We are just passing through and are not looking for any trouble." His voice was strong and he stood tall as he spoke. He showed no fear in his voice or change in his facial expression.

Fists clenched, one of the men approached Millard. Millard was ready. He'd noticed a wooden barrel of crowbars sitting beside him, and when the man made his move, Millard grabbed one of the crowbars and hit his opponent across the top of his head. The man fell hard to the floor and looked like he was dead.

John quickly hit the man nearest to him squarely on the jaw and the man went down. He attempted to get up, but it was very evident that his jaw was broken and a bad break at that. He could not do any fighting without risking dangerous injury. He groaned in pain and just sat where he had fallen. The injured man pulled his pistol from his shoulder holster, but John quickly disarmed him, knocking the gun out of reach. The man gave little resistance, due to the intense pain in his jaw. The two men left standing went at it fist to fist. They were pretty evenly matched, but Millard had no intentions of continuing an ordinary fistfight. He wanted to end the altercation quickly, and that he did. He snatched another crowbar and made an overhanded swing at the man, who quickly stepped aside, causing Millard to miss his head and strike his shoulder. He too was in tremendous pain. Obviously his shoulder had considerable trauma, and he could not continue fighting. He also reached for his pistol but changed his mind when he saw John pointing a gun at his face.

Only one man was left standing, and both John and Millard jumped on him, anxiously wanting to finish the fight quickly. But it was not to be. The man was solid as a rock and strong as a bull. They both hit him hard and fast, but he just would not fall and knocked both John and Millard down two or three times each. Finally, he started getting winded, and John and Millard were able to spin him around and push him as fast as they could through the store and run him into the biggest potbellied stove they had ever seen.

The strong man and the stove crashed to the floor, jerking the overhead stovepipe loose and pouring a deluge of soot down on the man and the stove. Millard and John jumped aside, dodging the large amount of soot still falling when they ran from the store.

As they ran for the truck, soot was bellowing out the door, and they could hear the owner yelling and cursing them and demanding payment for damage, but that was all they heard. They jumped in the truck and took off as fast as they could go.

Both Millard and John were short of breath, so they just drove for miles without saying anything. Finally John said, "Damn, I didn't expect that one. Where do you think them damn fools came from, Millard?"

"I don't know, but they were not locals. They appeared to be from organized crime, considering their dress and that expensive car they were driving."

"That was the impression I got," John replied. "Let's just think about it for a while and let our heads clear. Right now, I am a little shook up. If you had not found that barrel of crowbars, it might have been us lying back there on the floor instead of them."

Millard shook his head and bit his lip. "I might have killed the first one I hit," he said, turning to John, almost to the point of tears. "He fell awful hard and didn't move after that. If he is dead, we might be in a heap of trouble." Millard wiped the sweat from his brow with his sleeve. He was relieved to see his lip was no longer bleeding. "Let's park the truck where it can't be seen and go inside," he said, gesturing to a café on the side of the road.

John agreed. "We need to rest a little while and eat something."

Inside, they found a secluded booth in the rear of the café and ordered sandwiches and coffee. They had hardly finished their meal when they heard a siren go past the café. Millard's eyes grew wide, and he leaned across the table. "That might have been a patrol car trying to chase us down."

When they paid their bill, Millard asked the waiter what that siren was all about. The waiter replied that he did not know and didn't give a damn. "We are aggravated to death around this part of the country by the law and the crooks, and it's hard to tell which is which," he remarked. "They shoot and cut and fight constantly around here. You men are headed for the mountains I'll bet. If you are headed toward Asheville, I would go north toward Virginia and then swing back down to the part of the mountains where you come from. It might save you a lot of trouble."

"That's what we will do then," replied Millard as he paid the bill and left a hefty tip.

"Stop by anytime you can when you pass this way. I will always help you any way I can."

"That was a lucky stop," said John, "and probably good advice as well."

"I think so too," answered Millard, "but just to be sure he is not in with the local crooks and the law, let's just vary a little in our return route home. What do you say we go north until we get close to Knoxville and then around to the left and above it before heading straight for our section of the mountains? We would miss Maryville and Sevierville and just maybe get home without any more trouble."

"That's sounds fine to me," said John. "And if that bunch comes over looking for us, they will get more than they bargained for."

"We have a lot of planning to do after we get home," Millard remarked. "We have to sort out our enemies and determine how to complete the expansion of our business to Chicago. If we can get these troublesome situations straightened out, I see nothing but good money and good fortune ahead. But we have got to get these hellfired people off our backs in order to fully succeed."

"That's right, Millard, and you and me are just the team to jerk the line straight. I'll bet Walter and Jackson is doing intelligence work every day to find out what we are up against."

"What do you say we drive straight through without stopping except to eat and gas the truck?"

"I like that idea," said John. "But I would like to continue to switch drivers every two hours so we don't get so tired. This is a good truck, but it beats the hell out of me when we drive too long without stopping or switching drivers often."

"Let's give it a try," said Millard with a slight smile on his face.

Their plan worked perfectly. They had no trouble and reached Spruce Willow before daybreak. As they pulled into Newbarn and stopped, they both slumped down in their seats and went immediately to sleep. They woke up with Jackson banging on the locked door.

"Damn, boys, I didn't expect you back until much later in the day or even tonight. Your trip must have gone very well."

"It did until yesterday," Millard replied with a look of concern on his face.

"Hellfire, what has happened this time?" asked Jackson, looking a bit disgusted.

Millard summed up what had happened for Jackson. "Now ain't that one hell of a tale to bring home with us," he concluded.

"It goes with the territory," Jackson replied. "Tell you what! You boys go home and get some rest. You look like you are half beat to death. Come back after you have rested awhile, and we will get with Pop and discuss your trip and some things Pop and me have that you need to know. If we have time, we will do some planning as well."

John and Millard did not argue with Jackson. They were weary, and John went home and straight to bed. Millard went to Salem's to see his little family. He walked into the house, and as quickly as he had kissed Flora and the children, he went immediately to bed and to sleep.

It was late in the afternoon when he awoke. He told Flora that he must return to Walter's for what he hoped would be a short meeting. Flora inquired of him about his trip and why a meeting had been scheduled for late Sunday evening. She knew something was going on from the way he looked and acted.

"We have some urgent business to discuss before the week begins," he told her. "Don't worry about me."

"I do worry about you," she answered. "When you came home this morning, I could see you had been in a fight."

"Our trip went well except for one small incident," he told her. "I will tell you all about the incident later when we have time to talk."

"My Lord!" she said. "Couldn't you for one time just tell me what happened instead of putting me off until later? And I can tell at a glance you have been in more than one small incident. I am a part of your life, and I have a right to know about what happens to you." She turned, with clenched fists indicating her frustration and anger. "Don't do me this way again!" she said in a loud voice. "I have heated a pan of water so you can wash yourself off here in the bedroom." She said no more.

"I must look a fright," he said. "I am sorry about neglecting you like this, and I will try not to do you that way again. How are the children?" he asked.

"Walter is asleep as usual, and Cameron is out playing. Cameron wants to see you, but he will be all right until you return."

Millard went directly to Walter's home, where Jackson and John had just arrived. Walter was his usual charming self and shook hands with each one as they entered his elegant home. His wife had individual trays, each laid out with sandwiches and delicious red wine. She knew, due to the lateness of the evening, that the men could eat and discuss the issues at hand and still return home and spend some time with their families.

Millard and John took turns relating their very successful trip to St. Louis and the large amount of money they'd received from happy, friendly customers. "That is the most successful city we have encountered both financially and socially. We found many customers and friends in that great city. John and me found nothing but the best of situations there and we believe we can count on them in the future," Millard concluded.

"Now we will tell you about our unpleasant return trip."

Again, John and Millard related in minute detail what had occurred at the store where the fight had taken place and how they'd dodged around Knoxville to avoid trouble and arrive home safely.

"Are you reasonably certain that you killed that man you hit with a crowbar?" Walter asked.

"It is very possible that I did," replied Millard. "All I can say for certain is that I hit him across the head, and he went down hard and did not move."

"There is nothing we can do but wait and see what happens," said Walter. "I have no reliable contacts in that area, and anything we might try to do now would probably just stir up a mess. The man might be all right, Millard. Let's just allow this one to pass for now."

They all agreed, but the uneasy feeling had not left Millard's mind, and he was certain that he would not rest easy until he knew the condition of the man he had hit.

Jackson gave a glowing report on the financial condition of Newbarn. "We do well everywhere we go, and in spite of the Depression, our cash flow is tremendous. Except for our expansion into Chicago, our reorganization is now complete. We will have to hire a few more men and buy more trucks. This entire reorganization has gone beyond our expectations, and if all continues we should be finished in a few months. Chicago will be our biggest test. It is a rough place for people in our business, but folks in that city also want to make fast money. If we move cautiously, I think we can make more money there than any two of the other cities we now serve."

Walter then reminded all that he was no longer in the business, except when needed to serve in an advisory capacity. "You boys are doing well, but we all know how times change, and this business cannot go on forever. Make all the money you can and keep things going well, and in a few years, go into legitimate, lawful business. Begin thinking about what you want to do, and when the time comes, go after it. I say this with every man in this organization in mind. It can be done. Just keep thinking in advance and plan carefully."

After Jackson and Walter finished talking, John asked the question most on his mind. "Have you found out who the men were that tried to kill us this side of Maryville on our return from St. Louis?"

"No, but we are working on the problem," Walter replied. "I was positive that Homer Cash was involved, but he had nothing to do with it. Someone or some organization is interested in our expansion and feels threatened. I can't imagine why, but I believe that to be the case. We will know soon what is going down. Jackson has hired a detective to follow the long-haul deliveries so we can put an end to this nonsense. He is very professional, and you won't even know he is around until his job is completed. He moves like a shadow and will find out everything that is going on and give us advice about what we should do to rid ourselves of those numbskulls."

"I think there is more than one group after us from Maryville, and I don't think they are connected to the four men that jumped on us yesterday," said Millard.

"I know," said Jackson. "It won't take our detective long to find out about the Maryville bunch, but the other four men are a different story. The detective will be around tomorrow, and I will get an opinion from him."

"John and me will need as much information as we can get before leaving for Chicago next week. If possible, I would like for us to talk to him with you."

"I like that idea," remarked John. "We need his advice and expertise in handling another bunch like that. We would prefer to avoid any confrontation on a trip for a change."

"I will ask him, but if he does agree for all three of us to talk with him, he will probably want you to swear not to reveal his name or anything about him. If he didn't operate that way, he wouldn't last long on this earth."

Millard and John could see Jackson's point and were well aware of the need for a detective. Keeping the Newbarn organization expanding and the customers served, along with fighting an enemy they did not know was becoming considerably more difficult and dangerous.

"I want to tell you that we have another new truck coming in tomorrow," Jackson informed them. "It's all yours for the Chicago trip if you want it."

"We need to decide what day we should leave next week," said Millard.

"The truck won't be ready and loaded until Tuesday or later."

"Might we make it Wednesday?" Millard replied. "I could come in and work tomorrow though. I am anxious to talk to that detective. I could use Tuesday to take my family back home. I might have to hire a lady to stay with them for a week or two. Flora is fine, but she had a very hard time with the delivery. I don't want to have any more children. We almost lost Flora and the baby due to a very difficult birth."

Jackson was looking forward to Sally giving birth to their first child, but with a little dread. He knew many of the dangers and complications involved in childbirth. He put his thoughts behind him.

"Oh yeah, guess what we named the little fellow," said Millard.

"We could never guess," said Walter, "but I believe we will soon find out."

"Walter Jackson Watson is his name, and I am happy that he will be called by that name all his life."

"Millard, you have honored me more than you know, and I am sure Jackson has the same feeling."

"Indeed I do," replied Jackson, "and I thank you kindly."

"Before you men leave, let's drink a toast," Walter said as he refilled their glasses. "May Walter Jackson Watson live to a good old age with good fortune by his side and happiness aplenty."

"I thank you, sir," Millard said in a humble voice. "My best friends are in this room, and I thank you all."

The house was dark and quiet when Millard returned from the meeting. He quietly opened the door to the bedroom and undressed for bed. Flora was not asleep and pulled the warm covers over him as he got into bed. Her soft, gentle touch was a comfort to him after such an unanticipated active week. They remained quiet until sleep came.

The house was still dark and quiet when Millard awoke. He knew this was an important day, and he needed to be at work early. He woke no one, not even Flora. He stopped for a breakfast sandwich and arrived at work before anyone else.

He did not have to wait long however. Soon, the Newbarn headquarters was buzzing with activity. The men were rushing to load up and get started on their assigned routes. Millard was amazed at how smoothly and well organized things went. It did not take long at all until the men were gone. There wasn't even much talking. Millard keenly observed how everything was operating. It made him acutely aware that he must learn quickly everything new and keep up with changes. He knew that, after he and John had successfully achieved their goal in Chicago, he would no doubt move to a more active role in management. With all that was going on now and the place still growing like it was, he found it hard to believe how Jackson was holding everything together as he was. Millard knew, however, that Walter kept a watchful eye on things and helped some in cases of emergency. What a great father Jackson had, and Millard was looking forward to the time when he could help Jackson and allow Walter to retire fully, void of stress as he richly deserved.

Soon John and Jackson arrived. John and Millard immediately began helping Jackson tidy up the place and putting things in order. They enjoyed helping in that way because, in that business, they did not know when they would be required to completely manage the affairs.

THIRTY-ONE

Later in the morning, everything was exactly as it should be. The truck was being checked out at Sam Burns's place, and Jackson showed Millard and John the exact procedure for handling all cash from the time it was received until it was placed in the vault. "At that point, the way we handle the money is very secretive and rather complicated. When we have more time, I will teach you both the entire process. Chicago is next on the agenda, and we don't know at this point how to proceed until we see how things turn out there. I think we all know that we can make tremendous amounts of money there, but we also know that Chicago can be a very dangerous place. Your trip there this week will be a critical point in the future or our organization. If all goes well, our expansion goals will have been completed. Of course, everything will have to be fine-tuned to run smoothly, but that sort of thing never ends. There will always be policies and procedures to revise or troubles to contend with. We have done well this morning, boys," Jackson continued. "I have run my mouth much of the time without giving you two a chance to ask questions."

"When will the detective arrive?" John immediately asked. "I would like for me and Millard to get to know him before he gets started on the case."

"We could probably provide him with information that would be helpful to him," Millard added.

"I wanted us to meet over at Pop's, but I don't know whether or not the detective will agree. He is very secretive, and I promised him our full cooperation. He will let us know today what to expect. It would not surprise me if he has been watching this place and the surrounding area all morning. He might wait until dark, after everyone has left except us, before he appears. We will just wait and see."

Finally, just before dusk, a late model Buick slowly drove up. It was an ordinary-looking black car, but it was obvious the engine was not ordinary. It had a powerful sound but was not noticeably loud. It appeared to provide both comfort and speed.

Millard watched a tall man with black hair get out of the car, put a cigarette in his mouth, and stand up straight while lighting his cigarette and looking about. He appeared to be over six feet tall, with a well-toned, muscular body. His face was tanned, and his square jaw complemented his white teeth, and he looked as though he could handle himself well in any situation.

Jackson made proper introductions, and Millard could tell by shaking his hand and looking in his eyes that the detective was a strong, intelligent man.

The detective introduced himself as Robert Swink. Millard and John felt confident that Robert was the man they needed. They doubted that Robert Swink was his legal name, but they were satisfied in knowing that Jackson undoubtedly knew the man's real name and trusted him.

"We have been looking forward to meeting you," said Jackson.

"My pleasure, gentleman," Robert replied.

"If you don't mind, we will go to my father's house to talk business and make plans," Jackson continued. "You will understand why we need his presence as we talk. He has a comfortable home, and it is a very secure place." Jackson no doubt had his reasons for trusting Robert.

The men left immediately for Walter's house and were greeted enthusiastically as Walter answered the door.

Robert seemed very impressed as they started their discussion with a glass of superb wine. As the meeting progressed, everyone became involved. They gave Robert a history of the business, starting with the reorganization process and ending with the current operation. He listened intently, specifically to the details about the encounter Millard and John had with the four men on their return trip from St. Louis.

For a few minutes, Robert stared out the window, sipping his wine deliberately. "I will begin sorting things out tomorrow by going to Chattanooga by your usual route and returning tomorrow night. My next step will depend upon what I find out tomorrow.

Whatever is going on between here and Chattanooga can be eliminated without too much trouble, but from there to Chicago might cause us problems, if not bad trouble. I don't like the way those four men came after Millard and John the way they did. Hit men from well organized crime act that way, and those four men had no intention of leaving you alone and probably would have shot both of you if you had given them the chance. You men did well by giving them a dose of their medicine before they got to you. And don't concern yourself about that man you hit with the crowbar, Millard. He has probably killed and injured people time and time again without remorse.

"If I don't return by nine o'clock tomorrow night, don't concern yourselves. I will be here for another meeting Wednesday morning, if that is agreeable with you, Walter."

"That's fine with me," Walter replied.

"I am impressed with your attitude, gentlemen," said Robert. "I will be on my way now. I might head for Chattanooga sometime tonight."

Millard arrived at home just before everyone was ready for bed. Martha brought Millard a piece of apple pie for a bedtime snack, and they decided to remain up and talk for a while. When morning came he and Flora would be going home with Cameron and Walter, but Flora had assured her parents they would return often. Millard thanked Martha for taking such good care of Flora and the children.

When they went to bed, Millard was asleep before Flora could talk with him or ask him any questions or even say good night.

The sun was shining brightly through the bedroom window when they awoke. The baby was crying, and Martha had come into the room to help out. Cameron had long since been up and was outside playing.

"I had no intention of sleeping this late," said Millard. "We should have been up long ago."

They quickly ate breakfast and prepared to leave. Millard tried to pay Martha for doing so much for them and delivering the baby, but she would not hear of it. He knew her better than to force the issue, so he let it be.

Salem was standing on the front porch soaking up the morning sun. He suffered from rheumatism, and the warm sun was of considerable relief to him.

"I hate to leave like this, but I have a very busy day ahead. I do want to talk to you as soon as possible though. I want to bring you up to date on the progress we are making in the whiskey business, and I also want to get your advice and help about building a house I have been planning to build. You are a fine carpenter, and I would like to get your advice and help with the entire construction."

"I might like that, Millard," Salem replied, a pleased look on his face. "When you decide to get started, we will make plans and get down to business. I am already looking forward to it, and with a bit of excitement I might add. You be careful in that business you are in."

On their way home, they decided to stop and visit Millard's parents, who still had not seen the new baby, and they did not want to deny them that pleasure any longer. When they arrived, Dad and Ma came out into the yard to greet them as fast as they could, and Grandma came out on the front porch. What a joyful occasion it was.

Millard immediately held the baby up and introduced him as Walter Jackson Watson. Dad insisted on carrying Walter into the house, where they could talk and take turns holding him. Millard and Flora brought them up to date on all the happenings since their last visit. "Walter is still too heavy, but he has lost about two pounds since his birth weight of over ten pounds," Flora told them.

"My goodness," said Ma. "Not many babies are born that heavy, but he looks very healthy."

"He certainly is a beautiful child," Grandma said when it came her turn to hold Walter. She had misplaced her glasses and could not see him well until she held him gently in her lap. "I believe this child will live to a good old age and will bring much happiness to our family. I will pray for him diligently every day, as I know we will all do."

Cameron had scrambled out of the car as soon as they'd arrived and climbed to the top of an apple tree in the yard to pick as many of the unusually delicious, light-colored apples as he could carry. He came into the house after putting his apples in the car. Everyone immediately turned their attention to him. They did not want him to feel neglected because of a new baby in the family.

Actually he had shown some jealousy shortly after Walter was born but he had gotten over that in just a few days. He now called Walter his baby brother and was very happy with him. He talked much about what fun the two of them would have when they could run and play together.

After lunch, the family gathered on the front porch for conversation and to catch up on recent happenings and gossip. Flora was very happy to be there to share the peace and happiness that was always there with family.

She missed Lewis, but the sadness was now gone and his endless suffering was no more.

Before they departed, Millard managed to place a five-dollar bill in the hands of Dad and Ma and Grandma. They each knew it was a gift of love and said nothing. He gave it to each of them in secret, and that made it even more acceptable to them. Before the foursome left for home, all formed a prayer circle and each said a prayer asking God to keep them all in his care.

Flora had a feeling that sadness was to descend upon the family in the not too distant future. She hoped she was wrong, but the feeling was there and she knew in her heart that it would not go away, not when it was so strong. They drove away with everyone waving to each other.

They soon arrived home, and after they'd lit the lamps, everything seemed to return to normal. They were happy to be home and were thankful for such a wonderful day. They did not have a cradle for Walter Jackson, so he would have to sleep with Millard and Flora. They dared not put him in bed with Cameron, knowing his habits of tossing about and kicking and talking in his sleep.

After the children were asleep, Flora noticed that Millard had become very quiet. He sat on the edge of the bed, and she knew he wanted her to sit beside him. She did so and gave him her full attention.

"Flora, I will be going to Chicago tomorrow, and I do not know what to expect during this entire trip. We have had trouble during our trips ever since we began making long hauls and have made enemies in doing so. We have a detective hired to locate the source of our trouble. He is very good at his job, and we are hopeful that he can help us solve our current problems.

"We are leaving in the morning, and it might be sometime next week before we return. John and me will take the load to Chicago. We work well together, and I feel much better having him along. We'll meet at Walter's in the morning before leaving. I hope that detective will have something to tell us then. He is a real professional, and we have complete confidence in him."

"You have surely made a wise decision," Flora remarked. "I hope the detective will be successful in helping you solve this terrible situation so that everyone can do business safely." She looked rather perplexed and was now realizing the full extent of the danger involved in Millard's work.

"This trip to Chicago will be the end of our reorganization and long-haul plans," Millard reminded her. "We have no plans to expand any farther. But we do intend to make deliveries to Chicago, and that decision is final. If we have to fight our way in, we will do it. I have not been told this, but I know that is how it will be. We will not cause trouble for anyone, but we have felt from the very beginning that we have as much right to do business there as anyone else does."

"Well, here is where my worries will start up again," said Flora.

"Don't worry too much," replied Millard. "I have prepared you for the worst, but we know how to handle ourselves, and we might have no trouble at all."

"That is what I will pray for," Flora remarked as he held her close.

There was no more talk. They were prepared for the next day.

THIRTY-TWO

Morning came quickly as though there had been no night. Millard dressed quickly and then picked up his overnight bag and quietly left the house. Flora watched him through the curtains as he carefully checked his pistol and tucked it under his belt. Then, before getting into his car, he turned and looked toward the house, as though he did not want to leave. Flora knew he was saying a short, silent prayer for them. That was his way and another reason she loved him so.

Millard drove slowly up the road, passing by the site where he intended to build a new house for his family and then moved onto the highway toward Spruce Willow. He drove at a moderate speed, giving him time to think and anticipate the events of the day. After stopping for a sandwich, he proceeded on to Walter's home as planned.

Walter was there, and soon John, Jackson, and Detective Swink arrived. The others were anxiously waiting to hear what Mr. Swink had to say. Small talk almost ceased after they sat down and coffee was served by the maid. They all knew this was very serious business.

Mr. Swink told them he had followed every lead based on the information that had been provided to him. "I have rambled all over the place between here and Chattanooga," he told them. "On my return trip, I made it a point to patrol the areas where you have had the most trouble. I even traveled up a steep rocky road to the top of a ridge where I could get a view of anything unusual going on below. It was a good spot and might be of value to us later on. I decided not to check out the place where you fought the four men on your last trip. Time was getting short, and I returned late last night."

"I hope you have some good advice for us," John said.

"The only advice I have for you men is to proceed with your business just as before. And don't reveal my name or anything about me to others not in this room. I have already told you more than I usually tell anyone, but you gentlemen are very smart and honorable, and I don't mind revealing things to you as necessary. As we leave for Chicago this morning, just travel on as usual. I will be somewhere behind—sometimes close and, at other times, several miles back. You had best not depend on me for anything because I will be busy seeking out potential trouble spots and possibly talking to people who might provide information or stopping at one of those old country stores for a sandwich and listening to gossip that some of the old-timers like to pass around. You would be surprised at how many times I have found information that proved to be very valuable to me by doing just that."

"Actually, Millard and John are ready to leave now," Jackson said as he nodded at them. "We will leave here and go directly to Newbarn."

"I wish you Godspeed," Walter said to them as they stood up to leave. "I plan to do all I can to help. I wish I could go with you, but I am well aware you can do much better without me in ventures such as this."

"Yes, but we know that smart mind of yours will be constantly working overtime figuring out ways to help us as you always do," John remarked.

With that very appropriate remark, they all shook hands and departed.

Millard and John quickly checked their loaded truck and other things they needed for the trip. John had his two 8-gauge shotguns ready to place behind the seat, and both he and Millard had their .38-caliber pistols in their belts.

When Millard saw John's shotguns he said, "Oh my Lord, I forgot to bring cotton for my ears. I will surely be deaf before we return."

Jackson ran into the office, got out a small box of cotton, and, with a broad smile, handed it to Millard. "I hope you will not need that," he said.

Most of the men, who were preparing for their local deliveries, did not know what was going on. It looked to them as though

Millard and John were headed off to a war of some kind, but they knew it was Newbarn-related business. Word about the trip would get around soon enough, and no information would be announced until necessary.

The new truck was smooth riding, and its engine was very powerful. Jackson had purposefully ordered it that way. He knew a powerful truck could give Millard and John a distinct advantage in their first long-haul run to Chicago if it turned out to be a city of trouble as he had heard spoken many times. It also could haul a heavier load than most trucks in existence that he knew of.

Soon, Millard and John were very much enjoying the familiar route to Chattanooga. They expected no trouble, and so far they'd seen nothing but blue sky and beautiful scenery. Stopping only for lunch and gas, they continued on at a rapid pace, hoping to arrive at Chattanooga before day's end.

The lights of Chattanooga were a welcome sight. The continuous day's drive had started to take its toll on them. They decided to stop at a boardinghouse with an adjoining café. They enjoyed a fine supper, followed by a very comfortable night in the clean, attractive boardinghouse, which provided feather beds filled with goose down feathers as an added attraction and comfort. It was not as plush and well-furnished and decorated as some they had stayed at, but it looked nice enough.

After breakfast the following morning, they left the city determined to once again cover as much distance as possible. "You know, I believe we will reach Memphis much earlier than we did the last time we were here. I would like for us to stop and visit Antonio Vitally for a few minutes. He was our first customer in Memphis, you know."

"I would like that," replied John. "We could keep on going after we leave his place and still be ahead of where we expected to be at this time."

They continued on after filling their tank and eating lunch. They were still making excellent time. Several hours later, they passed Somerville and knew Memphis was not too far away.

They drove directly to Antonio's only to find he was not there. Two men who introduced themselves as Jonathan Orders and Ford Simpson came out and informed them that Antonio had gone on a business trip to Chicago and would return in a day or two. John and Millard introduced themselves and informed Orders and Simpson that they were the deliverymen from the mountains and were headed for Chicago as well. "We just stopped for a friendly visit with Antonio and to assure him that all is going well with our business arrangement."

The two friendly men were aware of their agreement with Antonio and said that all was going well. "All deliveries of that fine whiskey you sell have been right on schedule," said Jonathan as Ford nodded his head in agreement.

"We will keep on going now," John said. "We want to go as far along as possible toward Chicago before we stop for the night."

"We hope to meet you gentlemen again as we travel this way," Millard added as they shook hands.

As they proceeded on toward Chicago, they found little encouragement to bolster their desire to reach that famous city. Traffic was getting heavier, and signs of hard times were getting worse. Everyone, whether riding or walking, seemed to be in a hurry.

"Wonder why the hurry?" Millard remarked.

"I don't know," replied John. "As a matter of fact, I have never understood why Walter and Jackson have been so hellfired determined to expand this far from home. From all I have read in the papers, Chicago is a place to run away from, not one to go to."

"I think I know exactly why," Millard remarked. "We will probably haul money back to Newbarn by the truckload. You know how we all are anxious to make all the money we can as quickly as possible. We have been unbelievably successful in making money since the very start, but I don't think we can keep it up indefinitely. Things could turn sour on us next week."

"I know," said John. "We have discussed going into legitimate business when the time is right. I would like that a lot. I suppose I am feeling a little uncertainty about this venture that I have not felt before. If we had more intelligence information, it would be of tremendous value."

"John, you know we will do what has to be done when we reach Chicago. Fate, or what have you, seems to steer us in the right direction. But I have the same uncertainty as you about the place. It is a dangerous place, and we will have to stay alert at all times. We will do our job and do it right; you'll see."

They increased their speed to keep up with the traffic as they moved toward their destination. The day was fading as they saw the lights of Chicago far in the distance. What an impressive sight. Both Millard and John were now feeling the excitement that was undoubtedly awaiting them. "Let's stop at the first place we come to that looks safe and secure," John suggested.

"Good idea. I'm getting hungry, and I hope the place where we sleep has a goose down feather bed."

They drove on until they came upon a very attractive-looking two-story boardinghouse, which was located in a residential neighborhood and served meals in a comfortable, attractively decorated dining room. After a fantastic meal and a glass of red wine, they decided to go directly to bed.

During the night, the owner of the establishment knocked on their door. They quickly answered the knock, and the owner informed them that a gentleman who said he knew them was in the parlor and wanted to see them. Both Millard and John knew who the owner must be talking about. They asked that he allow the gentleman to come to their room.

They were right. Robert Swink came into the room and sat down in a soft chair between the two beds. "I will make my stay as brief as possible," he said. "It will probably take me two or three more days to figure it all out, but for now I need to ask you about a person you met in St. Louis named Antonio Vitally. I was close by when you stopped at his place yesterday. I suspect that place is anything but legitimate and used often for gatherings of mob leaders, gangsters, and even politicians."

"What has Antonio done other than be a good customer for Newbarn?" asked Millard.

"We see no conflict where he is concerned," added John.

"I will contact you again when I find out more, but for now, stay away from anything you suspect might be connected to Antonio," Robert said, his voice relaying a stern warning. "I feel for your safety, and that is my purpose for contacting you at night like this. Wherever you go, I probably won't be too far away."

"We intend to succeed in setting up deliveries here on a permanent basis and no doubt will need all the information you can get."

"It very well could mean your life in this vile place," said Robert. "You two will probably find ways of making more money than Newbarn can hold. But you must be cautious and deliberate and not stir up trouble. Now here is the name of a gentleman I can, with a clear conscience, recommend to you as a good potential customer. His name is Edward Brown, and his office is located in a large building on Lake Michigan. I will keep in touch." Just like that, Mr. Swink was gone.

Millard and John had lost a little sleep, but he had made them feel like they were in control again—a feeling they had not had since they left St. Louis.

They were awake early and, after having their coffee and breakfast, were speeding along, closing in on the city limits of Chicago. As they entered the city, they stopped at a place called Joliet and bought a map, just as Robert had suggested. Using the map, they drove around a part of the city and stopped at a nice café for an early lunch. They spread the map out on their booth and studied it carefully until they were reasonably satisfied they could find their way around to a moderate degree.

After lunch, they set about to find Edward Brown, the businessman Robert had recommended to them. The map was a good one, and they easily found the address they were looking for. It was just a few blocks from Lake Michigan in a large, attractive building that could have been a warehouse or manufacturing plant of some kind. The grounds were neatly landscaped, and the interior was a series of luxurious offices and waiting rooms. They were promptly greeted by a very pretty, neatly dressed young lady with blonde hair and deep blue eyes. Her face was especially beautiful.

When they asked to see Mr. Edward Brown, she politely told them that Mr. Brown could see them, but it would be an hour or perhaps two before he could do so.

"We are new in Chicago," Millard said to her. "Would it be an inconvenience if we left our truck parked here and walked down to the waterfront while we wait to meet Mr. Brown? We are very excited about this famous city, and the waterfront, as it appears on our map, looks like a great place to visit."

"That will be just great," she assured him.

Millard and John walked quickly to the waterfront and just stood there for a while, astonished at all they were seeing. Ships were being unloaded and loaded with everything imaginable. Large warehouses were located all about, housing things from foreign countries to be delivered by rail and truck to places all over the country. Machines, cranes, and barges steadily moved for one purpose or another. There seemed to be no end to it all.

"I guess we are looking at a giant country at work," said John. "No wonder I have heard and read so much about America and the powerful nation it has become. Where do you suppose it will all end, Millard?"

"I don't know, but I keep hearing about Europe being stirred up like a hornets' nest by a crazy man named Hitler. We might need all the power we can muster to whip his ass in a few years."

They quietly turned and walked slowly back to their meeting with Mr. Brown, thinking as they walked.

They did not have to wait long until Mr. Brown appeared and personally invited them into his office. He was a very nice-looking man and was much as they had expected. He appeared honest and forthright, just as Robert had said he was. He was well dressed and mannerly, and when asked a question, he answered without hesitation—a good sign that he had nothing to hide. They were very relaxed and comfortable in his presence. After they'd introduced themselves and explained how Robert was helping them out, he knew immediately what they were all about.

"I know Robert very well," he said as he lit up a Cuban cigar and sat back in his chair. "He is very professional in his work and honest in all his dealings with others. He has helped me out several times. I understand you have access to plenty of good, old mountain corn whiskey and are willing to sell some of it to us city slickers. He rambled on and on about it, so it must be mighty fine whiskey."

"We do have good, clean mountain whiskey and would like to find a market for it. We are trying to get through these hellfired hard times just like most people these days," Millard explained.

"I know where you are coming from. As you drive around Chicago, you will understand what I mean. The front streets don't look so bad, but in the back alleys and poor side of town, everything is just awful. The crime rate is high, and the soup lines are long and constant. The poor get poorer and don't know what to do. In other places, the rich get richer, and there are no soup lines. I do what I can to help, but there isn't much I can do. Honestly, I could sell everything I own and give it to the poor and it wouldn't help much. I keep my businesses running and create as many jobs as I can and give money to the church where the people are doing all they can to help the poor. I know we will come out of this sooner or later, but who knows when.

"As soon as Mr. Swink told me about you gentlemen, I immediately began thinking about how we might be of mutual benefit to each other and strike a deal wherein we both can prosper. And like you mountain people, I don't want to buy a pig in a poke. If you will bring in a sample of your product, perhaps we can do some business."

No sooner had he made that remark than John was out the door and had returned with two quarts of whiskey, which he placed on Mr. Brown's desk.

"I can tell at first glance that this whiskey is probably of fine quality. You make it clean and clear, which usually produces a good product. Both jars are very clean, and the contents look like clear spring water." He opened a jar and took a moderate-sized drink, swishing it around in his mouth to see how it soothed his palate. "I will take another drink if you don't mind," he said. "Damn, that is good whiskey—the best I've ever tasted, white or bonded."

"We have heard that remark many times before," said John. "I don't remember ever hearing a bad report."

"I hope we can do business with you," Millard said with a smile. "I do believe things would go well for all concerned."

"I will buy your entire load, and you can start delivering to my establishments immediately if that is agreeable with you."

"I know a good deal when I see one, and this is a good deal," replied Millard.

Millard quoted their prices, and Mr. Brown considered them to be quite satisfactory with him. I will give you a map showing all my places. They are numbered, and to save time, I want you to make your deliveries starting with number one and proceeding from there. We can then calculate approximately how often and how large our deliveries will need to be in order to keep us well stocked."

"That is agreeable with us. But the way our business is run, John and me will not be making the deliveries once we've gotten everything established and running smoothly and have ensured that your deliveries are being made just as you want them to be. We will visit you regularly to assure you are being served well. Don't worry about the other employees who make your deliveries. You will never meet more honest and honorable men. You will have no trouble with any of them. We do business by handshake, leaving no paper trails," continued Millard.

"I like that way of doing illegal business like this. It has another advantage as well. If either party wants to end our agreement or can't continue for some reason, we can just resolve the matter in a gentlemanly manner and not worry about suing each other or anything like that. Gentlemen, we have a situation where no one can lose, unless some very unusual situation beyond our control should occur. After you have made your run, come back here, and I will pay you for the entire load."

"One load less one crate," Millard added. "That crate is for your personal use, sir, and it won't be the last one for you either."

They all had a hardy laugh and passed the open jar around, each drinking several large swallows.

Millard and John left Mr. Brown's office knowing they had probably made the best deal they had made since working for Newbarn. The map Mr. Brown gave them was easy to follow. The first stop was a nice hotel with an elaborate dining room. They went to the hotel lobby and were greeted by a very nice gentleman. They told him their business after introducing themselves, and he invited them into his office. He said that Mr. Brown had called about his business arrangement with them and instructed him to fully cooperate. "He said for me to take a shot of real mountain corn whiskey—the finest he had ever tasted."

THIRTY-THREE

The man introduced himself as Cliff Banister. He was a man of medium size with a little extra weight around his middle. His manner was exceedingly cordial. Cliff opened one of the jars and took a rather large swallow of the clear liquid. His reaction was immediate; a pleased look appeared on his face. "No wonder Mr. Brown was so excited about this good old mountain dew," he said. "I suspect we will be doing business for a long time to come."

"You are our first customers in the great city of Chicago," Millard announced loud and clear, "and we look forward to coming here often. This seems to be a very friendly place, contrary to what we have heard in the mountains and elsewhere."

"Well, it is and it isn't," replied Cliff. "As you get to know this city, you will know what I mean. Just be careful and stay alert. When you let your guard down is when you can be vulnerable to all sorts of misfortunes. I wish you well. Call on me anytime I can be of help to you. I know how to read people pretty well, and I believe you are two good and honest men that I would like to have as my friends."

"We thank you kindly, sir," John replied.

Millard and John continued on their way, feeling very pleased with their first customers and the warm welcome they'd received.

Stop number two was less than five blocks away and they were in and out in less than twenty minutes. It was a large, fancy bar and pool room combined and very crowded and busy. The manager of the place recognized them quickly and came directly to them. He made it very clear that he had no time to socialize other than introductions and handshakes. "Mr. Brown called and explained everything, and that is enough for me," he said and then ordered twelve crates, one of the largest orders they had every received at one stop. The manager looked tired and overworked and had no desire to even sample the whiskey. Everyone in the place seemed to be having a great time. There were no signs of the Depression here. Millard and John thanked him and left, after assuring him they would be stopping in on a timely basis.

On they went, stop after stop, rarely having to remain over twenty-five minutes at each establishment. They were tired and hungry when the streetlights came on and decided to end the day. They ate supper at the last café stop they'd made and began looking for a place to stay the night. The advice of Mr. Brown and Mr. Banister about being cautious and alert was on their mind, and that was enough.

As they were discussing where they should stay, their first delivery stop came to mind. It was a very nice place, and they agreed that it was a safe-looking place as well. They enjoyed the evening very much. They sat in the lobby, where they listened to the evening news on the radio and enjoyed a couple of beers at the dining room bar. It had been a wonderful day, and they slept safe and sound on the second floor of that place they would never forget.

When morning came, they could hardly wait to get started. They dressed nicely, ate a nourishing breakfast, and were off. Beside their first stop was a men's clothing store. Brimmed hats were very fashionable in Chicago, and they decided to buy one each to put themselves in line with other well-dressed men of the day. They both tried one on and, after laughing a bit at themselves, considered that they had made a wise decision and went out of the store looking very stylish.

They did not complete servicing all of Mr. Brown's stores. By midafternoon, their truck was empty—something they did not want to happen. To compensate, however, they decided to visit the remainder of the stores to make themselves known and promise to make deliveries to them at the earliest possible date. They only had about thirty establishments left, and they managed to visit every one of them—a decision which would prove valuable when they returned.

Without exception, every potential customer welcomed them and appreciated their apologies for not making deliveries to them as they wanted to do. Millard and John promised to return to Chicago at the earliest possible date, and most customers said they would look forward to their return. One manager told them that he was not accustomed to people going out of their way just to be polite and make such an appropriate apology.

The day was exhausted, and rather than start the return trip home, they decided to stay the night at stop number one and leave in the morning. They also hoped Robert Swink would pay them another visit before they left. He might very well possess valuable information that would save them trouble on their return journey.

They woke rested and hungry and somewhat apprehensive about their trip home. Robert had not made contact with them, and that made them wonder if something was going on that had delayed him.

They should have known better. As they entered the lobby, there he was, reading the morning paper while he waited for them to come down on their way to breakfast. What a welcome sight he was.

As they were drinking their morning coffee, he told them what he had found out. "A meeting is taking place here in Chicago, and it is exactly what I expected. It is indeed a meeting of organized crime and a big one at that. One item up for discussion is the bootlegging competition they are getting from other sources, and Newbarn is at the top of the list. The competition is cutting in on their profits, and they don't like it at all. Antonio Vitally is there and is probably one of their sources of information. I am going to stay here until I can get all the information I can about what goes on during their meeting, especially the deadly decisions that are made. They are not playing games here, and until all this business is settled, I must keep abreast of all that is happening. The meeting will probably adjourn Saturday, and after I have done all I can here, I will be back at Newbarn, likely on Sunday or Monday. Keep all that I have told you secret, and above all, don't go near Antonio Vitally. We will take care of him in due time.

"I might scout around the edge of the Blue Ridge where you have been having so much trouble on my return trip. That's about all I can report to you for now. As you go home, dodge around as best you can to keep from having any more shoot-outs."

"We haven't been able to avoid trouble yet around that rat hole," remarked John.

"That's a fact," added Millard. "We always try to stay clear of trouble, but they leave us no choice. John and me are tired of being pushed, and we have the firepower with us this time to teach them some manners. If John agrees, we will split Maryville and those other little places wide open. As John has said, this is a free country, and we have a right to do business just like everyone else. We will not play the dodging game anymore."

Robert smiled a little at Millard getting so riled up. "I know you mountain men are stubborn, but sometimes it is best to wait until the iron is hot before you strike. Please tolerate as much as you can until I complete my investigation, and then you will have ample opportunity to strike back when the time is right."

Millard and John thanked him for his successful work in Chicago and for confiding in them.

"Our intentions were to leave for home this morning, but after talking to you, I wonder if you will be safe here alone. We will gladly remain here with you if you have any doubts or concerns," said John.

"No, I have no concerns, and I am accustomed to working alone."

With those words, they shook hands and departed.

Millard and John immediately drove to meet with Mr. Brown on their way home. He was very happy to see them and congratulated them on the glowing reports he had received from his employees. "Our verbal business agreement has worked extremely well, and I look forward to your return trip."

"We will have to bring two trucks on our return trip to assure we have enough to go around. We had rather bring more than we need than to run short before we have delivered to everyone," Millard reassured him.

"That will be fine," said Mr. Brown. "We can make adjustments as needed."

He then handed Millard a large amount of cash in a leather bag with a strong zipper. Millard and John carefully counted the money in front of Mr. Brown. It was the exact amount of $875, as they had known it would be, and it was a small fortune, considering that an ordinary frame house could be built for $500. "It is a pleasure to do business with such a man as you," Millard said warmly. "We will make every effort to never disappoint you, and we will return at the earliest date."

They shook hands and departed on the best of terms.

As Millard and John departed the city, they both felt a sense of achievement. They had accomplished their goals for coming to Chicago and with such ease and enjoyment they could hardly believe their good fortune. Masses of people were traveling toward the city—some in old, beat-up, open-bed trucks, some in horse drawn wagons, and others walking with heavy burdens of farm produce on their stooped backs.

"I will never forget such scenes as this as long as I live," John remarked. Though rough as could be in many ways, John was a softhearted man. "The plight of the poor is almost unbearable to me at times. I never thought I would see such as this."

"Try to forget it, John," said Millard. "It has been going on for years and probably won't end for many more. We didn't see where these people go when they get to the city, and I don't think I care to."

Chicago was beginning to fade into the background, but they still drove past many businesses along the highway. After they had traveled ten miles or so, they were getting into open country and John had dozed off. Many of the farms were very large with elegant, well-kept homes. The barns and fences and other structures were brightly painted. The region was much like similar places in Kentucky. Millard did not wake John. He saw no need to disturb him. They would be reaching St. Louis before the day's end, and they would need to be very alert and cautious from there on to the Blue Ridge Mountains.

He wondered about the men who had been assigned to make deliveries to the other cities he and John had organized. He hoped that he and John and Robert could help the Newbarn organization plan strategies sufficient to provide all drivers safety in their work. He hated having to defend themselves with guns everywhere they made deliveries outside the Blue Ridges.

But he knew very little about such security measures. Robert Swink would know how to lead them in that direction. Having him with them in Chicago had made the trip far better than it would have been otherwise. His suggestion that they contact Edward Brown had cut their work in half, and just knowing he was working in their interest was the primary reason for their most successful trip ever.

John woke up and could not believe how far they had traveled. "Why didn't you shake me awake?" he asked.

"There was no reason to wake you up," replied Millard. "Now you will feel much better as you drive for a while."

"I might have known there was a motive there somewhere," John said as he yawned and stretched his arms. "Since we are this close to St. Louis, let's drive on through and stay the night somewhere on the other side of that fair city."

"I agree," said Millard. "That would even put us farther ahead of schedule than we are now."

"Do you think we should take Robert's advice and take an alternate route instead of going through Maryville and those places that usually cause us so much trouble?" John asked.

"I don't rightly know," Millard said, shaking his head. "Let's sleep on it and make a decision in the morning."

Darkness was approaching when they passed through St. Louis. The center of the city was well lit and exceptionally beautiful. The poverty there was hidden from sight in the back alleys and slum areas, where unfortunate homeless people could seek shelter as best they could. Millard and John drove on through and were soon on the outskirts and headed on toward Memphis.

They kept on going until they came to a small café with a gas pump in front. They filled the truck with gas and then went inside. It was a one-man operation, and he was just about out of food. Beef stew and hot dogs was all he had left. They settled on a delicious plate of beef stew with biscuits and coffee.

Soon they were back on the road keeping an eye out for a place to stay the night. They drove about forty miles before finding a decent-looking boardinghouse. It proved to be a better than average place to stay, and they slept well.

In the morning, they quickly readied themselves for the day, and after breakfast at the boardinghouse, they were on the road again and anxious to get as far toward home as possible before stopping for the night. It was the Sabbath, and church bells were ringing as they passed through small villages during the morning. Businesses were not open on this day, and they knew hunger would catch them before they found a place to eat.

They had driven a far distance before coming upon a town where eating establishments were open. Apparently, the larger places had no laws forbidding businesses to open on Sunday. They ate a meal at a nice café and continued on their way. Luckily, they found one place with a gas pump open at the edge of town. A full tank would probably last until they reached Memphis.

"I suppose we should make a decision about taking an alternate route home as Robert suggested," Millard said, looking at John for input.

"Well," said John, "taking the alternate route is farther, and it being Monday may lessen the chance of trouble if we take our regular route. All considered, I believe our regular route would be all right."

"Let's just go that way then," said Millard. "Surely those hoodlums won't try anything this early in the week and during the day no less."

They completed their trip to Memphis much sooner than they expected. They had planned to stop there and spy on Antonio but decided that was a bad idea. That was Robert's job, and there was always the possibility they might get recognized by one of the men who worked for Antonio, which could hamper Robert's plans. Instead, they decided to gas the truck, buy some sandwiches and colas, and speed right along to Chattanooga and spend the night there. The plan worked perfectly well. They took turns driving to prevent road weariness and made it to their destination in plenty of time to eat supper and stay the night.

When they got into the truck the next morning, they were hoping trouble would not find them. They lowered the rear door as a precaution. They did not want to damage the new truck that Jackson had ordered with a special door that could be opened or closed from inside the truck. It worked very well and provided safety for the truck and any cargo that might be inside.

"We are on our way now," said Millard, "and if all goes well we should reach home sometime tonight or early morning. I hope our luck holds as it has during this entire trip."

As they continued, they talked little, staying alert for anything out of the ordinary.

"Actually, I don't expect trouble," said John, "but we should be careful around the Maryville area and on toward the mountains. If something does occur beyond Maryville, I have a plan that might quickly turn the tide in our favor."

They wasted no time as they crossed Tennessee toward the mountains. All was now becoming familiar territory to them, having traveled this route many times before. The shabby little towns and villages were interesting—each one having its own personality. They stopped nowhere except to eat or fill the gas tank, usually doing both at one place. When they did stop, John would stay with the truck close to his shotguns and Millard would go inside for sandwiches and drinks. They wanted no more surprises of fine automobiles and fancy dressed men with broad-brimmed hats, and it would be wise for such no-accounts to keep their distance.

It was late in the afternoon when they passed through Maryville, and dark had fallen when they drove through Sevierville.

"We will soon know if trouble is brewing ahead," said Millard.

"Damn their sorry hides; they had better not try to ambush us. I won't hold back this time; I will shoot to kill if they fire one shot," John replied in a harsh voice.

Millard started increasing speed as they approached the bottom of the mountains. He wanted a good momentum as they started gaining altitude. Millard hoped they would cross over the mountain and arrive at home in peace.

It was not to be.

THIRTY-FOUR

They were rapidly moving up the mountain and were almost past the area where trouble usually struck, but as they rounded a sharp curve, they could see the outline of a vehicle.

"Oh hell," said Millard as he reached in his shirt pocket and pulled out a piece of cotton. He had already pulled his pistol out of his belt earlier and placed it beside him.

When the vehicle showed up in plain view of their headlights, it was what appeared to be an old car stalled in the road. John had one of his shotguns ready for action as Millard brought the truck to a halt.

At first, the two sides seemed to be in some kind of standoff. Millard thought it best to let the other side make the first move, but he had no intention of backing up.

Finally the car backed up a few feet as if to allow the truck to pass on by. Not so; as soon as the car came to a stop, a hail of gunfire erupted from the vehicle.

The shooters had just made a bad mistake. John was ready with his 8-gauge shotgun and gave them a broadside with both barrels. The gun roared like thunder, and flames immediately came from the car's front end, spreading quickly throughout the vehicle. The flames lit the area, and at first sight, John saw the engine laying on the ground and the car slowly rolling backward into the woods. Several men quickly exited the vehicle and ran into the woods without further gunfire.

As soon as there was room enough to get around the burning vehicle, Millard left the scene as fast as he could. Just for good measure, John emptied his pistol into the woods in the direction the men had gone.

"What message are we supposed to get from that fool trick?" Millard asked, without really expecting an answer.

John was so busy reloading his weapons and trying to assess the situation that he did not comprehend what Millard had said.

They rapidly climbed on up the hill until they reached a pull-off point near the top of the mountain and then stopped and waited to determine what, if anything, was going on behind them. They could see flames getting higher down below where the shooting had occurred. "Damn," said John. "That blazing, old car must have set the woods on fire. Let's get our asses out of here and fast."

"We're gone," replied Millard as he pulled onto the road and left the scene as fast as the truck would go. "Did any of that lead hit you, John?"

"No, but I don't know about the truck. It might have thirty or forty holes in it."

"Hell, I hope not," Millard replied. "I won't rest easy until I know."

He immediately pulled to the side of the road, and both men went around the truck striking matches and counting holes. They discovered twelve holes on the right side but none in the cab.

"That's not too bad," said John. "I can patch those holes, and no one will ever know the difference."

"Whoever attacked us should find another line of work; all that shooting and so few hits," Millard replied. "Let's get back to Newbarn as quickly as possible and go home before the working day begins there."

They arrived at Newbarn and, after leaving a note to Jackson, went home, leaving the truck locked in the loading area.

Millard went directly home, hoping to get a few hours' sleep before being disturbed. Flora and the boys were still asleep. He went into the house as quietly as possible.

Flora was awake and began asking questions faster than he could answer. He asked her to wait until later, and he would explain things as best he could. Just a few hours' sleep was all he wanted. He had done most of the driving during the night and was very tired. She said no more and kept his breakfast warm until he awoke.

Before noon, he was out of bed and preparing for work. Cameron was up and wanted him to pick him up. He did so and walked around the house while talking to him. "Let's go in and see little Walter," Millard said as he carried him into the house.

"I don't want to see Walter. He sleeps all the time and won't play with me one bit."

"When he gets a little older and stronger, he will learn to walk and he will play with you then. You were the same way when you were his age. You slept just about all the time like he does now. Just hug him softly and kiss him, and he will like you very much as he gets older."

"That is just what Mama keeps telling me, so I guess that is what I will do."

Millard ate and left for work, still leaving Flora without answers to her questions. She didn't mind much though. She knew he would get around to talking with her in due time.

Millard wanted to get to work as soon as possible. His curiosity about the events of the previous night and what Detective Swink had discovered during his investigation was overwhelming. He went directly to the office at Newbarn, and when he arrived, he found, to his delight, that John, Jackson, and Detective Swink were all there. They greeted each other with enthusiasm and a few funny remarks.

"Sorry to be late," said Millard.

"That's all right," said Jackson. "John just arrived, and Robert just before him. We haven't talked business yet. Do you guys want to talk here or meet at Pop's this evening?"

"I think we should meet where you and Walter would like to meet," John said.

"Well, Pop would probably like us to come over there after we finish the day here. He has been feeling a little poorly of late, and I think meeting at his house would cheer him up."

"I will stay around here and help you catch up with your work until the meeting then," Millard said.

"Count me in as well," John said. "Millard and me have been concerned about you having so much work to do with both of us gone all the time."

"I agree," said Millard. "That is another reason we want to get our reorganization completed."

"I sure could use your help; I won't deny that," Jackson remarked.

It was a pleasant afternoon, and everything at Newbarn was in good shape when they left for their meeting at Walter's. They started the meeting at once, and they were all looking to Robert Swink and Jackson for answers about all the troubles they had experienced since they'd begun making long hauls.

Walter was his old hospitable self and, as always, made sure everyone had a helping of his expensive wine in a fancy glass. He loved his home and never failed to adequately welcome all his guests.

Jackson assured everyone not to concern themselves with formalities. "We are all here to discuss issues of mutual interest and share information that we hope will be of benefit to us. We have reached the end of our long-haul plans. We have some problems to solve, but we will take care of them as we must do. Robert Swink is with us, and I have asked him to report his latest findings. Then he will give us an opportunity to ask questions."

Robert remained sitting as he related what he knew with the group. "Fellows," he said, "I have traced your long-haul route from Spruce Willow to Chicago. I see no problems between Spruce Willow and the foot of the mountains. All the gunfire has taken place around the area of Sevierville back in this direction. I don't believe the men responsible for the shootings intend to come across the mountains; they just don't want you men to come down into what they consider their territory. They are a selfish bunch and you are intimating the hell out of them."

He pushed his chair back from the table to get some notes out of his pocket. "The word is out about the quality of your whiskey, and they don't want you to start peddling it through their territory all the way to Chicago as they know you intend to do. So far, you have stoutly turned them back at every attack they have made," he said as he stood up, looking at his notes.

He lit a cigarette and, after a short pause, continued on. "I gave Homer Cash another look, but after watching him and his men come and go, I am convinced he is not the leader of your attackers from down below. He was responsible at first, but I am confident he does not want to be involved in such mischief any longer." His face stern, the detective looked directly at each man, as though he expected them to not believe him. "Cash is just a small cog in a large wheel. From what I have determined, several leaders are involved in the whiskey business between here and Chicago. Each main leader has many small dealers under his control. Homer Cash is one of those small dealers, and I feel certain that he knows the large dealers, certainly the one over him. I think I can get Homer to reveal the names of the ringleaders, and that is where you can start putting some restraints on them and protecting Newbarn.

"What I'm suggesting sounds hard, but it really isn't that bad. They scare just as much as other people. You just have to find their weak spots and use that leverage to put them on the defensive." He smiled as he made that statement; he could see that he had the men's attention and had gained their respect. He knew they needed that reassurance. "That should get things settled on this end first, and I will get what I've proposed started for you if you decide you want me to get involved in your business to that extent."

Robert paused to take a big sip from his wine glass and then continued, "One of the leaders is somewhere between Sevierville and Chattanooga, and I am confident there is one in Chattanooga. One we already know is Antonio Vitally in Memphis, who is a snake in the grass and greedier than most.

"The next one I found out about was Jim Henderson, a very dangerous character who lives near St. Louis in a place called Dexterville. I could not find that place, and it is not on my map."

Walter quickly expressed his doubts about Jim Anderson being involved in anything like that. "He is too old, like me. The last time I talked to him, he was still in St. Louis. I have heard of a wild bunch operating in that area, but that is all I know about them. Dexterville might be just a fictitious name made up for some unknown purpose."

Robert nodded and then continued. "Chicago, of course, is one of the worst places you will have to contend with. The gangs and mobsters there deal in everything that brings in large amounts of cash. One mobster has found out about your whiskey. He wants to control your business, and you can bet he will contact you pretty soon. He will want to talk to you and work out some kind of business deal, but he won't attack you like these hoodlums at the bottom of the mountain. He only gets rough when there is no other way to get what he wants."

The pleasant expression on Robert's face and sincerity in his voice seemed to have captured the attention of the men. They knew they had a new friend, and he had the pleasure and belief that he could help these good men. "You might do business with him in some way, but one way or another, he will end up with the lion's share of the profits. He will provide you protection though, so that could be of some comfort to you. I just wish I could provide you with his name, and I will as soon as possible. Just talk to him if you want to, but don't allow him to bully you. Agree to what you want to do and nothing else. To hell with him is all I can say. He can be dealt with just as anyone else. That is about all I can report to you for now. You are the finest, most honorable group of men I have ever dealt with, and I will help you in every way possible."

"How do you think we should proceed from here?" asked Millard. "Our automobile delivery routes have been established from Virginia to the foot of the mountains."

"My advice is to keep things going as they are here in the mountains and then plan a strategy starting from that point on to Memphis. Expect troubles along that stretch because there are at least two big wheels to contend with, and in Memphis, there will be old, sly Antonio Vitally. Keep doing business with him until we determine what to do about him. After that will be good, old St. Louis and then the biggest prize of all, Chicago. Then if you can compromise or conquer what you are after there, you will have your entire organization in place. I hope you succeed, and I believe you will. But make no mistake; there will be troubles ahead.

"Oh yes, consider arming yourselves with those shotguns like John has. That scares the hell out of just about everybody. I talked to a man in Sevierville who heard some of the shooting, and he said it sounded like another Civil War battle was being fought over there."

In keeping with his word to leave things to Jackson, Walter had listened carefully to the report without comment. Walter then looked at Robert and said, "After hearing your report, I now have some doubts that we could be as successful in our long-haul operation without your expertise. You are a good man, Robert, and Jackson was wise to hire you."

"I thank you for your confidence, and I will put forth my best effort to help with the organizational plans at Newbarn."

No more questions were asked, and after some interesting conversation and another glass of wine, the men shook hands and departed for home.

Millard reached home after dark. He could hear guitar music playing before he reached the door. Flora was entertaining the boys. Cameron was delighted with the beautiful sound, and Walter was on a quilt on the floor with his eyes wide open as though he wondered what was going on.

Millard picked the baby up and held him closely, being quite aware that he had not given him the attention he deserved since his birth. It would not be long now until he would be crawling around and getting into everything.

After the boys were in bed and Flora had served Millard a warmed-over supper, they retired to the front porch to talk and look at the stars. It was a crisp, clear night, and the stars were a magnificent display of grandeur. No moon was shining, and that caused the skies to display even more and brighter stars than usual. "Perhaps someday we will know more about what is up there," Flora remarked.

"I have wondered about that since I was a small boy," Millard replied.

"I do not expect to ever know the secrets of that heavenly body," Flora continued. Jesus told us he will descend in a cloud from above to take us to heaven someday. When he does come for us, I want you and the boys and me to be together."

At that point in the conversation, Millard seized the opportunity to change the subject. He did not want to get involved in a long conversation about religion. To Millard, religion had its place, business had its place, and politics had its place. "I promised to tell you about how my work is progressing, and I don't know where or how to begin without going into much detail. Suffice it to say, our Newbarn organization has now reached Chicago, and we are making more money than I have ever dreamed possible. Our organization now reaches from Virginia to Chattanooga and on to Memphis, St. Louis, and Chicago. We have no plans to go any farther, but we have made many enemies, most of which we don't even know. I hope the detective we have hired will help us find out their identity. We have had many fights, but so far none of us has been seriously injured. John and me are carrying the heavy load right now. We might succeed in going into legal business ventures sooner than I thought. Now, how does that sound to you?"

"It sounds wonderful," Flora replied, "and I believe it will happen, but I sense a lot of trouble ahead before it does. I have never completely accepted this way of life you have chosen. I have tried many times to persuade you to consider less dangerous work, but you had your mind set, and that is always that."

"We take chances every week, and I know it will continue this way for the foreseeable future. A cautious, steady move ahead is what I have in mind, and I think the others feel as I do," said Millard. "We will plan our next move tomorrow morning and waste no time in getting started. That's about all I can tell you for now. Maybe I will have more to tell you tomorrow night—that is, if I come home. Things are so unpredictable now that I don't know what will be decided tomorrow." Millard looked very concerned.

"Millard, I haven't mentioned anything about Dad yet. Lee came by and told me that he had another spell with his heart. He wouldn't go to Dr. Burleson as Lee tried to get him to do. The pain finally stopped, and he seems to be all right for the time being. I think he is taking terrible chances with his heart health. If something should happen to him, I will get word to you as soon as possible," she promised.

"I don't know what I should do now," Millard said. "I am glad you told me about him, and I would go to him now, but I know he will not follow any advice I could give him. If I can avoid a long trip, I will do so, and we will go over there and stay with him all day."

After a restless night, Millard thought he was dreaming when he woke to the smell of ham frying. Flora had decided the night before to fix him a breakfast of ham and eggs with all the trimmings.

"What is going on?" Millard said as he walked into the kitchen.

"You are going to get a nice breakfast for a change," she told him.

"I cannot wait for a lengthy breakfast," he said. "I have to get to work early."

"Sit down and eat," she said. "They can wait on you for a few minutes. You have deprived yourself long enough, and you are going to make yourself sick if you don't start eating nourishing meals."

He said no more; the smell already had his undivided attention. He ate without rushing and then kissed Flora and the boys and was off to work.

As he walked in the door at the office, everyone was there but him.

"Where have you been?" Jackson asked. "We have been waiting on you."

"Well, I won't lie to you. I woke up early, but Flora had got up even earlier. She had a breakfast of ham and eggs and all that goes with such a fine breakfast and demanded that I sit down and eat. I could not refuse. If I told you I am sorry, I would be lying."

All laughed loudly.

"I told them you could not tell a lie," said John. "Actually, we arrived just before you got here. We just wanted to have a little fun."

"I will pay you all back sooner or later," Millard said and began laughing even louder than the others.

"Fellows, I think we should get right down to business," said Jackson. "I have a feeling we don't have a lot of time to lose if we all want to become very rich and fight back the competition that seems determined to ruin us. We need to get started today and move right along. We purchased a new, heavy-duty truck like the one Millard and John broke in last week. This one is like the other one, including a retracting rear door. We will get the two other trucks modified the same way today."

"At this point, I think you should run all four trucks during this week," answered Robert. "That will shake up the people who are after you enough for me to find out who they are and where their home base is. I know approximately where they are, but I need more time to trace all of your routes. There may be more locations where separate groups connected to the mob operate that I have not found. It will be a busy week and maybe a dangerous one. I will keep in touch with all four trucks as often as time and distance permits."

"The new truck is already loaded and ready to go," said Jackson.

"John will have the holes in the side of the other new truck repaired shortly, and it will be loaded and ready to move also," Millard announced.

"Speaking of the holes," said John, "Robert, did you find out anything about the four men in that old souped-up car that came after us with guns blazing the other night? Millard and me did not know what to make of that incident. We didn't know what to expect after we blew it all to hell and set the woods on fire. They might be still burning for all we know. I hope the men who bailed out and ran away were not injured, but we did not invite them to attack us, and I shot to kill to be honest about it. We are tired of people trying to kill us like that."

"I was a far distance behind you when I heard all the noise, but I didn't know what was going on when I saw fire blazing up through the trees. I think the law knew what was going on though; otherwise, how would they have been ahead of me when everything started?

"When I arrived on the scene, they allowed me to go on through. A good number of men were fighting the fire. I don't know where the firefighters came from, unless there are some houses around there. Normally, the law officers would have ordered me to stop and help fight the fire. That's all I know, but I will scout around and try to determine who was behind that stupid act."

Millard had noticed Jackson shifting his feet and acting ill at ease. He immediately suggested that they prepare for the trip and be prepared to leave as soon as possible. He suggested they double-check everything and move out at intervals of two hours, the first truck leaving at six in the evening and the last one at twelve noon tomorrow.

No one objected, and Jackson nodded his head indicating his approval.

After the others left the office area, Millard asked Jackson if he could help ease his load in any way. "You seem to be working too hard. You carry a heavy load of responsibility, my friend, and I want to help if I can."

"There is nothing you can do right now except be in the fourth truck tomorrow. You and John can handle things, and if there is trouble ahead, you two could intervene in some way and keep everything from getting out of hand."

"We will do just as you say," Millard replied. "I just want things to go well for Newbarn, and they will. You can count on John and me, and all the other men also.

"Is Sally doing well?" Millard asked.

"She is," replied Jackson, "and Mom and Pop are standing up well too. I know what you are getting at, Millard, and I will handle things here. It's just that we have so many men in our organization and so many things going on at one time, it just gets to me sometimes."

"Well, after this trip is over, we can get our heads together and make things easier for you," Millard replied with obvious sympathy in his voice. "Oh, I didn't tell you," he added, "Dad is having episodes with his heart again. I will have to check on him soon after we return. He is a tough old-timer. I am worried about him but not overly so at this time."

THIRTY-FIVE

The first truck left Newbarn at six o'clock. The men involved in the long-haul ventures, including Horton Pritchard and Jefferson Platt who were scheduled to take the first haul, had worked feverishly all through the afternoon. As they'd worked quietly and efficiently, the tension had been apparent. Horton and Jefferson were taking one of the two older trucks that Sam Burns had been modifying to accommodate retractable rear doors. Now they could retract the doors and see directly behind them, giving them a better shot at anyone shooting at them from behind.

Robert Swink had left the area in front of the first truck, which would make deliveries in and around Chattanooga. He wanted to determine whether Horton and Jefferson were being observed by any suspicious characters—be they local people, law officers, or even mobster soldiers. He had his ways, and he intended to put these people in their place once and for all. After Horton and Jefferson had made their deliveries, he would follow them, in his own way, back to the top of the mountain beyond where the ambushes usually occurred.

He would pick up the trail of the second truck after the first truck had safely crossed the mountain. If all went well, he would scout for the second truck in the same way. He would have to drive all night and part of the next day, but he had done so before and did not mind. It was just a part of the job, and he loved it.

Horton and Jefferson had been briefed by Jackson and Millard before they left. They were confident they knew exactly what was before them, and they intended to do a first-rate job. They knew what it meant to them and to the organization. On they drove, very carefully and at a modest speed. They intended to reach the delivery areas with time to spare and follow the delivery list of customers and directions with utmost caution. No customer must ever be missed. And every customer was to be treated with utmost respect.

As they reached the bottom of the mountain, seemingly out of nowhere, Robert passed them and motioned for them to stop. They immediately pulled off the road, and Robert walked back to talk with them.

"So far, everything is all clear up ahead for about twenty miles," he said. "Did you men notice anything I should know about on your way down?"

"Nothing," said Horton, who was driving the truck. "Actually, it has been an enjoyable trip down the old mountain."

"Good," Robert replied. "Just keep a sharp eye out. I will be close by and stay with you until you are back across the mountain as we planned. Good luck," he said and was gone as quickly as he'd appeared.

The second truck, driven by Raymond and Dennis, departed Newbarn at twelve o'clock, headed for Memphis. He was surprised that Horton and Jefferson had experienced no trouble during their run; except for a sheriff's car that had followed him for a short distance and two old, souped-up cars that had been roaming around, he had noticed no suspicious activity all day. He had passed the vehicles by as though he had noticed nothing.

From this point to Memphis, he intended to contact Dennis and Raymond at least once, but if he didn't, he would use his detective skills and experience to find anything that would be helpful in solving what was turning out to be an unexpectedly complicated case. He had learned from past experience that practically all cases were solvable if you were persistent, very observant, patient, and alert. He drove at a rather smooth, rapid pace but not so fast as to attract undue attention. Doubtless, he would have to stay the night somewhere this side of Memphis.

He had previously stayed in a town named Lawrenceburg located between Chattanooga and Memphis. It was a row of small, one-bedroom cottages and a perfect place for him to stay. Dennis and Raymond were either somewhere in front of him or he had missed them somewhere behind.

The latter turned out to be accurate. They had stopped for supper, and he had passed them by. Luck was on their side, however, and as he reached the cottages where he intended to stay the night, they were not far behind. They noticed his car and immediately stopped to see what he was about. Actually, he was about to turn in for the night. They were happy to find each other, and Dennis and Raymond decided to lodge at the same place. What a comfort it was to be near Robert.

He was like a security blanket to them, and he knew it. They were fine, smart men, but they had not had experience in what they might be about to get into.

Morning came as it always does, and when the truck pulled out, Robert waited a few minutes and then followed them. He stayed far back enough to just keep them in sight. They ate their breakfast at a small café, and Robert reminded them not to tarry anywhere. "The less you are seen, the less the chance for trouble.

"As you know," he added, "Antonio Vitally will probably be in his warehouse. By all means, don't let on that you know anything about him other than that he is a good customer. Be real nice to him and give him a quart of whiskey as a bonus. Laugh and joke with him and act like the true mountain men that you are. Just act natural, and that will do what you need to accomplish. I know Millard and Jackson have briefed you very well, but I want to emphasize the importance of this man. We don't know what his reaction will be later on; it may stay the same for a while. We do know that he is a dangerous man with mobster connections; indeed, he is part of organized crime—the kind that will kill anyone considered a threat to their way of life. If we are as patient and clever as they are, who knows, perhaps we might witness them being sentenced to life in prison or executed sometime in the future. After working around such people as I have, I have developed hatred toward them and everything they stand for." That Robert had experienced many bad confrontations with such people was clear, and it was also clear that he wouldn't hesitate to kill them if provoked. The hatred flashing in his eyes cooled a little, and he concluded, "Well, here I am preaching to you. Let's just get on with our day and do our job well. I will keep in touch as usual."

Robert knew the individual places where Dennis and Raymond would be going that day. The one that worried him, however, was the first and most unpredictable of all in Memphis. He decided to park his car and walk as close to the warehouse as possible without drawing attention to himself. He checked his pistol and carefully placed it in his shoulder holster. If Antonio or his men suspected anything at all, Robert knew there would be trouble—the kind that might end up with Dennis and Raymond at the bottom of the Mississippi River. But they would not end up there if he could prevent it.

He saw no way he could get close enough to the warehouse to work his way inside. The next and only thing he could do was wait and watch, for the time being at least. If those two fine young men were not out of there within one hour, he would take his chances and walk in, pretending that he needed directions to some familiar place in the city.

It was fifty-five minutes before their truck came out of the warehouse. They looked okay and were acting normal in every way. He waited until they were safely away from the warehouse and then carefully made his way back to his car. The boys must have done well, and he was glad. Being a detective for many years had caused him to recognize his intuitions, which experience had taught him to never ignore. Robert was confident Dennis and Raymond would do well that day. He knew of no dangers that might be lurking now that they had left Antonio's place.

Robert knew very well that Antonio had plans for Newbarn and was carefully gathering every bit of information concerning their operation. Perhaps he might have been a friend of Walter's years ago when things were different and people could be trusted, but he was a clever snake now and no friend to anyone who he could use to further his ambitions.

His time will come, thought Robert. During the day, he scouted the city and trailed Dennis and Raymond part of the time. He wanted to be absolutely certain that no harm came to them. They were smart and capable, and he had no doubt about their future in completing successful long-haul runs for Newbarn.

Confident that all was in hand, Robert decided to return to the mountains and do some scouting along the way. One place of particular interest to him was the place near Chattanooga where Millard and John had the big fight with the four strangers driving the fancy car. In Chattanooga, he gassed up, ate a light evening meal, and then proceeded to scout the city very carefully for suspicious-looking places that might serve as a haven for gangsters. He detected nothing that remotely caught his attention. If the mobsters were from Chattanooga, doubtless they had a place in the country where one would least expect. Robert knew that the store where the confrontation had taken place was on the east side of Chattanooga and decided a visit might be a good thing.

The store and post office were both open when he arrived, and several people were there, some buying store items and others doing business in the post office. He bought a snack cake and sat down near the large stove. No one seemed to pay any attention to him or even speak for that matter.

As he stood up to leave, he heard men talking and, upon further observation, noticed stairs in the rear of the store leading to a second floor. He walked to the bottom of the stairs, and sure enough, that was where the voices were coming from. Apparently the men who were talking had failed to close the door to prevent being heard or didn't care who heard what they said. Robert believed the former. He could only hear parts of the conversation, but he did detect enough to determine that it was a serious meeting of unscrupulous men with evil plans and motives. Words indicating the elimination of all competition from Chicago to the Blue Ridge Mountains and on to the East Coast were voiced, but he could only hear bits and pieces of the conversation. Their conversation included many organizations, but he heard only one vague reference to Newbarn.

Robert stood under the stairs until someone shut the partially open door, and the voices from the room were totally muffled. He was very pleased to have discovered, quite by accident, another enemy in the chain of enemies that the Newbarn organization would have to deal with sooner than later. If he was correct, he had only two or perhaps three major obstacles to flush out and identify before they could clear the way for their bootlegging trucks to travel unmolested from Newbarn to Chicago. He was very anxious to accomplish that task.

Robert immediately headed away from Chattanooga, hoping to find a spot to rest and possibly link up with the third truck bound for St. Louis. Jackson and Millard had selected Cecil Garner and

Foster Holmes to take the third truck out. They both had proven themselves many times in places of trouble, outrunning other cars, including the law in some cases, and still making their deliveries and returning to Newbarn safely.

Robert waited about one hour and was about to doze off when he saw Cecil and Foster pass by. He quickly followed them, and when they saw a secluded field ahead, they left the road and stopped to talk. Robert reported to them what he had located in the store near Chattanooga. "I believe that is a bad area around there, and it would be to your benefit to avoid trouble if you can. You don't know how many men you might have to tangle with. Keep your shotguns ready. That could end up giving you a much-needed edge."

"I will be glad when we can make our runs without having to watch for trouble all the time," said Cecil.

"That ain't going to happen until we find out who our enemies are and show them that we are not to be taken lightly," answered Robert.

"I am looking forward to such a time as that, when we can make our long—and short-haul runs and make plenty of money and have fun too," said Foster. "Actually I enjoy working like this, even with all the trouble from other people. They might not know it, but we can get just as mean as they can if we have to."

"Hell yes," Cecil said in a determined voice. "Let them lowlanders bring it on. We can give them tit for tat without giving one inch."

They all laughed at that remark.

"Well, boys, if you don't mind I am going to turn back toward the mountains and see what happens. I intend to find the bottom of this foolishness no matter what it takes. Just take it easy, and I will see you back at Newbarn."

As Robert was driving away he thought, *What a damnable name for a business—legal or illegal. I need to find out how such a name came to be. I think I should put that in my memoirs someday.* He kept on driving a few miles and then realized that he should start anticipating possible trouble ahead. A store with a gas pump was just ahead, and he elected to fill his tank before going any farther.

As he paid the store owner, he asked him how the roads were up ahead and across the mountains.

"The roads are fine so far as I know, but there has been a lot of hell rising from Maryville on up the mountains. They say it sounds like a war is going on up there some nights. I suspect bootleggers are settling their differences in the worst kind of way. Have not heard of any killings though. Still, if I were you, I would go north and circle around Knoxville to avoid getting involved."

"I might just do that," Robert replied and thanked the man for his advice.

As he drove away, he looked in his rearview mirror, and the man was watching him closely. *That might be an informer's hut, and I will keep him in mind*, thought Robert as he drove away. *Legitimate store owners do not usually watch their customers drive away like that.*

Of course Robert had no intention of going any other way than across the mountain. It was early enough that he might just see something that would be of help to him in solving this case, which was getting more and more complicated. He increased his speed and headed directly toward the mountains. After passing through Sevierville, he started carefully watching for anything unusual. He remembered Millard telling him about being ambushed from the fields at the bottom of the mountains. After circling around the area and even driving into the fields, he could see nothing that attracted his attention.

Cautiously he began the trip upward. At every turnoff, he would stop and just get out of his car and look and listen. He detected signs that cars had been spinning around and tracks where they had left the road. Places where fire had burned both on and off the road could be seen, and pieces of metal from cars were lying around where they had been overlooked as wreckages had been removed. Several miles up the mountain, he noticed an old chimney at the crest of a ridge at the left of the road.

The road leading to the chimney site was rather hard to find and washed out, leaving only rocks that revealed no tracks. It was narrow and had arbors on either side, scarcely leaving room for a car to pass through. Robert managed to reach the chimney, where obviously no house had been for many decades. It was a creepy place and gave him chills. But plenty of car tracks revealed that it had been visited often and recently. He quickly decided to leave the site, since the sun was getting low and he would be boxed in that place if some rowdy devils decided to come up that road with evil on their minds. He would be in a precarious position to say the least.

THIRTY-SIX

After leaving the spot, Robert drove up the mountain a ways to a place where he could observe the old chimney site without being noticed. He saw nothing.

After waiting until dark, he then made his way toward Newbarn. The information he had accumulated on his journey was valuable, but linking it all together was a different matter. His suspicions and observations needed to be confirmed. He suspected the chimney place was probably used as a meeting place for some of the devils who were hell-bent on destroying Newbarn. Secluded places near roads and rented houses and barns were very important hiding places for such bastards. He would find them soon, and then all scores could be settled. Robert felt the key to this type of situation was patience.

When he returned to Newbarn, it was far too early for anyone to show up. A nap in the car did him good, and by the time he woke up, the place was swarming with men loading up enough whiskey to sink a ship. Jackson seemed very happy to see him and was very anxious to learn about his trip.

After the men left and things had settled down, Robert accompanied Jackson into the office where they could talk over a cup of coffee. He went over his notes with Jackson, taking care to miss nothing.

Jackson was very impressed with the work Robert had done. "I will go over this information with Pop, and things might start making sense.

"Millard and John left at twelve, and they will probably return with a wealth of information," he added. "As soon as they return, we should all compare notes and observations. Then we will be ready for action of some kind. They are going into a dangerous place as you well know. Their last run was easy, but this one might be different."

"Not to worry," said Robert. "I have observed those two in action, including their work in Chicago. They are very professional and show kindness to everyone they meet. Every person I saw them approach liked them right off. Their mountain manner went over big, but they did not deliberately flaunt it to impress anyone."

"I don't expect them to return before late Wednesday or sometime Thursday," Jackson remarked. "It could be even later if they experience trouble."

"Say, you wouldn't have one of those big shotguns like John has been using and recommended to the drivers, especially those making long hauls?"

"I don't have an extra one, but you can use mine if you like," said Jackson.

"I would like to borrow it and some of those shells with extra slugs and black powder," Robert said enthusiastically. "Late this evening, I intend to patrol that mountain from the bottom up to the old chimney I told you about. That place gave me the creeps, and I do not look forward to going there again."

"Here you are," John said as he handed the gun to Robert, "and here is a box of ammunition, which I loaded with my own formula."

"I know that will make me feel much more at ease, provided I can lift it while I use it. I have never held a gun this heavy," Robert remarked. He lifted it up and down, trying to hold it to his shoulder.

"Just practice lifting it, and you will quickly get accustomed to how it handles," said Jackson with a grin on his face. "Take it out and fire it one time though. Then you will really know how it handles."

"I would rather have it with me than be without it," said Robert, "even though I can see how amused you are about it all."

"You will be all right with it," Jackson replied. "I was just amused at the look on your face when you first started handling it."

"I am going to take another nap in the car and then return to my hunting spot near the chimney. I will return in the morning, unless things of interest compel me to remain there longer. Otherwise, I will head west and try to intercept our trucks as they come this way and watch out for them. They might have information that would be of value to us, and I will need to do some concentrated detective work before returning here. I want to solve this troublesome situation for you soon. It has been my experience that the longer a case goes on, the harder it is to solve."

"I wish you well, and I wish I could go with you. Good luck!" said Jackson.

Robert slept several hours and then left Newbarn for what he suspected might be a long night and perhaps another long day. After he'd reached his intended parking place, he took a small saw to cut down some small, bushy trees, and camouflaged his car. He was satisfied with his position and settled back to wait. Every so often, he would scan the area with his binoculars.

Only a few cars had passed, and he did not think any of them had noticed his presence. Hour after hour, he waited with only some hoot owls and other night birds making a sound. Shortly after three in the morning, he thought he heard a sound. He listened carefully, and indeed it was a sound, and a familiar one at that. It was one of those old cars with a loud, souped-up engine. It turned up the road to the old chimney area where he had been watching all night.

No sooner had the engine stopped than he heard what sounded to him like one or perhaps two more high-powered cars. Both had come up the mountain and also turned up the chimney road. Something was up, but he did not know what. After thinking for a few minutes, the answer came to him. *One of our trucks is coming up the mountain and is about to be ambushed.* He heard the three cars creeping down the chimney road, and he knew he must act fast. He quickly removed his camouflage to permit a quick exit from his position.

Soon Robert heard the unmistakable sound of a truck whining up the mountain in a low gear. *It's bound to be Horton and Jefferson,* thought Robert, *and I doubt that they have the slightest suspicion of the danger ahead. We have never had any trouble up this far on the mountain before, and those boys probably think they are home free.*

At that instant, he heard car doors open and close. He knew then what he was up against. The men were leaving their cars and lying in wait between the chimney road and the highway. He had only one option left. He would take his weapons and cross the road on foot and circle around behind the place where the ambush was about to occur. The truck was coming closer, and he placed himself as best he could where he would have the best line of fire at the ambushers. His heart was pounding, but that didn't bother him much. His mind was solely on the thought that Horton and Jefferson could be killed if he didn't do something to save them.

Just as the truck was a few yards away from the point of ambush, out of thoughtless reflex, he fired his pistol in the air. That slowed things down, but neither side knew what was going on, and both were completely surprised. Horton and Jefferson were now at the spot of the ambush, but the shot had alerted them in time to grab their guns.

Suddenly, all hell broke loose. The ambushers started shooting high-powered rifles and shotguns and probably pistols as well. Robert fired his double-barreled shotgun, sending slugs and shock waves through the bushes. That probably helped Horton and Jefferson more than anything else he possibly could have done. It gave them time to determine where their enemies were, and they bailed out the opposite side of the truck, opening fire into the bushes and brush, now knowing where to aim their fire.

Intense gunfire was coming from all over the place, but no one had a clear target. Robert knew none of the men involved knew exactly where he was, and he wanted it to stay that way until he could figure out what to do. The men in the bushes were trying to pick a target without hitting one of their own.

Finally, the firing slowed and Robert could hear low talking and moving about. He knew they were either trying to find better cover or get back into their cars. Some of them had been hit, and painful groans could be heard.

He heard sounds from the other side of the truck also—sounds that made him believe Horton and Jefferson were in pain and needed assistance. In a very risky maneuver, he circled back around and crossed the road, from which point he could best reach the truck. He knew very well that he could be shot dead before he sprinted across the road, but he also knew very well that he had no choice. Both those good men might be in critical condition, and seconds could mean life or death.

Horton had been hit in the shoulder, and Jefferson had taken a shotgun blast to his leg, but Robert did not think he'd taken a full load. He had two or three slugs in the fleshy part of his right leg. As best he could determine, the wounds were not life threatening. Both told him they would be all right.

The shooting had almost stopped from the other side of the road, and Robert did not know what to make of that. He asked Horton and Jefferson to remain where they were and let him have their shotguns. He knew the shotguns were very effective in /this thick, brushy area, allowing him to sweep the entire area with heavy buckshot. If the devils did happen to try running across the road, Horton and Jefferson could pick them off with their pistols. Robert worked his way up the road, crossed it, and moved in behind the ambushers, but not as close as before. He could hear two or three of the men groaning with pain; one sounded as if he was doing badly, and someone said they should get him to a hospital.

"We can take them to a doctor after we kill them bastards," a voice replied. "There are only three of them, and I am for taking them out. I mean kill every damn one of them."

That was the last straw for Robert. He knew they would not stay where they were for long before they started searching for them. Very quietly, he moved behind a nearby rock. No more talking could be heard, just unintelligible noises. He would wait no longer. He fired both barrels of his 8-gauge, aiming at the gas tank of the middle car. Return fire came at him, and he felt a burning sensation in his left cheek. He quickly grabbed one of the other shotguns and blasted the car parked behind the other two.

The middle car should have exploded, but obviously he had not hit the gas tank. He had, however, hit a gas line and started a fire that was spreading quickly. Suddenly, both cars blew up, and flames rose high. The first car was started up and escaped the immediate scene. It proceeded up the road a short distance and then swerved off the road and into a ditch. Horton and Jefferson had found cover behind a large oak, and when the car came out into the road in front of the tree, they emptied their pistols at the vehicle, doing much damage including flattening of both right tires and causing the car to plow into the ditch again. Robert had already moved farther back into the woods and was shooting at everything that moved.

Suddenly everything quieted except for the roaring of the fire. Robert took the opportunity to make his break and ran as fast as he could. Down the road a little ways, he crossed the road, expecting bullets to come at him any second. He found Horton and Jefferson and at first thought they were seriously injured. "Are you boys all right?" he asked.

"Our injuries are not bad," answered Jefferson. "We have not been hit again."

"Thing is, how are you?" Jefferson asked, seeming a bit alarmed.

"Just a crease," answered Robert.

"Let's get our asses out of here while we have the chance," Jefferson said in a low voice.

"What happened to the ambushers?" asked Horton.

"Don't know," answered Robert. "I couldn't see where they went, but they sounded like a herd of deer running through the woods."

Robert waited until Horton and Jefferson made it to their truck. The truck had been damaged, but apparently it was only sheet metal bullet holes. It started normally, but they checked for gas leakage before moving the truck forward. They were glad that they were mobile enough to move around. Robert's car also started, and he pulled out right behind them.

They wasted no time making their way to Newbarn and were overjoyed to get there in pretty good shape. They could do nothing now, except wait for the others to arrive. They didn't have to wait long until Jackson arrived, along with several of the other men.

Jackson could see at a glance that things had gone wrong, but this was no time to sort things out. He explained nothing to the men loading up to make their daily runs. But he would respect their curiosity and explain things to them later.

Robert, Horton, and Jefferson followed him into the office area. Financially, their trip had been excellent, and they had enjoyed their trip. Robert explained the entire episode—giving in minute detail every seemingly insignificant part—of what he referred to as "the war on the mountain." Jackson listened carefully. He knew that, to Robert, patience and details were of utmost importance in solving cases.

Robert took Horton and Jefferson to a physician who lived only a few miles away. The physician examined them very closely and decided to remove the bullets in his office. He said there was no point in taking them to the hospital when he could remove them using his own surgical instruments. The procedures went well and the physician instructed them to keep the wounds clean and bandage them every day until the soreness was gone.

Robert needed no special care other than cleaning what amounted to a long scratch on his face. The wound was not deep enough to leave a scar and required nothing more than a sterile cleaning. The physician gave him a small bottle of a blue-looking liquid to help it heal quickly and keep infection away.

As they left his office, he told them that he would not mention their visit to his office or keep any records. "I know you boys have been in a shooting ruckus, and it probably was not your fault. Please do not mention my name, but one of the men who were probably connected to this situation came in before you men with a wound too serious for me to manage in this office. I sent him to the clinic in Spruce Willow. He said several others were wounded but they had gone down the mountain for treatment where they lived."

"Did you get the name of the man you treated here or where he lives?" asked Robert.

"His name was Samuel Flint, and he lives on Goose Creek. He said he would have nothing else to do with that bunch from down under the mountain and that he had no idea when he got involved with them that they were outlaws and killers. He also said they wanted him to help them find where the whiskey stills were located up in our mountains and offered to pay him well. I tell you this to help you keep that outlaw gang away from here."

Robert thanked him and told him the information was very valuable.

Jackson was in the office when the trio returned to Newbarn. The name Samuel Flint was familiar to Jackson. "We will deal with him when the time comes," he said. "Let's just sit tight until all the trucks have returned from the long hauls, and then we will compile our information and move on. Robert, we will need your input then. I hope you will stay with us and continue your investigation. You are the professional here, and when you say the time is right for the hammer to strike, we will take care of things the mountain way. I expect Millard and John to have helpful information when they return from Chicago, but I don't know when that will be. It could be the end of the week before we see them. We will just have to be patient and wait."

Sure enough, it was late Friday night when Millard and John returned. Jackson had waited up in anticipation of seeing them. He felt strongly that, if they did not return Friday night or Saturday, something must be wrong. When they pulled into Newbarn headquarters, he could not have been happier. They looked very tired, but otherwise, all seemed well. The truck didn't even have bullet holes in it. Jackson asked them about their trip.

"It went well," said Millard. "We sold every jar of whiskey we had and could have sold more. Our only trouble was when we tangled with some drunks in a bar where we made a delivery. One of them called us a couple of mountain mules. That didn't sit well with us, especially John. He ordered the man to apologize, and that only brought a fist being thrown at him. John promptly spread the man's mouth all over his face by a very hard blow. One man standing there started to hit John from behind. It was a bad mistake for him. I just about knocked his head off in one hard swing. The other men started to move in on us but changed their minds. I guess they decided that, if we were mules, they didn't want to get kicked."

Jackson laughed and said, "I never know what to expect from you guys; always something new and different, that's for sure." He filled them in on what had happened to Horton and Jefferson.

"You should go home now and get some rest," Jackson continued. "Come by tomorrow, and we will discuss our future plans as far as possible. I am anxious for everyone involved in the long-haul operation to meet either tomorrow or Sunday and continue our plans. I am well aware that Robert will need to complete his investigation, and he will need all the information we can provide that will speed his investigation along. The longer we stay in limbo as we are now, the more dangerous things will become and could even jeopardize our long-haul ambitions."

THIRTY-SEVEN

Millard and John immediately left for home after talking to Robert on the way to their cars. They wanted him to know their desire to work as closely with him as possible. He knew exactly the message they were conveying to him. The help they could provide him, along with his working alone, would probably be the course of action. It wasn't that he wanted to exclude the other long haulers; they just did not have the experience that was needed, and three was enough for now.

As John and Millard started toward their cars, John paused for a moment and looked at Millard in a strange way, as though something important was on his mind that he wanted to say before they went their own way, but he said nothing. John drove away without another glance.

Millard drove away but not with a happy feeling inside. After stopping for a sandwich for lunch, he continued on home, realizing how nice it would be to see his family again. He had been away so much of the time during the last month or two; he had given them little thought. Soon he would be home, however, and all would be well.

As he drove down the driveway, he knew something was wrong. No one was at home—he found only a note on the door telling him that Dad was very sick and to come soon. Flora had signed the note with a PS, "Please hurry."

Millard immediately drove away without entering the house. When he arrived at Dad's home, Dad was lying propped up on a pillow covered with a sheet. His breathing was labored and raspy. Millard approached the bed and placed his hand upon Dad's chest. "How are you doing, Dad?" he asked.

"Not so good, son. You told me not to push myself too hard, but I have disobeyed you. You know what a stubborn old fool I am."

"I can't deny that you are stubborn, but you are not a fool and never have been," Millard replied as he looked him in the face and smiled. "Has Dr. Burleson been to see you today?"

"Yes, and he told me without hesitation that the outlook of my condition was not encouraging. He did give me some new kind of medicine, though, and I feel slightly better after taking it."

"Would you agree for me to take you to a good hospital where they might give you better treatment?" Millard asked.

"I would if I knew it would do any good, but I know it would not. I can feel myself slipping away, and I know there is no way of stopping what is to be. Don't worry; I have no fear of dying. You are a fine man, and all I ask of you is to see to the family as best you can. Now I think I will take a little nap."

Millard stood and looked around the room. Ma, Flora, Lee, and Grandma were sitting in the room. Cameron and Walter were both taking a nap in the room where Millard and Flora had slept after they were married. Millard walked out on the porch and Flora followed.

"He is dying, honey," she said. "Dr. Burleson said a few hours at most. He has severe heart failure, and short of a miracle, nothing more can be done."

Millard sat down on the porch and did not move for about two hours. Then Flora came and told him that Dad was gone. He still remained seated without saying a word. Flora sat down beside him. She knew nothing else to do but try to comfort him with her presence. She knew that Millard and Dad had always been very close. He had told her many times that never had so much as a harsh word come between him and Dad. Finally, she left him sitting there and set about helping Ma. She was so heartbroken Flora knew she would need her help.

The family sat for a little while, leaving Dad lying just as he was, with closed eyes and a peaceful look on his face. Flora did not know the secrets of the Holy Spirit, but she imagined that it might be lingering with him for a little while.

Finally, Millard came into the room, and after viewing Dad for a few moments, he pulled the sheet over him. Surprisingly he showed no emotion other than a painful expression on his face. Lee began sobbing quietly. He and Millard and Dad had always been very close. Now that wonderful triangle had been broken. They were a strong family, and their strong faith would pull them through just as it always did in times of sadness.

Flora decided to take the responsibility, at least for now, of helping the family with things that must be done. Millard drove down Birch Creek and notified some of the neighbors. The news spread quickly, and soon neighbors began arriving, bringing in food for the family and helping in every way possible. As was the custom, several of them would remain all night. The family gathered in the kitchen along with their preacher to make funeral arrangements. The most skilled carpenters and wood carvers in the community were waiting outside the room, knowing they would soon be called upon to construct the casket.

Flora helped as needed but did not interfere with decisions the family made. She watched Cameron and Walter to prevent a disturbance.

The funeral would be held on Sunday afternoon. Ma had one unusual request; she asked Millard to sing one of his beautiful hymns a cappella. She wanted the choir to sing also, but she insisted that he sing one final song for Dad. Dad had always looked forward on Sundays for Millard to sing with the choir, but sometimes someone in the congregation would request for him to sing a song a cappella while standing in front of the church. He never liked doing so, but he never refused because he would notice the smile on Dad's face while he sang.

Saturday morning came, and Millard decided to drive over to Newbarn and leave a note telling everyone what had happened and see what was going on over there. Jackson was there and told him he should remain with his family and not worry about things there. "I was not certain if anyone had notified you about Dad, and besides I needed to get away for a little while. This loss is mighty hard to take, and I didn't expect it."

"You never do expect something like this," replied Jackson. "And there is just no way to prepare yourself for the shock. I lost my brother many years ago, and I thought it would kill me. It took a year for me to start getting over it, and I still miss him."

"I wish you guys well, and I will return on Monday morning. I hope to hear good reports from what you have learned. I am especially optimistic about Robert. I have observed him work, and he does good work, real well. I hope we cooperate with him in every way possible. He is capable of leading us out of this unending mess that seems to haunt us so often. We already know we can hold our own with whoever is after us. They should know that by now." Normally this would bring on a good topic for conversation, but this was not the time for Millard. "Well, I will go home now and endure this sad weekend. I do wish Dad could have lived a few more years. I was going to take him on a trip out west. He always wanted to go there. I never could afford to do anything like that before."

As Millard was walking away Jackson called, "Millard, I just want you to know, as I have told you before, I sure am glad you are my friend."

"Same goes for me too, brother," replied Millard before he drove away.

Millard drove up the road to his old home place, where he and Dad had done so many things together. A sad feeling accompanied him, but in another way, he had reason to be happy. He had always heard that death was a part of living, and he believed that now. It should be a time of celebration—for having had such a wonderful father.

As he drove up in the yard, a typical scene greeted him. Neighbors and friends and relatives were sitting on the porch and inside the house. Ma had insisted upon making the detailed arrangements, which seemed to give her special closeness to Dad, and that was good.

As Millard entered the room, he was very impressed. Dad's body had been placed in a beautiful, white oak casket, with beautiful carvings of holy figures. The inside was lined with soft material and covered with silk. A veil covered the upper half of the casket and gave Dad's face an unusual ash color. Perhaps it was caused by the black material that had been placed behind the casket to seal out the light from the window behind where the casket had been placed. Millard thought the setting was very unique and appropriate. *Such sadness humankind must endure while passing through life on this earth on the trip to eternity*, he considered. Now Dad's journey was over, and this would be his last night here in his simple home he'd loved so much.

As morning came, so did the dread of the day for the family. In keeping with tradition, a few neighbors had remained up all night to comfort the family. Plenty of food had been placed on the table for all who wished to eat breakfast. Ma encouraged everyone to eat to provide sufficient strength for the day. Grandma ate very little, just what she considered enough to get by.

The church bell rang loud and clear up the valley—a reminder that church was about to begin and an invitation to all to attend. The family listened quietly, realizing that, when the bell sounded again, it would not ring but would sound the toll for Dad's last service—one toll for each year of his life. Millard had hired a sleek new hearse to carry Dad's body to the church and a limousine for the pallbearers.

It was the fanciest funeral procession anyone in the community had ever witnessed. The pallbearers wore black suits, and black suited ushers seated all who entered the church. Even Preacher Brown was a little subdued and sophisticated in his sermon. Not so with the choir; they sang songs with the utmost enthusiasm. The final song before everyone left the church was Millard's. It was Dad's favorite hymn—"Rock of Ages." He was a little nervous about singing at his own father's funeral, but Dad had asked him to sing that particular hymn at his funeral several years ago. Millard sang it superbly. Flora declared that she could hear it clearly as it carried down the valley and beyond the river. The sound was not abnormally loud, but it seemed to echo a holy message to all who heard.

After the service, the pallbearers carried Dad's casket slowly around the front of the church and to the cemetery, where four funeral home employees lowered it into the ground. Those gathered around the gravesite sang another hymn, and Reverend Brown spoke the last rites.

All was now complete. Dad was at rest near Lewis, and as Millard looked over at Lewis's grave, he was reminded of the thought he had when Lewis was buried. *Dad now belongs to the ages.*

Millard drove Ma and Flora and the boys up the road to the home where Dad had lived most of his life. How sad and empty the house seemed, although many of the neighbors and family members were there and a meal was being prepared for the family.

Millard did not want to remain there, and after quietly notifying Ma, he took Flora and the boys home. He wanted to be with his own little family, which he had been neglecting for much too long. They ate a quiet supper, and after the boys were put to bed, he and Flora went to the porch to relax and talk before going to bed.

Millard was well aware that Flora deserved to know far more than he had been telling her; she had every right to know what a dangerous game he was now involved in and that he had every reason to believe things would probably get worse before they got better. She knew he was involved in expanding their whiskey business all the way to Chicago and that they were using large trucks to make deliveries. He had told her very little about the recent trouble they had been having, and he could not reveal the full extent of what was going on until after tomorrow. She avoided harsh words that might cause Millard more pain. Robert, along with everyone involved in the long-haul expansion, was trying to figure things out, and Millard hoped they would be successful in their efforts.

They talked until late about Dad's death and family matters and then went to bed. Sleep did not come easily.

Morning came all too soon, though, and as the alarm clock sounded, Millard wondered how the events of the day would influence the days to come. He drove to work with almost overwhelming sadness. Dad's death was just now coming to bear, and it was taking its toll more than he'd expected. As he approached Newbarn's headquarters, he pulled off the road for a little while, just to pull himself together. He felt tears filling his eyes and rolling down his cheeks. After he'd composed himself, he proceeded on to work. His heart was heavy, but his face and eyes were clear. Dad was now a wonderful memory, and he would leave it that way.

When Millard reached Newbarn, he immediately entered the office area, where he was greeted and treated with utmost respect. Jackson, Robert, John, and Walter were present. Walter was there at Jackson's request. He was the most knowledgeable in the business, and Robert was the finest detective that could be found. With those present in the room, all should go well.

Everyone was waiting to hear what Detective Robert Swink had to say. They knew he was probably the key to the success or failure of their reorganization, especially the long-haul phase in which they were now so deeply involved.

Robert knew they were depending on him to solve the problems confronting them. He had been through similar situations many times but none as puzzling as this one. Jackson asked him if he would begin their discussion, and he immediately reached into his briefcase for a notebook labeled "Newbarn." It was obviously a very detailed compilation of his work since the first day he was hired. He did not have to fumble through anything to find what he wanted to present to the small group.

"Fellows," he said, "the motive of your opposition is not difficult to detect. I can sum it up in two words—power and greed. In a very short time, you have accomplished what they have been trying to do for many years. You have organized well and continue to do so. You have a fine whiskey that they cannot duplicate, and they are mad as hell."

"They can go to hell as far as we are concerned," said John.

"They want control of everything that makes large sums of money, and they are after you and will stay after you until they accomplish their goal," Robert continued.

"I hope you can help us keep them from their goal," said Jackson.

"The final decision will be yours, but I would not like to see them succeed in their efforts."

"You are telling it like it is," replied Jackson, "but if we were not willing to fight for what we have accomplished, we would never have started this expansion."

"If you want to continue as you are and establish your operation to Chicago, I believe you should show no signs of weakness or slowing up. Keep up the pace you have established and let them know that you will not be deterred," Robert continued. "You have about six or seven groups to contend with between here and Chicago. The first place you will have to sweep clear is where the most trouble has occurred from the very start of your long hauls, and that is from Maryville across the top of the mountain, where Jefferson and Horton and me had the battle with the men at the old chimney near the top of the mountain. I heard one of them say they were going to kill every damn one of us, and I am certain he meant what he said. They did wound us, but we put them on the run through the woods, leaving their cars ablaze. Some of them were wounded, including Samuel Flint from Goose Creek. Samuel didn't know they had an ambush planned, or he would have not been involved I don't think."

"Maybe we should consider giving him a break," said Millard. "He might be of help to us now that he knows about that bunch he was in with from down the mountain. He did not like them, and I think we can persuade him to provide us with information about the damn fools. Once we find out who the leaders of that group down there are, we can end their mischief rather quickly, in my opinion."

"Judging from their actions against you, I doubt they are very well organized," said Robert.

"The second hurdle we have to cross is in or near Maryville," he continued. "The leader of the men causing the trouble for us is in Maryville. The men who work for him are not very smart, but he keeps his identity well concealed. He might be connected to a line of leaders reaching all the way to Chicago, but my guess is his boss is Antonio Vitally in Memphis. Vitally is the big dog that controls everything from Memphis to St. Louis and on to Chicago."

"He sure had Millard and me fooled," said John.

"When the time comes, perhaps we can negotiate with Antonio and convince him, in a peaceful way, that we don't mean him or anyone else any harm," suggested Millard. "We'll explain that we just want to make long hauls from Spruce Willow to Chicago; we have no plans to expand any farther, and we doubt we will make a dent in his business. I doubt he will go for it, but it won't do any harm to try," Millard concluded.

"I will attempt to arrange a meeting with him and try to talk things out, and we'll see what happens," Robert said. "Just remember, we will be on the border of showing a degree of weakness here. I will try to convince him that working with us would be in the mutual interest of everyone and that he will end up making more money than ever before. I won't try to explain every detail to you now, but I will make no agreements with him without your approval. I have done this sort of maneuver many times before, and it often works. By the time we get through talking, I will convince him that we intend to continue running the same routes as we are now and that he is dealing with good, honest people.

"If everything goes well, he will be convinced that he has much to gain and nothing to lose. He will agree with nothing at that time. His mob bosses in Chicago run everything and will have given their consent to all agreements before he can meet with me again. If we get in good terms with the mob in Chicago, we will have no more trouble. Of course, we will always have to contend with small operations, which will be of little consequence.

"There might be larger mob-type operations that we do not know much about, such as that mean, unprincipled bunch who operate between Memphis and St. Louis, in Dexterville. Walter has been told that they intend to take over the whiskey business for hundreds of miles around. They intend to organize in our direction all the way to Asheville."

"They will play hell doing that," said Jackson.

"Well, I have plans for them, which I will provide for your consideration, that will take care of them very well if they make a move on this Newbarn organization," said Robert. "We have things moving along now, but I must now identify who we are up against. I have much information, but we cannot move to control our competition until we know the names and location of those devils. I will find out this information for you as soon as possible and report to you again. I thank you for allowing me to be a part of this group, and I will complete my work as rapidly as possible."

All Robert had said seemed to fall into place, except for the discouraging information he had reported about Antonio Vitally. Walter appeared perplexed about this man, who had been his friend for many years. "I would like to talk to him before we get involved in possible action against him. We are now doing a whale of an amount of business with him and his friends. I just want to go see him alone and determine what has happened to him. I will go over there tomorrow, and then we will know where he stands one way or another."

"I would not advise you to go over there alone, Dad," Jackson remarked.

"I will be all right," said Walter, "but if one of you men wants to drive me over there, I would be pleased. If Antonio has turned into an enemy, I want to know it. If he is somehow still a friend, I do not want to lose him."

"Things are changing fast," said Jackson. "From what I have heard, some people around Memphis and Chicago, mobsters mostly, will meet with you and laugh and talk and drink wine with you; then as soon as the opportunity presents itself, they'll shoot you in the back of your head."

"Damn," said Walter, "things are changing. Perhaps I had better pack my pistol when I go over there. I am going though, come hell or high water."

"I thought you were retired, Dad," replied Jackson, hoping Walter might change his mind about going.

"Well, just this one more little venture," Walter replied.

"Did you hear what he said?" Jackson said to Millard.

"I did, and I am not surprised at all," said Millard with a slight smile on his lips.

The meeting then ended with little more to say. Robert left immediately to continue his investigation. He knew the remainder of his work must be done with utmost secrecy. The chain he needed to fit together had an unknown number of missing links, and he intended to find them quickly and efficiently and fit them securely into place. Only then could he provide the leaders of Newbarn the information they must have in order to succeed in completing their reorganization and put an end to the harassment they had been subjected to. If he did not do his job well, Newbarn would be bombarded more and more by outside forces; failure would be inevitable.

The men at Newbarn did not understand all these factors until he could somehow identify their enemies and help them with a plan of action. They could handle the Blue Ridges, but from the bottom of the mountains on to Chicago would take clever doing. It could be done, and he had already decided to stay close on this case until it came to a successful conclusion. He had grown strong feelings for these good men and would not let them down.

He had changed his mind about how to approach this problem. Instead of starting at the foot of the mountains and working his way to Chicago, he would start at Chicago and work his way back from there. He desperately needed to know the names of all those involved in actions against Newbarn and exactly where Newbarn fit into their plans. If Newbarn still topped the list of concerns of too many bad characters, he might have more of a problem than he anticipated. Too many problems were coming to mind, and he did not want to overburden his mind. He decided to ease up, find a nice place to stay the night, and have some fun.

THIRTY-EIGHT

Robert continued on his journey early the following morning. He could be in Chicago by evening, allowing for three or four stops along the way.

He wasted no time after arriving at his destination and drove directly to the finest hotel in that fair city. The place was large and filled with well-dressed guests. Even the employees were neatly dressed and wore uniforms. The furniture was beautiful, and the windows, designed beautifully with colors in keeping with the hotel decor, were draped in the finest fabric. Deep, plush carpet covered the floors everywhere, keeping noise to a very comfortable level. In the very large dining rooms, people were well served on decorative tables with expensive-looking china and silverware. Everyone seemed dignified both in movement, manners, and conversation. It was like a place designed for the future. Such a grand place was perfect for what he had in mind.

Robert knew right off that he could move around pretty well unnoticed. The bar and dining room provided plenty of places to observe and meet important people and possibly establish contacts that would serve his purpose for being there.

The night he arrived he made no attempt to approach anyone. There were people in that building that could help him in every way. The problem was his to solve, and he would do so.

Morning found him sitting at the table. He had dressed well for the day, wearing a brown suit; a beige tie; well-shined, brown shoes; and a Stetson hat. He sat in the largest of the three dining rooms in the hotel at the time most businesspeople were having breakfast and readying themselves for the day.

He observed and tried to memorize as many people as he could. Then, with briefcase in hand, he left for the day. Determined to waste no time, he began moving his way around the most important section of the city, most of which was located reasonably close to the hotel where he was staying. There seemed to be no end to establishments only the rich would have reason to frequent. Luxurious theaters, grand operas, restaurants, rare antique shops, large banks, tall insurance buildings, and investment firms were only a few of the places where the wealthy could buy almost anything they desired and make financial transactions that could further enrich them. Robert knew he was in the place he needed to be. He was in the middle of a place of not only material considerations but a place where he could find the information he needed.

Late in the evening, he returned to the hotel with little to show for his efforts of the day, but many ideas had come to mind. After dinner, he went directly to his room to listen to the radio before going to bed. After double-checking the locked door and placing his pistol under his pillow, he enjoyed a comfortable night's rest.

The wide, thickly carpeted stairs and beautiful paintings were obvious to him as he descended to the dining room. He had no specific plan in mind, but he positioned himself where he could best observe goings-on that might be of interest or concern. After leisurely eating breakfast, he lingered over his coffee while pretending to read the morning paper. So far, he had noticed nothing unusual, but he knew that, when people began leaving, he would need to be alert and ready to move.

He didn't have to wait long. Businessmen who were probably traveling alone and men with their wives were leaving rapidly. As the crowd thinned out, he noticed a large number of men exiting the room and heading up the stairs, presumably to the same place.

After allowing some time to pass, he followed in the same direction they had gone, careful not to lose track of where they were going.

The men entered a room midway down the hall and locked the door behind them. Undoubtedly, something special was going on in that room, and Robert strongly suspected it was a meeting of some importance. He stood for a moment outside the door, but not a sound came through. The room was surely constructed to ensure that what was said inside remained inside. If it was a meeting, he must work fast to find out if it concerned Newbarn.

This avenue was a long shot, but he decided to pursue what was going on behind those locked doors using all his detective experience. He quickly went to his room and found an instrument in his suitcase that might just be the useful item he needed. The long, thin, metal tube was larger on the receiving end, and when placed in the outer ear, it allowed the user to hear voices or noises otherwise muted by things like heavy doors.

It worked; however, the sounds were only slightly audible. If he could find a secluded place to work with the device and successfully maneuver it into the room undetected, he might just hear what he'd come to Chicago to find out. He knew he must work fast, or all would be lost. He searched frantically for a small room or closet that would suit his purpose. After finding nothing on the same floor, he went to the next floor up.

Luck was surely with him. He soon found a storage closet directly over the meeting room below. He could remain there all day, and the material in the room was arranged perfectly to allow him to hide undetected if someone should enter. Using his utility knife, he cut a small hole between the floor and wall, working the knife all the way down until he could feel that it was very close to penetrating the meeting room ceiling. He withdrew the knife and very skillfully inserted the tube down the hole, slowly rotating it until he penetrated the ceiling. He went no farther, fearing dust may flake into the room and be noticed by someone.

Practically no voices could be heard when Robert placed the tube to his ear. Ever so carefully, he moved the device in a circular motion, hoping to clear any obstacle preventing him from hearing voices. It worked! He could now hear low, clear voices, and he readied himself to take notes.

Nothing but readings of financial reports and discussions that meant nothing to him came through. Anyone else in his position would have been discouraged, but years of such work had taught him patience.

His patience paid off after lunch; only then did he realize why the morning had been a failure. Lunch had not entered his mind, but everyone in the room below left for the dining room at the usual lunch hour.

Robert had heard such talk—almost a dialect all its own—before. Italian, Irish, and Yankee accents were almost always prominent. The morning group had taken care of the lesser important business, leaving the bosses to get right down to business without small talk and without wasting time.

Different mob bosses spoke, covering varying subjects of crime and even murder.

Midafternoon brought a familiar name and voice. "What do you have for us, Mr. Vitally?" boomed the voice of the man who'd been conducting most of the afternoon session.

"Moonshine whiskey is flowing out of the Blue Ridge Mountains like a mountain stream," Antonio told the men. "An organization called Newbarn is now expanding its operation out of the mountains at Chattanooga on through Memphis, to St. Louis, and on to Chicago. They work the mountains in high-speed automobiles, but they are using trucks to make long-haul deliveries. My sources tell me they do not intend to expand any farther than this city. They are hard to compete with because they have perfected the best quality moonshine I've ever tasted. Bonded whiskey is no match for that clean, pure stuff, and it always tastes the same. They have four trucks on the road at this time, but I am sure they will have more going soon in order to keep up with their ever-increasing demand."

"We have no choice but to stop them now," said one of the men in a loud, coarse voice.

"I believe you are correct, sir," replied Antonio. "But we must discuss all options and plan carefully before proceeding with this important issue.

"I am one of the customers of Newbarn. I have their whiskey stocked in both my warehouses and have permitted the organization to sell to all my businesses. I did this for a purpose of course. They came to me early, and I was one of their first long-haul deliveries. I knew we had to get them under our control or get our soldiers to wipe them out to the point that they no longer want to venture out of the mountains to steal our business."

Robert heard a few cheers, indicating an interest in the matter.

Then Antonio continued, "I know that most of you gentlemen have already picked up on the situation and what a problem we're facing—what allowing these mountain men to proceed could cost us. At this time, I would like to open this matter for discussion and possible solutions. Right now, Newbarn is our number one potential problem. What say you, gentleman?"

Not one word was spoken or proposal made; Robert heard only some mumbling sounds and feet shuffling.

Antonio clearly had the attention of everyone present. At first, Robert was surprised at the lack of response from those men he'd listened to so casually discuss murder. But then a surge of pride rushed through him. He was certain that the men in the room below him knew what they were up against—mountain people who could not be taken for granted.

Finally, Antonio broke the silence. "We could negotiate with them in areas of mutual interest. Or we could block their routes in various places until they give up and then offer to leave them in peace if they stay beyond Chattanooga. If they refuse to either follow our rules in our areas or stay out of our areas, then we might make an all-out assault on their headquarters and the locations where they make their whiskey."

One man spoke up. "I do not advise that one at all. The mountains are not our terrain. If we assault them there, we would be in a guerrilla-type war, and I do not know what the outcome would be. They probably would pick us off one by one with their expert marksmen."

One other man, whom Antonio addressed as Jeff, replied with a snarl, "Our organization is quite capable of destroying that two-bit mountain operation. We have always protected what is ours, and we still can. If we scout out the area and plan well, we will put things in order just like we always have."

"Oh, we could handle them if we took enough men along and scouted out the place well before going in," Antonio replied. "But blood would flow, and that's for sure. Best we stay away from that line of thought for now."

Other men in the room voiced agreement with his opinion.

Once the room was quiet again, Antonio continued. "We must take care of them soon, however, or we will lose larger sums of money fast, more than we are now."

The men all began talking at once, and then Antonio interrupted. "It doesn't look as though we can solve this problem today," he said. "Let's take care of other outstanding business and wait until our big boss, Gordon Piker, is present later on."

Even though he was a bit uncomfortable, Robert decided to wait where he was. He wanted to wait for Piker to arrive. He waited patiently for an hour or more, listening to boring gangster talk of no interest to Newbarn business.

After a while he heard the door open and men enter the room. The boss was now there, along with three or four other men whom Robert determined to be bodyguards, as he could detect different and separate voices as Piker entered the room. Robert knew from experience that bosses such as Piker always had bodyguards with them.

After clapping and handshaking and all the formalities, Piker quickly took charge, as though he were in a hurry. "I know you gentlemen have had a busy day and have covered numerous subjects in the interest of our organization. I do not have time to hear reports of all the issues you have covered today, but I will start at the top of the list. I know that the thorn in our side and festering is that hog hollow bunch of assholes in the Blue Ridge Mountains of North Carolina. I also know that they have developed a way of making white whiskey that people find hard to resist. They sell it at a reasonable price and still make enormous profits. They have just reorganized and set their sights on our fair city. They do have nerve, but I doubt they know what they are actually getting themselves into."

"Perhaps an early grave," called out one of the men.

That caused the men, including Mr. Piker, to laugh loudly.

"The solution to this problem might be rather simple," Mr. Piker said. "Suppose we visit them and make the offer that usually works for us. Explain our position to them and then offer them protection from others who will undoubtedly want to cut in and take control of their business. Then, based upon those terms, offer them safe passage from their mountains to and including Chicago for 80 percent of their profits. All who agree with this arrangement, please raise your hands."

The room went silent, and then Mr. Piker said, "Good." Robert assumed that everyone had raised his hands.

Mr. Piker continued, "Mr. Vitally, you will arrange a meeting with their head man and me in Memphis. Do you see any problems with doing that?"

"No, sir," said Mr. Vitally. "I think I can persuade them to meet in Memphis but no farther this way. They will probably want you to meet him on their turf in the mountains."

"We will not do that," said Mr. Piker. "If we go up there and something goes wrong, we might very well, from what I have heard, find our vehicles ablaze or wrecked and our asses filled with buckshot. Still, we cannot allow them to get away with things the way they are.

"After you talk with Jackson Stamey, their head man, report back to me, and while you are in the mountains, get a list of all their men in leadership positions and the areas where each one is in charge. I have been through situations similar to this several times before, and I have found, without exception, that when you determine your competition's organizational plan and the names and locations of all their leaders, you can easily confuse and defeat them."

Antonio answered, "I already have such a list of their names in my office in Memphis, and I believe it to be entirely correct. I anticipated the need for such a list after their first truck came to my office. I also have an up-to-date list of our distributors and soldiers between here and the North Carolina mountains."

"Good man, Antonio," said Mr. Piker. "Now let's take the second order of business."

Robert had heard enough, and not wanting to make any mistakes in getting clear of the storage room and on through the hotel to his car, he meticulously exited the cramped place where he'd spent most of the day. He carefully removed the listening device and covered the hole with a small piece of white tape, smudging the color to prevent discovery of that important little place. He suspected that he might need that hole again at some future date.

Carefully, he cracked the door open enough to see that the hall was clear. He went directly to his room, picked up his luggage, and headed straight to his car.

A large, black Cadillac limousine with curtains tightly drawn over the rear windows was parked near the hotel entrance. It obviously belonged to Gordon Piker. A chauffeur waited patiently, keeping watch at the same time. He was dressed in a black suit and was wearing the typical Stetson hat with the brim pulled down in the front.

Robert knew the man had seen him leave the hotel, and he quickly moved his car in the direction of the parking-lot exit and found a more secluded spot to park. The chauffeur could not see him, but he had a perfect view of the hotel entrance.

It was getting late in the afternoon by the time Mr. Piker and the men with him came out the door. Piker looked much as Robert had imagined him to look. He stood about six feet tall and had a large build; his suit, along with his alligator shoes, probably cost a fortune, and to top everything off, he was wearing an ever popular Stetson hat and smoking a large cigar. *Typical mobster and a sorry bastard at that*, thought Robert. *He considers himself to be king of a very large part of Chicago. He probably thinks we are like flies that he can swat away at his convenience.*

Robert had not forgotten Antonio Vitally and his lists of names of all the leaders of Newbarn he'd so proudly spoken of in the meeting. He needed those lists for Newbarn, and he intended to get them as soon as possible. He did not want such a list to remain in Antonio Vitally's office. Also, he wanted to know who had provided Antonio such a list.

It took him only a short time of get out of Chicago, and he was soon bound for Memphis at a high rate of speed. Realizing that he was feeling the effects of the day both physically and mentally, he slowed down and relaxed. Memphis was too far to expect to make it there before dawn, but he could get there tomorrow and, if his luck continued, steal those lists from old Vitally and be on his way to Newbarn.

When he arrived in St. Louis, he passed on through with no desire to stop. After driving about fifty more miles, he stayed the night at a small boardinghouse in a small village, and after sleeping about four hours, he continued to Memphis, stopping only for gas and a MoonPie and an orange Crush.

After reaching Memphis in record time, he thought he might have arrived early enough to complete his urgent mission before dawn. Dawn came and spoiled his early morning plans, forcing him to wait until later in the day. He dared not even drive past the warehouse until the time was right. He parked his car behind some woods near the warehouse and waited.

Soon, he heard cars drive up, and after peeking through the bushes, he knew they belonged to Jonathan Orders and Ford Simpson, who worked for Antonio Vitally. Traffic to and from the warehouse was brisk all morning. Then at noon, Jonathan and Ford promptly locked the doors and left for lunch. *It's now or never,* thought Robert.

He wasted no time in selecting the right illegal entrance key and opened the door. The warehouse office was directly ahead. It was not locked, thus allowing him quick entry. Surprisingly, he saw no sophisticated filing systems evident. A row of filing cabinets filled with folders alphabetically filed, a very large safe, and two desks were the only items of interest.

Robert went immediately to the filing cabinets and began looking through the folders. A folder labeled Newbarn almost jumped out at him. It stood up higher than the others, as though it had been used frequently. He quickly opened the folder, and right in the front was exactly what he was looking for. He flipped the folder open. To his surprise, the folder contained two lists: one containing a list of Newbarn leaders, and one list labeled "Newbarn Enemies." Just then, Robert heard a car pull into the driveway. He ran to the entrance door and locked it to avoid suspicion that there had been entry since he had been gone. An iron pipe was in the corner, and he decided to use it. He did not want his identity revealed if at all possible. A man entered and closed the door behind him; Robert hit him soundly across the top of the head. The man fell to the floor, and Robert saw that it was Jonathan Orders.

He returned to the filing cabinet and flipped through the folders looking for anything else of interest. He found only one document that seemed to be related to Newbarn. It was labeled "Walter Stamey." He did not have time to copy the document, so he decided to steal it as well. He returned the folder to the cabinet, careful to leave it exactly as he'd found it. He rapidly exited the building, leaving Jonathan unconscious.

Briskly walking to his car, Robert reached safety just in time. Three cars drove up to the warehouse just as he ducked behind the bushes. Well pleased with what he had just accomplished and happy to get away, he left Memphis as rapidly as he dared drive. He had no time to accomplish anything else.

When he was far enough away from Memphis to feel safe, he stopped at a small restaurant for lunch and to rest a short while. He had intended to travel at a moderate speed to consider all the information he's gained and see if he spotted anything else suspicious along the way.

Damn, he said to himself as he scanned the list of Newbarn's leadership. His name was the last one on the list. Someone somewhere had fingered him, and he wanted to find the person responsible. Lists such as this were always important, just as in this case he discovered that he had been identified by someone in the Mafia. The list might prove even more important when the men at Newbarn viewed it. He knew it would be dawn before he could reach Newbarn.

Robert's trip to Chicago had been a tremendous success, far more so than he had expected. He had found the origin of the trouble and identified most of the people determined to take control of Newbarn, and he had completed his mission without being detected.

On through the night he drove. It was now raining, and fog was setting in as he approached the mountains. He welcomed the fog. It shielded him from danger, even if it did cause him to drive slowly to avoid wrecking in one of the deep curves. When he crossed the mountains the fog lifted, revealing a bright moon and a beautiful, starry sky. He was glad to be returning home. Actually it was not his home, but he was beginning to consider it so. How could one not love such a place so beautiful with people so kind and wonderful in every way?

Robert reached Newbarn before light. He was surprised to find Jackson there readying things for the day. As he entered the door, Jackson was all smiles and seemed very glad to see him. "I didn't expect you back until tomorrow or later," he said as he walked forward and gave him a stout handshake. "For some reason I have been a little concerned about you. I knew you were going into dangerous places with no one covering your back. I didn't like it, but I know you like to work alone."

THIRTY-NINE

Shortly after dawn was breaking, John and Millard came in. Both were delighted to see Robert. No one asked him any questions. They were well aware that he had information but would not reveal it until a more suitable time.

Within a few minutes, the other employees were entering the storage area to load their cars and begin their route deliveries. One could easily see how happy they were in their work and how well organized things were. The reorganization of the short-haul system was working perfectly. Now if they could get the long-haul operations working as well, all would be just fine with Newbarn. Robert sat watching the well-oiled operation and considered that he would help these good men fulfill their ambitions.

After things had settled down around Newbarn and Jackson was satisfied that all the delivery routes were being covered, he came back inside. "This is a busy place as you all know," he remarked as he removed his hat and fanned his face with it.

Millard and John agreed. They had been waiting for Robert to return before taking long-haul runs and had been very aware of the amount of work Jackson had to do when they were not there to share the work. "We are mighty glad to see you return in good shape," said Millard. "I think everyone here has been a little concerned about you, and we are mighty glad to have you back."

"Was your trip successful?" Jackson asked.

"It was very successful," answered Robert. "I found very valuable information in a very short time. Luck was with me all the way, except that my name was on a list I obtained for our use. Someone has fingered me, but I will find out who it was in due time. I am positive that I was not noticed while I was in Chicago. I will give you all the details of my trip from start to finish, but I would like for Walter to be present when I do."

Jackson immediately left the room and, in a short while, returned with his father.

Walter came in and, after being greeted by everyone, took a seat at the table. "What is all this about?" he asked, a bit of concern in his voice.

"Robert just returned from his trip to Chicago," replied Jackson, "and he has important information that might be useful to us. It might help us make quick and important decisions. We did not want to continue without your knowledge and advice."

"I thank you for that consideration," replied Walter.

"Robert is going to give us the complete details of his trip, and we will go on from there," said Jackson.

Robert thanked Jackson for proceeding without delay. He then reported to Newbarn's leaders the complete details of his trip. They were all amazed at the way he'd managed to maneuver his way around in the hotel in Chicago and listen to such an important meeting without being detected and equally amazed at the way he'd obtained the information from Antonio's warehouse without getting shot.

At one point, Walter said, "You are luckier than a billy goat in a field full of nannies."

That remark brought laughter from all, especially Robert.

"The list of names is worth its weight in gold from my point of view. I can learn everything about your enemies that you want to know. It gives us a tremendous advantage, considering that they do not know we have such information. I could hardly believe they would leave such sensitive information so open to scrutiny with no measure of security. In a way, it tells me that they have gone for a long time without being challenged—so long that they have become very lax in their business and about their own safety.

"I could not resist removing the document pertaining to Walter from Antonio's files. I was afraid it might contain the names of his old girlfriends and he would never forgive me."

That again brought on much laughter, especially from Walter.

"What are we going to do with you?" Walter remarked. "You have more fun in dangerous situations than anyone I've ever known. Now I will pass the paper you gave to me around for you men to read. Antonio and I have been good friends over the years in other business ventures, and I wanted him to be aware that our organization is now making long hauls of fine whiskey and that I would like for him to try it out. He replied and invited us to stop by. His letter sounded like the same old Antonio, and I had no reason to doubt his sincerity. That goes to show how people change these days and turn from friend to foe. It appears that he is now running with the wrong crowd."

"Well, you know about him now and how close he is with at least one of the top mobsters in Chicago. I believe he will be contacting you come Monday," Robert replied. "He will not be aware of the amount of information we have on him and the Chicago bunch, and that will give us an advantage in any future contacts, that's for sure."

Jackson suggested that, for the moment, they do nothing except continuing on with business as usual, keeping their guards up. He asked the other men in the room to give their opinions and ideas.

"Millard and John made the first delivery to Antonio and liked him very well as I recall," said Jackson.

"I don't like the sorry bastard now," said Millard. "And I would like to deal with him and his employees in a rough way. I have no doubt but that they are all in this together."

"I feel the same way," John added. "And I don't like people trying to make fools out of us."

"We have sold a whale of a lot of whiskey through him," said Millard. "I am anxious to find out what he has to say when we meet him again."

"If we do indeed arrange a meeting with him, I want all in this room to be present," said Jackson. "Antonio might not agree, but we will try to maneuver him into saying yes. After the meeting, I believe we will be in a position to plan our strategy to rid ourselves of the entire bunch, unless something could be worked out to our advantage. We will just have to wait and see."

"Matters such as these are not settled overnight," Walter reminded them. "We will have to move cleverly and cautiously. After we finish up our day here, let's all go home. We'll return Monday if that is agreeable and there are no other questions."

As Millard drove home, he pondered the problems of the most wonderful job he had ever had and wanted to keep. Many men who were desperately poor were making good money now, and their families were experiencing happiness and relief from this hellfired depression. His mind wandered from his personal family life to his job, considering one situation and then another.

He was very happy to see the lights in his lovely little cabin. It hardly resembled the place they had first moved into; Flora had worked so diligently to improve it. He had helped with much of the outside work, but she had succeeded in making the entire place both useful and beautiful. As he walked through the yard, he smiled as he heard a guitar playing and three voices singing. Flora and Cameron were doing well, and Walter was doing as best he could. His sweet little voice blended in well, and his attempt at words were just fine too.

When he entered the room, they all laughed and clapped their hands. What a wonderful welcome it was.

After supper, they read stories and sang songs and played games until both boys were ready for bed.

Millard and Flora were wide awake and had no desire for bed. Millard wanted to discuss with Flora the possibility of building his dream house. "I have the money now, and I think we could build our house with a considerable amount of money left over," he told her. "And the property below us is for sale real cheap—almost a giveaway. There is a lot of acreage there too. What do you say about going ahead with it?"

"My word, honey," she said. "You hit me with so much so fast. I want to build it, but give me a little time to think about it."

"Is overnight enough time?" he asked. "I am thinking of going up to see your folks tomorrow so I can talk to Salem about it. We discussed the house some time back, and he agreed to help me with the building. I know he is a fine builder, and he could boss the entire construction. He seemed to want to do just that when we decide to build."

"I will be happy to visit them, and so will the boys," she said.

"Let's listen to the radio a little while and then go to bed," Millard replied.

The following morning, they ate breakfast and were anxious to leave. Millard and the boys were in the car, and Flora was lagging behind. Cameron and Millard both called for her to hurry.

"Wait," she said. "I will be there in a minute." She returned to the house to get extra clothes for the boys. She knew accidents always happened when they visited grandparents. Cameron especially could be depended upon to fall in cow poop or tear his pants while crawling through a barbed wire fence or some other situation.

Up the road they went, happy as could be.

When they reached Grandpa and Grandmas' house, everyone came out to greet them. Cameron was soon off to visit all the farm animals and chase the chickens and investigate everything, especially the blacksmith shop. Flora went inside to be with Martha and her sisters. Walter went with her and was passed around from lap to lap.

Salem and Millard walked around the pasture and kept watch on Cameron, making sure he didn't get into something he couldn't handle. There were some mean roosters around who would knock him down and peck him and jump up and down on him if they took a notion.

Eventually, Salem and Millard made their way to the woodshed, their favorite place. As they passed the car, Millard reached in and pulled out a quart jar of whiskey he had brought as a present to Salem.

Salem quickly opened the lid and sampled the good stuff. "Just seeing if the quality is still the same as the last," he said.

"I know what you mean," said Millard, and they both had a good laugh.

They each sat down on a chopping block and began whittling on pieces of stove wood. They talked at length about the problems at Newbarn.

"It sounds like men could end up hurt or killed if you don't come up with some kind of settlement in your negotiations," Salem said. "I don't have a good feeling about this, Millard. You be damn careful until things are in hand."

"I will be very careful" said Millard. "I always feel better after I talk to you about things like this."

Salem suspected Millard would be approaching him about building a house, so he wasn't surprised when Millard changed the subject.

"You know, Salem, other than wanting to enjoy your company, I came out here to ask you about an entirely different subject. I am ready to build that big house I have wanted to build all my life. Are you still interested in supervising the construction of the building? I don't want you to be concerned with labor on the place. I know how skilled you are in home construction among other things, and it would please me to no end if you would boss the entire project."

"I would indeed," replied Salem. "In fact, I have already given it some thought. I have a book of house plans and pictures of the kind of house you want to build. Study it over and you might find one that suits your fancy. I have never built a house quite as elaborate as those in the book, but I think I can do the job. Besides, I have all my farmwork pretty well caught up and I would like to try something else for a change."

"We will look at your book this week, and as soon as all arrangements can be made, we will be ready to begin," said Millard. "The only things that might hold us up would be conditions at work and the possibility of an early winter. If possible, I will come up next weekend and let you know how things are progressing."

On their way home, Millard told Flora the gist of the conversation with Salem.

"Are you certain about going on with this building with so many serious things going on at work at this time?" asked Flora.

"Building materials are cheap now, and labor is even cheaper. If we don't go on with the building now, it might never happen. I am convinced now is the time. I have this book about houses that Salem gave me, and I would like for you to study it closely this week and decide on one that you like. We will decide next weekend and begin building as soon as all the details have been worked out. I will wait no longer, Flora."

He was in one of those moods where he would not take no for an answer. She would say no more and do as he said. *Besides*, she thought, *it will be something indeed for poor folks like we've been to own such an elegant home overlooking a beautiful farm.*

Sunday proved to be a very pleasant, restful day. Sunday school and church services were a delight to the children and adults as well. Millard did not sing in the choir, to the disappointment of many. He wanted to sit on a bench with Flora and the boys for a change.

Walter did not understand why he was not in his place in the choir. He kept grunting and pointing at where he thought his father should be. Millard knew what he was indicating. He smiled and placed Walter on his lap.

After church, they drove Ma and Grandma home. They all missed Dad but only spoke of him in ways that brought pleasant memories to mind. Grandma was a little pale but otherwise happy and well.

Lee and his wife joined them, and they had a very nice lunch together. It was the first visit they had shared together since Dad had passed.

Millard and his family went home at midafternoon. Millard wanted to rest and think about his job and what he might do to help solve some of the problems they were encountering.

✶ ✶ ✶

As morning light appeared, Millard prepared for work and left the house without waking anyone up, not even Flora. As he drove slowly up the hill to the spot where he intended to build his house, he stopped to look about. He was very fond of that place, especially the view of the area below, which sloped toward the river and gave him such a peaceful feeling. *I will always cherish the thoughts I have here.*

He then continued on toward Newbarn, his mind quickly turning to his work and the day ahead. He wanted to have at least one sensible idea when he arrived at work, but so far, he'd come up with nothing. Perhaps something that would be of value would come to him during the morning meeting.

When he arrived at work, the route deliverymen had loaded their cars and were leaving for the day. Millard and Jackson arrived at the same time, followed by John. Millard had been taking more of the responsibility, and they were working well as a team. They completed the morning office work and prepared for their meeting. John checked the trucks over, including the new one. They would meet as soon as Walter and Robert came in.

Soon, all were sitting around the table in the office. Robert was the first to give an opinion. He wanted to take Walter to meet with Antonio Vitally. The fact that the two had been friends and that Antonio had immediately wanted to deal with Walter led Robert to believe that there might be a degree of goodwill still there. It would be a good starting point and could prove to be useful. He said to the group, "I suggest we leave as soon as possible and work with Antonio as best we can. I have other plans in mind, but some of them depend upon what happens at Walter's meeting with Antonio."

"Truly it should be Jackson making such a trip, but due to my past acquaintance with Antonio, it would be best for me to go," said Walter. "It would do little good for anyone else to negotiate with him. We will leave early in the morning, Robert, if that is all right with you."

"It might help if John and me could go along in case some extra muscle is needed, but I know Jackson needs my help. He has been overworked far too long, and John needs to keep these long-haul trucks on the road, or we will be right back to hauling with cars only," Millard remarked.

FORTY

Walter invited Robert to spend the night at his house, where they could prepare for the following day. Robert needed to fully orient Walter about what they might encounter during their trip to Memphis and what could happen at a meeting with Antonio.

Jackson was opposed to his father going off on what could be a dangerous trip, but he took comfort in the fact that Robert would be Walter's companion.

Walter was no fool, and he was aware of his intellectual assets. *We will just see how this turns out*, Walter thought to himself. He concluded that his meeting with Antonio could prove to be an interesting battle of wits.

Millard and John helped Jackson during the remainder of the day, and while working, they discussed Newbarn's progress and the options open to them after Walter and John met with Antonio.

At the end of the day, everything in and around Newbarn was in good shape. If one of the long-haul trucks returned, Millard and John would probably have to take the next long haul out. It was imperative that all new long-haul deliveries be made in a timely fashion no matter what. In spite of the adversities the organization had encountered, Newbarn was prospering—for the most part, due to the will and collective determination of the entire organization. All the workers were beating poverty, and they would not turn back.

To the surprise of his family, Millard showed up at home that evening. Flora and the boys were happy to have him home in time for supper, and they all received hugs and kisses.

It was a delightful evening, and they decided to take a short walk even though there was a chill in the air. The fire Millard had built in the heating stove made the house very cozy, and after reading a nice story to the children, they were ready for bed.

Flora asked Millard about his day, and he gave her a full report. She was not pleased with the way things were going and told him so. He paid little attention to her complaints. Plans had been made concerning his work at Newbarn, and he saw no reason to hash things over again.

"I have made a decision today," she said. "I went through the book of houses as you asked me to do. I found a house that is so beautiful I can't foresee us ever building it, but I think we can build it at a lower cost than most of the others. I want you to see it right away," she added, reaching for the book near the bed. She quickly turned to the page and pointed to the house she had selected.

"Wow," he said as he held the book closer to the lamplight. "This one would suit me just fine. We will show it to Salem soon, but I know we will want to study each one in the book many times before we make a final decision. The one I am looking at now is the one we will select I'll bet."

Again, Millard left for work early. He could feel the stress of too many things happening that needed his attention. He had no stomach for breakfast. Coffee and a donut at work might do well later on in the morning. When he arrived at work, the whole place was busy as could be. He wondered what was going on. Jackson was inside the office, and he wasted no time in going in to talk to him.

Jackson gave him a puzzled look and said, "I know what you are going to ask, and I do not know the answer. Let's go out and talk with the men."

It did not take long to find out why the men had all came to work so early.

"What's going on, fellows?" Jackson asked.

"If there is going to be a fight over Newbarn with some people from Memphis, Tennessee, we want to be in on it," Cecil Garner said with a convincing tone in his voice. "We don't want to seem out of line, but we want to help when and where you need us."

"I thank you men for you offer and dedicated service to Newbarn, but I hope we will avoid any violence. Walter and Robert are in Memphis talking with a man there who could cause us trouble, but we expect no problems. If we do, you good men will be notified, and we will take whatever action is deemed necessary. We are a team who looks after our organization, and that will continue. We have no intention of giving up our hold on the territory we have worked so hard to develop, and we know that we can depend on you good men."

As Jackson tried to put the men at ease, he could only think of what a fine, loyal group of men they were. "We will keep you informed of new developments. I know one thing; if there is any fighting to do, I would not like to be on the other side. We know you can fight and you can shoot. It sure is a comfort knowing we are all together in our work."

"We thank you for your confidence in us; you can be sure we will do our part," said Cecil.

Seemingly satisfied, the men began loading their cars. As the men drove away, they waved and voiced complimentary words to Jackson and Millard.

"Now, I wonder who told the men what is going on in Memphis," said Millard. "We haven't discussed the situation anywhere outside this room, other than any discussions Walter and Robert had after they left for Walter's home."

"No way of knowing," said Jackson. "One of our men could have been standing outside and overheard something, or it is possible that we have a spy from down under. In any case, we need to be very alert and make an all-out effort to find and get rid of any mole we might have in Newbarn."

"I honestly do not think we have a mole here," replied Millard. "If there is, we will find him; I have no doubt about that."

"John is very impressed with the new truck we purchased," Jackson told Millard. "He is determined to make our long-haul expansion a success no matter what it takes, and if one of our trucks runs into trouble while making a routine delivery, he wants to immediately go to the rescue and make certain that delivery is made to every customer on that route. The three of us will talk it over and decide if such a move would be wise."

"I think we should wait until Walter and Robert return before we decide," said Millard. "Their talk with Antonio might be very helpful to us in making further plans. We will carry on with business as usual until you return."

With that said, they proceeded to carry on with business as usual while waiting on Robert and Walter to return.

★ ★ ★

As it had many times before, Robert's fast car came in handy. Walter was amazed as they cruised along at eighty miles an hour. Robert had his reasons for such speed. He wanted to find Antonio before the day's end and arrange the meeting for the next day. He reached Memphis much earlier than even he had expected. Walter was showing signs of being road weary and prompted Robert to find a nice place for them to stay.

Walter recovered quickly and was anxious to find Antonio. Robert drove directly to the warehouse, where they were greeted by Jonathan Orders and Ford Simpson. Jonathan had a bandage around his head. The men looked rather puzzled but relaxed when Walter told them who he was, mentioning his friendship with Antonio as the reason for their visit. They all exchanged handshakes and the men did not act as though they were aware of the things that were going on between the mob and the mountain whiskey business.

Ford Simpson was apologetic and said, "I wish Antonio were here. I am sure he would be glad to see you gentlemen, but he won't return until late tonight. He has gone on a business trip, but we do not know where. He will contact me in the morning, and I am sure he will want to arrange a meeting with you."

"We are staying at the Marcus Hotel," Robert told them. "We would be grateful if someone here would inform us when the meeting has been arranged. That will give Walter a chance to recuperate from our long ride over here today."

"We will indeed," replied Jonathan.

Walter and Robert bid them a good evening and departed to eat supper and return to the hotel.

"Why in the hell did you tell them I am in need of rest?" Walter asked.

"I wanted to lure them to us rather than find conditions we don't expect if we meet on their turf. You do need to rest, and so do I. Our day was not exactly easy, you know."

"Oh shit, I might have known you had a reason for speaking up, and I'm glad you did," said Walter as he looked at Robert.

"Your face is red, and you look tired," said Robert.

"Detectives are a clever breed of people, and I am glad you are with me," said Walter, a little sadness in his voice. "I'm getting old, Robert, and this is going to be the last time I get involved in such as this. I have said that many times since I first announced my retirement, but this time I mean it." As he spoke, he looked off into the distance. "You young bucks need to take over things now. Jackson, Millard, John, and Horace Blue are more capable now of running things than I am."

"Now, I wouldn't go so far as to say that," replied Robert, "but you deserve to retire after many years of hard work and do fun things like travel or whatever you enjoy most."

✳ ✳ ✳

True to his word, Jonathan Orders knocked on the door early the next morning. He came with a message from Antonio, stating that he would prefer to meet at his warehouse office. "Antonio says that his office is quiet, secure, and a perfect place to discuss any issues without being heard by others. Most hotels like the Marcus are usually the opposite."

Walter cut his eyes at Robert before giving an answer. "We will be there within the hour," said Walter.

"I think you will be satisfied with this arrangement," said Jonathan.

"I think his office will be just fine," said Robert.

After Jonathan departed, both Walter and Robert agreed with the decision they had just made. "I really don't expect trouble, and that is a good place to meet," said Robert. "If we smell a rat, we will do what we have to."

They hurriedly ate breakfast and went to the warehouse office. Antonio met them very cordially, and everything started off in a very relaxed tone. Robert visually scanned the place as they sat down to talk. He saw nothing to be concerned about but was very alert—a trait he had become automatically accustomed to since becoming a detective.

"How are things going on the Blue Ridge?" asked Antonio.

"Things in the mountains were going very well, until we started expanding our organization," Walter answered. "We have been having some nasty trouble with people we know very little about. As you know, we now have some trucks hauling our whiskey from our mountain location to Chicago. We make a good-tasting, clean whiskey, and we have no interest in being hoggish in trying to sell it or running anyone out of business. You were our first customer in Memphis, and we have been making deliveries to you ever since.

"We thought, since our whiskey went over well here, we would try to make some sales routes in Chicago and then stop our expansion there. We have no interest in going any farther. We wanted to get your opinion about our plans. I have known you for many years and would appreciate anything you have to say about our situation. We are aware that you have connections with a mob boss in Chicago who wants to sell all the whiskey and make most of the money. We have no desire to do anything but sell some whiskey and make some money. But we will not allow him or anyone else to shove us around with intentions of taking over our business."

At that point, Robert offered a suggestion based upon the fact that he knew far more about him and the mobsters than they knew about Newbarn. Walter immediately caught on to what Robert was trying to accomplish and allowed him to continue. "Why don't you try to persuade your contacts in Chicago to meet with us on our territory in the mountains? Perhaps we could work out a business arrangement and have some fun at the same time.

"We could get acquainted and make things work out to our mutual benefit. Seldom is anything but injury or even death and loss of money gained by fighting and quarreling. And we can't forget we are operating under hard times—damned hard times."

Antonio sat listening without any reply, but Robert and Walter could sense that he was listening and thinking intently. He wondered how Walter and Robert had obtained so much information about him and the mob, and at the same time, he was considering how he might maneuver a meeting in Memphis instead of in the mountains as Robert had suggested. He concluded that his only option was to meet in Memphis. All considered, he decided to lean on his past friendship with Walter, and there was probably only two ways to accomplish that. Either he would lie like hell or he'd tell them the truth about his involvement with the mob. He decided on the latter.

"Would you be willing to meet somewhere in Memphis if I can talk Mr. Piker into doing so?" he asked. "I will tell him that you want to meet him on your turf, but I know that he will not agree. He has asked me to arrange a meeting with you folks in Chicago, and I told him I doubted you would come any farther than here in Memphis. He will expect to meet with Jackson Stamey, as head of your organization, and he will attempt to dictate the number who can attend and anything else he can get by with. I'll tell you right now, he is one dangerous son of a bitch."

At that point of the conversation, Antonio almost choked up. It was noticeable to Walter and Robert that he had been under a lot of pressure in the past and was especially so now. "I wish I had never become involved with Piker and the mob, but it is too late now." His voice shook slightly. "But I can try to help out every way I can without getting myself killed. Walter, I am so very sorry about all of this mess. I was sincere when I saw the chance to stock your fine whiskey in my warehouses and help you contact good customers. It was a good arrangement for both Newbarn and my people here in Memphis."

Neither Walter nor Robert knew exactly what to say or do at that point. Antonio did seem sincere and humble. But they were not convinced that he could be believed. After lying in a storage room all day listening to such evil men in a meeting followed by their boss, Gordon Piker, Robert was skeptical. He knew that, if things went wrong, he and Walter could very well end up in a back alley with their throats cut or shot.

"I see no other way but to invite Piker to the mountains for a meeting. If he refuses, we will meet here in this room, but there will be conditions on our part. We do not intend to drive over here and walk into an ambush like the mobs in Chicago are famous for. If they try something like that, your boss best purchase caskets for himself and those with him. Is that agreeable with you, Walter?"

"Yes, I agree, Robert, but I would like for Antonio to sincerely try to persuade Piker to come to the mountains. Tell him he will be safe and treated kindly among our people."

It was a good meeting and a friendly ending. Antonio walked with Robert and Walter to their car and assured them he would be in touch with them within two weeks or earlier if Piker was available before then. "He is a very busy man, and everything has to be done at his convenience. That is the way he is, and I do not have the authority to change policies that he has in place," said Antonio.

Before they departed, Robert said to Antonio, "Can you give us any assurance that you are not trying to deceive us? Over the years, I have concluded that it is best not to trust anyone completely."

"You can't," Antonio replied. "I am somewhat a skeptic myself, and I understand how you feel. I watch others, and they watch me. We have come to a sad part of our lives when we realize that we have only a handful of people in our lives we trust and that they are usually close family members or the people we work with—people who have proven themselves to us over and over." His answer left a sad look on his face as he turned toward his office.

"In a way I wish I had not asked him that question," said Robert. "But people like me have to set our standards and stick by them if we are to survive."

"I know," replied Walter. "I could easily have turned to that way of thinking when I was young, but I didn't, and I am glad. The world has turned unfriendly and much colder since I was a lad."

"We have had a very interesting, important day," said Robert, "and I hope it proves to be a fruitful one."

Robert and Walter encountered no problems on their return home. They wondered if word had gone out, notifying those who ordinarily wanted to harm them to back off. It was a relief to enjoy their return trip without shots being fired or some other such mischief.

They reached Newbarn in the early morning hours on Thursday. Everything at Newbarn appeared in perfect order.

Jackson was extremely glad to see them and anxious to hear a good report about all that had happened in Memphis.

"We will tell you everything later on, but we would like to go home for a little rest. We drove straight through without firing a shot," said Robert.

"That's a first," said Millard.

John was behind him and was hoping to find out what had happened in Tennessee, but he would have to wait until later in the day or early Friday.

Millard and John had both been making some short deliveries in their cars during the past few days. They were filling in for some of the men who had been sick and unable to make their rounds. An outbreak of the flu was wreaking havoc on many homes and villages, and deliveries of the men who were ill with the flu had to be made and would be.

Evening came without Walter and Robert returning to the office. Although Millard was working long hours, he had been managing to go home each night. That was of considerable comfort to him and his family. He hoped that the flu epidemic would end soon. He was second in the chain of command of Newbarn, and he had wanted to fill the position full time without so many interruptions. He had numerous ideas for improvement of their organization and wanted to implement them without further delay. John was of the same mind and wanted to help Jackson and Millard improve the business and add some his own ideas as well.

They all went home intent on returning early the following morning.

★ ★ ★

It proved not to be a promising evening for Millard. He could tell something was wrong when Flora did not greet him with her pretty smile.

"What's wrong?" he asked.

"It's Grandma," she replied. "I believe she has contracted this devilish flu that is going around everywhere. As usual, Lee came and told me. He knew I would not want to take the children over there because this flu has caused several deaths since it began."

"You made the right decision," Millard replied. "Actually, I have not had that killing flu that makes an appearance every so often."

"I have had it," said Flora. "It was a terrible time as I am sure you remember. I don't think I should go over there and chance getting the flu myself or bringing it home to the children."

Millard looked thoughtful and then said, "I could take us over, and me and the children could wait down below the house in the car. I think that would be the best thing we could do considering the dangerous circumstances. After supper, we will do just that."

Dark was approaching when they arrived at the old home place. Flora went in but did not stay very long. Grandma was sleeping, and she did not want to disturb her. Ma said she had been sick during the day. Flora did not want to remain in the house any longer than necessary due to the possibility of getting flu germs on her clothing. She made no attempt to touch Grandma, even though it saddened her not to do so.

Millard was very concerned. He asked Flora if she would mind him taking the children to her parents to stay the following day so he could bring her to help out with Grandma until he returned from work. She was very happy with that arrangement.

Millard slept uneasily and expected a difficult day.

They followed their plan when morning came. The children were delighted to visit with Grandpa and Grandma.

Flora found Grandma awake but sick. She tended her every need as best she could. Nothing they did helped, thus helping them make the decision to get a neighbor to go for Dr. Burleson. Grandma did not object, and Dr. Burleson came a few hours later. They heard his horse snort near the porch, and slowly he walked up the steps. Flora met him at the door. He was an elderly gentleman with slightly hunched shoulders; however, he looked stout and healthy.

He went directly to Grandma's room and smiled at her as he peered over his glasses. After reminding her that he had no interest in her anatomy other than for medical purposes, she allowed him to proceed with his examination but insisted on his not looking at or touching any private parts. Her examination consisted primarily of her lymph nodes, heart, lungs, abdomen, throat, blood pressure, and temperature. Dr. Burleson examined her lower extremities for swelling, as occurs with congestive heart failure. He found her to be in essentially good health considering her age and flu symptoms.

Her heart was moderately weak with murmurs; her temperature was elevated, and she had some swelling of her feet and ankles and a very swollen throat.

Dr. Burleson returned to the living room and told the family that Grandma had the flu but that it was not the kind of flu that spreads and kills like some of the epidemics in the past. He ordered continued bed rest and cough syrup, along with rubbing ointments from his own formula, aspirin, sassafras tea, and plenty of liquids. He would take no fee and left riding the same old horse that amused Grandma so much every time he came.

✷ ✷ ✷

During the morning Walter and Robert came to the office and gave a full report on their mission to Memphis. Millard, Jackson, John, and Horace Blue were astonished about what they had heard, but they did not attempt to make suggestions or express ideas or concerns about what they had heard. Now was not the time.

"There is nothing we can do about anything until we hear from Antonio," Walter told them.

Jackson decided to make as many deliveries as possible while waiting on Antonio. "While they are making decisions, whether good or bad, they are not likely to harass us. If they take two weeks to contact us, we will have a two-week window to sell a lot of whiskey," he said.

"There is one precaution we should take, and soon," Millard said. "We need a twenty-four-hour watch on Horace's whiskey making operation. If they should decide to sabotage his operation or obtain his formula for making such fine whiskey, we would have a tremendous problem."

"Damn right we would," said John.

"Well, I know one thing that will help us," Horace replied. "The formula is in my head, but having said that, they might try to beat it out of me. So I guess we need a guard or some way to protect my still and me."

"We will find someone for that job this very afternoon," Jackson quickly answered.

"See, Robert, I have been telling you what a sharp group of leaders we have in this organization," said Walter. "If one doesn't pick up on an important issue, another one does."

"Well, I think we should sell our whiskey and wait for Antonio to pay us another visit," Jackson concluded.

"Amen," replied Horace, and laughter ended the meeting.

After the meeting, John suggested to Jackson and Millard that he and Millard make a trip down the mountain past Maryville, as though they were making routine whiskey deliveries in that area. "The point being," he said, "we can determine whether we are being watched and see if they make any hostile actions against us as we return. Things are in good shape here, and I don't think it would create a hardship if we are away the remainder of the day and possibly most of the night."

"I like the idea," said Jackson. "It would provide us with information any way you look at it."

"I agree," replied Millard. "If nothing unusual occurs, I think it might give us an indication as to how the chain of command is being controlled from Memphis to points in this direction."

"It is possible that you guys could be caught up in another gun battle," said Jackson. "If and when bullets start flying, serious trouble or injuries could happen."

"We are willing to go if we are all in agreement," said Millard.

"Go as soon as possible," Jackson said. "I will inform Pop and Robert if they come by while you're away."

FORTY-ONE

Millard and John left immediately in Millard's car. Millard drove at a moderate speed down the mountain and past Maryville. From that point, they began driving through the countryside where they had established delivery routes and continued the procedure as they slowly returned to Maryville, putting themselves in noticeable places.

The following evening, as they were leaving Maryville, a police car that was very familiar to them passed them by. The two policemen in the car showed no interest at all.

"What do you make of that?" John asked Millard.

"I don't know," replied Millard. "But we had best be alert for anything to happen. These are some crazy fools over here."

"If we have no trouble from here on up the mountains, I think it will be an indication that they have received orders to call off the dogs," said John.

"I think you have got it right," said Millard. "What do you think about driving about halfway up the mountains, backing the car into the woods, and waiting for half an hour or so to see if anyone suspicious passes?"

"Sounds reasonable to me," replied John.

Millard increased his speed, and on up the mountain they went. It wasn't hard to find a good place to park and observe the road. Their many trips up and down those mountains had taught them every curve and parking place. They stopped about halfway up at a very secluded spot, where they could observe all the comings and goings without exposing themselves to passersby.

After about twenty minutes, they could see a vehicle approaching from down below. It moved unusually slow, as though the travelers were expecting to meet someone or just cautiously scouting their way up the mountain to see if anything was going on.

"I believe they are looking to see where we went," remarked John. "But why are they moving so slowly?"

"I think it is just a scouting mission and nothing else. Makes me think they have orders not to make contact but to keep check on our movements," said Millard. "Let's wait a spell and see if they return in a suspicious-acting way that might tell us something."

"Good thinking, Millard," replied John.

They waited, and sure enough, back down the mountain the same car came, moving at about the same speed.

"They are surely keeping track of us," said Millard. "Do you think they saw us, John?" he asked.

"I don't think so, but they could have. A shiny part of this car could have given us away," John replied.

They compared observations and after deciding they had accomplished all they could expect to accomplish, they returned to Newbarn.

As soon as they had driven into Newbarn headquarters, Jackson came straight to the car. He had stayed the night at the office so he could be there when they arrived. Millard immediately sensed something was wrong when he saw Jackson approaching with a solemn look on his face.

"Your brother Lee came by after you left and said your Grandma had died. I would have contacted you, but I didn't know where you might be."

"Oh my," said Millard, almost breaking out in tears. "She was a great benefactor to me and my family at a time when I was just about down and out. She took her Civil War check savings and bought the little farm and cottage where we now live. I need to go home and see what I can do for our family. Lord, what a shock."

"You go home, Millard, and do what you must do. Express my sympathy to you family and call on me if there is anything I can do," said Jackson.

"The same goes for me," said John. "I will update Jackson all about our trip and observations."

Millard drove home, harboring sadness he had experienced only a few times before. He drove home before going on to his old home place, where he had found both joy and sadness over the years. To his surprise, Flora and the boys were there waiting at the door. A wreath was on the door, and he wondered why. Flora had never done such a thing before. No one had died in their house.

Flora walked slowly toward the car to meet him. "You know about Grandma, or you wouldn't be here," she said, tears rolling down her cheeks.

The boys sat on the edge of the porch looking sad. Walter had no comprehension of death. Cameron had been introduced to death when Dad had died and knew that his grandpa had been put in the ground, but that was about all he'd understood. Now, he knew that Grandma had been done the very same way.

"What happened to cause Grandma to pass so quickly?" Millard asked Flora. "She was doing pretty well when I left, or I would not have gone away."

When they returned to the house, Flora explained what had occurred. "She died in her sleep the night before last. Dr. Burleson came over yesterday morning. He seemed as mystified as the rest of us. He told us he did not believe that people died of old age. 'Disease of some kind always takes us out of this world,' he said. And he seemed very confident in his theory. He had someone from the health department bring Dr. Sloop over to get his opinion. Ordinarily, there would be no need for a second opinion on a death of a person Grandma's age but many dreaded, deadly diseases have surfaced over the past several months. Dr. Burleson was concerned that Grandma might have contracted one of the deadly types of flu; however, she had shown no symptoms of that type of flu when he last examined her. When Dr. Sloop arrived, they scraped something from her throat and sealed it in a box to be sent to a laboratory in Asheville, I think. The man who took whatever it was wore a white coat and a mask over his face."

The two doctors had sat on the front porch until the man in the mask had returned, bringing bad news. Grandma had died with the worst type of flu known to humankind. Luckily, when they'd started ascertaining who'd had close contact with Grandma before she died, they'd determined that very few people with whom she'd been in direct contact hadn't previously been exposed to the strain and survived the epidemic. The two relieved and weary doctors had taken those who were in danger to the Spruce Willow Clinic to be isolated until the period of incubation had passed.

"The good people in this community hurriedly did everything to prepare Grandma for her funeral. I am sure you would have approved of the decisions that were made and the loving work that was done. We had graveside rites. It was much too late for a funeral inside the church, and no one wanted to bury her after dark. Beautiful songs were sung, and Reverend Brown preached a very appropriate, short sermon. I am sure Grandma would have approved. We did the very best we could do under the terrible circumstances. Ma grieved as always in her own quiet way."

Both Flora and Millard knew that the quietness of Ma's grieving did not truly reveal the grief she held inside. Ma had experienced many deaths and funerals during her long life and had learned her own quiet way of grieving.

Millard could not control his tears, even though he tried. Cameron had not seen his father cry before, but he knew how it hurt to cry. "It's all right to cry, Daddy. Mama told me so a long time ago."

They all sat on the porch until dark and the stars came out.

Flora lit a lamp, and they all went to bed without talking anymore. Their silence was saying enough. Even little Walter seemed to understand that something was different.

Millard slept sporadically, awakening often and then dozing again for short periods of time. Flora was aware of his restlessness and said a prayer for him.

The following morning, they left for the old place to be with the family. This was one of those times when families needed closeness and comfort. They stopped along the way to visit Grandma's grave. Millard was very distressed, and it showed. They did not remain at the cemetery very long before going to the home.

Grandma's chair by the fireplace was there, as though she had just gotten up to go sit on the porch. She was the last surviving Civil War widow anyone knew of anywhere in that part of the country and one of the last of a rapidly declining generation. She would not soon be forgotten.

Late in the evening, Flora found Millard sitting in Grandma's chair in a state of mourning and suggested that they go to her parents' home and stay the night. "We need to tell them about Grandma's passing. They were very fond of her, but I could not find the opportunity to get the news to them with so much going on around here."

Millard agreed immediately. "I feel like I am smothering just sitting here like this. We can come by here in the morning and take Ma home with us for as long as she will stay. I will ask Lee to stay with her tonight."

When they arrived at Flora's parents', Salem and Martha were preparing for bed and surprised to see them. Walter and Cameron were asleep, and Millard and Flora both looked very tired.

"Is something wrong?" asked Salem.

"Yes, Papa," Flora answered. "Grandma died suddenly of that horrible flu that has been going around recently. Millard was on a trip, and we had to bury her hurriedly before he came home."

FORTY-TWO

"I wish we had known of your loss; we would have tried to help out in some way," said Salem.

"Because of the spreading of that disease, I guess it was best that you did not come," Flora replied. "Dr. Burleson and Dr. Sloop wanted to prevent the spread of the disease as much as possible."

"It is a terrible loss, but Grandma had a very long life and died in her sleep. How could one ask for more?" Millard said, looking toward the floor and trying to hold back tears.

Salem went into the living room and started a fire in the fireplace. No one wanted to go to bed. The room was soon warm and cozy, and they talked of Grandma's life and all the happy and sad experiences she'd encountered during her long life. The most interesting parts of their discussion centered on the Civil War days when her husband was gone. They recalled her love for the Cherokee Indians and the sadness she'd endured when they'd been forced to leave. They knew that she never stopped praying for them every day until death intervened.

"I hope she is with them now and listening to them sing the songs as they did on that horrible day when they walked away from her home and disappeared from sight," Flora said.

It was far into the morning hours when everyone went to bed. It was a good thing they did, and Millard was glad he had brought his family there for the night.

It was the Sabbath day, but no one had the desire to attend church, even though it was the church Flora loved so well. They were still washed out from the previous day and from staying up most of the night.

After a good breakfast and lounging around for a while, they all felt much better. Cameron took off outside and tried to wreak as much havoc as he could until a big red rooster who was close by chased him and knocked him down. He was not hurt, but the tangle calmed him down a bit.

Salem and Millard went to their favorite spot, of course, the woodshed. Salem offered Millard a nip of the same whiskey Millard had given to him previously. "This might make you feel a little better. I know you must still be unnerved from the passing of you grandma. Let's just sit here and talk for a while," he said as he pushed a large piece of unsplit firewood toward his son-in-law. No sooner than they had sat down, Flora came out and sat down with them. They wondered what she had on her mind when they saw her coming.

"I came out here to remind you two that we are now ready to build our house." Actually, Flora's primary motive for coming to the woodshed was to turn Millard's attention in another direction, away from one of sadness, and toward the future and a project he had thought and dreamed of for many years of his life. He appeared to need uplifting, and the thought of his long dream coming to fruition did it. "Grandma is gone and we need to move forward," she said. "That is exactly what she would want us to do."

Salem watched Millard sit up straight and look up through the pasture.

"Oh hell," Salem said, "and I promised to boss the whole thing. What was I thinking about, Millard? You caught me at a weak moment most surely."

Millard laughed loudly, as he knew Salem could not wait to get started. Salem was a natural-born builder, among his other very proficient traits. "Flora and me have been talking about building, and she has picked out the house we like from the book you loaned us," he said to Salem. "When do you think we can start?"

"Maybe by next week," Salem answered. "The days are cooling down, and we need to get it under roof, unless you want to wait until next spring. If we can get it roughed in, we can work on the inside regardless of the cold."

Millard looked thoughtful and then said, "If we could get things going a week from tomorrow and you stayed with us for a week or two, it would put us ahead of weather. The only thing is, my work might get in the way. We are going through some troubled times over there, and things might get much worse."

"I am ready to start on the house in one week just as you said," said Salem. "I see no trouble at all, other than your problems at work. I don't think you could have picked a better time to start."

For the first time, Flora seemed genuinely excited about building the house. She knew Millard had wanted to accomplish many things and become a man of means since she'd first met him. She had thought these notions were just a product of a young man's ambitions. But knowing the good man that he was, she had since made up her mind to help him fulfill his ambitions—especially this one. He was the love of her life, and every day, usually in the morning, she stopped whatever she was doing and said a special prayer for him.

It had been a good day, even though the sadness of knowing he would never see Grandma again still lingered. The good thoughts and memories of her would remain in his mind, and that would make the difference as time passed.

Cameron wanted to remain another night at Grandpa's house, but Millard knew he needed to take his family home and prepare for another week. This week could be one of the most important weeks of his life, and he knew lives could be lost in the coming months if talks with the mob bosses from Chicago and perhaps other places did not turn out well. He knew the Newbarn men and leaders, including himself, would not back down from a fight if it came to that. In a way, he looked forward to tomorrow. Not knowing what to expect was a stressful situation to be in, and tomorrow might bring good news.

They returned home and went to bed soon thereafter. Flora did not try to initiate a conversation with him. She just held him close until he went to sleep. Afterward, she lay quietly, saying silent prayers. She had been sensing danger and knew he would be very involved in whatever was to be. She knew he was a man of leadership and never shirked his responsibilities.

He was up early and lit a lamp. He wanted to dress nicely and look the part of his position as second in command at Newbarn. Only when she knew he was ready to go out the door did she call his name and hug him tightly. She did not want to interrupt his thoughts, of which she knew he had many.

He walked to his car slowly, looking back at the house as though he had something to say. Before he got into his car, he checked his pistol and placed it under his belt. As he drove off, she watched him until he had passed the place at the top of the hill where they planned to build their new home. *Next Monday, we will start the home he has always wanted*, she thought.

As her thoughts centered upon the house, the icy fingers of fear went down her spine, and she could not shake the sense of danger. She heard Cameron begin to stir and put the thoughts in the back of her mind, resolving to consider them no more.

Millard proceeded on to work, passing the little place where he so often ate breakfast. He knew he would have little appetite until later in the day.

When he arrived at Newbarn, John was the only one there. "Howdy, Millard," he said.

"Morning, John," Millard replied.

"I didn't sleep much last night," said John, "and that does not happen to me very often. I usually sleep sound as a baby. Sometimes I wake up once to go pee."

"I suspect you were concerned about what this day might bring," Millard replied.

"Well, you are just about right. I am concerned about this day and how much I have become accustomed to Newbarn and all of the men who work here. I just couldn't find much sleep, so I got up and came on over here. My wife says I am going crazy over this place, but I am not. To be honest, I am concerned about all these good men who have families and depend on Newbarn to keep them from returning to the poverty they were suffering. I do have my blacksmith shop, but most of them have nothing."

"We have always thought the same way, John," said Millard. "I am one that had nothing until Grandma bought me that little farm I live on. She somehow got that deadly flu that is going around now. It was a blow to me, which I know will take a long time to overcome. She was fortunate in one way though; she lived one hundred years and then died in her sleep with very little suffering. That has been a comfort to our family."

Millard and John had hardly finished talking when Newbarn began buzzing with activity. The men hurriedly prepared to make their deliveries as usual and were quickly gone. They took their duties very seriously, and the success of their efforts was very obvious when the large amounts of money were counted at the end of each day. Jackson had come in and gone into the office to begin his daily chores. John and Millard helped him, and they soon had everything caught up for the morning.

When Robert and Walter came in later in the morning, they could hardly wait for everyone to gather around the table in the office and hear about the Memphis meeting. Even Horace Blue had decided to come over. He knew his whiskey operation could be in jeopardy, and he wanted to keep abreast of everything and attend every meeting until some sort of agreement or truce could be established between the parties involved. Horace was no fool by any standards, and he would protect his interests. He did not like meeting with crooks and mobsters—people he considered low-life bastards with no honor or integrity.

Robert gave a full report of the Memphis meeting, with Walter making remarks as necessary. "It was a good meeting," said Robert. "We did not expect things to go so well." He gave every detail of the meeting with complete accuracy. His remarkable memory was increasingly evident as the meeting progressed. The men were impressed and very pleased.

Now they had information sufficient to use collectively and make decisions necessary for the next meeting. Jackson was especially satisfied with the information, since he now knew that he would be the man facing Gordon Piker when they got the word from Antonio Vitally.

"Antonio will be coming over here after he receives further instructions from Piker," Walter commented. "We already know that Piker will be a hard case and want his way in every decision. It is my guess that Antonio will be over here one day next week, probably a week from today. They are concerned about us, and I don't think they will waste much time in making the necessary business decisions about us."

"One thing for certain," said Jackson. "They will not get 80 percent of our profits. Such an insulting offer could cause an end to the meeting right there, but I will be patient and hear him out."

"Debatable issues will come up," said Walter. "I have been in such situations many times over the years. You just have to feel each other out at the first of the meeting, much as prizefighters start out with a jab, and then gradually make decisions based upon what each one considers acceptable. In the end, everything usually turns out all right, but I don't know about this bunch of crooks. Jackson, you will just have to play your hand as the cards are dealt."

"If and when this meeting with Piker takes place, it sure would be nice if I had Millard and John with me or somewhere nearby," Jackson remarked. "It would make me feel better having those two old war horses to depend upon. But I know someone has to be around here to run the place, and I will do as Pop said about playing my hand as the cards are dealt. For now, let's go about selling all the whiskey we can while we are waiting for the meeting."

After the others had gone their separate ways, Jackson, Millard, and John remained in the office. "Boys, we need to do some planning and soon," Jackson said. "I did not want to reveal everything that came to mind at the meeting, but we need to take action on everything that was discussed.

"First, we need to hire a tough person to guard Horace's place at night. He has plenty of help during the daytime, but he is vulnerable at night. Do either of you know of such a person?"

"I suggest we allow Horace to pick a suitable person," said John. "Horace will know someone who lives close by and knows the country around there well. If you men agree, I will pay him a visit and work out a satisfactory solution with him."

"That will work," said Millard.

"We all agree then," said Jackson. "Thank you, John, for volunteering to handle that problem. Please go over there as soon as you can. We don't know at this time what might be coming this way with intentions to destroy our operation."

"I will go right now," said John, "and I'll return as soon as everything is well fortified over there."

"Next," Jackson continued, "we need to make a delivery to Edward Brown in St. Louis. Millard, would you and Horton Pritchard make that delivery? I am sure you will have plenty of time to return before Antonio arrives with news from Gordon Piker."

"We can move out this evening as soon as Horton returns from his daily route. He is a very cooperative man, and I am sure he will be glad to go," replied Millard. "He has recovered from his gunshot wound."

"Robert will be involved in his detective duties. We are depending on him to help guide us through these problems, and I don't expect to be disappointed," Jackson continued. "We are now in good shape until something else comes up."

"I will have the truck loaded and ready to go when Horton gets here," Millard replied.

He had a shotgun just like John's now and plenty of John's kind of ammunition. He hated the damn noisy thing, but he knew it was a necessary item at Newbarn. Every man working there now kept one in his vehicle, along with a pistol. He also went to a restaurant and bought some sandwiches and drinks. Having some food along would make the trip a little nicer, especially the first night.

He and Horton left for St. Louis shortly after Horton returned from his daily run. Horton looked tired from his many deliveries up toward Virginia, but he smiled when Millard told him of the trip ahead. He had wanted to continue on the long-haul operation from the beginning when he and Jefferson Platt had taken one of the first hauls.

Mr. Brown was not in the building, but his secretary soon contacted him, and he came over immediately from another part of town. He was very happy to receive his shipment and invited Millard and Horton into his office for a mixed drink. "How are things at Newbarn?" he asked.

"We are doing very well," answered Millard, "but we might have some trouble brewing with some people in Chicago. I can't tell you about it now, but I will fill you in later."

"When you say Chicago, you don't have to say any more," said Mr. Brown. "I have had trouble with that damn bunch ever since I first started into business for myself many years ago and still do sometimes. They don't want me to make any money at all; they want it all for themselves."

FORTY-THREE

That Mr. Brown had no use for the mob in Chicago headed by Gordon Piker was very evident. "If I can ever be of help to you good mountain men in dealing with Piker, I would welcome the chance to do so—even to the point of putting a bullet between his eyes. And I know several other men who feel the same way as I do."

Millard and Horton listened to him politely. They believed his every word, but they were reluctant to say too much for fear of revealing a bit of information that might be used against Newbarn at a later time. It was a joy to visit with him and hear some of the long stories he had to tell about the whiskey business and the good old days when things were not so complicated and men were honorable and true to their word. They made no attempt to rush their conversation with Mr. Brown and thoroughly enjoyed their time with him.

Their truck had been unloaded and was now parked in front of the building. The hour was getting late, but Mr. Brown insisted on taking them to supper before they departed the city. They accepted his invitation and enjoyed every minute they were with him. He even had a small glass of their good whiskey served with the meal. That was a thrilling experience for them, since they had never had their own product served in such a classy restaurant with a meal. They had a good laugh with Mr. Brown when the whiskey was brought to the table and they took their first sip. It was good whiskey and a fine meal, just as Mr. Brown wanted for them.

The sun was down when they departed from St. Louis. Their main interest was now centered on a safe return home. They had no way of knowing what to expect on their return trip. Again, they decided to travel as far as practical before stopping.

They passed through Memphis before gassing up and eating. They had expected no trouble but kept a close watch for anything unusual. They knew from the encounter with the four men at the store so many months ago that daylight did not provide immunity from danger. Millard adjusted the rearview mirror at an angle to keep watch on vehicles behind them. As they passed through, Memphis they were certain that Antonio Vitally was there with Gordon Piker and probably several soldiers as well. They reached Newbarn after dark.

Jackson was in the office when they arrived and was surprised to see them. "I didn't expect you guys to return until late this afternoon," he commented.

"We decided to return as fast as possible, considering things are somewhat unsettled right now," said Millard. "We had a very nice trip. Mr. Brown treated us with every courtesy, and we had no trouble at all. Crossing the mountains during the day might have prevented us from having a shoot-out. Either that or they have decided to ease up while Piker is deciding what he thinks he might do with us. Who knows what them devils are about? Guess we will know soon. Easiest trip we have made. Mr. Brown even had our truck unloaded while we sat in his office having mixed drinks."

Jackson was amused at their report of such good fortune. "Well, most of our long hauls have been peppered with blood, sweat, and gunfire. It's time we got a break for a change," he said. "I am glad you two are back," he added. "To be honest and unashamed, I say a little prayer every day for the safety of all the good men working at Newbarn."

"Have you heard from Antonio since we have been gone?" asked Millard. "I hoped he might come a little early, but I know you don't expect him until next week."

"He will probably be here about the middle of the week or maybe a little sooner," Jackson replied. "I don't like these waiting games, and I don't see the point in wanting to test people's nerves before negotiations of any kind. I have heard they think such nonsense gives them some sort of advantage. They will get no slack cut here if that is what they are expecting. The week is passing quickly, and we need to keep alert and ready to respond to anything."

Millard agreed and said, "Tomorrow is Thursday, and I will be here as early as possible to work with you in preparing for a big week ahead."

"I will come in early too, and you can depend upon help wherever I am needed," Horton added.

"How is John doing?" asked Millard.

"He has been with Horace since you left for St. Louis. He has gone over every detail concerning the security of Horace's operation. He found one entrance into the place that even Horace did not realize was there. John fixed that place with large timbers and boulders and even hung a bell connected to trip ropes all around the place. He has even been staying up most of the night keeping watch. Horace is well pleased with all that has been done. Tomorrow and Friday, John will train a new man named Ronald Barrier. After Friday, we should be as prepared for the days and weeks to come, be they good or bad."

"The day is finished and I think we should go home to our families for a change," Millard said, looking at Jackson and Horton for a nod of approval.

He quickly got one, and they closed the place securely and left for home.

Millard was halfway home before he realized how tired he was. His eyes were droopy as he reached the house. The lamps were lit, and he could hear a lot of noise inside. As he approached the door, he could hear Flora's guitar playing and two little boys singing loudly.

He softly opened the door, hoping to surprise them, but not so. They immediately saw him and tried to wrestle him to the floor.

Flora was so happy to see him she could not stop smiling and kissing him. When they quieted down, she brought him a plate of nice hot food.

"How did you know I would be home for supper?" he asked.

"I just had a feeling you would be here," she said.

Millard looked at her with love in his eyes and said, "Enough said. I know you have your feelings, and that is enough."

"I also know you have been to St. Louis, but that was not a feeling. Jackson came over and told me," she said to him.

After Cameron and Walter were put to bed, Millard and Flora sat close by the fire and talked. "Papa came over Monday morning shortly after you left and started measuring for our new house. He was very excited about the project and could not wait to get started," Flora said. "I wish Ma had not refused our offer to stay with us at the cabin. She would enjoy watching such a house being built, I am sure."

Millard nodded, and they shared a silence for a moment before Flora continued.

"Papa then went to the supply place in Spruce Willow and had enough material delivered to build the foundation. And that is not all; he worked all day Tuesday and part of today laying everything out and preparing to build the foundation. He intends to start the work as soon as he has an opportunity to consult with you. He was so happy and wants to build us a beautiful house. I know me and the boys will enjoy watching the construction work," she told him.

Millard was pleased with her comments. "If possible, I will get with him on Saturday and plan the first stages and then he can begin work immediately," he told her. "But now I need to get some sleep. Tomorrow will be a busy day, and next week we will have some serious business to take care of at Newbarn. Try not to worry about me when I don't come home at the end of the day or for several days without telling you in advance. I just don't know anything else to tell you now, except that, if you should feel unsafe around here, stay close to Salem."

They went to bed hoping everything would be all right. They held each other softly as they both prayed silent prayers that all would go well during the difficult days ahead.

When Millard arrived at work the following morning, Jackson, John, Horace, and Horton were already there. He looked at his watch to confirm that he was not late. He figured the others had not slept well and that, along with some worry thrown in, had prompted them to come to work early.

Soon the entire workforce was there and quickly loading their vehicles for their daily deliveries. Everyone in Newbarn was aware that trouble might be brewing—trouble that could interfere with Newbarn and their all-important jobs. They knew the Depression had not left, and they knew how lucky they were to have well-paying jobs. They would not go back into such poverty, even if preventing that meant risking their lives. They would protect Newbarn, and they were preparing for the worst. Their attitude was a comfort to Jackson as they worked so diligently and would not leave for home each day until they had assured themselves that everything was secure.

Horace returned to his whiskey-making after thanking John and the other leaders and expressed his confidence that they could keep the operation operating normally and secure from any invaders that might try something foolish.

John and Millard set about building a strong locust fence around the entire boundary of Newbarn. They hired two men who were especially skilled at such work to help. They built a fine-looking, stout gate with iron posts and locks capable of stopping most any trespassing vehicles.

After they were satisfied that all was well with Newbarn, they left for home and a relaxing evening. Millard and John decided to stop at the restaurant and bar where he used to stop almost every evening to do his paperwork and record his route locations. They both had a steak and a few beers and talked at length about Newbarn and what they could do to improve its operation. After drinking a few more beers, they left feeling a bit woozy. They had lifted a few more than they had intended.

When Millard got home, everyone was sleeping soundly. The house was dark, as it was not safe to burn lamps unless they were attended. He lit only one lamp to see by and then blew out the flame on the wick after getting into bed. That was all he remembered until Friday morning.

Millard had set the clock to alarm at five o'clock, and it promptly did exactly that. He was out of the bed quickly and set about dressing nicely. Flora shined his shoes and combed his hair and inspected him thoroughly for loose buttons or anything she did not like. "I feel like I am being dressed for church like you do the boys," he remarked.

"You are very handsome," she replied, "and don't you forget it."

He left for work without breakfast, hoping for a day that would bring good news and goodwill for the organization that was on the brink of providing him and his family the successful life he had worked for since the days when he was courting Flora and walking that long, dusty road to her home. He could not fail now, not now!

Flora watched him place his shotgun and pistol in his car and drive up the hill past the place they were already preparing to build the house of his dreams, and now hers also.

FORTY-FOUR

Millard and Jackson were still talking when John and Horace came in. Jackson briefly filled them in on what he and Millard had been discussing. They waited patiently until Walter and Antonio Vitally came.

Hand shakings and introductions were in order, and Antonio was given a chance to relax. They treated him with every courtesy, making him welcome in every way they could. He was well dressed and appeared to be extremely happy to be there. Coffee and ham biscuits were on the table, and everyone was eager to talk to him, making him even more comfortable. If he had been anxious about the meeting, his anxiety was now gone. "You men here in the mountains do know how to make a man feel at home," he said. "I thank you all for receiving me this way."

"No need to rush with our meeting," said Jackson. "We might just finish off these biscuits and coffee before we get started."

That was what they did.

Then Antonio started talking business. "Mr. Piker has asked me to visit with you and make an offer, which he believes will work well for all of us. He offers protection for you from here to Chicago. That means that he will not allow others to bother you as you cover the routes you currently have established. He will guarantee you safe passage all the way to and from Chicago. It will cost him considerably to provide this costly offer. Therefore, he will require 80 percent of your profits."

"Damn," said Jackson. "I believe he wants our entire operation. Did he give you permission to negotiate with us? His offer is almost insulting it is so lopsided in his favor."

"No, he did not give me an option to negotiate," replied Antonio; his voice lowering a bit. "I wish he had. I think we could work things out very well right here at this table and probably soon." He pounded the table lightly with his fist.

"Ask him to come over here and meet with us," replied Jackson.

"He has already told me that, under no circumstances, will he come over here for talks," said Antonio.

"Why not?" asked Jackson. "We will treat him kindly and drive him around to view the fall colors."

"No point in asking him," said Antonio. "He will not come. He said if he comes over here with some of his men and there is a dispute, they will be out of their territory and come back down the mountain with their cars ablaze and their asses full of buckshot."

That brought loud laughter from everyone, including Antonio and Jackson.

"He will be treated kindly if he comes over here, and I believe he would thoroughly enjoy the trip. We are civilized here in the mountains and do not like trouble," said Walter.

"He will not budge in this direction beyond Memphis for a meeting. This is the only way he will meet with you, and the meeting will be with your head man, Jackson Stamey. That is all I have been authorized to tell you; but I will tell you this, if I can see any way to make this situation easier and help make you a more reasonable offer, I will do it. I know he will be willing to make some kind of counteroffer, or he would not be willing to meet with you in Memphis. That is about all I can relate to you at this time. He might feel a little better about things when I tell him of your kind offer, but it is not likely."

"If that is the final word on his offer to meet with us, we will have to give him a reply," said Jackson. "What is your opinion, Millard?"

"I think we should meet with him, but with some stipulations. For one, there's no way you're going over yourself, Jackson, and we should not reveal who will accompany you," Millard concluded. "All Mr. Piker needs to know is that Jackson will have protection in case there is a serious dispute over that way. That shouldn't bother him too much."

"What about you, John? You are a man of wisdom," Jackson continued.

"I also think we should meet with him, but we need to be very cautious. I have heard how devious the Chicago mobs can be. They will smile at you and then walk behind you and cut your throat. Also, the 80 percent cut from our profits cannot be. But we should leave such issues open for negotiation and discuss them when we get to the meeting."

"Jackson," said Walter, "if Antonio will come to my home for supper, he can use my phone and call Mr. Piker and ask him when and where the meeting will be and tell him that you will be happy to meet with him at the place of his choice. That should answer all the questions in that regard."

"I believe that to be a reasonable course of action," answered Jackson. "I want everyone in this room to have a part in this decision," he added. "Everyone who agrees with what has been discussed here, raise your hand."

The vote showed all in agreement and well pleased with the decision.

"How soon might we expect an answer from Mr. Pike?" Walter asked.

"Probably tonight or tomorrow afternoon," said Antonio. "Believe it or not, he goes to church every Sunday. I will try to reach him tonight. If phones are working as they should and telephone operators get us connected through to Chicago, I might succeed in reaching him tonight."

"It is a good thing we have a telephone at my dad's. There are only a few around, and they are party lines, or should I say gossip lines. Conversations can be heard by anyone who wants to pick up the receiver and listen in," said Jackson. "Since this is Saturday and we have no other reason to be here, let's lock Newbarn down tight and go home."

Everyone except Millard and Jackson left quickly.

"Millard, what do you think will be the outcome of this mess?" Jackson asked.

"I believe that things will have to proceed in some sort of sequence. Antonio will have to inform us of times and places before we can make specific plans about how to proceed. I feel a little better about Antonio, but he is still a mobster and probably a loyal one, regardless of what he says. If he is a sworn member, he cannot leave the mob except through death. They would kill him in a heartbeat if they suspected he was becoming a little cozy with us. When we make our plans to go to Memphis, I do not think he should be present. Dealing with any of that mob is like dealing with the devil," replied Millard.

"I think you are right," replied Jackson. "We need Robert here to advise us. It occurred to me during the meeting that, if he could get information for us like he did when he spied on them at their big meeting in Chicago, it might give us the advantage we need. We could do that if Robert gets his ass back here before Antonio talks to old Piker."

"If you want to, go on home. I will stay here until midnight in case he comes in. If he does, I will let you know immediately," said Millard.

"That would be just fine if you want to do that, but I wouldn't stay here any longer than midnight. I will come by here early to see if Robert is here. We will just have to be watchful and very alert until we know more about what to expect," Jackson said before leaving for home.

Millard made himself a pot of coffee to help him stay awake until midnight. He did not expect Robert to return this late, but if he did, he would have something important to tell them. While he was waiting, he thought of his family and the new home he was building. His mind reverted back to the early years of his life and the hard life these mountains could force upon you without warning. Achieving success at this time in his life was, at last, not only fulfilling his ambitions but far exceeding his fondest expectations. He would continue his loyalty to Newbarn even if it meant his life. Everything had its price, and he was more than willing to pay his share for what life had graciously given to him during the last several years. Flora's prayers for him since they'd first met were being answered, and he had no reason to doubt her prayers for the future. His thoughts were causing his mind to drift as though he were in a boat at sea.

Suddenly he was awakened by a closing door in the storage area of the building. It was Robert, and the time was eleven thirty.

Robert looked as though he had been driving far too long and with little sleep. "I didn't expect to find anyone here at this hour," he said.

"I am glad to see you," said Millard, "and I know Jackson will be also. We were going to take turns waiting on you."

"Sounds like something is going on that I should know about," replied Robert.

"There is," said Millard, "but I will go fetch Jackson before we talk. No sense in going over things twice."

Millard left and returned a short while later with a sleepy-eyed Jackson. "Here he is for what he is worth," said Millard laughingly.

Millard immediately brewed a fresh pot of coffee, and along with some leftover donuts on the table, the coffee revived the trio sufficiently to carry on with business.

"What on earth is going on important enough to keep you guys up all night?" Robert asked.

Jackson couldn't keep from yawning, so Millard gave Robert a complete report on what had transpired since Antonio Vitally had shown up sooner than expected with instructions about the upcoming meeting in Memphis. "Walter invited him to stay at his home where he could use his telephone to talk to Piker and decide on a time and place for the meeting."

Robert looked puzzled and asked, "What is the urgency of all this? We can negotiate with them when a time and place is agreed upon. We need not worry about Piker's instructions and demands. All the give and take can be decided at the meeting."

"We know that, Robert, but we need your help in planning our strategy for the meeting," Jackson remarked. "Most importantly, we need more information about their plans for us and any information we can get that will help us know their intentions. In other words, we want you to spy on them again like you did before. Antonio Vitally seems to have warmed up a little in his attitude and has even hinted that he would like to be on our side. Of course, we know that cannot be. He is a mobster, and we doubt that he wants to get himself killed, which Piker and his bosses will do if he crosses them. We just feel like we are flying blind, and we need more light to work by in dealing with those hellfired bastards. We have already committed ourselves to our long-haul business, and if it takes fighting to hold on so be it."

"Give me a little time to make some decisions," said Robert. "I have been scouting all over trying to discover those responsible for attacking us as we drive up the mountains every time we return from a trip. I am closing in on them, but it is very important that I determine if they are working as an independent gang or if they have connections with others on farther west—even the mob we are trying to negotiate with now. We will discuss this in the morning if you don't mind. I will be here in the morning for a planning session."

"That sounds fine with me," replied Jackson.

"I will be here before the cock crows," said Millard.

With those words, they closed up Newbarn and departed.

Millard drove home slowly, giving himself time to think. He wanted to contribute to and influence the plans and actions taken over the next few days in a sensible, credible way. Jackson needed all the help he could get, and he would not let Jackson down.

It was past two in the morning when he reached home and eased into bed. Flora was awake as usual. She had little to say, sensing that he needed sleep to help him cope with the day. She did ask him if he wanted to attend church, although she knew he could not.

"I wish I could tell you about all that is going on, but that will have to wait," he told her. "I think I might be home sometime tomorrow, but even that is questionable. Just be patient and see to our little fellows, and I will be home as soon as possible."

"I know that, dear," she said, "and you didn't even have to say it. The boys miss you when you are gone, but I tell them you are at work, and that always seems to be enough to satisfy them. Papa came by today and looked over our site again. He is ready to begin construction on Monday as planned. He wants to hire two men who are good carpenters and fast workers Monday morning. He wanted me to get your permission, but I told him to go ahead. I knew we both wanted him to start construction as planned."

Millard gave her a quick kiss and said, "You are right, my darling wife."

Millard forgot to set the alarm clock, and he was a little later getting to work than he had planned. It didn't matter though. No one else was there either. He started making coffee and waited for more than an hour before anyone showed up.

Finally everyone drove up within minutes of each other. They had all overslept and made no apologizes at all. Jackson had gone by Walter's, only to find that Antonio had not contacted Mr. Piker.

"We will just have to wait, I guess," said Jackson. "Anyway, Mom sent us a lot of breakfast food to keep us from getting too grouchy."

"I hope this not a sign that nothing will get accomplished today," said Millard.

They waited almost another hour before Walter and Antonio appeared. They had finally talked to Mr. Piker. There had been a storm last night somewhere, and the phone lines had been down.

Everyone began talking at once before Jackson could get things started. "What did you find out?" asked Jackson after he had the others quieted.

"Did you ever see such an anxious bunch?" said Walter as he looked at Antonio.

"Don't believe so," answered Antonio, seeming amused at the group.

"Well," said Jackson, "let's allow Mr. Vitally a chance to inform us of what Mr. Piker has to say about our meeting in Memphis."

Antonio looked around at all of the men seated in the room and said, "I don't have very much to tell you except that he wants to meet us on Thursday of next week at my warehouse office at ten o'clock in the morning. He had no changes to make to his previous offer and says he will not compromise."

"To hell with him," said John and then caught himself and quickly apologized for his remark.

"We know these are just words and Mr. Piker will no doubt be flexible," said Jackson. "Do we agree to meet with him in Memphis?" he asked the men. "I know the final decision is mine, but I want your opinion."

The men all raised their hands in agreement, and Jackson asked Antonio to inform Mr. Piker of their decision.

"I will do so indeed," said Antonio, "and I will also inform him that he will be meeting with gentlemen; although he has indicated he will only meet with Jackson, I doubt that he will stick with that requirement."

After everyone had had his chance to express his opinion, Walter and Antonio left.

Robert had not actually attended the meeting. He was in a small room close by and could hear all that was said. After Walter and Antonio had left, he came out to talk with the group. He was overjoyed that Mr. Piker had set the meeting for the following Thursday. "That will give me time to do some spying in Memphis and then drive on to Chicago and spy on their meeting," Robert told them. "Hopefully I will have valuable information that will prove useful to you in the meeting with Piker. We have to keep ahead of these damned rascals, and this should help us to do so at a critical time. Actually, all I want to do in Memphis is follow Antonio around and see where he goes and what he does after he leaves here. I don't fully trust him yet and probably never will. He could easily get us killed if we are reading him wrong. Never trust a mobster or a former mobster."

Jackson was pleased with how the meeting had gone and how quickly they had accomplished all they had needed to do for the day. "Let's go home and relax and get a good night's rest. Then we'll return here in the morning."

Flora and the boys saw Millard coming down the road toward the house and began waving at him and running toward the car. What a wonderful afternoon they had. Millard could not talk the boys out of going to throw rocks and wading in the river. Afterward came the highlight of the day—ice cream and chocolate cake at their favorite place in Spruce Willow.

As they returned home, they were surprised to see Salem looking over the place where he would start building their home beginning on Monday. Salem wanted to look the place over again and talk with Millard and Flora to give them an opportunity to make any changes in plans before he got started. They wanted him to build it just as he had in mind.

Millard looked out over what would be fields and pastureland with a barn and outbuildings and the river winding around the lower ridge. He hoped he could purchase all the land he needed to complete the scene. He would bargain for the land the following week if he had time.

Salem ate supper with them, and after playing with the boys, he left for home.

"We will see you on Monday," they yelled as he left.

The sun was sinking as they returned to the cabin. "I don't ever want anything to happen to this house," Flora remarked. "I had rather live in it always rather than let it go."

"We won't let it go," replied Millard, "and that's a promise."

Millard and Flora went to sleep with few words to say. She knew he was mentally tired, and she wanted all this bickering about whiskey selling to stop soon. Millard had his heart in this dealing with the mob, and she just wanted it to go away. She had felt for a long time that there would be killings before it all ended.

FORTY-FIVE

"Antonio is leaving soon, probably after your mother persuades him to eat lunch and packs a bagged meal for him to eat on the way," Robert said with a smile the next day. "I will be waiting for him along the way, and I'll follow him all the way to Memphis. I want to keep a record of every place he stops, but he will not know I am anywhere near him. You know, fellows, I think we will bring this thing to an end reasonably soon. I can feel things coming together and see patterns established. We will just have to be patient and use our heads." He grinned. "If patience don't work, we can always get just as rough as we need to.

"Actually, we could assassinate Antonio and Piker if we have to and let the blame fall in some other direction. They are not as invulnerable as they want everyone to think. I discovered that during the day I listened to their meeting in Chicago. All that bullshit about everyone playing by the rules meant little to me. Actually, I could have picked off Piker as he left the hotel that evening and been on my way to St. Louis before they figured out what had happened, much less, who'd fired the shot. Over the years, he has become careless, making him very vulnerable."

As he turned to leave, Robert reminded Jackson not to be concerned about knowing how to contact him in Memphis. "I will find you when the time is right. See you in Memphis."

"We need to get our act together here at home, and then we will have accomplished all we can today and I will be glad," said Jackson. "Millard and me will leave for Memphis early Tuesday morning. I would feel better if John could go with us, but someone has to manage things here at Newbarn, and John is third in command, and very competent I must add. Is that arrangement agreeable with you two?" he asked, looking at Millard and John.

They both nodded in agreement.

"There would be fighting for sure if me and Millard both went with you. Fighting and shooting and such seem to follow us around when we are together," John replied with a laugh.

"We always take care of business though," said Millard, "and that is a fact. I always like my back covered in such a situation, but Robert will be there, and things will probably go well."

"If there is nothing else that needs to be talked out, I think we should all go home. We still have most of Sunday left," Jackson concluded.

Millard was delighted to get home in time for dinner and hurry on to see Ma. She was doing well and had been to church. The house had an emptiness about it, and Millard did not like the feeling.

Flora had a similar feeling. Lewis, Dad, and Grandma were all gone in such a brief time.

Millard suddenly asked Ma if she would like to go with them to visit Flora's folks. Flora thought it was a great idea, and Ma was very agreeable. "I have not been off this place in so very long, and it would be wonderful to see Salem and Martha."

They immediately headed up the road with little Walter gleefully sitting on Ma's lap.

Seeing the group pull up was a wonderful surprise to Salem and Martha, and they had a delightful visit together. Of course, Salem and Millard headed to the woodshed for their usual separate visit. The women had apple pie and tried to catch up on all the gossip.

Millard handed Salem a quart of whiskey, and after they'd each taken a snort, they started talking about the house.

Salem was still ecstatic about starting construction the next day. "Everything is ready to go," he said. "I would like the house to be completed by Christmas, but that would be hurrying it a bit, I suppose. I hired one more man to help out, and I think you will be pleased. He is the finest mason I know, and I hired him to construct the rock foundation and help put the sills in place only. After that, I will have to see how things are working out before seeing if we need another carpenter or two." Salem picked up his knife and began to whittle. "Millard," he said after a moment, "it is pitiful to see how this depression is hurting people. Every time I go over to check on something at the house site, several men come by desperate for work. It sickens me to turn such good, able-bodied men away. It is good that you will be providing work for a few of them for a short while."

"Temporary work is better than nothing," replied Millard. "I thought I would never find work. At times, I thought I was losing my mind, and I think I did get a little sick in the head a few times. I have seen so much poverty caused by this depression since I went to work for Newbarn I have actually gotten a little used to it." He sighed. "Speaking of Newbarn, I will be leaving for a meeting in Memphis this Thursday. The hell of it is, we are meeting with a big mob boss from Chicago. It is the first meeting we have had with him, and we don't expect trouble. We have a detective spying on them to get information that will be of value to us. I will get word to you soon after I return."

"Damn, Millard, you are getting in deeper and deeper in this stuff," said Salem. "I don't know much about mob activity, but I have read and heard bad things about them. From what I do know, they will kill you without blinking an eye. You be careful; even more, maybe you ought to quit before you get yourself killed."

"I can't, Salem. There is no going back to my old way of life. Don't worry too much. We might settle this dispute with the mob quickly and put it behind us."

After their visit was over and the children had received a dozen or more kisses, they were on their way home. They took Ma home and continued on their way. Millard had tried to get her to spend the night with them, but she'd declined, saying she needed to be at home to look after things. Millard had built a fire to eliminate the evening chill for Ma before they left.

"After we build our new house, I think we should move Ma in with us," Flora said to Millard. "She is getting too old to be alone, and I know we would enjoy having her live with us."

"I have been thinking about doing that for some time now," Millard replied.

After they arrived at home and put the children to bed, they sat on the front porch to watch the full moon and star-filled sky. "Flora, if all goes well, I will return home on Friday night or sometime Saturday. Jackson and me are going, but Robert will be watching out for us while we are there. I think trouble will stay away this time. I can hardly wait to return and see the house under construction."

Millard left for work early the next morning. Flora watched him with his small suitcase and guns. He did not know she was watching, but she was not only watching; she was praying a short, humble prayer for his safe return.

When he arrived at Newbarn, Jackson was ready to leave and seemed somewhat anxious to do so. John was also there, planning for the week ahead. Jackson and Millard wasted no time in leaving for Memphis. Millard drove his car. They might need speed, and his car was the fastest one at Newbarn. "We will reach Memphis easily by tomorrow evening," he said to Jackson. "I am glad we are not driving one of the trucks. They are kind of slow, especially when fully loaded, and if not held at a slow speed downhill, I think they would turn over if you enter a sharp curve too fast."

Meanwhile, Antonio Vitally was now well on his way to Memphis with Robert following, using maneuvers to prevent detection by Antonio. To his surprise, Antonio had stopped very few places so far. In Maryville, he'd stopped and talked to the store owner without making a purchase. The owner was the same person who'd acted very suspicious when Robert was there once before and had watched him as he left, showing an uncommon interest in him.

Antonio stopped several other places that were obviously of no concern. Robert continued following him to his warehouse and positioned himself where he could observe his activities and remain concealed. Antonio remained in the warehouse until dark and then went home. It was very important to Robert to know where he lived so that he could continue following him the next morning. The day had ended very successfully. Robert was exactly where he needed to be, and Millard and Jackson had settled in at a nice, little hotel close enough to reach Memphis the following day.

Robert dreaded tomorrow for some reason. He knew he probably would not have the luck he'd had when he'd spied on the meeting of the mob the last time. He had experienced similar feelings before when he knew he would be in a dangerous situation, so he just let his concerns pass. He decided to rise early and eat a nourishing breakfast to avoid discomfort from hunger during the day.

He did just that and returned in plenty of time to see Antonio come out of his house, dressed in an expensive-looking suit and hat and shoes. He was headed to the same hotel and probably the same room where the last meeting was held. Robert carefully tailed him, without stopping, and parked in the same place where he had watched Piker exit the hotel after the last meeting he had spied on. He walked directly into the hotel and ordered a light lunch to keep from drawing attention to himself sitting at an empty table. It was essentially a repeat of the way he'd handled things when he was on the previous spying mission.

As soon as the lunch crowd had thinned out, Robert slowly ascended the stairs to the hallway leading to the storage room where he had hidden before and listened to the ridiculous mob meeting. He entered the room and found the hole in the floor was just as he had left it; if anyone had disturbed the room at all, it was not obvious. He removed his pistol from his shoulder holster, installed the silencer, and placed it beside him, sitting down in the most inconspicuous place in the room to wait. An hour passed before he heard noises in the meeting room below. He quickly lay down with his ear over the hole in the floor.

This time, no one called the meeting to order as Antonio had before. Soon, the door opened again, and he could hear a grand entrance of several men as before, but this time he could hear Antonio talking. Robert knew the most important part of the meeting would be first, and it was.

Antonio called the meeting to order, and Mr. Piker began speaking. "We will discuss our whiskey business first," he said, "which brings me to the bunch of hillbillies in the Blue Ridge Mountains. Mr. Vitally has been over there to meet with them, so I will let him tell us of his mountain experience. I see no holes in him, so I suppose things went pretty well."

That remark brought loud laughter from the group.

Surprisingly, Antonio reported his meeting with the leaders of Newbarn just as it had happened. He told of how kindly and respectfully he had been treated and how he had enjoyed his stay.

He said, "They acted as gentlemen in every way and sent their regards to Mr. Piker. But make no mistake; they will not accept all that we want. They will come to the meeting and discuss each of our concerns and give a reply to each one. They did not say in so many words, but they implied that, after the concerns, negotiations would be in order. There was no mention of any agreement with any of our concerns or demands."

"Well, that ends that for now," said Mr. Piker, his tone sounding angry. "Antonio and I will meet with them at Antonio's warehouse in Memphis at ten o'clock on Thursday. Who knows? We might work out something without having to knock them off one by one. I have just about had all I intend to take from those hillbillies who have the audacity to think they can come over here in our country and negotiate with us on equal terms. To hell with them. They deserve no more attention from us at this time."

That statement made Robert angry to no end.

The subject of the meeting changed, and Robert stood to leave. Just then, a large, well-dressed man suddenly opened the door. He was a private security agent hired by the hotel to watch over every part of the hotel. He had discovered that someone had been hiding in the closet several days ago, and the hotel wanted to eliminate that security risk and the possible damage it could do to much of their business—especially with such groups as the Mafia, who met there regularly, depending upon the security the hotel provided.

The agent's gun was already in his hand, and Robert knew instinctively that the man was there to kill him. The man moved entirely too slow. Robert fired three shots in rapid succession. Two bullets hit the man in the head, and the third pierced his heart. Robert covered the man with a large piece of rug and tried to make it look as nothing was underneath. The silencer on his gun had prevented the shots from being heard.

His heart was racing as he started to leave the storage room. He thought someone was coming down the hall but listened carefully again and heard nothing. He walked very deliberately down the hall and down the wide stairway, stopping to buy a pack of gum as he walked toward the door. He was reasonably certain that no one had noticed him enough to have any concerns. When he reached his car, he sat quietly for several minutes—long enough to compose himself and clear his head from that musty closet he had been in most of the day.

His mission in Chicago was complete, and he sped out of that city headed for St. Louis. It was getting late when he reached his destination, and he was feeling the psychological effects of having to kill a man. It wasn't his first kill and probably would not be his last, but he had already concluded that it was something he would never get used to.

The first thing he did the following morning was to purchase a Chicago newspaper. He turned to the crime section, and there it was—the picture of a murdered man and a lengthy article about what an outstanding man and wonderful citizen he had been.

"Wonderful citizen like hell," Robert mumbled. *The world would be far better off without wonderful citizens like him. I will consider him no more,* he thought as he threw the paper in the trash can.

He took his time driving to Memphis, stopping every so often for snacks and relaxation. He arrived in Memphis in plenty of time to carefully check the area around Antonio's warehouse, looking for anything out of the ordinary that might make a difference in case of trouble.

He located Jackson and Millard, and the men met and went over their plan carefully. Then Robert took Jackson and Millard back to their hotel but decided it best that he find other quarters. He knew that it would be best for the three of them not to be seen together this close to the meeting and decided to make no contact until after the meeting was over.

A good night's sleep did them all good. Millard and Jackson were at Antonio's warehouse on time, and Mr. Piker and two overweight bodyguards arrived about half an hour later. Millard started to ask that one of the bodyguards leave the building but quickly decided that it was not a good idea. They had Robert outside, and that was enough. Mr. Piker was very cordial to them, but the bodyguards stood stone-faced, and Mr. Piker did not introduce them.

FORTY-SIX

"You have fine moonshine whiskey, and you seem intent on running us out of the whiskey business, I do believe," said Mr. Piker.

"We are doing no such thing," answered Jackson. "We have every right to make and sell our product the same as you, and we intend to continue doing so. We have expanded recently, but we have no plans to expand any farther than Chicago. We sell our whiskey over the Blue Ridge Mountains and continue down to Chattanooga and then across to Memphis and on up through St. Louis to Chicago. We are a small business compared to your organization, and I see no threat to you whatsoever."

As Jackson looked around, he could see that someone had created a pleasant atmosphere for the meeting. The table and chairs were expensive and sitting on a nice, large, plush rug. A sofa and chairs had been placed attractively around, and lamps sitting on small tables gave soft light.

"We will allow you to keep the same routes you have established, and we will allow no one to bother you as you cover the routes you have established. But providing such protection is a considerable cost to us. Other eyes are watching you with mischief on their minds, and they will not leave you alone unless you share with them," said Mr. Piker.

"Are you at liberty to share the names of those people with us?" Millard asked.

"Not at this time I cannot," answered Mr. Piker.

"We are often attacked when we do business west of the Blue Ridge Mountains, and we do not understand why," Millard continued. "There is plenty of business and no reason to quarrel. It seems to us that some people want all the business and intend to allow no competition. We do not believe things should be that way, and we will not tolerate such selfish behavior toward us."

"I am sorry you feel that way, but we intend to keep on controlling the white whiskey distribution, and that is all there is to it. We will, however, try to work out a fair deal with you, if you are reasonable and don't try to take over what we have worked for all these years," said Piker, his coarse voice intimidating and loud and a firm, determined look on his face. He did not smile, and his eyes glared as he looked straight into the faces of the men across the table.

"Tell us what you consider to be a fair deal," Millard replied. "I think we are all aware that this comes down to money and power."

"Yes, it does," said Jackson, a bit of anger in his voice, "and we believe you are a greedy and selfish man who wants it all—both power and money. Just how much do you have in mind to provide us with protection from predators and lazy asses who want us to do all the work and hand over most of our profits to them? I understand you have offered protection for the ridiculous price of 80 percent of our profits.

"Do you actually expect us to agree to your offer?" he asked.

Piker stood up and pounded his fist on the table. "You will or suffer the consequences," he growled.

Jackson and Millard stood when Piker did. Both looked him in the face but said nothing. The two bodyguards moved closer to the table in an intimidating manner. A silence came and Jackson tried to use it to some advantage in bringing order. "Let's remember our manners and discuss this like men of honor," he said, "and just maybe we can work something out. Our problem is the protection fees you are asking. We are aware that you have people stationed and doing business with you all along our route to the Blue Ridge Mountains. Some of the men patrol the route and look out for your best interest already. So you have nothing to lose and a lot of money to gain from us."

Piker sat quietly with no answer, as if he realized that they had him figured out and didn't know exactly what to say.

"We could use some protection but not 80 percent worth. The highest I will pay is 20 percent, and that is my first and final offer," said Jackson.

"Hell no," said Piker, his face getting redder and redder.

"Well then," said Jackson, "this meeting is over. If you change your mind, you know where to find us.

"Only one more thing," Jackson said as he stood up as if to leave and then turned slowly and menacingly back to face Piker, raising himself up to his full height and speaking slowly and clearly, "if you try stopping us from doing business along our present routes, I will make it so damned hard on you to do business from Chicago to our mountains that you will have to shut down your whiskey operation in the southeast altogether."

After they left Mr. Piker and his two goons sitting there, Millard and Jackson kept watch over their shoulders. As mad as Piker was, they thought he might send his bodyguards out the door with guns blazing. It would have been a bad move for them, though. Robert was close, and they both had their hands on their shoulder-holstered guns.

"If they come out that door with guns firing, shoot to kill," said Jackson.

At that time, Robert quickly pulled his car out from behind the tall bushes and motioned them to get in. "I will take you to your car," he said. "Three of Piker's men are in a car parked around the building. If trouble had started, I am sure they would have come straight after you, and you probably couldn't get away fast enough to prevent getting hit."

Robert took them straight to their car and advised them to head for home. "I will follow you but not too close at first. I want to spy on Piker and his men before they leave for Memphis. And we need to know more about Antonio and how Piker is using him against us. I will glean all the information I can from Piker and Antonio, but they will not know I am around, and then I will catch up with you before you reach the mountains."

"If you don't catch up with us, we will wait on you somewhere. We will not leave you in danger not knowing where you are," Millard replied.

Without saying a word, Robert was gone.

Robert could not keep his mind off Antonio Vitally. He knew he must discover what Antonio was about. After Millard and Jackson had left, he kept expecting Piker and his men to leave also, but they did not. Even the men waiting outside the warehouse left their cars and went inside. Fortunately, none of them had seen Robert when he'd come to the rescue of Millard and Jackson as they left the meeting and they had no idea he was even in Memphis. In fact, he was reasonably certain none of them actually knew him.

Soon Vitally, Jonathan Orders, and Ford Simpson showed up and went inside. Robert knew he desperately needed to hear what was being discussed in there. He wasted no time; it was now or never. He parked his car in a very secluded spot not far from the warehouse, where he could observe the front of the building from a side view. It was a perfect place to hide. He could see who came and who left the building clearly, but it would take a special effort to notice him sitting there. No one else came, and shortly, the entire group came out discussing where they should eat supper. From the gist of their conversation, it was obvious they intended to return to the warehouse office after supper.

Robert again knew he must move quickly. Many hiding places were inside that building, and he already had one in mind. He used his special key and let himself inside and used his flashlight to make sure everything was as he had remembered it. He decided to conceal himself about thirty feet from the meeting table behind the filing cabinets. He found an old quilt to cover him and to smother any noises he might accidently make, such as a sneeze. He checked his pistol and then placed beside him a .45-caliber submachine gun with a long fully loaded magazine holding thirty rounds of ammunition. He checked and double-checked everything. The machine gun gave him considerable comfort; he would have felt even better if he hadn't had only very little practice with it. But it was a rather simple gun to operate and very reliable.

The mobsters had been gone less than an hour when Robert heard them drive up. Lights came on, and they continued their meeting. Several belches and farts could be heard, probably from the two overweight bodyguards with Piker.

"We need to finish up with this meeting as soon as possible," Piker remarked. "I have business in Chicago tomorrow evening."

Robert recognized Antonio's voice saying, "What do you fellows think we should do with the mountain men? They are killing our profits. The big boys in Chicago are getting mad as hell about it."

"Well, no use wasting our time trying to flush them out of the mountains," said Piker. "I am in favor of stopping them after they leave the mountains. Their trucks will be fully loaded as they head for Memphis, and I think a well-planned ambush might just persuade them to confine their business within the mountains. Don't mess around with them. Blow their trucks all to hell. That would be a tremendous loss, and I doubt they could sustain such financial losses very long."

Antonio spoke again. "That would be the most drastic step of all, Mr. Piker. Perhaps if I contacted them again and offered them a 50 percent split instead of 80 they might just agree. Judging from the success with their whiskey sales, we might just end up making more than we are now. If they would sell us an agreed amount of their whiskey at below wholesale prices and hand over 50 percent of their profits, I believe we would come out on top and their profits would still be as much or more than they are now and without violence."

"No," replied Piker without pausing to even consider what Antonio had just said. "I have tried these sorts of negotiations before, and they never work out. We would be bickering back and forth a year from now while they are making money hand over fist, and the anger of our organization would be intolerable. It is a matter of principal as well. We just can't take that chance. Let's get this thing settled right away. Call Jackson Stamey tonight and tell him our offer is final, but emphasize that we will protect them from those who would do them harm and he can count on that."

The meeting ended with much less discussion than Robert had anticipated, but it was over. They turned out the lights, and as they locked the door, Robert stood up to leave. It was very dark, and as Robert walked toward the door, he tripped over something that made a loud clanging noise.

The men were getting into their cars when they heard the noise, and all came running to the front door. Robert stood close to the wall so he would have a chance to run after they came in. He was in a dangerous situation, and he knew it. But to his surprise, every one of the men ran inside the building and started fumbling for the light switch. Antonio had to squeeze himself around them to reach the switch.

Before the lights came on, Robert counted to three and took a deep breath. He barreled through the door, barely hearing it slam against the wall behind him. His jacket was blowing behind him as he dashed toward his car, and his footsteps echoed on the macadam.

The mobsters ran after him, firing their pistols. Robert jumped behind a tree and opened up on them with his machine gun. They ran in the opposite direction toward the other side of the building. Robert knew they would run around the building and fire at him from a better position. That gave him time to reach his car, but he did not leave until they came around the building, trying to find shelter and shoot in his direction. He fired another burst, spraying bullets all over the general area where they were trying to hide.

Robert's course of action turned out well for him. He'd bought himself just enough time to speed out of his hiding place and leave the area, squealing tires as he went.

✶ ✶ ✶

The mobsters made no attempt to chase after him; they knew from the sound of that car that they had no chance of catching him.

"Who in the hell could that have been?" asked Antonio.

"I don't know," said Piker, "but we need to find out."

"I don't believe it was one of the mountain men," replied Antonio. "They don't know this country well enough to pull a stunt like this, and it just ain't their style of doing things."

"Well," said Piker, "it was either a burglar, which I doubt, or someone with a specific reason for being here.

"It very well could be one of those wild bastards from Dexterville who have been bragging that they intend to take over the whiskey business for several hundred miles around," Mr. Piker added, "but they are so damned crazy I don't think they have sense enough to pull off something like this. The person who came out of that warehouse tonight was a professional, and a good one at his work too; that's for sure."

"I will try to put a mole inside their gang if I can and see what they are doing besides bragging," said Antonio. "We said nothing that would be of interest to them, but I agree with you, Mr. Piker; we do need to find out who it was and what they were after. I will do my best to find our spy."

FORTY-SEVEN

As Robert sped out of Memphis, he considered how lucky he was. He always managed to squeeze himself out of dangerous situations, but this was one of the uglier ones. If they had caught him, they would have either killed him or beat him until he told them everything he ever knew. Robert steadied his shaking hand on the wheel and took several deep breaths. His shirt was soaked, and he could feel rivulets of sweat trickling down his spine. He squeezed his eyes shut and tried not to cry as he thought about what would have happened if they had caught him.

Robert's heart was racing extremely fast, indicating that he was having a panic attack. He felt dizzy, and his eyes felt blurred. Robert pulled over to the side of the road, and after sitting a few minutes with his head leaning on the steering wheel, he could feel his heart slowing, and he began to feel better.

He was now tired but knew he needed to catch up with Jackson and Millard as soon as possible. He settled for coffee and a hamburger at a small roadside café and then headed for the mountains. Jackson and Millard intended to wait for him there, and he was going to be terribly late. Nevertheless, he knew they would be there or headed back to look for him. He set a steady speed and kept watch as it got later to avoid passing them in the opposite direction.

On through the night he drove thinking of the countless times he had, out of necessity, driven through the night all alone like this. He liked it this way, but this night was different. Somewhere up ahead, two wonderful, honorable men were waiting to see him safely home. He had not had a feeling like this since being on the battlefront in World War I when he and his comrades looked after each other as best they could. Most of the men he knew there were killed in that war or had died since. Maybe that was why he liked working alone. He did not want to relive those nights following the war when he would wake up worrying about them and the horrible dreams and nightmares about them and the events surrounding so many good men being killed. Even seeing the enemy soldiers die under such terrible conditions had been hard. But it was all over now. The dreams and nightmares were gone, and he hated the enemy no more.

✳ ✳ ✳

Jackson and Millard had reached the foot of the Blue Ridge Mountains now and were waiting for Robert. It was three in the morning, and he still had not showed. They both knew they would remain there in that secluded place beside the road until he came. They had been taking turns for over three hours dozing and keeping watch to assure he did not pass them by.

It was almost four before he came. They knew it was him by the fast approaching headlights of his speeding automobile headed for the mountains. They flashed their headlights to signal him their position.

He stopped and got out of the car to stretch a bit and speak to the boys.

"What has been keeping you so long?" said Millard. "We considered going home and fetching the coonhounds to help us find you."

"If you don't mind, one of us will drive your car to allow you some relief from that long drive," Jackson added. "In any case, let's go home and try to get some rest."

"That sounds good to me," replied Robert. "I just went through one hell of an ordeal."

They immediately headed across the mountain and on to Newbarn. They had not expected trouble as they drove home, and none came. What a relief not to hear gunfire coming in their direction. It would be nice when they reached the point where they could go into legitimate business like ordinary folks. But ordinary folks did not peddle moonshine and shoot at each other like they did. If unscrupulous men would leave them alone, they could accomplish their goal of legitimate business much sooner than they'd first thought.

It was past daybreak and the sun had started its journey across the sky as they arrived at Newbarn. The place was busy as a hive of honeybees. The cars were loaded and moving out to start their daily deliveries.

John came out to greet them with a smile and a handshake. "I sure was glad to see you men drive up," he remarked. "I had wondered why Jackson had been looking so poorly of late. This job keeps one moving all day long. It has been a learning experience for me and helped me to grow in this position. Did you have a successful trip?" he asked. "I have been uneasy about you ever since you left on what I considered to be a dangerous mission."

"We did get into some bad situations, but they turned out reasonably well," said Jackson.

"The three of us made a good team," Millard added, "and if you had been along, we would have had four good men."

"John, if you don't mind managing this place alone, we will take a few hours off and get some rest," said Jackson. "We will return this evening and give you and Walter a report on our trip. We need to make some decisions, and we best not wait too long."

"I don't mind at all," John replied. "You all look like you need to take a nap."

Millard was happy Jackson had made such a decision. He had been thinking of his family very often during this trip. Going home today was very special. Today, he would see his new house under construction.

As he left the highway, he could see that work on the house was well under way, and to his surprise, Flora and the boys were sitting on a lumber pile watching every nail being driven into the new house. The workmanship looked perfect. Salem had gone to Spruce Willow to have some building materials delivered. It was close to noon and the men were stopping to eat lunch.

Millard and his family drove down to the cabin. The boys were delighted to see him, and Flora could not stop smiling. Walter insisted on holding onto the steering wheel while sitting on Millard's lap. It was one of those rare occasions that would not soon be forgotten. Flora quickly prepared one of her nifty lunches that were always so delicious.

After lunch, they returned to watch the men work on the house again. Salem was there, and Millard shook his hand and thanked him for what he was doing. He also met the three men Salem had hired and thanked them for their fine work. Millard wished he could stay for the remainder of the day, but he knew he could not. He was tired and wanted to lay down until he felt rested for the upcoming meeting.

Salem and Flora understood and the boys were used to his coming and then leaving like that. He hoped that it would not be too long before he could have a regular schedule and be with his family more.

After a short nap and relaxing for a while, he was ready to return to work. Flora handed him a sandwich as he went out the door, and he was off. He waved at the men working on the house as he passed. He wished that he could stop and help out, but it was essential that he hurry along.

The day was winding down as he arrived at Newbarn. The men scheduled to attend the meeting were there, and to everyone's surprise, so was Horace Blue. John had gone by his house and asked him to come. His presence was always needed at meetings, but these days, he declined because of his busy schedule.

"You are looking well and prosperous," said Millard with a jovial laugh.

"That is because you men are selling so much of my good whiskey," Horace replied. "I have made so much whiskey this year I have been forced to have corn trucked over from another county to keep enough on hand. The local farmers have sold me about all they have to spare. Don't worry, though; I have an unlimited supply from other sources."

They all shook his hand and went inside for the meeting.

Before the men could get seated, Jackson asked for everyone's attention. "We can't have a meeting until Antonio Vitally calls me from Memphis. I expected him to call long before now. We have no phone here, so Pop has asked us over to his house where we can wait for the call there. It will be much more comfortable there, and

I thanked him for asking us over. Besides, the seating will be soft over there and won't punish our asses like these hard chairs do."

They all laughed and immediately closed Newbarn down and headed for Walter's nice home.

The men were warmly welcomed into Walter's home and waited for the events of the evening. Millard and Jackson alternately gave a report of their ill-fated meeting in Memphis, which made everyone there angry at Gordon Piker.

Robert then told of his trip and what he had heard at the meeting. "They have no consideration for Newbarn," spoke Robert. "Piker would not budge on his demand for 80 percent of our profits in exchange for protection."

"What?" said John. "We thought he would be willing to negotiate, at least some; otherwise, what was the point in a meeting?"

"Antonio tried to persuade him to offer a fifty-fifty split, but Piker remained firm. If we don't meet his demands, he intends to ambush our trucks as they leave the mountains, fully loaded, and blow them to hell. He thinks we cannot sustain the financial losses and will be forced to keep our business within the confines of the mountains. I still could not read where Antonio stands. He tried to soften Piker up without sounding soft himself. There is a possibility that we could talk him over to our side. I do get a feeling that he has had just about a bellyful of the mob and would like to be rid of them. But he has a problem—he may not be able to do so without ending up in Lake Michigan with cement boots on."

"The only chance he has to get away from the Mafia is to come over to our side and hide here in these mountains," Millard added. "Otherwise, he will never escape from the eternal torment that devil's gang have created for themselves." Millard let out a deep sigh. "What a hell of a mess to be caught up in."

"I will keep trying to feel him out though, if ever I can get an opportunity to meet him," said Robert. "That is all I can tell you about my trip and their respect for us."

"Disrespect nothing," said Millard. "It was disrespectful to nature when the men in the mob were born. They certainly make it easy for us to get mad at them."

Robert smiled. "Now I will tell you about the submachine gun I recently bought," he added. "It might have already saved my life. I think we should consider having each long-haul member of Newbarn carrying one. You are welcome to try mine and see how you like it. Our shotguns are perfect in these mountains and foothills, but if we should get into a shoot-out in close quarters in a city, I believe the submachine would prove its worth. Keep our shotguns, of course, and use them just as we have in the past, is my advice. We all know what they can do."

"I hated them at first, but I got used to them after I saw the damage they can do," said Millard.

"Well, gentlemen, what should we do?" said Jackson. "They do not know we are aware of their plans, thanks to Robert getting away and leaving them without a clue that everything they had said would soon reach our ears."

"They will have suspicions about us, but that is all. The Mafia does not have a habit of acting before being very certain about who they are facing," said Millard. "Antonio has not called Jackson yet, and by some miracle, they might have changed their minds in some way."

Shortly, the phone did sound two short and then two long rings, which was Walter's number. It was a large wall phone with a protruding crank on the side that could be turned the correct number of turns in order to talk with a person on another phone.

Jackson answered the phone quickly and exchanged friendly greetings. Jackson then asked Antonio if they could meet privately somewhere soon.

"I would like that very much," replied Antonio. "I believe such a meeting would be of mutual interest."

They agreed to meet in Chattanooga on Sunday at the Valley Inn.

Jackson said nothing for a few minutes after the phone conversation. Then he proceeded to continue the meeting. "Piker has held firm to his demands upon us—80 percent with guaranteed protection for us, and that's it."

"That bunch might be the ones needing protection if they keep up such foolishness," said John. "They are not the only people who can blow up things," he added. "I have enough dynamite and caps stored in a cave behind my house to level everything they have, and I can obtain as much more as we need."

"I hope it don't go that far," said Jackson, "but it's good to know we have a supplier among us. Millard, you have been very quiet, and I can tell you have been thinking during this meeting," said Jackson. "What say ye?"

"I have been thinking," said Millard. "We don't have many options available to us. We could accept their offer of 80 percent, which would be ridiculous. We could give up our right to travel the highways and do business like other people. Or we could risk having our trucks blown up. I believe we should reject everything they have put before us and make plans of our own. They don't know that we are aware of their plans to blow our loaded trucks up. I suggest sacrificing one truck to determine exactly what they have in mind. Load our oldest truck with jars of water and send it out as a normal delivery. Robert should help us plan the details. He knows best. Two men would be in that truck, and we don't want to risk their lives," Millard continued.

"I don't know about sacrificing trucks," John remarked. "I guess we could try it, so long as we stop with one old truck. The newer trucks are becoming more and more expensive."

"It could be worthwhile if it proves to give us an edge," said Jackson.

"We have to show them we mean business from the start," Millard replied. "But what I have said is just a rough idea. It would be a serious blow to the Mafia and get their attention."

"The only other option I can think of is to respond in kind if they blow up one of our trucks," Horton Pritchard said.

"You have a point, Horton, but that would have to be a last resort," Jackson replied.

"I can think of no other options left open to us at this time," said Millard. "If we should decide to follow my plan, we would have to make the plan work perfectly the first time and sting them enough to cause them to reconsider what they have in mind.

"I know we can defeat them greedy devils while keeping our present plan and continue Newbarn delivering whiskey just as we now have it organized," he concluded.

The men expressed other ideas, but none held up to close examination.

Robert was in favor of Millard's plan but not without much investigation and careful, step-by-step planning. "I will work on such a plan," said Robert, "and put it in writing for you to study tomorrow morning. Please think about everything we have discussed and be prepared to criticize and make suggestions that might be of value, no matter how insignificant they may seem to you. Some of us could get killed in a conflict with those people, and we certainly don't want that to happen. Neither do we want to kill or cause injury to anyone else. We just want to be left alone to conduct our business, and if we can convince them that we will accept nothing less, perhaps they will let us be or at least realize that they must negotiate with us reasonably and fairly without insulting us."

Jackson ended the meeting, and all went their separate ways knowing how much was at stake in their possible confrontation with the mob leaders in Chicago. But all knew how stubborn the mountain people were and how determined they were to do what was right and honorable. They conducted their business honorably and expected others to do the same. To have the mob demand the lion's share of their profits in return for protection was ludicrous to them and totally unacceptable.

They did realize that life was unfair, and at times, making deals that seemed a little unfair was not unreasonable. However, they were now dealing with men who wanted everything for themselves with no regard for anyone else. They forced themselves upon others and would not hesitate to commit murder to get their way. Getting their way for so many years had caused them to become so spoiled that they now considered it their right to be the privileged few. Well, they would not get their way this time, and they could just get the surprise of their lives. That crowd might just return to Chicago with their asses full of buckshot as Gordon Piker had predicted not long ago.

Millard was in deep thought as he drove home, and he figured the others who'd attended the meeting were too. He had planted a seed at the meeting and was convinced it would help their situation, especially with Robert planning their strategy. He would not worry about what might happen later. One step at a time was always best he had learned over the years.

As he reached home, he was still deep in thought. Flora knew he had something heavy on his mind to cause him to walk to the bed and sit down with his head in his hands.

He soon realized that he had entered his home without speaking to his family. He began laughing at himself, and so did Flora. The boys were playing and did not notice until they looked up and saw him sitting there.

"You look tired but otherwise all right," said Flora. "How was your meeting? I would bet a nickel that you were thinking about that meeting when you came in the door."

"The meeting went well, but we have many important problems that we must deal with over the coming days and even months that seem almost overwhelming. I am second in command of Newbarn, and that makes me feel very responsible for all that goes on there. We are in a disagreement with the mob in Chicago that must be resolved soon, and people could easily get killed in the process. But let's not talk anymore about my work until a different time."

Flora did not disagree. She called the children over, and they all sat in a row on the bed. The boys started asking questions so fast Millard could not keep up. They told stories and sung songs until past bedtime, and laughter filled the room more than it had in several weeks. What a wonderful evening.

Millard ate some leftovers and they all went to bed. Millard was almost asleep when he suddenly realized that he had not asked about their new house.

"Oh my," said Flora. "It is going up much faster than I expected. I did not know my own father knew so much about construction. And the carpenters are experts. They are cutting all those fancy angles and things that most houses do not have. They have been working feverishly to get it entirely finished outside before cold weather sets in."

"I will be gone before Salem gets here in the morning, so tell him how much I thank him for his work and ask if he needs more money at this time. Flora, I keep our money in a safe place, and I will show you where it is tomorrow if I don't have to leave for places unknown."

They quickly went to sleep, and the house was quiet.

As Millard left for work, he stopped briefly to take a quick look at the new house. He knew it was going to be one fine house that his family would spend many happy days in. *It is going to be even grander than I dreamed. Could it actually be true that the dreams of my young days are actually becoming a reality?* He entertained the thoughts about his younger years until he reached Spruce Willow.

When Millard arrived at work, Robert was busy writing at the table in the office. "Have you been working all night?" asked Millard, in a kidding manner.

"I feel like I have," answered Robert. "Actually I have been here about two hours pondering over what we should do about our enemies, and I mean enemies. You would agree if you had spied on them to the extent that I have. I think your idea is a good one, but I question if we should take so many men and vehicles and head that way just yet. As you know, Jackson and Antonio will meet on Sunday. Antonio would not agree to meet with Jackson if he had no purpose in mind. I recommend waiting until after their meeting before we do anything except make our deliveries as usual, except for the long hauls. With the weekend coming up, I doubt we will have any trouble until Monday at least. Then we will do what we have to do, depending upon what information Jackson has when he returns. That will probably be the time to act.

"If we do have to make our truck deliveries under guard, Newbarn will probably have to hire one car for each truck to run interference using a pattern that I will show them. Other considerations will be the cost of the four cars and salaries for eight extra men, possibly only four. The initial cost could be heavy, but later it might be less. It depends on whether our strategy works well. That's as far as I can go at this point, except that I might do some patrolling over the weekend to look for suspicious activity."

Millard listened carefully to what Robert had said and agreed with him fully. He was hopeful that Antonio and Jackson would come up with some intelligent business arrangements that would be acceptable to Piker and convince him that negotiating would be in his best interest and profitable to the mob.

Jackson soon arrived, and Robert handed him the short-term recommendations he had written.

Jackson agreed with Robert, just as Millard had, except Robert had not explained John's part in the plan. Robert had considered the possibility of bad trouble if they were attacked here at Newbarn. "I don't think one man could handle a large attack. Millard and John should both remain here to see that nothing like that happens."

"Maybe my expectations are too high, but I do have high hopes that me and Antonio can find some middle ground that will be acceptable to old crazy Piker and that we can all carry on our business without any more conflict," he said as he looked at Millard and Robert.

FORTY-EIGHT

Robert soon left to follow up on some sensitive information that might be useful to Newbarn. He did not want to take time to explain what he was about.

Millard and Jackson decided to put the office in order and then check everything outside. By noon, they had completed their chores. As they sat down to rest, Jackson said, "Millard, I have had enough of trying to pacify Piker and that damn mob in Chicago. I am going to talk with Antonio on Sunday, and we will see if anything comes out of it. If not, I believe we should continue exactly as we now have it organized. I do like Antonio, and I hope Sunday will be a good turning point for us. He was quick to agree to a meeting, and maybe that is a good indication."

"Is Robert going with you Sunday?" asked Millard.

"I will leave that up to him," replied Jackson. "He keeps ahead of us on everything."

"I will go with you if you think you might need a backup," said Millard. "I would have to keep out of sight, of course. You handle yourself well, but you could get into a dangerous situation where you would need help."

"That is always a possibility," said Jackson, "but I think things will go well. Besides, you need to be here Sunday to make double sure we are ready for whatever happens on Monday. Next week might be a decisive week for us, and we need to have one of our top three leaders here at all times.

"You are second in command of Newbarn, so if anything should happen to me during some misfortune, carry on and don't let up. I have legal papers addressed to you in Pop's safe. Either Pop or Mom will hand them to you as I have instructed. You will have a heavy burden on your shoulders if you should have to use them, but things will all work out."

"I wrote a sealed note to Flora and placed it on the shelf above our bed containing instructions for her to follow in case of my death," said Millard. "But I would appreciate you helping her get things settled. I never thought we would be having such a conversation as this," he added, "but we have been thinking along the same lines, and for good reason."

"Our families are the good reason you are talking about, Millard," Jackson replied. "We are considering them first, and that is the way it should be."

"I have faced death several times and know it can come without notice," Millard replied.

"We have accomplished a considerable amount of work and talk today," said Jackson, "and it is too late to start anything else, so let's help the men as they come in and then close up Newbarn."

Millard noticed that Jackson seemed very happy and even danced a little jig to top off his rather loud announcement.

As they ended the day, they checked to assure Newbarn was secure before starting home.

"Unless there is a need, I will not be here tomorrow. But I will be here early Sunday morning and remain as long as necessary," Millard said as he opened his car door.

"I intend to head to Chattanooga very early Sunday morning without coming by here," replied Jackson.

"You be careful," Millard called out as they drove away from Newbarn.

Millard was extremely happy to get home. Salem and the workers had retired for the day, but he could make out by his headlights that much progress had been made while he was away.

Flora and the boys were waiting patiently for him to arrive. Supper was being kept warm on the cookstove, and Flora was playing tunes on her guitar to entertain the boys. It was a wonderful evening. Flora played more songs, and the boys did their best to sing. Millard could only smile and sing a little. His bass voice just did not blend in. He told them about the trucks he drove, which he had not done before. They seemed to understand most of it and listened closely. He promised to take them for a ride sometime when he had time. After an evening of total fun, they all went to bed. Millard wanted to sleep well and arise early to see the progress on their new house.

In the morning, Millard was very surprised and happy. Except for a portion of the roof, the house was completely roughed in. It looked somewhat larger than he expected, and he knew it was going to look spectacular.

Salem soon drove up in his Model T Ford and seemed overjoyed to see Millard. "Well," he said, "how do think your new cabin is going to look?"

"Almost as good as your new Model T," answered Millard with a broad smile on his face. "I enjoy seeing it every time you drive up."

"There is one change I want to make, with your permission of course," said Salem. "I want to put two chimneys instead of just one for the living room fireplace; I would enjoy building another one for a fireplace in the master bedroom. I just know Flora and you will enjoy waking up in such a bedroom as that, not to mention the view overlooking the countryside and the river in the distance."

"I would indeed," replied Millard. "Build it just as I know you have in mind. Speaking of the view, I want to own that view," he added. "There are three or four hundred vacant acres leading down to the river. Mr. Smith owns it, and I suspect he would sell it to me. We have always been very good friends, and I would allow him continued access to the property. He is now elderly and has no heirs. I would help him in any way possible as he gets on in years. I will ask him soon."

"You have a perfect notion for this entire project," replied Salem. "Our carpenters have been working very hard, and I did not ask them to work today. We will complete the roof and begin work on the inside as well on Monday. A stonemason will be here also to begin the chimneys and fireplaces. I will build the rounded stairs leading from the foyer to the second floor. I have had considerable experience with such delicate work, and I enjoy doing it.

"If you have time, you and Flora go over the plans for the interior of the house and decide what kind of ceiling you want to use. Then while the mason works on bricking the outside, we will work on the inside."

"I have to be on duty Sunday, but Flora knows what we want. We have gone over it again and again," said Millard. "Depending on what goes on at Newbarn, I might get a chance to come home early one day," Millard continued.

"Am I wrong in sensing you people are having trouble at Newbarn?" asked Salem.

"You are exactly right," said Millard. "The mob wants to horn in and has demanded that we give them 80 percent of our profits in exchange for protection as we make our deliveries. We haven't agreed to their scheme and don't intend to. Jackson is going to meet one of the mob members in Chattanooga on Sunday. That's why I need to work Sunday, in case of an emergency. Jackson is going over there alone, and I wish he would not do so. Our detective will probably watch out for him though. I will keep you informed about things as I can."

He then gave Salem ten dollars for gas money, which Salem did not want. "You pay for my gas, and Flora cooks a nice lunch for me each day. I am doing all right," he said as he got in his Model T and started it up.

"Why don't you stay and eat supper with us?" Millard asked.

"Can't," Salem replied. "Got to get home; I still have some work to do."

Millard smiled as he drove off. That old, handsome car looked and ran like new. Millard had wanted Salem to spend each night during the week at the cabin to save him from having to drive to and from home. He'd said he would, but so far he'd declined to do so.

Millard hurried home to be with Flora and the boys. He had stayed longer at the construction site than he had intended. As he walked back down the road to the cabin, the thought struck him that he might be doing more than he should in building such a place. Just look at all the poor, desperate people he saw every time he drove to Chicago. With the money he had accumulated, he could help relieve at least some of that suffering he encountered almost daily.

When he saw Cameron and Walter playing in the yard, he thought how fortunate they were in every way. Many children were with their parents at this very moment searching for food and hoping for better days.

He played with the children all afternoon, trying to make up a little for the many times during recent months that he could not be with them. They had gotten used to his absence, and so had Flora. His absence was not due to neglect, and even when he was away, his thoughts were never away from Flora and the boys for very long. His sons' future was very important to him, and it was his desire that they grow into adulthood as well-educated gentlemen prepared to face the world, with a caring attitude for their families and their fellow human beings.

He had shared these thoughts with Flora many times. She prayed often, and many of her prayers centered on his philosophies of life and his unselfish wisdom. She had known that he would start criticizing himself for being extravagant before their home and the beautiful surrounding grounds—the fruition of his youthful thoughts—were finished. She did not think what he was doing was selfish at all, and everyone should have at least one or even several of their dreams fulfilled during their lifetime. This dream he was now fulfilling was materialistic in nature, while her dream was having a man like him come along in her life. Her dream had been fulfilled long ago and still sufficed. We are all different in our aspirations of life.

Their afternoon was filled with fun, and when evening came, they jumped in the car and were on their way to their favorite café in Spruce Willow. Large hamburgers and soft drinks were the main course for all, followed by chocolate cake topped with vanilla ice cream. What a delight and a sight and a mess after they were through eating. The table was covered with spills and smears of chocolate cake and looked as though it needed scrubbing with a brush. The waitress cleaned it all up, and Millard gave her a quarter, which was a nice tip and made her happy. Tips were not very common during such hard times.

Both Cameron and Walter were sound asleep by the time they arrived at home. It had been quite an evening for them, and they were quickly put to bed.

Millard made a nice, warm fire in the heater, and the house was soon nice and cozy. Millard and Flora sat up late talking about everything of interest. They both knew the situation at Newbarn and avoided talking too much about it. Ma still insisted that she intended to remain in her own house until the day she died. Millard was certain she would change her mind when it got cold and she saw how roomy and warm their new house would be.

"I will just insist that she move in with us," said Millard. "It is dangerous for an elderly woman to be alone over there, especially during one of our mountain blizzards."

"I do not want to be the one to try forcing her out," replied Flora with a laugh. "I would end up with bruises all over me."

"I will take care of her," Millard replied.

Flora reported that all was well with her family and that Salem was tickled to death about supervising the construction of their house.

They went on from one subject to another until well after midnight before going to bed.

Millard decided that he would not hurry to work the following morning. He wanted to eat a nice breakfast before leaving. As he was leaving after breakfast, he said to Flora, "I will be the only one there today, and I will not come home until Jackson returns and I know he is all right. If something unusual should surface while he is in Chattanooga, I might even have to make a trip over there for some reason." He then walked to his car and drove away, as if his thoughts were far away.

When he arrived at Newbarn, he made a pot of coffee and then proceeded to find work to keep himself busy. He and Jackson and John all liked to keep everything in its place and well organized. After drinking a cup of coffee, he set about doing just that. After he had finished, everything was in fine shape.

In the distance, he could hear a church bell ringing. What a wonderful sound to hear on a beautiful Sunday morning after all had been so quiet since he had arrived. He wondered about Jackson and Antonio, hoping they were planning something that would turn out well. But he knew the chance was slim to none, unless Antonio had something to offer. Millard waited all afternoon, dozing and eating snacks.

Dark arrived and still no Jackson. He did everything he could think of to pass the time, but nothing worked.

Hours had passed, and it was now after ten o'clock and no Jackson. Robert had not arrived from wherever he had gone either. As professional as Robert was, Millard decided that he had probably been shadowing Jackson to make sure no uninvited visitors were lurking about. If the mob had the slightest suspicion that Jackson and Antonio were having an unauthorized meeting, they would have men there to see what was going on. But Millard was reasonably sure that Jackson would cover himself and not allow that to happen.

It was four o'clock on Monday morning when Millard heard a car drive up. It was Robert, his lips pressed in a thin line and without his usual smile on his face. "Howdy," he said as he walked in the door.

"Have you seen Jackson?" asked Millard. "He should have returned hours ago; Chattanooga is not that far away."

"I followed him to the Valley Inn where they were supposed to meet. Their cars were there and were still there when I returned at two o'clock in the afternoon. I passed on by and returned again late in the afternoon. Antonio's car was gone, but Jackson's was still there. I went inside and asked the bartender in the restaurant if he knew where Jackson and Antonio were. He gave me a smart remark, indicating that it was not his business what went on among his customers. It was obvious to me that he knew exactly what was going on and was telling me a lie. I snatched him by the shirt collar and pointed my pistol right in his face before he began to realize I was not playing games. He then told me that he did not know where they'd gone.

"I asked him why Jackson's car was outside.

"'I don't know,' he answered, 'and that is the truth. Those men you're talking about came in at about eleven o'clock and talked for an hour or more and then ate lunch.' He told me that four men came in and sat down next to them, and some angry-sounding words were exchanged. He said they all stood up, and then he described Jackson to a tee and said Jackson knocked two of them to the floor. They all then grabbed Jackson and one of them stuck a pistol to his ribs and they went outside. Jackson got in the car with three of the men, and Antonio got in his own car with the other one of them. I asked him if Antonio helped force Jackson outside. 'No, I don't think he did,' he told me. He said that he did not see Antonio do anything to Jackson, and he was reasonably certain that the man who got into Antonio's car with him was pointing a gun in his direction. He said the car in which Jackson was riding with the other men was a large, black, fancy-looking sedan. I thanked him very kindly if he was telling me the truth," said Robert, "but I also told him that, if I found out that he was lying and something happened to Jackson, I would return and burn that place down around his ears with him in it. He assured me he was being as truthful as he could be.

"Millard, I don't know what is going on, but it probably isn't good. Usually when things happen like this, the first few hours are crucial. They might have kidnapped Jackson for some reason, and Antonio might be in just as much danger as Jackson. We need to get over there fast. I am going over to tell Walter about this, and then I will be back."

"I will see to things here, and I know we need to do something right away," Millard replied.

"After we get on the road, we will figure out our first plan of action."

As Robert was leaving the room, Millard said, "Robert, I would like to take John with us. He is the best fighter among us, and he has explosives, which both of us know how to use. Would you ask Walter if he would mind coming over to Newbarn and taking charge of things while we look for Jackson? Everything is in good shape here in the office and all the men are now well trained. He would just need to keep an eye on things and take care of the money. If he is not feeling well, don't ask him. We will figure out something else."

Millard was very uneasy about this situation. He knew he must keep calm and think things through while it was still quiet. John usually came in early, and he hoped he would do so this morning. If Walter could not help out, however, he would have no choice but to have John remain at Newbarn, and he and Robert would head for Chattanooga.

He would never express his thoughts, but he was surprised that Jackson and Robert both had exercised poor judgment to get themselves in such a predicament.

As soon as John came in, he would have him return home and fetch dynamite and anything else his clever mind could think of. If Walter came back with Robert, they would wait for John.

Robert and a sleepy-eyed Walter soon returned to Newbarn. Walter was very concerned about his son and wanted action fast. They did not have to wait long before they heard John drive up. Millard ran out and met him at his car and told him of the existing situation.

In less than an hour, Millard, John, and Robert, along with a boxful of John's dynamite and plenty of caps, were speeding down the mountain on their way to Chattanooga. Robert suggested they travel in his car to save time and effort in locating places where he had scouted before. They decided to begin their search at the most likely places east of Chattanooga and work their way westward.

The first and most logical place to begin their search was the Valley Inn where Jackson had been kidnapped. Jackson's car was no longer there. The same bartender was not on duty, but the current bartender on duty knew all about the situation involving Jackson's disappearance. When they asked him questions about the event, he seemed to hold nothing back. He said that two men had come by but had not come in, and he was sure one of them was Jackson based on the description by the bartender who'd witnessed the kidnapping. He did not know why they'd stopped. They had just talked for a few minutes and then continued on toward Memphis. He had caught a glimpse inside the car as they'd left, and the man with Jackson was holding a pistol.

Millard, John, and Robert decided to roam all around Chattanooga looking for either Jackson's car or the large, black sedan the four men had driven, and hopefully both.

They saved the last place they wanted for a specific reason. It was the large store where Millard and John had had the big fight with the four men dressed in fancy clothes, and from the description the bartender had given them, they concluded that it was the same large, black sedan.

They approached the store as though they expected to find what they were looking for. They cautiously drove around three sides of the building, saving the wooded back side until last.

They discovered nothing until they had driven around the rear. There they saw sixteen cars parked. Jackson's was parked well back in the woods where it would not likely be seen. And sure enough, the mysterious black sedan was there also.

FORTY-NINE

"Damn, what do you reckon is going on here?" Millard said with astonishment.

"I don't know yet, but you can be sure Jackson is in there," Robert replied. "I am going to park farther back in the shadows where we can see who comes and goes."

"I see only one window, but surely there are more," said Millard. "I'll walk around the building and try to determine what we're up against." He quietly opened the car door and disappeared.

His scouting did not take long. "There's nothing around the building except gas tanks," he reported when he returned to the car. "There are two barred windows on each side of the bottom floor. I saw only one window upstairs in front and the one here in the back. If we had a ladder, we could take a peek in this rear window and maybe see what we are up against."

John had said nothing so far and Millard quickly saw why. He was placing caps and fuses in sticks of dynamite and preparing them for use.

Robert continued to observe the building and contemplate strategy while Millard went searching for a ladder or something long enough to allow them to climb up to the window. He returned with a homemade ladder, which had rotten places in it, but he thought it might work. He tested it, trying to determine if it would hold him up and found that it was stronger than it looked.

All three men lifted the ladder very carefully up to the window, not wanting to make any sounds that would reveal their presence. "Well," whispered Millard, "I found the ladder, so I guess I should climb it—unless one of you wants the pleasure."

"We don't," said John. "Now climb your ass up there, and let's get on with the show. You know if I try going up, it will break that ladder all to hell."

Millard took one careful step at a time until he was eye level with the lower section of the window. He stood there quietly for about ten minutes or more before he eased slowly back down.

They returned to the car before any of them spoke.

"What took you so long?" Robert asked.

"There are two rooms up there. The men are all congregated in the far room. No activity is noticeable at the rear window, and that made it difficult to see who was in there and how many. There is a pool table there, and they are shooting pool and talking. I did not hear one word they said. Several of them are just lounging about. Jackson is there, with his back directly in front of the window and another man sitting directly beside him with a pistol in his shoulder holster. It appeared that he was guarding Jackson."

"Did you see Antonio?" asked Robert.

"No," Millard answered, "I did not see him."

"I checked carefully to see what firepower they had, and I saw nothing but pistols in shoulder holsters. If they had any automatic machine guns, I didn't see them. Of course, they could have had them placed in a part of the room where I had no view."

"They probably do have them," said Robert. "I believe them to be a mean bunch and capable of anything."

"I think so too," John replied, adding, "I have things ready to even the odds."

Millard knew Robert already had his strategy for rescuing Jackson in mind and listened carefully as he began telling them of his plan.

"Fellows, I think we agree that we do not intend to leave here without Jackson. We do not like killing, but if we have to, we will in order to get him out of there. Millard, I want you to climb the ladder again with your pistol and machine gun. John, you station yourself in front of the building, where you can blow the front door open when we are ready. I will move my car down beside the front porch and climb on the roof and station myself beside the front window near where Jackson is. When I am sure we are all in position, I will throw a rock on the roof of the building. I will smash in the front window as Millard knocks out the rear window. We want to confuse them as much as possible. Millard, you fire as many rounds with your machine gun as you think necessary, and I will tell them to remain still and they won't be hurt. All we want is Jackson. As soon as he climbs out on the roof, we will drive out of the way as quickly as possible.

"Millard, you keep firing until you see your way clear and then make your break. The last thing we need to do is blow up that place. John, when we are ready to drive away, blow open the front door of that damn devil's den and then throw enough dynamite into the lower floor to pretty well demolish it. We don't want to kill the men, so use your skills as best you can. It might do well to throw a stick through the store that will blow out the rear wall. That will allow them an escape route. Give them a little time to escape out the back and then blow the entire place to hell."

"I will be happy to take care of that job and do it well," replied John. "As you men well know, plans sometimes don't go as we want them to go. If something goes wrong, we will play it by ear and get out of here as best we can. As for me, I will not leave this place without either of you men. Let's get it done now."

Every man followed the plan precisely. Millard scurried up the ladder and positioned himself as securely as possible. Robert and John quietly drove the car to the porch, and Robert climbed on top of his car and was kneeling by the front window within seconds. John had his dynamite ready with two loose sticks for the doors and several sticks bundled together. Obviously, the bundle was for making kindling wood out of the building. He also had a small stick of aged pine wood called rich pine. Once lit, it would not go out, even if the wind was blowing. He took no chances of not having a reliable flame ready for lighting fuses.

They were all in place, and after peeping in the window, Robert threw a small rock on the roof. It bounced all the way to the ground.

Millard immediately smashed in the rear window and almost fell off the ladder when he did. He fired several short bursts from his machine gun, which caused those inside of the front room to scramble for cover. By that time, Robert had kicked the front window in and yelled to the men inside that no one would be hurt if they remained still and allowed Jackson to come out.

No one moved, and Jackson came out. The mobsters had all been caught off guard and had not had time to recover and figure out what was going on.

It was now time for John to blow the front door out, and that he did. After the smoke cleared enough, he lobbed a stick of dynamite across the merchandise in the store and hit the rear wall. That worked also, and the men upstairs scrambled down what was left of the steps and jumped toward the opening caused by the explosion. With no time to spare, John lit the fuse on the remainder of the dynamite and threw it directly in the middle of the store.

The explosion could be heard for miles. Their job was done. The four Newbarn men jumped in the car, and Robert took off and was out of sight before the hellish bunch knew what had happened. They were too busy saving their cars from the fire as the second floor started collapsing.

No one in the car said a word as Robert raced down the highway and turned off on a side road he had discovered previously that allowed them to travel about thirty miles before reentering the main road. It was a dusty road, but no one minded. In the event that someone had witnessed what they had done, that dusty road might keep them from being caught for thirty miles.

After that, Robert would have a head start on anyone trying to follow him and have a better chance of making it across the mountains to safety. They doubted that there was a car around that part of the country that could catch him anyway.

After they reached the main highway, Robert slowed down a little but kept a high rate of speed until they were across the mountains.

Robert drove them straight to Newbarn, where Walter was up and anxiously waiting. Walter could tell they had been through the rough but asked no questions. He knew they needed to rest awhile before reporting all that had happened. His son was home safely, and Walter was happy beyond words.

They were strong, healthy men in the prime of life, and it didn't take long for them to recuperate. As Walter watched them sitting around the room dozing, he could not help wishing that he could have been involved with them in whatever they had done.

He made a pot of strong coffee as he saw them start yawning and stretching and placed a large selection of food and desserts, which his wife had prepared for them, on the table. The men immediately began talking about what they had done and asked

Walter if he had received any calls or heard any news on his radio indicating trouble in Chattanooga.

"I have heard nothing," replied Walter. "Did something go wrong over there that would be newsworthy or important enough for one of my friends over there to call me?"

"Well, I reckon yes would be the right answer," Millard replied. "We blew hell out of that damned, old, big store where that hellfired bunch that has been causing us so much trouble was hanging out. It's the same store where John and me had that fight with the four men."

"You actually blew the place up?" said Walter, looking astonished.

"We did indeed," continued Millard. "It was blown to smithereens and burning when Robert got us out of there in a hurry. We made a way for all the men upstairs to escape though. We are reasonably certain that no one was killed or even seriously injured."

After Jackson had finished his nap, he told the men what had happened before they rescued him.

"I drove directly to the Valley Inn as we had planned, and Antonio was there sitting at a table. He shook my hand with a firm grip, and I rightly determined that he was happy to see me. He looked at me very seriously and said, 'I have much information I want to pass on to you—more than I can probably tell you in a short time. First off, I want you to know that I want out of this hellfired mob so much that I am risking my life to make my break. If you will help me discharge myself from that no-good, self-serving organization, I will explain to you how the mob works and everything about it. And believe me, I know just about everything there is to know.'"

The more Antonio talked, the closer Jackson listened. Antonio had said that he would make his break that very day if all his assets weren't located in Memphis. He wanted to work out a deal with Newbarn and promised that, if it worked, Newbarn would benefit very much. He said he could sell about half of what he owned to contacts in Memphis without the mob knowing.

"He then expressed a firm desire to sell the remainder of his business to Newbarn and then be a part of our organization," Jackson continued. "In any case, he thinks a deal can be worked out, but we would have to be careful—extremely careful. He then said, 'Jackson, if you think Newbarn is interested, I will have my lawyer list my assets that I can sell to Newbarn, and I will drive over one night and go over them with you and we can proceed from there. That is what came to my mind when you suggested that we meet.'

"I then told him I did have other reasons for asking him to meet, but after thinking about our relationship with him and his relationship with the mob, I now had doubts that we could accomplish anything—certainly not until we at Newbarn had considered his offer from every angle.

"I did, however, tell him that there was something about him that seemed different from the other men he was associated with. The mean streak just did not seem to be there. I knew Robert has heard his firm talk to other members of the mob, but I considered that was a part of his job and he had to perform efficiently or else. Robert is going to tell you about what he heard at the meetings he spied on in Chicago."

After nodding toward Robert, Jackson continued. "We had suspected that Antonio wanted to divorce himself from the mob, but there was no way out if he wanted to keep his head. He seemed to relax a bit when I told him I would discuss his proposal with Newbarn and get back to him soon, and he loosened even more as we kept talking. One important thing we both knew—if we at Newbarn work out an agreement with him, we will have to get him out of Memphis quickly to keep them from whacking him. He would be safe in the mountains.

"Just as we ordered lunch, the door opened and in walked four men. 'What is going on here?' one of the men demanded. 'Ain't you out of your territory, Antonio?'

"'No,' answered Antonio. 'Jackson delivers some of his good mountain whiskey to me on occasion. Piker knows about it, and he wants to negotiate with Newbarn about doing business together. We have talked about it one time and so far have not made much progress.'

"'You're a damn liar,' said the largest of the four men. 'We believe that you are planning to leave the mob and you are here scheming ways to betray the mob.'

"'You are the damn liar, and you don't know what you are talking about,' Antonio told him. 'I have always been a loyal member of our organization, and you have no reason to think otherwise.'

"'We will think what we please,' said the same big man, 'and we think we will take care of this asshole from the mountains while we have him cornered.'

"That's when I stood up and knocked the man standing near me to the floor and then hit the large man with the big mouth with a very hard blow on the chin. He took a hard fall to the floor.

"Antonio wanted very much to help me, but he knew if he made such a move the mob might have him killed. I knew it was a situation beyond our control, and we both knew it without having to exchange words. They restrained me, and one of the men held a pistol to my ribs. We all left quickly and they forced me into the big car. Antonio was ordered into his own car, and one of the men got into the back seat and sat behind him.

"They drove me directly to the building where you men found me. I was told to remain seated until they told me otherwise. I think they were waiting for orders from Piker or someone higher up about what to do with me.

"I don't know what happened to Antonio but I am certain they would not harm him without specific orders from above. Antonio is smart, and we will no doubt be hearing from him again.

"How do you men think we should proceed from here?" Jackson asked. "I have my own opinion, but I think we should all be a part of the decision, just as we have been doing."

"I don't see how we can do anything at this point except carry on with our business as usual," said Millard.

"I don't either," said John, "except that we need to collect information on all the people who are causing us such trouble and then make a major move on them. If we do have to make such a move, there will be weeping and wailing and gnashing of teeth."

"That is what I had in mind also," said Jackson. "Keep alert and cautious while Robert does his fine job of spying. I hope Antonio has not been killed."

FIFTY

Millard hurried home, hardly noticing the progress made on his new house as he passed. It was late when he arrived, and the boys were sleeping peacefully. But Flora was up waiting for him. Somehow he'd known she would be.

"I have been worried about you," she said. "You have been in danger, haven't you?"

"Yes, Flora, I have and so have Jackson, John, and Robert. I do not think our troubles are over with those mean devils. Things are fine for now, and we hope to have a normal work day tomorrow. Let's go to bed, and I will tell you more about our work problems come morning."

It was a restless night for Millard. He tossed about and woke up often—a problem not often familiar to him. Morning came and he told her nothing about their work problems. The last several months had been stressful, and he suspected his nerves as the problem. He made no mention of it to Flora, but as always, she knew.

Millard readied himself for work and was gone. Although no emergencies presently existed, the leadership of Newbarn needed to stay close to their responsibilities as long as the Mafia was on the prowl and remain alert. Their long-haul trucks were on the road and a cause for worry. He decided to make a quick stop at the new house to update Salem.

"Don't worry about things here," said Salem. "Things are going well. As you can see, we have the house weathered in. The mason is coming along faster than I'd expected on the exterior, and the two chimneys will be completed soon. The chimney mason alternates days working on them. That allows him to construct both of them as quickly as one. He can only lay a certain number of bricks before leaving them to cure. Otherwise, they might sink under the weight of additional bricks. The next day, he follows the same procedure on the other chimney. You take care of yourself, Millard. I eat dinner with Flora and the boys about every day now, mostly to keep them company. They miss you when you are away, and I do too."

Millard shook his hand and walked away. He wanted to stay with Salem and work on that house so very much. They could have had a fun day. He pushed the thought aside and drove on to Newbarn.

Everything was "normal" at Newbarn. The deliverymen were scurrying about to get started and headed for their varying delivery routes. Most of the men were very happy now that almost everyone had a routine established. Even the long-haul trucks had gone. They knew already the trouble they might encounter along the way, but it did not matter to them. They were tough and the money was good.

Millard just stood there watching the activity until Jackson called to him to come to the office area. "Everyone is accounted for, and Newbarn seems normal this morning, but I am worried about Robert," he said. "He came by my house after I got home last night and said he was going to find out what happened to Antonio. He gave me few details about where or what he was going to do. I am guessing that he was going to Chattanooga to pick up where we left off. Damn, I hope he locates my car. It was a good, fast car and I want it back."

"Knowing Robert, if the car isn't still at the store, he'll keep backtracking undetected until he finds it, and anything else he wants to know. Let's give him plenty of time, and if he fails to show up after a reasonable time, I will go looking for him," said Millard. "What do you think about that? I am learning some of his tricks of the trade, and maybe I could be of help."

"You might have to do that," said Jackson. "You would be the logical person to head west if we have to. The only drawback is that we need John here in case that mob should send some of their people over here wanting to fight or destroy our business here."

The men were thinking and acting as professionals, and their decisions were continuously proving to be correct.

"The main objective right now, other than finding Robert, is to keep our organization in place just as it is and miss not one delivery," Jackson continued. "We promised our customers prompt delivery, and to do less would probably be the downfall of Newbarn."

"I think so too," said Millard. "We have made some wise decisions in a short time. John is coming now, and I believe he will agree with us also.

"Come in, John," Millard said with a smile. "We need your wisdom and counsel."

"I will tell you all I know, such as it is," replied John.

Jackson and Millard told him about Robert and the decisions they had made. "If you have other ideas about the situation, we would like to hear them," said Jackson.

"I don't see anything we can or should do at this time," said John. "But things might change before the end of the day. I think we should leave things as they are for now. I saw the last truck going out as I came in, so this should be an interesting day."

"We should keep close around here because things are so uncertain," said Millard. "We are concerned about Robert, but he is probably doing what he enjoys the most—spying and collecting information on our enemies. We also should notify Horace Blue about all that is going on. He might want additional security coverage. I will go by his house after work and talk to him. I enjoy going over there and watching his operation. He is continually making improvements that increase production."

Millard did not like sitting around waiting for something to happen. He mentioned his unrest to Jackson and John, and they were of the same mind.

"Well," said Jackson, "we have everything in fine shape around here so maybe now would be a time to consider future plans and improvements."

"Let's take a walk around and look for things that might need attention as we expand," Millard said. "We need to build an addition to our whiskey storage area. The place is practically empty every morning after the men have loaded up, and sometimes we get extra orders to fill and have to go over to Horace's place for additional loads."

"Maybe we should wait until later to start anything new," said John. "We might have to do some fighting before all these troubles are settled."

"That would keep us busy sure enough," said Jackson. "We could walk around and prepare a to-do list that we could use later when the time is more favorable," he added. "That would be a good project for today, and if we have no word from Robert by tomorrow, we will have plenty to keep us busy."

Millard, Jackson, and John were the last three to leave Newbarn. As Millard was driving home, he decided to stop at the restaurant with the backroom bar. He drank several beers and just relaxed for a little while. He considered that he should have gone directly home and spent time with Flora and the boys. That would have been the right thing to do, but he hadn't, and somehow he did not feel guilty for not doing so.

He had promised to visit Horace on his way home, and he had no guilty feelings about not doing that either. A man needed a few hours to relax and be himself sometimes, and he saw no fault in that. As he drove by his new house, he could readily see the men were still making great progress. It was going to be a great place, but it did not capture his interest enough to stop and look about. That was not normal behavior for him, and he wondered why.

He slowly drove on down to the house where the boys were in the front yard playing. What a joy it was to see them laughing and playing with none of the cares of this world to be concerned with. He quickly got out of the car and picked them both up, holding one in each arm. Having four little arms around his neck made the day worthwhile.

Flora was watching them through the door but did not interfere. It was a joy just watching them. Millard did not have enough time to spend with them but that was well and good. She understood, and they would also as they got older and knew why he'd sacrificed so much for them.

They came in the house soon. The air was getting chilly, and tonight would probably be the first autumn frost. Millard built a fire in the wood heater with plenty of help from the boys, who handed him each stick of wood he used. In their cozy, little cabin, they ate supper and played until Flora got her guitar and played some songs. They all sang along, and it sounded good. They were all natural-born singers, except Millard's bass did not fit in very well. Millard noticed how Flora had improved her guitar playing. Millard had been acquainted with music all of his life, and he knew that

Flora was approaching professional status in her playing. "Wouldn't that be something if we could all get good enough to play and sing in church?" said Millard. If the boys showed an interest, he would buy each an instrument of his choice. *It might just happen someday,* he thought.

After the boys were tucked in bed, Millard and Flora sat by the fire and talked for a long while. He told her all that had happened at work. She had not heard anything about the kidnapping and arson and fighting and all the dangerous things that had been going on. She could hardly believe they were actually having trouble with the Mafia in Chicago.

"When will it all end?" she asked him.

"If they will negotiate reasonably with us, it might not take long. But we are prepared for the worst. I hope Robert will bring some helpful information to us. But if he has not returned by morning, I will be the one to go searching for him. Try not to worry too much about me though. Robert has taught me a lot about how to contend with danger without getting injured or possibly killed. I intend to be very cautious as I go about my business tomorrow and the days to come."

"I saw that last gun you brought in the car," she said. "Get rid of that thing," she screamed out. "What on earth will you do with it other than get yourself killed?"

"It is a machine gun, and it fires about five hundred bullets per minute. The other side has them, so we had to buy them for our people. Every man in Newbarn has one. We take our other guns with us as well. I will not use it unless I have to."

"That scares me to death, Millard," said Flora, her horror clear in her voice. "Get out of Newbarn if it means life or death."

"You know the answer to that, Flora," he replied. "I cannot. I am committed, and I told you that when I went to work with Jackson and Walter. I cannot and I will not get out."

"There is nothing else I can do," Flora said, but she knew that he had not heard her. This was always the case when he'd made up his mind. "I have had unwelcome feelings about all of this violence for some time now," she said, and then left it at that.

They went to bed with little more to say. Flora held him close and said, "Please be very careful, Millard. I do not know what me and the boys would do if we lost you. I had rather see that big house you are building go up in flames and live here in our cabin for the rest of our lives than lose you. The boys adore you. They mimic just about everything they see you do. They love your car and your guns and your way of life and vow that they will grow up to be just like you."

"That wouldn't be such a bad thing," said Millard. "And please don't make any of your predictions. Ever since you predicted that mine cave-in, they scare me to death."

With that exchange of words, they promptly went to sleep.

Millard wasted no time in getting to work the following morning. He knew very well what chore might be waiting for him. When he arrived only a few men were there. Jackson and John arrived very soon after, and Millard could see on Jackson's face that he had something to tell.

They went directly into the office and sat down at the table. Jackson immediately informed them that Walter had received a call from Robert. The call had been garbled and Walter had been able to understand very little of it. Walter guessed that he might be under some sort of attack or had been hit over the head. The only thing Walter understood was that he was in Memphis and something about Antonio being hurt.

"That ain't much to go on, but it is enough for us to take action," said Jackson. "Millard, are you prepared to leave as we planned yesterday?"

"I can be ready within half an hour or so," Millard replied. He turned to John and asked John to help him double-check his guns and let him have a good amount of dynamite.

"I will give you plenty of dynamite and two hefty bundles containing six sticks each in case you need to toss some like we did the other night."

"I think that will be fine," Millard answered. "I will repay the favor. It sure is a comfort knowing I have that stuff in case I should need it."

In less than half an hour, Millard was ready to go. His guns and ammunition and dynamite were placed on the front seat and camouflaged. He told John and Jackson that he would be in touch as soon as possible.

"Damn, he has guts," said John as Millard drove down the long driveway and on toward Spruce Willow.

"I guess we all do, John, or we couldn't survive in this business," replied Jackson.

"You are right Jackson," John answered. "I am just glad to be working with two men like you and Millard—two men I can totally trust. Of course, I trust Robert as well. I hope Millard finds him well and snappy as he usually is."

"Let's make the most of the day and hope for the best," Jackson remarked as they turned to enter the office building.

Millard drove at a moderate pace as he approached the steep mountainous road leading down to the towns and villages and farms below. He expected no trouble at this point and encountered none. On toward Chattanooga he went, dodging places where he might be noticed. He did not want to be overly cautious, but he did want to arrive at Memphis in good shape and ready to complete his mission.

When his gas tank started getting low he stopped at a very secluded little café with a gas pump in front. *This place will do just fine*, he thought. He had his gas tank filled first and then went inside and ate a delicious liver mush sandwich and ordered another to take with him. He had gotten thirsty while on the road, so he ordered several Royal Crown colas to take with him also.

The sun was getting high in the sky when he began seeing mileage signs indicating Chattanooga was not far away. When he approached the outskirts of the city, he had every intention of bypassing as much of it as possible, but he quickly changed his mind. He decided instead to drive past the places most likely to be of interest in his search for Robert and possibly Antonio.

He drove by the place they had destroyed with dynamite not long ago, keeping a healthy distance away from the remains of the building. All he could see was a few men in suits looking around, as though they were trying to find evidence or something. Millard considered that they were federal men, since dynamite use for blowing up buildings was considered a federal crime; so he had heard.

He checked out several places, including the restaurant where Jackson was kidnapped, looking for clues. He did not find anything to be concerned about and decided to continue on to Memphis.

FIFTY-ONE

It was well past dark when Millard arrived in Memphis. The days were getting very short, consistent with late autumn. He stopped for gas, which reminded him of Robert who had told him several times to always fill your tank when you enter a city where you might have to leave in a hurry. The long hours were catching up with him, and he was road weary as well. Yet, he had not traveled all this way for his own comfort. He decided to cover a few areas of the city looking for clues that might lead him to Robert.

The first place he picked was Antonio's warehouse, which was not far away from where he intended to stay the night. The place was dark, but there was a half-moon above, which was of great help. Just as he started to pass on by the warehouse, he noticed what appeared to be a vehicle of some kind parked next to the building. He cautiously drove around to get a closer look, careful not to be too obvious in case of the presence of a security guard. The closer he got the more familiar the vehicle looked. "Well I'll be damned," he said to himself. "I haven't been here an hour and I have found Jackson's car." He determined that, if he possibly could, he'd remove it and store it in a safe place. *I have had a good day*, he thought. *Now it's time to get some rest.*

He went directly to the small hotel that he had spotted earlier. After eating supper, he went to bed. Tomorrow might bring good luck or trouble, and he knew he needed a restful night. He carefully secured his car and hoped it would stay that way.

With morning came a bright sun and a degree of warmth in the air. After breakfast, Millard sat in his car trying to figure out just where he should begin his search. After considerable thought, he reasoned that Robert and Antonio were in Memphis. If not there, they had probably been kidnapped and taken to Chicago. He decided to drive by Antonio's warehouse and see if Jackson's car was still there.

The car was still there and had not been moved. I *will have to take chances or I will accomplish nothing on this trip*, he thought, *and the sooner the better.*

Apparently no one had reported for work at the warehouse this early, so he drove to the same place where Robert had parked and observed the front of the building. He did not have to wait long before Jonathan Orders drove in with Ford Simpson behind him. The two men parked and went directly inside without even looking around.

Millard immediately decided to confront them. He checked his pistol and placed it in his shoulder holster under his coat and removed his machine gun and hid it under his coat as best he could. The bottom of it stuck out, but that would have to do. When he entered the door he went directly to the counter where Jonathan and Ford were standing. They recognized him at first sight and bid him a rather cheerful good morning.

"Good morning to you, gentlemen," replied Millard. He kept a stern look on his face, and they knew he was not there to pass the time of day.

"How can we help you this morning?" said Jonathan.

At that point, Millard pulled the machine gun out of his coat, but did not point it at them. "I want to know why in the hell Jackson's car is parked here and why we received a call from one of our men indicating to us that he was in trouble and perhaps Antonio also. I want answers, and I don't want any bullshit."

"I wish we knew," Jonathan replied. "The car was parked there several nights ago. We have not moved it one inch. The doors are not locked, and the key is in the ignition. And we have not seen Antonio since the same night the car was parked here."

Ford then said, "We considered calling the authorities but decided not to do so—at least not yet. Sometimes Antonio leaves for several days like this, and we are always careful about what we do or say because of the people he deals with in Chicago. We know what he does, but we are not a part of it," he continued. "Antonio trusts us, and we trust him. We would go to his side at any time. He has always been square with us."

Millard pointed his gun toward the floor. Somehow, his instincts told him that Ford and Jonathan were telling the truth. Still, he could not afford to trust them. Anytime the Mafia was involved, trust and truthfulness were very often absent. If these two men were connected to the mob, one wrong move on his part, and he could easily end up at the bottom of the Mississippi River.

Millard explained that he was not there to hurt anyone but that, at the same time, he could not trust anyone. He wanted to find his friend or Antonio. "I want to walk over every inch of this building to look for evidence that might be of value to me in determining their whereabouts."

They turned and began walking up and down each aisle in the warehouse, the two others in front of Millard. Ford and Jonathan helped him search everywhere, but they found nothing that would be the least bit helpful. The warehouse was solid, heavy metal and very secure. The place was vast—it looked to be a hundred by two hundred square yards with a fifty-foot ceiling—and the sheer volume and variety of items stored there was astounding. It housed everything from stacks of new tires to boats and a new vehicle; he could easily overlook a vital clue. As he searched through the warehouse, Millard determined that, if he found nothing there, he would look over the grounds outside.

When he proceeded outside to search the entire area, Jonathan and Ford accompanied him and even pointed out one small patch of woods that he did not know was a part of the warehouse property. He found nothing that would help him in his search for Robert and Antonio. But he did have Jackson's car, which he had purposefully left for last, waiting to see if anyone might come for it while he was there. No one did, and he found nothing, even though he searched every square inch of the vehicle. He even scooted under the vehicle, looking for anything—just anything. The engine started normally and he decided to leave it just as it was for now.

He thanked Jonathan and Ford for their cooperation and asked them to leave the car just as it was, telling them he would have it stored in a secure place later. That car might yet prove to be helpful to him, and he had already decided that its presence meant something. He had every intention of watching it until he could determine no reason to leave it there longer. Then he would indeed store it at the most secure place he could find.

As he was leaving the warehouse area, he noticed that Jonathan and Ford were watching him with keen interest. After driving away, he decided to get some take-out sandwiches and coffee and return to the warehouse without wasting much time. He parked behind some bushes, which hid his car well, but not where he had parked before. He did not have a view of the entrance to the warehouse but could see the greater part of the parking area and, best of all, the back of Jackson's car.

Millard waited all afternoon but saw nothing more than obvious customers coming and going. It was past six o'clock before Jonathan and Ford came out of the building and locked the door. But there was something going on that made Millard sit up in his seat. Ford was dressed in cold winter attire, including a heavy, lined coat and fur cap. He carried even heavier clothing in his arms, including a winter suit, a warm-looking overcoat, and a Stetson hat. Ford put a large pistol in a shoulder holster and placed it on the front seat of Jackson's car. It was plain to see that he intended to travel north and not in his own car. He and Jonathan were having a serious discussion about something. Jonathan then drove out the gate with Ford close behind.

Millard knew without a doubt he was on to something, and it made him angry. They had done little more than try to make a fool out of him. If Jonathan and Ford were two lying crooks, he would spare them no mercy when he got a chance to deal with them. He hoped he was wrong about what he suspected. Millard pulled out behind them, taking care not to follow too close. Jonathan turned left at the next intersection, but Ford kept going straight toward the route leading toward St. Louis and no doubt on to Chicago.

This is going to be a long night, Millard thought. The lights in Memphis were fading far behind him. He would have to follow Ford possibly all night. Ford kept a steady speed—driving Jackson's car—Millard had no problems keeping him in sight but at a safe distance. He did not want to scare him off, so he took no chances. Finally, when they were through St. Louis and headed toward Chicago, Ford stopped at a rooming house and went inside.

Luckily, a small parking lot was located across the street, and Millard drove his car closely behind the other cars parked there. He was satisfied that he would not be detected in that spot. He was tired and hungry, but he would have to wait until morning to refresh himself. He dozed off and on most of the night. At one time, he slept soundly for about two hours and awoke startled, fearing he might have lost Ford. But all was well. Ford had not left the rooming house.

Millard was fully awake and had just combed his hair when Ford came out of the rooming house and continued on the same route toward Chicago. He had rested better than expected, but he was very hungry. Ford had eaten breakfast at the rooming house and probably had no reason to stop except for gasoline. As they passed through a small town, Ford did stop to fill his tank, which should be enough to make it to Chicago.

Millard waited down the road and then rushed up and filled his gas tank. He ran into the store to buy anything he could find to eat. The owner had a small grill and had just made some large browned biscuits filled with sausage, and two of those and a large tin cup of coffee put him back on the road.

It did not take him long to catch Ford, but he remained far enough back to avoid alerting Ford. They reached Chicago late in the afternoon. Millard began following his target as close as he dared. The traffic was heavy, and he was determined to follow Ford to his destination.

That did not take very long. Ford drove directly into the parking lot of the hotel where Robert had done so much spying and killed one man on his last spying mission. Millard had already guessed why Ford was going by the luxury hotel and the exclusive part of Chicago they had driven through to get there. He drove past the hotel and around the block before entering the parking lot. Ford had already parked and had gone inside.

The man's absence was a welcome break, as it allowed him to find a good parking spot where he could view the hotel yet remain pretty well hidden and unnoticeable. *What should I do now?* he thought. He had succeeded in following Ford to this hellhole, and now he honestly did not know what to do next.

He decided to sit in the car until he was ready to take some kind of action and also to give himself a break; he was very road weary. He felt no urgency to hurry now, other than to find a men's room somewhere. But he could wait a little longer, and he did.

He went in the front door of the hotel and directly to the dining room, where he took a seat at the most secluded table he could find. Ford was nowhere to be seen.

Millard knew exactly where he was going and that he was probably already there. He decided to give himself some time by eating supper while watching the doors and stairway in case one of the three people he was concerned about might pass through. Actually, there was very little he could do now because of the lateness of the hour. Enough time remained to allow him time to scout the hallways, but it probably would be wise to check into a room before doing so. He might cause suspicion if he wandered around without being a registered guest. Robert had told him about closets on each floor and they were labeled as such. He decided to check them out when he felt comfortable doing so.

Later in the evening, he entered every unlocked closet on every floor. Unfortunately, the closet he wanted to enter most was the one over the meeting hall where Robert had shot and killed the man who'd caught him spying. He knew it would be locked before he tried turning the knob, and he did not have one of those skeleton keys like Robert used.

Millard crept cautiously down the first-floor hallway, the smell from the gaslights still tickling his nose. He passed the burnished walnut doors of the banquet room and paused. Looking to be sure no one was coming down the hallway, he pressed his ear against the door. He couldn't hear anything but muffled voices that he couldn't distinguish. He knew without a doubt the men were somewhere in that hotel and he intended to find them.

He located one unlocked closet on the same floor as the banquet hall. There might be deadly mischief going on in that large hall, and he must act decisively and fast.

He went to his room and lay down on the bed for a few minutes just to allow himself time to think of some plan. He decided to enter the one unlocked closet on the first floor and peek out as often as possible. He was very careful to keep the crack narrow to prevent it from being noticed.

After hours of watching diligently, Millard had not seen one person who was remotely familiar come out of that door. As day was breaking, he decided on more drastic action. He went to the check-in desk and asked the one clerk on duty if the men he was supposed to meet there last night had checked in. The clerk denied any knowledge of them.

Millard knew the clerk was lying because he knew Ford was there. He decided not to push the clerk or cause a disturbance. He just smiled and told the clerk he would return later.

As he went out the front door he looked for Jackson's car and it was still parked where Ford had left it. He went to his own car and watched for a while. No one came out the front door, so he returned to the hotel dining room and sat at the same remote table that he had selected the previous night. He had just ordered breakfast when he saw Antonio come in the front door and proceed down the first-floor hallway. Millard walked to the hallway entrance and observed Antonio go down the hall and enter the banquet hall. Millard figured Antonio was likely attending a meeting of the mob and that Piker would no doubt be there as well. The fact that Antonio was there did not prove anything about him except that it was a must that he attend. To do less might cost him his head if he did not show up at this no doubt special meeting.

Time for action is approaching, thought Millard. He must contact at least one of the three men he was looking for. If he could just see Robert, he would consider things were in hand.

He worked together a scenario that he hoped was accurate. Robert was probably a prisoner in that room. Antonio had probably talked himself free from whatever was happening when Robert had called Walter the other night. And Ford had come at Antonio's instruction. He had driven Jackson's car because he knew the mountain men would more than likely follow him that way. Millard knew he was guessing and that was all. But he did believe he was in the place where their major problems were, and if he could figure things out, he might be able to solve some of them.

Millard had noticed the hotel manager's office on the first floor. If the manager was not also a mob member, he could be of great help. He walked to the office and knocked firmly on the door. No one answered his knock, and he could hear nothing inside. He was getting angry and frustrated but he knew he must keep calm and collected.

He then reapproached the desk clerk, who was busy and showed little interest in acknowledging his presence. When he finally looked up, Millard asked, "I was supposed to meet three friends of mine here yesterday evening. Would you kindly see if they have registered? Their names are Ford Simpson, Robert Swink, and Antonio Vitally."

Surprisingly, without even looking at the desk registry, the clerk said, "No, sir, they are not here."

"Please check your registry, just to make sure," Millard said. "We have an important meeting scheduled, and I do not believe they would have forgotten."

The clerk was noticeably nervous as he pretended to look for their names in the registry.

"Well, that's all right," said Millard. "I will keep checking with you regularly until they show up. Please tell them I am here if they show up while I am gone."

Millard turned and walked out the door and went directly toward his car, only this time he found a place where he could view the clerk to see what the clerk did after he left. The clerk immediately made a phone call. Shortly thereafter, a man came down the stairs and talked with him and then departed back up the stairs and disappeared down the hall.

Millard knew that Ford and Antonio were in that room, but he was very worried about Robert. If Robert was in this hotel, he was being held somewhere under guard. He had no way of knowing more than what he now knew. He would have to go with what little information he had.

Millard put his hat on the seat and sighed in frustration. *I might squeeze information out of that damn little worm of a desk clerk*, he thought. He tapped his fingers in agitation.

If that meeting adjourned, everyone would probably scatter in different directions and ruin his chances of finding any of the three men he was trying to contact. His mind was made up. He placed his machine gun and five sticks of fused dynamite in his overcoat and, with great care, folded his coat so they would not be noticed. Without hesitation, he walked to the hotel entrance and was at the desk of the clerk before he realized he was there. He leaned over and softly said, "I do not want to cause a disturbance, but it is very important that I find Robert Swink very soon. If you know where he is, I advise you to tell me now."

In a shaky voice, the clerk said, "Sir, I have no knowledge of his whereabouts, or I would tell you."

"Well," said Millard, "maybe you just forgot and need to be reminded." He then pulled his coat back just enough for the clerk to see the handle of his pistol protruding out of its holster.

"I really don't know where Mr. Swink is, but you might try knocking on the door of room 502 on the fifth floor, and please don't involve me any more in whatever is going on."

Millard knew the clerk would run for help just as soon as he was out of sight. "I think it best if you just walk calmly, in front of me up the steps to the fifth floor and you knock on the door of 502," said Millard. "If all is well with Robert you may return to your desk immediately, and no one will ever know this ever happened if you just keep quiet."

Up the steps they went, and the clerk was getting increasingly nervous. Millard wanted no hesitation in getting this chore completed, and he had no intention of allowing the nervous clerk to return to his desk alone.

The clerk knocked on the door, and after a few seconds, someone asked, "Who's there?"

"It is the desk clerk, and I have a message."

The voice behind the door didn't belong to Robert, and Millard drew his pistol from its holster, ready for action. He could hear the door being unlocked, and a well-dressed man with a moustache opened the door.

"This gentleman wants to talk with a Mr. Robert Swink," said the clerk.

"There is no Robert Swink in this room," the man replied.

Millard could see a faint shadow of someone in the room, but he said nothing.

"You best return to your desk and I will talk to this man myself," the man said to the clerk.

Millard then stepped beside the clerk and said to the man, "I don't think so. This man leaves when I do, and if anyone shoots in our direction, you're a dead man."

The man looked at Millard's .38 and slowly opened the door wide open. And there in the dimly lit room was a man sitting in a soft chair whose face he could hardly see.

"What in the hell are you doing here, Millard?" said Robert.

"Well, I might ask you the same thing," replied Millard.

"This fine man who you were prepared to shoot is Mr. Ransom L. Madison."

The desk clerk seemed to relax and breathe deeply when he saw there was going to be no trouble. Mr. Madison told the desk clerk to return to his work and not to report this incident to anyone else. Millard started to object, but Robert assured him that Mr. Madison was trustworthy. They went inside, and Robert formerly introduced them.

Millard was surprised to say the least when Robert told him that Mr. Madison was a federal agent. "Mr. Madison didn't come to arrest us old mountain men did he?" asked Millard.

"Not at all," said Robert. "He has no interest in us other than mutual friendship and mutual help where possible. He is slowly but surely gathering evidence on the Mafia and their bootlegging activities. He almost has enough evidence to nail old Piker, along with high-ranking members and many members of lower rank, to the wall. He is aware that times are hard and people like us mean no harm and are not dangerous, except to the Mafia people and others who try to harm us."

"We have been worried about you, Robert, after your call to Walter indicated you might be in danger and Antonio also. It was a peculiar message, and I have been on your trail ever since. We look after our own, you know."

FIFTY-TWO

Millard was happy to find Robert. They talked at length about what had happened since they'd left Newbarn. Millard was most anxious to learn about Ford Simpson and Antonio Vitally. "I followed Ford in Jackson's car from Antonio's warehouse to here. I know Ford and Antonio are in the large meeting room on the first floor, and I don't know if they are friend or foe. I got tired of this cat and mouse game, and I decided to find out what was going on in this place and where you were. I was certain that you were being held against your will somewhere in this maze of rooms."

He then unfolded his coat, and Robert and Ransom were amazed at what he had brought in.

"I had no intention of using the dynamite, except to bluff my way out of here if I had to leave in a hurry. I don't trust this place at all, and I intend to leave this devil's den alive."

That brought laughter from Robert and Ransom. "I know I wouldn't confront you with what you have there," said Ransom, pointing at the dynamite.

"What was going on and where were you when you called Walter?" asked Millard.

"Antonio and I were in Memphis. He had been in Chicago earlier but had returned to Memphis to take care of some business. I found him right away, and we went to a bar that, according to Antonio, was known as the place to find information on just about anything if you knew the right people to ask. Antonio knew the place well and had made contacts with individuals who were interested in purchasing part of his assets secretively.

"As he was discussing the sale with his contact, several men entered the bar. I knew right away they were looking for Antonio and I was right. They went directly to his table and snatched him up and headed out the door with him. The bartender and me knew what was going on and we, along with Antonio's contact, went to his aid. We had a hell of a fight, but they wanted to kidnap him rather than beat him up. They had a car parked near the door, and one of the men opened the door to allow the others to force him into the rear seat. We put two of them out, but there were just too many.

"If the barkeeper and Antonio's contact had not come to our aid, I don't know what would have happened. I probably should not have called Walter, but I had taken some hard blows and was not thinking straight. All I could think of was to contact Newbarn. When I called, something was wrong with the phone lines. I didn't think I had gotten through, but evidently I did get to say a few words, which probably didn't make much sense. I am sorry for the confusion I caused."

"Well, since I am here, I am willing to help out any way possible," said Millard. "I am puzzled about some things, but I know you will set me straight. I located Jackson's car parked beside Antonio's warehouse in Memphis with the doors unlocked and the keys in the ignition. I searched the warehouse and grounds thoroughly looking for you. Jonathan Orders and Ford Simpson cooperated with me after I pulled the gun out. They denied being members of the mob, but I am not convinced of that at all.

"I told them to leave Jackson's car where it was and then watched the place to see what they would do. Shortly thereafter, Ford drove the car toward St. Louis and then on to here. What I know now is that Ford and Antonio are in the large banquet hall on the first floor, and after intimidating the desk clerk, I found you and Mr. Madison here."

"You are right, Millard," said Robert. "Jonathan and Ford are members of the mob. The three of them are wanting out of the mob, but they will have to take it slow and easy in order to get out with their lives. As you know, Antonio has his plans made, but Jonathan and Ford have not figured a way out yet. They are moving somewhere out west. Coordinating a desertion like that without getting caught and slaughtered will take some doing."

"I'll bet they would like to join Newbarn," said Millard, "but we will not accept them. I will tell you that. If the decision were left up to me alone, I would not take Antonio into our Newbarn group either. These Mafia people are very convincing with their lies, and while I do find myself believing in him, I continue to have doubts. To rise to prominence in the Mafia as he has, he must have done some awful stuff. People do change, though, and I hope he has. We have indicated to him that we will accept him in our organization, and he says he intends to divorce himself from that hellish Mafia."

"Well, Millard, we are here and here we must remain until that meeting is over," said Robert. "Then we must act decisively and get out of here fast. Antonio and Ford will come up here to talk with us. Ford did get you to follow him up here by driving Jackson's car, just as you probably suspected he would.

"When we are ready we will leave here one at a time and meet at Antonio's warehouse back in Memphis. Ransom is going to Memphis also. He wants to know where he can make future contacts with us and become familiar with the layout of the area and the location of the warehouse. That information could prove extremely valuable to him should he get into a running battle with members of the Mafia. Anytime he is in more trouble than he can handle, the warehouse will be a temporary place of refuge for him. Ransom has agreed to help us in return for our help at certain times, and he has agreed not to implicate Ford, Antonio, or Jonathan as having any connection with the mob," Robert continued.

"What a relief," replied Millard.

About an hour later, the big meeting adjourned and everyone went his own way. Ford Simpson, Jonathan Orders, and Antonio Vitally came up to the room, and after some very interesting conversation and swapping of information, they left the building as planned and headed for Memphis. They had decided to delay stopping anywhere until they passed St. Louis. Antonio left first and Millard last.

Antonio knew of a large rooming house and considered it a safe place for them to sleep a few hours. They were up at first light and headed on toward Memphis. None of them had slept soundly, but all was well when they stopped at a café for breakfast. They were more at ease now and beginning to act more like old buddies. They had a smoke and told a few jokes in the parking lot and then headed on to Memphis.

Antonio and Ford were very watchful and alert as they drove along at a smooth pace. They knew what it could mean for them if mobster spies were watching them. Millard also kept a close surveillance by doubling back and then turning around to follow along behind again. So far he had noticed nothing suspicious.

When they reached Memphis that evening, they went directly to Antonio's warehouse. Mr. Madison was well pleased to have such a place where he knew he would be safe and could possibly be helpful to Antonio and his men in their efforts to leave the Mafia. Millard and Robert did not remain at the warehouse very long. Antonio had already briefed them on what was going on in the mob that would be of concern to Newbarn, and they would use that valuable information to its best advantage. They decided to keep only a short distance between them and drive straight through to Newbarn, stopping only for gas and something to eat. They were very watchful as they passed through Chattanooga and on toward the mountains. Nothing unusual happened during this stretch or from there on to Newbarn.

Everything was closed down at Newbarn, so they left a note that they had returned and went home.

The house was dark when Millard arrived, but a kerosene lamp was lit as he parked his car. Flora came to the door and asked, "Where have you been so long? I have been so worried about you; I didn't know what to do."

"It did take me longer than I thought it would, and I was in several dangerous situations," said Millard. "Robert was at a hotel in Chicago, in good shape. I won't try to explain all the things that went on, but we will talk things over in a few days as we usually do. Let's go to bed now. I will need to be at work on time tomorrow. We will need to go over some valuable information we brought home with us. Important decisions will need to be made that cannot be put off. I do want to look at the house before I leave in the morning though. How are things progressing up there?"

"Wonderfully well as you will see. Papa has been in his glory working on that house. He says it is the finest home he has ever constructed."

Millard had no sooner set the large alarm clock above his bed when it went off, shocking him awake. "I just set that thing," he mumbled from under the covers.

"Maybe you set it too early and your body is trying to tell you it needs more rest," Flora replied.

"Well, my mind tells me to arise and get to work," he said.

"Roll over on your stomach and I will rub your back," she continued. "That will help you relax and feel more rested."

He did as she said and sure enough, that did the trick. He sat up straight and got out of bed.

The boys got up wanting him to play with them, but all he could do was promise to play with them later. He could do little more for Flora than give her a great big hug and kiss, and after hurriedly eating a bite of breakfast, he hurried out the door.

He started toward his car and then turned and came back in the house. "Get me a clean change of clothes," he said. "I can't go into work looking like this. I hold a position in Newbarn, and I can't go in looking like a bum."

Flora did as he asked, and while she did so, he got a pan of lukewarm water and washed himself with a washcloth. "Not much of a bath, but I feel like I look better," he said laughingly.

"You had better go if you want to look at the new house before you leave," she said.

He started the car, wiped the dew off the windshield, and then proceeded on up the hill. The new house seemed bigger than a large barn looking down at him. It was completely enclosed, and the windows were beautiful. The chimneys were completed, and the doors Flora had picked out were just perfect. The upper half of each door was made of stained glass. He didn't have time to look inside, but he had seen enough to keep him excited all day.

Millard drove on to work. He realized the danger of becoming an obstructionist by disagreeing with changes without listening to others and their points of view. There must always be respect by the leadership or Newbarn would slowly begin to weaken and eventually fail. He decided that he would not allow himself to drift in that direction.

Jackson was the only person at Newbarn when Millard arrived. Before Millard said good morning, Jackson said, "Where is my car, Millard? I had a feeling when you left that I would never see my car again," he added.

"You look shaky and worried, Jackson; just calm down a little. Your car is in Antonio Vitally's warehouse in Memphis, safe and sound. He will bring it back over here soon. Besides, you have your fine old Buick to get around in for a few more days."

"I guess that will have to do," Jackson replied. "At least it ain't gone forever, I reckon."

Soon John and Robert came in. It was Saturday, and the other men were probably still in bed. Robert said he thought he was late, but if he was, it couldn't be helped. He'd had to explain to Walter, in detail, what had been going on while they were away.

"What all did happen?" asked Jackson.

Millard had brewed a pot of coffee and filled their cups before a lot of talking began.

Robert told the group about his recent experiences. "When I left here last week, I followed our usual route down the mountains to Chattanooga and beyond. I found nothing of interest, and that is saying a lot. I covered every familiar place and then did a back and forth coverage of the entire countryside. After that, I convinced myself that I could do no more and that, if there was anything to be concerned about, it was well hidden. I continued on to Memphis, covering every main road all the way and any side roads that appeared to be heavily traveled.

"In Memphis, things were more interesting. I went on to Antonio's warehouse and found him in his office, where I knew he would be. He knew I wanted to talk to him and made every effort to make me comfortable in doing so. We had several long conversations and many meals together. The more we talked, the more I came to like him and enjoy his company. He did not deny his past with the Mafia and the crimes he had committed over the years. 'I am now making plans to get away, and Jonathan Orders and Ford Simpson want to leave as much as I do,' he told me.

"'They will look for you for years and go anywhere to locate you and murder you,' I told him. 'That is why few people ever make it out of the Mafia or even attempt to do so.'

"That is when he told me of the next meeting of the Mafia in Chicago. I followed him to the famous hotel where the important meeting was to be held. He warned me not to acknowledge him or try to contact him while we were there and said that he would contact me when the time was right.

"I met Mr. Ransom Madison by accident as we were eating dinner at the hotel. One subject led to another until we decided we could be of mutual benefit, since he was a federal agent and I was a detective. We were both interested in the Mafia and wanted to see its downfall. We were waiting for a contact from Antonio when Millard found us on the fifth floor—with weapons and dynamite."

"How can we be certain he is a federal agent?" Millard asked.

"We usually don't meet by accident as Ransom and me did, but by our conversation and inquisitiveness, we knew rather quickly that we had a common interest. We were careful enough in this situation to carefully examine each other's credentials.

"Don't worry about Mr. Madison because he is, indeed, a federal man. He assured us that he has no interest in us mountain men and will do all he can to help us. He is soliciting our help also. You will be pleased when you meet him. He wants us to help him gather information that he can use as evidence to put the whiskey-selling, murdering mobsters behind bars. It is obvious that we have a no-lose situation here. We will be rid of that hellish Piker, and that will be a major achievement. When he goes, our main troubles will probably leave also, at least for a while. We will all benefit from such an arrangement," Robert concluded.

"One thing stands out in my mind," said Jackson. "Who were those men who tried to kidnap Antonio in Memphis and what did they want from him?"

"We have not figured that one out yet," replied Robert. "I am sure they will show themselves again though. The only men I can remotely think of are that bunch of fools near St. Louis who have vowed to take over the whiskey business for hundreds of miles around. We heard about them from Jim Anderson, one of our customers some time ago. We will have to wait and see what happens. I know of nothing else we can do now. Antonio might want to follow up on that strange event, but we cannot be certain that Newbarn was even involved."

"Millard, how did things go on your trip?" Jackson asked.

"I accomplished everything I went for," replied Millard. Millard relayed the details of his trip, and Jackson agreed that it went well.

"I suspect that we all have little doubt about having to return there again," he said.

"I think we will settle these matters before too long," said Millard. "I can see things coming together, but we will have to be very careful and very patient. What we have to do now is wait for Antonio and let him tell us firsthand what the Mafia knows about us and the hellish plans they have for us."

"This is Saturday, and I know we need some time off," said Jackson. "Unless someone has something they want to discuss, let's go home and return Monday. I doubt that Antonio will come over before then. We are geared for action and ready to move when he gets here."

They all departed and were delighted to have a free weekend.

Millard drove home quickly. He had many things he needed to see about, but spending time with the boys and Flora was foremost on his mind. Down the hill he went with a smile on his face.

Flora and the boys were in the yard playing ball, and little Walter was trying to bat. Every time he swung the bat, he threw himself off balance and fell down. They stopped playing and ran to him as fast as they could. He hugged and kissed them, and they went into the house and sat around the kitchen table.

"How long are you off?" asked Flora. "When you left this morning, I thought you might be gone all day and maybe longer."

"I am here for the weekend at least," he replied. "You three plan what we should do today and tomorrow while I listen. I might want to add a little something too. Maybe you could allow us to go up to the new house and look it over."

Flora and the boys wanted to do that first thing—as Millard's tour guides of course.

"Then we want to go for chocolate cake and ice cream," added Cameron.

Little Walter just gave him a big smile and a slobbery kiss on the cheek.

The house was well on the way to being finished. *It is certainly a grand house, no doubt about that*, thought Millard. "Maybe I overdid it some, Flora," he said. "I like it very much; it just seems so out of place compared to other homes in the area. What are the people around here saying about it, Flora?" he asked.

"They think it is a welcome addition to our community," she answered. "It makes them want to make our community something special like our house is. And you should not feel guilty for building it, as I believe you are doing."

"I don't feel guilty exactly. I just wish our neighbors had fine homes built just the way they would like them to be."

FIFTY-THREE

After Millard had thoroughly inspected the house, they were off to Spruce Willow for ice cream and chocolate cake and a cola of their choice.

Cameron then wanted to go wading in the river, but Millard explained that the water was much too cold and they would have to wait until spring.

Flora suggested that they visit Ma. She needed a visit from them. They all thought that was a great idea, and soon they were driving up to the house.

Ma was extremely happy to see them. The boys played outside most of the time, while Flora and Millard enjoyed talking with Ma. During the conversation, Millard asked Ma how she would like to live with them when their house was completed.

"I think not," she said politely.

Millard encouraged her to think about it, and they would discuss it again soon. "Ma, you just can't stay here alone, especially during the cold months. It would be dangerous for you. If you should go outside when snow and ice are on the ground and fall, it could be disastrous. It would be a joy to have you live with us and don't worry about the farm here. I will see that it is kept just as you leave it."

"I will think about it," she answered.

"We are going up to Bald Ridge to visit Flora's folks when we leave here. Would you like to go with us?"

That offer took no thought at all. She immediately said yes, and soon they were on their way.

When they arrived, Salem and Martha had heard them coming and were standing on the front porch looking pleased as could be. After laughter and an exchange of greetings—and the boys being kissed more than they wanted to be—they all went inside. Ma had not been to the house since her last visit with Millard and the family. Martha had cooked supper early, and that made everything fall into place just as though it had been planned that way.

After supper, of course, Salem and Millard went to their favorite spot in the woodshed to talk and sip a little shine. Millard replenished Salem's supply with a quart he had hidden in his car. "I knew you had some of that good, old moonshine when I saw you drive up. Just in time too; I was just about out."

Millard, as usual, brought Salem up to date on the happenings at Newbarn. Salem could hardly believe that they had accomplished so much without getting into bad trouble. He was mostly amazed at the dynamiting of the store in Chattanooga and also at Millard getting out of that hotel in Chicago without being detected.

"Damn, it appears you men at Newbarn don't fool around much," said Salem. "I still worry some about you, Millard."

"Don't worry, Salem," said Millard. "We have things in hand for now, and we are alert at all times. And we will negotiate with the Chicago people as long as they negotiate in good faith. They want 80 percent of our profits, and that cannot be. I think they will deal with us for their own sake. I get the feeling they are somewhat skittish about tangling with us old mountain men. They had rather have a fair deal than nothing at all." Smiling, he changed the subject. "It's difficult to think about work much while admiring this beautiful home. You are building a fine house, and I want it put to full use too. I didn't expect you to construct it in such a short time," said Millard.

"That is a big house," Salem agreed, "and I think you will need another chimney for looks and for comfort. You will have a wood cooking stove and a wood heater in the kitchen, and with all those fires going, you will have a nice, warm house to enjoy in any weather."

"Flora has a good eye for interior design, and she will show you the type of wood for the walls and the ceilings and the corner moldings and other niceties that will be appropriate for the house," said Millard. "She has bought books about such things, and I am sure she will get your opinion as well. Next spring, I hope to completely landscape the yard and pasture and sections set aside for woods and shrubbery. Later, outbuildings and a barn and perhaps even a blacksmith shop can be considered. Oh hell, one could ramble on and on about such, but I know that, at some point, the place will please my eye and it will be finished. I don't intend to work on it after that. But rest assured, Salem, that place will be a place where Ma and you and Martha and anyone in our families can come and always be welcome. If I can't accomplish that, I had rather stay in our cabin in the hollow below."

"I believe you mean what you say, Millard, and I thank you for saying those words to me. Thank you kindly. We should go into the house and visit with the family, I suppose," said Salem.

"Yes, we should," said Millard. "I don't come here often enough as it is, and I don't pay the boys enough attention either. The little fellows seem to understand and complain very little. I would like to take them and Flora to church tomorrow. They love to attend, and I love taking them, but Newbarn has taken so many of my Sundays recently that church has been out of the question. The next Sunday I am off, we will attend church up here. I love your church too, and they always insist on me singing in the choir every time I attend."

"I am not much on church myself, but if you come, I will go with you," replied Salem.

After a very happy visit, Millard headed home with his family. Luckily, he would have several hours to spend with Flora and the boys before bedtime. After supper, they all sat in a circle on the bed and told stories, and Flora read the Bible to them.

Millard told the boys about his work at Newbarn, but only the fun parts. They asked him many questions about Chicago and Memphis—to them, unimaginable, far-off places. They stayed up later than usual and then were off to bed with kisses aplenty.

After they were asleep, Flora wanted to know more about the dangerous situations she knew Millard had been in. He explained to her what he could without causing her to worry and promised that things would soon be stable and peaceful at Newbarn. She knew he had neglected to tell all, but she was content with what he had to say.

Millard set his clock with the dreadful alarm to wake him early and, as usual, it didn't fail in its duty.

Millard slid out of bed and quietly prepared himself for work. He rarely ate breakfast at home anymore, preferring to sleep a little longer and finding breakfast later in the morning. He had his guns and extra clothes in his car, as was the policy at Newbarn.

Sadly, he was beginning to consider himself an outlaw, but not in the true sense of the word. Newbarn was different from the outlaws attached to the Mafia at penalty of death if they strayed or abandoned their evil rules. Newbarn was an honorable organization and would always be that way. A handshake is all that was asked of new members.

Millard hoped that Antonio Vitally would come to Newbarn today but considered that it might be several days or weeks before they saw him. Vitally had a dangerous mission before him, and if the Mafia caught him in the act of abandoning the organization, he would probably never be heard from again. Ford Simpson and Jonathan Orders would witness the same fate. Antonio was very intelligent and clever. He might just be able to pull off his dangerous maneuver. In any case, Millard considered that the next month or two would be a time of turmoil and even injury and death. He was nearing Newbarn now and hopeful of good news and plans well made.

As Millard drove down the road to Newbarn, he saw few cars. He wondered why, until he realized how early he was. Only Jackson and John were present. The office was quiet with only a "good morning" to greet the day.

Millard decided to keep quiet until Robert and, possibly, Walter came in. He poured a cup of coffee that Jackson had brewed; it was almost too strong to swallow. He realized that Jackson must have his mind in deep thought or he would never have made coffee that strong. Millard could wait no longer without talking. It was making him tense and uneasy. "Has anyone heard from Antonio lately?" he asked.

"Not a word," answered Jackson, "and it makes me nervous. I know we have no reason to expect him this soon, but if he doesn't show by the end of the week, I am going over there to get my car. Will one of you fighting rascals go with me?" he asked as he looked around the room.

"Hell yes," said John. "I'll go. I am just in the mood to smack some heads about while we are over there too," he added.

Laughter filled the room, and everyone loosened up a bit.

"I just heard Robert drive up," said Millard. "I hope he has something to say that will urge us to make some decisions."

Robert quickly came in the door, and he did have something to say, but he hesitated to talk until he'd poured himself a cup of Jackson's strong coffee. "Who had the pleasure of making this coffee?" he asked.

"Now don't start picking on me," said Jackson. "I know the coffee is bad. I couldn't drink it myself. Have you had any word from Antonio?" he asked.

"Yes, we have," said Robert. "He called about three o'clock this morning. He will be over here one day this week to discuss the business at hand. Mr. Piker, he says, has agreed to allow us to keep 40 percent of our own money in exchange for his protection. Don't believe a damn word of it. He has no intention of giving you more than the 20 percent that was his original offer. Be ready for trouble. Ford and Jonathan have been lucky enough to make final arrangements and move out west. That helped Antonio I think, since he had not left and Piker does not know he is selling off most of his assets in secret. He also said he thought we would be safe to make our usual truck deliveries that way. Piker has no interest, so far as he could determine, in trying to stop you at this point. But he will."

Everyone sat quietly before speaking.

"You talked to Antonio, Robert," said Jackson. "Do you believe what he said?"

"Yes, I do," Robert replied. "He had a very sincere tone, and I detected enough fear in his voice to indicate he wants us to move quickly before Piker's lieutenants make plans on how they can wipe us out and kill him. I suggest we make our deliveries in that direction as we normally do. I will keep close watch and alert you if I see danger approaching or anything else important lurking in the shadows."

Each person in the room expressed his opinion, and they all came to the same conclusions, except for a few nonsignificant issues. Millard suggested that he and John take the run to Chicago. They had the most experience in long hauls and were very good at identifying and getting out of trouble. If their run proved to be successful, perhaps that would be a good indication that other trucks would get through as well.

Jackson announced that more than enough men had been trained for long hauls now. "Actually we have good, well-trained men for short and long hauls," he added. "It took a while to completely build our organization, but it is now completed. Our land and buildings are in excellent condition, and we have a complement of fine, dependable men; well-equipped vehicles; and enough firearms for a small army."

"You forgot what a fine product we have to sell," said John.

"You are exactly right," said Jackson. "Newbarn could not exist without our fine whiskey made by Horace Blue, the finest whiskey maker ever to walk these Blue Ridges."

Millard and John were ready to leave immediately. They checked their guns carefully, wanting to be prepared should trouble come their way, and John placed a full case of dynamite in the truck—"just for added protection." They went directly to Horace Blue's and loaded their truck to capacity. Horace wished them a safe trip, and they were off.

They followed the same route as usual, taking no extra precautions, other than staying alert and very watchful of the passing traffic and areas they knew were rough and often troublesome. Along the way, they stopped for food and gas and even some relaxation, and before long, they could hardly believe they were in Memphis and feeling great. They found a very nice rooming house, which had a room with a window that afforded them a plain view of their truck.

Morning revealed a beautiful, frosty day with a bright sunny sky. After a hardy breakfast, Millard and John decided to stop for a short visit with Antonio before heading on to Chicago. They drove to his warehouse.

It appeared that he had been there all night. He received them warmly but kept working, doing inventory and paperwork. Over half of the warehouse had been cleared out. "I have been working here since yesterday morning," he said. "I have been in constant touch with the people who are buying much of my solid assets, and they have been helping me load their trucks with items I have sold to them. We are making good progress, but it will take a while to complete the job."

"I hope the mob don't get wind of what you are doing and jump on you while you are in the middle of this move," said John.

"I am keeping myself pretty well covered," replied Antonio.

"We would like to help you," said Millard, "but we have a heavily loaded truck of moonshine to deliver to Chicago as you suggested the other night."

"Damn, I will be glad to see you leave this place and come over to Newbarn," said John. "You will be safe there, and we will have a new friend among us."

"On our return trip, we will stop and check on you, and if you have some things you want us to haul to the mountains, we will be glad to do so," said Millard.

"Please do," said Antonio. "I can tell you now that I will have all you can haul."

With firm handshakes, Millard and John were off toward St. Louis. They intended to drive straight through to Chicago without stopping for the night.

Memphis, as usual, was a beautiful drive. The signs of the Depression were very prevalent however. "My Lord, Millard," said John. "I don't believe this hellish depression will ever end."

"Don't seem so," said Millard, "but it will. I will never accept such suffering of the poor though; but the poor have been with us always, and I have been one of them. I know how it is firsthand. Seeing such misery bothers me, but I keep it out of mind as much as possible."

"I have never been poor like many folks, but I have been wanting at times, and that was a problem to me," John remarked.

On toward St. Louis they continued, stopping only for gas and food. As they neared St. Louis, they decided to stop briefly and pay Jim Anderson a visit. He was happy to see them. Business was good for him, and he was especially content with the relationship with Newbarn. "All the truckers that make deliveries to me and my customers are always reliable and courteous."

"We are on our way to Chicago with this heavily loaded truck," said Millard.

"How are things going up that way?" asked Jim. "Usually that damn place is little more than trouble."

"Well, it hasn't changed much except for the worst," said John. "We are trying to get along with the Mafia up there, but it appears to be an impossible undertaking. We have no intention of changing our ways of doing business, though, and they probably know it. Have you heard any more about that crazy bunch near St. Louis who was threatening to take over the whiskey business for hundreds of miles?"

"No, I have not," replied Jim. "I have asked about them, but no one seems to know. All I can guess is that the Mafia got them or they self-destructed." He chuckled.

"We have had no trouble with them," John remarked. "I just asked as a matter of curiosity."

"We will stop by every chance we get," said Millard. "We don't expect much trouble in Chicago this time. Considering that we are in the midst of some negotiations with the Mafia, we don't think they would try anything foolish now. We intend to stay alert to any situation, however."

"Good luck to you both," replied Jim as they shook hands. "I would sure like to come over and visit with you people some time," he added, "but it seems that all I get done is working my ass off over here."

"You would be more than welcome anytime you can see your way clear to come," replied Millard.

As Millard and John headed on toward Chicago, they talked very little. They enjoyed the scenic beauty but deplored the plight of the people they passed—people who scattered about achieving their goal of finding food for the day; some walked, and a few hauled anything they thought they could sell anywhere they could find a market.

When Millard and John reached the city, it was getting late and the lights were shining brightly. "I am hungry as a bear," said John.

"Me too," Millard replied. "Let's find a good place to eat and park the truck where it will be safe. I don't trust this place enough to leave the truck out of sight. Let's go to Cliff Banister's restaurant. He was our first customer in this city."

FIFTY-FOUR

After Millard and John left the restaurant, John said, "We have had nothing but good luck since we left Newbarn. If we return to Newbarn trouble free, it will be a first for us. We usually catch hell at every turn."

They stayed the night at the fancy hotel where they had stayed before. Again nothing happened out of the ordinary.

The next morning, John said. "All this good luck is making me nervous."

"Let's get this load delivered to our customers and be on our way home," Millard replied. "I will feel a lot better after that I hope."

Having established this route, they knew it well and were successful in completing it much faster than usual. They finished the day early enough to make the decision not to remain in Chicago another night. They knew they could make it to St. Louis before too late and then be home by tomorrow. It was not a difficult decision, and they soon were on their way. They thought of stopping to see Mr. Brown, but it was too late for that. Given the circumstances, they thought it best to make it home as soon as possible while their luck still held.

As they traveled on toward St. Louis, they took turns driving and sleeping. They had done this many times before. They made excellent time and arrived in St. Louis much earlier than expected. They found the same place they had stayed before and slept well.

They were up early, anxious to get on the road toward Memphis and home. Gas and food stops were all they made. They were getting road weary but decided not to stop, except at Antonio's warehouse for a load of his things to haul back to the mountains for him. Then on they went through Chattanooga and to the top of the mountains. When they reached the top, they stopped at a familiar parking place, and both went to sleep for a short while.

When they woke up, they were both groaning from being cramped up for so long. "I am never going to sleep in the truck again if I can help it—especially after traveling all day," said Millard.

"Neither am I, but we will probably do the same thing again sooner or later," John said as he groaned again.

"Have we ever done anything together that didn't involve some type of suffering?" Millard complained.

"Crank up that engine and let's get on home," said John.

They knew they would get to Newbarn before daybreak, but they did not expect anyone to be at the headquarters when they arrived.

The place was well lit, and a few people were inside. "Wonder what is going on," John said.

"I don't know, but I believe that something is wrong," Millard replied.

As they walked in the door, they quickly became acutely aware that something very unusual had happened. Jackson, Robert, and Horace were sitting at the table looking very sad.

Before they could utter a work Jackson said, "Dad died shortly after midnight this morning."

"My Lord," said Millard.

Neither he nor John could say another word. They went over and sat down on the couch. Silence filled the room. Jackson knew how they cared for his dad and wanted them to have time to adjust to the shock. Neither he nor the others had actually adjusted, but time had allowed them to accept the reality of the terrible situation. "Mom called me immediately. She heard him take a deep breath, and when she turned the lights on, his last breath was gone. I went over immediately, hoping against hope that perhaps something could be done. Mom had already called our family physician, and he was there before I arrived. It was his opinion that Pop had died peacefully in his sleep from heart failure with no suffering. He offered to have an autopsy performed in case he was wrong about the cause of death, but Mom and I declined."

The room returned to quiet again.

Finally Jackson broke the silence by telling them he was going to be with his mom and his family and he did not think he could bear to work until after the funeral. "We have made no specific plans yet, but we will soon. This is Friday, and I will leave this place in your capable hands," he said, looking at Millard, John, and Horace.

"You need not worry; we will take care of things here," replied Millard. "The men will be coming in after a while so we will tell them what has happened and complete this day as usual. One thing I might tell you that might ease your mind some. We encountered no problems at all during our trip to Chicago."

"That is good news," replied Jackson.

"If we can be of help, please call on us," John said to him as he was leaving.

After Jackson left, the others sat around the table and discussed what affect Walter's passing would have on Newbarn.

"My dad died not too long ago, and it was not an easy thing to experience," Millard remarked. "Jackson will be devastated, but the sorrow will pass, and life will go on."

As the deliverymen came in, Millard told each one what had happened. They were all sad beyond words. One of the younger men began crying; he told how Walter had befriended him and given him a job when he'd had no way to support his family and they'd had nowhere to turn.

The day went smoothly, but sadness among Walter's friends, Newbarn employees, and all those who loved him seemed to hover over them like a dark cloud.

They were all very tired and decided to go home and return the next day and determine how they could pay their respects. Millard knew that Jackson would include them in some way as final plans for Walter were made. When they departed from Newbarn, they left every light on.

Millard drove home, his heart filled with sorrow. Flora knew something was frightfully wrong. He explained to her the events of the day and the shock of coming home from Chicago and hearing the horrible news that Walter had died. "I think we should visit the family soon. They are very close to us and have been for a long time," he said. "I will go over to Newbarn tomorrow morning. I need to talk some things over with John and Robert and possibly Horace.

"Everything went well on our trip to Chicago," he told her. "There were no attempts to harm us in any way. If things go well over the next two months, I think we can settle our disputes with others and end this troublesome way of life. Don't get your hopes up though. Some of our problems could turn to violence."

"That is what I have been afraid of," remarked Flora. "It has been worrisome to me since you began expanding Newbarn toward Chicago. We are mountain folks, and those people are different from us."

"We will settle things pretty soon one way or another," he assured her.

Millard was restless all night, and the boys talked in their sleep. Flora did not feel rested when morning came, so they all slept later than usual.

Millard went to Newbarn after breakfast. He assured Flora that he would return after he had talked with Jackson. As he drove slowly toward Newbarn, deep in thought, he dreaded the day. To his surprise, Jackson was at the headquarters all alone.

"I am glad to see you, Millard," he said, wiping tears from his eyes. "Everything is so quiet down at the house. I would have stayed with Mom, but some of her friends are with her, and they seem to be doing very well. I am having a hard time with this, Millard. Everything seems upside down or something and I can't make myself do the things I want to do."

"Maybe you don't need to do much," said Millard. "The funeral director will do everything, if you want to go that way. When my dad died, the men and ladies in the community built a casket for him that was beautiful beyond words."

"The funeral director did come last night and helped us plan every detail concerning the funeral and burial. But you know, what you just described about the casket strikes a note with me. I believe that is exactly what Pop would really like. He was one of the old school and had an appreciation for things like that. Do you suppose we could get the people who constructed your father's casket to build one for my father?"

"Of course they would. They could have it completed before evening," said Millard.

"Go with me, Millard," said Jackson. "Help me get it done. That would be the greatest honor I could show my dear father." Millard detected a slight degree of joy in his friend's voice.

"I will drive you over there after you tell your family where we are going," replied Millard.

Just then, John and Robert walked in the door. Jackson quickly told them of their plans, and they volunteered to go along and help out. "I have helped build caskets many times," said John. "It would be an honor to help build one for Mr. Stamey."

Robert wanted to help too, so off they went without any hesitation.

When they arrived at the turnoff to Birch Creek, Millard stopped at the houses where he knew the fine carpenters and carvers lived, and not one refused to build the casket. The ladies volunteered their skills with the same enthusiasm as the men. One of the carpenters owned a large carpenter shop stocked with every woodworking tool imaginable. All the men assembled began working on the casket soon after they had discussed the details with Jackson and Millard. Basically, Jackson wanted his father's casket built like the one they had made for Millard's father.

As Millard had predicted, completing the casket took less than a day. It was almost a duplicate of the one they had built for Millard's father. They were a little short on white-oak lumber, but they had found enough to complete the job.

"What a beautiful piece of art and beauty," Jackson told them, running his fingers over the ornately carved vines along the side. "I know you do not charge for such labors of love, but I want to give you something in honor of my father. These are hard times, and it is my hope that you will accept it for your own use. But if you don't want to accept it for yourselves, please give it to a needy person or your church or some other place of your choosing."

The wonderful people did not refuse the substantial sum of money he left with them.

"I will instruct the funeral home to come for the casket, and I am very grateful to you."

As they arrived back at Newbarn, most of the route men were there looking as though they did not know what to do. They were obviously very sorrowful. Every man who worked at Newbarn had been befriended and treated with utmost kindness by Walter and Jackson Stamey.

Jackson talked with the men and welcomed them to come by Walter's house, where his body would lie in state. No other plans had been made past that point. "We are all family, and we will stick together through this time of sorrow and then continue the Newbarn business that my father founded many years ago. I am certain that is what he would want us to do."

The men seemed more at ease after Jackson spoke to them and expressed their desire to help in any way they could. Millard thought Jackson had handled the situation very well. Most of the men went home, and a few went by the house to pay their respects to Mrs. Stamey.

Everyone had left Newbarn except Jackson, Millard, John, and Robert. They decided to leave Newbarn and return in the morning. Robert did not say where he was going, but he mentioned that he had important information concerning Newbarn and he wanted to follow the trail. Millard wasted no time in getting home. He was tired and wanted to be with his family. He had just lost one of the best friends he'd ever had, and he was so sad he hardly knew what to do.

When he arrived at his little home he realized that he had not even checked on the progress of his new house. The last few days had taken more out of him than he had realized.

As he entered the house, two little boys were there waiting for him. They grabbed him by the legs and tried to wrestle him down. That alone made him start feeling better. He and the boys wrestled on the floor, laughing louder and louder as they went.

Flora watched, a smile on her face, enjoying their play. She had expected Millard to come home soon and had supper almost ready.

Soon, they were gathered at the table with Flora saying a very appropriate blessing; she thanked God for his wonderful care and for keeping them all healthy and safe and asked God to give the Stamey family peace and comfort.

After supper, they played games and sang songs while Flora played her guitar beautifully. The boys were very happy indeed.

After they were in bed, Millard explained to Flora that he would have to work for a short while the following morning to see that all was well and plan Monday's work schedule. "I will return as soon as possible, and we will go pay our respects to the Stamey family. I will no doubt need to spend far more time at Newbarn for some time; how long will depend on how quickly Jackson recovers from this ordeal.

"This is a great loss to Newbarn," Millard continued with sadness in his voice. "I know Walter had retired, but he was always there when we needed his wisdom and advice. No doubt my responsibilities will increase now that he is gone. He taught me much, and I always listened carefully. I anticipated that something like this might happen sometime, and I wanted to be ready to respond with unquestionable competence. I will not let Jackson down."

Flora listened to him patiently; she knew of nothing else she could do for now.

Millard dragged himself out of bed the following morning with a groan. The Chicago trip plus the shock of Walter's death had taken more out of him than he had realized. Nevertheless, he drove slowly to Newbarn, stopping only for a few minutes to view his new house, which appeared to be near completion.

All was quiet at Newbarn when he arrived, and no one came by while he was there. He was glad to be alone while he was working. Jackson had everything so well organized it made his chores easy. All short and long delivery routes were completely planned and assignments made for all drivers. Entries in some logbooks had not been made. He brought them up to date and returned them to the safe.

As he was checking things in the safe, he was amazed at the amount of money it was holding. Clearly, it was much more than should be kept there. He decided to bring it to the attention of Jackson and John, and the three of them could make decisions about where the cash should be deposited or invested. Jackson already knew, but Millard knew that he and John needed to know as well. Should an emergency arise, they needed to know what to do. When he was satisfied everything was in order, he returned home.

Later in the evening, after Millard had taken a short nap, the family headed out to visit the Stamey family. When they arrived at the house, they were greeted by Jackson, who introduced them to the small group gathered in the parlor. Walter's body lay in the beautiful casket at the far side of the room with the open part draped by a silk covering.

Millard and Flora and the boys quietly walked up to view the body. Flora had already explained to the children what had happened and why they were going to visit the Stamey family. She and Millard held them up to view the body, hoping to persuade them from forming abnormal opinions about death.

Millard reminded the group that little Walter was named after Walter and Jackson.

FIFTY-FIVE

The death of Walter had been a shock to Newbarn and all across the Blue Ridge Mountains. Not only did all in the Newbarn organization come by to pay their respects, but highly respected politicians and judges and lawyers and the upper echelon of law enforcement came by as well. People came from other areas outside Spruce Willow as well. Walter had become rather reclusive in his later years and had remained close by Spruce Willow, but he had always kept contact with business acquaintances and friends who'd benefited from their mutual interests. They had all profited immensely and had great respect for each other.

Jackson had asked Millard, along with Newbarn's other leaders, to serve as pallbearers. "Pop was never much on attending church and had no church affiliation, so we are having his funeral at the church where my wife and I attend. We will leave here at eleven o'clock in the morning. And, Millard, I have heard your beautiful singing voice. Would you sing a song for him during the service?"

"Lord, Jackson," Millard said. "It is a hard thing you are asking. I don't know if I can sing without a shaky voice. Would you mind if Flora plays her guitar as I sing? Maybe that would help me out. I will do my best either way, but I know it will sound better if she helps me."

"Of course, Millard, that would be wonderful. 'Shall We Gather at the River' was his favorite religious song."

"We will be here early, Jackson," said Millard. "I am grateful for the opportunity to honor Walter in this way."

"One more thing I need to ask of you," said Jackson. "Pop always said he wanted to be carried to his grave on the shoulders of stout men. I know he would want you to be one of those men."

Millard smiled at that request. "It would be another honor to me," he replied. Jackson had already asked Millard, but Millard did not remind him.

On the way home, the boys were very quiet. Millard and Flora had expected many questions about death, but none came.

"You know, Flora," said Millard. "Children are not stupid. They understand far more than we give them credit for. When we explain to them that death is an ordinary part of life and answer their questions truthfully, they grow up with a healthy outlook on life and death."

"You are so right," said Flora. "I believe God placed the burden of death upon us, but he also gave us the knowledge to understand it and a way to defeat it and have everlasting life through Jesus our Savior."

Few words were said during the remainder of the way home, and they were soon in their beds warm and safe.

It was the Sabbath day, but there would be no time for the Watson family to attend church services. After breakfast, they dressed in their best clothes and drove to be with the Stamey family and participate in the funeral services. Few people were at the house when they arrived, and few came afterward. Most of them had paid their respects the night before and would be at the church for the funeral service.

A sleek new hearse was parked on the front lawn beside a long limousine for the family. With the funeral procession in line, they drove out the driveway, taking Walter away from his beloved home for the last time.

It was the most impressive funeral anyone could remember. The church service was very appropriate. Several dignitaries, including the mayor of Spruce Willow, spoke, followed by the minister who gave a very comforting sermon. Millard sang beautifully, with Flora playing her guitar and singing with him on the chorus. It was a very dignified service, and the six men carrying the casket on their shoulders to the gravesite was a showing of the utmost respect for Walter. As is often said as life comes to an end, Walter now belonged to the ages.

The sad group of people slowly left the cemetery, leaving only the prevailing cold wind in attendance. The fascinating life of Walter Stamey was no more.

It was breaking day when Millard arrived at work the next morning. He immediately began preparing for the day. He thought that Jackson might take the entire day off but knew John would be in soon. The short-run drivers came and left on their routes almost before he could update his checklist to make sure all the drivers were there and all the delivery routes were covered. There was little talking, however, and one could detect a degree of sadness among the men. It was as if they wanted to show Walter how well they could do their jobs.

John looked sluggish and sad as he walked in the door. John was a strong, brave man with a kind heart. He usually could hide that wonderful part of his personality, but to Millard and Jackson, it made him even more special.

"I doubt that Jackson will be in today," Millard said as John poured a cup of coffee.

"I figured that as I drove to work," replied John. "He will probably have a lot of family business to take care of, both today and for a good while to come."

"We both know he will come to work tomorrow though," replied Millard."

"That is just the way Jackson is," John added.

"I noticed here on the schedule that you don't have any long-haul trucks heading west today," Millard commented.

"I don't," John replied, "but we have one going out to Memphis in the morning. I wish we didn't have any going out all week, or at least until Antonio or Robert provide us with some intelligence."

"I don't expect Antonio today, but I do think Robert will be here sometime this afternoon," said Millard. "He knows how important, and maybe dangerous, it might be for our drivers to be on the road this week. And he also knows we will put our loaded trucks on the road without hesitation according to schedule."

"If we hadn't made that commitment, we wouldn't be in business very long and that's for sure," John concluded.

The day was passing quickly, and Millard and John worked methodically, putting things in order at Newbarn. After lunch, they inspected the storage areas and walked around the entire property, examining the boundary fence line and entrance gate.

Soon the deliverymen began checking in and leaving for the day. Each expressed his concern and hopes that all was well with Jackson and his family and offered to help them and Newbarn as needed and work on into the night. Millard and John thanked them for their kindness and dedication and told them that the work for today was completed.

"I know Jackson will be pleased when we tell him of your unselfish offer," said Millard.

"Dark is settling in, and no sign of Robert," said Millard. "I expected him before now."

"Maybe we should wait for him until midnight at least," said John. "We both know he will probably bring important information to us."

"I think so too," replied Millard.

They made themselves as comfortable as possible, expecting a long wait.

At a little past eleven, both had dozed off, and they were awakened by screeching brakes and a car sliding to a stop. Before they could stand up, someone was knocking rapidly at the door. Millard quickly opened the door, and there stood Robert with his face swollen and a huge black eye.

"You look like you have been hit by a train," said Millard.

As Robert moved toward the table, he could hardly walk straight. John held him by the arm until he sat down.

"Don't ask me what happened until I get my head straight and feel like talking," said Robert. "Just bring me a towel and some warn water for now."

They did as he asked and immediately picked him up and laid him on the table flat on his back. He groaned loudly as they removed his shirt, and they could readily see why. From his waist up, he was blue and swollen. They examined him carefully and found three ribs with compound fractures on his right side and two on the left, along with many contusions. They gently washed him and held warm towels to his face and upper body to combat the swelling.

Fortunately the broken ribs had not punctured his lungs. He had no injuries below the beltline, but both Millard and John were concerned that he could possibly have internal injuries.

He refused to be taken to a physician. "I am not any worse than I was when I left Memphis," he said. "Just help me to the couch and let me sleep until morning, and I will be much better."

They did as he asked and remained with him until morning.

Millard and John decided to awaken Robert before the deliverymen or anyone else arrived. They needed the details of his entire trip without any interference from others. They walked to the couch and spoke to him softly, careful not to startle him too much.

He immediately opened his eyes, and as he sat up it was evident how much better he felt, just as he'd predicted before he'd gone to sleep.

"How about some hot coffee and something to eat?" John asked him.

"That would be great, and please go over to that little café near Spruce Willow and fetch me one of their nice big ham and egg sandwiches."

That brought a smile from Millard and John. They knew he was beginning to recover and would be up and about in a few days.

"We don't want others to know you have returned until we have heard about your trip," said Millard. "There is a large soft chair in the storage room, and you will be comfortable there for a while. We will go after your sandwich after you get settled, and we will keep close watch on you until we are convinced you are in no danger."

John went for the sandwich, while Millard moved Robert's car around back where it would not be noticed. Now all they needed to do was let the day run its normal course and wait for Robert to recover sufficiently to talk without too much pain. They knew it was very important to talk with him as soon as possible.

Robert slept most of the day and was quite alert and feeling better as evening approached. John and Millard decided to remain with him as long as necessary. After a few hours, Robert was walking around slowly with few complaints, except for his sore ribs.

"Do you feel like telling us about your trip?" asked Millard.

"I do indeed," said Robert, "and I will tell it to you as soon as we eat supper."

"I will make another trip to the little café you like so well and get us three plates of hot food and hurry back before it gets cold," replied John. "I'll get big helpings too," he added as he went out the door.

After supper, they moved Robert's chair near the table in the main office. Millard got a blanket out of his car and placed it around Robert without asking. "We want to keep your injured body nice and warm. We want to take no chance of you contracting pneumonia, and there is always that danger after injuries such as yours. Do you feel well enough to give us the information you discovered concerning Newbarn?" asked Millard.

"I think so," said Robert.

After coughing a little, he seemed to sound stronger and looked reasonably well. "After I left here, I traveled to the hotel in Chicago where the Mafia was holding its ever-important meeting in their usual meeting hall, where I shot and killed the security guard. I was nervous, but I couldn't let that opportunity pass.

"I lay on the floor all morning listening for any discussion about Newbarn. Finally after lunch, Antonio Vitally introduced the subject, and he, along with Gordon Piker, announced that decisions had been made—one change had been made to the last offer made to Newbarn located in the Blue Ridge Mountains.

"'We last offered them a twenty-eighty split of all profits with a guarantee to keep them safe from interferences in their operation,' said Piker. 'We have increased that offer to a twenty-five—seventy-five split. We think that is fair, and we intend to stick by our offer. We are sending Antonio Vitally over there in a few days, and if they don't accept, they will have to stop doing business at the bottom of the Blue Ridge Mountains on the west side of Chattanooga, or we will bring the hammer down.'

"Someone in the background then said, 'I am afraid there will be many bodies lying around and most of them from our side.'

"'We will get people who know exactly how to take them out before we make our move, so don't worry too much about that,' Mr. Piker replied.

"That is all that was said about Newbarn, but in my opinion, they will not wait much longer before they cause trouble. They know they cannot do the job and have hired others, perhaps mountain men, to do their work."

"Damned cowards," said John.

"I left there in a hurry and headed toward St. Louis and on to Memphis," continued Robert. "When I arrived in Memphis, I broke my old rule of never staying in the same place too often. I decided to sleep a few hours at the same hotel where I had stayed on the way over. That was one hell of a mistake, and it almost got me killed.

"After I checked into my room, I heard someone outside my window, and when I peeked through the curtains, I could see a man with a pry bar trying to ease the window open without making any noise. I immediately went out through the lobby and crept along behind the shrubbery to confront the man, but I didn't get the chance.

"Out of nowhere came a huge man and grabbed me from behind. I couldn't get back inside, so I ran for my car. I reached my car and tried to get inside, but I was too late. They both started hitting me and succeeded in knocking me down. I kept them away some by kicking their legs, and as they backed away a little I was able to get up. Before I could get set to defend myself, they were on me again, hitting me with very hard punches. I felt myself passing out, but fortunately they snatched me off my feet and slammed me over the rear of my car. I honestly think they intended to kill me right there where they could deliver fatal blows.

"Somehow, I thought of my old switchblade knife and slid my right hand into my pocket. I flicked it open as I was pulling it out. I began jabbing and swinging that sharp blade back and forth until blood was spurting all over the place. I think I cut those two suckers to the bone.

"The last I saw of them, they were staggering around the corner of the building, where their car was, I suppose. My senses were returning now, at least enough to find my pistol in the bushes where I had lost it at the beginning of the fight. Half-crazed, I got into my car, and that was a wonderful feeling. It's fast, as you know, and I used that speed to get away and outrun another car, which began chasing me as I left the hotel. I did not stop, except for gas and snack food until I got here.

"I am convinced that all of our troubles come from Memphis and Chicago They have an organized line of soldiers at strategic locations all the way to the foot of the Blue Ridges—places like that large store we destroyed with dynamite not long ago. Soldiers of the Mafia committed to the strength and growth of the Mafia are our enemies. I have found no others. There might be more problems yet to be discovered, but we will find them in due time."

"Are there no bright spots in all of this?" asked Millard.

"Yes, there is one big one," answered Robert. "The Mafia is vulnerable outside of Memphis and Chicago. I think we could defeat them so soundly in these mountains that they would just give up and bother us no more. They like to kill anyone who is a bother to them, but they do not like their soldiers to fall."

"How long do you think it will be before they try coming after us?" asked Millard.

"Soon, and we need to start preparing for them immediately. They are full of tricks, and we must be ready. Antonio will try to help us, but we cannot depend upon him alone."

"Well," said Millard, "we are narrowing things down to the point where we might just manage things more in our favor."

"That is true," said John, "but we need to hear what Antonio has to say before we began making any plans."

"He will be here this week if all goes well," said Millard.

"He does not know about my trip," said Robert, "and I suggest that you do not tell him until we check out his report and find no fault in him. Those Italian Mafia types are very devious and should not to be trusted in most cases, until what they have to say has been verified."

"I do believe Antonio will be a friend to us. However, we might never see him again; that is the way things are in their world," Robert added.

"There is nothing we can do until later in the week, so let's go home," said Millard.

"I agree," John replied. "We will not leave you alone here. Go home with me where I can be certain you are safe and comfortable."

"I will not refuse that offer, John, and I thank you very kindly."

They left for home happy that Robert had returned.

Millard was happy to be going home. As he turned off the highway toward home, he could see his new house with the help of a beautiful full moon. It looked even larger than he had thought it would, and it was even more beautiful than it had been in his dreams. He went on down the hill, easing along and looking back at the house as though it was an illusion.

Flora met him at the door with a hug and whispered for him not to make much noise. "I just got the boys to sleep. They thought you would be here and were determined to stay awake until you arrived. How are things going at work without Walter and Jackson being there?" she asked.

"As well as we could expect at this time," he said. "Robert returned yesterday all beaten and bruised. We have yet to determine what that was all about. We are expecting Antonio Vitally to come over later this week, and we hope he will have news to our benefit."

Flora had a worried look on her face and told him she did not have a good feeling about what was going on.

"Say no more," Millard replied. "I am scared enough without any of your predictions of doom ahead. Let's go to bed and let our troubles rest at least until tomorrow. I can't wait to see the house in the morning. I will get up early to see it."

FIFTY-SIX

After a sound night's sleep in their cozy, little, warm cabin, Millard had no dread of the day. He ate breakfast and played with the boys a little while and then drove up the hill to their new house.

Salem was just arriving, and Millard ran to greet him. "You are one of the best construction men I have ever seen," he said as he shook Salem's hand. "The house looks almost completed, and the columns look magnificent."

"I didn't stop looking until I found what I thought you would want. They are of solid oak and straight as an arrow. I found them at a lumber company in Asheville."

"Is the inside finished?" asked Millard.

"No, but it will not be long," Salem answered. "Inside work goes the slowest, you know."

They went inside, and sure enough the work was almost completed. The electrical wiring was in place, ready for the lighting fixtures, and two large chandeliers were ready to be hung in the foyer and large living room. Almost all the ceilings and walls were completed, and beautifully carved, chestnut mantels were perfectly crafted and fitted in place above the fireplaces. Salem had located a master carver who had designed and finished the mantels to perfection. No two designs were the same. Everything from biblical figures to Italian scenes stood out graciously on each mantel. Millard could hardly take his eyes off such works of art.

Salem watched him to assess his reaction. He was happy to oversee the construction of this beautiful home for the fine man his daughter had married and his grandchildren.

Finally, Millard looked at his watch and realized that he should have been at work already. He ran toward his car while looking back over his shoulder to thank Salem and assure him he would return as soon as his job would allow. "I need to talk to you again as soon as possible," he said as he drove away.

Millard rushed down the road and reached Newbarn just as the route men were preparing to leave. "I am sorry to be late on such an important day," he said to John.

"I was a little late myself. I didn't want to bring Robert out without breakfast. He seems to be worse today than yesterday."

"I have had injuries such as his, and that's the way they usually react," Millard replied.

"After breakfast, he went back to bed," said John. "He said he would be over here about noon."

"I hope Antonio shows up today or tomorrow," said Millard. "This not knowing is driving me crazy. You have two trucks going out tomorrow, and I think we both have reservations about them leaving until we have more intelligence about their routes and what they might encounter."

"I know what you mean," replied John, "but we made the decision to serve our customers come hell or high water. We have done just that so far. We will just have to wait and see how things develop and hope for the best."

Shortly after they set about the daily chores and putting everything in order as Jackson had been doing so meticulously, in the door he came. He was in a surprisingly good mood. "I see you two are keeping things straight," he said with a smile. "I would have stayed out another day, but there is nothing I can do. I am executor of my father's estate, but I am not ready to tackle that just yet."

"You probably should have stayed out at least another day," Millard told him. "Mourning goes on for months or longer. My dad has been gone for some time now, and I still get sinking feelings about him that just come out of nowhere, and then sadness follows and lasts for hours."

"Yes, I realize that," said Jackson. "I will have to get through it, and I might as well start today. Mom is doing well with Sally there with her.

"What is all that stuff stacked behind the building?" Jackson asked.

"It belongs to Antonio," John answered. "He is getting ready to leave Memphis and the Mafia. We helped him out a little by hauling some things for him. He will probably rent a storage building when he comes over here this week."

"I got a call from him last night," said Jackson. "He will be here sometime tomorrow. He worries me some. If he makes it out of Memphis and gets settled over here, we can count him a lucky man. I have heard that the Mafia will follow you around the earth if you break the organization's code. They haven't discovered that he is leaving yet, but if they do before he gets out of Memphis, he will end up in the river over there or buried in some swamp. He said he has some information for us when he gets over here."

"We need more information badly," said Millard. "We are at a standstill as to what to do. Two trucks headed out this morning fully loaded, and two more are leaving tomorrow. If we have trouble today, we might have to reconsider our plans for tomorrow. Hell ain't it."

"I instructed the drivers to haul more things for Antonio on their return trip if they could but not to take any chances," John explained.

After lunch, Robert came to the office. He looked much improved. Much of the swelling was gone from his face, and he could walk slowly without groaning. He took his shirt off to show his black and blue trunk.

"I want you to go down and show Mom your condition. She keeps an old-timey remedy handed down through generations that works like a miracle," Jackson told him. "You will think you are on fire when she first rubs it on you, but within hours, the soreness will begin to ease. The fractures will take some time to heal, but she has remedies to help them also. Just do as she says, and you will do just fine."

Millard had been thinking about his new home frequently all day. He stopped on his way and walked all around, looking at the building from every angle. He then went inside and went into each room, giving each the same close examination. The dreams and plans he'd had as a young man were unfolding before his eyes, and the home was even more elegant than he'd expected during the hours he and Flora had spent studying plans and pictures before construction began. He was looking forward to talking with Salem about the home and several other subjects. Perhaps he could find time this weekend for a woodshed talk and sipping a little moonshine.

He drove on down the hill to the cabin. As he stood in the yard, he looked up the hill, and the new home looked even more spectacular. When the yard was landscaped and the land cleared down to the river, it would be a special place of beauty that he hoped would be passed down to his children and grandchildren, giving them a desire to excel in life based upon their youthful desires and dreams. And he hoped that all poor people would soon be lifted above their present status in life and would find their hopes and dreams far above the level of this terrible depression.

As Millard turned to go inside, he saw Flora standing on the porch silently, watching him with a slight smile on her face. "I know your thoughts, and I agree with all of them," she remarked.

"You are not getting one of your feelings are you?" he asked.

"It has been gone for over a year, but it is back again stronger than ever. And I saw those bright lights that I used to see when we lived with Dad and Ma. I saw them last night far down in the swamp below the house. It was as though the lights were following, wanting me to understand their purpose here. It doesn't bother me anymore, and I know that I have nothing to fear."

"Damn, I do," he said. "Let's go in the house; this talk causes me to shudder."

They went inside where the boys were playing marbles on the floor and fussing about some aspect of the game. Millard picked them up and gave them both a hug at the same time. They began laughing, and their fussing ceased. He got down on the floor with them, and they played marbles until supper was ready.

They stayed up late and played games and sang songs and wrestled on the bed until the boys finally got tired and lay their heads on Flora's lap and went to sleep.

"That was fun," said Millard. "I hope it will not be too long before I can come home each evening and be off every Saturday and Sunday and live like normal folks."

"That would be great for all of us," said Flora. "I miss church a lot; we seldom attend anymore."

"This has been a good day," Millard replied. "Let's not get into any serious conversations and mess it up. I might have information tomorrow that could help us feel better about things. Or it could be news that could turn out bad, very bad. Some sort of climax has to surface out of all this trouble sooner or later and I will try to keep telling you about it."

Morning again arrived, and Millard was on his way to work after briefly slowing down to admire his house. He wondered what it would be like to live in such a place. Actually, he liked the cabin they lived in now, but he knew this house would be much better and something to be proud of. He also was confident that the house would serve many good purposes for many years on into the future. The house was his most important youthful dream now come true.

The work day began surprisingly routine. Millard hoped it would remain that way. Little did he know, Antonio was already on his way from Chattanooga to Newbarn. Behind him was a large truck he had bought to expedite his move from the warehouse. It was fully loaded with things he intended to keep somewhere in the vicinity of Newbarn.

Actually, John had already located a very large barn with many outbuildings all around. It was for sale, and he'd asked the seller to hold it for Antonio for a few days. John hoped Antonio would live long enough to use it, but he said no such words to anyone except Millard.

"I have serious doubts that he will. I am afraid that damned Mafia will find a way to assassinate him sure as hell," said Millard.

"But you know," said John, "we are pretty much aware they are somewhat afraid of us in these mountains. What do you say we make them very much afraid? They are people just like us, only mean as the devil, but we have an advantage up here. Most of the men who work here at Newbarn can appear and disappear in seconds, just like the Cherokees of old. I read a book once that explained about guerrilla warfare. That type of fighting could be used to defeat those who are trying to intimidate us and boss us around, and our men could do well using their knowledge of these mountains."

"You can't shoot what you can't see," replied Millard. "I think you have a good idea, John. We have a few men who fought in World War I also. Let's keep it close in our minds in case we have to defend ourselves."

The morning work was done and everyone had had lunch when Antonio finally drove up to Newbarn, looking tired and bewildered. All the leaders of Newbarn ran out to greet him.

"How was your trip?" asked Jackson.

"It went well, except we are almost exhausted. It wasn't so much the trip but the pressure we were under, not knowing what to expect. We had to keep constant watch for an ambush or something bad. Apparently no one in the Mafia has discovered what I am up to. After all, Mr. Piker did give me the authority to come over here and negotiate with the leaders of Newbarn. But we do not know what he has found out about me since then. I hope nothing, but ears are everywhere. I have loads of stuff still in my warehouse that I want to bring up here."

"We will settle the most important things first and deal with the rest as we must," said Jackson. "Come in and rest, and we will get down to business later."

The man driving the truck remained in the truck. Antonio gave his name as Wayne Farmington from Memphis.

"Ask him in for coffee, and we will make him welcome, except we won't accept him in any meetings or negotiations," said Jackson.

"I knew you wouldn't," answered Antonio, "and I don't blame you for not doing do."

"Well, you men rest up and take a nap if you want to. Then after supper, we will talk business. Or if you want to wait until later, we can just sit around and shoot the bull, as the saying goes here in the mountains."

"That sounds good to me, especially the nap," replied Antonio.

Millard had hoped to make it home at a reasonable hour, but that was not to be. After Antonio and Wayne were rested, the entire group went out for supper at the restaurant where Millard used to stop in the evening on his way home. They had a very pleasant time and, while there, decided to return to Newbarn to have a few drinks and discuss business.

As of yet no one except Antonio knew for certain what Gordon Piker's instructions to him were. Robert had listened in on the meeting, but that did not necessarily mean what he'd overheard were final instructions. Some big bosses above Piker could have changed things around to suit themselves. They were an unpredictable, vast organization, and only they alone knew how large they were and who had veto power and the ability to make unchangeable decisions. The Newbarn leaders dreaded dealing with such an unknown and large threat, but they had made their decision; they would not back down or dishonor themselves.

When the group returned to Newbarn headquarters, Jackson sat at the head of the table. "Do you men want to talk business now?" he asked.

Everyone said yes.

"Well then, I think we should have only a couple of drinks until the meeting is over and drink all you want afterward."

All agreed, but Robert said in a low voice, "This will be a short meeting," causing laughter.

"All right, who is the smartass?" said Jackson, who was laughing himself. "Now, if there are no more remarks, let's get down to business.

"We have had Robert's complete story about being jumped by two men in Memphis, but we will discuss that later. Now let's hear from Mr. Vitally what message Mr. Piker has sent us."

"Mr. Piker's message is not long, but he was very emphatic about what he wants out of our negotiations," said Antonio. 'He offers a twenty-five-seventy-five split. He considers his offer fair and final and advises you to accept it."

"Did he say what his intentions are if we don't accept his offer?" asked John.

"Piker intends to send men to put you out of business. He didn't say it, but I think he's actually a bit afraid to send men over. And I know you don't want to do it, but for the record, if you were to drop your long-haul routes and stay east of Chattanooga, I think he'd drop the matter and leave you alone."

"Millard, what do you think we should do?" asked Jackson.

"Offer him 10 percent of our profits from our long-haul runs and tell him to take it or leave it. Actually, he will be doing nothing for us to deserve even 10 percent. All he would have to do to protect us is tell his own organization to leave us alone. Tell him we intend to keep six trucks hauling our whiskey on the same routes we are now doing and nothing more. He has our word that we will expand no further, but we will sell our whiskey to the Mafia at a 10 percent discount as a goodwill gesture."

"Damn, Millard, you have been giving this some thought I do believe. What about you, John?" asked Jackson. "I know you have some ideas in that head of yours that you want to share."

"I have been thinking along the same lines as Millard, but I have one addition; tell them we will not back down. They have a chance to put a considerable amount of money in their pockets for doing nothing, and that should be sufficient. We want to get along with them and all make good money, but if they start shooting at us and force us to fight, we will kill him first."

"My Lord," said Jackson. "I did not expect ideas for such forceful action. Do you have any advice for us, Antonio?"

"Very little," Antonio replied. "Right off the cuff, I suggest you offer him 20 percent of long-haul profits. I know they do not deserve one cent, but it might save much trouble, and he might accept your offer. He is a big blowhard, and you are sending him a strong message. He will not relish the thought of your big guns throwing slugs of lead at his ass. That is just an old fool's opinion though."

"Robert, we are anxious to hear what you have to say about this."

Robert looked around the room and said, "I agree with Millard and John, and I wouldn't offer him more than 10 percent. But I think there is more to this than we think. I need to make another trip to Memphis where I tangled with those two men. That is a problem that must be solved. If they were from the Mafia, we could put it to rest with our dealings with them, but I do not think they were Mafia soldiers. They were too dumb. Nothing they did made sense. I will go over there as soon as I heal and find out what is going on. I would go sooner if I had a man to ride shotgun and cover me while I do the detective work. I don't think I could stand another fight now. But I suggest we send Mr. Piker our return offer as soon as possible. Otherwise, he will think we lack confidence in our intentions."

"Would someone volunteer to go with Robert to Memphis as he has asked? I too think it is very necessary. If we have other enemies, we need to know who they are and what they are about," said Jackson.

"I will be glad to go," said John, "but I can't leave before Saturday or maybe Monday because of personal business I have been neglecting too long."

"Let's just set the day for Monday," said Jackson. "We all need a weekend without so much aggravation; then on Monday, Antonio can leave to deliver our message to Mr. Piker, and Robert and John can leave for Memphis. Tomorrow, Millard and John and me will make our final decisions about things. But I do not anticipate any changes from what we have decided here. Now let's have a few more drinks and then go home."

Millard went directly home, stopping only to look at the new house. Flora had not expected him home tonight. Too many things were going on at Newbarn recently to know when she would see him again. They talked briefly and then went to bed.

"I need a restful night," he said. "There is always the possibility of having to make a trip, and that could come at any time the way things are going now. We will make some important decisions tomorrow, and that is all I can tell you."

The morning brought rain and fog, and Millard got stuck in the mud as he drove up to the highway. He thought how lucky he was not to drive a truck out. *There are some very distinct advantages to being second in command at Newbarn other than making plenty of money,* he thought.

Just as he drove up to Newbarn, Jackson opened the door and motioned for him to hurry inside, as though something was wrong. "I got a call from someone who would not give his name. He said he was calling for Mr. Gordon Piker and wanted to speak to Antonio Vitally and the message was very important. I put him off by telling him that, due to a severe storm here, I could not reach him until the storm let up. I do not feel right about that call, and I want us to stay close all day. Other than the employees here at Newbarn, I trust very few people where our business is concerned."

"I know," said Millard. "Robert has said to me several times that he did not trust Antonio completely. I think he is wrong about that. We have every reason not to trust him. He is now risking his life to remove himself from the Mafia just to find refuge and peace in these mountains. His knowledge of the Mafia might prove valuable to us."

"You are probably right," said Jackson, "but my point is that, if either of us has the slightest suspicion that something is wrong, we need to be alert. Pop was that way, and few people ever pulled anything over on him."

"I will do exactly as you say. We have nothing to lose by being careful," replied Millard. "You know, you are talking and acting and even looking more like your father all the time."

"That is one hell of a compliment, Millard, and I thank you," Jackson said with a big smile.

Within a few minutes John, Robert, and Antonio came into the office. Jackson immediately told Antonio about the phone call. Antonio said he had no idea what the call was all about, and he was curious as to why the caller would not leave his name. He said he would wait a while and then make some calls to Chicago and try to find out who would do such a dumb thing. He also said Piker never went into his office this early or he would call him now.

FIFTY-SEVEN

Considerable tension was in the air at Newbarn among the leadership. It was a normal day for the short-haul deliveries but even the haulers sensed something was wrong. Jackson reassured them that there was nothing for them to worry about, and that seemed to settle them down. Jackson, John, and Millard set about completing the routine chores and anticipating what Antonio might find out when he called Chicago.

After lunch, Antonio began making his calls. He made numerous calls with no success; those he talked to either knew nothing or wouldn't talk. He did not want to call Mr. Piker's office, but he finally came to the conclusion that he had no other choice.

One of Mr. Piker's trusted aids, Oliver Francisco, finally answered. Antonio asked him about the late-night phone call.

"It was me," Francisco admitted. "I could not make contact with any of the higher-up bosses. You know how they do things to protect themselves."

"Well, what is it all about?" demanded Antonio, a little anger in his voice.

"Gordon Piker is dead," he said. "I passed by the office on my way to an opera, and his car was sitting there. And when I returned and it was still there, I knew something was wrong. I looked in the car, and he was lying on the rear seat with his throat cut. His chauffeur was dead in the front seat with his neck looking like he had been strangled with a fine wire or small rope. It was a horrible sight. I didn't know what to do, and that is why I tried to find you. Your number was on a notepad on his desk.

"I knew better than to call the police without orders from the higher-up bosses. After I finally contacted one of them, he did not seem very surprised and told me to forget everything I had told him. The matter would be taken care of with no police involvement.

As a matter of fact, the bodies were removed and disposed of while it was still dark. I got the impression that the car and both bodies are now at the bottom of the lake. For God sakes, don't repeat what I just told you. I wish you would come back from your trip and help me deal with this. I could make one mistake and end up as fish bait too."

"Don't panic, Oliver; you know things like this happen in the Mafia. You should be used to it by now. Just go about your duties just as if nothing had happened. Be careful and alert as we all have to do always. Now, tell me if Mr. Piker left you any instructions about my negotiations with Newbarn in the Blue Ridge Mountains," Antonio said.

"Yes, he did. What do you need to know?" Oliver asked.

"Tell me everything you know about what is going on. I need to know everything," Antonio said, with some urgency.

"There is now an agreement among the bosses that they will accept 20 percent of the profits but no less. Piker is now dead, and they are talking big. I think they will follow through with some of their threats, but they would be very reluctant to come over there to do harm. The only thing against the mountain men is that the Mafia could possibly stop the truck runs they are making from Chattanooga."

"When will you see the bosses who have made the 20 percent offer?" asked Antonio.

"Anytime now," answered Oliver. "They won't fool around with this. They will erase all traces of both murdered men, and the newspapers will report some story about two outstanding citizens being killed in an unfortunate accident, with little evidence to support their story."

"Well, when you see them, ask them to contact me as soon as possible. The leaders of Newbarn have a reply to their terms for a negotiated settlement regarding their long-haul trucking. They want no trouble and believe that such a small matter can be handled easily by phone. It is important for them to not delay the matter, however."

"I will give them your message, but I think it will make them mad as hell. I don't think they will consider this a small matter. They will consider it a threat to their organized business. They hate competition," said Oliver, his voice shaky. "Don't even let on that you are aware of Piker's death, as the answer will be directed to me."

After Antonio talked to Oliver, he turned to the leaders of Newbarn, who had been listening, and said, "I wonder why they killed old Piker. I have worked as his assistant for many years and never once thought of them killing him. He did something that made them mad."

"Do you think it might have something to do with us?" asked Jackson.

"No, and I think I would have known if that was the case. But maybe that is the reason I have no knowledge about the killing. I was too close to Piker. They usually cover all bases, and all killings are carried out methodically. They will invite you to dinner and pour you the finest wine, and all the time, they know, as they smile at you, that you will be murdered that very night as they drive you home. Now you see why I want out of that evil organization. I hope I make it out alive."

"Stick with us, and we will try to see that you do," said Jackson.

Other than Antonio's phone call, the day proved to be quite normal. At the day's end, the leaders of Newbarn decided to remain in the office area and drink some beer and play a little poker to pass the time. They were disappointed that they had received no calls from a member of the Mafia or even Oliver. They agreed to stay all night if necessary.

Shortly after midnight, the phone rang. The man introduced himself as Ransom Mann. His accent was very Italian, and he spoke in a high-pitched voice. He apologized for calling so late but stated that a person in their organization had expired and had caused a much disorganized day. "We were all very fond of him."

"I am sorry to hear that," said Jackson.

"Mr. Jackson, I have been informed that you have a counteroffer you would like to present for our attention. I am ready to begin if you are, sir."

"I am indeed," said Jackson, "and I'll get to the point rather quickly. We are willing to hand over 10 percent of our profits from our long hauls west of Chattanooga to Chicago. We will expand no farther in your direction than we are as of this date. We will keep six trucks on the road or enough to make deliveries to our present customers. We will sell some of our fine whiskey to you gentlemen at a 10 percent discount as a goodwill offer. In our opinion, this is a very generous offer."

"It is not a generous offer, and we cannot and will not accept it," said Ransom Mann. "It costs us a fortune to protect you and allow you to expand into our territory. No! That will never do."

"Oh, come off that rigid stance," Jackson countered. "We might be mountain men, but we are not fools. We are offering you 10 percent of our profits for doing nothing but instructing your own men to stop harassing us, which they have been doing since way back when. And you do not own everything westward any more than we do. There is plenty of business for all of us. We are not greedy. All we want is a market for our fine product, and we will not back down from this very fair offer."

Ransom Mann's voice got louder as he said, "All I can say now, Mr. Jackson, is that you will be hearing from us soon, and you will wish you had accepted our offer."

"If you change your mind, you have my number, and I do not at this time consider your language as a threat. We wish you well and hope that you will reconsider our generous offer," Jackson concluded and hung up the phone.

"Well, we have our answer," Jackson said. "Did everyone hear our conversation?"

"You held the phone just perfect for us to put our heads close together and hear everything," replied Millard.

"Now how do you deal with such a numbskull?" said Jackson.

"Like you would deal with other men who are just like spoiled brats," said John. "Just give them a good ass whipping."

"We don't know when they will come or from which direction," Jackson replied.

"I have an idea," said Millard. "Robert is an expert in such matters. Let's let him decide what our options are and consult with Antonio as well. I will wager they will figure things out within a few days."

"Sounds like a reasonable approach to me," replied Jackson.

"I don't think we should fret about it unnecessarily," said Robert. "I will attack this matter as best I am capable and form a plan that will free us from these devils as fast as possible."

Antonio nodded in agreement.

"Let's all go home," said Jackson. "We all need to think on these complicated matters before we make any final decisions. The Mafia will aggravate us to no end until we take some drastic action."

Millard was at his wit's end. *Somehow, someway, all this nonsense has got to come to a close*, he thought as he drove home.

If I have my say, Monday will be a day of decisions. In my opinion, we have almost enough intelligence information to proceed with our plans. If I know Robert, he will be working his brain to provide us with a plan of action, and Antonio will provide assistance by anticipating the plans the Mafia will probably make.

As Millard kept thinking, he realized that the main problem was the men who attacked Robert in Memphis. "When we find out what is behind that situation, we will be very close to making solid decisions," he reasoned aloud. "Then we can go on the offensive against them and clear these mountains of any soldiers of the Mafia, should they be foolish enough to come after us in our own territory. I wonder what advice Walter would have if he were with us. I miss that wonderful, old man."

Millard was in sight of his new house before he realized how deep in thought he had been. He knew he must take the next two days to rest his mind and enjoy the weekend.

The boys met him in the yard, begging him to take them for a ride down to the river.

"It is cold down at the river," Millard explained to them. "The water is cold, and the air is cold. Why don't we ask your mother if she wouldn't like to eat out at our special café in Spruce Willow?"

"That will be okay," Cameron said, and Walter smiled at the thought.

They entered the house and before they could ask Flora, she said, "I am almost ready."

The boys laughed loudly. They did not know she had been listening to their conversation.

It was a fun time and a fun evening. Each one got to order what he or she wanted, and after they got home, they played jack rocks on the floor and then sat on the bed and sang songs. What a great evening they had.

On Saturday, they were all anxious to do fun things. First, they visited their new house. The carpenters had almost completed the inside. It was sealed inside with differing types of smoothly sanded lumber waiting to be painted or stained. The foyer and parlor was of factory finished mahogany Flora had chosen. It was looking more and more like the mansion that was in Millard's dreams as a very young man.

Millard was satisfied, and the family headed to Salem's to tell him how pleased they were with the home. When they arrived, the entire family sat on the front porch to enjoy the unseasonably warm, sunny day. Neither Salem nor Martha could remember a winter so mild and warm.

Millard did not get to have his usual woodshed talk with Salem. While they were talking, Millard had fallen asleep. Flora started to awaken him but Salem motioned for her to not bother him. "I talk with him pretty often, and I know his work is becoming increasingly dangerous and without regular working hours. I have told him that I am concerned about his safety and even suggested that he consider quitting. I mention it no more. He would never quit under any circumstances. It is all for you, Flora—you and the boys. He is not a selfish man."

Soon Millard awoke, looking embarrassed for having gone to sleep. As they walked to the car, Flora removed a paper sack from under the car seat and handed it to Salem. It was a half-gallon of whiskey. "I know Millard brought this to you, but his nap caused him to forget. Also under the seat was this envelope." She did not say what it was, but she knew a sizeable amount of cash money was sealed inside.

"I am sorry to be such a deadhead," said Millard. "I wanted to talk to you, but I will return next week, if possible."

"You take care of yourselves," Salem called to them as they drove away.

Salem looked at the items Flora had handed to him and slowly walked toward the woodshed. His movement seemed to indicate sadness.

Millard and his family drove home without stopping anywhere. Flora asked Millard why he did not stop to visit Ma.

"We will visit with her tomorrow," he replied. "Now I want to take the boys to the river, where they wanted to go yesterday. I know it will be chilly down there, but we can sit in the car and just watch the river pass."

They sat in the car for a long while and enjoyed every minute they were there. They talked of the beauty of the river and took turns guessing where they thought the river lived and where it was going. It proved to be much fun, and they laughed as little Cameron remarked, "What a silly game this is. Some of the river comes from our spring above our house, and it is all going into the ocean. Someday, I am going to look at the ocean. I have seen pictures of it, and it is too big to see across."

"I will tell you something, Cameron," said Millard. "When I do not have to work so much, I will drive us all to the ocean, and maybe we'll stay several days. We will swim and play in the sand and even go fishing on a boat. We probably can't go this coming summer, but the next summer we might just get to do that."

"You have given them something to talk about for a year or two," said Flora with a smile on her lips.

"If there is any way to make it happen, I will," Millard replied.

Though they'd been by the river for some time, Millard lingered. He couldn't pinpoint what it was, but something was tugging at him to stay there, watching the river. He was aware that when he got the house completed and the land developed, they would have a view of the river down to the water's edge. But it was something else that caused him to want to remain at the river longer. After sitting for a while longer, he realized that nothing would come to mind. He slowly drove back to their cabin, thus ending a very happy day for his wonderful family.

What a wonderful night's rest ensued. The entire Watson family awoke early the next morning and almost at the same time. *We surely want another fun day like the one that just passed*, thought Flora. She decided to start the day right by cooking a delicious breakfast.

They hurriedly ate breakfast and dressed for church. They wanted to take Ma to church, and if they did not hurry, she would be gone before they got there. She had started down the road when they pulled up. A few minutes later, and she would have left the road and been walking on a not often used path through the forest that was a shortcut to the church.

Millard hurried to the church, hoping he would arrive in time to take his seat among the choir, but he was too late. A nice-looking young man was in the seat, seeming a little nervous. Millard did not let on that he even noticed. He took a seat in the congregation with Flora and the boys. He hoped the young man would do well, but sadly he did not. The service went well, however, and it helped Millard feel lighthearted and happy.

As they drove away from the church, Millard told Ma that they were all going to Spruce Willow to a special little café for supper. She did not like the idea much but gave in without refusing to go. They had a wonderful time and the boys talked to Ma to the point of aggravation.

"Stop talking so much," Flora said rather harshly. "Your dad and I want to talk to Ma too."

As they were driving home, Millard told Ma that their new house was almost finished. "We want you to go with us and see how you like it."

"I guess so," she replied. "I haven't seen it, but everyone is talking about it around this part of the county. Some say you are getting too big for your britches, and others say you have gotten uppity."

"Not true on either account," said Millard. "I have always wanted a nice home and to rise above the level of poverty most mountain folks endure. Everyone should strive for something in life, be it something small or large. Maybe they are jealous, but some are probably like me—wanting to get ahead. The others are content with things as they are and will grow old that way."

They arrived at the house and Millard looked lovingly at Ma and said, "You will be living here soon with us, and don't start that no business."

"I think not," replied Ma in a sassy voice.

That ended the conversation, but Millard could readily see that she was in awe when he showed her the bedroom she would occupy—one with a fireplace and plenty of room for her to sew and quilt and do whatever she wanted to do.

After Ma had expressed her reluctance to stay the night, they took her home, ending a most wonderful day.

Millard took a nice nap after they returned home while Flora played games in the yard with the boys. Dark came, and sleep followed.

FIFTY-EIGHT

Millard was awake before the clock alarm went off. His first thoughts were of the difficult week or two ahead. Their case was beginning to fall into place, and they did not intend to be threatened and intimidated without taking action. He was very concerned about the entire matter. Men were going to get killed unless some agreement with the Mafia could be reached. He had great confidence in the skills of Robert and Antonio as well since he had been proving himself again and again. *We are prepared for the worst, and what has to be will be,* he told himself.

He wasted no time in driving to work. He was the first person there, but within fifteen minutes, all employees had arrived, both for work and to find out what was happening to the organization they loved. So many rumors were being voiced among the men that Millard discussed the situation briefly with Jackson. He then called the men into a group and explained to them how things were developing and told them not to be too alarmed. "Just consider this a normal day; you will be informed of any changes at the day's end," he concluded.

That calmed the men down, and everyone went about his business.

Shortly, Robert and John came by on their way to Memphis. They were loaded for bear from the looks of Robert's car. Millard saw four 10-gauge shotguns, shoulder holstered pistols, and an enormous amount of dynamite. Jackson came out and asked them what their plans were after they got to Memphis.

"We intend to go straight to the hotel where the two men attacked me and start from there," said Robert. "I am in no shape to fight yet. That is the reason for so much armament. We will try to contact you if and when we find out anything."

"I am worried about your trip, boys," said Jackson, "and I know Millard is too. If you can find out where this trouble is coming from and put an end to it, then all we will have to deal with is the Mafia. I suppose it is the not knowing that bothers me so much about your trip.

"I wish you luck," he said as they drove away.

"They lose no time when they start something," said Millard. "I thought they would wait until today to make plans for Memphis and Antonio would give his advice as well."

"The three of them decided to start planning early. They are independent rascals, and I don't mind one bit so long as they know what they are doing. Antonio headed for Memphis to settle his business there. He wants to make his move over here and be done with Memphis and maybe St. Louis and Chicago," Jackson continued.

"He might have to move to the other side of the world to get away from them," said Millard.

"Let's help him all we can," Jackson replied.

"I think we should also," Millard agreed. "I would hate to be in his shoes with no aid or comfort. I think he has plenty of money, but a man needs friends at a time like this."

★ ★ ★

Antonio had left for Memphis earlier than Robert and John. He wanted to reach his warehouse and hoped the two delivery trucks from Newbarn would come by his warehouse before noon on Tuesday and take a full load to his storage barn near Newbarn, which he had rented for that purpose. He would wait until noon, and if they had not come by then, he would have to call a moving company and have them move as much as possible Tuesday night.

The trucks did show and the Newbarn drivers loaded them quickly, locked the warehouse, and headed toward the mountains. He hoped no one concerned would notice the trucks from Newbarn leaving from his warehouse. He stopped outside Memphis and called the individuals to whom he had agreed to sell a large number of items in the warehouse and they agreed to take delivery on Thursday. If all went well, he would hire the moving company and have them load the remainder of his goods stored there and leave for the mountains Thursday night. He was reasonably certain they could manage to move the rest of his items in one load.

If not, to hell with the rest of it. He would give the remainder to the individuals who had bought the large volume of items for delivery on Thursday. He was getting very nervous. If he was not successful in moving to the mountains, this could well be his last week alive. How he wished he had never gotten entangled with those Mafia sons of the devil.

✴ ✴ ✴

Robert and John reached Memphis not too far behind Antonio, but not soon enough to do much about their mission. Come morning, they would stake out the place where Robert had been attacked and go from there. A cold wind was blowing, and they had no desire to do anything but eat supper and find a warm bed. Their day had been a pleasant one with many topics up for discussion. They had tried to anticipate what they would be up against when they reached Memphis but had decided upon nothing specific.

As they were eating supper, Robert's detective skills came through, just as John knew they would. "There is a parking lot at the hotel and places where we can park almost out of sight but still see most of what is going on. We will stay there a little while, and if nothing of interest occurs, I think we should go inside and question the manager. Sometimes just being blunt and bold works out very well."

"Sounds reasonable to me," John replied.

They were up before daybreak on Tuesday and went directly to the parking lot. People came and went, but they saw nothing suspicious.

They went into the lobby and approached a nicely dressed man who appeared to be the manager. Robert told him what had happened to him at that hotel, giving him all the sordid details.

The manager did remember the incident and had called the police but all parties involved were already gone when the police arrived. "After questioning some of our guests," the manager said, "the police reported that the evidence showed that a car with a

Chicago license tag was parked behind the building. Two men came around the front of the hotel and one stayed in the car with the motor running. The manager and guests heard a fight going on. Then two men returned, running back to the car, and left very fast. The police were amazed at the amount of blood on the ground and said that, if all the blood came from one man, he was probably dead. That is all. I have not heard one thing about it since that night."

He thought a moment and then continued, "Oh yes, one of the policeman said that, in his opinion, it was an attempted homicide."

"Sir," said Robert, "you have provided us with some valuable information, since it was me who was apparently the intended victim."

As they were walking away, Robert returned and asked the gentleman if, by any chance, anyone at the hotel had identified the automobile.

"It was a very new-looking black Buick," the manager replied.

"What does that remind you of?" Robert asked John.

"Mafia-type vehicles," replied John. "I think we need to head for Chicago."

"Are you serious, John?" asked Robert.

"Hell yes," replied John. "Why should we come all this way without kicking some asses? You never know what we might find just by driving up there and looking around," he added. "You know the place pretty well; after all, you knocked off one man up there."

"Don't remind me of that, John," said Robert.

"Why not?" said John. "I think you did a good deed in that case."

Robert was not hard to persuade, and soon they were on the way to Chicago. John did the driving as he had been doing the entire trip. Robert was almost healed from the injuries he had sustained in the fight.

"If we should get into a rumble, do you think you can hold up all right?" asked John.

"I am a little weak, but I think I could help out pretty well. Certainly by tomorrow I should be in good shape," replied Robert. "I always have my pistol and my switchblade, which should even things up in a have-to situation."

They passed right on through St. Louis in record time and stopped for gas and food at the north side of the city.

"How do you feel now, Robert?" asked John. "We will drive on to Chicago if you say so, or we can stay the night here."

"Let's stay here," said Robert. "With a good, long night's rest, I believe I would be in even better condition."

"I agree," John replied. "We will be in Chicago tomorrow either way, and you won't have to push yourself."

Morning came and they felt wonderfully rested. The hotel had feather beds, and both men had slept like fallen trees. After a good breakfast, they were on the road again.

Robert rested and napped part of the way to Chicago, taking advantage of the extra time to regain his strength completely.

Chicago was less than one hundred miles away when they were about to make an important decision. "Where should we stay tonight without getting our throats cut?" asked John.

"I have been pondering that decision since we left Memphis," said Robert. "And I have come to the conclusion that we should stay in the same hotel the mobsters always stay, dangerous as it is. When we arrive, we will park as much out of sight as possible but where we can observe the front entrance to the place. It has always worked just fine."

"Surely they will recognize you immediately," John replied.

"I don't think they will, John. You can get us a room on one of the upper floors, and when I see several people entering the building, I will just mix myself among them and walk right on in. After I get inside, I will steer myself around people who might recognize me. It works every time."

"All right, I am ready to follow your advice and directions," John agreed. "You are the detective, and I am your body guard, so to speak."

Robert directed John directly to the fancy hotel frequented regularly by mobsters. They wasted no time parking in a perfect spot. They sat watching people come and go for a while and settled themselves down for the chore ahead.

I doubt this will be a cakewalk, John thought to himself. He proceeded to the admitting desk, and the clerk on duty rented him a room on the third floor, just where he wanted to be.

It was over an hour before Robert showed. "I thought a sizeable group would never appear, but one finally did. I walked in close behind them with no trouble at all. I had never seen the admitting clerk before. If I had known, I could have been here much sooner."

"What do we do now?" asked John.

"We go down to the lobby and read the newspaper and wait. We are looking for two or three men who appear to be traveling together. We will follow our intuitions, and for gosh sakes, don't let them get the slightest hint that we have any interest in them."

When supper time came and groups of all sizes came in, it was very difficult to make any distinctions between individuals. After waiting as long as they dared, Robert and John left to sit in the car. Even in the car, they wasted no time. They looked at every car in sight, trying to spot a late model black Buick. They saw one, but an elderly couple soon came out and left in it.

"We are beating a dead horse sitting here," John remarked.

"I think you are right," replied Robert. "Perhaps we can try this again in the morning. But for now, let's canvass a few restaurants and bars close by. We have some time on our hands. In detective work, time is your best friend."

"You know, Millard and me brought the first load of whiskey to Chicago, and it was one more lucky day. We met Mr. Edward Brown, and he was so impressed with our whiskey that he wanted all he could buy from us and also directed us to his many restaurants scattered about. The first delivery we made was to a very nice restaurant and bar. I know exactly where it is. As I recall, his place is located about two blocks over."

They decided to eat supper at the restaurant and attempt to locate the men they were searching for later. They received the same warm welcome as Millard and John had enjoyed and almost ate themselves silly. Edward sat with them much of the time while they dined and kept their wine glass filled. As they left, they promised to return at every opportunity.

As they were returning to their car, Robert motioned for John to stop. Robert had noticed a black Buick, and they stepped into the shadows. The car was empty, but they remained quietly in the shadows, hoping to determine who returned to it. They waited for over an hour before three men came down the alley by the restaurant and drove away.

"Let's get on their tail fast before we lose them," said John.

The men went directly to the hotel where John and Robert were staying. John drove the car into the same place where they had parked earlier, and the Buick parked on the far side of the parking lot.

"Now maybe we can determine who they are and if they are who we are looking for," said Robert.

"You don't suppose we could be lucky enough to locate them this easily do you?" asked John.

"You never know," Robert replied. "Sometimes it takes less than one day and, at other times, a week or more to find a person."

The three men sat in their car for a few minutes and then went into the hotel. John and Robert followed but waited outside until they thought it advisable to go inside. They went to a back corner table and ordered wine and cheese to keep from being obvious to anyone. They could observe the three men well, and the more they watched, the more convinced they were the men they were looking for. They could see numerous injuries on two of the men. The other one showed no sign of any cuts or bruises. He must have been the driver.

"What do we do now, Robert?" asked John.

"Wait and see what happens for now," answered Robert. "They won't remain in the same place too long."

"Robert, have you noticed the one sitting closest to us. He looks unusually pale, and the other one looks even more so. I think they're wearing skin-colored makeup covering facial scars too. Maybe they have been to a beauty parlor." John snickered.

"You are getting good, John," said Robert. "I cannot see what you are describing."

"I think the lights are shining brighter from my view," replied John.

"I think if they leave, we will follow. But we will stay here as long as they do, unless you have some other idea," Robert said as his eyes kept scanning the room.

When the dining guests began to retire to their rooms or depart for home, John and Robert decided they must make a move also.

They left as the others did and went to their car. Sitting low in their seats, they observed the front entrance of the hotel. Their three suspects were still inside, and their black Buick remained where it was. They waited and waited, but nothing happened. John had sneaked around to a side window and peered inside.

The three men were sitting in the same place and the dining room was closing down. "What in the hell is with these men?" said John.

"If they are going anywhere, they will be out shortly," said Robert. "They might not be at their best physically, but that don't mean they can't plan a sneaky mission and complete it. If they have an order, they will carry it out."

Robert was right; at one in the morning the three men came out the door, looked around as if expecting to see someone, and then left. John started the car but did not turn the headlights on until he'd pulled out of the parking lot and the other car was far enough away not to pay much attention to anyone behind them.

"Where do you think they are going?" asked John.

"I have a suspicion they are going to Gordon Piker's office for some reason or maybe to the office of one of the other Mafia bosses," answered Robert. "The office is about a mile away, and those men are going in that direction. We will know soon."

Robert asked John to pull over a block before they reached the dead man's office. It was a perfect night to case the place. They each armed themselves with a 10-gauge shotgun, and John took two sticks of dynamite with fuses in place. They walked lightly among the shrubbery along the sidewalks until they were near the office and saw that something was going on.

Lights were on and at least a dozen men were inside. The black Buick and other fancy cars were parked behind the house.

"Let's wait among these thick shrubs until we can figure something out," suggested Robert. "They might have a soldier or two guarding the place. If they do, we need to know exactly where they are posted. You stay here, and I will circle the entire perimeter."

"Damn, be careful," said John. "I have a feeling we are not going to a prayer meeting."

Robert disappeared without making a sound.

After a while, he returned as silently as he'd left. "I saw one man guarding the place, and he is just milling around in dark areas. Inside, they are having a meeting and drinking pretty heavily. We need to find a place where we can hear their conversations. That guard has to be silenced before we can find a way to conceal ourselves and hear all that is being said."

"I noticed a small building behind Piker's office," said John. "If you could manage to open the door and find some heavy tape or cloth, I will restrain him so that he cannot move or talk. I am sure you can do it since I just saw you move around like a ghost. If you can do that, I will take care of the rest."

Again Robert was gone and returned again as before. He had a large roll of tape and a small piece of rope.

"That will do just fine," said John. "Now I will locate the guard and silence him."

John moved around behind the shadowed area and knocked the guard out cold. Using both the tape and the rope, he did a nice job restraining the guard, should he come to.

Both men began working their way in opposite directions around the house behind the shrubbery. Robert quickly found a large hole in the foundation, but after seeing something moving inside, he returned and found John. "I found a large hole, but there is something moving around in there."

John quickly followed Robert to the hole. He shined his flashlight inside and whispered, "It's a damn snake." He grabbed it and threw it far across the yard.

"Thanks," whispered Robert. "Snakes scare the hell out of me."

They both crawled in and went directly to the fireplace chimney, where some light was shining through from above. They could hear the conversation above as if they were in the room.

They listened but soon came to realize that many subjects had already been discussed before their arrival.

Finally, they heard the man who seemed to be conducting the meeting say, "Now that the subject of putting old Piker where he belongs has been settled, let's move on to the present gnat in our eye—Newbarn up on the Blue Ridge Mountains. Our new boss tried to negotiate and talk some sense into their heads earlier this week but got nowhere. They want to give us 10 percent of their profits to leave them alone and accused us of harassing them."

Laughter immediately erupted in the room.

"Damn fools," whispered John to Robert.

"They don't know the definition of harassment until we get mean and go after them," someone in the room said, his words slurred from too much booze.

"They also want to sell us their fine whiskey at a 10 percent discount and promise to expand their current distribution in our direction no farther."

"Five percent would be too much for the bastards," said one man with a harsh, loud voice.

"We have worked hard to build our business, and they want to take it away in one short swipe," said another man with a Spanish accent.

Several voices could be heard opining about the 10 percent offer. They all sounded furious, suggesting death to all the damned sons of bitches.

"They also had the nerve to say that we do not own the west any more than they do. We have allowed them to have their way so far with just a smack on the wrist now and then as a warning. We cannot tolerate them any longer. Old man Walter Stamey died recently. He had retired, but he was still the brains of the outfit. They are well organized but have only four leaders. Walters's son, Jackson, is now in charge. I doubt they can withstand the pressure we are about to put upon them. Their delivery routes that affect us most start in Chattanooga and spread out to Memphis and then north to St. Louis and on to Chicago. That is the direction they think we will come from to put them out of business, as you all know. I suggest that we make plans right here and now to take action against Newbarn."

A man with a high-pitched voice spoke up and said, "I have been thinking about how best to end this problem since I tried to negotiate with Jackson several nights ago. It seems to me quite simple now. I think we should send about a dozen well-armed men to deal with those bastards."

Someone in the room said, "With all due respect, I doubt that a dozen men will be enough to handle them, sir."

"Sir, I propose we have at least twenty men when we go, or maybe more. That country is heavily forested, and the men are scattered all about," another man added.

"You make a good point," said the boss. "And we will consider it carefully as we continue."

"The new boss is Mr. Mann, the man who talked with Jackson a few nights ago," Robert whispered.

"I believe you are right," John replied. "That Italian accent comes through very clear from here."

Robert nodded, and they listened to another man suggest, "Our men could travel down through Ohio, Kentucky, and Tennessee, and rent a place in Asheville, North Carolina. Asheville is less than sixty miles from Newbarn. I doubt they will be expecting us to come up through the Cumberland Gap and on to Asheville."

"We will consider this further before we act," said Mr. Mann. "Remember, when the detailed plans are being put into place, we do not want to stir up any more publicity than necessary, and Newbarn probably feels the same way. That is the reason for being so secretive. We don't need to do anything with the short deliveries either. They are carried out within the Blue Ridges and present no problem to us. Their long-haul operation is the problem. I want to consider all opinions, but as of now I believe we should determine for certain the identity of all the leaders and then do everything on one dark night. We must burn Newbarn's headquarters and the houses of every one of the Newbarn leaders—put the torch to all cars and trucks and then get the hell out of there, leaving no connections to ourselves."

A pause followed, and then Mann said, "What is it, Ellis?"

"We will have a hard time keeping publicity down with so much burning and destruction and maybe killing. Would that not put local, state, and federal authorities on our asses?"

"No doubt it will, Ellis," said Mr. Mann, "but we will scatter the soldiers who do the work to Florida until things settle down. I will send a detective over to scout the countryside prior to your leaving. I want this task completed within the next two weeks. If we are met with armed resistance, kill them all. Again I say, we must first plan carefully."

That brought a loud response from all across the room, indicating approval of the firm remark Mr. Mann had just made.

Robert and John remained very quiet until the meeting was over. From the sounds coming from the room, the men inside were pretty well intoxicated when they began leaving the office. Robert and John were happy to hear them all leave. But now they must get out quickly and quietly and release the guard. He was still tied and bound just as they'd left him.

Robert apologized to him for the discomfort he had endured. "We are federal agents and are gathering evidence on those who murdered Gordon Piker and his chauffeur. In cases like these, if we don't find solid evidence right away, the chances of solving the case are practically nonexistent."

Robert showed him his fake badge and identification to assure the guard he was being truthful. He then asked the guard if he or anyone he knew could help find eyewitnesses or factual information that would help solve this case. "Murder is a terrible thing, my friend, and any information you can give us will be held in the strictest confidence. And you will not be involved in any way."

The guard looked scared but said, "I will admit that I do not like the new boss, Ransom Mann. Mr. Piker was not a good man either, but he did not deserve to be murdered like he was. I think Mr. Mann killed him to move himself into the higher ranks in the Mafia. But I have no way of proving what I think."

"I believe you," said Robert. "We might contact you again just in case you should hear something useful. Thank you for your help. Please do not tell anyone about us being here or talking to you."

"I will do as you say," said the guard.

"You really laid it on thick and I feel sure he believed you," said John once they were back in their car.

"I had to," Robert replied. "If the hellish gang in that room gets one hint that anyone from Newbarn knows their plans, they will cancel everything, and we will have to start over from scratch. It might cause some of us to get killed as well."

"It is much too risky. I will check us out of the hotel, and unless you have some other business here, let's head for home."

"We will do just that," said Robert, "but it might be advisable to return home by taking the more northern route across the

Cumberland Gap. We have accomplished more than I expected, except we did not find out the names of those characters that beat on me."

"Beat up on you," replied John. "It looked to me like it might have been the other way around."

'It might look that way, but believe me, it was not that way. My knife is all that saved me. I will get them later, one way or another. My work for Newbarn will be somewhat restricted at least for now, however. They know who I am and who I am working for. Apparently, I have been successful in interrupting their plans for Newbarn; they want no interferences from anyone, and we might have our hands full with them soon."

John continued to drive after they left the hotel. Robert insisted he was quite able to carry his load now, but John would have none of it. "We need you in the best of health in the days to come, so why should we take chances?"

"Oh, I know," said Robert. "I do great wonders and eat rotten cucumbers."

John laughed loudly. "I haven't heard that one in many years, since I was a kid."

"We haven't had much fun on this trip," said Robert, "Let's stop for the night in Lexington and have some good food and fun for a change."

"Sounds fine to me," replied John. "We couldn't make it home tonight anyway."

John drove at a steady speed, making good time. The weather was getting very cold, and dark clouds seemed to forebode snow.

"Let's just change our direction a little farther south toward Nashville and drive until we feel like stopping," Robert suggested. "We might have less chance of getting into a snowstorm."

John was in full agreement. He had no desire to drive in snow.

As they made their way south, the air did begin to get warmer, and some blue sky could be seen. They traveled on until after dark and then stopped at a tavern with several adjoining rooms, which were quite adequate for the night. They were satisfied at how the day had turned out, but after a few beers, they were ready for bed.

At breakfast, they estimated they would arrive at Newbarn well before midnight, and after stopping for gas and meals during the day, they arrived at eleven o'clock. Since tomorrow was Saturday, they decided the information they had acquired on their trip needed to be shared with the leaders of Newbarn. Decisions needed to be made the following day, and Robert volunteered to contact everyone early in the morning. He knew John must be tired after driving practically all week long.

"Do not forget to notify Horace Blue," John said. "He of all people needs to be on the alert."

★ ★ ★

All the men were present and on time at the meeting Robert had called. The smell of freshly brewed coffee was strong, and the men were filling their cups. Robert thought the meeting was important enough to invite Horton Pritchard and Jefferson Platt to the meeting. If more bad information surfaced at the meeting concerning the Mafia, they might need more leadership.

Millard did not have a good feeling about these happenings, seemingly without end; in fact the entire buildup of trouble was making him nervous, but that would pass. As he had driven to Newbarn, following Robert's summons, he'd thought about how great it would be if they could work without having enemies. Even better, he'd contemplated the possibility of once again reorganizing Newbarn, only this time shaping it into a profitable, legitimate business. They had talked about doing just that before but, adverse circumstances had prevented them from doing so and this depression lingering on might push such a plan even farther behind.

Before the meeting started, excitement was very prevalent; but the conversation and funny jokes ended when Jackson called the meeting to order. Jackson asked Robert and John to tell them about the events of their trip.

"We will if someone will stoke up the fire a bit. It's cold in here, and my teeth are beginning to chatter," said Robert.

Everyone laughed, and Jefferson quickly had the fire getting hotter.

"We were lucky at first," said Robert. "We found the three men involved in the attack on me, and sure enough, they were Mafia men. John followed them directly to the hotel where the Mafia usually meets. We maneuvered and dodged around the place without being recognized. The three men who attacked me in Memphis were there.

"We followed them when they left the hotel to the building where Gordon Piker had lived and worked. It was a meeting of many of the Mafia leaders. We concealed ourselves under the house and listened to most of what they said. They spoke of Mr. Piker being where he belonged—in the lake of course.

"Nothing was said about Newbarn until near the end of the meeting. They intend to put an end to our business and probably within the next two weeks. They intend to come up through the Cumberland Gap to Asheville. From there, they'll make their attack. They plan to burn our headquarters here, along with the homes of every one of our leaders and our trucks and cars, and then leave fast. They want to do their mischief with as little publicity as possible, and they have little interest in our short runs within the boundaries of the Blue Ridge Mountains, so they said. I doubt they will keep their word about that. We actually make about as much money with our short runs as we do the long-haul trucking business. Anyway, they were just about drunk, and after they sobered up, they might have changed their minds. But I believe they will follow their plans put forth at the meeting."

"Well, I believe we should keep watch for them to arrive in Asheville," said Millard. "Asheville is not that large, and we might just locate them before they know we are near.

"If we do find them all congregated in Asheville, let's jump on them like ducks on June bugs and give them such a beating they will all have a bed in Asheville Hospital."

That brought on more laughter.

"Damn, Millard, you are a violent man, I do believe.

"By the way," Robert continued, "would someone turn the damper down on that stove? My ass is burning now."

That brought on even more laughter.

"You shouldn't stand so close to the stove," Jackson said.

"Now, back to business," Robert continued. "They will be driving fancy black cars and will stay in one of the finest hotels.

Heaven forbid that they should lodge in a boardinghouse; that would be far below their dignity."

"I agree," said Jackson. "We should have at least two men scanning the city to locate them when they get here and notify us when they arrive."

"That is my job," said Robert. "I know exactly how to go about it in Asheville, and I will locate and follow them if you men agree. I will spend about a third of my time patrolling that narrow, curvy road across the Cumberland Gap."

Everyone agreed that Robert was the expert professional to handle that part of the job.

"Be sure to take your switchblade with you, Robert," said John. "You might just turn them around at the Cumberland Gap and send them back toward Chicago with their britches cut off."

Everyone laughed.

They knew how proficient Robert was with his knife.

"We know they are not foolish men, and we should assume that we are going to be raided," said Jackson. "They probably have scouts watching us, just as we will be watching them. And what should we do if Robert discovers where they are and when they are coming?"

"I believe we should keep someone in the office here at all times," Millard replied. "I doubt they will try anything at all during the day, except snooping around. We should make a list, and if Robert finds that they are on their way here at night, he should notify the man on duty, who will notify the next man on the list. As soon as a man is notified, he should report for duty here. We all know Robert will take whatever action he feels is necessary if he sees a surprise coming our way."

"We must protect Horace Blue at all cost," said John. "They might know the location of his stills by now."

"I don't think they do," said Horace. "They couldn't destroy my operation if they tried. I am protected behind by the high water and rough terrain. I have men at the stills at all times and four bulldogs that could eat intruders for breakfast."

"I would consider it an honor to help you out," said John. "I know the Mafia will try to harm you, maybe murder you. That is the way they are. I keep plenty of dynamite, and I know how to use it. They will regret the day if they try anything with me around."

"Do you want his help, Mr. Blue?" Jackson asked.

"I do want his help; I would be foolish to turn him down. Thank you, John," said Horace.

"I think we all understand what is going on now and the task before us. We will save Newbarn and go on with our business. Perhaps it would be reasonable to think about our situation, and Monday we will put our plans in place as much as possible," Jackson concluded.

"We should all go to church this Sunday," Millard said as they were leaving the room.

He got no reply but the men looked at him as though they agreed that prayer might be a good idea.

As Millard drove home, he was feeling nervous again. *We are dealing with professional criminals*, thought Millard, *and they will not hesitate to kill us just as they do in Chicago and St. Louis and Memphis and any other place where they have their tentacles attached.*

They do not want publicity, however, and they are somewhat fearful of us old mountain men. Maybe everything will turn out better than we expect, he reasoned.

Flora noticed the stressed look on his face as he entered the door and knew something was wrong. Cameron and Walter wanted to wrestle, and with all the commotion, he began to look relaxed and pleased to be home. Flora had pinto beans and cornbread for lunch, and that was sufficient to please anyone and lift their spirits high.

After taking a short nap, Millard wanted to see the progress on the new house and go visit Salem. That immediately pleased everyone. As Millard drove up the hill to the house, he was amazed at the beauty of the place. Since the temperature remained rather mild at midday lately, the carpenters had been painting the woodwork on the outside, and it was looking fantastic. He briefly walked through the inside of the house. Everything was progressing nicely.

On they went to visit Flora's folks. Millard wanted to discuss the Newbarn situation with Salem. When they arrived, they received their usual warm welcome, and the boys took off to the barn to play in the hay stored there.

Later, Flora made them come into the house because of their chasing the chickens.

Salem and Millard headed for the woodshed to talk and sip moonshine. "I'll declare, Horace Blue seems to improve on the quality of his whiskey every time I taste a new jar," Salem remarked.

"It does seem that way, but actually the taste and quality stays the same," said Millard. "And that is one of our problems with the Mafia. They are jealous and want us to give them 90 percent of our profits for any long-haul deliveries we make beyond Chattanooga, to protect us so to speak. In other words, they want us to pay them to keep their own soldiers from harassing us, which they have been doing all along. They want everything for themselves without competition."

"Have you responded to their demands?" ask Salem.

"Yes, we have offered them 10 percent of our profits, promised not to expand our runs beyond what we are doing now, and threw in a goodwill offer to sell our whiskey to them at a 10 percent discount. They would not negotiate with us, and we expect them to attack us soon. We will be ready and are going to keep watch and take precautions to keep them away or suffer the consequences. John and Robert overheard them planning to burn Newbarn to the ground, along with the houses of all the leaders of Newbarn. What would you do in such a situation, Salem?" Millard asked.

"Seems to me that you men have done about all you can do until you find out more information. I would keep vigilant continually and wait for their next move. I don't think they will come over here for very long. From what I have read, they have things like this going on regularly and probably can't watch everything at once. They have limits also. One thing I can do is watch your family at night when you are away. I will take my guns and plenty of ammunition. Don't worry about either house. I will hide some dynamite in the right places, and if they show up, I will light the fuses as they are needed. I didn't fight in World War I without learning a few things."

"You don't know how good that makes me feel, Salem. I thank you, sir."

They finished their visit and went home earlier than they ordinarily would, but Millard knew he needed to spend time with his family this evening. Salem and Martha understood without question.

The boys wanted to go for ice cream and cake, but Flora insisted that they go home. She wanted to fix them a pot of soup and cornbread and a glass of cold milk from the spring box.

After supper, she surprised them by placing a nice chocolate cake that she had baked on the table. A large piece of the cake, along with another glass of milk, made them glad they had come home instead of having just cake and ice cream.

After the treat, they gathered around the kitchen table to put together a picture puzzle, something they had not done before. Millard thought how amazing it was that Cameron and Walter could find a small piece of the puzzle and place it in the right spot. When they had finished, the puzzle showed a very pretty picture of a farm surrounded by mountains and a river and a lake with ducks swimming around. What fun that was, and Millard was amazed at how quiet they had all been while they were putting it together. Millard promised to make a frame to hold the picture together and hang it on the wall. It was a very unusual evening, and the boys were getting tired and sleepy.

"To bed with you," said Millard as he carried the boys toward the bed, one under each arm. They were as happy as any two small boys could be.

After the boys were asleep, Millard and Flora talked at length of the worsening situation with the Mafia. He explained to her all that had happened from the very beginning of the trouble to what now seemed to be turning into a violent situation that could end in injuries or even death.

"Get out of it, honey," Flora pleaded.

"I cannot do that," Millard replied. "I am committed to our cause, and there is no turning back. Don't ask me to leave my job again."

"What about our boys and their safety?"

"No, Flora, you and the boys will be safe. We expect something to break within the next two weeks, but we have no way of knowing for certain. Salem is going to come over and stay with you and the boys if and when trouble starts. He has a plan to protect you based on his experience as a soldier."

"You must get out, Millard, before you get killed," Flora insisted.

"As it stands now, we at Newbarn are going to continue our work as usual while keeping scouts watching for any signs of the Mafia coming over here to cause trouble. Don't worry; we will have plans in place to cope with them if they come across the mountains."

"Me and the boys cannot take losing you. I don't think we could ever get over it," she said with tears in her eyes.

"Well, I don't intend to let that happen. But if the worst should come, you would have to go on with your lives. Time heals all things, and we have no assurance of one more day on this earth. I worry about you and the boys when I am away, but I can't allow that to keep me from doing what I do. I have made provisions for my family in every way in the event I should leave."

"Everything except your presence with us," Flora replied.

"I know," Millard replied, "but we could talk all night and nothing would change."

They had little more to say on the subject. They just sat quietly for a while and then went to bed. They slept the entire night holding each other closely as they usually did when uneasy feelings persisted.

FIFTY-NINE

When the clock alarm went off, Millard wasted little time in getting dressed. He expected a normal day but took time to dress appropriately in keeping with his position in Newbarn. His shoes were polished but not shined. His pants were nicely ironed with a crease in front, and he wore a neatly ironed, button-to-the-top, wool shirt and a nice hat. Due to the chilly weather, he put on a waistcoat. After kissing Flora and the boys, he drove rapidly up the hill, hardly noticing his new home.

He stopped for a breakfast sandwich to go, and to his surprise, he was the first one to arrive at work. Robert was soon to follow, and then all of the other leaders of Newbarn, including Horton Pritchard and Jefferson Platt, arrived. They hardly had time to discuss any weekend activities before the routemen came in.

The men did not want to depart on their routes until Robert had told them about any unusual activities during the weekend.

"We will probably have trouble with the Mafia, but I have no way of knowing exactly when or where," he explained to them after some effort in getting them to assemble in a group.

They reminded him that they could be counted upon to help out in any way, including in any fighting to be done. They loved their work at Newbarn. It had pulled them out of poverty and hard times for their families, and they were anxious to show their appreciation and loyalty.

Jackson came out and thanked them for what they were doing. He always referred to them as gentlemen when he spoke to them, and they knew he was sincere. They were then off on their daily runs, confident that things were in hand.

Jackson and Millard and the other leaders of Newbarn quickly gathered around the table inside to discuss and make plans based upon available information.

Robert had not lied about the Mafia to the men he had just spoken to, but he had thought it best not to reveal any more than was necessary. He saved much of the information he had obtained over the weekend by traveling the area from the Cumberland Gap to Asheville numerous times. Now was the time to reveal his findings to the leadership of the organization. "Men," he said, "we might have more trouble on our hands than we can cope with unless we are very clever and cautious and secretive. I spotted two men who have been scouting the entire area I just described. I followed them as they drove all around Asheville, probably finding lodging for their soldiers who are coming over and also trying to gather all the information they can about us and how you operate your business. I really don't think they know where this place is just yet, but make no mistake, they will find us. As soon as they get over here and get organized, they will probably spread out to locate the homes of our leaders and this place in particular. I am sure they will try diligently to locate Horace's whiskey-making operation, but even if they find it, they will wish they hadn't. I think you know what I mean about that."

Robert stopped to take a drink of his coffee and then continued, "I have a parking place near the top of the Cumberland Gap from which I can see every car that passes, and I have already detected three large, black cars with five men in each car. They make no effort to conceal anything and appear oblivious to the fact that we are here and probably watching for them. They stand out like a sore thumb with their Cuban cigars; black, four-door sedans; and expensive suits, topcoats, and Stetson hats. Some of the locals might become suspicious and confront them if they go round far off the main roads wearing expensive clothing."

Most mountain men wore bib overalls, heavy shirts, boots, and coats. In the cold of winter, they often wore two layers of clothing, long underwear (long johns), and a heavy coat.

"I have no doubt that they will bring a horde of their soldiers over here—as many as they think they will need and then some. We should start preparing today. They are. Newbarn is blessed with enough intelligent men to form a plan of action and turn this entire crisis around in our favor here at Newbarn," he concluded.

John then brought up an import point to be considered. "If those bastards are coming across the Cumberland Gap, others could be coming up the mountain from Chattanooga, the route we usually take. I think it would be wise if we have one or two men watch that road until we get this mess settled."

"I will ask the county to patrol that mountain from the bottom up with at least two patrolmen in the car," replied Jackson. "I will give them the full details of what might happen, and I will only ask officers who can be depended upon to do the job. We have known all along that many officers, who are not in our pocket, both state and county, have been receiving compensation from somewhere. Now we know for certain the Chicago Mafia has been reaching farther and farther in this direction, intending to take over our organization and probably other territories all the way to the Atlantic Ocean.

"I wondered why they would begrudge us old mountain boys making a little money up here on the Blue Ridges. They didn't seem very interested until we began establishing truck routes and making large amounts of cash. I say to hell with the Mafia. Before we leave here today, we will put our plans together as best we can and be alert at all times."

Jackson continued, "The day is rapidly moving, and we should busy ourselves immediately. First, I think we should make a speedy trip home to check on our families and make certain they will be safe and well cared for. Each one of us must be responsible for our families and for keeping our homes from being burned to the ground. Actually, I do not think they will attempt to burn our homes, but they did make that threat. They would have nothing to gain by doing so, and the bad publicity would be tremendous."

Robert excused himself from the meeting. "I must return to my duties of tracking those criminals. Now that we have a telephone, I can call here and keep you informed regularly."

The men left for their homes quickly as Jackson had directed. Millard volunteered to remain at Newbarn while the men were gone. He knew Salem was watching after his family and both houses. He guessed, and correctly so, that Salem had prepared his defenses early this morning.

Millard arrived just as the family was preparing supper and managed to take enough time to eat with them. They talked very little before he headed out the door. As he was walking swiftly across the yard, he called to Salem to inform him that they might have unwelcome visitors at Newbarn soon. He knew Salem knew what he meant and would explain the meaning to Flora.

When he returned to Newbarn, the deliverymen were returning and asking questions about what had transpired during the day. Jackson and Millard had previously decided to keep the men informed as much as possible without giving out information that might be damaging to Newbarn if it was leaked to the Mafia. They did not believe that even one spy was in their organization, but they had not totally ruled out such a possibility. Money could cause men to do things they would never ordinarily consider, but that one man could do enough damage to cause the destruction of Newbarn.

They informed the men of necessary information and made them aware that their help might be needed soon if the present situation worsened. Millard asked them to be prepared and stay close to home in case they were called upon to help defend Newbarn.

They responded as though they would welcome such a call and their reaction would be swift.

Jackson seemed especially moved by their reaction and said, "Don't think for one minute that your devotion to Newbarn is not appreciated. We are all family here, and that is the way it should be and will continue to be."

The men left for home quietly, and Millard could easily detect that Jackson had struck a comforting note with them.

The days were getting shorter and the temperature colder now. The leaders of Newbarn went inside and started a fire in the stove. Horace decided to return home and help his men keep the many whiskey stills running and the mash cooking. It took a lot of fire to make whiskey in this weather, even though shelters with chimneys were built to keep the men warm.

All the other leaders remained near the warm fire waiting to hear from Robert. They had done all they could for now.

It was near midnight when the phone rang out one long and two short rings, which were the correct rings for their phone. It was Robert calling from Asheville.

Millard answered, and the first words from Robert were, "Tell John he was right in getting us to patrol the road from Chattanooga. Sure enough, several cars full of their soldiers were starting up the mountain when our officers headed them off. They left in a hail of bullets, and the lawmen forced them to retreat back toward Memphis. I stayed on watch at the top of the Cumberland Gap until after dark. Three more Mafia cars passed by before I left, and I followed them to a hotel here in Asheville. I am going to drive around Asheville until I locate where all of them are staying the night, and then I will try to get in a few hours of sleep myself. I will sleep in my car somewhere near them. I will call you again in the morning, but I have no idea what time it will be."

"Well," said Jackson, "I think we should try to sleep as much as we can before morning."

"This damn floor is hard," said John. "My ass went to sleep hours ago. It is nice and warm in here though, so we should be thankful."

Tuesday came and nothing had happened during the night that they knew of. Millard prepared a pot of hot coffee, and Horton went for breakfast sandwiches.

"We need to get prepared for the day," Jackson remarked. "I hope we hear from Robert soon, or we will have to go to Asheville and try to find him."

"I am willing to do that now if you consider it a good move," said Millard. "If we can keep that mob from getting ahead of us in carrying out some wild plan they have in mind, we would be far better off."

"You might just have something there, Millard," Jackson replied. "You and John work amazingly well together. John, would you be willing to go with Millard as he has caused us to consider?"

"Sure," said John. "I think we should stay right on top of them as much as possible. Don't give them time to breathe. They are a sorry bunch and used to being ahead of everyone and having their way. We know that much about them already."

"Call us when you get up there, or we will get concerned about you two as well," said Jackson.

"We will be on our way in a jiffy, as soon as we tidy ourselves up a bit," said Millard.

Within a few minutes they were spinning their wheels out of the driveway.

As they entered the city of Asheville, they began canvassing one street at a time, beginning near the center and working their way outward toward the French Broad River. The center of the city covered about thirty blocks and was fairly modern. The remainder of Asheville had widely spread roads with some of them paved. The trees along the roadside made for a nice-looking city, and the houses were well kept. The landscape was mixed with hills and hollows, and the French Broad River was impressive, swift, and dangerous-looking. There was one large mansion that covered many hundreds of acres, known as the Biltmore House. Undoubtedly, it was the largest and most elaborate mansion in the United States. It had taken millions of dollars and years to build.

Millard and John were hoping to find Robert first and save a lot of searching for the Mafia. They were close to giving up searching and finding a place to call Newbarn when they rounded a curve in the road and there was Robert eating a snack beside the road.

"What luck," said Millard as they approached Robert. "We were about to give up and call Newbarn."

"I located the hotel where they all stayed last night, and I have counted sixteen cars. Each car was filled with four or five Mafia soldiers. They have leadership and a plan, but I do not know what it is. We have our work cut out for us. I think we might have underestimated them a little. They know I have been following them and that we are waiting on them to make a move."

"We have a mole among our ranks then," said Millard. "John and I have discussed the possibility."

Robert continued, "I did hide among the bushes late last night and heard two of them talking as they stood outside the hotel. All I heard was a few words about burning Newbarn. I will find out more after I get on their trail again. I don't have time to discuss the situation further. Call Newbarn for an update, and I will meet you in the center of the city as soon as possible. Don't leave if I am late in meeting you. I don't think we have much time before those bastards make their move to harm us, probably in more ways than one."

Millard and John decided to do exactly as Robert had said. They headed uptown where they had seen a pool room and went in to make a phone call to Newbarn. Jackson answered the phone. Millard quickly updated him on all that had occurred in Asheville and promised to call them again later. "After we meet Robert," he said, "I believe we will know of their intentions."

Jackson told Millard that the road up the mountain from Chattanooga was blocked off now, thanks to the law officers who had helped them yesterday. That was good news for John and Millard; it was comforting to know the law officers were going to be of value to them. *We pay them well but, they are with us when we need them*, Millard thought to himself.

"Nothing else for us to do now except wait for Robert," said Millard. "I hope we don't have to wait too long, but I think he had his reasons to ask us to wait for him."

They'd waited over an hour before Robert appeared. He approached them with a worried look on his face. "You know I had a feeling that the Mafia had not left the hotel, and I was right. I went to the rear of the building and went inside. I heard laughing and talking going on as though a group was having a party. It made me mad as hell, and I intended to get to the bottom of things then and there. I returned to my car and loaded my pistol with hollow-point bullets; as an added measure, I fused three sticks of dynamite and tucked them in my coat.

"When I returned, I looked for a room next to the large room where the noise was coming from. I found none, but I did find the ladies room and put an Out of Order sign on the door. After I got inside and locked the door, I easily routed out a small hole in the corner of the room and could hear conversations and some short speeches.

"I know the Mafia is capable of almost anything, but what I heard was sickening. They intend to do exactly what they came here to do, including burning homes."

"Sons of bitches," growled Millard, his fists clenched.

"I know we are prepared for this, but I did not believe they would carry out such a threat," John said. "Good thing we did take them at their word. What the dynamite I have rigged around my house don't get, the men I have hired will. I tell you truly, I intend to kill every damn one of them without mercy." John's voice was harsh with a terrible anger.

"I will help you with that job," said Millard, who was staring in the direction of his home with a sad look on his face.

"They sounded as though this was a small job to them," continued Robert. "I know they were drinking and might not have meant all of what they said, but they have convinced me. It crossed my mind to toss all three sticks of dynamite into that room, but I knew that would never do. We need to alert Newbarn about this. The three of us should get on their trail again and follow them everywhere they go. We will just have to play things by ear until we determine what has to be done. Damn, what a situation to be in.

"They are hanging around the hotel and the surrounding area waiting for nightfall. Let's drive around up there until we locate them again and then stick on their tails without letting up."

"I think you are right," said Millard. "And let's try not to allow them to know how close we are after them, but I don't know if that will be possible."

The hotel clerk said a group of men from Chicago had left over an hour ago. Robert, Millard, and John sat on a bench in front of the hotel to discuss their options. None of them believed the Mafia was anywhere in Asheville, and even if they were, they did not have time to look for them.

They called Newbarn and then immediately headed for the headquarters, one car behind the other. They drove as fast as they dared over the sharp, curvy roads until they reached Newbarn. John was out the door before Millard had even come to a complete stop, and Robert was close on his tail. They quickly went inside to discuss the situation, which was growing rapidly more complicated.

Jackson met them at the door, and Robert filled him in, giving a rapid but accurate report of recent events.

"What do you men think we should do now?" asked Jackson. "Surely they are now in this area someplace."

"My guess is they located a secluded farm with a barn large enough to hide their cars before they came here from Chicago," Robert answered. "I suspect they have persuaded someone in our group to pass on information to them. Either that or they have a detective like me keeping abreast of everything that has been going on recently and doing a good job of it."

"One thing is certain; we must find them soon," Millard remarked. "We have no choice but to believe what Robert heard them saying."

"Let's get organized and get to work," said Jackson.

"I think it best that we notify all of our people to come help us out," Millard said. "It shouldn't take long for them to get here, and when they arrive, we should utilize everyone here to the best advantage."

They agreed, and Jackson began making calls to those who had telephones, asking them to notify others who ordinarily would not know they were needed until much later.

"I think we should proceed now in spreading ourselves out around our grounds and buildings here in case that damn bunch should try to burn our headquarters here first thing," John remarked. "With so few men here now, we will be spread thin."

John and Millard advised everyone where he should position himself.

SIXTY

"That is about all we can do for now, Millard," said John. "One thing we might do is guard the front gate ourselves."

"There is good cover behind those big trees over there," Millard replied. "We both know what to do if they show up, and my ears will be even worse afterward."

"Damn, Millard, you never will let me forget that first time I had to defend us with my shotgun."

"I will, but my ears probably won't."

That brought laughter from both men, but it was low and subdued.

Robert had already left to locate the Mafia men. He had been feeling somewhat guilty for letting them out of his sight after he'd first found them. He intended to remedy that mistake and quickly. The mob was close around. He was certain of that. And if they succeeded with their plans, they would head back to Chicago as quickly as possible. To avoid anyone making a connection between the Mafia and the damage they intended to inflict, they'd get it done as quietly and rapidly as possible, avoiding if at all possible the excessive noise of shotguns, dynamite, and the like. He guessed the trouble would be tonight, based on his previous detective work. Also, Robert had overheard them indicate they would pick a dark night to complete their work. This was a very dark night with no moon during those hours.

Recent events were rapidly coming to mind. He thought of Antonio's barn in a valley several miles north of Spruce Willow. If the Mafia higher-ups did have a spy in the area, they would surely know of Antonio's betrayal by now. He considered their anger and was certain their foot soldiers would head straight to take Antonio out. He had to move quickly if he were to have any chance of saving Antonio's life.

He drove directly to the barn, which was in view of the main road, and cut up a dirt road that dead-ended at a spot above the building. It was dusky dark when he parked and partially hid his car. He decided to creep through the tall weeds to the barn.

He was just a short distance away when he heard noises inside. He also heard another noise close by that he did not like; a bulldog was making its way through the tall grass and coming directly toward him. He decided to stand perfectly still; the strategy with dogs had worked for him before, and he hoped it would work this time. Sure enough, the dog came up to him wagging its tail and licking his hand. Apparently no one paid any attention to him. The dog went on his way after Robert patted him on the head a few times, and then Robert continued his pace toward the barn.

Now was the time he dreaded. He looked through a crack in the wall, and there they were—a large number of black cars and at least fifty men in the cars. Candles burned all through the barn. He thought about setting fire to the barn but quickly decided that would not be a good move. He started to back away slowly but hesitated when he saw two men lying on the floor partly covered with hay. No doubt about it; they were dead. His heart had been racing before he approached the barn, and now it was beating so fast he was short of breath.

Robert slowly made his way back to his car, drove slowly back to the main road with his lights off, and then headed to Newbarn at top speed. More men were guarding the place.

Millard and John came in right after him.

"I hope you have good news for us," said Jackson.

"No, I have information but nothing good. I found where the Mafia men are hiding. They are holed up in that enormous barn Antonio Vitally rented up in the valley north of here. All the cars and men are there as best I could estimate the numbers. Before I left, I saw two dead men lying in the floor covered with hay. I could not identify who they were.

"I usually handle danger, but this trip shook me up a little. These men seem like ministers of Lucifer who came from hell rather than Chicago."

"Well then," said John. "We might just send them back where they came from and stoke the fire a bit hotter for them."

"I think about all the men who have been contacted are now here," said Jackson, "but perhaps we should group together for a head count. We don't want to lose anyone."

It took only a few minutes to complete the count.

"The night is young, and there is no moon," Robert said after they had all gathered inside. "Let's take advantage of the long, dark hours left before daybreak. I think we should go over to that big barn, see if they're still there, and do what we have to do. You are all good men, and I don't think any of you actually want to kill or be killed. Of course, the decision is with you and your leaders."

"Does anyone here have a better idea?" Jackson asked. "This could be one of the most important decisions we will ever make. If no one has any answers or different ideas, I will say that I believe Robert has the only logical solution. This could mean serious injury or death to one or several of us, so don't hold back if you have something to say."

"I do," said Robert. "I have two other considerations we should cover. First, if they attempt to ambush us, we need to get out of the trap as soon as possible and assemble back here. Second, we must keep a third of our people here to guard Newbarn. If they determine that we are well defended here, I do not think they will attempt to force their way in. They will know they are at a disadvantage. I know Jackson will hold things down here while the remainder of us assess what is going on at that damned old barn."

"I think our plan is the best we can do for now," said Jackson. "Stay as close to Robert as practical and head back here if the danger is too great. We do not want anyone killed."

Millard and John were listening to every word. They traded glances, knowing that if the group got into a bad spot, the heavy lifting would no doubt fall on their shoulders. Neither said so, but they knew they were the best two fighters in Newbarn, without exception.

As they drove out the gate, Millard felt a strange but transient feeling of sorrow inside. He was aware of this feeling but forced himself to pay it no mind. The men kept a comfortable distance between the cars to keep from drawing undue attention. Their drive to the barn was very deliberate and cautious. When they arrived at their destination, they drove with their headlights off from the turn-off point to the dead end behind the barn. They approached the barn fully armed and expecting gunfire at any moment, but none came. The barn and the entire area was deathly quiet; not even a night bird could be heard.

Robert inched himself forward ever so slowly, until he could touch the barn and then dropped to the ground and turned his small flashlight on to look inside. Only the two bodies covered with hay remained inside, along with the cars.

"There is no one here, men," said Robert in a low voice. "Let's go inside and look the place over."

The barn door creaked open when Robert cautiously gave it a slight push. They eased on in as quietly as possible, just in case there might be others in that vast place. "Wonder where the murderers of these two men have gone and why they've left all these cars unguarded," he said softly.

"I'll bet one or more men are somewhere around here watching us now," replied Millard.

John and Millard went directly to see if they could identify the bodies. When they removed the hay, they were both aghast at what they saw. "Hellfire," said Millard. "It's Antonio Vitally and Homer Cash." Blood was puddled around the bodies.

"Good Lord," said John, "they were executed, and in a brutal way too."

"Their throats have been cut and cut deep. Their heads are almost off," said Millard in a loud voice.

"Hey, Robert, what in the horse's ass do we do about this?"

"God bless," said Robert as he leaned over the bodies. "Legally, we should call the sheriff to investigate, but given our situation, I suggest we leave them until tomorrow sometime. By then, maybe we will have enough information to give the sheriff a more logical explanation, or we might find it more to our advantage to just leave things as they are and let someone else find the bodies."

"I think we should report this to the sheriff when we return to Newbarn," Millard replied. "I can't abide leaving them here for rats or other varmints to violate their bodies."

"Yes, of course," said John. "No offense, Robert, but we would be lowering ourselves to the level of the scum we have to deal with."

"You are quite right," said Robert. "Sometimes I forget that I am working with decent, honorable men. Let's leave here quickly and get on with what is ahead of us on this horrible night."

The trip back to Newbarn was rushed and worrisome. Most of the men had never experienced violence and murder, which was so common among organized crime people. For some strange reason, Millard experienced that same feeling he had when they'd left Newbarn a few hours earlier.

He was soon to find out why!

When they drove up to Newbarn, everything was different. A few men were quietly waiting outside, but most of them were gone.

"What is going on?" asked Millard. "Things seem different from when we left."

Jefferson Platt was sitting on the steps near the door of the office. He replied not one word; he just pointed inside.

Millard knew before he stumbled through the door that something had happened to Jackson. There lay Jackson on his back inside the door. He had been shot once through the head and once in the chest—a typical Mafia killing. It appeared that Jackson had gone to answer the door and someone had shot him.

John then walked up and immediately said, "They assassinated him as sure as hell."

"Do you know what happened, Jefferson?" asked Millard.

"No," said Jefferson. "They got through our lines somehow. We didn't take our eyes off the place and ran down here as soon as we heard two shots. That was only about half an hour ago. I heard more shots up there, and I think our men are chasing whoever was doing the shooting; I just don't know any more than what I have said. We would be up in the woods ourselves, but we just couldn't leave Jackson here alone. If they can be caught, our men will catch them."

Millard and John just stood there speechless. Millard could feel his heart pounding in his chest so loud and fast he could hardly get his breath, and he was uncontrollably shaking.

John shined his flashlight on him and could see how pale he was turning. "Sit back and relax as best you can, Millard. You are having a panic attack and bad. You think you are dying, but you won't. I have had several of them before."

Millard followed John's instructions, and after a while, he could feel his heart slowing, and his breathing gradually returned to normal.

"You are in charge of Newbarn now," John said to him, "and you have some important decisions to make. I will help you all I can, but they have to be made, and fast."

"I know, John," said Millard after he had regained most of his strength and composure. Tears were in his eyes, but he knew what he had to do, and he would not fail. Jackson would have wanted him to carry on the organization in a responsible and professional way. "Let's remain inside and think things through for just a few minutes," he added. "Can you think of anything we should do to cover ourselves and our organization before I call the county sheriff?"

"No," said John, "and he needs to know right away. I assume he is one of our paid officers."

"I am most certain he is, but I will open the safe and double-check our records." Millard opened the safe and brought out a record book, which did, indeed, have the name of Harold Cope, Sheriff of Madisonville County, along with dates and amounts of money paid.

Millard immediately called the sheriff at his home in Spruce Willow. When Sheriff Cope answered the phone, Millard told him that he should come to Newbarn immediately as murders had been committed. Cope replied that he would be there soon.

"The gate will be open, and we will be watching for you," Millard said and hung up the phone.

The sheriff arrived shortly, and he came in with no flashing lights and no sirens sounding. He probably wanted to investigate as much as possible before the break of day. Millard and John had decided not to move Jackson's body, and the sheriff seemed quite shocked to find Jackson lying on the floor as he came to the door. "I expected to find a murder, but not my friend Jackson Stamey. Please cover him with a blanket so he won't be so exposed. I want to find the person who murdered this good man, and soon."

"I will help you in every way I can," said Millard, "and I know John Hughes here will do the same. I am in charge now, and John Hughes here is second."

"I am glad to meet you, John," the sheriff replied. "I know we can solve this case, knowing each other as we do."

"We have much more to tell you about this situation, Sheriff Cope," said Millard. "You see, two more murders have been committed this day. We discovered the bodies at that large barn located in the valley north of here. The names of the dead men are Antonio Vitally and Homer Cash. I know that I am probably confusing you, but there are so many complications in this case that we will have to start from scratch and tell you what has occurred over the past several months."

"I already know much of what has been happening," said Sheriff Cope, "actually over the last several years. Walter and Jackson have kept me informed in case something might happen that would include my office, especially serious matters. We have had a good working relationship, and I could never imagine having better friends. I will tell you many wonderful stories about them later on."

He paused, as if momentarily recalling those stories before continuing in a solemn tone. "There is a professional photographer in Spruce Willow, and I have been using his services. I will call him now and have him come over and take photographs of all three bodies. I will need both of you with me some of the time until we solve these cases."

The photographer arrived with his tripod camera shortly after the sheriff called him. Millard felt his heart starting to pound when the sheriff removed the blanket for the photographer to take the picture, but he turned his eyes away and that prevented him from having another episode like before.

They wasted no time in driving to the barn where the bodies of Antonio Vitally and Homer Cash lay. They carefully uncovered their pale, stiff bodies, and the photographer did his job.

"God, how pitiful," said Millard.

"I know," said the sheriff. "All decent people abhor such scenes as this, knowing that life does not have to be this way."

They returned to Newbarn, where the sheriff called the funeral home and the coroner. Millard then quickly related enough information to help the sheriff search for the men who had committed these crimes.

Suddenly, they could hear noises in the woods above Newbarn; it sounded like a coon hunt from all the dogs barking. The Newbarn men had not been wasting their time in their pursuit of the devils guilty of coming onto Newbarn territory with such evil intentions and threats of burning down homes and destroying everything.

Then, out of the darkness of the night and the heavily treed area round the property five Newbarn men appeared, marching two men at gunpoint, who appeared almost totally exhausted. From the looks of the two captured mobsters, they had been roughly treated and had little fight left in them.

Sheriff Cope called all his deputies, including those who worked during emergency situations, and blocked the Cumberland Gap and all other major exits from the Blue Ridge Mountains, especially those near where the Mafia might try to escape.

Every one of the Newbarn drivers had found out what was going on by now and they were all scouring the woods and hiding places with their dogs hot on the trail of the fleeing men they were looking for. Apparently, the stragglers had been left behind by their Mafia brothers who were supposed to drive by and take them away to some other place. Their plan to get away clean had not worked. Newbarn men were after them and would not give up until they were caught. Every now and then, the sounds of dynamite could be heard; probably Mafia cars had been blown to smithereens. The mountain boys had scruples and would never blow up a car with occupants inside unless there was no other way to defend themselves. The Mafia would probably not have been so kind to them.

Millard began talking to Sheriff Cope, briefing him on recent occurrences that had caused much trouble and possibly the murders. Millard told him that it was commonly understood between the Mafia and Newbarn to avoid publicity, and Newbarn would prefer to avoid publicity even now. "We want no one killed, and we would like to remain in business. We do not want the state or federal authorities to get involved."

"I intend to keep everything as quiet as possible and within my jurisdiction, but doubtless there will be publicity. Too much has happened to keep it all quiet, and we don't know what else will happen before this is all over," the sheriff explained. "Please call your employees in and send them home."

The Newbarn leaders hesitated to reply to Sheriff Cope but then told him they knew they could not call the employees in until they decided to come in themselves.

"Well, get them to come in when you can; that will probably contain most of the trouble near Newbarn and the surrounding area," Sheriff Cope continued. "We will handle that Mafia crowd if they have not already escaped back across the Cumberland Gap, but your boys seem to be close on the trail of several of them. I intend to arrest and jail all those we catch and decide from there what we should do."

"I intend to kill the bastard that murdered Jackson the minute I find him," Millard said.

"Don't do that, Millard," the sheriff warned. "It might force me into a situation where I would have to arrest you, and that would complicate everything even worse. I will call the funeral home and have Jackson's body removed from here. That might make everyone, including me, feel a little better. I am leaving now for the Cumberland Gap to help my deputies, but I will return here as soon as possible."

Millard and John immediately began organizing and putting things in order. Newbarn had never been in such a crisis, and it was up to them now to take command of the situation.

The hearse arrived shortly thereafter.

"Stand close with me, John," said Millard. "This is killing me."

"It is killing me too, Millard," said John. "We will just stand together as we always have."

Aided by Horton Pritchard and Jefferson Platt, they gently carried Jackson's body and placed it in that morbid-looking vehicle. Few words were exchanged, and Jackson was gone from Newbarn forever.

SIXTY-ONE

They reentered the building and sat down at the table to discuss what needed to be done.

"We can't remember what all must be done and in what order," John said. "Let's get one of those journals from the safe and write what we have done this night and what must be done in the future to put things right as Walter and Jackson would want us to do."

"Good idea," Millard agreed. "Let's list them in order of importance; otherwise we will run in circles."

Soon the men from Newbarn came in with three more captured Mafia soldiers. They had bruises, torn clothing, and brier scratches and looked as though they had been cuffed around more than a little. They swore they had not been informed of Jackson's death. Their purpose for being on the grounds of Newbarn was to burn the buildings and destroy everything else they could find, especially the long-haul trucks and cars used for hauling whiskey.

Millard and John instructed their men to go home and get some sleep and report for work as usual the following morning. "It is especially important that we make our assigned deliveries without missing a customer. That policy has been in place since I first came to work here. I know we will need to make some policy changes now that we no longer have Walter and Jackson, but we will keep this organization progressing just as they would have us do."

Sheriff Cope was late in returning to Newbarn, and so was Robert Swink. They had reached the Cumberland Gap ahead of the Mafia soldiers and had captured most of them and locked them in jail. Deputies took the other five being held at Newbarn and placed them in jail as well.

Sheriff Cope had never used dynamite before against criminals, and he liked it. Robert had a lot of it, and they'd had no choice but to use it. Robert had signaled the sheriff's men to stop before they reached the Tennessee line. He thought the Mafia was behind them. No sooner had they set up a roadblock then the Mafia automobiles came at them at a high rate of speed. The mobsters obviously intended to run right through their roadblocks, and the sheriff and his deputies had made it equally obvious they did not intend to allow them to do so.

Some of the drivers had wrecked their vehicles trying to get stopped once they realized that the deputies were throwing sticks of dynamite in front of the heavy roadblocks and Robert was tossing sticks of dynamite from behind. They were trapped, and they knew it. Just about all of the men who had come over the mountain were jailed.

As Sheriff Cope talked to the Newbarn men, he seemed a bit bewildered about all that had taken place in Spruce Willow in such a short time. Finally, he told the men he knew they were facing far-reaching, important issues and bade them well. After telling them he and his deputies would return in the morning prepared to help them in every way possible, he departed.

Millard and John stood as though they were partially in shock. They knew they had to think and gather their senses before making further decisions.

"We never did complete our list of important things we must do," John finally said.

"We still need to complete it," said Millard. "But I believe what we need now before anything else is to visit our families and give an account. I doubt that any of them have been notified yet. We should not feel guilty, though. We had to concern ourselves with the most serious things first. I think we should go home and talk with our families and then sleep a few hours before we return for the sheriff's meeting in the morning. I will inform Jackson's wife and mother."

"You are right," replied John. "Otherwise, we might not have our wits about us enough to absorb what the sheriff has to say and provide our input."

"Before we go home, however, we must allow the men who have been up all night to leave for home and officially appoint two new leaders."

Horton Pritchard and Jefferson Platt were sitting at the table and were anticipating such a move. Millard asked Horton if he would assume the position of third in command at Newbarn and then asked Jefferson if he would assume the position of fourth in command. They both said, "Yes," in very firm, convincing voices.

"Well, that settles that," said John. "I thank you for accepting, as I know Millard does, or he would not have appointed you."

"I think you men should go home and see to your families now. I will notify Jackson's wife and mother and will leave a note on the door for the sheriff so he will stay here until I return," said Millard. "After our meeting with the sheriff, I will go home and explain things to my wife."

The men all agreed on the need to go home but promised not to linger.

"God, how I dread this day," remarked Millard. He drove directly to the elegant home Walter loved so much. He could not help standing there just looking in admiration of the home and thinking of Walter. As he proceeded up the walkway, everything looked exactly as Walter always kept it. The lawn was beautiful, as were the beautiful statues and fountains and manicured shrubs and well-trimmed trees. The large, white columns across the front porch completed the stately look of the beautiful mansion.

He knocked on the door, and a very tearful Mrs. Walter Stamey answered the door. "I know what you came for, Millard. I heard some of the details on the radio early this morning. Oh, what will we do, Millard?" she managed before breaking into uncontrollable sobs.

He held her in his arms, attempting to console her, but it didn't help much.

"I am going to tell Jackson's wife now, and if she is agreeable, I will bring her and Benjamin over here to stay with you until you and she make necessary decisions."

She agreed and Millard quickly left to see Sally. She too needed no explanations and was sitting on the porch swing trying to decide what to do.

As Millard climbed up the steps and looked at her, he had never seen such agony in one's face in his entire life. She was totally devastated. Millard put his arms around her, but his comfort did not help her much either.

After he'd talked to her, she agreed to stay with Mrs. Stamey so they could discuss things and console each other as best they could. She had one request. "You go to Flora and ask her to come over and be with us. I know her presence will be a great comfort to us."

As Millard drove down to the house, Flora and the boys were sitting on the front porch looking sad and forlorn.

"The radio did not give us good news this morning," Flora said.

"I know," said Millard. "I wanted to come home sooner, but I just couldn't get away until now. This has been a bad night, but I can't tell you all the details just yet. I went to see Sally, and she wants you and the boys to come over to the Stamey mansion and be with her and Mrs. Stamey, maybe for several days; I don't know for sure. Get ready quickly, and I will take you and the boys over there as I go. I have to meet with the county sheriff this morning to make important decisions."

Flora knew Millard was under great stress so she wasted no time in doing as he asked.

As they drove up the hill, there stood Salem. Millard left the car to shake his hand and apologized for practically abandoning him so long.

"Oh, you don't have to apologize to me. I have been listening to my old Philco radio regularly and know most of what has been going on. I am glad to own my radio. Not many people are lucky enough to own one. Now that a few people are managing to get one, all the neighbors who do not have one gather in to listen to it in the evenings. I have listened carefully since news started to come in about your organization and the Mafia. I made certain your family and this great house would come to no harm. No one has tried to burn your houses or bother us in any way. I have enjoyed Cameron and Walter every day. They think they are full-fledged carpenters now. The house is completely finished now, and Flora is making plans to decorate the inside."

Millard thanked Salem and then said, "I don't think anyone will be around to bother you now, but keep an eye out for a few more days, just in case. I have a meeting with the county sheriff shortly, so I will leave you again, bad as I hate to. Sally wants Flora and the boys to come over and be with them for a few days, so they are leaving you too. I will make all this up to you as soon as I can."

Millard made it back to Newbarn just in time. The sheriff had called and said he would be there within the hour.

When Sheriff Cope arrived, it was a perfect time to hold an uninterrupted meeting. All of the routemen and long-haul drivers had left on their deliveries. Although sad at heart and tired in body, they were determined to keep the business going just as they had decided hours earlier.

Millard started the meeting by asking Sheriff Cope to contribute whatever information he had and promised the leaders of Newbarn would do the same.

"Men, I did all I could during the night with all my competent deputies helping in every way. We decided to go straight to the horse himself by making a call to Ransom Mann, head of most of the Mafia organization in Chicago. I asked him what in the hell he was thinking when he sent a horde of his men over here to murder and destroy like some kind of a fool. He hesitated to even discuss the matter with me and did not call me by my correct title. He claimed to have talked to Newbarn leaders who were willing to negotiate until they wanted everything for themselves. I explained to him that they have left themselves with little negotiating power because you men have evidence that could well put him and a horde of his soldiers in federal prison until they have long, gray beards and rheumatism.

"I asked if they were ready to negotiate or not. He clearly was not, but there was no other choice for him to make. He said he would accept your terms as stated by you previously and wouldn't mind buying a little of your mountain whiskey now and then, with the ten percent discount of course. We ended our conversation at that point by him agreeing to talk with Millard if Millard would call him at his office before five o'clock today. He was trying to save face by acting a little huffy."

"Well," said Millard, "I suggest we accommodate him by calling him just as soon as we have made our decisions and we are all in agreement. I will talk with him this time, but only if Sheriff Cope is in the room with us in case we need his advice or intervention. He is our friend, and I would appreciate him being our legal expert."

"I will do that for you good men. You have never caused me any trouble, and I know I could count on you should the occasion arise."

"We all miss Jackson," said Millard, "but Sheriff Cope has already advised me not to avenge Jackson's death by murdering his killer."

"What should we do about the jail full of Mafia soldiers, Sheriff Cope?" John inquired.

"I will allow most of them to return to Chicago, but those who have committed serious crimes will have to face charges in this county. The one who murdered Jackson must be tried here for murder. I will talk to Ransom Mann and make every effort to convince him that we will settle for nothing other than justice in this case. He might have an idea about another acceptable way, but I doubt it."

Millard whispered to John, who was sitting beside him, "They need not concern themselves about a murder trial for Jackson's killer; I intend to kill him myself."

"Not unless you get to him before me," replied John.

"Sheriff Cope is no fool; he knows that man who killed Jackson is a walking dead man."

There was nothing to discuss at this time, so Millard proceeded to call Ransom Mann. Mann answered the phone, and the conversation began without any pleasantries. Harsh words were exchanged, with neither getting an edge over the other. Ransom was clearly in a bind, however, and Millard could detect it in his voice. He was a Mafia boss, but he did have over him men of high power whose names were unknown to all except for a select few. Apparently, Ransom had been taking on too much authority too quickly. Gordon Piker had been dead only a short while, and Ransom had made the decision to take on the Newbarn organization without adequate consultation with the top echelon. He was getting too big for his britches. The longer Millard and Ransom talked, the more conciliatory Ransom became.

He agreed with everything Millard wanted but would not name Jackson's killer. He said he could not comply without breaking one of the strictest laws of his organization. If he were to provide a name, he wouldn't live to see another day after the big bosses in the mob found that he had broken one of their most sacred laws.

Millard agreed to press him no more on that issue. It would be like asking him to commit suicide.

"What can you tell us about Antonio Vitally and Homer Cash?" asked Millard.

"Vitally broke another law," said Ransom. "He was in the process of leaving the Mafia, and that is forbidden. Homer Cash is an old mobster who was of little value to the Mafia except for providing information about people who were threats. He thought he was someone of importance, but he was an old, worn-out bag of horseshit. I think he was killed because he was observed talking to Antonio, and that was enough. They didn't trust him anymore. Anyway, I have no idea who killed either of the men. It would take a month of Sundays to sort out all the entanglements causing trouble for Newbarn between Chattanooga and Memphis. Why don't we leave that job up to your sheriff? He seems to be a pretty good man."

"Tell you what," said Millard. "We have solved many of our problems by the agreements we have made here on the phone. If you keep your part of our agreement, we will keep ours. One thing, however, we will never forgive the murder of Jackson Stamey; and I intend to kill the man who killed him sooner or later."

Millard and Ransom ended the conversation by agreeing to keep future discussions confidential and talk often until attitudes changed and things got better.

"Millard, from what I could detect, you handled that conversation very well, except the part about killing the man who murdered Jackson," Sheriff Cope said. "We don't know who the man is yet, but I suspect that he might already be in my jail. Once I discover who the killer is, I will work on getting the man tried and convicted and, if I fail at that, I'll turn my back." Before Millard could reply, he continued, "My deputies and me will follow this case closely, and if we find any Mafia people in this county, we might just shoot first and ask questions later, as the old saying goes. I have other matters that I must attend to, so I will leave you men to carry on the affairs of Newbarn. But we will be checking by here often until all is well."

After the sheriff left, Millard asked the men to contribute any ideas or suggestions or just say anything that came to mind. Not one man had anything to say. The room was very quiet, and Millard considered that it would be a good thing for them to just sit quietly for a little while—if for no other reason, to honor the memories of Jackson and Walter.

The men seemed worn out and a little in shock. It was a good thing Millard did.

At the day's end, Millard and John went by to pay their respects to Jackson's family and then went home. It was a rough night for both men. Their sleep was restless and interrupted by unpleasant dreams.

Salem was at the new house but was not roused when Millard came home.

Morning could not come too soon for Millard. He awoke at dawn and prepared for the day. Again he passed his new house without even noticing a light in a window. Salem observed him passing and wanted to discuss what was going on. He kept hearing bad news on the radio about the Mafia being in the county and people being shot—some true and some untrue.

The day began surprisingly normal. The deliverymen departed on time. They knew the importance of things going on at a normal pace. One long-haul truck left for St. Louis as well. John talked to the drivers about being careful. They had little experience, but John thought they would do all right since they would not be going on to Chicago. They were smart, strong young men, and that was always especially important on long hauls.

With the morning chores completed, Millard, John, Horton, and Jefferson proceeded to the Stamey mansion to visit with the family. Such a dread it was to enter that wonderful old house where they had always been so welcome and treated with such respect and where they had enjoyed so many jovial times.

They wished that Robert was with them, but they knew he was someplace searching for the person who murdered Jackson. He would not be deterred from that task. Even though he was aware of what Sheriff Cope had said about Jackson's killer possibly being in his jail, he also knew that not all the Mafia men had been captured, and the murderer might still be on the loose.

The leaders of Newbarn made every effort to conceal their despair as Flora seated them in the parlor and served hors d'oeuvres and fruit punch, but it was obvious to everyone in the household that, while they were there to console the family, they needed consoling as well. Soon they were surrounded by family and friends, and the men realized that Jackson would have wanted it just that way.

Jackson had been a practical man in life, and they would treat his memory the same in death. His body would be placed in that room later in the afternoon to lie in state until the funeral on the following day. Jackson, like his father, had left a simple note directing that his funeral be conducted exactly as his father's, including that he be carried to his final resting place on the shoulders of six stout men. Strangely, according to Sally, he had written that note just a few days before his death.

Flora and the boys accompanied Millard back to Newbarn. She'd decided not to stay another night at the Stamey home. The men had returned from their daily deliveries and were outside the office waiting for a report on the events of the day. Millard had very little to report, except for the funeral arrangements. He also told them to pay their respects to the family before going home if they felt so inclined. That ended the day at Newbarn. Two of the men agreed to watch over the place through the night.

When Millard, Flora, and the boys reached home, they talked very little before eating a light supper and the boys were put to bed. Salem soon came down from the new house and stayed for a while. Millard told him of all the recent happenings, which took quite a while. Salem had dismissed the builders but had remained for security purposes. Millard asked him to stay for at least two more nights until he could be there himself. "This entire disturbance is probably not over, but I think it will be a good, long time before anything else flares up."

"Cross your fingers," said Salem as he went out the door.

After they were in bed, Flora knew something was on Millard's mind. "I believe you want to talk with me about something," she said as she caressed his chin and snuggled close to him.

"Well, I do," he replied. "What do you think of that letter Jackson wrote concerning his own funeral?"

"Just a premonition," she answered as she rubbed her hand over his hairy chest and tickled his stomach lightly. "They are not that uncommon, but I do not think most people like to discuss them, especially if they affect them."

"Why not?" he asked.

"Because few people like to think of themselves in death, but they do want to have a say in what happens after they're gone," she said, giving him a sincere answer.

"You are just teasing me," he said.

"I am not," she said. "I would never tease you over something as important to you as what you asked."

"Then, do you think all this trouble and killing is over now?" he asked her.

"No," she answered, "especially the killing. I feel there will be more, but who knows how many, maybe just one or perhaps dozens."

"Hellfire, I wish I hadn't asked," he replied.

"I do know one thing," Flora added. "You will not be one of the dead."

Millard breathed a sigh of relief and said, "That is a comfort to me, but I wish you would tell me a little more comforting stuff."

"I cannot do that," she replied. She kissed him on the cheek, and they went to sleep.

★ ★ ★

Millard had set his alarm clock to wake him early. When the alarm went off, Millard was up quickly so he would not turn over for a few extra minutes' sleep. He knew it would be a very sad, stressful day, and he wanted to be prepared for whatever he must do. The funeral was the first thing on his mind. It would be sad, and he and Flora both knew they would be asked to sing one or two songs during the service. He did not especially dread that part; it was putting his friend away for his eternal rest that seemed more than he could bear. But bear it he must, and he would not fail.

This too will pass, he thought; just like all the tragic events in his past had, it would be healed by time and trampled upon by determination.

Salem came down, and they all had breakfast together. Salem volunteered to keep Cameron and Walter with him until they returned. "You need not hurry," he said, "me and my grandsons will keep things in order around here."

That was a great help to Millard and Flora, and soon they were very nicely dressed and on their way.

Millard knew John would be there seeing to the morning routine. Knowing what to do and working together allowed them extra time to be with Jackson's family.

The funeral director was busy arranging every detail to the satisfaction of the family. Sally was a very brave and courageous woman. She had had Jackson's casket constructed in minute detail by the same people who had prepared Walter's casket. Everything in that elegant room was arranged as it had been when Jackson's father lay there in death not so long ago. Sally asked Flora and Millard to sing at the funeral—one song during the church service and one at the grave site. Flora, of course, had anticipated a guitar accompaniment, and after some practicing, they were prepared.

The funeral procession moved slowly to the church. A large gathering was already present for the funeral service—an indication of the many friends Jackson had left behind. Millard and Flora sang a beautiful rendition of "Shall We Gather at the River" followed by a very impressive sermon by the preacher. The congregation sang several songs, and then came that long, always dreaded march to the gravesite.

Six strong men from Newbarn carried the casket on their shoulders and ever so gently lowered it into the grave. Not one sound could be heard. Sally whispered to Millard that he shouldn't sing a farewell song—that quiet respect shown by his friends was enough.

The people gradually departed after the grave was closed and flowers were placed upon the grave by flower girls as was the custom. Millard and John stood by the grave with a sadness they could not express. There lay Jackson, interred beside his father to remain throughout eternity with the unrelenting night breeze, the cause of which had never been explained.

When they all returned to Newbarn, everyone wanted to join in and complete the chores. They had no desire to leave for home until they'd ensured that all was in order, just as Jackson had done every evening before leaving.

Millard realized that, although all seemed peaceful, the peace would only last momentarily. He assigned one man to serve as night watchman, with instructions to shoot trespassers if he considered them to be a danger and call the sheriff immediately.

This long sad day was over, and the Newbarn men went home with an emptiness lingering among them still. Tomorrow would be another day.

SIXTY-TWO

When Millard and Flora reached the turn-off, their new home stood there tall and beautiful. Construction was now complete in every detail. Salem and the boys were sitting on a rock in the front yard looking proud and happy. Flora decided to go to the cabin and cook a good supper for her men. She knew Salem and Millard had many things to discuss about financial matters and other considerations to be satisfied within the near future.

Millard had not borrowed one cent to build the house, and Salem had gone to an insurance company the day before and purchased insurance in case of damage or destruction of such an expensive asset. They decided to proceed with landscaping the yard and clearing the land down to the river for a good view and to provide pasture for livestock and outbuildings, including a large barn. Millard had given the plan due consideration and had come to the conclusion that labor was now very cheap and he had a lot of cash money. As usual, he wanted Salem's opinion before making important decisions. He explained exactly what he had in mind, and Salem agreed without exception.

"It will not be a very difficult job, seeing that the land lays well and there is no heavy timber to cut. It will not take long to complete, and you can provide your neighbors with some temporary work.

"This depression will not last forever, but when it ends, I believe the cost of everything will go up. You have a good head for planning Millard; there is no doubt about that."

"I am going to do something special for your hard work and attention to building this house," said Millard.

"No need," replied Salem. "You have paid me every week and provided me with plenty of good moonshine, and that is sufficient. This has been a fun job for me."

"Nevertheless, I intend to do something special for you."

"I see sadness in your face, Millard. You buried one of your very best friends today. Why don't we go for supper and some relaxation and talk business another time?"

It was a joyful evening, although the loss of Jackson still lingered heavily on Millard's mind. The same was true for Flora, but she had her way of handling grief most of the time. She did so by strongly concentrating on the negative thoughts, but not so much as to remove the sad thoughts entirely from her memory. Millard knew he would always have strong thoughts about Jackson, but as time passed they would be happy thoughts.

"Millard," said Flora, "we have been talking while you seem to be in a trance."

"Sorry," he replied. "I suppose the last several weeks have taken more out of me than I realized. I think I will go to bed now. I trust tomorrow will be a better day."

Morning came as it always does; the only difference in this morning was that Millard did not know what to expect. He dressed slowly and left for work. As he drove up the hill, he noticed a light in the room where Salem slept and stopped to bid him a good morning. As he reached Newbarn, he found all the men reporting in and carrying on their duties, just as if Jackson were there. He was in command of Newbarn now, but he had no illusions that Jackson's shoes would be easy to fill. *Lord, how I wish he were here*, he thought as he walked into the office.

John soon came in, followed by Horton and Jefferson. Since Jackson had made out the schedules and duties a week in advance, Millard had time to think and put things in perspective before making any changes of duties and plans. He was feeling a little better about his first full day in charge and was now ready to proceed with enthusiasm and much-needed confidence.

After discussing some issues that Horton and Jefferson needed to be involved in, John and Millard decided to take a walk around the property of Newbarn. They were both aware that they needed to talk about many things involving the organization.

"John, I know we have many problems that must be solved, and I hardly know where to begin. The security of our people and our Newbarn organization comes to mind first, and I sense that something is not right. Where in the hell are Robert and Sheriff

Cope? They seem to have vanished at a time when we need them most."

"I have had some suspicious thoughts about that as well," said John, "but I know of nothing we can do now except give them more time to show."

"The next thing that we need to be thinking about," said Millard, "is ownership and management of Newbarn. As we know, this organization is held together by verbal contract only. All properties were owned by Walter and Jackson and will go to their wives. They cannot manage the place, but we can. What sort of arrangement or offer do you think we might make them to keep Newbarn in business?"

John said he had been thinking hard about the same thing. "Offer to buy them out by a partnership arrangement between you and me, with you still at the top," he suggested.

"That answer sure didn't take long," replied Millard with a broad smile. "I had the same thought in mind, but not with me remaining at the top. I wouldn't argue at all if you wanted to manage Newbarn."

"I know, Millard," said John, "but you are well educated, and I am a blacksmith with a third-grade education. You know how to handle business."

"I have a sixth grade education, and that is all," replied Millard. "In any case, we could split all profits and then consider going into a legal business should the opportunity arise. We will discuss it further later."

The remainder of the day went surprisingly well, considering the mental trauma of losing Jackson. In fact, the entire week was successful in every way. Only Millard and John were aware of the disappearance of Sheriff Cope and Robert.

On the Monday morning following the horrible week of fighting and killing, John mentioned it to Millard to remind him of the situation.

"Have you considered any action we might take at this time?" Millard asked.

"No," replied John, "but I do know we must act soon or we will have hell of some sort to contend with."

"I think you are right," replied Millard. "If Sheriff Cope and Robert do not come around within a few days, we will know something is very wrong and we will be compelled to ask for an investigation into their disappearances by high-ranking state law officials. That is all we can do at this point. Obviously the sheriff is not here, and we have had little contact with his deputies. Our authority is lacking. All we can do is file a missing persons report as any other citizen would do," he concluded.

As Millard drove home, he could not keep his mind off Robert and Sheriff Cope. *People do not just disappear*, he thought. Something was wrong, and he knew it. Too many things had gone wrong lately, and he was starting to become suspicious about everything.

As soon as he arrived home, he explained his recent feelings to Flora.

"Millard, I am not a fortune-teller. All I can tell you is what I told you before—that all the troubles are not over and one or more people will die before it all ends."

"Don't tell me that, Flora. You have told me too many things that have come to pass."

"If I knew the answer to what you are asking, I would tell it to you," she replied. "I wish that what I believe about more deaths wasn't true."

"I know you would," he said. "I was just hoping against hope, I guess."

He played with the boys, and after putting them to bed, he and Flora talked until long after midnight. Talking to her all that time was soothing to his mind, and he slept well.

All the following day and week passed without one problem surfacing. *How can this be?* Millard kept asking himself.

The only change that had been made since Jackson was killed was assigning a night watchman. To Millard, however, Newbarn seemed like a strange, different place with Jackson gone, and the disappearance of Robert and Sheriff Cope made everything even stranger. There was an answer somewhere, and he intended to find it.

John returned on Friday.

"I didn't expect you back until Monday," said Millard as John walked in.

"I finished my work at home, and I just couldn't stay away any longer. I knew that neither you nor me would be satisfied with Sheriff Cope and Robert Swink missing. I drove by the sheriff's office yesterday and asked to see him. The deputy on duty said that he was on vacation and that he didn't know when he would return. I did not believe him, and I told him so. I asked other people around town, and no one even knew he was gone."

"The mystery remains," said Millard, "and there is nothing we can do now. We have no detective to sort things out like Robert did; and we have to keep our customers served or risk losing Newbarn. Monday morning, I will travel our short-haul routes and hope to find some trace of Robert. Perhaps we should let the county handle the sheriff, unless his disappearance involves Newbarn in some way. I will travel our long-haul truck routes later if we see the need. Traveling both routes without a break would be tough and perhaps produce nothing but danger."

"If Jackson were here we could make the trip together," said John.

"That would be great," replied Millard.

It was Friday evening, and everyone at Newbarn was feeling better, even though thoughts of Jackson remained with them.

Millard went home in a somewhat jovial mood. He took his family, including Salem, to supper in Spruce Willow. They had a wonderful time, and when they returned home, they played games and sang songs until past bedtime.

Salem slept in his room in the new house as usual. Millard and Flora stayed up late making plans to buy furniture and decorate their new home. Since Millard knew he would be traveling during the week, he asked Flora if she would mind selecting the furniture and appropriate decorative items for the windows and walls. "I will go with you tomorrow and help you get started," he explained.

"You do not have to do one thing," she replied with a pretty smile on her lips. "What do you think I have been doing while the house was being built? Every time I could get Papa to go with me, we went to a large furniture store in Asheville and selected some things. I planned what I needed for the entire house before I started making purchases. It all went very well, and all will be delivered by truck next week. I thought that was the least I could do for such a dear husband who has worked so hard for so long. Tomorrow we will go to the store and give you an opportunity to select any special items you want. Papa won't go if he can get out of it. He seemed in misery every time I insisted he take me over there."

The next day went just as Millard and Salem knew it would go, although Millard did enjoy looking at the beautiful furniture and the other items as well.

While they were walking through the store, Flora said, "I hope you won't mind, but I asked the professional decorator who works here to help me. She is coming over one day next week, and I am glad. I am just a country girl, and I did not feel up to the job. That beautiful house deserves to be decorated by a professional interior decorator. She does not charge too much either."

"How much?" asked Millard.

"Oh, I have to go to the ladies room," she said and was off in a flash.

"See what I mean Millard," said Salem. "I didn't much want to come over here."

"Yes, I know what you mean, and I won't ask her any more questions."

Salem and Millard were obviously amused.

"I definitely am glad they had a ladies room in this fancy furniture store," said Millard.

"You know," said Salem, "I have noticed that most fancy places do have indoor toilets these days. I doubt one was needed in this case, however," he continued with a controlled laugh.

Cameron and Walter had to show off the things that would go in their bedroom as well, which was also amusing.

When they returned home, Salem decided to go home. "Since I know things will be all right with you being here tomorrow, I will check on things at home and return on Monday morning."

Sunday always had been the most important day of the week in the Blue Ridge Mountains. There was nothing special about this Sunday, except it was to be especially joyful. The church service went very well with a fiery sermon and beautiful singing with Millard at his very best.

After the service, they drove Ma home and visited for a while. Later, they made a short visit with Grandpa and Grandma. Millard wanted to return home to relax and do some reading. He did not know what the coming week would bring, but he needed his mind clear and a time to sit on the porch and meditate before days end. It had been a wonderful Sabbath day.

Early Monday morning, Millard was up thinking about the uncertain week that was now upon him. He planned to spend this day and maybe most of the week traveling the area, covering as much territory as he could, taking notes as he needed, and especially searching for any signs of Robert or even Sheriff Cope. He knew he could cover the territory at a fast pace, not having to actually make deliveries and talk with customers. Thoughts of Jackson kept occupying his mind, but that was all right. He could deal with flashes of the wonderful times and experiences they had encountered over the years.

He traveled all day without noticing anything unusual; rather, he saw some faces of nice people he had met while working those territories. He knew that country, and after circling Spruce Willow, he kept traveling north. Few places existed where he could stay the night, but he knew them all. When dark started approaching, he stopped at a nice little farmhouse that had two rooms for travelers like him.

He was up at daybreak and off again, still going toward Virginia. The notes he had made when establishing those routes were very helpful to him. He traveled all the way past Galax, Virginia, before turning back. The left to right and back pattern he had developed still looked the same. It caused him to smile when he found that every establishment, whether it was a general store or a honky-tonk, was still in business and seemed to be doing well.

All day he drove, canvassing about two-thirds of the Blue Ridge Mountains that they considered Newbarn territory. He stayed in a nice hotel in Asheville and continued on the third day, driving the route south of Asheville, which he took credit for discovering. It was there that he'd first found places to sell their whiskey all on his own. The section did not take long to cover. The establishments were few, but they always bought large amounts of moonshine. Tourists were wild about the good stuff.

Millard then traveled back across the mountains and ended the intended part of his trip in Chattanooga. He was very interested in that town and the smaller towns he would encounter on his return trip.

On the outer west edge of Chattanooga, he thought he saw Robert's car and rushed full speed to catch up with it, but it roared out of sight. He was reasonably certain it was Robert's car. Millard knew of no other car that much faster than his own.

Another strange episode, another riddle he could not solve, and another problem on his mind that he could do nothing about.

He returned to Newbarn late in the evening. During his entire three days of scouting, he'd come up with nothing concrete to show for his efforts except for the possible sighting of Robert's car. And he had not seen whether anyone else besides the driver was in the car. Most observers would probably say it was not Robert, but Millard took nothing for granted and kept his mind open to the possibility that it was Robert.

Flora was awake when he arrived home. She had not been to sleep and admitted to Millard that she had been worried since he'd left Monday morning. Her concerns were not necessarily about him; they were just uneasy feelings that she had not experienced before. "Something is wrong," she said. "I could be wrong but I don't think so."

She wanted a response from her husband, but none came. He was asleep and she doubted that he had heard what she had said. *If only he would stop exhausting himself when troubles come*, she thought.

She did not awaken until she heard Millard getting ready for work. She could not get out of bed quickly enough to engage in any conversation or ask any questions.

"I will be home this evening as soon as possible, barring any diversions," he said as he shut the door behind him.

"God bless this day," she said as she heard him drive away.

She wanted to show him what she had accomplished in the house, but that would have to wait. The interior decorator would be here soon and would probably complete her work today or certainly no later than tomorrow. *I know Millard will be thrilled when he sees one of his dreams of younger years come true.*

Soon she saw the decorator's car at the new house. The boys were ready for the day and anxious to get started. Both Cameron and Walter claimed to have built part of the house outside and were now completing the inside work. The decorator amusingly bragged on how smart they were and how helpful they had been.

Millard stopped for breakfast and was at work in plenty of time. Tom Helton, who had been on watch during the night, had nothing unusual to report. John soon came in just ahead of the entire crew of drivers. The drivers loaded their cars and were ready to head out. They only hesitated for a moment to ask Millard and John if there was any news about Robert and Sheriff Cope. A brief answer was sufficient and they went roaring off.

"How did things go, Millard?" asked John.

"I have only one thing of interest to report to you. I think I saw Robert's car near Chattanooga, but I did not get near enough to confirm if it was Robert or even anyone was in the car other than the driver. Whoever it was took off very quickly, as though they did not want me to catch up with them. I viewed it as being very suspicious."

"Sounds suspicious to me," said John.

"Have you heard anything about Sheriff Cope?" asked Millard.

"Not a damn thing," replied John. "The people around here don't know, and the deputies either don't know or won't tell. I thought about calling the attorney general in Raleigh but decided against it. We have enough to contend with here at Newbarn. Everything is in good shape here. We have had no problems at all since you have been gone," he concluded.

"An idea just occurred to me, John," said Millard. "We have some extra time today; let's go visit with the Stamey ladies. Our time has been limited since Jackson's death. While we are there, if the timing seems right, we could ask them about making an offer or proposal about Newbarn and give them the pointers as we discussed several days ago."

"We should do that," said John. "They might appreciate talking about the business, and they might have some questions they want to ask us."

Both ladies were at the Stamey home. Millard very appropriately brought up the subject of Newbarn and explained to them the options available concerning the organization and property. The ladies knew Millard and John were very busy, and they knew the importance of making a decision about the place, and quickly.

Sadness was apparent in everyone's faces as the four talked. "We have been discussing this matter, and we are glad you men have been giving it consideration also," said Sally, and Mary nodded in agreement. "Walter established this business, and I would like for Mary to tell you what we have decided."

Mary looked closely at both Millard and John and said, "We want you men to settle on a price for the entire organization, including everything, and we will sell it to you for that price. We can't manage it, and you gentlemen can. That is our firm word, and we will abide by it."

"My word, I did not expect such an easy way of making a decision," said Millard. "If John agrees," he added, "we will accept your offer."

"I think your offer would serve you ladies and Newbarn very well," said John.

After all was said about the agreement that needed saying, they all shook hands and both Mary and Sally kissed them on the cheek.

"We are almost like family, you know," said Mary.

"That is true for me also," replied Sally, tears rolling down her cheek.

"We will see you again soon, and we will always remain close as families do," said John as they departed.

Millard and John silently returned to Newbarn and, once there, began discussing the many issues that must be settled before transacting the business at hand. They agreed to complete every detail the following week while everything was fresh in their minds.

At the end of the day, with everything going as it should, everyone departed for the day. Millard and John decided to visit Horace Blue and see how his operation was doing and answer any questions he might have about Newbarn.

They were amazed to see the changes Horace had made. All the technology one could find to make whiskey efficiently was there. He had plumed the entire operation from the base of the water source—a big time-saver over carrying water in buckets. Large waterproof wooden containers were systematically placed as holding tanks to contain the whiskey until the men could get it bottled and crated. A contraption had even been installed above each distillery to filter the smell of mash cooking. Large open sheds with high ceilings, fireplaces, and cooling fans protected the entire operation from the weather and allowed the men to work in comfort under all conditions. Also, Horace now had the capacity to keep several distilleries operating continuously. Horace was very proud of his operation and happy to hear that Millard and John were going to purchase Newbarn and continue the operation.

Horace wanted to know about Robert and Sheriff Cope and was very puzzled about their disappearance. "Cope has been an asset to Newbarn since Walter Stamey established it many years ago," said Horace.

"We will keep you informed of important information every day or two," John told him as they shook hands and departed.

SIXTY-THREE

When Millard arrived at home, Flora and the boys were waiting at the new house and waving for him to stop. He knew something pleasant was up when they revealed such big smiles. When he got out of his car, he was met with big, tight hugs and then led to the front door of the house.

When the door was opened wide and he was led inside, he could hardly believe what he saw. The interior decorator and Flora had completed their jobs and what they had done was fantastic. Every room in the house was appropriately and tastefully decorated. Except the Walter Stamey mansion, Millard had never been inside a house so beautiful, and his wasn't far behind it. Magnificent chandeliers were in the parlor, dining room, and foyer. The walls were decorated with paintings in hand-carved frames. The bedroom walls were covered with beautiful cloth wallpaper selected individually to suit each bedroom. The entrance foyer, parlor, dining room, and hallways were of finished mahogany. The window draperies were cleverly designed to suit each room and, except for those in the kitchen and other less important places, were of velvet material. Clocks and ornamental items were hung on the walls throughout the house. Standing just inside the foyer was a grandfather clock, which chimed every hour, graced by a large oil painting of Thomas Jefferson. The home was not overly decorated, but just as it should be to look its finest.

Millard walked through the house several times before sitting down in an elegant chair in the living room to rest. As he sat there looking about, he considered it to be more of a palace—a palace for his family and for him. It was an achievement kept alive by hope and accepting nothing less.

Millard had never wanted that beautiful place to show off or appear to be above anyone else. He simply wanted to beat the cycle of poverty that had beaten him down so many times during his life and become a man of means and stature. He did not accept the meager existence these mountains had to offer and wanted to inspire others to realize that they too could do the same, if they just kept working and hoping. Millard had told Flora many times that God gave everybody hope and all should grasp it and never let it go. What a wise man she had married.

The evening was indeed a happy one for the family. They went to Spruce Willow for supper, which included their favorite dessert of chocolate cake and ice cream. When they returned to their cabin, they sat on the bed and played games and sang songs. Flora played her guitar beautifully now, and Cameron and Walter insisted that she play several songs each night.

The evening ended when they noticed that Walter had gone sound asleep without their noticing his sudden silence. Millard went to bed with a clear mind and a thankful heart.

The following day, being Saturday, was crammed full of activities. Millard had no need to check on Newbarn for any reason. John, along with the assigned watchmen, was going to keep a sharp eye on things during the weekend. The family went to the river and washed the car, and Millard and the boys got in some fishing time.

After their picnic lunch, which Flora had prepared, they visited Ma. They did not remain there long because they had other places to go and the air was turning cold. They wanted to visit with Salem and Martha. Millard wanted to pay Salem his wages for the week and talk with him for a while.

The two men went to the woodshed to spend a little time together, but they did not stay long. The air was getting cold and uncomfortable. "I forgot to bring you any moonshine," said Millard. "I will make it up next time and explain the troubles we have been having at Newbarn."

"I probably know much of what has happened," said Salem, "but I would like to hear it all from you. Much of what I have heard is probably not true."

As Millard and his family left for home, the air was getting colder rapidly. "Feels much like snow to me," said Flora. "Maybe we had better go directly home, and I will fix us some soup and sandwiches for supper."

They all agreed and Cameron said loudly, "I want to go to our new warm home."

"New warm home?" said Millard.

"I should have told you, I guess," said Flora. "We wanted to surprise you, so we planned everything yesterday so we could stay at the new house tonight."

The new house was chilly inside but not too cold. It warmed up quickly when they lit all three fireplaces. Wood shavings with heavier wood on top warmed and brightened the house. It seemed very strange to turn on electric table lamps and have everything so bright. Their entertainment for the evening proved to be making another tour of each room and looking at everything and enjoying sitting on the floor in the living room in front of the fireplace.

The boys were soon put to bed in their own room and did not seem to like it very much. They were used to sleeping in the same room with Millard and Flora. They would get used to the change soon enough.

Millard and Flora sat by the fire for a while longer and then decided it was time for bed for them also. Their upstairs bedroom was nice and warm, and they laughingly decided they were in a happy room. Their bedroom window exposed their little cabin below. As they stood there looking down at the dark, little place so dwarfed and lonely looking compared to their new home, Flora felt a little sad and sentimental about it. They had had so many good times there.

She told Millard how she felt about it, and he said, "Let's keep it just like it is, and when we take a notion to go down there and sleep, we can do so," said Millard as he gave her a kiss on the cheek.

"What a wonderful idea," Flora replied. "I have a feeling we will go down there often, especially when we are alone." She giggled and tickled his feet with her toes as they sat in the middle of the bed.

They slid under the covers and talked for a while. "I still have lingering unhappy feelings about Newbarn," she said. "I honestly think that death has not departed from that organization. Lead it well, Millard, and protect those who work for you in every way possible. For it is among them that death lingers, not you. Death is indeed not far away and will not go away for a week or two I believe, maybe longer."

Millard lay silent and listened intensely. He knew from the sincerity in her voice that much trouble was probably waiting for him. After such a happy day, they both slept in an uneasy state of mind.

Morning came, and Flora shook Millard with all her might. "We should look out the front door," she said. "Something is terribly wrong."

He knew something was terribly wrong when he heard fear in her voice. He took her by the hand, and they descended the cold stairs together, tripping along in their bare feet and holding to the stair railings to keep from falling.

"Let's go back and get our shoes on," said Flora. "If we need to do something outside, we can't do so with frozen feet."

"Oh no," he said. "We can't return until we see what is outside."

They opened the door to find that the wind from the night before had stopped blowing and well over a foot of snow had fallen. As Millard's eyes scanned the porch, he could see what looked like two people lying there completely covered with snow. "That looks like two people there."

"It is two people lying there," replied Flora, "two dead people. Oh my God," she screamed, wringing her hands.

Millard quickly pulled the two stiff bodies into the house. His heart raced rapidly, and his face turned pale. He could see that both men had been shot twice in the back of the head. He turned both bodies face up, and as he looked down, he could hardly speak. He was in a state of panic. It was Robert Swink and Sheriff Harold Cope.

A note was pinned to Robert's chest. It read, "Here is the man who killed Jackson Stamey."

Another note was pinned to Sheriff Cope's chest. It said, "Here is the man who murdered Robert Swink."

Millard staggered, almost falling to the floor. "Oh my God!" he groaned, holding his chest. He looked at Flora and said, "The Mafia has returned."

After standing near the bodies for a few minutes and allowing himself to calm down, he sat down on the bottom step of the stairs. He had regained his composure now, and his sharp mind cleared.

The entire scene began coming into focus, and he instinctively knew what had occurred.

"I doubt the truthfulness in these notes," he said to Flora as she sat beside him with tears in her eyes. "Look," he said, "both men are shot twice in the back of the head. The man who shot them is the same man who shot Jackson Stamey. I believe Robert Swink and Sheriff Cope went somewhere together after the fight we had with the Mafia. At some point, they stopped, and while they were out of the car, the guilty man managed to lay down on the floor behind the front seat, concealing himself. When they took off again, he waited until they stopped at some remote place and then shot them. Robert and the sheriff were probably getting hot on his trail, and he knew it. These two bodies and notes were just placed here to confuse us and give him some time."

"He is still close by," replied Flora.

"Are you sure?" Millard asked.

"I am sure," Flora said. "I am positive of it."

Millard ran up the stairs and quickly put on warm clothes and a heavy coat and hat. He ran back down the stairs to his car and was gone. He drove carefully to keep his car from skidding off the road as he made his way toward Spruce Willow, the only logical way to even attempt travel on such bad roads. As he traveled along the treacherous road, he kept close watch for anything suspicious.

He had not driven over five miles when he looked off to the left and saw Robert's car off in a deep ditch. Next to it was a man working feverishly to get it out. "Well, I'll be damned," said Millard. "There the son of a bitch is, sure as hell."

Millard got out of his car and headed straight for the stranded car. The man smiled as he saw Millard coming. "Can you help me get out of this ditch?" he asked.

"I can help you all right," said Millard, "if you know Robert Swink."

The expression on the man's face changed from a smile to a look of sinking fear. He knew the trouble he was in, and his hand quickly reached for the pistol in his belt. He was too late—far too late.

Five booming gunshots rang out from Millard's pistol and echoed across the valley. The sound seemed to go on forever.

Millard knew he had committed a deadly sin and this echoing sound would haunt him forever. Millard stood over the body of the man he had just killed, feeling no remorse, sorrow or guilt. The man lying there killed without reason. Millard then slowly walked to his car and drove home leaving the man, whose name he did not know, lying facedown in the snow, as he had left his friends, Robert Swink and Sheriff Cope.

ABOUT THE AUTHOR

Ken Ollis is a native of the Blue Ridge Mountains of North Carolina. He was born in 1935, at a time when the Great Depression was running rampant. After leaving for many years, he returned to the mountains, where he and his wife, Jackie, live in their comfortable home on a mountain called Gingercake. They raised two sons and have three grandchildren and three great-grandchildren.

After traveling abroad, living over much of the United States, and serving in the US Air Force, Ken concluded that the Blue Ridge Mountains were unsurpassed in beauty, solitude, and rich history. He considers living here a privilege that inspired him to write this book concerning unique episodes of times and circumstances. Since his retirement, he has published one other book, *Seasons of Poetry*.